"THE SITUATION ON DOCK TWO is deteriorating. Send all available staffers," Rachel ordered.

"Already done. Ops called. Now kindly remove your esteemed self from Section B."

"Can't." Rachel cut the connection to the Safety warden.

Rosita shouted, "Benjy! Behind you!"

The distinctive thunder of falling cargo containers shook the deck plates of Earth Port Station.

"Kill!" a Phi-Nurian rasped. "Kill, kill, kill!"

Rachel peered around the tractor's metal chassis. Benjy lay pinned beneath a heavy canister, Captain Allos reared over him in triumph, claws flexing.

"Damn!" Rachel vaulted onto the tractor and started it up. The powerful engine thrummed to life beneath her feet. She seized the steering stick and swung the vehicle onto the loading area, leaning into the turn.

In the center of the fracas, Rosita and Chen pushed themselves between their helpless colleague and the attacking Captain Allos. Modesto desperately heaved at the canister on Benjy. Brandishing cargo hooks and crowbars, the Rofan swarmed over the barricade.

Heart in her mouth, Rachel roared toward the assembly at full speed. . . .

GRASP THE STARS

Jennifer Wingert

DAW BOOKS, INC.
DONALD A. WOLLHEIM, FOUNDER
375 Hudson Street, New York, NY 10014

ELIZABETH R. WOLLHEIM
SHEILA E. GILBERT
PUBLISHERS
www.dawbooks.com

First Printing, July 2004
1 2 3 4 5 6 7 8 9

For John and Martha Wingert

Special thanks to Mickey Zucker Reichert,
Genya Freeman, Becky McKee, Juanita Mitchell,
and Beth Nachison.

I grasp the stars and take the light to heart. I walk like plush and teach the rabbits how. I weep sweet diamonds and drop the sparkles one by one. There is nothing to learn and I learn it very well. I stand alone and fill my arms with wind. I grasp the stars. I grasp the stars.

—from *The Collected Flights of Prudence Clarke*

CHAPTER ONE

THE JANGLE and bash of alien music echoed over the cavernous dock, mingling with the squeal of heavy machinery. Beside an overflowing refuse bin, Meris crouched within a pile of broken shipping crates. Dried traces of procreative fluids still clung to her silver fur, tainting it with the stinking reminder of her would-be rapists. *Can't let them find me.* Terror stretched her nerves taut, and she curled her tail tightly against her body, focusing her awareness on the rapid rhythm of her three hearts. *Need to hide. Stay safe.*

Safety, however, seemed a rare commodity aboard Igsha Reey Spaceport. Freighter crews and merchant captains of several species thronged the dock, shouting to make their voices carry over the uproar. Lights flashed from the garish advertisements that covered the curving bulkheads between berths; gigantic depictions of ground cars, drug inhalers, and bejeweled knives arched up to disappear into the overhead maze of loading cranes and power conduits. The scent of decontaminant spray swirled through the hot air, drifting from the dispensers mounted over access hatches, but it failed to compete with the gut-churning odors of refuse, Phi-Nurian dung, and Human secretions.

Close at hand, a Rofa screeched a string of curses. Certain she faced a fresh attack from unknown quarters, Meris bared her claws and shifted to find a better peek-hole.

At a nearby berth, a Rofan crew scrambled into position

along a cargo conveyer. Meris watched them tensely, bracing herself for action, but the Rofan seemed entirely unaware of her presence. She noted that their smooth russet pelts and round eyes marked them as members of the childbearing gender. This made them less likely to commit a sexual assault, but more likely to challenge her to a death match with knives.

Still huddled within her nest of broken crates, Meris listened carefully to the crew's talk, trying to determine how much time had passed since her family had sealed her into a stasis unit. She heard no clues regarding the current date, nor did she detect any gossip concerning her home world of Jada or the resolution of its dangerous political tensions. In a native tongue redolent with trills and hisses, spiced with invective, the Rofan crew conversed about work schedules, cargo mass, and sex.

Discouraged, Meris let her ears droop. Somehow, her stasis unit had been spirited from Jada to Igsha Reey Spaceport, where it had fallen into the hands of Rofan criminals. There had been three of them, and they had not even spoken to her. One had said something to its partners about having fun first. Then they pinned her, stripped off her jewelry, and began mouthing her privates.

Meris feared that, somewhere on the station, her attackers sought to recapture her. If they found her, they would not underestimate her physical strength again, repeating the careless error that had enabled her to escape. They would kill her. *After they finish.*

The mere thought robbed Meris of the will to move. Limbs weighted with terror, belly roiling with nausea, the Treasure of Jada lay in filth, peering out through the shattered slats of a plastic crate.

Meris desperately wished she could access the full range of her memories. She was quite certain that, as the most ancient member of a long-lived species, she possessed a familiarity with the martial arts or some measure of expertise with weapons. She cursed the drug overdose that had caused her amnesia and reduced her active memory to a brief span of twenty years, limiting her to an adolescent's capabilities.

A six-legged Phi-Nurian scuttled by, the light gleaming on its mottled carapace. It left a trail of dark green droppings behind it, each about the size of her foot. The Phi-Nurians could not control their eliminative processes, she recalled reading, and their dung was malodorous in the extreme. Though greedy and bureaucratic, they were not violent unless provoked. They traded raw ores in exchange for Jada's synthetics. Wringing out her slender store of knowledge, it occurred to Meris that a Phi-Nurian captain might agree to provide passage back to Jada in exchange for the promise of a reward.

Several Humans followed the Phi-Nurian at a careful distance. Though two-legged and upright, they lacked the beauty and dignity of the Rofan and Jadamiin. The Humans' gestures, gait, and even the flashing movements of their eyes were unnervingly swift and erratic. Meris studied them with growing distaste, noting their various heights and shapes, trying to recall if the divergent colors of their manes denoted gender. Bodily secretions soaked the aliens' hairless hides and unimaginative garments. As they passed, their sour scent overpowered the odor of Phi-Nurian dung.

Revolted, Meris swept her tail up to her face and buried her nose in its tufted tip. Instead of her own comforting smell, however, she inhaled the stink of Rofan sexual spume. Nausea nearly overwhelmed her, and she gagged. As if triggered by the tiny noise, a bit of ruptured tubing slid from the trash heap and hit the deck plates with a thump.

One of the Humans whirled with freakish speed and glanced toward the bin. Meris' mane and the heavy ruff around her shoulders rose up in hackles. She forced herself to stay silent and flexed her clawed hands. She would fight if attacked. She was slightly larger and, she hoped, stronger. The Human made a remark in its sloshy language to its companions, and the group moved on.

Meris shuddered, hearts beating in a rapid triplet thrum. Jada traded with all systems but one: Eartha. The Jadamiin could not tolerate the denizens of that damp and odorous world. The Humans, with their restrictive government and conformist society, represented all things repellent to the artistic and sensitive Jadamiin. Meris shook her ruffled fur into place, finding that the bout of revulsion had cleared her mind somewhat.

She needed to go home, but it seemed unlikely she would

find someone of her own reticent species at port. She peered out at the dock, wondering again if she might somehow seek passage aboard one of the Phi-Nurian vessels.

It would be difficult to manage, since she carried nothing of value. Approaching any Rofa would be folly, since she recalled reading that Igsha Reey Port was notoriously rough. Even if she evaded ravishment, if she inadvertently offended a Rofa, she would find herself in dire peril. Under certain circumstances, Rofan society did not consider it a crime to kill, and dueling was a popular pastime.

From the nearby berth, a very young Rofa spoke in a tone of protest. "But, Eeya, I can too help. I'm big enough. Almost six."

A myriad of hairlike vibrissae on Meris' brow rose up in an involuntary response to the sound of a child's voice. She peeked around the side of the bin.

An adult Rofa carried a child toward a low stack of canisters. Both wore layers of rich tunics cut in varying lengths, which was typical garb for the merchant class. The adult lifted the child to the top of the canisters. "Jhaska, we need you to help by staying up there," Eeya said. The Rofa bore the unmistakable insignia of a dockside brawler, notched ears and a puckering scar across its muzzle, but it handled the young one gently. "Stand guard against cargo thieves."

Jhaska's diminutive ears flicked back. "But I want to move crates."

Eeya did not argue, but reached into a sleeve and produced a fist-sized item wrapped in orange plastic. Meris recognized it as a popular brand of commercially packaged candied fruit.

Jhaska's ears flicked forward, and it reached for the treat with both hands. "Sweet-sweet!"

"You cannot eat this and move crates at the same time," Eeya said. "Tell me whether you want to stand guard or load cargo."

Jhaska looked from the rumbling conveyors to the package of fruit, then spoke in a cagey tone. "Eat-and-guard."

Eeya raised the fruit to within easy reach, and Jhaska snatched it away. The Rofan always took what was theirs; Meris found it charming to see this sense of confidence instilled in one so young.

"Remember," Eeya said. "Stay up there."

Jhaska ripped open the package with its teeth. "I'll remember."

Eeya walked away without another word to join the others at the conveyor. Jhaska tore off the plastic wrapper and threw it on the floor. The sticky-looking piece of fruit was dyed an unnatural shade of yellow. Undaunted, Jhaska sank its sharp, little teeth into the delicacy and yanked off a bite.

Entranced, Meris sank to her haunches to watch. With its blunt snout, liquid eyes, and sweet lack of self-consciousness, Jhaska's face seemed soft and babylike. Meris longed to pick up the engaging little creature and snuggle it under her chin. Strange how something so appealing would one day become a swaggering Rofa with a narrow, triangular face and a penchant for dueling.

Jhaska busily chewed its bite of fruit, round eyes glittering, head bobbing in obvious pleasure.

So adorable.

Somewhere on the dock, a Rofa shouted. Meris found her webbed ears redirecting themselves toward the sound. More voices joined the shouting. Jhaska glanced up, licking its nose, and stared.

Inwardly cursing her stupidity, Meris tore her gaze from the child and peered around the crates. The crew at the conveyor stopped working and stood in attitudes of wary excitement. It was probably only a duel, but she could not be sure from the sound alone.

The commotion moved closer. Little Jhaska bounded to its feet, still clutching its candied fruit. "Dútha!" it cried. "Dú-Dú-Dútha!"

Meris recognized the name and caught her breath. A *gukka*, or hired duelist, Dútha was a deadly fighter of unimpeachable honor, reaching legendary heights at a young age. If Dútha still lived, then her sojourn in stasis must have been brief.

The conveyor crew stepped out onto the dock, blocking Meris' view entirely. She shifted within her hiding place, trying to find a better peek-hole.

An iron grip closed around her left arm. "Got you!"

Meris' gut lurched. She flung herself forward, scrabbling on her hands and knees, dragging her captor through the broken crates.

It snarled and twisted, but did not release its hold.

Panting, she glanced back at it. The large Rofa bore a jagged scar across one eye. Distinctive patterns of white marked its golden pelt, and it carried a knife in its free hand. She recognized it as one of her attackers.

Mad with panic, Meris lunged to her feet and ran onto the dock, still pulling the Rofa. It tried to slash at her with the knife, but she jerked her arm violently to keep her attacker off-balance and stumbling. A wall of stacked canisters loomed. She swerved abruptly. The one-eyed Rofa hissed and regained its footing. Meris swung her arm, throwing her whole weight into the move, and slammed One-Eye into the stack of canisters.

It lost its grip on her and fell in a sprawl. Meris turned to bolt, but found herself in the middle of a tight ring of Rofan. There were dozens of them, and from their excited cries, she knew that they were enjoying her struggle to survive.

Her hearts galloped. Meris spun back toward her attacker.

One-Eye lurched to its feet. It approached her cautiously, knife ready.

"Coward!" someone called in weirdly accented Trade. "The Jadamii is unarmed!"

The gathered Rofan lapsed into startled whispers.

One-Eye whipped its head toward the voice. "Who spoke?"

"I did. Bailey of Eartha." A Human shouldered its way through the crowd. The alien's long, unruly mane glistened with varied hues of orange and red, and its hairless face dripped with moisture. Baring its square, white teeth, it pointed at One-Eye, adding insulting gestures to its accusation. "Coward."

The fur down Meris' spine rose, prickling. No Rofa would ignore so many offenses, especially the charge of cowardice. She could not imagine why the Human wished to draw an attack upon itself.

One-Eye spoke in a tone of utter scorn. "Human, you're of a species without valor. Your words mean nothing." It returned its attention to Meris and continued its deadly advance. "Jadamii, I shall taste of your blood."

Her three hearts beat so hard, Meris could scarcely draw breath. She watched her enemy approach, trying to make herself flee, knowing the Rofa would kill her.

"But Bailey of Eartha is correct," called a new voice with a Rofan accent. "The Jadamii has no weapon."

The spectators growled in agreement.

A Rofa stepped into the ring. It was a tall individual whose buff-colored pelt shaded to white at its throat and breast, and it wore only a loincloth and a knife.

Meris' tongue felt thick. This was not the rangy youth that she recalled seeing in pictures, but an adult in its prime. "Dútha?"

"Yes." The *gukka* regarded her calmly, its dark eyes bright with an odd amusement. "You have no weapon." Its tone was dry and indulgent. "No?"

Meris slowly lifted her trembling hands, showing them empty. "No."

The spectators hissed in disapproval and glared at her attacker. A single word whispered around the ring: "Coward. . . ."

One-Eye stopped, licking its teeth uneasily. "Very well," it said. It bent and laid its knife on the floor, then kicked the weapon over to Meris. "There. Now the Jadamii is armed." It looked at Dútha. "I'm not afraid to fight bare-handed."

Meris stared at the weapon by her feet.

Dútha gestured casually. "Pick it up."

"I can't," Meris whispered. She raised her hands beseechingly to the gathered Rofan. "I don't know how to use it."

Dútha tilted its head. "Then it was foolish of you to accept the challenge to duel."

"But I didn't!" Meris blurted wildly. She mentally dithered, then decided not to mention the attempted rape. "That Pathless monster simply attacked me! For no reason!"

Dútha turned toward her assailant. Its eyes glittered, but its tone was amused. "Really?"

One-Eye's ears swept flat. "She insulted my ancestors."

Meris sputtered in mingled fury and terror. "I don't even know your ancestors!"

One-Eye shouted: "Pick up the knife!"

"I don't know how to use it!" Meris shouted back. "I don't know how to fight!"

Heavy silence fell over the watching Rofan.

Gulping for air, Meris turned a gaze of entreaty toward the *gukka*.

Dútha repeated slowly: "You don't . . . know how to fight?"

Meris feared that such an admission would brand her as a nonentity, but she could not pretend to a skill she did not have. "No."

Dútha studied her, its ears flicking thoughtfully. "I do," it said finally. "And my services are for hire."

"But—" A violent trembling seized Meris. "I don't have any means to pay."

"You have . . . yourself."

Meris could not breathe.

"You would make," Dútha continued, "a most attractive possession."

Her joints went limp with horror. Meris thought she might faint. The Rofan were omnisexual, regularly active with the Jadamiin, and even going so far as to couple with Human and animals. "I—" *By the Three Great Paths, this cannot be happening!* She glanced at One-Eye, then at Dútha. *Rape and death. Or rape and slavery.* Meris swallowed and said unsteadily. "Very well. I'll hire you."

"Most sensible," Dútha said. It pulled the knife from its belt and pressed the hilt into her hand. "Hold this for me."

Numbly, Meris wrapped her fingers around it. The knife felt heavy and toollike. Whispers spread among the watching Rofan.

Dútha pointed to a spot in the crowd. "Stand over there until I'm finished."

Meris turned to obey.

Snarling, One-Eye dived for its knife on the floor. The crowd of Rofan broke into outraged cries. "Unfair!" "Coward!"

Locked in fear, Meris stood rooted.

In a series of neat, clean moves, Dútha stepped on the knife with one foot and used the other to kick One-Eye in the face. Her enemy went rolling.

Surprise replaced terror, and Meris stared at the *gukka*.
"How did you do that?"

"Stand over there," Dútha repeated in a patient tone.
"Where you won't get hurt."

Her legs and shoulders shook as Meris walked to the
indicated place. She recognized the individuals around her
as the conveyor crew. Eeya stood nearby with Jhaska in its
arms. None of them spared her a glance; but with offhand
courtesy, they shifted to give her plenty of room. For the
first time since awaking from stasis, Meris felt somewhat
safe. She took a more comfortable grip on the knife and
returned her attention to the fight.

Within the ring, One-Eye climbed unsteadily to its feet.
Blood soaked the fur around its snout and dripped from
its mouth.

Dútha waited, seeming composed and relaxed. "You
really aren't skilled enough to fight me, so killing you would
bring me no glory." The *gukka's* voice still carried a note
of amusement. "Forfeit the duel, and I'll spare your life."

One-Eye gingerly touched its bleeding nose, then glared
at its opponent. "Never."

"You answered too quickly," Dútha said. "Better think
about it."

In a flash, One-Eye leaped for Dútha.

Meris gasped.

Dútha appeared merely to step to the side and raise its
fists. Something crunched.

One-Eye collapsed on the metal deck plates at Dútha's
feet. Blood puddled up around its head.

Meris stared. *It's over? Just like that?*

The gathered Rofan burst into shrill cries of approval.
"Dútha!" they shouted. "Dú-Dú-Dútha!"

Meris' pulse thundered in her ears, and she again found
it difficult to breathe. *What happens now?*

Dútha stepped back warily from its fallen opponent and
raised its gaze to Meris. For a long moment, it simply
looked at her as if memorizing her appearance, then it
beckoned.

The crowd broke up, drifting back to normal work as if
nothing unusual had occurred. Bailey of Eartha seemed
ready to approach her, then evidently reconsidered and

turned away. Four Rofan picked up the body of her former
assailant, hauled it to the refuse bin, and unceremoniously
heaved it in. Feeling sick, Meris edged her way through the
press of aliens to stand beside Dútha. She wondered if any
of One-Eye's companions had witnessed the fight, and if
they would dare to challenge the *gukka*.

Dútha regarded her with ears up. "My knife." It extended its hand. "If you please."

Meris passed it over, wishing she could disguise the
trembling in her fingers.

Dútha took the weapon and sheathed it, bowing politely.
"Most gracious."

Meris returned the bow. "Most honored." Realization
hit. "You—?" *Asked for your own knife.* She fell silent,
afraid of offering an insult.

Dútha seemed to read her mind. "You think I'm passably
polite for a Rofa."

"You seem to know Jadamiin manners."

"I had a distinguished instructor, one who taught me that
courtesy comes in many forms." Dútha paused, and its tone
became oddly gentle. "I fought your duel. Are you prepared to pay my fee?"

"Yes, but—" Meris did not know if she ought to finish
her thought. "Do you know who I am?"

Delicately, Dútha tapped the tip of her nose and whispered: "You are Meris, Mother of Multitudes, Treasure of
Jada." Amusement returned to its voice, along with a certain shade of intimacy. "And you are mine."

Full of dismay, Meris stared at her new surroundings. The
Rofan preferred vivid colors, and they usually arranged
rooms to lead from one to the next, like beads on a neck-
lace. The interior of Dútha's ship was a sterile white, however, and a single compartment contained the living
quarters.

Tufted tail sinking to the floor, Meris turned in a slow
circle, taking in the whole nightmarish layout. A galley area
filled one corner, an inner bulkhead contained a built-in
bunk, and only a simple partition separated the sanitary
facilities from the rest of the room. "All Paths," she
whispered.

"Not much to look at," Dútha said casually. The Rofa

squatted in front of a storage locker on the floor and opened it. "But comfortable."

All edges were hard and straight; all shapes geometrical. In growing uneasiness, Meris sought a flowing line upon which to rest her gaze. "What kind of ship is this?"

Dútha pulled a bath comb from the locker. "It's a new type of courier ship. Nothing's faster."

Meris turned another circle, seeing only bleak utilitarianism. "But it isn't a Rofan ship, is it?"

Dútha peered at her over the locker's lid. "What do you mean?"

"The design." Meris waved her hand vaguely. "It's strange."

"Prototype." Dútha shut the lid and stood. "Only one of its kind."

"Really?" Meris asked, without thinking. "Then why do you have it?"

Dútha's large, triangular ears swept back.

Her hearts picked up tempo. "Forgive me," Meris said hastily. "I meant no offense."

"None taken. I had simply forgotten how curious you always were."

Confused by the comment, Meris did not know how to respond.

Dútha handed her the comb. "I suppose you'll want to clean up."

She held the comb in both hands and bowed. "Most gracious."

"Most honored." Dútha pointed toward the partitioned area. "The bath pit is in there." It gazed at her, seeming to consider its next words. "I have this ship," it said, "because I'm an agent for the Legitimacy."

Meris had never heard that the legendary *gukka* served the ruling clan of Igsha Reey. "Since when?"

"Almost always." Dútha's voice turned soft. "But you wouldn't remember that."

Meris' webbed ears drooped. It no longer troubled her that perfect strangers knew about her Phenox overdose and the resulting memory loss, but she found her host's manner unsettling. Dútha clearly wished her to believe it once knew her personally. "I . . . I've been in stasis for a while. I don't know how long."

"Galactic date is five-fourteen-sixteen."

Only twelve years. A guarded hope shimmered through Meris. "And affairs on Jada? My family? Do you know how they fare?"

"Your clan prospers, as always."

Relief robbed her of strength, and Meris longed to sink to the floor.

Dútha gestured toward the bath. "Get cleaned up, you'll feel better. I'm going to tell the station to bump up our departure time." The Rofa strode toward the bridge, then paused at the door. "And don't be afraid, I won't let anyone harm you. You're safe, understand?"

She wanted to believe it, wanted to believe that the nightmare was over, that she would soon find a way to return to her family. "Yes."

"Good." Dútha flicked its fingers imperiously. "Go bathe."

Meris hesitantly approached the partitioned-off area, then paused and looked over her shoulder at the single bunk. The fur down her spine rose and shifted. *Safe?*

CHAPTER TWO

T HE ONLY LIGHT on the bridge came from the main
view screen, which displayed an image of the station's
gray-and-white exterior in the harsh wash of flood lamps.
Operational chatter flowed from a speaker on the control
panel. Dútha sat hunched in the pilot's couch, moodily
gnawing a thumbnail.

Uncertain of her welcome, Meris paused in the doorway.
"I've finished."

Dútha slowly turned its head and studied her for a moment. "Much better."

Meris glanced down at herself. Her silver pelt seemed to
sparkle in the dim light. "I had to cycle the sand through
three times before the smell came out."

Dútha continued to gaze at her. "I would imagine."

Meris waited for the Rofa to say more, but it did not
move. "So." She hoped she would not regret her next
words. "What do you want me to do now?"

"Mm?" Dútha said absently, then seemed to come to
itself. It pointed at the copilot's couch. "Sit there. If you
please."

Hesitantly, Meris crossed to the indicated seat and eased
herself onto the couch. Though covered with a soft synthetic material, its contours felt strange against her legs and
buttocks. *Not designed for someone with a tail.*

Dútha opened a small storage compartment in the arm

of the pilot's couch and pulled out a plastic bag. "Do you like *ksh-ksh*?"

"I'm not sure." Meris kept her tone quiet and courteous. "What is *ksh-ksh*?"

"Something to eat." Dútha handed her the bag.

Wary, but trying to conceal it, Meris opened the bag and peered in. She found thin brown chips with a savory odor. "They smell good. What are they?"

"Marinated mushrooms, sliced and dehydrated. Quite nutritious."

Meris picked one out of the bag, nibbled its edge, and discovered it was both spicy and crisp. "It's good!"

"Don't sound so surprised," Dútha said mildly. "Did you expect me to feed you something bad? I have more pride than that."

"Forgive me." Meris ate the chip and reached into the bag for more. "But I don't know you. I don't know what it means to be . . . your possession."

Dútha's ears flew back, but Meris now recognized it as a startled expression, not one of anger. "It means I take care of you. What else?" The humorous tone returned to its voice. "Isn't that how you treat your valuables? Or do you leave your fragile and irreplaceable antiques out in the snow?"

Meris found her nose wrinkling with amusement in spite of herself. "Are you calling me an antique?"

Dútha settled back on the couch, folding its arms behind its head. "Only as a term of vast respect," it said slyly. "But you can't deny your advanced age. Of all Jadamiin, you're the oldest, yes?"

"Yes." Meris ate another chip. *Delectable.* "Our scientists estimate that I'm over eight thousand years old."

"Eight thousand," Dútha repeated. "What stories you must know."

Wariness returned. "Are you mocking me?"

"Just a little." Dútha rolled its head to look at her. "I know about the Phenox overdose." It paused, and its tone became gentle. "How far back can you remember? Just a few decades?"

The fringe of fur down her spine prickled with uneasiness. "About twenty years, yes."

Dútha looked interested. "Really? Do you remember me?"

"Well," Meris said politely, "I remember hearing about you." She tried to keep her fur from lifting, concentrated on the *ksh-ksh*. "You were becoming a celebrity even on Jada."

Dútha studied her for a long moment. "I imagine," it said finally, "that you must deal with a lot of strangers who approach you, claiming to be old friends."

"Yes." Meris struggled to keep her webbed ears from folding back and failed. "You keep hinting that you know me. Are you also going to claim friendship?"

Dútha settled again and closed its eyes. "No. I shall not claim it. I shall prove it."

Meris found the burst of Rofan arrogance refreshing and oddly reassuring. She scooped a handful of chips from the bag.

Dútha remained lying still with its eyes shut. "While you bathed, I received some . . . interesting . . . business proposals. It would appear we have a number of antique collectors on the station."

Her hearts began to pound.

"Rofan, Phi-Nurians, and Kamians have all offered to buy you."

Meris' gut clenched. Kamians were not even oxygen breathers. Insectile, ten times the size of a Jadamii, they were the most technologically advanced species in the galaxy. "Kamians?"

"And the Human ship at the next berth has sent a blistering manifesto on the right of sentient beings to live free of the bonds of slavery. They say I should be ashamed of myself and that I should release you. The knowledge that I have saved your life should be the only recompense I desire."

Suddenly queasy, Meris returned the uneaten chips to the bag and folded it closed. "They want to buy me, too?"

"No. They simply want you to be happy and free."

Meris recalled how the Human had tried to draw One-Eye's attack upon itself. "Why? Why should they bother? I don't understand."

"Neither do I, entirely. But I rather suspect their concern

is sincere. It fits the pattern, and they enjoy meddling in the business of others. A most peculiar species." Dútha abruptly sat up and turned to face her. "Do you know what else is peculiar? There is an envoy ship from Jada's High Assembly berthed on the upper dock. And it has sent no word, no offer to ransom you back. Why is that?"

"I—" *An envoy? No offer?* "I don't know."

Dútha's tone became serious. "You must be honest with me. Hiding information at this point will only hinder my efforts to protect you." It leaned toward her. "Tell me. Why did you take the Phenox? Why were you hidden away in stasis? And why does it seem that your own family wishes you dead?"

Shock robbed Meris of self-possession. She pressed her hands against her throat. "That's not true! They love me, and they—" Sudden realization hit, and she struggled to prevent her voice from shaking. "It must be the Guardians."

"Guardians?"

"Or so they called themselves." Meris paused, wondering how to explain. "A branch of the family. After my Phenox overdose, they wanted to take me away from my direct descendants, claiming I needed better custodians."

Dútha grunted and glanced away. "They wanted the political power of your name."

"Exactly." Meris closed her eyes, remembering the grim meeting, her pleas, and the sternly impatient replies of her caretakers. "Elders within the family decided that I should go into hiding in stasis. For the safety of everyone."

"Mm."

"The Guardians were making threats. I suppose the situation has only deteriorated while I was . . . away." Meris opened her eyes and regarded Dútha earnestly. "Please. Let me contact my family."

"Not yet."

"But—"

The *gukka* kept its gaze averted. "Understand me. I'm not trying to be cruel. But until I know why other species wish to become involved in a Jadamiin power struggle, I think it's best not to draw attention to your family."

Meris drew a breath to protest, then released it silently, seeing Dútha's point. "Very well."

"To complicate matters," the Rofa continued, "the Legitimacy has given me orders to return you to the Jadamiin envoy. Of course, I have no intention of obeying."

Meris stared at Dútha. "But you said—you're their agent!"

"Yes. If they discover that I plan to betray them, I'm dead." It returned its gaze to her. "But that doesn't matter. The planets are shifting in their orbits."

"I'm sorry, but what are you talking about?"

Dútha slid off the couch and paced a few steps. "I can understand the Jadamiin feud to claim custody of you. But interested parties from every part of the galaxy also seem to want possession of you—even at the risk of invoking Jada's ill will."

"But I don't—"

"I'm thinking," Dútha said slowly, "it may have something to do with the reason for your overdose."

The fur on Meris' spine rose and her ears rolled back. "The reason?"

Dútha leaned against a console and seemed to gaze at the main viewing screen. "I was there when it happened. Didn't your family tell you?"

"No."

"I was the one who found you."

"You?" Meris could not keep the skepticism from her voice. "Don't tell me that you were a member of my household."

"Just a visitor. A courier, actually, with tidings of friendship from the Legitimacy to the Immortal Meris."

Possible. Meris recalled receiving several Rofan couriers within her span of memory, and it pleased her to entertain them as guests. "And do you know why I chose to erase my memory?"

"I don't—" Dútha's tone became soft and faintly edged with pain. "I don't think you planned to erase your memory. I believe that you intended to die. The Phenox overdose was an attempted suicide."

"*What?*"

"Think about it. With Jadamiin physiology, Phenox has a three-stage cycle, correct? Sleep, awake, sleep."

"Yes, but—" Meris heard the tension in her own voice and paused to compose herself. "But we can't remember

what occurs during the second stage. It's as if Phenox puts
a chemical 'lock' on the brain, making it impossible to recall those events until one is again under its influence."

"Exactly my point. The memory is only affected for a
specific amount of time. Phenox doesn't erase memories; it
partitions them."

"But it erased mine," Meris pointed out. "I had to re-
learn how to walk and speak and feed myself."

"Ah, yes." Dútha lowered its gaze from the view screen
and stared down at a control panel. "Yes, you took a massive overdose."

"But why would I take Phenox, if I wanted to die? Why
wouldn't I take a known and effective poison?"

"Because the Phenox was most available." Dútha opened
a recessed storage compartment in the panel and absently
stirred through its rattling contents. "I was a guest in your
household at the time, and I had a large supply with me."

"But—"

"Phenox works differently on the Rofan. For us, it's fun.
Makes us feel good." Dútha finally looked at her. "I think
you panicked. Something from the past resurfaced, something dreadful that you could not bear to endure."

Meris stared helplessly at the Rofa, as everything she
thought she knew about herself abruptly took on a different meaning.

"I've been thinking about it for years," Dútha continued.
"Piecing events together, listening, watching for clues." It
picked up a small piece of equipment from the compartment, rolled the object around on its palm, then tossed it
back. "When I visited Jada, twenty years ago, the news was
full of a recent archaeological find. A research team had
uncovered traces of Jada's ancient and highly advanced civilization under the ocean."

Meris' ears went limp in bewilderment. "But I knew all
about the past. I lived in it, cherished it. Why would an
archaeological discovery trigger a suicide attempt?"

"Because of the Guardians." Dútha picked up another
item from the compartment. "They were actively seeking
custody of you even before the overdose. I was only a visitor, but I saw things . . . heard things. . . ."

"The Guardians." Troubled, Meris climbed to her feet.
"Tell me. Please."

"As far as I could gather, they wanted you to decipher something. Evidently, one of the most important items uncovered during the dig was a badly damaged time capsule. It contained an engraved piece of metal that—"

Uneasiness gave way to confusion. "Wait," Meris interrupted. "Are you talking about the Artifact?"

"So. You know about it."

"Everyone knows about it. Thousands upon thousands of replicas exist. It's a standard feature in most schools."

"But, back then, you refused to even look at it. The Guardians were threatening drastic measures, and tensions were running high within your household."

Utterly confused, Meris searched for words. "But that doesn't make any sense. The Artifact is merely an archaeological relic. It's just an old—"

"Eight thousand years old," Dútha interrupted in a colorless tone. "You must have known what it was, to take such an adamant stance in your refusal to study it."

Meris struggled to fully weigh the *gukka's* words. "My family never told me any of this."

"Perhaps your family is a set of conniving, Pathless monsters."

Meris' ears snapped back. "How dare you call—"

"They buried you alive in stasis and hid you away." Dútha's voice remained calm and empty of emotion. "The Guardians claimed you were dead, and they demanded that your remains be placed in a public shrine." It paused, as if deciding whether or not to continue. "Jada's High Assembly is racked by instability and could topple with the merest breeze, leaving the two factions of your clan in a war of domination for the planet."

"But—"

"And now intelligence reports indicate that someone has partially deciphered the Artifact."

Meris flung out her hands. "So what?"

Dútha's voice darkened. "It seems that the Artifact is a set of equations dealing with the structure of time and space."

"It can't be."

"Really? Then why did your own family arrange for you to be discovered and murdered aboard Igsha Reey Spaceport?"

"I—" Meris' breath caught. *My own family?* "I don't believe it."

"Could it be they feared that, at some point in your long life, you had seen the original Artifact in its undamaged state and could reproduce it?"

"But my memories were erased."

"Really? What if you were drugged with Phenox again? Wouldn't that provide you access to your full range of memories?"

Growing frightened and angry, Meris struggled to keep her ears up. "I'm telling you that the Artifact is nothing more than a historical curiosity."

"You know, the Legitimacy has ordered me to return you to Jadamiin custody. I believe this is tantamount to a death sentence. Both sides of your family would benefit from having you eliminated. Once you achieve the status of goddess, there's no risk of the equations falling into the wrong hands, and each can accuse the other side of your murder."

Meris made a noise of protest. "Murder?"

"Yes. And if I thought that the current crisis could be dealt with so simply, I would obey my superiors' orders to return you." Dútha met her gaze without flinching. "But I believe that your death would resolve nothing."

"Most gracious," she said faintly.

"Don't thank me yet. It isn't over. And you may not like the course I take to preserve your life." Dútha approached her slowly. "To start, we need to find the mathematician responsible for partially deciphering the equations. Who is it? Do you know?"

"Don't you?" Meris asked unsteadily. "You seem to know everything else."

Dútha laid a hand on her shoulder. Though startled, she prevented herself from jerking away. If the *gukka* wanted to harm her, it would have already done so.

Something hard and cold pinched Meris' neck; a medicinal sting filled her nostrils. Her pulse lurched. "All Paths!"

"I wish there were another way, dear friend."

Meris' vision wavered, sound dulled. Frantically, she attempted to cling to consciousness. "Poison?"

"I would never be so cruel," Dútha said. "It's Phenox."

Her eyes drifted shut. "No," she whispered.

"Please. . . ."

Handling her carefully, Dútha gathered her into its arms. "Don't be afraid. When you wake up, you'll have a friend by your side."

Meris awoke gently. For a few drowsy moments, she lay with her eyes closed and allowed the memories to sweep through her. The faces of lovers and children long dead, cities gone to dust, sorrows, burdens, small triumphs; all returned to her with aching clarity. She longed to savor her lost lifetime, but the drug's memory "window" would soon close. She would again fall into a deep sleep and remember nothing but a bare score of years filled with a web of lies.

Dútha was lying beside her, warm scent heavy in the air, breath stirring the delicate hair on her ears. *I shall not claim it. I shall prove it.* Whatever blame her family carried for recent events, they were absolutely guilty of hiding her past relationship with the *gukka*, her best friend, lover, and champion. *Unforgivable.*

Meris opened her eyes and discovered that they reclined together on the bunk in the ship's common room. Sighing, she rolled to face her friend.

Dútha did not move or open its eyes, but murmured: "Remember?"

Meris laid her head on Dútha's shoulder. "I've missed you terribly, without knowing why. Only that something important was gone from my life."

"They wouldn't let me near you. I didn't know how to get a message to you."

"Not your fault."

Dútha wordlessly caressed her face, ran a tender hand through her mane.

Bittersweet memories and the looming tragedy of losing her friend again shadowed the moment. Then the full weight of the present struck; as Dútha had surmised, someone in her family had betrayed her, setting her up to die at the hands of Rofan assassins. She forced herself to draw away and sit up. "How long did I sleep?"

"Ages." Dútha also stirred and climbed from the bunk. "Perhaps we should eat while we talk. We may not have another chance for some time." It crossed to the galley. "While you slept, some of the antique collectors on station became insistent about purchasing you."

Meris stretched and shook her fur into place. "Really?"

"Shortly after I dosed you, a group of Phi-Nurians broke into station offices and shot the place to pieces." Dútha's tone was matter-of-fact. "They may still be at large. Station com has been off-line ever since."

Meris stared at Dútha, her ears bolt upright in terror. "But how—?"

"Also, the mystery of the Jadamiin envoys' silence has been answered. They're all dead. Station authorities were calling it life-support failure, placing the blame on the ship."

Shock held Meris motionless.

Dútha unlatched a storage cupboard and pulled out two foil packets. "The Legitimacy believes I have the bodies on board. They have officially sent their apologies and condolences to the High Assembly, and they've informed them that I'll be transporting the remains—and you—back to Jada."

Meris remembered the Guardians' threats: that her perfectly preserved body displayed in a shrine would serve their purposes as well as her living presence. "But I can't go back to Jada."

"I agree."

Meris drew a breath to speak, then let it out again, finding no words.

"Choices are limited." Dútha tore open the two packets and squeezed their contents into a bowl. "I believe that Eartha is our only option."

Meris' spine bristled at the thought of the nearly hairless Humans and their reeking bodily secretions. "No!"

Dútha's ears flicked back. "Why not? They're a passive species, you would be safe."

"They're disgusting."

Dútha's tone was mild. "Perhaps. Perhaps not. They take a little getting used to, but I find them rather . . . charming."

Meris stood up. "You can't be serious. They—" She gestured impotently. "They make me sick."

Dútha measured water into the bowl and stirred the mixture. "A Human designed this ship."

She glanced around again at the rigidly geometric lines of the common room. "Is that supposed to impress me? They stink."

"Did you know," Dútha said calmly, "that Humans don't require a targeting scope on a gun? Not that they commonly use such weapons." It wiped up a small spill. "But I find it fascinating that the same subtle neural connections that allow you or I to guide the movements of our hands, have somehow translated into an ability to accurately guide the trajectory of airborne objects. They make games of it—throwing and catching things—bandying them back and forth."

Meris shuddered, fur prickling as if covered with insects. "They're freakish. I loathe them."

"So far, they're the only oxygen-breathing species who have not threatened to claim you through violent means." Dútha tasted the mixture in the bowl. "And besides, I think I may need their help to track down the perpetrator of the true problem, the mathematician responsible for partially deciphering the Artifact."

Abruptly, the memories of eight thousand years ago avalanched through Meris' mind.

The Jadamiin had reached an advanced technlogical state, but their society was brutal and militaristic. She was an experimental genetic construct, designed as a "reproductive machine," and her intended function was to spawn large numbers of offspring to serve as soldiers.

Then it was discovered that she, and a handful of others like her, did not age. The Jadamiin had intended to carry their warfare to the stars against their own colonies, but instead began fighting among themselves over the handful of "machines" with the immortality factor. Their advanced civilization fell, and the population was reduced to a primitive existence.

Three of the "machines" had been placed in stasis, and these were discovered six thousand years later, when Jada's civilization had finally reached the second dawn of its industrial age. One of the units had been damaged by a rockslide, and its occupant was dead; but Meris, and her "sister"

Orha, became celebrities. Soon they had families and were living relatively normal lives. They made a pact to keep Jada's warlike past a secret, and so spun a lovely fairy tale of noble ancestors. They said they had volunteered to be put into stasis in order to bring knowledge of the Three Great Paths to the future. They claimed to have no idea what caused the demise of their own civilization. Orha died in a traffic accident several hundred years later. Meris lived on, doing her best to slow the progress of technology, fearful of a return to the ancient ways.

Soon it became evident that she was not aging. Her family became something akin to royalty, styling themselves "the House of Meris," and they did their best to protect her from accidents. And so she lived on and on and became known as the Mother of Multitudes, and everyone loved her.

Eventually, in spite of her efforts, technology reared its head. The carefully preserved stasis units fell under new investigation, and Jada took a leap forward into quantum physics. They rapidly redeveloped space flight, contacted the Kamians, whom they mistrusted, and the Rofan, who became firm allies. Meris herself fell under scrutiny, and although scientists found the immortality "gene" impossible to replicate, they were able to enhance the typical life span of their species.

Eager to learn more, scientists began combing the world for archaeological remains of the former advanced civilization. For a long time, they found only tantalizing clues. Then a badly damaged time capsule was found. It contained a single artifact: a sheet of metallic alloy, engraved with a series of strange hieroglyphs.

Recalling its appearance with all her memories intact, Meris supposed that some of the characters might represent numbers. She had been illiterate in her first life, confined to a gray cell in a subsurface military base.

Panic reared, and Meris turned away to hide her agitation. "I've told you, forget about the Artifact. It's not important."

Dútha's voice held a neutral tone that conveyed strong control. "You still insist upon that, though you have your memory? Interesting."

Meris did not turn around. "I never saw the original Artifact, but it can't be those dangerous equations. Think about it—numbers would be easy to decipher, wouldn't they?"

Dútha did not reply immediately, but continued to putter about in the galley. Meris tensed. Listening to the click of utensils, the whirring oven, she wondered if Dútha could smell the lie.

"Very well," Dútha said. "The Artifact is unimportant. But no one else knows that. How do we persuade them that the equations are a fraud, and that your death is unnecessary?"

"I don't know. Perhaps all we need is time. Give the equations to everyone, and let them try to make them work. They'll soon enough discover the truth."

Her friend stayed silent. Meris finally turned to look.

Dútha stood with its back against the bulkhead, ears up, gaze steady. "Is that wise?"

Meris felt a touch of doubt, wondering if the Artifact could actually be as dangerous as Dútha feared. "It can't hurt anything. All we need is a safe place to wait."

"Eartha."

"No."

"But it's the only safe place available. You know, the Humans haven't committed a violent crime in over four hundred years."

Meris made a noise of disgust. "They claim. When did you become so gullible?"

Dútha seemed to think for a few moments. "Meris. Have you ever murdered anyone?"

Her vibrissae rose in surprise. "No."

"Eight thousand years is a long time. Are you sure? You've never killed? Not even in self-defense?"

Meris hunched her shoulders in irritation. "Of course not. I follow the Three Great Paths."

"Then . . . do you know anyone who has committed murder?"

"You."

"I don't count. Do you know any Jadamiin?"

Meris spoke stiffly: "I don't consort with criminals."

Dútha's nose wrinkled in a parody of Jadamiin amusement. "Me."

In spite of her irritation, Meris' nose wrinkled, too. "You don't count." She waved her hands impatiently. "I see where you're going with this argument. But crime is a condition of sentient life. Even if the Humans followed the Three Great Paths, they would still—"

"But they do," Dútha interrupted in a gentle tone. "I've been studying them, you see. The Jadamiin call the Three Paths: 'Hand,' 'Mouth,' and 'Eye.' The Humans name them: '*Baadii*,' '*Mynnda*,' and '*Ssóla*.'" Dútha approached her slowly. "You see? A civilized species, a safe place to wait. You will go to Eartha."

"But they stink."

Dútha placed its hands on her shoulders. "You will go to Eartha. I will make you do it, even if you hate me for it."

The words stung. "I would never hate you," Meris said, her voice trembling. She slid into Dútha's embrace, wrapping her arms around its sinewy body. "You are brave. And truer to me than kin." She pressed her nose into its neck. "I don't want to forget you again."

"I know," Dútha murmured.

Meris' pulse throbbed in her ears. She wanted to cling to Dútha forever, to always know such perfect trust. "There is a Fourth Path," she whispered. "The Path of Friendship."

"You'll go to Eartha."

"Yes," she breathed. "I'll go."

CHAPTER THREE

WITH A BRIEF nap substituting for a full night of sleep, Deputy Rachel Ajmani paused on the threshold of Dock Two's Operations booth and rubbed her bleary eyes.

Rose and amber light slanted down from the overhead panels, simulating daybreak. It threw a pastel sheen over the control console and well-worn chairs, lending an air of faded elegance to the scuffed woodwork and threadbare upholstery. A built-in vid on the right wall played a muted newscast from Earth, flashing images of the World Council in session. On a low table along the left wall, a highly polished brewer glowed like molten brass. Beside the brewer sat a rack of clean mugs and a platter of churros.

Feeling a bit queasy, Rachel averted her gaze from the fried pastries and passed a brown-skinned hand through her hair. Her fingers encountered a bewildering number of tangles in the long, black curls. Drawing her brows together, she unsuccessfully tried to recall using a comb after her hasty shower. It did not bode well for her state of mind. *Another twelve hours to go,* she thought. *God help me.*

On a normal morning, the booth would be full of cargo techs waiting for their shift to start, drinking coffee and chatting about their children. At the moment, however, only the Operations manager for the late shift appeared to be on duty. A young woman with a terra-cotta complexion and stylishly shaved scalp, Lafiya DuChamp sat at the control console, evidently listening to someone on her headset. "Uh-huh," she said in an unconvinced tone. She fidgeted with her writing stylus, her delicate features set in a sullen frown. "Uh-huh."

Positioned in front of a large, one-way window, the control console commanded a panoramic view of dockside activity. Cargo techs on reach-forks flashed past in seemingly random traffic. In the distance, a crane on the overhead gantry lowered a pallet of plastic canisters onto the flatbed of a truck, its gigantic grapple maneuvering the load with eerie precision. Struggling against a sense of disconnection from reality, Rachel wandered to the middle of the booth and tried to focus her thoughts.

Hovering over the console, burning with the lucent colors of a stained glass window, a holographic docking chart displayed the wheel-within-a-wheel image of Earth Port Station. A purely mercantile facility, the station served as Earth's only port of call for out-system freighters. Three new blips appeared on the chart, passing Jupiter's orbital plane, shifting to approach vectors.

It took Rachel's tired brain a long moment to remember that the flashing points of color signified ships, which boosted the tally of unscheduled arrivals to fourteen. The entire ungainly mess of her previous workshift abruptly returned to memory: more alien ships at dock than the station could handle, urgent calls to nearby mining colonies for backup personnel, and a disappointing canvass of Earth freighters for extra crew. *Three more.* "Damn," she whispered.

Lafiya glanced over her shoulder at Rachel, and her face went blank with surprise. "Hold on." She hit the mute key for her headset and peered at Rachel. "Deputy Ajmani, what are you doing here?"

Suppressing a yawn, Rachel nodded at the chart. "Andrew in Docking Control called me."

The station operated under the auspices of the Port Authority, whose deputies administered everything from daily business to extra-species jurisprudence. As one of three silver rank deputies, Rachel possessed ambassadorial power, able to dictate policy with Earth's alien visitors. With the swelling influx of unscheduled arrivals, a state of emergency existed, and she needed to be on hand.

"Andrew said—" Rachel once more slid her fingers through her hair and vigorously massaged her scalp, trying to fully wake up. "Said—" A yawn almost escaped, and she paused to battle it back. "—more company coming."

Lafiya glanced at the clock on her console. "You weren't gone very long," she said. "Did you catch any sleep at all?"

"Oh, sure." Rachel dredged up a smile, lines of exhaustion and habitual good humor mingling around her mouth and eyes. She was forty-two years old; and her dark skin, tall build, and proud carriage evinced a Padma ethnic heritage, which was a fusion of bloodlines that originated in the region between the Nile and Ganges Rivers. "Plenty of sleep."

"But you've already worked a couple of twelve-hour shifts." Lafiya rubbed the back of her smooth head. "Can't Deputy DelRio or Deputy Omar relieve you?"

Rachel's gaze drifted to the vid, but the images of the World Council's chambers had given way to a weather map. "Both of my silver rank colleagues," Rachel replied carefully, "and the head of Port Authority are in that meeting with the World Council's Committee on Xeno-Relations."

Lafiya's face clouded with indignation. "I still think that stinks. Why didn't the XRC include you?"

Rachel kept her expression pleasant. It was hardly an honor to be summoned to a procedural audit. Especially since the head of the XRC, Councillor Weber, had made an unprecedented and highly publicized trip to the station in person. Some of the councillor's colleagues had recently fallen under investigation, and Rachel suspected the visit was a tactic to divert the media's attention. *Searching for a sacrificial lamb.* "I don't mind."

"But—" Lafiya abruptly seemed to reconsider her intended words and broke off with a sigh. "Shall I have Medica bring up a cot for you?"

"No, thank you. I'm fine. Really." She gestured loosely toward the brewer. "Just need a little coffee."

Lafiya raised her brows. "Coffee?" she repeated in a doubtful tone. She studied Rachel, seeming to take in her determinedly cheerful manner. With a kind of sympathetic tact, Lafiya flicked her gaze to the brewer. "I don't know, Deputy. Wu made the last batch. It's pretty awful."

At the mention of the Safety warden's name, Rachel widened her smile. "Don't worry. I know all about Wu Jackson's coffee."

"Then enjoy." Lafiya grinned and returned to her phone conversation. "I'm back," she said. "Now. About that linkage program. . . ."

The brewer chuckled and purred, going through a reheating cycle. Relieved of the need to converse, Rachel strolled to the low table and found a clean cup. Hoping the caffeine would clear her mental fog, she held her cup under the spout and turned the spigot. An oily, black, and evil-smelling potion flowed out.

Rachel smiled privately. The warden was renowned for three things on the station: his relentlessly playful personality, his unorthodox love affairs, and his blithe lack of expertise with a brewer. *What doesn't kill you,* Wu always said, *will wake you up.*

A modest gallery of crayon drawings hung on the wall over the brewer; artwork contributed by the station's children. A new picture caught Rachel's eye. Blowing on her coffee, more to delay the moment of drinking the stuff than to cool it, she studied the lively rendering.

A woman with an hourglass figure and long eyelashes stood in the picture's center. Dressed in the indigo blue of a Port Authority deputy, she appeared to be offering purple roses to the two aliens who flanked her: a Phi-Nurian and a Rofa. The young artist portrayed the Rofa as a bright orange, minklike creature dressed in green and yellow garb. The Phi-Nurian, looking like a six-legged crab, wore its mandibles flexed in an impossible smile. A neat label in the picture's lower right corner read: " 'When I Grow Up' by Erica Injasuti, Age 10."

Amused and touched by the child's idealism, Rachel slowly shook her head.

Named by early Human explorers, the planet Phi-Nu hosted a species that communicated primarily through olfactory signals. Phi-Nurians required vocoders to speak aloud; and they politely, if somewhat bemusedly, permitted Humans to label them with classical Greek appellations. Easily startled, any Phi-Nurian offered roses could conceivably mistake the action as a threat and fall into an instinctive, self-protective frenzy.

A Rofa would not wait for an offer. If it wanted the roses, it would simply grab them.

Still on the phone, Lafiya made an impatient noise. "Fine," she said tightly. "Go ahead. Ignore me. But I'm telling you, we don't have enough people."

Rachel drifted to the console, continuing to blow on her coffee, and looked at the holographic display. Close enough for the long-range relays to identify, registry information for the three ships appeared on the chart. One of the vessels hailed from Phi-Nu, the other two from Igsha Reey, the Rofan home world. Rachel narrowed her dark eyes in thought.

Though Earth engaged in regular trade with Phi-Nu and Igsha Reey, most of the station's traffic was Human. In-system freighters, supply ships to the mining outposts on Ceres and Pallas, and transports to far-flung science colonies filled the majority of berths. Non-oxygen-breathing aliens, such as the hive-minded Yhiu or the enormous Kamians, did not disembark, and the station accommodated these merchant clients on Dock Six. The Rofan and Phi-Nurians required more exhaustive attention, and Earth Port preferred to contain them on the specially equipped Dock Two. *We're running out of room.*

"I am not exaggerating," Lafiya insisted. "You're not listening to me. It takes six hours to—please, just listen. It takes six hours to activate a berth. We need to—" Her face turned brick red. "Because we have to run checks on all the linkages!"

Leaving Lafiya's work undisturbed, Rachel activated a secondary holographic screen and brought up the listing of Port Authority bulletins. Reviewing the events of the last few hours, she discovered a disturbingly long list of personal injury accidents, including the nasty explosion of a chemical battery. *Damn.* There was also a notice that the welcoming fete for the new surgeon had been postponed for the second time.

A flashing line caught her eye: "Priority message for Rachel Ajmani—confidential." Wondering why it had been posted among the general bulletins, she tapped in her ID and opened it. It was from her mother. Alarmed, Rachel braced herself for news of a medical emergency, but the message was nothing more than a typical letter full of reproach and recrimination. Evidently, Rachel's father had begun dating a younger woman; and, though divorced from the man for over thirty years, her mother was in a seething rage. Sighing, Rachel deleted the message. *Too tired for this.*

She hurriedly skimmed the other bulletins, but found no fresh information on the influx of alien traffic. All arriving ships told the same story: the massive station at Igsha Reey was warning off incoming vessels, claiming some vague life-support emergency.

Rachel lifted the cup to her lips, then lowered it again without drinking. If the Rofan required several days to clamp down the emergency, and if most of the freighters diverted to Earth, then the current crisis would be merely the first few drops of a monsoon. Not only would the station receive an unprecedented amount of traffic, but also a large number of Rofan ships might need to berth at Earth Port for weeks. Given the unpredictable and chronically belligerent nature of the Rofan species, it would be difficult to prevent violence from erupting.

Rachel sighed again. *Really. Too, too tired for this.*

Scowling, Lafiya pulled off her headset and tossed it onto the console. "Stupid!"

Since bad moods were contagious and frequently fatal in an enclosed environment, the station discouraged its personnel from any physical displays of temper. Rachel shaded her voice with light warning. "Trouble in paradise?"

Lafiya glanced at her sidelong. "That was your friend, Andrew, in Docking Control. Long-range relays just picked up some new arrivals."

Rachel winced inwardly. "How many fell out of the barrel?"

"Ten." Lafiya spoke in a flat tone. "Ten more."

Rachel wished she also had something to throw. She speculatively regarded her cup of coffee, thinking of the satisfying mess it would make. "Hmm."

Lafiya jumped up from her chair and stalked to the brewer. "And, of course, Docking Control issued approach instructions. It's stupid."

"Tempting as it is," Rachel pointed out, "we can hardly turn them away."

"Why not?"

Rachel remembered that Lafiya had a lot of Isleño in her, a fiery mix of bloodlines that resulted from a massive dislocation of various Latin and Celtic populations during the Last War. "Well, they can't all be Rofan. Some are undoubtedly from Earth."

"Keep telling yourself that, Deputy."

"And besides, it would cause us an incredible amount of long-term inconvenience." Keeping her face straight, Rachel nodded toward the holographic chart. "All those freighters would run out of fuel, and their crews would die. Just think of the debris in our approach lanes."

Lafiya grunted and poured coffee for herself. "Just think of the debris on Dock Two when ten ships full of Rofan pirates—"

An indicator light on the operations console flashed red. Rachel picked up the headset. "Take a break," she told Lafiya. "I'll get this." She slipped the phone over her ear and tapped the line open. "Ops. This is Deputy Ajmani."

"Oh. Well—" The young man on the other end sounded flustered. "Deputy Ajmani, I wasn't—" He cleared his throat. "This is Carl Stein, on the loading gantry."

Rachel looked out the window. Two massive towers joined by a steel framework bridge, the gantry spanned the dock, riding overhead along a set of parallel tracks. The cagelike operator's cab perched on top of the bridge, forty feet above the floor. Rachel noticed that the main crane hung motionless, a pallet of shipping canisters in its grapple. "Hello, Carl," she said. "Stuck again?"

"Well," he confessed, "yes. But I—"

He was new, she recalled, still fresh from a big commercial operation on the Moon and no doubt accustomed to state-of-the-art equipment. "Try nudging the drive train into neutral while very slowly engaging the taxi belt."

"I've already tried that, Deputy. It won't—"

"Very . . . slowly," Rachel repeated. "Remember you're on Earth Port Station, we have a very small budget, and so everything here is an antique. That gantry could be your great grandmother."

At the brewer, Lafiya snorted derisively.

Carl's voice went up in pitch. "But, Deputy, it's not working. I'm trying, but it won't—"

"Yes, it will." Rachel cautiously tasted her coffee and found it unbelievably brackish. *Wu, my friend, you've surpassed yourself.* "Do it slowly. You ought to be able to feel when it kicks over."

"But—" The crane jerked. Carl's tone turned jubilant. "Hey, it worked! Thanks, Deputy."

"You're welcome," she said. "Be safe." She cut the connection and pulled off the headset.

Lafiya sauntered back to the console. "I hear the Kamians have developed some new system for moving cargo." Returning to her chair, she took the phone from Rachel. "Uses gravity fields or molecular restructuring or something."

Rachel raised her brows. "Do tell." The Kamians were sticklike creatures, ten times the size of an adult Human, but so fragile they required a zero gravity environment. Inveterate gadgeteers, and unabashedly fascinated by their tiny neighbors, Kamians constantly offered new technical products to the unreceptive natives of Earth. "Is this anything like those bizarre communications systems they're always pestering us to try? Miniature phones clipped to our ears like jewelry? Microscopic computers planted in our brains?"

Lafiya grinned. "Some of their ideas make sense. Like those free-floating surveillance cameras. We could make Dock Two a lot more secure with a few of those flying eyeballs zooming around."

"Oh, sure." Rachel waved to the air beside the holographic chart. "We could have the images piped in here. Just a couple more things for you to watch. Just a little extra work, but nothing you can't handle."

Lafiya flung out her hands in surrender. "No, no!" she laughingly protested. "I take it back. The cameras are a rotten idea."

Wishing to encourage the return of Lafiya's good humor, Rachel eased the topic in a different direction. "They're using them on Pallas, aren't they? To shoot that real-life drama?"

Over the past decade, in an effort to compete for viewers, vid broadcast companies had begun to record the events of everyday life aboard science and mining colonies. Not only did these programs glamorize difficult and dangerous occupations in space, they made celebrities of ordinary technicians and miners.

"That's the worst part of working this double shift." Lafiya made a woeful face. "I'm missing the latest episode."

Rachel smiled. "Oh? Is it getting good?"

"It's pretty juicy. I think today's the day that Dan will finally tell Lars about his fling with Natalie."

Rachel looked down into her coffee cup, wondering if Dan, Lars, and Natalie realized just how deeply this would affect the rest of their lives. A few years earlier, during a real-life drama set aboard Earth Port Station, Rachel had found herself the center of worldwide attention. The notoriety still lingered, making her infrequent furloughs to Earth awkward and uncomfortable. "Hmm."

"Dan and Lars are so cute together, I hope they don't break up because of—" Lafiya abruptly seemed to focus on a dockside occurrence. "Oh, great."

Rachel turned to look. About fifty feet from the booth, a cluster of Phi-Nurians surrounded a couple of Safety staffers.

The Phi-Nurians scuttled in circles around the two Humans, flexing their claws in obvious agitation. Dressed in bright blue and green uniforms, the staffers shifted to put their backs together. One was a blond young man, the other a petite woman with her dark hair done up in short braids. Rachel recognized neither, which was strange; and she could not recall hearing of new Safety people.

Lafiya breathed a curse. "Glance away for half a second. . . ." She tapped in a code for her headset. "Safety? This is Dock Two Ops. Got a situation at berth 14-B. Request additional staff to that area."

Out on the dock, more Phi-Nurians scuttled from the access tube of their ship to join the first group. A throng of Rofan crew members at the next berth stopped unloading pallets and shifted closer to watch. Their ears pricked forward, and they sinuously bobbed their heads in excited pleasure. Rather than attempting to defuse the tension, the two staffers drew their guns.

Rachel inhaled in a sharp hiss. Though the weapons, known as "stingers," inflicted only a nonlethal electric shock, Wu authorized very few of his people to carry them.

Most of his staffers were trained specialists, some with degrees in xeno-psychology, and he preferred that they rely upon wit and diplomacy to maintain control in difficult situations. By drawing their stingers, the two staffers broke every procedure in the manual.

"Thank you, Safety. Will relay immediately." Lafiya plugged in a new code, her expression sour. "Priority one broadcast to all cargo techs, Safety advisory: Section B closed until further notice, place all work orders for that area on standby. Relay and confirm, please." Across her board, amber indicator lights began to glow one by one. On the holographic docking chart, the restricted section turned a flashing red-orange.

Four more staffers converged on the area. Rachel recognized them as two sets of partners: Rosita and Benjy, Chen and Modesto. They moved in a casual manner, as if out for a stroll. As they approached, the unknown staffers bolted, breaking through the surrounding Phi-Nurians and disappearing down an interior cargo ramp.

"Damn!" Rachel launched herself toward the door.

"Deputy, wait!" Lafiya called after her. "Don't—!"

The door sealed behind Rachel, cutting off Lafiya's voice. Outside the booth, a long air lock nicknamed the "front porch" stretched in both directions. To the right, it led to a set of lifts that ran up to Safety's headquarters. She turned left, passed through another air lock, and stepped onto Dock Two.

Cold, damp air enveloped Rachel, stinging her nose with the odor of plastics and hot metal. Cargo hoists squealed, and a tractor rumbled by, pulling a string of empty carts. Following a pathway demarcated in black and white, Rachel started toward the trouble. She knew the staffers were more than capable of handling the problem; but with the meddling XRC aboard, she wanted to be in a position to take responsibility should events go awry.

Berths filled both walls of the dock. The large freighters enjoyed access hatches set at floor level. The station relegated smaller vessels to higher berths serviced by a system of ladders and catwalks. Frantic crews of technicians worked on every level, trying to activate berths that had not been occupied for years.

As Rachel approached 14-B, one of the Phi-Nurians

raised its synthesized voice. "Outrage!" Stacked cargo pallets interrupted her view, but she heard the normally breathless quality of its species' vocoder transmission dissolve into a harsh buzz. "Intolerable outrage!"

While attempting to maintain dignity, Rachel lengthened her free-swinging stride. Phi-Nurians were timid beings, but they reacted violently when frightened. It was instinct, the Phi-Nurians maintained, an involuntary reaction that often caused them great dismay.

There had been some discussion within the World Council of breaking ties with Phi-Nu. But such a shortsighted action would not only destroy the trade-based economy of Phi-Nu, it would leave Earth without a close ally in the Galactic Trade Association.

Benjy's velvety baritone held no note of uneasiness. "Describe what happened, Captain Allos. I'll make a full report."

"Threats!" Allos buzzed. "Violence to my egg-mates!"

"Please be specific, honorable Captain. Who threatened you?"

Rachel paused beside a stack of plastic crates and studied the scene. In the loading area in front of an access tube, Benjy and Rosita faced a contingent of ten Phi-Nurians. Chen and Modesto nonchalantly approached the excited Rofan, several of whom had climbed the shoulder-high barricades that separated the loading areas.

Allos stood upright on its lower set of limbs, which was a typical response to perceived danger. "Must protect eggmates!" It erratically waved its upper and middle set of limbs. "Outrage!"

Heart pounding, Rachel held her breath. It was important for Benjy to keep Allos' rational mind engaged, to keep requesting concrete information, or the Phi-Nurian would fall into a frenzy and its primitive "under-mind" would gain control. The fact that its vocoder produced short, declarative bursts was a bad sign.

Benjy's expression remained implacably calm, and his arms hung at his sides in a nonthreatening manner. "At what time did this outrage occur, Captain?"

The Phi-Nurian hesitated, claws still flexing, but answered in a less strident tone. "Moments ago."

Rachel released her pent-up breath. *Good job, Benjy.*

She reached for the phone in her pocket, and only then realized that she still carried her coffee. *Stupid, stupid, stupid!* Fingers trembling, she carefully set the cup down on the crate beside her.

Balancing on top of the barricade, a Rofa hissed and chittered, its beady eyes full of malice. "Human," it called to Benjy, "fight the stinky thing! Fight!"

Evidently reacting to the taunt, one of the Phi-Nurians whirled toward the Rofa and blundered against a stack of loaded pallets. The stack rocked, and three canisters tumbled to the floor, booming as they landed.

All ten of the Phi-Nurians reared up, madly flexing their clawed upper limbs. Some of them passed fist-sized nodules of dung, and an acrid stink cut the air.

"Kill!" Allos buzzed. It lurched toward Benjy, weaving to bring him into better focus with its single eyepad, snatching at him with all four upper limbs. "Kill!"

Rachel choked back a cry of warning and clenched her fists. To break through the Phi-Nurian's frenzy, Benjy would need to somehow offer a larger threat that would reengage Allos' intellect.

Benjy deftly avoided the Phi-Nurian's grasp, dodging around cargo containers, and kept up a steady stream of talk. "You can't win this fight." His voice stayed even and reasonable. "All I have to do is call for more help, and then you'll be outnumbered. Be wise, honorable Captain."

"Kill!" Allos buzzed. Its mandibles clacked in excitement. "I shall kill!"

Crowding against the barricade, the Rofan crew screeched in their native tongue and gestured invitingly at the berserk Phi-Nurians. One Rofa, dressed in layers of pink and orange, kept a hand on something concealed in its sash. It was not a gun, Rachel knew, for the Rofan disdained projectile weapons as cowardly. *A knife.*

The possibility of a riot loomed in her mind. Feeling thick-witted, she bit her bottom lip. *Get a grip.* Sweat rolled down her sides beneath her uniform. Councillor Weber and the XRC would roast the staffers unless she could successfully intervene. The event might also reignite the debate over breaking ties with Phi-Nu. *Think!*

A Phi-Nurian careened in her direction, claws snapping. Rachel scrambled from her open position and crouched behind a parked tractor. Breathing in gasps, she listened for pursuit. The XRC was not the only problem. Wu would never let her hear the end of this. He would make up one of his annoying little songs about her current escapade and teach it to the station's children. Hands shaking, she pulled out her phone and keyed Safety.

"Checkpoint. This is Wu."

As usual, he seemed buoyantly cheerful. She felt her brain begin to work again at the sound of his voice. "This is Rachel. The situation on Dock Two is deteriorating. Send all available staffers."

"Already done. Ops called."

"Thank God."

"Thank God for Lafiya DuChamp," Wu purred. "And while on your knees, take time to remember that the Rofan at berth 15 are new to Earth Port—never docked here before. They might not recognize the exalted status of a silver rank deputy, so kindly remove your esteemed self from Section B."

"Can't." Rachel cut the connection and pocketed her phone.

Rosita shouted: "Benjy! Behind you!"

The distinctive thunder of falling cargo containers shook the deck plates.

"Kill!" a Phi-Nurian rasped. "Kill, kill, kill!"

Rachel peered around the tractor's metal chassis. Benjy lay pinned beneath a heavy canister. Captain Allos reared over him in triumph, claws flexing.

"Damn!" Rachel vaulted onto the tractor and started it up. The powerful engine thrummed into life beneath her feet. She seized the steering stick and swung the vehicle onto the loading area, leaning into the turn.

In the center of the fracas, Rosita and Chen pushed themselves between their helpless colleague and the attacking Captain Allos. Modesto desperately heaved at the canister on Benjy. Brandishing cargo hooks and crowbars, the Rofan swarmed over the barricade.

Heart in her mouth, Rachel roared toward the assembly at full speed.

For a second, the Humans, Rofan, and Phi-Nurians stood frozen in a tableau of shock. Then the Rofan scattered, a few scrambling up the sides of stacked pallets. Captain

Allos and its cohort turned as a group and scuttled toward the access tube of their ship.

Swooping past the staffers, Rachel stomped on the horn pedal. It blared like a trumpet. The Phi-Nurians collided at the tube's portal in a tangle of clawed limbs, each scrabbling to save itself. She aimed the tractor straight at them. With a final frantic heave, the last Phi-Nurian scrambled inside. The access hatch slammed shut.

Rachel jerked the tractor into a sharp turn to avoid smashing against the hatch and cut the engine. Not allowing herself to feel anything but rage, she jumped from the vehicle before it stopped rolling, stormed past the staffers, and charged the group of staring Rofan.

"You!" Rachel flung her arm in an imperious sweep, her long hair flying with the violent motion. "Return to your ship!"

A few Rofan hunched their narrow shoulders in submission and backed away, but most held their ground, their eyes bright with challenge.

Rachel continued toward them, banishing any thought of fear. The Rofan could smell it. She pitched her voice to a deep bellow capable of cutting through the deafening racket of the main gantry. "Now!"

The single word echoed and reechoed over the dock. More Rofan lowered their heads and uneasily slunk back. The one in pink and orange stood firm. "I shall taste of your blood," it snarled.

The threat was a standard opening for the ritual exchange of insults preceding a duel. Rachel marched directly up to the Rofa until they stood just inches apart. "I'm from Port Authority. Are you the captain of this ship?"

The Rofa's small ears flicked flat. "I shall feast upon your guts."

"If you don't answer my question, I'll take away your docking bonus." Refusing to dwell upon the knife in its sash, Rachel stoked her anger, knowing the Rofa could smell that as well as fear. She put her hands on her hips, scowling. "And if you threaten me again, I'll confiscate your cargo."

The Rofa tilted its head, and its flat, triangular face displayed an almost Human surprise. Then it swept its hand away from its belt in the manner of a dismissive shrug. "I am Captain Akya."

"I am Deputy Ajmani. Remember my name, because if you or your crew interfere again with the safe operation of this dock, I will personally order your ship off the station."

Akya's tone was scornful. "Big talk."

"I'm not bluffing." Rachel pointed at the captain's nose, knowing the Rofan considered the gesture offensive, and punctuated her words with repeated stabs of her finger. "You go to your ship. You study Earth Port's regulations and learn them like the names of your kin. You teach them to your crew."

Akya's eyes burned with undisguised menace. "You insult me."

"I'll do a lot more than that, if you make trouble," she promised. "Ask other Rofan captains about Deputy Ajmani, and they'll tell you that I mean what I say." Rachel's anger attempted to sweep away her self-control, and she fought to rein it in. "Now. Return to your ship."

Akya growled deep in its throat, but took a half step back. "Deputy Aja-mani. I shall not forget this."

"Better not."

It abruptly turned and swaggered away. Screeching to its crew, it waved them all toward their access hatch. Breathing hard, Rachel watched until they disappeared inside.

Behind her, Wu spoke brightly: "Well, isn't this nice? Now we're all good friends."

Rachel slowly turned.

In his fifties, cherubic, and crowned with a mop of black hair, Wu regarded her with a sunny smile. "Good morning, Rachel. I believe this is yours?" He handed her a cup of coffee. "I found it on that crate over there. We mustn't leave this stuff unattended, you know. The last thing we need is a dock full of hyper-caffeinated Rofan."

Suddenly numb, Rachel stared at the cup of cold coffee, then looked past Wu to Benjy. Surrounded by a ring of concerned-looking staffers, he sat on the floor, holding his side. "Benjy, are you all right?"

"I'm fine." His expression was calm, his deep voice reassuring. "It just knocked the wind out of me."

His partner, Rosita, crouched beside him with her arm

around his shoulders, her face hard with worry. "We'd better go to Medica," she told Wu. "He may have some broken ribs."

"No," Benjy said.

"Yes," Wu contradicted in an enthusiastic tone. "I hear the new surgeon is very pretty."

The tension drained out of Rachel, and she began to shake. Coffee slopped over her fingers. "Wu—"

"Oops," he said. "Sorry. Let me take that." He relieved her of the cup.

Rachel struggled to collect her thoughts. "I have a complaint to make against two of your staffers."

Benjy and his colleagues exchanged knowing glances.

Wu raised his brows. "Oh?" He took Rachel's elbow and steered her in the direction of the operations booth. "Why don't you tell me about it while we walk?" He looked back at the staffers. "Rosita, please take Benjy to Medica. If he resists, shoot him."

Benjy made a noise of protest. "But I—"

Wu gave no sign he heard. "Chen, please notify Ops that the advisory is lifted. The rest of you, make sure the fire is well and truly out."

Rachel yanked her arm from his grasp. "I'm serious, Wu. I don't know who they are, but they pulled stingers on the Phi-Nurians. Once Captain Allos calms down and thinks the whole thing through, we may have a lawsuit on our hands."

"I'm serious, too, Rachel." He motioned to the black-and-white walkway. "If you please?"

Sighing, she started toward the Ops booth with him.

After a few rolling steps, Wu looked around, then spoke under his breath. "We have two unknowns aboard the station, posing as staffers."

His words made no immediate sense to Rachel. "Pardon?"

"Impostors. Posing as staffers." A reach-fork hummed past. Wu smiled and waved at the driver. "I don't know who they are, and I don't know why they're engaging in this masquerade. But until I apprehend them, I'm trying to keep news of their existence off official channels. Can you imagine how our valued merchant clients would react, if they caught wind of this?"

Rachel's stomach went cold. The aliens might refuse to cooperate with any of the staffers, claiming they did not know if they dealt with authorized personnel. "We'd have chaos."

"Unparalleled," Wu agreed. "So we can't publicly disavow their actions."

"But—then we're liable!"

"Oh, yes. Isn't it fun?"

Rachel blew out her cheeks and tried to think the problem through. "How did they get aboard?"

"I'd rather not say."

She stopped in her tracks and glared at him. "Wu—"

"But I'm not sure," he protested. "I may be wrong."

"Tell me."

Wu glanced around again, then casually pressed his fingertips against his upper lip and spoke behind the cover of his hand. "It appears they arrived with the Xeno-Relations Committee."

Rachel blinked. "Why would the XRC bring a couple of miscreants with them?"

Wu shrugged and started walking again. "I don't know. Why would they show up for a surprise audit and demand the attention of almost all ranking officials, even though the station is facing one of the most difficult crises in its history?"

Rachel reflected upon the full implications of his question. "Because they're idiots?"

"I actually hope that's true." Wu took a swallow of cold coffee. "Mm. Yummy."

Rachel smiled grimly. "Maybe I'd better have a talk with Councillor Weber."

"Please don't."

"But—"

Wu paused and gently clasped her shoulder. "Deputy Ajmani, listen to me." He dropped his voice to a whisper. "Please . . . be careful. Watch and wait."

She drew a breath to argue, but something in his eyes stopped her.

"Please?" Wu repeated. "Take my advice, just this once?"

The moment lengthened. Rachel's tired mind grappled with political maneuverings, World Council duplicity, and how her dearest friend hid his misgivings behind a show of breezy good cheer.

Watch and wait.

Rachel released her breath with a sigh. "Very well."

"Thank you." The habitual smile returned to Wu's face. He dropped his hand from her shoulder and motioned to the end of the dock. "Now, let's get to the Ops booth, where it's warm. I'll make some fresh, hot coffee. Just for you."

Still inwardly reeling, Rachel resumed her walk beside him, following the safety grid. She wondered what else he knew and, in an unfamiliar and unwelcome flash of suspicion, what else he was hiding.

"Coffee?" Rachel carefully copied his playful tone, telling herself that the deepening cold in her gut was only the lapse of adrenaline. "Honorable Warden, you make the worst coffee in the known galaxy!"

Wu's grin turned wicked. "What doesn't kill you," he told her, "will wake you up."

CHAPTER FOUR

RACHEL RUBBED the back of her neck and struggled to remain mentally focused. It had been four long hours since her last cup of coffee with Wu. *Eight hours to go.*

In contrast to the cold and mechanized lower level where the actual exchange of cargo took place, the upper level of Dock Two extended civilized amenities more conducive to business negotiations: warmth, soft light, and bubbling fountains. Access hatches lined the walls, and the stalls for licensed arbitrators stood in a row down the center of the richly tiled floor.

At the moment, Rachel stood in the newest stall, a confection of brass, polished wood, and stained glass. Captain Deiras crouched beside her. One of Earth Port's regular merchant clients, the Phi-Nurian displayed remarkable calm for a member of its excitable species. It clutched a calculator in one clawed hand and a printout of weight specs in the other.

The accused, an arbitrator named Sanderson, lolled in his upholstered chair and spoke in a round tone of immaterial percentages.

Rachel's phone chimed. She stifled a sigh. "Pardon me." She pulled the handset from her pocket and raised it to her ear. "Deputy Ajmani."

"It's Kepler." The coordinator of Safety Checkpoint sounded anxious. "Rachel, I just got word that Captain

Akya is out on the upper level of Dock Two, looking for you."

Kepler Thai was not a man to flinch at imaginary threats. *Marvelous.* "Thank you, Safety," Rachel replied formally. "I'll take that under advisement."

Kepler continued. "I'm pulling a staffer off . . . the special project . . . to send your way."

It took Rachel a few seconds to grasp his meaning. Wu evidently was maintaining the communications blanket on the impostors, and he had also placed all available staffers on the hunt for them. "Thank you, Safety," Rachel said, "but that's unnecessary."

"Rachel, please—"

She spoke gently: "Be safe." Resisting the urge to look over her shoulder for the irate Captain Akya, she pocketed her phone and returned her attention to the arbitrator. "Please repeat that."

Sanderson stared at her reproachfully, fair brows rising. "I said the margin is immaterial, Deputy. Due to a system error, we calculated the tonnage to nine decimal places."

Captain Deiras clicked its middle set of claws. "Galactic Trade Association guidelines dictate that all percentages must be figured to ten decimal places." It brandished the printout like a weapon. "The creature admits its dishonesty."

Sanderson gave a bark of laughter. "Dishonesty? It was a mistake!"

"Brigand! Pirate!"

"It's an immaterial amount!"

Rachel kept her expression neutral. Though Sanderson's arbitration firm had been in business for merely a fortnight, it had already incurred a warning from the head of Port Authority. "An immaterial amount in whose favor?"

Sanderson's face darkened with a flush of red. "Now, hold on, Deputy. What are you suggesting?"

Rachel permitted herself a slight frown. "I suggest nothing. You need to—" Her phone chimed. She bit off her intended words. "Excuse me." She pulled the handset from her pocket and answered it. "Deputy Ajmani."

Port Authority's computer clicked as it verified her identity, then it spoke in a cool, genderless voice: "Priority message recorded, log time delta-five-three-two, from inbound Kamian freighter 2624 to Deputy Rachel Ajmani."

Rachel shivered. She had no idea why one of the immense aliens would choose to contact her personally. The computer clicked off. A whirring sound filled the silence, then the soft noise shaped itself into the filtered whisper of a Kamian vocoder. "'I grasp the stars and take the light to heart.'" The computer clicked on. "Transmission complete. Awaiting instructions."

Baffled, Rachel squinted in thought. The message sounded vaguely familiar, like the first line of an old poem. "File message in Port Authority log and my personal log." She returned the phone to her pocket and mentally groped for the thread of her argument with the arbitrator. "Margin of error."

Sanderson sputtered: "A tiny fraction of nothing!"

"But in your favor?"

"I'm telling you, it's immaterial!"

Rachel regarded the man narrowly. "Not when applied to tons of raw ore. Not when accrued over a standard business year."

"But—!"

Rachel's phone chimed.

Sanderson gestured impatiently. "Ignore it."

Allowing her frown to deepen, Rachel pulled the phone from her pocket again. "I'm on duty," she reminded him, then answered the call. "Deputy Ajmani."

A woman spoke in an imperious tone. "Rachel?"

"Speaking."

"Rachel? Is that you?"

"Yes, this is—" Then Rachel recognized her mother's voice. The minimal lag time in transmission indicated a hyper-light link, which made it an extremely expensive call from Earth, but her mother never counted the cost when it came to having her own way. A series of conflicting emotions battled for supremacy within Rachel. Exasperation won, but mindful of Sanderson and Deiras, she managed to keep it out of her voice. "Yes."

"Well, you could have said so." Her mother said in a scalding tone. "I suppose you're going to tell me that you're busy with something terribly important."

Rachel clenched her jaw. "Yes."

"What could be more important than calling your own mother?" She didn't wait for a reply. "I wish my dear Sasha were still with me. He always had time to talk, and he had a much busier schedule than you."

Pain eclipsed Rachel's irritation. Her older brother, Sasha, had always been quick to respond to their parents' demands, taking their every criticism deeply to heart. To earn their praise, he had pushed himself to the limits of his physical endurance. The autopsy following his fatal car accident revealed high levels of amphetamines and euphorics in his blood. It had been over ten years since his death, and Rachel missed him intensely. "I can't talk now."

"You can *never* talk, can you? Someday, I'll be gone, and you'll wish you—"

Shaking with rage, not trusting herself to speak, Rachel cut the connection.

Sanderson climbed out of his chair and folded his arms. "Could we finish this business without further interruptions? Please?"

Trying to hide her agitation, Rachel carefully pocketed her phone. "Very well, I'll make it quick." She met his gaze. "You will correct the percentage calculation in your system, so this problem won't occur again."

"I've already taken steps to ensure that—"

Rachel flashed up a hand. "And you will make restitution to Captain Deiras in the amount of the error margin."

Sanderson's pale eyes glinted, but he smiled broadly. "Of course, Deputy. But you *do* understand that the margin is immaterial?"

Rachel hardened her voice. "Then you won't mind paying it."

Sanderson broke into bluff laughter. "Anything to keep the Port Authority happy."

Rachel paused, weighing the man's reaction, and recalled that his business already had a warning on file. "You will also pay a fine. Five percent of the original invoice, with the money to reimburse Captain Deiras for time and aggravation."

Sanderson turned bright red and made a choking noise. "A fine? But it was a mistake!"

Rachel looked at the Phi-Nurian. "Captain Deiras, do you believe the judgment to be fair and reasonable?"

"Most satisfactory," Deiras said. It bowed, making a concession to the Human form of courtesy. "Honorable Deputy."

Rachel bowed in return. "Honorable Captain Deiras." She continued speaking to the Phi-Nurian, but flicked her attention to the arbitrator, measuring the effect of her words. "Port Authority shares your dismay over this incident, Captain. If we find that this firm does not fully comply with my judgment, we shall file a new complaint on your behalf and take disciplinary measures."

The tone of Deiras' vocoder transmission turned caressing, and it bowed again. "Honorable Deputy Ajmani."

Breathing hard, verging on the apoplectic, Sanderson glared at her. "You can't do this."

"I can."

"You don't have the authority."

"I do. In fact, I can cancel your license now."

"You—" Sanderson broke off with an audible swallow. His voice took on an oily friendliness. "I'm sorry if I seem on edge, Deputy. But you can understand why I'm upset about paying a fine, can't you? It was an honest mistake."

"Then pay an honest penalty." Battling against her own rising temper, Rachel bowed curtly to the arbitrator, turned, and stalked away, heading for the lift. *Avaricious fool. Expecting me to let him off easy. And at a client's expense.*

Rachel took deep, calming breaths as she walked. She passed a whispering fountain of smooth river stones that occupied a spot between two arbitrators' stalls. Phi-Nurians clustered in and around it, clearly enjoying the damp air. Water polished their usually dull carapaces, revealing subtle shadings in the mottled hues of green and brown.

The sight eased some of Rachel's anger, and she slowed her pace. Farther along the dock, she spotted three Rofan crouched near an entry hatch. They hissed at each other, ostensibly arguing in their own language, but they also passed a fresh peach among themselves, displaying the typical Rofan blend of hostility and camaraderie. Juice dripped from their hands and muzzles, and their heads bobbed with enjoyment.

Rachel smiled privately. If Earth Port could keep the situation under control, it stood to gain a great deal from the current crisis. Besides a broader client base, there would be increased goodwill and understanding, perhaps mutual cultural exchange programs.

I grasp the stars and take the light to heart. In her exhaustion, Rachel almost spoke the words aloud. She pulled out her phone, keyed into the station's computer, and sent an inquiry regarding the Kamians' message. After a disconcertingly long search, the computer informed her that it was a quote from a work by Prudence Clarke, one of the first experimenters of the "flight."

Rachel clicked off and pocketed her phone. From her school days, she recalled that a flight was a poetic form that described a moment of revelation or private ecstasy by cataloging evocative details. "Laundry lists," one of Rachel's teachers had called them. *I grasp the stars and take the light to heart.*

Rachel had no idea what Human poetry would mean to a Kamian. The enormous aliens tended to be quite direct in their communication, and their messages usually sounded more like recipes than sonnets. At any rate, to her recollection, they had never quoted a text as obscure as Prudence Clarke. Rachel resolved to consult the xenological indexes before the inbound freighter docked.

Her phone chimed.

The muscles in Rachel's shoulders clenched. For a long moment, she thought about not answering; it had to be her mother. The phone chimed again. She pulled it out, clicked it on, and said without warmth: "Ajmani."

Lafiya spoke hesitantly. "Deputy. Sorry if I'm interrupting anything important, but I thought you ought to know right away. Mid-range relays picked up IDs on those ten incoming ships."

Suddenly alert, Rachel felt her hands go cold. "And?"

"Four of them are ours. Two are from Yhiu. Two from Phi-Nu. One Igsha Reey. One Kam."

It could have been much worse. "Excellent."

Lafiya's tone became more circumspect. "That's the good news, Deputy. Bad news is that long-range relays have picked up another sixteen ships."

Rachel could scarcely draw a breath. "Sixteen?"

Lafiya sounded apologetic. "Just thought you ought to know. Docking Control posted it to your message board, but I was afraid you wouldn't find time to check."

"Thank you," Rachel said numbly. "Be safe." She put the phone away and started walking again, trying to convince herself that sixteen incoming ships did not necessarily signal disaster.

Someone fell into step beside her. "Found you."

Rachel thought the voice seemed vaguely familiar. She glanced in its direction and discovered Captain Akya.

The Rofa still wore its layers of pink and orange tunics, and perhaps it still hid a knife in its sash; but its ears were up, and its manner seemed peculiarly relaxed and companionable. "I am studying Earth Port regulations, as you directed."

Surprise eclipsed the first stirring of fear, and Rachel paused. *As I—?* She abruptly remembered telling Akya to learn the station's rules and guidelines like the names of its kin. Only a Rofa would take such a figure of speech literally. "Good."

"Confusing, at first. But I think I now begin to understand."

Rachel wondered what the Rofa planned to do. "Yes?"

Akya tilted its head in a considering fashion. "Humans do not fight with knives. They fight with words."

Prepared for threats, Rachel fumbled to recalibrate her thoughts. "We prefer not to fight at all, but to cooperate."

Akya flicked its fingers in disparagement. "Your species loves to fight, Deputy Aja-mani."

"We love to argue. Not the same thing."

"Words." The Rofa seemed to think it had scored a point. "You, yourself, are a *gukka* with words."

Rachel began to deny it, then had to admit that the comparison was not only apt, but that it also pleased her. "Thank you, honorable Captain. But, unlike a *gukka*, I don't fight for myself or my own honor."

Akya's small ears flashed back in a sign of confusion. "No?"

"I'm a government official, sworn to uphold the law."

Akya seemed to meditate upon her reply, its round eyes narrowing in thought. "Human law is strange. But taking an oath? That, I understand."

Rachel's phone chimed. "Excuse me, honorable Captain." Sighing, she pulled it out and answered it. "Deputy Ajmani."

Wu's tone was bantering. "What's this I hear about you marrying a Rofa?"

Rachel stifled another sigh, knowing that Wu was attempting to tease her into accepting help. A staffer arriving as a bodyguard at this moment, however, would only send the wrong message. "Is this important?"

"My spies tell me that Akya found you. Is it true that you've charmed the honorable captain's pants off?"

Rachel scowled. "I'm hanging up now."

"Just remember—in bed, Rofan bite."

"No one knows that better than you," Rachel replied crisply. She clicked off and returned the phone to her pocket. "Sorry for the interruption, Captain. You were saying?"

Akya's attention appeared fixed upon her pocket. "Your communicator is surely an antique."

Rachel blinked at the sudden change of topic. "Yes. Quite a bit of the equipment on Earth Port Station is antique."

Akya gazed at her, furrowing its brow in an almost Human expression of bafflement. "Why?"

Rachel drew a breath, then held it, wondering where to begin.

In spite of complaints about budgetary restrictions, most station personnel voted against replacing outdated equipment. It was more than a distrust inherited from the survivors of the Last War, a deep-seated cultural suspicion of technology for its own sake; and it was more than a frugal sense of conservation, a reluctance to squander the Earth's precious resources. She did not suppose the Rofan had a word to express sentimental attachment.

"Humans like antiques," Rachel said finally. "We enjoy surrounding ourselves with things that remind us of our history."

Akya tucked in its chin, staring at her.

"And it's not just objects. We also practice ancient customs." Rachel almost launched into a description of the Freeholds, historic preserves where the lifestyle had not changed since the end of the Last War. Freeholders worshiped their ancestors, exercised ritual cannibalism, and engaged in group marriages. Reminding herself to keep it simple, she returned to the previous topic. "And our laws have extremely ancient origins, from before the written word, handed down orally."

Akya appeared to be deep in thought for a long moment. "And you, Deputy Aja-mani—" It peered at her, its little ears pricked forward. "—you are sworn to uphold this law? This great burden of uncounted years?"

So strange to consider it in that light. "Yes, honorable Captain, I am."

Akya hunched its shoulders somewhat, in a mildly submissive manner. "I must study further."

Rachel spread her hands. "Call me if you have more questions."

Akya threw her a dubious glance and walked off without another word.

Closing her eyes, Rachel swayed a bit, suddenly exhausted since nothing claimed her attention. *So tired. Need coffee.*

A man with a deep voice spoke. "Deputy Ajmani?"

Blinking, she raised her head and discovered staffer Benjy Oso gazing down at her in concern. "Benjy?" Wu never would have sent an injured staffer onto the dock. "What are you doing here?" And then she realized how that might sound. "I mean, are you all right? Shouldn't you be in Medica?"

Benjy nodded in deference to her rank and replied somewhat formally. "I am well, Deputy. Thank you for asking."

Rachel could scarcely credit Benjy's rapid recovery. "I take it, then, that the canister didn't crack any ribs."

Benjy smiled, but his smile was also formal. "I was fortunate in the extent of my injuries. I'm not yet ready for regular work, but I imagine that accompanying you for a stroll on the dock would qualify as light duty."

Rachel slowly continued toward the lift, maneuvering through the groups of aliens and Humans wrangling business agreements. He must, she realized, have heard about her refusal of protection from Captain Akya, and had taken it upon himself to assure her safety. "And I imagine," she said, "that coming with me to cadge a cup of coffee from the Ops booth would qualify as even lighter duty."

Benjy replied in a serious tone: "Unless Warden Jackson made the coffee."

Rachel grinned, then had to fight the urge to laugh. In her current state of mind it could only too easily develop into hysterical giggles. "So," she said. "How was the new surgeon? As young and beautiful as everyone says?"

Benjy frowned a bit. "Doctor DeFlora is young, certainly, but he seems to have Medica's staff well in hand. A quite . . . dynamic . . . personality."

Rachel raised one brow. "Oh, really?"

"And he's a competent surgeon. I had five broken ribs, and it took him less than an hour to weld them."

"Broken?" Rachel stopped in her tracks and stared up at Benjy. "Shouldn't you go lie down? Give them a chance to set solid?"

Benjy regarded her calmly. "I did lie down."

"For what? Ten minutes?"

"Deputy, we're too short on personnel for me to take time off."

Rachel snorted. "If you incapacitate yourself, Staffer Oso, the warden will have your head in a basket."

A few yards away, near the entry hatch of a ship, a young man stood conversing with two Rofan. He wore the traditional garb of the Northern Freeholds, which consisted of a patchwork kimono tucked into rugged canvas trousers, a collection of scarves around his neck, and a serapelike cloak over one shoulder.

Rachel's scalp prickled. "That's odd," she murmured. "I was just thinking about Freeholders."

Benjy made a polite noise.

Then Rachel realized how peculiar she must sound. *Sorry, Benjy. Humor me.*

Abruptly, the Freeholder whirled and looked straight at Rachel. His eyes were copper-colored, bright with intellect.

Rachel experienced a sudden shock, like that of recognition. She stopped short and stared at him, only distantly aware that Benjy spoke.

The stranger stared back. His hair was long, stained an

unnatural shade of orange, and it framed his narrow face with a mass of unruly curls.

Rachel found she could not glance away, could not shake the feeling that she knew him.

The Freeholder took leave of the two aliens, dismissing them with an arrogant flick of his long fingers that was purely Rofan, and sauntered toward Rachel.

Benjy tapped Rachel's shoulder. "Deputy?" He sounded as if he had been trying to get her attention for some moments. "Excuse me? Deputy?"

Rachel jerked to self-awareness. "Sorry." She looked at Benjy, noted that he appeared uneasy. "What's the matter?"

Benjy cleared his throat. "I asked if this were a friend of yours, if you wanted privacy."

Rachel considered it, then recalled the impostors. Their presence on the station cast a suspicious light upon any Freeholder who seemed well-versed in the customs of Igsha Reey. "No. Stay close."

Benjy turned a wary gaze to the approaching stranger. "Yes, Deputy."

Rachel also watched the fellow walk toward them, noting his free-moving grace, and wondered why her heart beat so rapidly.

The Freeholder grinned, displaying a somewhat crooked set of teeth, and his aura of keen intelligence evaporated. "Zo," he said, as if the word were a greeting. "Narsh day, zint—?" He broke off, grimacing, then pulled what appeared to be a dental appliance from his mouth and unceremoniously shook spittle from it. "Sorry. Forgot I had it in." He spoke with the singing accent of the Northern Freeholds. "Nice day, isn't it?"

Both appalled and amused, Rachel continued to study him. His age, she supposed, could be anywhere from mid-twenties to late thirties. His nose was large and prominently curved, giving his profile a distinctly convex outline. His jaw was strong, his eyes were deeply hooded, his fingers were long and weirdly attenuated; but he moved with a dancer's poise, and radiant energy suffused his visage. Rachel could not decide if he were the homeliest young man she had ever seen, or the most beautiful.

He continued speaking, clearly oblivious to her silence. "I'm Trabail Rye. But everyone calls me Bailey."

Benjy stirred. "You?" he said with thinly disguised incredulity. "You're Professor Rye?"

Bailey blinked. "Uh . . . yes." He cleared his throat. "You've heard of me?"

Rachel turned to Benjy and raised her brows inquiringly.

Benjy nodded toward the Freeholder. "Professor Rye holds multiple degrees in xenology and xeno-linguistics." He returned his attention to the young man, and his deep voice gained an admiring tone. "I read your recent monograph on the etymology of the Rofan word *hjeina*."

Bailey gaped at Benjy with an expression of inert stupidity. "Eh?"

Benjy nodded. "Interesting. Your supposition that *hjeina* derives from the root word for laughter."

Slack-jawed, Bailey blinked. "Rofan don't laugh." He turned his baffled gaze to Rachel. "What I actually said, to put it briefly, was that *Hjeina* is the name of a folk deity. And that when a Rofa calls you *Hjeina*, it doesn't just mean that you're crazy, it means you're a crazy god." He grinned suddenly. "I also drew some tenuous parallels between *Hjeina* and the Freehold term *heyn-na*, or 'weirdo.' All rather spurious, actually, but the editor likes that sort of thing, and I needed to publish."

Benjy's voice warmed considerably. "Professor Rye. An honor." He offered his hand. "Benjamin Oso."

Bailey shifted his stare to Benjy. "Eh?" Then his brows lifted, and he grinned. "Oh, I get it. You were testing me, to make sure I was who I said I was. Very tricky." He reached for Benjy's clasp, then evidently recalled that he still held the appliance. He switched it to his left hand, wiped his wet fingers on his kimono, and completed the handshake. "Zo."

Trying to hide her inner battle between mirth and distaste, Rachel folded her arms to preclude any invitation to a saliva-coated handshake and offered a bow. "Deputy Rachel Ajmani. Earth Port Authority, silver rank."

Bailey ducked his head in an abbreviated bow. "Zo."

He looked back and forth between Rachel and Benjy. "Tell me, up here on Port Station, do you often run into many people who've assumed false identities?"

Rachel maintained an impassive expression. "No, but your presence is enough to warrant cautious curiosity."

"Eh?"

"I mean that you're a long way from a Freehold, Professor Rye."

Though Bailey still smiled, his gaze turned cool. "You're mistaken, Deputy. I *am* a Freehold."

Rachel's thoughts darkened.

Responsible for over eighty percent of the Earth's food production, the Freeholds maintained a long-standing tradition of neutrality and political independence from the World Council. During the Last War, corrupt governments had seized control of the food supplies, causing widespread famine. The Freeholds' autonomy was intended to act as a check against the World Council's nearly absolute power; and their citizens could, technically, claim exemption from the jurisdiction of civil authorities.

Rachel wondered if Bailey had mistaken her remark as an oblique threat, for his assertion of personal sovereignty could only be interpreted as a courteous warning. "I understand, Professor Rye."

There was an odd challenge in his bright eyes. "Please, Deputy. Call me Bailey."

Rachel returned the challenge. As if facing down a hostile Rofa, she jerked her chin up, trusting that he would grasp the gesture on several levels. "Rachel."

Bailey's lips parted. For a long moment, he studied her with an admiring expression. "Rachel," he repeated softly, hitting the 'r' with a subtly exaggerated Freehold accent.

Or a Rofan accent. Rachel smiled in spite of herself. "Very good," she said. "I'm impressed."

Grinning, Bailey clicked out a strange phrase. "That's Farnii for 'thank you,' " he explained. "It literally translates as 'you're most gracious.' "

Farnii was the official language of the Jadamiin, a species who refused to recognize Humans as sentient beings. "So," Rachel said, "you also speak Farnii?"

From an entry hatch several yards away, Captain Akya stepped onto the dock. He caught sight of the Freeholder and made a commanding motion for him to approach. "Bai-al-ly!"

"I'm quite fluent in Farnii." Bailey slipped the appliance

in his hand back into his mouth. "In fact," he continued
with a flawless Rofan accent, "I speak all languages.
Fluently."

Captain Akya snorted with impatience. "Bai-al-ly!
Come!"

Rachel set her mouth askew. "All languages? That's
impossible."

Akya raised its voice to a screech, clearly pushed past its
tolerance. "Bai-bai-bai-al-ly!"

"Impossible? Really?" Bailey grinned, fully exhibiting his
crooked teeth. "When you want me, Rachel, I'll be on the
Rhu Dakha." He turned and loped to where Akya waited.
The two of them passed within the hatch without a backward glance.

Rachel stood frozen, thinking through her earlier encounter with Captain Akya. The Rofa had somehow gained
an alliance with a Human genius, a Freeholder whom no
one on Earth Port Station could legally touch. Moved by a
sudden impulse, Rachel pulled out her phone and keyed
into the manifest of the *Rhu Dakha*. Professor Trabail Rye
was listed as the sole passenger, incoming from Igsha
Reey Port.

Frowning, Rachel cut the connection and pocketed the
handset. She considered calling Wu, then an unsettling
sense of doubt seized her. *Watch and wait.*

Benjy cleared his throat. "Deputy?"

She gazed up at him and tried to sound casual. "So. What
do you think of Professor Rye?"

"I'm not sure," Benjy said in a neutral tone. "What do
you think, Deputy?"

"I think he's an alien." Rachel had intended to sound
sardonic, but her own words reverberated in her mind. She
again recalled the impostors running loose on the station,
perhaps conveyed to Earth Port by the World Council.
Cold seized her. "Come on," she said, heading once again
for the lift to the lower level. "I need a cup of coffee."

CHAPTER FIVE

H ER DARK EYES wide with equal measures of excitement and apprehension, Concha Singh paused outside Councillor Weber's office and carefully adjusted the silken folds of her teal-blue sari. Her heart pounded, and trembling robbed her slender limbs of strength. *Relax,* she told herself. *Just breathe.*

Concha had been hired as an aide only the day before Councillor Weber's celebrated departure for Earth Port Station. The decision that she would also make the trip had been handed down to her only several hours before the shuttle left. After the desperate rush to prepare, the trip aboard *Gaia's Love,* flagship of the World Council, had been a nightmare of inactivity. No one on the councillor's staff had the time, it seemed, to explain her duties. After repeated and futile attempts to make herself useful, Concha had spent the weeklong trip in her cabin, watching the old, real-life drama of Earth Port Station over and over again.

But the councillor and the other members of the Xeno-Relations Committee were currently taking a break from their marathon meeting, and Concha had been summoned to the main office aboard the ship. Steeling herself, she pressed the door buzzer.

There was no answer, and the door remained closed.

Upset that she had clearly interrupted the councillor in the midst of something important, Concha waited.

Several minutes passed. Three elegant young women, all

aides like herself, strolled up the narrow corridor, indignantly discussing someone's insulting remarks. Concha stepped aside to make way for them and smiled. "Good day."

They completely ignored her.

Sighing, Concha returned her attention to the door. She heard the aides continue up the corridor until they stepped onto a lift.

Abruptly, the door shot open.

Concha jumped.

Like every other room aboard *Gaia's Love*, the sterile white office seemed little more spacious than a closet, though it was equipped with a small desk and chair. Councilor Weber stood in front of her desk, turning off a phone. "Sorry to keep you waiting." She smiled and beckoned Concha into the room. "But I received an unexpected call."

As always, Councillor Weber looked impeccably groomed and utterly composed. Her tall, angular frame identified her Euro bloodlines, as did her chestnut hair and hazel eyes. According to the available biographies, the councillor was in her early sixties, but she looked several decades younger.

Warmed by her employer's friendly tone, Concha stepped into the office and bowed. "Please don't apologize, Councillor. My time is yours."

Councillor Weber's smile widened. "Why, thank you. I can use all the time I can get. My schedule has been somewhat . . . hectic . . . lately." She turned to the desk, set the phone down, and picked up a printout. "We really haven't had the opportunity to talk yet, have we?"

Concha ducked her head in an abbreviated bow, recognizing the question as rhetorical.

Councillor Weber glanced over the printout. "I have your *vita*, here. You're a fully licensed spacecraft pilot. And you've spent three years with Governor Adana's office as a confidential courier."

Concha nodded deeply again. "Yes, Councillor."

"Did you ever visit Earth Port Station?"

"No, Councillor. I only flew a lunar shuttle." Impulsively, Concha added, "But I think I've memorized the whole drama series."

Councillor Weber's face lit up, melting the mask of com-

posure to reveal boundless enthusiasm. "Hav____
you, really? So have I!" Obviously mimicking W____
she adopted a comically evil leer. "What doesn'____
will wake you up."

All of Concha's accumulated distress and worry va____ed
from her memory, and she laughed. "Yes, yes! That's
perfect!"

Councillor Weber continued speaking in a rush: "And
what about Deputy Omar? When she chased that Rofan
smuggler over the catwalks?"

"The first time I saw it, I thought she was going to die."

"So did I." Councillor Weber's smile faded. "And to
think that I've spent the last two hours arguing with her
about the procedures for enforcing dock fines." She returned Concha's *vita* to the desk. "I suppose it just goes to
show, you don't really know someone until you spend time
with them. You can't learn who they are by reading about
them, or by watching them on the vid." Her gaze seemed to
turn inward. "And sometimes . . . you never know them."

Concha's breath caught in her throat. She supposed the
councillor referred to the scandal involving most of her
longtime colleagues. One of them, William Smyth, was facing impeachment proceedings for charges ranging from sexual misconduct to misappropriations of funds. A World
Council member usually held the post until death or voluntary retirement; if the impeachment went through, it would
be the first in over a hundred years.

Suddenly, Councillor Weber seemed to come to herself.
"Sorry," she said, smiling again. "I'm a bit tired."

Filled with sympathy, Concha crooked her brows. "Councillor, is there anything I can do to help?"

"Not unless you can arrange for me to be in two places
at—" The councillor broke off and studied Concha with an
abruptly alert expression. "Tell me, Aide Singh, what is
your opinion of Deputy Ajmani?"

Concha mentally floundered in the sudden change of
topic. "Well, just from watching the series, I'd say she was
amazing. I can see why there was a nomination petition
circulating."

Most members of the World Council started their political careers at a local level, working their way up from city
to prefecture to region, until they caught the attention of

the World Council's secret Nominating Committee. With the advent of real-life dramas, however, ordinary citizens were becoming global heroes, and the number of nomination attempts by petition was growing.

Councillor Weber nodded. "Deputy Ajmani appears to be exactly the type of person we need to serve upon the World Council: energetic, innovative, with unshakable integrity." She paced a few steps, steepling her fingers. "Of course, that's all based upon the series. For all I know, she may possess nothing more than a photogenic face and a knack for disguising her inadequacies. Like that wretched fellow on Brontos. What was his name?"

"Um, Basil Tampere?"

"That's it." The councillor frowned. "He looked very good on the vid, too. And yet, what a disaster he caused."

A real-life drama had been recorded on the Brontos mining colony. Basil Tampere, the handsome and charismatic director of the project, had caused such a stir of interest that the vid company returned a year later to record a follow-up series. But while they were there, the unthinkable occurred, and the main shaft collapsed. Nearly three hundred people lost their lives in the disaster. Most of the fatalities had been caused by the lack of simple maintenance procedures overseen directly by Director Tampere. Most heartbreaking was the failure of the escape pods filled with the colony's children.

One of Concha's coworkers at the time had lost her daughter, son-in-law, and grandchildren on Brontos. Poor Marla had hunched over her desk, weeping uncontrollably and clutching her daughter's wedding portrait. Distressed by the memory, Concha swallowed. "Wasn't there a petition for his nomination?"

"There was, indeed." Councillor Weber studied her intently. "Did you know anyone on Brontos?"

"No, Councillor, but a friend of mine—" Concha's eyes misted, and she had to look away and blink hard. "A friend lost her entire family."

"I don't think anyone was left untouched by the tragedy," Councillor Weber said. "And we must never allow anything like it to happen again. So I want you to—"

The phone on the councillor's desk trilled. "Excuse me,"

she said to Concha, then picked it up. "Yes?" She listened for a moment, then said: "Five minutes."

Concha began to withdraw, but the councillor turned off the phone and smiled at her. "Well, I guess I'd better make this speedy. I want you to fill in for me, Aide Singh."

"Pardon?"

"Governor Adana praised your discretion, so I feel I may trust you with a highly confidential matter." The councillor leaned back against her desk. "I made this trip as a member of the Nominating Committee, and my purpose is to ascertain whether or not Deputy Ajmani is fit to serve on the World Council."

Words failed Concha, and she stared.

"In order to judge her worthiness, it's been determined that she must overcome a set of secretly engineered ordeals. We call it Operation Starcatcher." Councillor Weber paused, seeming amused by Concha's obvious shock. "I have two field operatives in charge of setting up the tests, and Warden Jackson is offering covert assistance. I, myself, was to personally accompany Deputy Ajmani and gauge her responses. However, another crisis is in progress, and I cannot undertake my portion of the operation. So, Aide Singh, I want you to go in my place."

"Me?" Concha repeated faintly.

"As the Advocate Observer, yes." Councillor Weber smiled reassuringly. "Don't look so frightened, my dear, you've got the easy part. Rife and Jardín will handle the difficult elements. All you have to do is follow Deputy Ajmani around as she works through the Starcatcher ordeal, and observe events as they happen. Can I trust you to do that?"

Numerous questions tumbled through Concha's mind. "Of course, Councillor, but I—"

"Excellent." Councillor Weber started for the door. "Now, remember. This is an entirely secretive operation. You may not, in any way, clue Deputy Ajmani as to its existence. You may not speak of Starcatcher to anyone else outside of the people I've already named. And if you have any questions, you must go to Jardín or Rife for guidance. Do you know who they are?"

Concha recalled meeting them only once during the flight to the station. "Yes, but I—"

"Fine, fine." Councillor Weber went to the door, opened it, and motioned for Concha to leave. "You've lifted a great weight from my shoulders, Aide Singh. Thank you."

"You're welcome." Reeling inwardly, Concha wandered over the threshold. "But what if I need to contact you?"

"You cannot." Councillor Weber smiled. "Good luck. And don't let Deputy Ajmani bully you. You're acting on behalf of the World Council, so use any means necessary to carry out your duties."

The door whisked shut, leaving Concha alone in the corridor. For a long moment, she stood motionless, trying to think, then she slowly turned and started back toward her quarters.

Concha wanted to feel proud to be entrusted with such an important responsibility, but an unexpected shudder racked her slender frame. *Any means?*

Break time, and technicians filled the ops booth. Smiling, Rachel wove through the conversing groups on her way to the brewer. Everyone appeared in high spirits, but she thought she detected a strained note in the laughter, a tension that matched her own state of mind. *Second wind. Another six hours, and we'll all be in trouble.*

Lafiya DuChamp still sat on duty at the console, though her relief should have arrived hours ago. Her smile fading, Rachel motioned Benjy to continue without her and moved toward the operations manager.

Lafiya's eyes were shadowed with fatigue, but she held her shoulders in a rigid line. "Please relay and confirm," she said into her headset and turned an inquiring gaze to Rachel. "Ops standing by."

Rachel spread her hands. "Where's Tóma?"

Lafiya hit the mute switch. "Summoned to the procedural audit. The Xeno-Relations Committee thinks it might want to ask him something."

"You're not serious."

Lafiya picked up her coffee cup, found it empty, and returned it to the holder. "They've also called in Mariko, Geophrey, and Trish," she said sourly. "At this rate, Deputy, you and I will be the only ones left to run the station."

Rachel carefully hid her indignation. The XRC was going

too far. "Fine. But *you* have to be head of Port Authority, not me. Gold rank Deputy Lafiya DuChamp."

"Okay. Do I get a raise?" Lafiya released the mute. "Hey, Carl? Awaiting your confirmation. Please respond."

Rachel picked up Lafiya's empty coffee cup and crossed to the brewer to refill it. Her phone chimed. Still thinking about the XRC, she pulled it from her pocket and answered. "Ajmani."

Wu spoke blandly. "Just wanted to let you know, I'm circulating a petition to nominate you to the World Council."

It was an old joke. The World Council was a self-nominating body; but, in theory, any adult on Earth could gain a seat. The first requirement in the process was a petition with five million signatures.

Rachel grinned. "Really? How nice." Several years previously, in the afterglow of Earth Port's drama series, some well-intentioned viewers had started a petition to nominate her to the World Council, but nothing had ever come of it. "How many signatures so far?"

"Just two. Mine and God's. I signed first."

Chuckling, Rachel held the coffee cup under the brewer's spigot and filled it. "A few of the current World Council members have worn out their welcome. Perhaps you ought to focus your attention on a petition to initiate impeachment."

"Say that three times, real fast."

Rachel turned and started back toward Lafiya. "Is there a reason for this call?"

"Oh, yes. Need to make an appointment to see you."

"When?"

"In six minutes. Where are you?"

Rachel fought to quell a sudden apprehension, and her hands began to shake. She set the cup in the console's holder before she spilled it, trying to tell herself that Wu only wished to discuss a matter too sensitive to risk over the phone. "Ops booth. Dock Two."

"On my way. Kindly keep your esteemed self off the dock until I arrive." Wu cut the connection.

Her thoughts whirling, Rachel pocketed her phone.

Still on her headset, Lafiya sighed. "Carl. Listen. No,

just—" Her voice roughened. "Just shut your big mouth and—"

Raising her brows, Rachel stared at Lafiya. "Hey!"

Lafiya hit the mute on her phone. "Deputy, the idiot's stuck again. Says he's going to climb out onto the gantry to fix the drive train himself."

Rachel closed her eyes and pinched the bridge of her nose. Physical displays of anger, she reminded herself, were unacceptable. "Tell him . . . not to."

"He isn't listening."

Rachel pulled the phone out of her pocket. "What's the number?"

"G-twenty."

She keyed it and listened for the line to click open.

Carl was in mid-sentence. "—what I'm doing! I used to do it all the time on—"

"Technician Stein," Rachel said. "This is Deputy Ajmani."

Carl choked and fell silent.

"I categorically forbid you to engage in unauthorized repair procedures."

"But, Deputy—" Carl's voice rose in pitch. "There's a kink in one of the drive belts. That's why it keeps sticking. If I just—"

"Did you hear me?"

"But I—" He swallowed audibly. "Yes, Deputy."

"Good. Be safe." Frowning, Rachel keyed the cutoff and pocketed the phone. "I'm the one who's short on sleep. Why is everyone else going insane?"

Lafiya's grin was tired, but mischievous. "He's young. Don't you remember what it was like to be that young?"

"I was *never* that young."

Lafiya noticed her fresh coffee. "Deputy, did you bring that? Thanks." She took an appreciative sip, favoring Rachel with an odd mix of compassion and critical assessment. "You look awful."

Rachel tried to smile, though she suspected it appeared more like a pained squint. "I'm fine, thanks."

Lafiya snorted derisively.

Relenting, Rachel shrugged one shoulder. "The morning after a party—curried prawns, rum punch, dancing till dawn. You know the sludge on your tongue when you wake up?"

Lafiya regarded her sidelong. "Uh-huh."

"It's coating my brain."

Lafiya clamped her lips together and looked away, appearing to scrutinize the dockside activity. "You ought to hear what they're saying about you out there, Deputy. You're quite the hero."

Rachel shrugged again. Her real concern lay in the upcoming meeting with Wu, and a sudden fear that his banter about the World Council had been a veiled warning. The episode on the dock had become a hazy, disjointed memory. "Some hero. I've made Earth Port liable for a couple of lawsuits." She could just imagine the reaction of Port Authority's head, coming out of a procedural audit only to hear about a certain silver rank deputy's antics on Dock Two. "Lois Jimanez-Verde is going to cane me."

"I doubt it, Deputy."

"I chased a dozen valued merchant clients onto their ship with a cargo truck."

"A tractor, as I recall." Still looking out the window, Lafiya grinned wolfishly. "It was fabulous."

Wearily, Rachel settled her folded arms on the top of the Ops console. "Fabulous," she repeated bleakly. "Heaven help us."

"Cheer up, Deputy. Merely seven-and-a-half hours to go." A call red-lighted on Lafiya's board, and she punched it in. "Ops."

With a sigh, Rachel rested her head on her folded arms and closed her eyes, letting the background conversation wash over her. *I grasp the stars and take the light to heart.* Her phone chimed. For a moment, the raw effort of making the necessary moves to answer it seemed too monumental to undertake. *Sixteen incoming ships.* With a mental groan, she pulled the handset from her pocket. "Yup."

The woman's voice was middle-aged and harried. "Deputy Ajmani?"

Rachel's eyes refused to focus. She closed them again and rubbed the heel of her hand between her brows. "Yes? Speaking."

The woman coughed apologetically. "Fran Swanson, here. Senior cargo tech. Got a problem at berth 12-C. A diplomatic kind of problem."

"I have a meeting in a short while, Fran. Could someone else possibly help you?"

Fran made a protesting noise. "I've been calling all over the place for ten minutes, Deputy. The whole Port Authority office is at that damned audit, and every single staffer is—"

It was too much. Hysterical laughter strained for release. Rachel emitted a squeak before she suppressed it.

"Deputy?"

"Sorry." Rachel pulled herself together. "A diplomatic problem. Phi-Nurian? Or Rofan?"

"Uh . . . the second."

The problem was undoubtedly standing at Fran's elbow. Battling for self-control, Rachel wandered to the brewer and poured a cup of coffee, trying to think. "Let me guess. It's a new client who demands to go pull its order itself."

"Not exactly, Deputy."

The Rofan practiced complicated systems of ownership, which made the transference of cargo a laborious process. They took what belonged to them, and so considered it a deadly insult to have the goods delivered.

Over time, the station had developed a procedural compromise, in which a variety of merchandise in excess of what the Rofan had ordered was conveyed to a neutral space on the edge of their loading area. The Rofan were then free to claim their cargo, selecting what they wanted and disregarding the rest. Regular merchant clients were familiar with the routine, but with so many Rofan ships docking at Earth Port for the first time, there were bound to be difficulties.

Rachel sipped her coffee. It was rich and delicious. Someone had adjusted Wu's brewer settings. "Well, Fran, what shall we do?" *A diplomatic problem.* She reminded herself that Wu had suggested she stay off the dock. "Do you want me to come out there?"

The Rofan claimed to possess seven distinct genders. However, since they violently objected to any type of medical investigation, and they abhorred the Human habit of identifying individuals by procreative functions, it was difficult to gather scientific support for their assertion. Most xenologists agreed, from studies of Rofan language and behavior, that there were actually six gender-types that seemed to be hermaphroditic combinations of basic male/female reproductive roles and one neuter-type with no reproductive abilities at all.

The Rofan who most commonly came to Earth Port were the self-impregnating type who, as Rachel understood it, formed a dominant segment of Igsha Reey's population. Captain Khanwa of the *Eyk-Eyk-Tu* was not one of these.

Instead of the usual smooth russet pelt, Khanwa sported thick black fur patterned with bursts of orange; and its ears were large and jackallike, not small and round. In addition, the captain did not wear the typical layers of clothing. Its only piece of adornment was a lushly embroidered sash slung low around its hips.

As Rachel followed the grid across the dock, she glanced up at Benjy who walked beside her. "Well," she said in an undertone. "These types tend to be less aggressive."

Benjy's mellow baritone made his correction sound mild. "Less violent, perhaps, Deputy. But more aggressive."

Rachel grinned tiredly. "I meant that the honorable captain wouldn't offer to feast upon my liver."

Benjy kept his face impassive. "No, Deputy. But it will undoubtedly offer to feast upon—" He broke off with a cough. "—it will offer other . . . challenges."

Three of Khanwa's crew gathered around their captain, lounging against stacked cargo, casually draping themselves over each other. They all possessed exotically long and silky-looking fur; shades of cream, spotless white, and brown with black ticking. Their ears and the shapes of their snouts were all somewhat different, and Rachel wondered if this connoted different genders, or if it were merely a result of the Rofan's bewildering genetic variety. Like their captain, the crew wore only sashes in lieu of clothing.

Fran, the cargo tech, was a slightly stooped woman who wore her silver hair in a tidy bun atop her head. In her coveralls, burdened with an oversized invoicing workboard, she seemed small and drab standing among the crowd of Rofan.

As Rachel approached the berth with Benjy, Khanwa sinuously twisted its head around to watch. "Look there," it murmured to its crew with a rolling purr of an accent, "more pretties."

The other Rofan bobbed their heads in amusement, licking their teeth.

Rachel took a stance beside Fran and folded her arms. "I'm Deputy Ajmani from Port Authority."

The Rofa's eyes were orange, matching the splashes on its inky fur, and its gaze traveled over Rachel's body with prurient intensity. "I am Captain Khanwa."

Fran cleared her throat. "The honorable captain is interested in purchasing this canister." She rested her hands on a waist-high drum of battered dura-plastic. It was part of a collection of dummy cargo the dock kept, reusing it for Rofan transactions. "I've explained that I need your permission to open it."

Rachel peered at Fran. *You do?* Then she turned her attention to the canister. Someone had scrawled '500' on its side with a fluorescent green marker. *Heavy. A mass dummy.* "What's in it?"

Fran stared at her in clear confusion. "I don't know, Deputy. No one's ever opened it before."

Rachel glanced at Benjy, raising her brows. He shrugged calmly. "Probably sand, Deputy. Sand or rocks. Certainly nothing hazardous."

Rachel turned to Fran. "Very well. Open it so the honorable captain may examine the contents."

Fran appeared upset. "But, Deputy," she said in a tone of protest, "what if they want to buy it?"

"Then we'll sell it."

Fran made a choking noise. "We can't," she blurted. "What will we use instead?"

Then Rachel understood. Members of the Human species often acquired habits of thought, making them blind to new concepts. "What will we use instead?" she repeated. "Almost anything else."

"But—"

"Fran." Rachel made herself speak gently. "It doesn't matter. We aren't . . . required . . . to use dummies."

Two pink spots appeared on Fran's cheeks, and she dropped her gaze. "No, Deputy," she mumbled, reaching for the canister key on her belt. "I suppose not."

Rachel kept her expression somber, fearing Fran would misinterpret a smile as condescending amusement. *Too, too tired.* She looked at Khanwa.

It still regarded her with interest. "So pretty," it said, as if continuing an interrupted conversation. "And you talk pretty."

Rachel thought Khanwa's Trade seemed unusually good for a newcomer to Earth Port. "Thank you, honorable Captain."

Khanwa lowered its voice intimately. "Smell pretty, too."

Oh, dear.

"When this business is done, you will come to my ship?" Khanwa gestured graciously toward the access hatch and added temptingly: "I have Eartha food. Grrapes. Yes? P'chez. Do you like p'chez?"

"Yes," Rachel said politely. "I like peaches."

"What else do you like, Deputy Aja-mani?" Khanwa purred. "I want to know."

Feeling the heat of embarrassment rise up her throat, Rachel avoided Benjy's gaze.

"Big, soft bed?" Khanwa continued. "Soft touches?"

Rachel reflected that she possessed a few thought-habits of her own. She knew how to deal with Rofan threats, but not with outrageous flirtation. "I'm flattered, honorable Captain, but I hear that the Rofan bite. I don't want to get bitten."

Khanwa lowered its voice. "But I bite . . . nice. You will like."

At that moment, the canister released its lid with a pressure-laden thump. Fran straightened, replaced the key on her belt, and then lifted the lid. "Honorable Captain."

Relieved by the interruption, Rachel turned to look. The canister contained tumble-polished stones. She identified agates, garnets, and marble-sized spheres of rose quartz. "Ah," Rachel said. "You were right, Staffer Oso. Rocks."

Khanwa stood motionless for several moments and stared at the stones. Then the Rofa picked one up, breathing a word in its own language, and held it to the light. "What is this?"

Rachel studied the purple crystal. "That's an amethyst, I believe."

The crew gathered closer to their captain, whispering among themselves and gazing at the stones.

Rachel gestured toward the canister, hoping Khanwa would be distracted enough to forget its efforts to seduce her. "These are only semiprecious, you understand, and were undoubtedly graded as unsuitable for jewelers' requirements. But they might make interesting curiosities on Igsha Reey. If you're willing to make an offer, we'll contact the—"

From behind Rachel, a young woman spoke in a breathless rush: "Deputy Ajmani, where have you been?"

Shocked by the interruption, Rachel paused, then decided that her business with a merchant client outweighed chastising ill-mannered behavior. "We'll contact the comptroller's office to obtain a release for—"

The woman interrupted again. "Deputy Ajmani. I need to talk with you right away."

Irritated, Rachel nodded respectfully to Khanwa. "My apologies, honorable Captain." She turned slowly, raising her brows, and injected low fury into her voice. "What?"

The stranger looked to be in her early twenties, with the shaved scalp that so many young women seemed to favor. She was slender, willowy, and the teal of her silk sari set off her dark skin and lustrous eyes. On one shoulder, she wore the badge of the World Council with its insignia of the Earth encased in a diamond. "We must speak privately."

At the end of her patience with the meddling XRC, Rachel looked the interloper straight in the eye. "Just who do you think you are?"

The young woman stiffened. "My name is Concha Singh. I am the personal aide of Councillor Weber, and I—"

Scowling, Rachel deliberately interrupted. "I don't see your visitor's pass."

Concha's eyes widened. "I don't need a—"

"Do you have any identification?"

"Identification? I'm the personal aide of—!"

"Staffer Oso." Rachel folded her arms and looked at Benjy. "I want you to take Concha Singh into custody. Detain her in Checkpoint, pending verification of her credentials, and file all applicable charges against her."

Benjy nodded impassively. "At once, Deputy." He gestured for Concha to precede him down the grid. "If you please?"

The XRC and Councillor Weber would be furious, but Rachel's actions were all by the book, especially in light of the impostors' presence on station. *Release my colleagues from the audit*, Rachel thought with grim satisfaction, *and I'll release your aide.*

Concha looked ready to explode. "Deputy, I must protest!"

Deliberately, Rachel turned back to Khanwa. "Sorry for the interruption, honorable Captain."

Its eyes glinted, as if amused by the interlude. "You are really, really mean. I like you."

Rachel sighed inwardly. "Well, I didn't intend to—"

Halfway down the dock, the main gantry issued an ear-shattering squeal of metal on metal.

Squinting against the noise, Rachel whirled to look.

The steel framework bridge twisted, as if wrung by invisible hands. A six-inch-thick cable snapped and whipped through the air like a striking snake. Forty feet above the floor, Carl Stein clung one-handed to the gantry's buckling frame, dangling precariously over nothing.

CHAPTER SIX

RACHEL TOOK one hesitant step toward the main gantry, keeping her gaze fixed on Carl's wildly kicking figure, and asked to the air in general: "Is he wearing a harness?"

Carl made a frantic grab for a support strut with his free hand and managed to gain a hold.

Still looking up, Rachel drifted closer to the gantry, trying to discern the fluorescent orange of safety tackle against Carl's blue coveralls. She did not see it. "Oh, God," she breathed. "Oh, God."

Without making a conscious decision, Rachel broke into a flat run. She blundered around cargo canisters and nearly collided with a Rofa, always keeping her attention focused tightly upward, as if her concentration would prevent Carl from falling.

All along the dock, technicians stood frozen, staring in horror at the man hanging from the gantry.

A shadow loomed across her vision.

With a sudden jerk of awareness, Rachel realized she had run in front of a reach-fork. It had swerved to miss her.

Eyes flashing with anxiety, the driver stopped his machine and stared at her. "Deputy, are you all right?"

The fork bore a pallet, making a stable platform upon which to stand. Rachel leaped onto the pallet and grabbed hold of the fork's back brace. "Gantry! Go!"

The driver continued to stare at her. "What?"

"Go," she called frantically. "Go, go, go!"

"But, Deputy, I can't—"

"Do it!" Rachel's voice dropped to a hoarse shout. "Move!"

With a doubtful expression, the driver shoved the vehicle into gear and swung it toward the gantry.

The pallet beneath Rachel's feet jiggled every time the wheels hit a seam in the deck plates. A bubble of nausea rose in her throat, but she returned her gaze to Carl. He seemed to have thrown one arm over a support strut. "Hang on," Rachel said through gritted teeth. "Help's coming." Without looking behind her, she reached through the back brace, rapped on the window of the cab, and motioned the driver to raise the fork.

For several moments, the pallet remained at the same level, as if the driver debated whether to obey. Then the reach-fork whined, and the pallet began to lift into the air.

Though still some distance away, Rachel felt reassured by the gained height. She took a tighter grip on the back brace with her left hand and reached out for Carl with her right. "Hang on! You can do it!" Rachel called, hoping he could hear her. "Just six more seconds!"

The pallet had nearly reached its maximum extension, but there was still a lot of floor to cross. *One.*

They sped closer. With new horror, Rachel noticed that the main gantry's frame was shuddering as the drive units continued to winch the cables tighter. *Two.*

The reach-fork slowed. They were almost there. Carl locked eyes with her. He seemed shockingly young, his black hair tousled, his mouth open and panting.

Rachel extended her hand even farther, leaning off-balance, praying it would encourage him. *Three.*

They reached the gantry. The pallet was nearly ten feet below Carl's swinging legs, and several feet to the left. *Four.*

The driver carefully maneuvered the reach-fork to place the pallet directly beneath Carl. Rachel stretched toward him, as if sheer will could close the gap between them. *Five. . . .*

Someone cut power to the gantry. It was the right thing

to do; but released from the cables' tension, the frame groaned and bucked. With a shriek of despair, Carl lost his grip.

He fell fast. Rachel had no time to react.

Carl struck the pallet crosswise. The force of his landing shook the fork. Rachel lost her grip and fell to her knees, grunting with the impact.

Carl tumbled toward the edge of the pallet.

"God!" Rachel flung herself over him.

They were both falling.

"No!"

Rachel then realized that the pallet was still solidly under them, and the driver was lowering it toward the floor.

Rachel's vision dissolved into sparkles. She felt hot, then cold, then nauseated. She wondered if she might faint. She wanted to be sick.

Carl whimpered.

Rachel raised her head, panting, and forced her eyes to focus. "Are you hurt?"

"My legs," he whispered. Sweat spangled his blanched features. "Can't . . . feel my legs. . . ."

The pallet settled on the floor. Swallowing hard, Rachel sat back on her heels and stared up at the ring of solicitous faces.

Benjy detached himself from the group and crouched beside the pallet. "Are you all right?"

"Call Medica," Rachel said. Her joints were like wet paper, and she still felt the urge to vomit, but she kept her voice steady. "Carl says he can't feel his legs. Don't move him. Wait for a medic."

The senior cargo tech, Fran, stepped from the encircling crowd of observers and knelt beside Carl. "You're going to be all right." Her motherly tone expressed calm conviction. She pulled off her coat and laid it over Carl's torso. "Just rest."

The crowd shifted and murmured. Concha Singh stood among the techs and aliens, shivering in her silk sari, gazing openmouthed at Rachel.

Feeling queasy again, but determined not to make a further spectacle of herself in front of an XRC aide, Rachel slowly stood and leaned back against the reach-fork. Her hands stung. She lifted them and noticed her palms were scraped and bleeding. *How did that happen?*

The driver disembarked and swung around to face her. For a long moment, he stared at her with somber brown eyes, then spoke in a direct and earnest tone: "I want a drink."

Amusement lifted some of the haze from Rachel's mind. "Me, too." She tried to recall the driver's name, thinking it was Roberto-something. "Good job, by the way. You get my vote for this month's safety award."

"Me?" Roberto said incredulously. "Not me. I didn't do anything, Deputy."

A sudden shakiness seized Rachel, but she made herself grin. "How do you figure that? What could I have done without you? You think I can fly?"

Roberto made a hapless noise. "Fly?" he repeated. "Wouldn't be a damned bit surprised!"

Rachel laughed weakly. "Not even on my good days."

Still lying on the pallet, Carl began to cry out in a feverish manner. "No! I need tell her! Need to—to tell her!"

Rachel jerked her gaze toward the injured man. Benjy and Fran both knelt beside him. Fran held Carl's hand, murmuring comfortingly. Benjy glanced up at Rachel. "Deputy, a moment, if you please?"

Rachel gave Roberto a thumbs-up by way of farewell, then turned to the pallet. Sweat ran in rivulets from Carl's face, and he tossed his head restlessly.

Sorry for his pain, Rachel crouched beside him, ignoring the protests of her aching legs. "It's all right," she said. "You're going to be—"

Carl opened his eyes. "Deputy—" He seemed to have trouble catching his breath. "I'm sorry. Sorry. I should've listened—"

Rachel swallowed hard against a sudden lump in her throat. "Just rest, now. Take it easy."

"Tried to fix . . . drive train—" Carl grimaced, clearly in pain. "Climbed out. Tried to fix—"

Sick at heart, Rachel sighed. So he had disobeyed her explicit instructions, after all.

"I'm sorry," Carl repeated. "I'm sorry."

Rachel ran her hand through her hair, trying to think.

"Technician Stein. We all make mistakes. No use fretting." It sounded patronizing, so she added: "Remind me to tell you sometime about a mistake I once made with a power cable."

Carl closed his eyes and subsided into silence.

Rachel studied him doubtfully, wondering if she had actually reassured him, or if he had simply run out of strength.

Fran's brow furrowed with worry, and she adjusted her coat to cover Carl more warmly. "Medica ought to be here soon."

Benjy glanced up and tensed. "Deputy, watch out!"

Khanwa spoke in Rachel's ear, breath warm on her cheek. "What are you waiting for?"

Rachel barely managed not to jump. She had not realized the captain had crouched beside her. "For a medic." She braced herself for a negative reaction, fully aware of the Rofan prejudice against medical intervention. "Someone who knows how to take care of the injury."

Khanwa's ears flicked back. "Maybe I do not understand. You wait for a *gukka*? To do the mer-ci-ful thing?"

Evasiveness would accomplish nothing. "For a healer. To heal the injury."

Khanwa abruptly stood, its black fur fluffed in agitation. "That is—" The Rofa made an obvious effort to regain its self-possession. "That is wrong."

Wearily, Rachel also stood. "It is the way of our species, honorable Captain."

"Your way is bad. Cruel."

Rachel sighed inwardly. She had held this argument countless times in the past with other Rofan. There was no way to convince them that medical science was not a revolting travesty against nature. The Rofan did not practice any form of medicine. They used and abused a wide variety of drugs, but only as a form of recreation, never to treat a disease or to prevent infection. "It is a matter of custom, honorable Captain. According to the laws and traditions of Earth, dueling is bad and cruel."

"It can be," Khanwa conceded. "Sometimes." The Rofa tilted its dark head. "But that is why there are the *gukka*, to fight for those who cannot. At Igsha Reey Port, I watched a duel between an unarmed Jadamii and a—"

The crowd around the reach-fork stirred, and Wu's voice broke over the assembly. "Greetings, everyone," he said buoyantly. "What's this I hear about our new gantry operator and a certain silver rank deputy?"

A startling sense of relief washed over Rachel. Troubled by the intensity of her own reaction, she folded her arms as she turned. "Over here, Warden Jackson."

Beaming, Wu edged through the press of techs and aliens to stand beside the pallet. "Hello, Benjy. I see you're up and about. Instead of in Medica, where I told you to stay. You're on report."

Benjy drew a breath, as if to argue, then evidently realized it would be a mistake. He nodded, managing to look both contrite and dignified. "Yes, sir. I completely understand, sir."

Wu bent to scrutinize the injured man. "Carl? It's mean ol' Warden Jackson. Can you hear me?"

Carl's eyes slitted open.

"There you are!" Wu tilted his head sympathetically. "Having a bad day?"

Fran glanced up. "Says he can't feel his legs."

Carl's lips moved soundlessly at first, then he whispered: "Sorry. . . ."

Wu's voice softened. "Just rest easy, Carl. The medical team's on its way." He straightened and looked at Benjy. "And you, Staffer Oso, are on your way as well. Hoppity-skippity, back to Medica."

Benjy stood with an air of dutiful resignation. "Sir."

"Shoo!" Wu said. "Hie thee hence. Your partner, Rosita, is due on the dock any second. Very much anticipating the joy of taking statements from all these witnesses. If she finds you here . . ."

Benjy turned away and started toward the lift, slowly shaking his head.

Wu raised his bright eyes to Rachel. "Deputy Ajmani. We had a date. You stood me up."

Rachel smiled thinly. "You should be used to that. You must get stood up a lot."

Wu made a facetious noise of outrage and reproach. "Oh, that hurt."

"Good."

Wu approached her with a menacing roll in his gait. "So you're looking for a fight, eh? Well, I—"

At her side, Khanwa issued a low growl and stepped between Wu and Rachel. "I shall not permit you to fight Deputy Aja-mani."

Wu prudently eased to a halt and raised his brows in mild inquiry. "Deputy? Another love interest? I sense song material in this."

Rachel was wistfully tempted to let the Rofa throw a few punches, but interposed herself between her friend and Khanwa. "Honorable Captain, please do not harm this person. He is not a threat to me."

Khanwa kept its orange eyes wide and fixed upon Wu's slightest movement. "Deputy, I am not finished with you."

"Oo, yes," Wu said. "A happy, bouncy, little song. Something that can double as a jump-rope rhyme. Like: 'Rachel, Rachel, dressed in blue—' "

Rachel found herself wishing the gantry would fall on her. Or on Wu.

At that moment, Rosita appeared, leading a medical team with a gurney through the crowd. Her expression was set and implacable. "Stand back," she grated. "Give us room."

Glad for the interruption, Rachel moved to a clear spot beside a loading area. She leaned against one of the shoulder-high metal barricades. It felt cold against her back, but solid.

Khanwa followed. "Deputy, there is the matter of the cargo to be settled."

Rachel felt a touch of embarrassment. The Rofa had not attempted to protect her from Wu; it had simply reasserted its business concerns. "Of course."

Concha Singh pushed forward. "Deputy, don't waste any more time on these petty affairs. You must—"

Rachel whirled toward her. "What are you still doing here? You're under arrest!"

Strolling over, Wu raised his brows and spoke in a mild voice. "Ah, Deputy? She's a World Council aide. We can't arrest her."

Concha presented Rachel with a smile of exasperated satisfaction. "I told you, I don't need—"

Scorched by frustration and anger, Rachel glared at Concha. "And I don't need your interference. Shut up."

Wu drifted to Rachel's side, feigning an interest in the

paint job of the barricade, and pitched his voice to a low undertone just for her hearing: "Told you to stay off the dock."

Rachel scowled at him. "You may also shut up."

Wu chuckled.

Khanwa gestured toward its ship's loading area. "Name your price for the cargo."

Rachel wearily ran her hand through her hair, again wondering about Councillor Weber's real agenda, and muttered to herself: "How about a few answers?"

Khanwa licked its teeth. Its voice turned reasonable and interested, as if Rachel proposed a commonplace transaction. "Ah, so you wish to trade the cargo for information?"

Rachel drew a breath to refuse, then recalled how Captain Akya had evidently purchased a Human adviser. With all the incoming traffic from Igsha Reey, it would be an incredible benefit to the station to have a Rofan consultant. Rachel cleared her throat. "Truthful information."

Wu spoke in a tentative tone. "Deputy, what are you—?"

Khanwa's ears lifted. "Deputy Aja-mani, please state your exact terms."

Rachel kept her eyes on the captain. In the space of three heartbeats, she mentally sifted everything she knew of Rofan psychology, wondering how to legally bind an alien into behaving as a loyal friend. *I must be insane.* She cleared her throat. "Honorable Captain, in exchange for the canister you've examined, you will provide me with truthful information." Her knees began to shake, but she plowed on. "To be specific, you will answer any question I ask you, without taking offense; you will supply unsolicited advice and explanations; and—" Rachel hesitated, but she had to insure that the Rofa would obey her implicitly. "—and you will swear your personal allegiance to me."

Concha released an explosive breath. "Deputy Ajmani, are you certain—?"

Khanwa's orange eyes were bright. "For how long would my ob-li-gation last?"

"For the duration of your stay at Earth Port Station."

Khanwa appeared to give the offer consideration. "Agreed. Make out the invoice now. I will sign."

Rachel looked around the dock. Fran still stood near the pallet, watching the medics strap Carl onto the gurney. In five strides, Rachel crossed to her. "Fran. I need to write up an invoice."

Fran seemed to come to herself with a start. "Oh. Deputy Ajmani." Looking bewildered, she unhooked the computerized workboard from her belt and handed it to Rachel.

"Thanks." As Rachel walked back to the Rofa, she hastily jotted down the terms of the agreement on the invoice screen and signed it. She held up the workboard. "Honorable Captain?"

Khanwa snatched it from her hand, read the agreement, and also signed. "I want a hard copy." Before Rachel could offer to help, it tapped the command to print. The workboard hummed, then extruded two copies of the invoice on colored film. Khanwa carefully compared the printed version with the agreement on the workboard, then peeled off the top copy.

The Rofan always took what was theirs. Following protocol, Rachel grabbed the workboard back. She stuffed her hard copy of the invoice into her pocket.

Concha folded her arms. "Deputy—"

Wu leaned close to the aide. "Shh."

Khanwa ignored everyone but Rachel. "I swear myself to you, Deputy Aja-mani, by my blood, my knife, and my kin. What do you ask of me first?"

Rachel could scarcely believe her own actions. "First?" she repeated blankly. "Well, I—"

Wu's tone was light, but it carried a note of uneasy warning. "Deputy . . ."

Concha regarded her in stony silence.

Rachel sighed inwardly. She had already provided the XRC with the grounds to initiate an investigation, to continue talking with Khanwa would only compound the damage. "I'll contact you later, honorable Captain. In the meantime, you are free to conduct business as usual, provided you obey all station regulations. Also—" She hesitated, but her need to know was too great. "I shall want information concerning the shutdown of Igsha Reey Port."

"Ah, yes." Khanwa gave her a shrewd, sidelong glance. "I shall get it for you, Deputy Aja-mani."

"Thank you, honorable Captain."

Khanwa turned and walked off in the abrupt way of the Rofan.

Rachel turned toward the XRC aide, but Concha was already striding across the dock in the opposite direction, undoubtedly to make an unflattering report. Rachel sighed. "Oh . . . damn it."

Wu stepped up beside her. "So. You've bought an informant. Dare I ask how you intend to pay?"

Tension began to splinter into exhaustion. Still laden with the workboard, Rachel wrapped both arms around it and hugged it close. "With shiny rocks." She looked toward the damaged gantry. Technicians were gathering to assess the needed repairs. Rosita was taking a statement from Roberto, the reach-fork driver. Carl was gone. Evidently, the medics had wheeled him away. "Think Carl will be okay?"

"Hope so. Poor kid." Wu touched her shoulder. "And now . . . my turn."

Rachel waited until they were alone in the lift to Safety Checkpoint. "Yes?"

Wu sucked his teeth, making a noise of disgust. "I told you to stay off the dock. I don't trust that little minx from the XRC."

Rachel frowned. "Why?"

"Animal instinct, or something—I don't know. But I *do* know that I *told* you—"

"Wu—"

"—to stay off the *dock*!" He put his hands on his hips in a facetious posture of scolding. "When are you going to listen to me?"

Rachel recognized the real anxiety behind his playful facade. "I'm listening now."

Wu regarded her with an abruptly serious expression. "The Earth freighter, *La Vaca*, just put into port, inbound from Igsha Reey."

Rachel mentally fumbled with the sudden change of topic. She knew the *La Vaca*; it was a regular visitor. "Marj Mendez, Captain."

"And nobody's fool. Rather than risk the station's lines being tapped, the honorable captain sent a sealed message to me, carried personally by her senior pilot."

Rachel made a wry face. In the normal course of daily routine, such precautions would seem laughably paranoid. But with so many concurrently running crises, she could only applaud the freighter captain's discretion. "Please tell me that she just wanted to arrange a romantic rendezvous."

"I wish." Wu did not smile. "Seems honorable Captain Mendez has a stowaway on board: A Jadamii."

For a moment, Rachel had trouble drawing her next breath. She tried to remember what Khanwa had said about a Jadamii at Igsha Reey Port.

Wu regarded her warily. "Rachel?"

"A Jadamii," she murmured. A nebulous connection began to form, just beneath the surface of thought. She recalled Bailey's words. *"That's Farnii for 'thank you.'"* Rachel turned to gaze at Wu. "Why would a Jadamii steal passage aboard an Earth freighter? The Jadamiin despise Humans."

Wu shrugged. "Add those to your list of questions to ask."

"My list?" Rachel said. "I can't take the case."

"Oh, but you must."

"Are you nuts? I'm baby-sitting Dock Two."

"Captain Mendez has her uninvited guest secured. Says she'll wait until you're free." Wu seemed to focus his attention upon the air in front of his nose. "Says she won't release custody of the Jadamii to anyone but you."

"Me?" Rachel peered at Wu. "Why me?"

"She likes you."

Rachel snorted, suspecting that the captain's attitude reflected the subtle influence of a certain Safety warden. "Likes me? She has a funny way of showing it."

Wu spoke blandly. "Should I turn the whole thing over to the XRC?"

"You fight dirty."

"So you'll take the case?"

Rachel clenched her jaw, not trusting herself to speak. Again, she tried to recall what Khanwa had said. *A duel between an unarmed Jadamii and a what?* Rachel abruptly realized she still carried Fran's workboard. She glanced down at the invoice still glowing on the screen. Below her name, instead of Khanwa's signature, were scrawled three words: *Danger Starcatcher Here.*

Khanwa had not signed the invoice, which rendered the agreement void. Rachel wanted to believe the Rofa had simply swindled the station out of a barrel of rocks, but it had taken the oath. The tension of a half formed intuitive leap shimmered through her mind. *Starcatcher.*

Wu peered at her. "Rachel?"

"Something's going on," she said distantly. She could almost see it, catch the glancing edge of it with the periphery of her mind. "Something . . . big."

"Rachel, please," Wu said in a plaintive tone. "Don't go spooky on me."

The portentous sense of a far-reaching web of events faded, and Rachel realized just how odd she sounded. Acting on impulse, she submitted the invoice to her own personal account, then cleared the screen. *Watch and wait.* "Sorry." She grinned at Wu. "Too much coffee."

"No such thing."

"Not enough sleep."

"I'll accept that."

Still smiling, Rachel studied Wu, noting the sag of fatigue in his shoulders. Her oldest and best friend, Wu had been a part of her daily life for nearly twenty years. She wanted to trust him, wanted to tell him about Kamians who quoted Prudence Clarke, Freeholders who spoke Farnii, and Rofan who broke contracts and kept their promises with the selfsame act. "What would I do without you?"

Wu's brows shot up. "Pardon?"

The lift glided to a halt, and the doors opened. A crowd of staffers and technicians waited to board, along with silver rank Deputy Sonría Omar. Rachel gaped at her colleague. " 'Ría!"

In her late fifties, Sonría wore her graying hair in a conservative shoulder-length style. "Audit's canceled," she announced, her dark blue eyes virtually disappearing in the creases of her smile. "We're back on the job."

Wu feigned terror. "Run for the hills!"

Rachel stepped off the lift to allow everyone else on, nudging Wu ahead of her. "Audit's canceled?"

"Yup. I got Dock Two. Alfie's handling administration. You're officially off the clock." Sonría pointed at the workboard in Rachel's hand. "Hey, what's that? You've been promoted to senior cargo tech?"

Rachel groaned. "It's a long story."

Sonría laughed. "I can always tell when you're tired, Rachel. You start carrying weird stuff around."

"I do not!"

"And you get argumentative."

Wu chuckled.

Rachel scowled at him.

Wu assumed an expression of wounded innocence. "I didn't say anything."

"You—"

Sonría tactfully interrupted the exchange. "Rachel, since I'm going down, you want me to return that workboard to its rightful owner?"

Rachel passed it over. "Thanks. Belongs to Fran."

A courteous technician held the doors. Sonría backed toward the lift. "So. What's it like down there?"

Rachel smiled weakly. "Busy."

Wu bounced on his toes. "And the main gantry is out of order."

The lift doors slowly closed on Sonría's expression of dawning alarm.

In Checkpoint, the monitor area filled a large, open room. Holographs hung from ceiling projectors like sheer, glowing curtains, detailing reports from the Environmental and Docking Control offices. The auxiliary and long-range communications banks ran along the left wall. To the right, a hallway led to a complex of offices, the lift to Station Central, and the detention block. A small lounge consisting of an old couch, a vid, a brewer, and a couple of armchairs occupied a back corner of the room. In the middle of the floor, the Checkpoint coordinator, Kepler Thai, sat on a swivel chair in the center of a circular console.

Wu waved a cheery greeting as he entered. "Kepler. Got those leaking chemical batteries handled?"

Kepler glanced over his shoulder. His grizzled brows were knotted, and his lined face drawn with concern. "No, unfortunately. Three more turned up. We can't seem to trace the problem."

Rachel drifted toward the lounge, wishing she had more time to rest and eat before dealing with a Jadamiin stowaway. A plate full of cornbread crumbs rested beside the brewer. She brushed the crumbs into the palm of her hand and funneled them into her mouth. "Say, Kepler—" She nearly choked before she remembered to chew and swallow. "Why was the audit canceled?"

Kepler pulled off his headset. "As I understand it, Rachel, the XRC had an emergency meeting with a delegation of ambassadors from Phi-Nu."

"Ambassadors?" Rachel brushed stray crumbs from her uniform and frowned in thought, mentally reviewing the latest list of incoming ships. "From Phi-Nu? I wasn't notified."

Wu crossed to a projection and studied it. "Their Excellencies got in about forty minutes ago, but the XRC insisted upon a communications blanket. How stealthy. They even arranged for an expensive docking, so that Their Excellencies could be conveyed in secrecy to the meeting." Wu paused, rubbing his chin with his thumb knuckle. "Seems they also insisted upon slotting the ship to one of those fancy, premium berths on Dock Two. Oopsy. Rather indiscreet, don't you think?"

"Rather." Rachel suspected that every merchant client aboard the station would be discussing the ambassadors' arrival. "Where's the meeting?"

"Dunno." Wu raised his brows expectantly at Kepler. "Please don't tell me it's in Station Central. We just put new carpet in our nice conference room."

An unexpected chill caught Rachel.

Alien visitors were always confined to special docks designed to meet their particular needs. In the case of the Rofan and Phi-Nurians, it was a matter of high priority to disallow contact with Humans who were untrained in xenorelations, and so they were never permitted access beyond Checkpoint. Aliens were violent; Humans were not. To allow Phi-Nurians into Station Central, full of families with children, was unthinkable.

Kepler shook his head. "They're all meeting aboard the World Council's ship. They took Deputy Jimanez-Verde with them." He blew out his cheeks. "I sent Kemi and Pat to wait outside the hatch of *Gaia's Love*, in case of trouble."

Wu grunted. "Good thinking."

Trying to hide her growing apprehension, Rachel turned

and looked at the brewer. "Well, maybe this meeting is a godsend. It will keep the XRC busy while everyone else gets some work done." She found a clean mug. "Now, if I don't receive any more phone calls . . ."

"You won't," Wu said. "I put your phone on lockout."

Rachel whirled to stare at him. "You can't do that!"

"I can." Wu dropped his voice to a darkly overblown baritone. "I have the power."

"I'm on duty!"

"Not anymore."

Fighting for patience, Rachel clutched her mug in both hands. "But I *was*."

Wu's eyes sparkled, and his mouth stretched into a thin-lipped goblin smile. "You were a mile high without a safety harness." He set his hands on his belt. "Which reminds me, I ought to put you on report for that stunt."

Kepler cleared his throat. "It's okay, Rachel. I took your calls for you. Your mother sends her regards."

Rachel exhaled through her teeth. "Damn."

Kepler continued, tactfully ignoring her reaction. "There was also some routine station business and several inquiries from the XRC regarding your whereabouts. Nothing important. It's all on your message board."

The XRC? A fresh brush of cold trailed over Rachel's skin. She drew a steadying breath and forced herself to smile at Kepler. "Thank you." Wu had locked up her phone to prevent the XRC from contacting her, she was certain of it. Wondering what part the stowaway Jadamii played in his decision, Rachel turned back to the brewer and filled her mug with spice tea. Her hands shook. *Danger Starcatcher Here.*

Behind her, Wu resumed questioning Kepler. "So. No trace on the batteries. What about our 'special project'?"

Kepler sounded worried. "They've definitely tapped into the communications links."

Wu sighed. "Oh, goody."

"And we might have a missing sanitation tech."

Her attention caught, Rachel turned and moved to stand beside Wu at the console. "Missing?"

Kepler nodded. "Maury Long. He's new to Earth Port." He keyed in a command, and one of the holographic curtains displayed an image of a rugged looking redhead in

white coveralls. "Last seen on his way to deep storage.
We're guessing he's lost down there."

Wu crooked his brows, clearly uneasy. "I really . . .
really . . . don't like that," he murmured. "We're hunting
two unknowns. We're patrolling for unstable chemical batteries. And now we have to search for a missing tech?"

Rachel frowned. "Do you have enough people?"

"No," Wu said. "And it bothers me that we're becoming
so overextended." He looked up at the ceiling in thought,
rolling his tongue around in his mouth as if savoring a hard
candy. "Kepler. Keep our staffers on the special project.
Organize search parties from off duty volunteers. Get ac-
countants, schoolteachers, whoever can be spared. Groups
of twos and threes. No one goes alone."

Kepler clicked off Maury's image and pulled his headset
on. "Got it."

Wu looked at Rachel mournfully. "And this started out
as such a nice day."

She set down her untasted tea. "Guess I should go to
the *La Vaca* and get out of your way."

Wu shook his head emphatically. "Oh, no, Deputy. You
will not be our next missing person."

"Wu—"

"You're not going anywhere alone. Not ever again." He
crossed to a recessed panel in the wall above the communications bank and unlocked it. The panel slid aside to reveal
a storage compartment with a rack of laser pistols. Wu
selected one weapon and belted it on. "In fact, my esteemed Deputy Ajmani, I plan to personally escort you
everywhere." He drew the gun and checked the safety
switch. "Even to the loo."

Rachel's skin prickled, and she wished his pledge of protection did not sound so much like a veiled threat. "You
know," she said, attempting a casual tone, "you're completely overreacting."

Wu grunted, peering at the laser's charge level. "I'm
funny that way." He holstered the pistol, shut and locked
the compartment, then presented her with a bright smile.
"Ready?"

Rachel's heart began to pound. "I'm not—"

A young man dressed in lavender surgical scrubs strode
from the hallway into the main monitor area. Silky, blue-

black hair slid over his forehead and overshadowed his dark eyes, and a golden Medica badge gleamed on his left shoulder.

Rachel stood motionless, her protests forgotten, and stared at the station's new surgeon. Wu, she recalled, had described Doctor Tigre DeFlora as "pretty."

A severe understatement.

Tigre's fine-boned features were extraordinarily graceful, saved from feminine delicacy by a hint of sharpness in the nose and chin. His hands appeared muscular, oversized compared to his slight build. His caramel-colored complexion suggested an Isleño background, as did the unmistakable storm of temper that brewed in his widening eyes.

Tigre stepped up to Kepler's console. "Wu Jackson?"

Wu stepped forward. "Here."

Tigre whirled. "You!" His voice was thick. "You have a lot of nerve!"

Wu raised his brows, smiling. "Why . . . thank you."

Tigre stalked closer. "What kind of idiotic game do you think you're playing? I've got a facility full of chemical burns, and you—"

Wu turned to Rachel. "Deputy Ajmani," he said in a light tone, "allow me to present the new head of Medica, Doctor Tigre DeFlora."

Tigre's face went brick red with sudden fury. "Don't get cute with me, you rotten bastard!"

Wu bounced on his toes. "Ah. Abuse. How delicious."

Tigre's eyes blazed. "You're just standing around cracking jokes? You need to by God find those leaking batteries!"

Rachel drew her brows down. "Doctor, Warden Jackson is doing everything in his power to—"

Tigre rounded on her. "Are you defending this incompetent shit? Twenty personal injury accidents in as many hours, not counting the seventeen acid burns from an exploding battery. And a few minutes ago, I had to narcotize some poor kid who fell off a—" Tigre's attention abruptly fixed upon Rachel's hands, and his voice rose in volume. "What the hell happened to you?"

Rachel had completely forgotten about the scrapes from the reach-fork's pallet. She clenched her fingers into tight fists. "Nothing."

Wu tilted his head. "How is Carl, by the way?"

Tigre returned his glare to Wu. "Are you a relative?"

"No, but—"

"Then it's none of your goddammed business!"

Wu's chuckle was low and purring. "But I am the Safety warden."

"Safety warden, my ass!" Tigre shouted. "It's your fault Carl fell off that—"

The heat of anger scorched Rachel's cheeks and throat. "Now, just a minute! You can't blame—"

Tigre ignored her, pointing at Wu's pistol. "Is that a gun?" His mouth framed several silent words, before he seemed to find his voice again. "Do you actually intend to shoot someone?"

Wu beamed at him. "Only if necessary."

Tigre's rage seemed to boil away. He stood staring and motionless for a long moment, then spoke very quietly: "You're finished." He backed away a few steps, as if from a large predator. "I'm notifying the authorities on Earth."

Rachel folded her arms. "About what?"

Tigre turned, swinging one slender arm in a violent gesture of finality, and strode off down the hallway toward the lift back to Medica.

At his console, Kepler raised his brows and puffed out his cheeks in silent comment.

Her pulse beating in her temples, Rachel glared after the surgeon, disgusted that she had initially found him attractive. "Why . . . the overbearing, foulmouthed, little piece of—" Fighting for self-control, she broke off and glanced at Wu. "You're fully licensed for that weapon. He has no grounds to report you."

"Stimulating, isn't he?"

"Not the word I'd choose," Rachel said. "Did he come all the way from Medica for the sole purpose of throwing a tantrum?"

"Evidently." As he gazed after Tigre, Wu's lips parted in a peculiar smile, and he adjusted his gun belt. "I think I'm in love."

CHAPTER SEVEN

CONCHA SINGH stood just inside the entry hatch of *Gaia's Love*, flagship of the World Council. The air lock's featureless, white walls offered no distraction from the pounding realization of her demoralizing failure. Half sick with shame, she wondered how Councillor Weber would react to her gross incompetence. *She was counting on me.*

The ventilation filters whispered softly as the system cycled out possible contaminates from Earth Port's odor-laden air. The smell of Dock Two, however, seemed to cling to Concha's silk sari. She grimaced ruefully. The entire station stank. She had expected some of it as a consequence of antique life-support systems, a sealed environment, and an endlessly recycled atmosphere; but nothing in the vid series had prepared her for the raw pungency of Earth Port.

Concha sighed and passed an unsteady hand over her shaved scalp. Everything about the station veered to the extreme, even the people. She recalled the nameless dock tech who snarled because she interrupted his work, then offered his coat because she looked cold; the fractious gantry operator, casually risking his life to repair a piece of outdated equipment; the warden, his nimble mind clearly evinced by his witty banter.

Rachel Ajmani. Concha had been unprepared for the peculiar force of Rachel's personality: icy and aloof in one instant, compassionate and protective the next. Concha sighed again. *And now she hates me.*

The air lock's inner hatch chimed, signaling the completion of the filtering process and granting her access to the ship. *Should be on the station, not here.* For a moment, sheer frustration held Concha motionless. "Idiot," she whispered to herself. "Do something."

The inner hatch hissed open, and the ship's purser stepped through, carrying a locked diplomatic satchel. A thin, bug-eyed man, Terrell always seemed to taste something bitter. When he saw Concha, he jumped, then laid a hand over his heart. "Good heavens, you scared me," he said. "Don't you have anything better to do than lurk in the air lock?"

His question rankled. Concha could offer no concrete reason for returning to *Gaia's Love*. Her mission involved observing Rachel, not retreating in failure. She walked around the purser, onto the ship. "Sorry."

Terrell sniffed with disapproval. "Check your shoes. I think you stepped in something."

The hatch closed, sealing him off from any reply. Humiliation flared through Concha, chased by anger, followed instantly by perverse amusement at her own expense. *I'm such an easy target.* Smiling sourly, she strode toward the galley. *Let's see if I can annoy anyone else.*

Like every compartment aboard the ship, the galley was white and sterile and bleak. Two Safety staffers in vibrant blue and green uniforms sat across from each other at the long table.

Surprised, Concha paused in the doorway. Then she abruptly recognized her partners in Operation Starcatcher, Jardín Azul and Rife Meier. Concha had not yet spoken to them, but she supposed the two would be as unfriendly as Terrell. Feeling both awkward and defiant, she walked into the galley without offering a greeting.

Rife appeared to doze, his head pillowed on his folded arms, his golden hair veiling his face. Jardín tinkered with a small particle welder, about the size and shape of a paring knife. Her heart-shaped face grew stern with concentration as she delicately twisted a probe, and she spoke without looking up. "The odor of Phi-Nurian dung clings."

Heat climbed Concha's throat, but she tightened her grin.

"So. You think I stink." She crossed to an upright stasis cupboard, opened it, and glanced over the wide array of unappetizing packaged sandwiches. "Terrell thinks so, too."

Jardín's tone was matter-of-fact. "No. I meant that we stink. I was warning you of the smell."

"Oh." Concha's shoulders slumped. "Sorry."

Rife stirred. "Terrell said you—?"

Concha grabbed a package at random. "Not in so many words, but he got the point across." A sanitizing lamp hung in a waist-high alcove beside the cupboard. She passed her hands under the blue light, enjoying the pleasant tingling across her palms. "I must admit, Terrell has talent. He can turn the most inane comment into an insult."

Rife chuckled sleepily. "Ignore him. He's perturbed because Councillor Weber made him fetch lunch—something yummy from the station's cafeteria, instead of these terrible sandwiches. And he thinks running errands is beneath him."

Concha found herself liking Rife. She settled into the empty chair beside him. "That's what the satchel was for? Groceries?"

"Probably." Rife laughed again. "Don't let him get to you."

"That's right," Jardín said, still involved with the welder. "Terrell's meanness is just a cover for a shocking lack of intelligence."

Concha savored the tart remark like a lime drop, its astringency washing away her sense of inner inertia. "After today's fiasco, Terrell will seem like a genius compared to me."

Rife snorted. "Doubt it."

Jardín asked quietly, "Trouble in paradise?"

The phrase was an Earth Port-ism. Concha grinned in spite of herself and unwrapped her sandwich. "It's just that—" The bread felt soggy. She peeled it apart and studied the lumpy green contents. "Chopped vegetables, I hope." She took a bite and discovered that the main ingredient, broccoli, had attained a bitter edge. "It's just that things aren't going as planned."

Rife grunted. "You can say that again."

Concha stared down at the sandwich, steeling herself for

another bite. "Not that I knew what the plan was, really. Councillor Weber didn't have much time to go over the details before she sent me out."

Rife raised his head and rubbed his eyes groggily. "Sent you out?"

"To be the observer in—" Concha glanced toward the door and dropped her voice. "—Operation Starcatcher."

Rife sat up, suddenly seeming wide awake. "You?" he said in a tone of vast disbelief. "She sent . . . you?"

Confused by his reaction, Concha glanced back and forth between Jardín and Rife. "An important matter came up, and she couldn't go."

Rife drew his golden brows together, his gaze seeming to turn inward. "And she sent you? To observe Deputy Ajmani?"

Swallowing hard, Concha set down her sandwich. "You mean, the councillor didn't tell you?"

"No."

Jardín murmured: "Rife, why are you so surprised? This is typical, really."

"True." Rife seemed to abruptly return to himself, and he grinned at Concha. "So, welcome aboard, partner."

Jardín kept her attention focused on the adjustments with her probe. "Yes, welcome. Perhaps I might offer a more comprehensive briefing?"

Some of the tension eased from Concha's shoulders. "Thank you. I'd appreciate your guidance."

"The premise of Starcatcher," Jardín said, speaking in a bookish manner, "is actually quite simple. In order for a candidate to prove their worthiness, they must work through a series of carefully orchestrated ordeals while under close observation. They are deprived of their usual support resources, such as the assistance of friends or colleagues, in order to insure that all vital decisions are the sole responsibility of the candidate."

Rife settled his head on his arms again. "It's a pretty good system, all in all."

Jardín nodded slightly. "The true difficulty lies in keeping the process a secret. I trust the councillor has at least stressed the importance of that?"

"She has," Concha said. "She told me I could speak of it only to you two. And Warden Jackson."

"Excellent." Still intent upon her work, Jardín shifted the angle of the welder. "To bring you up to speed with Operation Starcatcher, we've just discovered that Councillor Weber has canceled the procedural audit. Which means that Deputy Ajmani has her support people back."

Concha shifted uneasily. "That's bad, isn't it?"

Rife spoke into his folded arms. "Yeah. But it could be worse. At least we still have Warden Jackson on our side."

Flinching inwardly, Concha recalled her narrow escape from arrest and detention. "The warden helped me out just a few minutes ago."

Jardín raised the probe and carefully blew on its tip. "Without the warden's unconditional assistance, the Starcatcher mission would be impossible," she said. "I doubt, however, that he thinks of himself as our ally. I'm certain that his only consideration is Rachel Ajmani's nomination to the World Council."

The drama series had vividly portrayed the friendship between Deputy Ajmani and the warden. Concha smiled. "True."

Jardín peered intently into the welder. "A delegation from Phi-Nu arrived about an hour ago, and Councillor Weber canceled the audit to meet with them. That's why all subpoenaed support personnel were released to return to work. And, incidentally, why she sent you out as an observer."

Trying to understand, Concha drew her brows together. "But, if Deputy Ajmani is supposed to be alone and without help, then why—?" She floundered, uncertain that she knew enough to ask a coherent question. "Didn't you say that all the decisions had to be hers? Shouldn't we abort the operation?"

"No," Jardín said. "Starcatcher continues as scheduled."

Once again, Concha looked back and forth between her two colleagues. Their calm detachment helped her to keep her own emotions from rising. "But that makes absolutely no sense. What is the councillor thinking?"

Rife murmured into his elbow. "Glee Weber is a clever woman. I'm sure she has reasons."

"Yes, but—" Concha gestured helplessly. "Everything you're doing—the ordeals, or whatever you call them— aren't they pointless unless Deputy Ajmani resolves them?"

Rife sighed. "Yeah."

Jardín nodded pensively. "Worse than that. Rife and I have engaged in—well, if they're not crimes, then they're certainly activities of dubious legality. Without the justification of Starcatcher, we're nothing more than troublemakers."

Concha jumped up. "I'm going to call the councillor."

"Don't," Rife said. "Don't bother her. That meeting is pretty important, I think."

Concha spread her hands. "But she can't mean for the mission to continue. She doesn't—"

"She can," Jardín said in her soft voice. "She does."

"But—"

Jardín raised her gaze to Concha. "We have to consider the best use of our time and resources. A trip like this, aboard the World Council flagship, costs a great deal. We simply cannot waste the taxpayers' money."

Feeling foolish, Concha sank into her chair. The trip to Earth Port had received a huge amount of media attention. As things stood, Councillor Weber would undoubtedly take some heat for canceling the audit. "Oh. Of course."

"Speaking of waste." Rife sat up and looked at the remains of the broccoli sandwich. "If you're not going to eat that, may I have it?"

"Please." Concha pushed it toward him, still trying to think. "So if the audit is off, and Starcatcher is now merely an ordeal for the Safety staffers, where does that leave me? I'm supposed to be the observer."

Rife wolfed a bite of sandwich and shrugged. "You still are."

Jardín set aside the probe and closed the cover in the welder's slender handle. "In fact, I think it may be up to you to salvage the mission."

"Don't say that." With a pang of guilt, Concha recalled her reasons for retreating to the ship. "I'm failing. Deputy Ajmani won't let me near her."

Rife regarded her earnestly, speaking through a mouthful of bread and broccoli. "Keep trying. Stand up to her. Be tough. She'll respect you for it."

Concha shook her head. "You want me to 'out-tough' Deputy Ajmani? Can't be done. At least, not by me." She then remembered how Rachel interacted with the staffer and the cargo tech, how respectfully she had treated the underlings. Concha narrowed her eyes in thought. "But maybe I can 'out-weak' her."

Rachel walked briskly along the upper level of Dock One, which serviced only Earth traffic. The arbitrators and Human merchant clients were relaxed, their expressions and behavior friendly. Many of them sat together at small tables, sharing an early midday meal.

Rachel reflected that she ought to find the nonhostile environment soothing, but instead discovered that she resented everyone's complacency. She glanced at Wu, who strolled by her side.

Though Wu wore a pistol on his belt, and his gaze flicked alertly over passersby, he did not present the visage of a man who expected trouble. A soft smile lifted just the corners of his mouth. He noticed her scrutiny. "Yes?"

Rachel shrugged one shoulder. "Nothing."

Wu chuckled. "You're mad at me."

"Maybe." Amused, though not sure why, Rachel looked away to hide her sudden grin. "You're still thinking about that little spitfire."

"Tigre." Wu made a soft and lascivious noise. "Yes."

Rachel kept her attention fixed in front of her, still battling to hide her amusement. It was a common occurrence, for Wu to seduce an adversary, and the penchant occasionally led him to sleep with Rofan. Instead of a means to physical pleasure, or as an expression of love, Wu usually employed sex as a form of conquest, and the gender of his prey seemed inconsequential to him.

It was this tendency that prevented Rachel from viewing Wu as anything more than a good friend. "You're after him, aren't you?"

"Tigre? Absolutely. What doesn't kill you, will wake you up."

"I thought that only applied to coffee."

"Applies to anything hot. And drinkable."

Rachel snorted, but found companionable reassurance in Wu's cheerful lechery. She reached into her pocket and withdrew the blue invoice copy. "What do you think about this?" She handed him the sheet. "At the bottom. On the signature line."

Wu took the invoice and read. "Danger. Star—" He jerked to a halt. "—catcher. . . ."

Caught off guard, Rachel walked on a few steps and had to backtrack. "I almost brushed it off as a prank, except the honorable captain—"

In an instant, Wu ripped the signature line from the bottom of the invoice, wadded it into a small pellet, and swallowed it.

Aghast, Rachel stared at him. "What the hell—?"

A glitter of perspiration covered Wu's upper lip, but he offered a bright smile. "Needed salt."

Rachel also broke into a sweat. Beneath her uniform, the drops trickled down her sides like ice water. He had destroyed evidence.

Wu handed back the rest of the sheet. His hand shook. "It was nothing."

Rachel found her voice with difficulty. "Nothing?"

"Nothing," he repeated in an intense tone. "Trust me."

Rachel pocketed the invoice, deciding not to make a scene on Dock One. "You don't make it easy."

Wu avoided her gaze. "I'll explain later."

"Damn right, you will." Still in shock, not knowing what else to do or say, Rachel resumed walking. Wu fell into step beside her. Neither spoke.

When they reached the La Vaca's access hatch, Rachel pulled out her phone and keyed the berth number.

A surly male answered. "La Vaca. Night watch."

"Port Authority Deputy Rachel Ajmani requesting permission to—"

The watch officer interrupted eagerly. "Oh, thank God, you're here, Deputy!" The access hatch slid open. "Please come aboard. Captain Mendez will meet you at the air lock."

Rachel raised her brows. "Thank you." She stepped through the hatch, putting her phone away. Still pretending that she felt no strain in her friendship with Wu, she added casually: "Watch officer sounded glad to see us."

Wu followed her aboard, then waited for the hatch to close. "Really?"

Rachel shivered at his tone of voice. He was pretending, too.

The air lock began to cycle, then hummed to a halt,

ventilators bumping with the sudden pressure change. Rachel then realized that someone had overridden the sequence, evidently unwilling to wait an extra forty seconds.

The interior hatch opened. A woman with blonde braids and anxious blue eyes stood with her hand still resting on the control panel. "Deputy Ajmani? I'm Captain Marj Mendez."

Rachel stepped in. The captain, she noticed, was barefoot and wore a red flannel robe over white pajamas. *Night watch.* She nodded respectfully. "Honorable Captain." She glanced at Wu. "I believe you know Warden Jackson?"

Marj seemed not to hear her. "The Jadamii is in the upper aft hold. This way." She started walking down a curving passage, still talking. "It yelled a lot, at first, when we locked it up. But then it got quiet."

Rachel followed the captain. "The Jadamii?"

"Right." Marj sighed edgily. "It stayed so quiet that I got nervous and looked in on it."

Walking behind Rachel, Wu groaned. "Marj. What did I tell you?" Exasperation and worry infused his voice. "It's an unfriendly alien. It already attacked Pete. Do you honestly believe—?"

Marj interrupted. "It was lying on the floor. I watched to make sure it was still breathing, and I tried talking to it. I think it's unconscious."

As she followed Marj along the passage, Rachel's stomach clenched. The stowaway no longer occupied the realm of an abstract problem. Real, unavoidable, it displayed all the early warning signs of a diplomatic nightmare. "Honorable Captain, please think carefully before you answer. Did you touch the Jadamii?"

"No."

"You're certain?"

Marj's voice sharpened in anger. "Of course, I'm certain. I stayed near the door, in case it was playing possum." They reached an inner hatch, and Marj turned to confront Rachel. "Don't patronize me, Ajmani. I make a regular run to Igsha Reey Port, and I've seen things that would turn your hair white. I know the score, here. I know where Earth stands with Jada. I know where you stand with that damned XRC. And I know that this situation—" She gestured toward the hatch. "—this is *bad.*"

Rachel relaxed fractionally and offered Marj a tired smile. "Glad someone else appreciates the scope of this problem."

Wu drew his pistol and checked the setting. "I'm not only appreciative, honorables, I'm terrified." He grinned at Rachel. "Let's get this over with, before I need to start breathing into a bag."

Rachel nodded. "I'm ready. Open the door."

Still grinning, Wu placed himself between Rachel and the hatch. "Me first."

Rachel stepped back and spread her hands in surrender. Wu pushed the control panel's intercom button and stood motionless for a long moment, head slanted, listening, a wary expression stealing his smile. Then he keyed the hatch open, and braced his pistol in both hands, his aim sweeping for a target.

Rachel tensed.

Wu stepped cautiously into the hold, keeping his pistol aimed at something on the deck plates, and sidled toward the wall.

The Jadamii lay on its side, stretched out in a limp sweep of silky silver fur.

Trying to judge its size, Rachel swallowed. "Big. About seven feet?"

"At least." Marj spoke grimly. "Maybe closer to eight."

Wu kept his attention on the Jadamii. "It's still breathing."

Rachel edged into the hold, and Marj followed.

Except for the rise and fall of its breath, the Jadamii remained motionless.

Marj spoke quietly, as if in a sickroom. "It was lying in this exact position when I last saw it."

"Mm." Rachel could not tear her gaze from the alien. Though she knew it was a person, animal comparisons forced their way to mind, perhaps because of its unclad state.

The Jadamii possessed a mane like a lion's, which grew in a tapering fringe down its spine to the plumed tip of its tail. Fanning larger than a man's spread hand, the large ears resembled bat wings, with velvety membranes stretched over delicate webbing. From what she could observe of its face, half buried beneath an arm, it conveyed none of the rodentlike qualities of a Rofa. The Jadamii sported more whiskers than a baby seal, but the charcoal patterns around its eyes and snout suggested the facial markings of a timber wolf.

Rachel murmured, "Beautiful, isn't it?"

Marj made a noncommittal noise. "That's what Pete said, even though it slashed his shoulder open."

Rachel glanced around the hold, noting that the cargo seemed to consist entirely of stasis units. One of the units had been removed from its crate, and it rested on the deck like an open coffin. "Honorable Captain, please tell me again what happened here."

Marj leaned up against the bulkhead near the hatch, and spoke as if relating a well-worn story: "Crewman Pete Glenrow came in to run a routine cargo check. The Jadamii jumped out from behind some crates and grappled with him, clawing open his shoulder. Pete broke free, ran from the hold, and secured the hatch behind himself. He then notified the watch and reported to sick bay." Marj shrugged. "It's all in my statement. Doc says you can talk to Pete when he wakes up, if you don't upset him. He was pretty shook by the whole thing."

Rachel nodded, trying to think. The stowaway had obviously used the stasis unit for the hyperspace jump. "And when did the Jadamii lose consciousness?"

Marj regarded her narrowly. "I don't know, Deputy. Like I said, it made quite a racket when Pete locked it in the hold. But I don't know if it stopped yelling and sulked for a while before it took a nap."

"When did you notice its silence?"

"About three hours ago."

Wu backed slowly from the Jadamii, his gaze darting over the deck plates as if searching for something.

Rachel turned her attention to the alien, trying to imagine the vulnerable figure engaged in hostile or agitated behavior. "You said it was 'yelling,' honorable Captain. What did it say?"

Marj blinked, clearly finding the question unexpected. "Didn't recognize the language. Wasn't Trade, or any of the Rofan dialects, so I suppose it was Farnii." She rubbed the back of her neck. "We tried talking to it, but it didn't seem to understand. Just kept yelling. Wish I'd thought of recording some of it."

"Well, yes," Rachel said mildly, "it might have been useful. Or it might have been an earful of expletives." She wondered why the Jadamii had shouted, why it had attacked the crewman in the first place. She knew nothing of Jadamiin psychology, so could not guess a motive. The fact that it dared to steal passage aboard an Earth vessel suggested it knew how reluctant Humans were to resort to physical violence. "Too bad it didn't try to explain itself in a quiet, rational fashion—" Rachel broke off with a shrug.

"Yeah." Marj grinned ruefully. "If it had done that, Deputy, I probably would have forgiven its trespasses, taken it to the galley, and filled it to the ears with hot cider. I've always wanted to meet a Jadamii."

Rachel returned the smile. "Me, too."

Wu stood beside the stasis unit. "Deputy?"

Rachel glanced at him and saw his attention lingering on the interior of the stasis unit. Circling the figure on the floor, she crossed to Wu. "Find something?"

Keeping the pistol trained on the Jadamii, Wu deftly used his free hand to slip a pair of tweezers from his belt. "Think so." He reached into the stasis unit with the tweezers. "Under the headrest."

Rachel looked where he directed and spotted a curving edge of yellow plastic. "A drug cartridge?"

Wu coaxed the item from beneath the headrest and held it up. A finger-length tube of plastic, the disposable injector displayed Rofan glyphs in orange and green. Wu beamed and repeated in a satisfied tone: "A drug cartridge."

From her place near the hatch, Marj made a noise of disgust. "Phenox. See it everywhere at Igsha Reey Port."

Wu grunted. "See it here, too, unfortunately."

Marj folded her arms. "You'll dust it for prints, right? I want it proven that my crew had nothing to do with this."

"Standard procedure, honorable Captain." Wu peered at the cartridge, as if trying to decipher the Rofan, and added in a distracted tone. "It's a sedative, actually manufactured on Jada, but the Rofan take it for fun." He glanced at Rachel. "As I understand it, Deputy, Phenox has an unusual cycle with the Jadamiin. Sedative-stimulant-sedative, in a single dose. On the Rofan, it acts as an aphrodisiac. Popular stuff."

Rachel released a pent-up breath and found some of her tension draining away. "So the Jadamii's current condition is self-induced? This is the second sleep phase?"

Wu nodded. "In my considered opinion. It's rather countersurvival to sedate oneself when at the mercy of so many potential enemies. And the necessity to escape the hold while still between sleep phases would explain the Jadamii's agitation."

Rachel had to admit Wu's reasoning seemed valid. "Though it doesn't explain why the Jadamii drugged itself in the first place."

"Maybe," Marj said tensely, "so it could pin the blame on us. Claim it was abducted."

Wu shrugged one shoulder. "Maybe, but to what purpose?"

Rachel felt an unexplainable touch of cold at his words. "We'll dust for prints. And if the Jadamii doesn't fall unconscious again, then we'll know this was the second cycle." She inclined her head toward Marj. "If that evidence is in our favor, then Jada's government can't claim it was a result of assault."

Marj smiled dryly. "They want to talk assault, they can look at pictures of Pete."

Suddenly weary, Rachel rubbed her face, mentally reviewing the next line of action. The sedative might be wearing off soon. "With your permission, honorable Captain, I'd like to get a team in here. Port Authority will take custody of the Jadamii and transport it to a supervised detention facility."

Marj's gaze traveled over the Jadamii. "Are you sure you want to do that, Deputy? It seemed . . . high-strung. Maybe you could leave it here on the *La Vaca.*"

Rachel began to answer, then paused to consider. With the continuous arrival of unscheduled traffic at Earth Port, the situation on Dock Two would probably deteriorate. Checkpoint detention was already crowded. Placing an excitable Jadamii in a cell next to frenzied Phi-Nurians or belligerent Rofan might be disastrous. However, leaving it on the ship was legally untenable.

Evidently encouraged by Rachel's silence, Marj spoke in

a reasonable tone. "We've got a guest cabin. Could put a lock on it, rig up some way of slipping food in."

Rachel replied slowly, an idea forming. "That's a generous offer, honorable Captain. But may I suggest another plan?"

A little over an hour later, Rachel stood in the center of the station's combat arts arena. Heavy padding covered the walls and floor of the small, square room. Cameras, intended to provide holocasts of the various tournaments, occupied numerous recesses in the ceiling.

Wu followed Rachel into the arena, glancing around doubtfully. "Please tell me you're joking."

Rachel gestured toward the wall opposite the door. "We can put a bunk there. And keep an eye on things via those cameras. The Jadamii will be perfectly safe and comfortable until we return it home."

"Safe and—?" Wu put his hands on his hips. "My esteemed Deputy Ajmani. May I respectfully remind you that we're in the heart of Station Central?"

Rachel regarded him stonily. "Conveniently close to the Port Authority offices."

Wu's brows shot up, and he retorted with unusual heat. "Conveniently close to the nursery."

"Don't try to—"

"What if our guest breaks out and decides it's in the mood for a snack?"

Rachel clamped down hard on her anger. "It's your job, Warden Jackson, to ensure that doesn't happen."

Shaking his head, Wu started away, then turned back to her. "Put the Jadamii in Checkpoint."

Frowning, Rachel folded her arms. "No."

"Please."

"Why? So you can eat its paperwork?"

Wu's hand went to his cheek, as if she had slapped him. "Rachel—" He appeared at a loss for words, and his dark eyes held a feverish brightness. "You have to trust me. There's more going on here than you realize. More at stake than just—"

Rachel's fury escalated. She clenched her jaw and spoke through her teeth. "Then fill me in, Warden Jackson. Tell me what I need to know."

Wu's shoulders sagged, and he lowered his gaze.

"Well? I'm waiting."

Wu sighed heavily. "Put the Jadamii in Checkpoint. This whole thing has the feel of a major galactic incident. Let me share some of the blame."

Sorrow tinged Rachel's anger. "Is that what this is about? Laying blame?"

Wu crossed to a wall and turned his back on her, running his hand over the gray canvas cover of the padding. "Yes. Entirely. Laying blame."

Rachel kept her voice steady with effort. "Is that why you insisted upon my involvement? To bear the blame?"

Wu dropped his forehead against the padded wall. Misery suffused his normally buoyant tone. "Rachel. Please—"

A hesitant tap sounded at the arena's door. Rachel turned to look.

A young woman with a shaved scalp stood on the threshold. She wore a pair of orange technician's overalls that were obviously borrowed; she had turned the cuffs twice, and the belt cinched at least eight inches of excess quilting to her slender waist. The woman's doelike eyes were wide with anxiety, and she spoke timidly. "Deputy Ajmani?"

Only at that moment did Rachel recognize the World Council aide, Concha Singh. Surprise robbed her response of irritation. "Yes?"

Concha swallowed loudly. "Excuse me, Deputy. I'm sorry to interrupt, but I need to talk to you—" Her gaze trailed nervously to Wu. "—as soon as possible."

Wu studied Concha, and a wintry grin thinned his lips. "What happened to your pretty sari?"

Concha glanced down at her ill-fitting overalls and plucked at its baggy folds in an apologetic manner. "This is more practical for the dock."

Rachel found herself countering Wu's chilly expression with a friendly smile. "I have a bit of time now. What do you need?"

Concha squared her shoulders, swallowing again, and looked Rachel in the eye. "I have instructions from Councillor Weber to accompany you as an observer."

"Oo," Wu said, glancing sidelong at Rachel. "Orders from on high. Can't argue with the World Council."

Rachel drew a breath to explode, then released it silently.

The aide was not to blame. It abruptly occurred to her that with Concha present, Wu could not blithely destroy more evidence. "I see," Rachel said with measured calm. "Somewhat unprecedented, isn't it?"

Concha tensed visibly, evidently expecting a verbal battle. "Yes, Deputy."

"Am I . . . under investigation?"

Concha appeared to consider several replies, then shook her head slightly. "I don't know, Deputy. Councillor Weber didn't mention that to me."

Rachel sorted through her growing doubts and misgivings. "Did Councillor Weber's instructions come about in response to the events you witnessed on the dock?"

"I—" Concha dropped her gaze. "I haven't yet reported on . . . your activities . . . with the Rofa."

Wu snorted. "Oh, really?"

Concha shot Wu a reproachful look, then returned her attention to Rachel, speaking in a rush. "Deputy, I just want to say, off the record, that I realize this is awkward for you. But I won't hamper you, I promise. I just—I just—" She knotted her fingers together. "I'd consider it an honor to watch you work."

Rachel forced back a skeptical reply and remained courteous. "Thank you." She gestured toward Concha's attire. "Do I understand that you wish to begin immediately?"

Concha's expression relaxed, and she edged through the door. "Yes, Deputy. If it's not too much trouble."

"Not at all." Inwardly tense, outwardly smiling, Rachel waved a hand in Wu's direction. "In fact, your presence will relieve Warden Jackson of bodyguard duty, so he can pursue more pressing investigations."

Wu's eyes darkened with alarm. "No."

"Yes." Rachel hardened her voice. "I insist. Go."

Wu glanced around the arena. "But we haven't resolved who gets custody of the . . . stowaway."

"I do."

Concha glanced back and forth between them, clearly confused.

Wu closed his eyes, as if struggling for patience. "Then I'll have no choice but to file a written report."

Rachel's smile turned brittle. "File any report you like. But be careful. Paperwork has a way of disappearing."

Wu sighed in exasperation and clutched the top of his head. "Please—"

Rachel walked past him toward the door, sweeping Concha along with her. "Excuse me, Warden. I have to contact a translator."

"Translator?"

Rachel paused and looked over her shoulder, carefully measuring Wu's reaction. "Professor Trabail Rye is aboard the station. Perhaps you've heard of him?"

Wu's expression flashed through a medley of emotions, then settled upon incredulity. "Bailey Rye? The fellow's an imbecile."

Rachel recalled Bailey's laserlike intellect. "I've met him. He's a genius."

Wu laughed. "He's a ninny."

Concha cleared her throat diffidently. "I've heard of him, Deputy. Though a Freeholder, he's something of a Renaissance man. Teaches physics and languages, designs spacecraft as a hobby."

Rachel smiled at Concha, then turned her back on Wu. "I'm not surprised to hear that. Right from the start, Professor Rye struck me as multitalented."

Only half listening as the aide continued to list Bailey's accomplishments, Rachel led Concha toward the Port Authority offices, feeling worse with every step away from Wu.

In the past, their quarrels had always ended in reconciliation. Anger and sorrow once again scorched Rachel's heart. She wanted to trust Wu, she wanted him to come after her and explain everything, but he betrayed her again. He let her walk away.

CHAPTER EIGHT

DÚTHA'S PURRING voice echoed in Meris' memory. *"Don't be afraid,"* the Rofa had said, gathering her in its arms. *"When you wake up, you'll have a friend by your side."*

Meris rolled over and opened her eyes. She found herself on a narrow bunk in a small, cube-shaped room. She was alone, and the stink of Human secretions filled the air.

Wildly, she pushed herself into a crouch and stared at her surroundings. Heavy, gray padding covered the walls and floor. A plastic bowl filled with liquid sat on the floor near the door. A large, empty basin sat in the opposite corner. Holographic cameras in the ceiling emitted a high-pitched whine, which indicated they were in operation.

In a flash of panic, Meris scrambled off the bunk and ran to the door. Like the rest of the room, it was also covered with padding. She scrabbled at its edges with her claws, searching in vain for a latch mechanism, and then she noticed the sticky matter coating her right hand.

Gingerly, Meris sniffed the unfamiliar substance. It smelled intensely of Human. In horror, she realized that the revolting aliens had laid hands on her person. Their rank odor clung to her silver fur.

Dútha had drugged her; and, while she slept in the grip of Phenox, the Humans had somehow claimed her. She was their prisoner. They were probably watching her on the cameras' transmissions.

"All Paths!"

Meris bolted across the cell and dived under the bunk. The space was narrow and shadowed, offering barely enough room to roll over. She felt much safer, though she distantly realized that the urge to hide stemmed from pure instinct. Seeking some relief from the stink of Humans, she curled her tail close and sniffed its tuft. The fur smelled of her own scent, overlaid by Dútha's warm odor. With an unaccountable sense of loss, Meris buried her nose in the tuft's silky depths and inhaled deeply.

She wondered where Dútha was, and if it had sold her to the Humans. Then she recalled that the Humans had not offered to buy her; they had merely exhorted Dútha to set her free. The other alien species wanted her, even the Kamians, for her supposed knowledge of the Artifact.

Meris' hearts began to thrum, but then it occurred to her that the Phenox had not erased her memory. She remembered everything up to the point of the drug taking effect. At least, she thought that she remembered everything. There might be gaps in her memory, but she was not sure how she could remember forgetting.

Wearily, Meris closed her eyes and pushed the confusing cycle of ideas from her mind. The facts that she could recall were more than enough to deal with.

According to Dútha, the Artifact was not merely a historical curiosity. A mysterious mathematician claimed to have deciphered it, which revealed the Artifact as a set of equations describing the structure of time and space. A preposterous notion, yet it caused her family to plan for her death, to prevent the knowledge from falling into the wrong hands. To complicate matters, alien governments also seemed to want possession of her for their own purposes.

Or, Meris was forced to consider, Dútha had lied from the start.

For whatever reason, she was a prisoner of the noisome Humans. At the very least, she would finally discover what they intended to do to her.

Meris closed her eyes and tried to calm the rapid, triplet beating of her hearts. Slightly heavier gravity added fatigue to her joints, which were already weak with terror. Outside the cell, a bell chimed once. Her eyes flinched open in an instant of panic, and the whiskerlike vibrissae on her brow lifted in an involuntary response to the sound. She stretched her webbed ears wide and listened.

Two Humans started up the corridor outside her cell, clomping along in the hurried, graceless way of their species. Even with the floor padding, Meris felt the vibrations of their heavy footsteps in her collarbone and pelvis. Both terrified and furious, she tensed, fluffing out her lustrous silver-and-charcoal pelt. Her silky mane stood up in a crest. The thick ruff that grew in a tapering fringe down her spine rose up in hackles.

The Humans passed her door and continued on their way up the hall. Still suspicious, Meris waited. They did nothing worse, however, than start a conversation. Tilting her ears, she listened intently. Long vowels and slushy consonants filled the incomprehensible phrases. Meris shuddered her fur in distaste, recalling how the Humans' bodily secretions soaked their clothing. *Even their language is wet.*

Their voices faded in the distance. Meris relaxed a bit in relief and shook her ruffled mane back into place.

She remembered Dútha's remarks concerning the Humans: *They simply want you to be happy and free.* Meris wondered how they had deceived Dútha, who had not seemed an overly trusting individual. Without a doubt, they were a species of damp and smelly liars.

Miserable with fear, Meris rolled onto her side and pulled her arms and legs close. The scent of Humans threatened to overwhelm her. She again curled her tail up so its tufted tip covered her nose, but it no longer provided protection from the stench.

The stink of Humans drifted to her on every air current, it breathed from the padded walls. Even the plastic dish of fluid in its place by the door seemed to exude a distinctly saline odor. Nausea bubbled through her empty belly. Within her span of available memory, she had never felt so physically wretched, not even when fleeing her attackers on Igsha Reey Port.

She was the Immortal Meris, Treasure of Jada, and Mother of Multitudes. But her children only saw her as a means to political power, and she would serve their ambitions better dead than alive.

A Human spoke in the corridor outside her cell, jerking Meris' hearts into an uneven gallop. She opened her eyes and fixed her gaze upon the door.

There were perhaps a dozen Humans, by the sound of it, all talking at once. Rage and bitter terror bristled the fur down her spine. Meris shifted and braced her back against the wall. She followed the Three Great Paths, which meant she could not attack, but only fight to defend herself. She flexed her fingers, extending her claws, determined to do anything necessary.

The door slid open to reveal a crowd of trousered legs, the upper halves of the Humans' bodies being hidden by the overhanging bunk. Meris listened but did not detect the hum of weapons.

Four pairs of legs stepped into the cell, moving cautiously. Meris clamped down tight on her fear and forced herself to lie still. The foremost Human in the group settled down on the floor so it could see her. Lost in a rising state of panic, Meris tensed, believing it planned to drag her out into the open.

As if sensing Meris' thoughts, the Human made no move toward her, but merely propped itself up on its elbows. The alien had a curly black mane, black eyes, and a smooth brown hide. Like most of its species, it wore simple garments of rough fabric, and its hairless face excreted moisture. The pelt on Meris' flanks twitched in loathing, but her breathing leveled out.

At that point, the Human slowly pulled a black box from a pocket. In a moment of sheer terror, all three of Meris' hearts froze and then beat together in a single stroke that jolted her entire body.

The Human's device was not a weapon, however, but a recorder, a compact model manufactured on Kam. Meris owned one just like it at home. She nearly swooned with relief.

A second Human stepped from the group and also lay down on the floor. Unlike its partner, it had a red mane, its hide was a lighter shade, and it wore its colorful clothing in layers like a Rofa. Though propped on its elbows, the alien kept its hands folded and its eyes cast down in a polite posture remarkably similar to that of a young Jadamii in the presence of an elder.

Meris studied the two, speculating that the differences in their coloring and garb indicated gender. The Human with the red mane reminded her of the creature aboard Igsha Reey Port who had attempted to intervene on her behalf against the attacking Rofa.

The first Human, moving with deliberate care, started the recorder and placed it on the floor. "Galactic date is thirty-two-fourteen-sixteen," it said in Trade. "Earth date is six-twelve-thirty-one."

Meris hunched her shoulders and wondered why the aliens wanted her to know the date.

The second Human raised its gaze and spoke in a faintly accented version of Jada's official language, Farnii. "Galactic date is thirty-two-fourteen-sixteen. I implore you, pretend you don't speak Trade. Earth date is six-twelve-thirty-one."

Being more adept at auditory signals than visual cues, Meris immediately recognized the alien's voice. This was her would-be rescuer, Bailey.

"I am Rachel Ajmani," stated the first Human, "a silver rank deputy of Earth Port Authority. With this statement, and in accordance with Galactic Trade Association laws, the following complaints are made against you by the Mendez y Mendez Trade Company: Unauthorized entry of the deep space freighter *La Vaca*, stealing passage aboard said ship and thereby defrauding said company of rightful profit, unauthorized use of a hyperspace stasis unit, and assault of a crew member. How do you plead?"

Stunned and confused, Meris could only stare at the deputy.

Bailey spoke swiftly. "She's Rachel Ajmani from Port Authority. You're in terrible danger, Mother of Multitudes. Your enemies are now here, meeting with corrupt members of our planetary government. I want to help you. Mendez y Mendez. Do you have friends I can contact? *La Vaca*. I'm a politically immune individual, and I can give you sanctuary, if you request it. Don't answer in Trade; there is a government observer in the room. How do you respond to the charges brought against you?"

Meris' ears twitched in confusion, and she wondered which line of thought to pursue. The charges were more than false; they were ludicrous. She would never steal pas-

sage aboard a freighter filled with disgusting Humans, she
did not know how to operate a stasis unit, and she would
only use her claws in self-defense. And yet, the gap in her
memory confounded any opportunity to provide an alibi.

To complicate matters, Bailey, as a translator, was obviously working to its own agenda. It knew who she was,
since it used a common honorific, and it offered her appropriate respect. It had put itself in danger for her sake
aboard Igsha Reey Port, and even Dútha believed its motives were altruistic. Lashed into a sudden decision, Meris
concluded that she would follow Bailey's lead. "I'm coming
out," she said in Farnii and motioned the Humans to move
away. "Give me room."

Bailey repeated her words in Trade to the deputy, and
both Humans stood and stepped back.

Though her joints felt weak, Meris climbed out from beneath the bunk, trying to maintain as much grace and dignity as possible. She shook her fur into place and sat on
the bunk, sweeping her tail to the side.

Bailey continued to behave with seemliness and deco-
rum, sinking to its knees and dropping its gaze to its folded
hands. With its motion, a hint of Rofan scent drifted from
the folds of its garments. The other Humans in the cell also
shifted positions. One crossed to stand by the door and a
second stepped closer to the deputy. Their movements were
repulsively quick and erratic, like the random skittering
of insects.

Hiding her distaste, Meris surveyed the aliens. With the
exception of the translator, traces of moisture appeared on
the Humans' hairless faces. A sharp reek filled the air. She
supposed the secretions were an instinctive defense mechanism, intended to repel threats. Perhaps the production of
odor was outside the Humans' voluntary control.

Reluctantly yielding to the charitable thought, Meris
forced her ears up and schooled her expression to something more polite. If she frightened them, they would only
smell worse. "The last thing I recall," Meris said in careful
Farnii, "before I awoke in this prison, is that an agent of
the Rofan Legitimacy drugged me with Phenox against
my will."

Bailey repeated Meris' words in Trade. The deputy

folded her arms. "Ask the detainee to clarify its statement concerning—"

Bailey interrupted. "Excuse me, Rachel. The Jadamii is not an 'it,' but a 'she.' A female."

Human vibrissae were quite short and lay in smooth arches over their eyes. Rachel raised her vibrissae at Bailey. "Very well," she said. "Ask her to clarify her statement concerning the Phenox."

Meris' fear ebbed, giving way to rising curiosity. A dozen questions regarding Human society crowded her mind.

Bailey looked at Meris. "What shall I say?" it asked. "With that observer in the room, I'm not sure we ought to tell the truth."

Meris glided her hand through the air in a palm-out gesture of formal reproof. "Of course, I shall tell the truth," she said. "Though not necessarily all the truth." She studied Bailey for a moment, then compared its appearance with that of the other Humans in the cell, again wondering about its gender. "And why did you tell her that I'm female?"

Bailey squirmed a bit. "Our species is obsessed with sexual identity, Mother of Multitudes. We find it difficult to relate to an individual as a person if we don't know their gender. In fact, if we—"

Rachel interrupted sharply. "Wait. What did she say? And what are you telling her?"

Bailey spread its hands, answering in Trade. "I translated what you said, then she asked what I said before that. And I told her that Humans are obsessed with sex . . . though not exactly in those words." Bailey let its arms fall limp. "A little free give-and-take is part of the translation process, Rachel. If you don't trust me, then you shouldn't have asked me to come here."

Rachel forcibly exhaled, clearly exasperated. "Just keep the 'give-and-take' to a minimum. Understood?"

Bailey slowly bobbed its head. "Yes, Rachel."

Meris stared at Rachel, letting her webbed ears flatten slightly. "Bailey—" She paused, wondering why she cared. "Are you in danger?"

Bailey shook its head. "No. As I said before, I'm politically immune, and I'm powerful in my own right."

Rachel made a guttural noise.

Bailey looked up at the deputy. "The detainee only asked me if I am also a female. And I said that, no, I'm a young, unattached male." His voice gained a strident tone. "Now, will you let me continue? Please?"

Rachel stiffened, but bobbed her head in assent.

Bailey held the deputy's gaze. "And kindly don't clear your throat again, it sounds too much like growling."

Uneasiness returned to Meris. "Perhaps we should discard this pretense. She already seems suspicious, and I'm afraid I'll make a mistake and answer you in Trade."

"You're doing very well," Bailey said. "Now, what shall I tell them about the Phenox?"

Meris curled her tail close, crossing it over her lap, and gave the question fierce consideration. "Tell them exactly what happened: I sold myself to a *gukka* in exchange for protection from an enemy. When my new owner got me aboard its ship, it drugged me with Phenox. I can't answer to the charges brought against me, because I'm unable to remember anything I said or did while under its influence."

Bailey again glanced up at the deputy and repeated Meris' words.

Rachel drew her vibrissae together. "Ask the detainee to clarify her statement that she was drugged by an agent of the Rofan Legitimacy."

Bailey turned to Meris. "I thought you went off with Dútha, not an agent of—"

Meris picked up the end of her tail and stroked its tuft. "Dútha claimed to work for the Legitimacy." She glanced around the cell at the Humans. Their eyes and the muscles beneath their hairless faces were in constant motion. She wondered if these twitches signified nonverbal communication and, if so, what they said to each other. Uneasiness hummed along Meris' nerves. "That's all I know, and I don't think I ought to say any more without the advice of a legal advocate."

Bailey raised his vibrissae at her, then looked up at the deputy and translated Meris' statement.

Rachel regarded Meris silently for a few moments. "Very well. Thank the detainee on behalf of the Earth Port Authority for its—her—cooperation. Assure her that we will notify her planetary government of the situation via hyperlight transmission, but we need to keep her in custody until we receive a reply."

Traces of moisture appeared on Bailey's upper lip. "Mother of Multitudes, I beseech you, let me help. Your government wants to erase you; other species want to use you. Earth's government is, at this moment, plotting against you." He paused and swallowed. "I can take you to a safe place. Just give me your consent, and I'll arrange everything."

Confusion welled within Meris. She recalled Dútha's words, just as it injected the Phenox: *When you wake up, you'll have a friend by your side.* Perhaps Dútha had meant Bailey. "Very well," she said unsteadily. "Do as you think best."

Bailey looked up at the deputy. "She says that she understands."

Rachel visibly relaxed. "Good. I have a few more questions for her, solely for the purposes of maintaining health and well-being. Her answers will not and cannot be used against her in a court of law."

Trying to keep the prickle of uneasiness from lifting her ruff, Meris glanced at the translator.

Bailey licked his lips. "This could be a ruse, Mother of Multitudes. I'm not sure what she intends to ask, but she may be trying to trick you into revealing too much. I beg you to be careful."

Rachel bent down, picked up the recorder, and switched it off. Then she looked at Meris. "What is your name?"

Meris felt a touch of indignant surprise. She was the Treasure of Jada, the Mother of Multitudes. She had assumed Rachel knew her identity all along.

Bailey carefully repeated the question in Farnii. "What is your name?"

Then it occurred to Meris that the questions were a test for Bailey, to determine if he were actually translating. "My name," she said, "is Meris."

Bailey glanced up at the deputy. "Her name is Meris."

Rachel straightened alertly. "Really? Off the record, Bailey, isn't that a figure from Jadamiin legend?"

Bailey spread his hands. "Yes, but the name is common."

"Hmm." Rachel studied Meris for a moment. "Ask her if she needs medical attention."

Horror shot through Meris at the thought of reeking Human hands, and she almost blurted the answer. She waited tensely, trying to calm her churning insides, as Bailey relayed the question. "No," she told him. "I am in excellent health."

Rachel watched her as Bailey repeated her answer. "Ask her if the food is adequate."

Meris barely managed to refrain from looking at the basin by the door. She fixed her attention on Bailey and concentrated on appearing calm and interested, as he translated. "What food?" she answered. "If the deputy means that container of reeking fluid, then I must say no."

Bailey appeared startled. "That's fruit juice. I thought you would like it."

Meris' ears folded. "It smells like animal urine."

Bailey stared at her. "But the Rofan drink it."

"Not," Meris pointed out, "from buckets on the floor."

Bailey ran a hand through his mane. "No," he said. "I apologize for that." He looked up at the deputy. "Meris says she resents being treated like an animal. She prefers her beverages served in a civilized drinking vessel, not a pet's water bowl."

Meris cut in. "Rofan foodstuffs are generally palatable, if that's what you have on hand, though I'm not fond of fruit. *Ksh-ksh* is better."

Bailey dutifully translated. Not waiting for Rachel to respond, Meris continued: "Also, this cell contains no bath pit. If I am to remain incarcerated here, I must have some means to keep clean. And I require a certain amount of privacy when I relieve myself. Does the deputy actually expect me to squat over that basin with the cameras running?"

Bailey repeated her words. Rachel's vibrissae shot up, and she said, "Tell Meris we will take steps to alleviate these problems."

Bailey looked at Meris. "I will come for you in just a few hours."

Meris felt drained and empty. She remained seated, but inclined her head in a slight, formal bow. "Thank you."

Bailey said to Rachel. "You're most gracious."

Holding the recorder in both hands, Rachel returned the bow. "Honored."

Bailey said in Farnii, "Be ready."

Rachel spoke to the other Humans and they all backed out of the cell. The door snapped shut, and Meris was alone.

She felt numb, absolutely used up. She listened to their footsteps as they hurried down the hall, carrying her future with them.

All the unnerving noises of an alien space station reclaimed her attention. A bell chimed somewhere far away. In any other place, Meris would have considered its tone soothing; but as a prisoner, she worried what it might signal.

The gravity pressed down on her. Exhausted, she sank onto the bunk. She knew she ought to try drinking the juice, but the thought made her queasy.

In spite of her anxiety, Meris fell into a fitful doze. Her mind drifted. She recalled that, before her long sojourn in stasis, she had left an unfinished game of "Hunter" on her bedside table. She wanted to go home and complete it. Her slumber deepened.

With Bailey, Concha, and Wu in her wake, Rachel tottered through the door of the temporary monitor room. A small conference table, surrounded by a ring of chairs, occupied the right-hand third of the floor. Grape stems and dirty teacups from a hasty midday meal still littered the table's surface, though over two hours had passed since then. In the far left corner, a wheezing brewer perched on a makeshift stand of plastic storage crates.

Two staffers, Chen and Modesto, sat in front of the centrally located monitor, watching an image piped in from the cell several corridors away. The redheaded Chen spoke without looking up: "Recorded the entire arraignment, Deputy. No problems."

Rachel's pulse still hammered in her temples, and the dregs of an adrenaline rush sparked through her limbs like an erratic series of electrical shocks. "Thanks." She sank into the nearest chair. "Let's get this wrapped up. Any objections to doing the evaluation now?"

Bailey shifted. "Uh . . ."

Rachel looked up at him. "Well?"

He blushed. "I really need to pee."

Rachel stifled an irritated sigh. "Can't you wait?"

"I did wait. I had to go before, and you wouldn't let me."

Rachel drew her brows together. Bailey had gone to the loo twice in their previous hour of preparation, getting lost on both expeditions. *What is he up to?*

Wu pointed. "That way, in case you've forgotten. Around the corner, fifth door on the left."

Bailey nodded and fled.

Wearily, Rachel closed her eyes. "So much for wrapping things up."

Wu crossed to the brewer. "Well, you can have my evaluation now, Rachel. I'd say it went perfectly."

Concha hovered near the door, as if uncertain of her right to enter. "Oh?" she asked in a shaky voice. "It did?"

Wu poured two cups of tea and carried one to Concha. "Indeed, it did." He handed her a cup. "Nobody died. Perfect."

Rachel massaged her forehead. "I wouldn't say perfect. It had its odd moments."

Wu sipped his tea. " 'Odd' is the only word for Trabail Rye." He sauntered over to stand beside Rachel's chair and continued *sotto voce*: "Even at this very moment, your boy genius is probably taking a wrong turn—"

Rachel sighed with irritation. "Wu—"

"—and soon will be hopelessly lost in the wild jungles of the administrative offices."

Rachel pushed herself from her chair and stalked to the monitor console. Wu was undoubtedly right. During the earlier preparations, Bailey had been determinedly eccentric, constantly interrupting the procedural briefing with tales from Hoshino Uta, his home settlement on the Freehold. He had babbled about veneration of the dead, his fervent belief in nature spirits called *eulies*, and the common practice of group marriage.

At first, Rachel had tried to think of his distractibility as a sign of genius, but she soon found it difficult to manage her growing frustration with him. Concha, on the other hand, had been an interested and often helpful presence. Though still suspicious of Councillor Weber's motives, Rachel had decided that she rather liked the aide.

Standing behind the staffers' chairs, she studied the image on the monitor. Meris lay motionless on the bunk.

Rachel's breath caught in her throat as she recalled that Phenox had a second sleep cycle. "What the—?"

Chen glanced up at her. "It's all right, Deputy. The detainee is just sleeping normally. She moves now and then, which she didn't do while drugged."

Rachel's sense of certain disaster slid away. "Oh, thank God."

Concha edged closer to the monitor. "The Jadamii fell asleep?" She turned her gaze to Rachel. "Why would it do that? Hasn't it had enough sleep?"

Rachel ran both hands through her hair and found the dark curls appallingly sticky with sweat. "Probably some sort of stress reaction. The poor thing's had a hellish day." Rachel looked down at Chen. "Wait until Meris wakes up from her nap before you institute the changes she requested."

Chen nodded. "Yes, Deputy."

Returning her gaze to the monitor, Concha spoke with surprising candor. "When it climbed out from under the bunk, I thought it was going to eat us."

Rachel recalled thinking something similar. At her slightest movement, Meris had puffed up like a badger. She grinned. "Me, too."

Concha spoke as if confessing something shameful. "I was . . . scared."

Rachel repeated: "Me, too."

"So was I," Wu said enthusiastically. "I was more scared than either of you."

Concha extended her free hand, displaying how it trembled. "I'm still shaking."

Trying to hide her amusement, Rachel held out her own quivering hand. "Strange, isn't it? How each finger vibrates independently?"

Wu joined the game, making his hand flutter like a pigeon's wing. "I win! I win! I'm still the undefeated champ!"

Concha smiled shyly.

A complicated resentment knifed through Rachel. She folded her arms, refusing to allow Wu's silliness to charm her. "Warden Jackson," she said with overstated courtesy, "kindly go to the loo and fetch our translator."

Wu answered in a sugary tone. "Trying to get rid of me, Deputy?"

Rachel smiled. "Yes."

Without a word, Wu set down his tea, made an overly theatrical obeisance to Rachel, then swept out the door.

Rachel paced a few steps, suddenly feeling keyed up. It was a debilitating emotional habit, to rely so heavily upon Wu's presence, she told herself, a form of weakness that she needed to overcome. "This is ridiculous. So close to being finished, just to be delayed by an overactive bladder."

Concha watched her for a moment, nervously sipping her tea. "Is there anything I can do, Deputy?"

Rachel walked to the brewer, then found the tea's spicy scent cloying. "We're at a standstill, I'm afraid. God only knows when Warden Jackson will return. You might use the time to file a report with Councillor Weber."

Concha shook her head, dropping her gaze. "The councillor doesn't—" She broke off and shook her head again. "Never mind."

Rachel's instincts red-lighted. Pretending to search for a clean cup, she began with a neutral statement. "I've never met Councillor Weber. She hasn't accompanied the audit team before."

Concha smiled stiffly. "Perhaps I'll have the opportunity to introduce you."

"I'd like that." Rachel peered at the interior of a cup and smelled it. "It must be interesting, to be a World Council aide."

Concha shrugged one shoulder. "I'm sure it's not as interesting as working at Earth Port Station."

"You think not?" Rachel smiled warmly, pressing for a more telling response. "Then perhaps I'll steal you from the councillor."

Concha returned her smile, though it appeared somewhat strained. "Perhaps you will."

Obscurely ashamed of her attempt to pump Concha for information, Rachel set down the cup and resumed pacing. She had a lot of reports to file, and she also wanted to contact the Kamian freighter about its cryptic message to her. *I grasp the stars and take the light to heart.*

Rachel circled the monitor, studying the holographic image of the detainee from every angle. *Meris.* There was something distressing about seeing her stretched out on the bunk, some quality in her supine sprawl so eloquent of despair. Rachel could easily imagine how Meris felt, alone among aliens, with no friend, no one to trust.

Rachel activated a small side screen on the monitor and replayed the arraignment, keeping the sound soft. She watched herself and the others enter the cell. Then came the first exchange and that terrifying moment when Meris emerged from beneath the bunk. Rachel noted how Concha had scrambled toward the door, and how Wu had moved closer to provide protection. The arraignment continued, leading to the brief squabble over "free give-and-take."

Then Meris looked directly at Bailey and spoke his name.

Stunned, Rachel hit the controls and replayed the segment, wondering why she had not noticed it during the arraignment.

"Bailey," Meris said, followed by a phrase in Farnii.

Rachel paused the recording and looked at the staffers. "Did you hear that? She knew him!"

Modesto rubbed his square jaw in thought. "Could be a coincidence, Deputy. Simple transliteration."

"Maybe." Rachel considered the possibility, but her uneasiness remained. "We'll have a chat with Bailey when Wu brings him back."

As if summoned by her words, Wu strode through the door, talking on his phone. "Really? That's good. So Maury's okay?" He lifted his chin from the mouthpiece and said to Rachel, "They've found our missing tech."

She nodded. "Good. Where's Bailey?"

"He—" Wu broke off and listened to his phone, narrowing his eyes. "Right. On my way."

Rachel crossed to him and grabbed his arm. "Where's Bailey?"

"Not in the loo." Wu hastily shut off his phone and pocketed it. "Maury had been locked in a storage closet by two playful staffers. I think you know who." He gave Rachel a meaningful glance. "He's unharmed. But we have five more missing people."

Rachel stared at him. "Five?"

"Six. If we count Trabail Rye."

Rachel tightened her hold on his forearm. "This can't be happening."

Wu gently laid his hand over her clutching fist. "I need to go. With your leave, Deputy Ajmani?"

Making a concentrated effort, Rachel released her grip. "Of course."

Turning toward the door, Wu drew his pistol and checked the setting.

Rachel spoke without meaning to. "Wu?"

He paused, holstering his weapon, and glanced over his shoulder.

Rachel blurted: "Please be careful."

Wu smiled at her softly, as if they were alone. "You, too." He sauntered out the door, his hand casually resting on the butt of his pistol.

Rachel stood motionless, wondering what had possessed her to speak like that. The moment seemed to stretch.

Concha set her empty teacup by the brewer. "Deputy, I—" She broke off, as if reconsidering her intended words. "I'm not sure I understand. Where's Professor Rye?"

Still feeling as if time were out of joint, Rachel regarded Concha. There was a pattern. Bailey had been on Igsha Reey Port, and so had Meris. The two were caught together, perhaps as victims, in the same web of events. She wondered if the Freeholder had covertly attempted to alert her, that an explanation lay buried in his ramblings about the power of unseen spirits and the blessed influence of the dead.

Someone else was working to a plan; Rachel could sense it, like the telltale bulge of a trip wire beneath a cover of dead leaves. The XRC auditors, the impostors, Concha Singh, Wu Jackson, everyone was connected.

Concha's expression grew concerned. "Deputy, are you all right?"

Rachel smiled. "Fine." She stuffed her hands in her pockets, curling the remains of Khanwa's warning in one fist. "I need to find Bailey Rye."

CHAPTER NINE

RACHEL STOOD on the threshold of the temporary monitor room and watched Wu walk away. His gait lacked its usual rolling quality, seeming more purposeful. Using the same quick and economical movements he displayed with a gun, he pulled out his phone and keyed in a code.

Rachel waited until he disappeared around a corner, then started after him. After a moment's hesitation, Concha followed. "Deputy. Where are we going?"

"I've already told you. To find Bailey." Rachel strode along the corridor, glancing through open doorways for a lanky Freeholder with an unruly mop of red curls. "We'll start with the loo."

Looking perplexed, Concha fell into step beside the deputy. "But didn't Warden Jackson already—?"

"Yes, but I want to see for myself." Pinching off her rising impatience, Rachel glanced at Concha. "Especially on something this important."

"Yes, Deputy. But surely it's beneath your rank to—"

Rachel shook her head. "It doesn't work that way. Not on this station."

"But you—" Concha gestured helplessly. "I'm sorry, Deputy. I wasn't questioning procedures. I just don't know what's happening."

Rachel paused and glanced around the corridor for listeners. A tired-looking man in a green Docking Control

uniform wandered by, eating a piece of corn bread. His
mouth was full, so he nodded in greeting. Rachel smiled
and nodded back, then turned to Concha. "Didn't you hear
Wu's report? Someone is abducting station personnel.
Given the circumstances, I can't dismiss the possibility that
they've taken Bailey."

"They've taken—?" Concha's face betrayed nothing but
outrage. "That's illegal!"

Noting Concha's complete lack of disbelief, Rachel felt
a touch of cold. Violent crime was rare on Earth. Most
Humans would insist that a mistake had been made, that
no crime had been committed, that Bailey was merely lost.
Rachel resumed walking again. "Yes. Illegal. And I want
it stopped."

Concha sounded shaken. "Who would do such a thing?"

"You tell me," Rachel said. "They arrived on your ship."

Concha jerked to a halt. "What?"

Rachel turned, keeping her expression and tone neutral.
There was a possibility that Concha did not know about
the impostors. "We have two unknowns aboard the station,
masquerading as Safety staffers. They've been making all
sorts of dangerous mischief, and now it seems they are kidnapping people and locking them in supply closets. Evidence suggests that the two arrived on *Gaia's Love*."

Sweat glittered on Concha's shaved scalp. "What makes
you think that? What evidence?"

"It isn't hard to trace," Rachel said. "This is a space
station. Our troublemakers didn't walk here."

"But—"

Rachel flashed up a warning hand. "I'm not saying that
you're involved, but I don't think I ought to discuss the
matter with you in great detail. Not until I know more."

They reached the loo, and Rachel stepped through its
open door. Concha paused outside, seeming ready to flee.

Rachel studied the tiled walls and floor, though not really
sure what she hoped to find. As Concha had pointed out,
Wu had been over it already.

Concha cleared her throat. "Anything?"

"No scuff marks. No strands of bright red hair." Rachel
pulled out her phone and keyed in the code for the temporary monitor room.

"Chen."

Rachel spoke quickly. "Assume this call is being tapped."

"Right."

"Any changes?"

"None," Chen said. "If anything happens, I'll call."

"Thanks." Rachel clicked off the phone and pocketed it. "Could be worse, I suppose."

Concha waited, raising her brows in anxious inquiry.

"Though I'm not sure how."

"Deputy?"

Rachel studied Concha, wishing she had the authority to question her. "We'll catch them, you know, your friends from *Gaia's Love*."

Concha's forehead puckered. "Deputy, I don't know what you mean."

"No?" Again, Rachel scrutinized Concha and saw only frightened confusion. She wondered if Wu had been mistaken in his suspicions toward the visiting members of the World Council. Until she gained concrete information, she would have to proceed with more delicacy. "Sorry." Feeling deceitful, she manufactured a rueful smile and rubbed the back of her neck. "It's the sleep deprivation talking."

Concha seemed to select her words carefully. "Are you quite sure that Professor Rye didn't just wander away? He seems rather prone to . . . distraction."

"Perhaps." Exhaustion reasserted itself. Rachel sagged against a wall and ran her hands through her hair. "For his own sake, Bailey had better be abducted. If I find him in the cafeteria, drinking tea, I'll—" Rachel's phone chimed, and she pulled it out. "Deputy Ajmani."

"It's Ría." Her colleague also sounded worn down. "Or what's left of her."

"Trouble in paradise?"

"Phones are tapped." Sonría snorted. "Boy, are they tapped. Everyone is eavesdropping. I'm tempted to start broadcasting station business. Jam all frequencies. Force them to listen, whether they want to or not."

"The 'Ría and Rachel Show?"

"Don't scoff. For the tiniest excuse—for just a box of rocks—I'd do it."

Rachel's scalp prickled, but she made herself chuckle. The remark clearly alluded to the bargain she had struck

with Captain Khanwa, and Rachel wondered if the other
deputy had news to pass along that could not be spoken
over the phone. "Do you need to meet somewhere to discuss how to sell advertising?"

"You know me so well. How 'bout the detention area
in Checkpoint?"

"On my way." Rachel clicked off and put the phone in
her pocket, then she turned to Concha. "I'm going to
Checkpoint."

Concha followed her back into the corridor. "You're
going there? Can't you just call?"

Still walking, Rachel flung her a look of irritated bewilderment. "Aide Singh, aren't you paying attention? The
phones have been tapped."

"Yes, but surely someone else can—"

Rachel slipped a hand into her pocket, finding Khanwa's
invoice and holding it like a talisman. "No. I've taken personal custody of the detainee. I'm responsible."

"But—"

"Concha. I'm going to level with you." Rachel skirted a
raised planter filled with fragrant hyacinths, then resumed
her quick pace toward Checkpoint. "I have someone from
another planet locked up in a converted rec room. This
makes me feel awful, because I can only assume that this
person is terrified." Rachel glanced at Concha as she
walked. "After all, that's how I'd feel if I were a prisoner
on an alien space station."

"I never—" Concha's brow furrowed. "I hadn't thought
of the detainee in those terms. Not as a prisoner, or someone who might be afraid. I mean, you haven't imprisoned
it. You've only detained it. Pending notification of the authorities on its home world."

Rachel shook her head. "I doubt," she said, "that Meris
would understand the distinction you've drawn."

Concha made a convulsive little shrug. "You're not mis-
treating it," she insisted. "You're attempting to keep it
comfortable. It really has no reason to be afraid."

"Doesn't she?" Rachel stopped to study Concha, wondering about her complacent lack of compassion. "She's a
prisoner. She's locked up."

"What choice did you have? Galactic Trade Association
laws forbid the use of personal restraints."

Rachel drew a breath, then realized the futility of further argument. "Never mind," she said, and started off toward Checkpoint again at a rapid clip. "This way."

Following, Concha continued speaking. "You can't even provide medical attention without the detainee's full consent." Her voice grew breathy with exertion. "Deputy, with all due respect, you're suffering from worse deprivations than the detainee. I happen to know you haven't slept in forty-two hours, and you haven't eaten a decent meal in ten."

Rachel sighed, trying one more time to make Concha understand. "That's immaterial. What matters now, is that Meris is alone and frightened. And I've lost track of the translator."

"Professor Rye." Concha jogged a few steps to draw even with Rachel. "You say the detainee knew him? That it called him by name?"

"Sounded that way on the recording, but I didn't catch it during the actual arraignment."

"Then that Freeholder tricked us." Concha nodded as she walked, narrowing her eyes. "Something else is going on, isn't it? Something we don't know about."

Us? We? For a moment, Rachel's weariness faded in a wash of gentle amusement. "I'm so glad that I'm not the only one who's feeling paranoid."

Concha made a self-deprecating noise and shook her head. "Everyone is an expert at something. My forte seems to be paranoia."

Rachel laughed softly. "Don't say that too loudly around the Port Authority offices. They'll deputize you."

They reached the lift. Rachel signaled for a ride to Checkpoint, then leaned against the bulkhead, settling her head back and closing her eyes. "After everything that's gone wrong, I'm wondering now if Captain Mendez didn't have the right idea. Maybe we should have left Meris on board the *La Vaca*."

Concha spoke hesitantly. "Deputy, please forgive me if this sounds impertinent, but you seem to be siding with the detainee."

"Someone has to."

"Deputy?"

A comfortable sleepiness stole over Rachel, enveloping

her thoughts in a golden haze. She forced herself to keep talking. "We've made contact, so far, with thirty-six sentient species in our galaxy. Only eleven of them are space-faring, and only five of those have consented to engage in trade. Now, take those five and count how many of them are environmentally compatible with Humans. Three: Phi-Nurians, the Rofan, and the Jadamiin."

Concha still sounded puzzled. "But the Jadamiin won't talk to us."

"Exactly. Our ancestors dreamed for centuries of contact with intelligent aliens, and they'd find our current state of affairs a distinct anticlimax."

Concha cleared her throat. "So what are you expecting, Deputy? I don't see how we can forge an alliance with Jada based upon the misadventures of one Jadamii."

Rachel felt virtually intoxicated by exhaustion, lacking even the energy to shrug. She wanted to say something to Concha, but could not remember what. The intention to speak hung in her mind, slowly revolving like a planet in space. Perhaps, she thought, she had already said what she wanted to say.

Concha persisted. "Maybe I'm misunderstanding you, Deputy. But is it possible that you hope to make friends with the detainee?"

"Could be." Rachel dragged her eyes open and pushed herself upright. "And why not?" *After all, I want to make friends with you.* The lift arrived. Rachel beckoned. "Let's go."

A Human shouted in the distance. Meris jerked awake and lay motionless on the bunk. Even though the language was strange, the cry had conveyed unmistakable urgency. Alertly, Meris glanced around her padded cell. Her ruff bristled. She held her breath and extended her vibrissae, straining to hear more.

The sound of running feet pounded in her ears. A Human issued a strident string of commands. Alarmed, Meris rolled to her feet.

A thin, wailing cry sliced the air. Shock blanked her mind and froze her limbs. *It can't be*, she thought wildly. *It can't be a baby. What is a baby doing on a space station?*

Piping shrieks echoed down the hallway, each scream

rose higher and higher as if the infant suffered increasing pain. Meris' gut wrenched in horror and pity. Babies only cried out like that when in torment. She did not care that it was a Human infant, it needed her help. Instinct took over. She was at the cell's door the next moment, scrabbling at its padded surface. Someone was torturing a baby. She had to stop them.

The canvas covering on the door's pad was rugged and smooth-woven. Desperately, Meris ran her claws along the edge, once again seeking a way to get at the lock mechanism.

The baby's shrieking grew louder and so did the thump of running feet. They were carrying the baby up her hall. Meris dug at the padding with both hands like a frenzied beast.

One of her claws caught in the canvas and broke off at the bone. The pain shot from the tip of her finger to her spine. Meris gasped in anguish, clasping her injured hand to her chest. Her sight turned to red shadows. Unconsciousness loomed.

The baby keened with every breath it took. Dizzy and sick, Meris flung herself shoulder first at the cell door. *Don't let me faint*, she prayed. *By all Paths, don't let me faint.*

The infant's weeping faded as it was carried away from her cell. A ferocious grief welled up in Meris, and she threw her full weight against the door. "Stop it," she shouted in Farnii, forgetting Trade in her anxiety. "Stop hurting it. It's only a baby."

The little one's cries were lost to her hearing.

Meris' horror deepened. Her pulse raced until the three separate beats became a continuous thrum. She backed up and took a running leap at the door. The heavy padding absorbed most of the impact. Maddened with frustration and rage, she flung herself at the cell door again. "Filthy Humans! Stinking, Pathless monsters!"

Outside her cell, the normal noises of the space station resumed. A bell chimed twice. Machinery hummed.

Crazed, Meris slammed herself against the padded surface. "Bring it back! Do you hear me? Give me that child!"

There were rapid steps in the hall outside, approaching her cell. Meris was lost in fury. She snatched up the dish of juice and dashed it against the door. "Give me that child! Give it to me!"

The door flashed open and revealed four Human guards. Meris felt a surge of killing rage, and she launched herself at them, springing into the hallway outside.

The guards moved like a team. One clutched her knees, one wrapped its arms around her waist, and one caught her arms. Furiously, she struggled to use her teeth and claws as they lowered her to the floor. "No!" she shouted defiantly. "I have to save that baby!"

The guards conversed in calm, everyday voices as they bound her with soft straps. Feverishly, Meris continued to fight. She tried to break free of the bonds cinched around her legs, to loosen her arms from her sides. "Please," she begged her captors. "Please. It will die if I don't save it."

One guard discovered her injured hand and examined it gently. Meris' stomach heaved at the touch of its hairless fingers. She jerked away from the Human's grasp, and her shoulder joint cracked out of place. Pain spread through her body like liquid fire. Meris gagged.

Murmuring, another guard smoothed her silky mane with its hand, as if trying to reassure her. Revulsion joined the agony. Meris retched again and brought up a bitter mouthful of gastric fluid.

The Humans conversed softly among themselves. One grunted and pressed something hard and cold against the nape of Meris' neck. Terror washed through her. *All Paths!*

There was an icy pinch near her spine. An acrid, medicinal smell filled her nose. Meris' mind went white-hot. She tried to hunch away from the injection. "No!" she gasped. "You can't do this!"

A Human crooned alien words and stroked her shoulder. Desperately, Meris struggled to remain conscious. Her arms and legs went numb. The pain in her shoulder melted away, and her head grew too heavy to lift. "The baby," she breathed. "The baby. . . ."

Meris' eyes closed. Fear and anger slipped from her mind, lost in the echoes of Dútha's last words. *When you awake . . . you'll have a friend . . . by your side. . . .*

The detention area was located in a converted office space in Checkpoint. It normally served as more of a waiting room than an actual prison block, and captains came there to reclaim errant crew members. Equipped with restraint fields, small holding cells lined two walls. These were reserved for only the worst offenders or for individuals who might harm the other detainees. At the moment, the detention area held a crowd of Rofan, Phi-Nurians, and staffers who were all talking at once.

Still leading Concha, Rachel stepped through the door and blinked. The smell of Phi-Nurian dung and Human sweat was appalling.

Captain Akya and three of its crew claimed the center of the area, completely ignoring a staffer's attempts to usher them to one side. Akya spotted Rachel and immediately swaggered over to meet her. "Ah, Deputy Aja-mani." It blocked her path. "I heard a rumor that you would be here. I have questions for you."

Rachel stifled a sigh. *A rumor? You listened to my phone call, you miscreant.*

Akya's crew gathered around Rachel and Concha. The Rofan remained silent, offering no insults or threats, but stared fixedly. Concha shivered and moved closer to Rachel.

Ría stood on the opposite end of the area, beside a holding cell. She caught Rachel's eye, then pointedly glanced at the cell's occupant. Khanwa waited behind the shimmering restraint field.

Rachel nodded. Her Rofan informant had clearly needed to get a message through to her and had enlisted Ría's help to arrange a meeting. Rachel casually returned her attention to Akya. "I have only one question for you, honorable Captain: Where is Bailey Rye?"

Akya waved dismissively. "Don't know." It stepped closer. "Explain 'witness.' "

"What—?" Then Rachel remembered Akya's determination to study Earth's laws. "A witness," she said, "is an individual who observes an event."

Akya's small ears flickered with obvious impatience. "I understand that. What I do not understand is the reliance placed upon them within your legal system. It seems unwise to trust the word of strangers."

Across the area, Khanwa spoke to Ría. She looked doubtful, then shut off the field. Khanwa strolled out of the cell toward Rachel and Akya.

Rachel struggled against distraction. "That is why we try

to find many witnesses. Even if their accounts vary, there will still be details upon which they agree."

Akya placed all its fingertips together. "Many witnesses," it said reflectively. "Many witnesses."

Khanwa stopped behind one of Akya's crew and delicately sniffed the back of its neck.

Worried that a fight could erupt, Rachel bowed, planning to excuse herself and draw Khanwa away. "Honorable Captain, I must—"

Akya fixed its bright gaze upon her. "And this forms the basis of the community pardon?"

Startled by the question, Rachel paused. The community pardon was an old practice, stemming from the Reconstruction after the Last War. If there were mitigating circumstances surrounding a crime, the village sometimes voted to pardon the accused. She wondered if it was even still on the books.

"Yes," Rachel said, "it does." The connection was tenuous at best, but she wanted to wrap up the exchange. "You're very clever, honorable Captain, to draw that conclusion."

Akya seemed to expand with the compliment, exuding an air of self-satisfaction. "You do yourself credit," it said indulgently, "to admit my excellence."

With a purring growl, Khanwa abruptly bared its teeth and bit the crew member's left ear.

Concha gasped and clutched Rachel's arm.

Rachel tensed to intervene, then realized Khanwa's victim offered no resistance. Instead, the Rofa squealed with pleasure; and though still growling, Khanwa inflicted no damage, mouthing the ear with mock savagery. Akya and the others completely ignored the playful exchange.

Rachel gently pried Concha's fingers loose, then bowed to the newcomer. "Honorable Captain Khanwa."

It straightened, licking its teeth. "Honorable Deputy Ajamani." It released the other Rofa, sauntered to Concha's side, and gave her a speculative sniff. "Pretty smells everywhere."

Concha moved to duck behind Rachel, and her voice quavered. "Deputy, please—"

Rachel respectfully gestured for Khanwa to keep its distance. "Kindly do not frighten this young person. She doesn't know how to play your game."

Khanwa cast a lingering glance over Rachel. "So . . . you . . . know how to play?"

"I—"

Before Rachel could react, Khanwa lunged forward and pressed its mouth against her ear. "Come away from these others," it whispered urgently. "You reek of Jadamiin."

For a split second, the Rofa's words made no sense to Rachel, then she recalled lying on the cell's padded floor less than an hour ago. *Damn.*

Khanwa tugged on her sleeve. "Come away, Deputy Ajamani. I want to play."

It was as good excuse as any to leave. Rachel sighed inwardly, then bowed to Akya. "Honorable Captain, if you will submit all your questions to my message board, I will answer them as quickly as my other duties permit." In Rofan fashion, she turned without waiting for a reply and headed for the door. "Concha, follow me."

Once into Checkpoint proper, Rachel found an empty conference room with a scuffed table and some plastic chairs. She closed the door and regarded Khanwa levelly. "I'm not here to play, you understand."

Khanwa inclined its head. "I understand. You want information." Its golden eyes glinted. "You smell like the Jadamii who died at Igsha Reey Port."

Rachel folded her arms. She had no intention of admitting that the Port Authority held a Jadamii in custody. "The one killed in a duel?"

"Not killed in a duel, she died later."

"How?"

"I do not know. But you smell like her." Khanwa tapped the side of its muzzle. "Very distinctive scent."

Rachel inwardly berated herself again for not changing her uniform. It was a ridiculous mistake. She knew better.

Khanwa continued, speaking slowly. "Some Phi-Nurians wanted the Jadamii. They vowed that if the *gukka* in possession of her body refused to surrender it, they would raid station control."

Rachel frowned thoughtfully. "What happened?"

"The *gukka* refused. The Phi-Nurians killed over sixty station crew."

Concha made a soft noise of distress and dropped into a chair.

Khanwa kept its attention on Rachel. "These same Phi-Nurians are now at Earth Port, speaking to members of your government."

Rachel tensed. "Why do you say that?"

"Because it is true." Khanwa gestured languidly. "I have my communications people monitoring all messages."

"That," Rachel pointed out, "is illegal."

One of Khanwa's ears slanted back. "You wanted information."

"Yes, but—"

Khanwa went on, its tone strangely earnest. "Deputy Aja-mani, I must tell you. These Phi-Nurians will destroy your station to claim the Jadamii's carcass."

Rachel paced a few steps, thinking fiercely. "What does this have to do with Starcatcher?"

"Nothing." The Rofa spread its hands, mimicking a Human shrug. "Starcatcher is a plot against you, Deputy Aja-mani."

Rachel stared. "What?"

Concha shot to her feet. "Deputy, I must protest!"

Khanwa ignored Concha. "You have found favor, Deputy Aja-mani, with the people of your planet. They wish to elevate you to membership of your World Council. But a small faction of those in power, led by Councillor Weber, fear your—" Khanwa paused and appeared to think. "What is the word? Your *rhu*. Your bravery. Under the guise of testing your worthiness, they seek to dishonor and discredit you."

"No!" Concha insisted. "That's not true!"

Khanwa turned its golden gaze to Concha. "Poor child. The others in service to Weber despise you. They plan for you to share in Deputy Aja-mani's downfall."

Concha whirled toward Rachel. "Deputy, I don't know what this—"

Khanwa interrupted. "You should ask, young one, how many have faced the Starcatcher ordeal in the past. And then ask how many have succeeded."

Sweat glittered on Concha's scalp and upper lip. "That's not—"

Khanwa pointed at Concha's face in a Rofan gesture of superiority. "None." Its voice dropped to a husky growl. "Starcatcher: A trap for those who shine too brightly."

Reeling inwardly, Rachel stood frozen.

Concha clutched Rachel's arm. "Please, don't listen to this—"

"circulating a petition," Wu had said, *"to nominate you to the World Council."*

"all about laying blame—"

I grasp the stars—

Rachel looked pointedly at Concha's hand.

Flinching, Concha released her. "Deputy, please—"

Rachel spoke tonelessly. "I think you'd better go. For your own protection."

"But—" Concha's shoulders slumped. She gazed in obvious misery at Rachel, then turned and left the conference room.

Khanwa stirred. "Was this wise?" it said. "That young one might betray your knowledge."

"Perhaps. But I could hardly arrest—" Rachel's phone chimed. She hastily pulled it out. "Yes?"

Wu said: "It's me. Come to the monitor station of the rec room."

"On my way." Rachel clicked off and returned the phone to her pocket. "Your pardon, honorable Captain, but I'm needed elsewhere." She turned to the door, then paused. "About that Jadamii. Why do the Phi-Nurians want its body?"

Khanwa glanced away, flicking its ears. "I should not say."

"You swore to answer all my questions."

Khanwa hunched its shoulders submissively. "According to rumor, the Jadamii is a criminal who escaped the custody of an agent of the Legitimacy. The Phi-Nurians want the body in order to buy favor with the Legitimacy."

Rachel's lips parted in surprise. "A criminal?"

Khanwa gazed at her steadily. "You are so beautiful, Deputy Aja-mani, and so strong. I wish you—" The Rofa fell silent and turned away.

"Honorable Captain?"

"You have no reason to trust me, I know. You would be a fool to do so."

Rachel spoke quietly. "Maybe."

Khanwa sinuously twisted to look over its shoulder, its eyes burned gold against its black pelt. "To save yourself from Starcatcher, to save your station, give me the Jadamii's body and say that I stole it."

Rachel blinked. "What?"

"Say I stole it," Khanwa repeated, turning fully toward her. "I will go back to Igsha Reey. The Phi-Nurians will chase my ship and leave Earth Port in peace. You will embarrass your political enemies, and I—"

"You," Rachel finished, "will be richly rewarded by a grateful Legitimacy."

"Indeed, yes." Khanwa slowly reached out and touched the back of her hand. "Think about it. I swore my oath freely. I am your friend. Would I say it, if it were not true?"

Rachel strode into the temporary monitor room. "All right, what's going—?"

The monitor was off. Chen and Modesto were gone. Wu sat alone in the room, sipping tea. "Hello, Rachel," he said softly.

Something in his voice made Rachel change her intended words. "What happened?"

Wu's round face grew worried as he gazed up at her. "Rachel, are you all right?"

Rachel laughed angrily. "No, I'm not all right. I'm walking in my sleep." She gestured dismissively. "It doesn't matter. What happened to Meris?"

Wu's hands tightened around his mug. "Meris is injured. While trying to batter down the door of her cell, she ripped out one of her claws and—well, maybe messed up something in her shoulder."

Rachel dropped into Chen's abandoned chair. "Great."

Wu studied her somberly. "I take it you didn't find Bailey."

"No." Rachel ran a weary hand through her hair. "Oh, well, it could be worse, I suppose. A broken claw isn't—"

Wu shook his head. "The claw isn't broken. It's ripped

out. Doctor DeFlora says the injury is comparable to a smashed finger on a Human."

Rachel slumped back in her chair, searching among her tumbling thoughts for a comprehensive reply. "Damn." Then Wu's words sank in. "Wait a minute. Doctor De-Flora—?"

Wu lowered his gaze into his mug of tea. "We took Meris to Medica."

"To Medica?" Rachel repeated, leaning forward. Meris could not provide consent without a translator, and Galactic Trade Association laws categorized unrequested medical treatment as torture. "What for?"

Wu seemed disconcerted, then he smiled sheepishly. "Force of habit."

Rachel settled back and folded her arms. "You'd better give me the whole story now."

Wu's smile faded. "You're not going to like this, Rachel."

"That's a stupid thing to say," she snapped. "I already hate it, and waiting longer will not improve my temper. Give me your report, Warden Jackson."

Wu set his mug on the floor between his feet. "Noni Mead's two-year-old daughter fell down and cracked her head against a table leg."

"What?" Concerned, Rachel's eyes widened. The Meads were her next-door neighbors. "Little Saja? Is she going to be all right?"

"Tigre says so." Wu clasped his hands together and rested his chin on his folded fingers. "At any rate, Saja was bleeding a lot. A new fellow on the nursery staff ran her down to Medica, carrying her past the rec room."

"But we had closed that corridor. We had signs posted—"

"Yeah, well, he was justifiably more concerned with taking the shortest route," Wu said heavily. "And he carried a screaming child past Meris."

Rachel made a noise of helpless exasperation. "And?"

"And Meris flew into hysteria." Wu met her gaze levelly, and his tone was carefully devoid of accusation. "A high-strung personality, it seems. But then, we knew that."

Rachel frowned, recognizing the implicit criticism. If she had placed the Jadamii in Checkpoint's detention area, she might have averted the current crisis. "Go on."

"By the time we got to the cell, Meris was as frenzied as a Phi-Nurian, shouting and throwing herself against the door. I was afraid she might hurt herself even more, so I thought—" Wu broke off and shook his head. "I thought that a physical confrontation would subdue her."

Rachel stared at him. Confrontation worked most of the time with agitated Rofan, but a Jadamii would respond to an entirely different set of behavioral triggers. "That was an idiotic assumption."

"Well, yes, I know that now," Wu said mildly. "She attacked us."

Grieved and furious, Rachel felt her voice thicken. "Was anyone hurt?"

"Not a scratch." Wu paused, then continued reluctantly. "We had to use restraints."

Rachel drew a breath to curse, but failed to find an expletive potent enough. "Restraints?" she managed to choke out. "You tied her up?"

Wu shrugged unhappily. "We had to. She was out in the hall. If she had broken free. . . ."

Fighting for calm, Rachel slid her hands up to her temples. "Is this when the shoulder injury occurred?"

Wu nodded. "She kept fighting against the restraints, and I heard something pop. It had to hurt—she got rather sick, I'm afraid." He swallowed. "Tigre can't tell if the injury might cause a permanent disability."

Rachel also felt a bit queasy. "Is Meris still in restraints?"

"No." Wu's face went impassive. He reached into his pocket, pulled out a small item, and displayed it between thumb and forefinger. It was a yellow transdermic cartridge with orange and green letters. "I dosed her with Phenox."

In disbelief, Rachel stared at the cartridge. "Dosed her?" She lifted her gaze to his. "You just happened to have Phenox in your pocket?"

"I've been carrying it with me ever since we brought Meris onto the station."

Rachel surged to her feet. "You illegally drugged a Jada national? And it was premeditated?"

Wu suddenly seemed dispirited, and his shoulders slumped. "I didn't know what else to do."

For a moment, Rachel was too angry to speak. She turned her back and paced a few steps on legs almost too wobbly to hold her up. "Do you realize what this means? Do you?" She turned to glare at Wu. "We could find our ships barred from every port in the galaxy."

Wu rolled his tongue around in his mouth. "I could have shot the detainee dead in self-defense," he pointed out. "That would've been perfectly legal."

"I can't believe you did this," Rachel whispered. "What if you've overdosed her? What if she dies?"

"Rachel. She could also die from an infected broken claw. And don't forget that was a self-inflicted injury."

"I can't believe you're talking this way." Rachel's voice shook with barely controlled rage. "I can't believe this is happening."

"Do you want to hear the rest of my report? Tigre put Meris on a medical scanner."

"A scanner? But that's—"

"Illegal. I know. I authorized it anyway. It's noninvasive, Rachel. The Trade Association's review board won't even notice it, next to the restraints and the Phenox. And besides, I thought Tigre was going to kill me." Wearily, he passed a hand over his face. "You, of course, must issue a warrant for my arrest."

His words hit like a dash of cold water. He was deliberately sacrificing himself, Rachel realized, and attempting to shift the blame away from her. For a brief eternity, she stood frozen, staring at Wu, trying to think. His mishandling of the Jadamii demanded an arrest; she saw no alternative. If she ordered his arrest, she stood a chance of exonerating herself.

The thought made her sick. "Oh, no, you don't," Rachel said. "You got us into this; you help dig us out." She returned to her chair and collapsed into it. "And when this is all over, and Earth and Jada are enjoying a thriving friendship, I'm going to make you climb all eight hundred and forty-three steps of the Last War Memorial on your hands and knees. And I'll follow behind you, kicking your ass with every step."

For a moment, Wu's expression remained grim, as if he had not heard her. Then he drew up one corner of his mouth in a faint ghost of his mischievous smile. "Very noble, Deputy Ajmani, but I see no reason for you to destroy your career."

"I won't."

"You will, if you don't have me charged. Your career is—"

"My career is not the issue."

"I'm afraid it is."

"You're not listening. I need your help. I can't have your help if you're locked up in detention." Rachel studied Wu, noting the anxious light in his eyes. "Someone is laying a trap for me, trying to box me into a set of limited choices. The best thing for me to do is make an unexpected move, right? I won't arrest you."

"Rachel—"

Without fully intending to speak, she said: "I know about the Starcatcher ordeal."

Wu's brows shot up. "The what?"

To give herself time, Rachel bent down, picked up Wu's mug from the floor, and took a large swallow of spice tea. "Maybe," she said reflectively, "I ought to start kicking your ass now."

Wu's features abruptly relaxed, and he chuckled. "Are you trying to get me all hot and bothered?" He reached for the mug. "Gimme my tea, damn it."

The bantering exchange induced a tremulous longing within Rachel, a desire to forgive everything and return to her close friendship with Wu. Smiling stiffly, she passed him the mug. "According to Captain Khanwa, Councillor Weber serves on the World Council's secret Nominating Committee. Only she doesn't like me, so she's set up some sort of trial by fire, hoping I'll go down in flames."

"According to Khanwa."

"You disagree?"

"Nope."

A drifting sense of betrayal mingled with Rachel's bittersweet emotions. Keeping her expression neutral, she leaned back in her chair and studied Wu from beneath lowered lids. "Why didn't you tell me?"

"Lots of reasons." Wu dropped his gaze. "Because I was ashamed. I let them deceive me into cooperating with them."

"And now, I want the truth."

One corner of Wu's mouth twitched. "Because I planned to sabotage their efforts so that you could sit on the World Council. And I knew you wouldn't approve." He shrugged with his eyebrows. "Also, I was hoping to shield you."

Rachel snorted. "Thanks a lot. Your confidence in me is overwhelming."

Wu finished his tea, sighed, and set the cup on the table. "So arrest me."

"Not a chance. Bend over."

Grinning, Wu met her gaze. In a single instant of shock, Rachel realized just how much he meant to her.

A faint sense of panic seized her. She hastily rifled through her memories, searching for evidence to the contrary. All she recalled, however, were the years of friendship. Her days were filled with work, but lightened by the sudden mention of his name or the happy necessity of requiring his assistance. She loved spending time with him in her off-duty hours; she never tired of his company, always finding comfort in his presence.

And even though Rachel received many sincere and serious overtures from other men, she never took lovers. She had always maintained that she never had the time for a relationship, and that her own parents' unhappy marriage made her cautious, but the truth of the matter was unavoidable. *My God, I'm in love with Wu.* The heat of panic gathered around her heart. *What am I supposed to do now?*

Wu spoke as if continuing in the natural flow of conversation. "Councillor Glee Weber is already facing investigation for her association with corrupt members of the World Council. Do you know what that means? She will do anything to clear her name and remain in power. Anything."

"Yes." Inwardly shaken, Rachel paused, trying to shove her emotions to the background of her mind, to focus on the crisis at hand. "And that's why we've got to gather solid evidence. She must be stopped."

Wu blew out his cheeks. "And will we do . . . anything . . . to stop her?"

"No. If we stoop to her tactics, then she's won."

"A noble platitude."

"Perhaps." Rachel wearily pulled herself to her feet. "But it also happens to be true."

Wu also stood. "It won't be easy, Rachel. The councillor has two pet sociopaths. They—"

"And I have you," Rachel interrupted. "So the advantage is mine."

"Flatterer."

Rachel ran her hand through her hair, attempting to think clearly. "You go round up the honorable councillor's pets. Once they're in custody, we'll gain some breathing room and a bit of bargaining power. Then find Bailey Rye."

Wu nodded. "What about Meris?"

Rachel crossed to the door. "According to Khanwa, Meris is a criminal who escaped custody at Igsha Reey Port." She paused, considering her informant's assertion. "But I think the honorable captain may be mistaken about that."

Wu raised his brows inquiringly. "And?"

Rachel shrugged. "And I'm going to go share in the blame. You authorized the scanner, I'm going to authorize medical intervention."

"Rachel—"

She stopped with her hand on the door and looked over her shoulder. Wu stood with his hands hanging empty at his sides, and his eyes were filled with pain and the need to be forgiven. Rachel searched for words, but her own confusion and her lingering sense of betrayal charged the moment.

Wu swallowed hard. "Be careful."

Remembering their last parting, Rachel managed a smile. "You, too."

CHAPTER TEN

RACHEL paused outside the temporary monitor room to gather her resolve. To her left, the corridor led to the quarters for station personnel and their families. To her right, it opened onto classrooms and the main cafeteria. Belatedly, Rachel recognized how justified Wu's actions had been with the Jadamii. If Meris had broken free, she would have been at large among personnel who were not trained to deal with an alien intruder.

Rachel drew a steadying breath and urged her aching body into a slow walk. Foot traffic in Station Central was light, since it was near the start of the second shift. Two women dressed in scarlet saris strolled toward personnel quarters. A teenage boy rode by on a battery-powered cleaner, his wide eyes conveying the earnest sense of responsibility he felt about operating a large piece of equipment.

Children's laughter drifted to Rachel as she passed a night care facility. Alone for the first time in twenty-four hours, she felt an odd pang of isolation. It was more than the loneliness induced by the unique burdens of high ranking authority, and she realized just how much she had come to depend on the presence of other people to help her stay centered in the midst of a barrage of crises.

The clock of Station Central chimed the half hour, and Rachel quickened her pace. She had no idea how long it would take before the first reports reached the office of

gold rank Deputy Lois Jimanez-Verde, but Rachel wanted
to order the medical treatment before she found herself
suspended.

As she walked, Rachel pulled out her phone to check
her message board. There were over twenty calls from Captain Akya, who still seemed obsessed with the concept of
gathering witnesses' testimonies. It was a pity she had no
time to respond fully to Akya's inquiries, since the Rofa's
curiosity presented a unique opportunity to increase interspecies goodwill. Reluctantly, Rachel sorted the calls into
a separate file, planning to review them as soon as she had
the chance.

There were five calls from her mother. Tightening her
jaw, Rachel deleted all of them.

There was also a personal message for her from out-
bound Kamian freighter 2420, delivered in the whirring
whisper of a vocoder: "I grasp the stars. I grasp the stars."

Rachel shivered. It was another line from the poem.
Hastily, she keyed into Docking Control's records. The ship
had passed through the system without requesting approach
coordinates. The Kamians had evidently entered transmission range for the sole purpose of sending a cryptic greeting
and farewell to Deputy Rachel Ajmani.

Her hands were cold as she returned the phone to her
pocket. She wondered if the Kamians were trying to warn
her of Starcatcher, or if the poetry of Prudence Clarke held
some other meaning for them.

Without warning, Rachel's right heel and instep began
to itch and burn. Her uneasy thoughts concerning mysterious alien messages evaporated in a burst of alarmed surprise. "What the—?"

She bent her knee to inspect the bottom of her shoe.
The rubber sole appeared bubbly, melted. Rachel hastily
kicked off the shoe and inspected her foot. The skin on her
instep looked red and irritated, and there was a cluster of
little white bumps on her heel, as if she had stepped on a
nettle. "Good God."

A maintenance tech passed, pushing an equipment cart.
He paused and raised his brows in concern. "Hurt yourself, Deputy?"

"I don't know what happened," Rachel said. "One second I was fine, and the next—"

An older man with a craggy face, the tech peered at her foot, then exhaled explosively. "Battery acid!" He straightened and made a dozen indecisive movements. "I've got to c–c–call this in," he stammered, fumbling for the phone case clipped to his belt. "Alert Safety. Get you to Medica. Get this—"

Rachel studied the forest-green carpet and noted a trail of dark spots. "There. Look." She pointed. "A kid on a cleaner just went by."

"A kid? You mean Jordie?" The tech's eyes widened in alarm. "If the battery on that thing blows—!" He stared at his empty phone case. "Aw, hell, I forgot. I loaned it to the search party. I need to—"

The man seemed poised to run after the cleaner. Rachel pulled her phone from her pocket. "Here. Use mine." She pressed it into his hand. "I'll get myself to Medica. You go after Jordie and call Safety on the way."

"But, Deputy—"

Rachel smiled encouragingly. "Stay calm. Move fast. And don't step on the wet spots."

"Yes, Deputy." The tech broke into a loping run down the hall.

Wanting to provide at least a minimum of warning for passersby, Rachel limped to the maintenance cart. She found a few strobe beacons, set them to flash green for biohazard, and placed them beside the acid spills. Then she put her melted shoe in a chemical-proof disposal bag and dropped it into an empty metal refuse can on the cart.

The skin on her heel simmered with itchy heat. Rachel checked the bottom of her foot again and discovered that the blisters were spreading. Sighing, she resumed her interrupted trip.

The lift doors opened onto Medica. Preoccupied with her own thoughts, Rachel nearly bumped into a couple waiting to get on. "Oh, I'm sorry—" she began, then recognized Carl Stein. The gantry operator's face appeared tight with exhaustion, but he stood upright. A gray-eyed young woman clung to Carl's arm, as if to help him walk, though it was actually unclear who supported whom. A shadow of guilt and worry faded from the background of Rachel's mind, and she smiled. "Carl! How are you?"

Carl stared at her. "Oh. It's you. Didn't recognize—" He paused, blinking. "I mean—"

The young woman glanced apologetically at Rachel. "He's still a little groggy. Doctor DeFlora says he needs to go home and get twelve hours of sleep."

Rachel stepped off the lift. "Sounds wonderful," she said. "Wish he'd prescribe that for me."

Carl's escort maneuvered him onto the lift, while he continued to stare at Rachel. As the doors slid shut, he turned his gaze to the young woman and calmly told her: "She's the one who saved my life."

Relieved they had not asked about her one bare foot, Rachel limped into Medica. Three hallways fanned out from the facility's reception desk by the lift. A mobile hung over a small waiting area, the delicate movement of its pastel rings driven by drafts from the ventilation system. The yeasty odor of regeneration compounds and the stinging scent of antiseptics drifted through the air.

Glancing around, Rachel found the hallways empty. "That's strange," she muttered. "Who's minding the store?"

The itch had faded from her foot, replaced by the hot irritation of an ordinary burn. Rachel leaned her shoulder against the wall for support and checked her heel again.

The little bumps had merged into one large blister, fish-belly white and oozing fluid. "Great. Just great."

Thinking she ought to check her other foot, she limped to a chair in the waiting area, sat down, and pulled off her left shoe. The rubber sole showed no sign of chemical damage. Rachel twisted her newly bared foot around and studied the bottom for blistering. The skin looked unbroken and healthy. Sighing, she slumped back in the chair.

A medic in powder-blue scrubs walked briskly from a room in the central hallway. She was an older woman, and she wore her graying hair pulled back in a low ponytail. When she saw Rachel, her thoughtful expression slid away into a frown. "Deputy Ajmani. What are you doing here?"

It was an odd question. Rachel thought for a moment, trying to recall the medic's name. "Hello, Nothando," she said. "I need to see Doctor DeFlora."

Nothando's mouth tightened. "The doctor doesn't have time for Port Authority politics."

Rachel stared at her. "What?"

"I think you ought to leave."

"Leave?" Rachel echoed. "But I have a—"

"Deputy Ajmani." Nothando's brows drew together. "The doctor is a very busy man, and right now he's with a patient."

"I see." Rachel wondered how she had upset Nothando. "But I need—"

"I'm sorry," Nothando said firmly. "But it's impossible to interrupt him."

Impatience sparked through Rachel. "Then maybe you can help me. I need some—"

"I'm afraid I can't be of assistance, Deputy," Nothando said. "I'm due on Dock Four to supervise patient transport."

Rachel angrily lurched to her feet, still gripping her shoe. "This is ridiculous!"

Nothando spoke crisply. "Deputy Ajmani, may I remind you that—" She paused, studying Rachel, and her expression turned serious and alert. "Are you all right?"

"Fine," Rachel snapped. "Peak of health." Maddened by frustration, she twisted to look down each of the three corridors, searching for another medic. The numbered doors all appeared identical, no telling which were examination rooms and which were closets. Rachel's concern for her own injury dissolved when she realized that no staffers seemed to be on duty. "Which room is the detainee's?"

Nothando's tone returned to its previous hostility. "Doctor DeFlora gave orders that the patient from Jada wasn't to be disturbed."

Scowling, Rachel looked at Nothando. "I don't want to bother her. I just want to know where the staffers are posted. They shouldn't be in the same room with her, she might—"

Nothando's brows came up. "Doctor DeFlora had your staffers removed from Medica."

After the first blank moment, Rachel felt inclined to laugh. Nothando's statement seemed like the wildest nonsense. "What do you—?" She caught herself gesturing with the shoe and paused to shove it into her pocket. "What do you mean 'removed'?"

"It was felt," Nothando said carefully, "that their presence disrupted medical efficiency."

"Oh, really?" Nothando's earlier attitude suddenly made sense to Rachel. Everyone in Medica was probably braced for a battle with Port Authority. "Well, let me tell you something. A couple of highly trained staffers are not nearly as disruptive as a dangerous alien who—"

Nothando folded her arms. "The patient is not dangerous."

Rachel laughed furiously. "What do you mean, she's not dangerous? She's got claws like a—!"

"The patient is still sedated—"

"And when she wakes up?"

"We'll know the moment she regains consciousness," Nothando said with a clear note of condescension. "We have her on a scanner."

Rachel fought the urge to shout. "I fail to see," she said in a careful, quiet voice, "how a scanner signal will prevent the Jadamii from shredding someone like a cabbage."

"Deputy, we know what we're doing."

Rachel snorted. "No staffers, no detainee." She reached for the familiar weight of the phone in her pocket. "I'm going to call Warden Jackson and have him move Meris back to her holding cell."

Nothando stiffened, obviously affronted. "You can't do that."

Instead of the phone's smooth case, Rachel's fingers encountered heavy canvas fabric. *My shoe.* Embarrassment brought heat to her face, and she had just enough presence of mind not to pull the thing out of her pocket. Her phone, she recalled, was in the possession of the jittery maintenance tech.

Nothando seemed unaware of Rachel's distraction, and she continued speaking in a crisp tone. "You don't have the authority to countermand Doctor DeFlora's—"

"Like hell, I don't!" Rachel stabbed the air with her finger. "You tell Doctor DeFlora that I—"

A door in the central hallway opened softly. Rachel froze and watched.

Doctor Tigre DeFlora came out and regarded her calmly. "Tell me what?"

Following the surgeon, a medic stepped into the hall with a sleeping child in his arms. Little Saja's head rested on his shoulder, and she wore a gray-green regeneration patch taped to her scalp.

The medic spotted Rachel, then looked uncertainly at his superior.

Keeping his gaze fixed on Rachel, Tigre spoke in a low, controlled voice. "Paul, please take Saja to the blue room and get her settled in one of the cribs."

"Yes, Doctor." The medic cast an uneasy glance at Rachel, then carried the child to a room at the end of the hall.

Nothando took a step toward Tigre. "Doctor—"

Tigre made a gently silencing gesture. "Nothando, I believe you're needed at the transport."

"Yes, Doctor." Nothando appeared both relieved and chastened. She crossed behind the desk and summoned a lift.

Tigre waited until the doors closed on Nothando and they were alone; then, with a weary sigh, he leaned his back against the wall, letting his head roll to one side and his arms hang loose. His lavender scrubs were as rumpled as if he had slept in them, although the dark smudges under his eyes suggested he had not rested in some time. "Deputy Ajmani," he murmured. "I didn't make the connection until just now—you're the lunatic who rescued Carl Stein."

"Yes." Undeceived by his outwardly relaxed manner, Rachel tensed for another argument. "That's me."

Tigre looked her directly in the eye. "You're here because I chased the staffers out," he said. "And you think you can bully me into letting them come back."

"Not exactly." Rachel tried to recall her original reason for visiting Medica, casting her thoughts back through the layers of intervening frustration and worry. "I came to authorize treatment for Meris of Jada."

Tigre smiled derisively. "I don't need your authorization. I have my Hippocratic oath and Meing's Vow."

Rachel returned the smile. "How nice for you." Then the implication of his words struck. "You've already—?"

"—rendered treatment?" Tigre finished. "Yes."

Rachel found it difficult to speak, her dislike for Tigre battling with her sense of responsibility. "Then you're guilty of torture under Galactic Trade Association laws."

"But not under the laws of the World Health Agency."

Tigre straightened, his dark eyes widening dangerously. "In fact, I've notified my superiors at the Agency, and I'm acting upon their instructions." He advanced on her. "Meris of Jada is my patient. Mine. You, Deputy Ajmani, are relieved of custody."

The edge of Rachel's vision sparkled. She thought of Kamians who quoted poetry, a Freeholder who spoke in alien tongues, and a Rofa who sought to fight with words instead of a knife. Long-established lines of power were shifting. In a flash of peripheral insight, she saw the World Health Agency attempting to reset certain political boundaries, and how the World Council would react to this challenge to its authority. "Doctor, you don't know . . . what you're getting into."

Tigre's fine features twisted with sudden rage. "Oh, really?" His voice dropped to a harsh murmur. "Well, let me tell you something. I've seen a mess like this before. A World Council audit. Mysterious and untraceable equipment failures. A rash of accidents and injuries."

"Doctor—"

"So don't talk to me like I'm some green kid who—"

Rachel's scalp crawled. "Seen it before?" she interrupted. "When? Where?"

Tigre clearly mistook the questions for a challenge, and his eyes blazed. "Two years ago. On Brontos."

Three hundred and twenty-seven people lost their lives when the mining colony's main shaft collapsed. The director of the Brontos project had been found guilty of criminal incompetence and sentenced to life on a penal farm.

Realization pierced Rachel. *Starcatcher.*

There was a phone on the reception desk. Rachel whirled toward it, intending to call Wu. Strained from bearing all her weight, her right knee buckled.

Frantically, she clutched the edge of the desk, but lost her grip. Her body twisted, off-balance, wrenching the muscles in her back. "Damn!" She tried to grab the desk again. Her right heel landed heavily on the floor.

Rachel felt the thin skin over her blisters adhere to the cold tile, then rip like wet tissue paper. Her right foot skated out from under her, leaving a smear of bloody fluid. She fell, slammed her shoulder into the side of the desk, and tumbled to the floor. Pain exploded from every point of impact: hip, elbow, head.

"Deputy!" Tigre slid into a crouch by her side. "Are you hurt?"

Angry embarrassment eclipsed Rachel's physical discomfort. "I'm fine," she answered automatically. "Just fine." She rolled onto her stomach and tried to push herself into an upright position. A white-hot pain knifed through her elbow and bruised shoulder. She inhaled sharply through her teeth and eased herself to the floor.

Tigre gave a heavy, exasperated sigh. "Are ... you ... hurt?"

Surprise filtered through Rachel's humiliation, as she realized that he actually wanted to help her. "My shoulder is killing me," she admitted, "but I'm positive nothing is broken." She wiggled her fingers to demonstrate. "See?"

Tigre gave no sign of hearing her reply. He gazed, obviously appalled, at the smudge of blood-tinged fluid on the tiled floor. "What the—?" He leaned closer to Rachel and bent to study her face. His silky hair fell over his forehead, and his eyes filled with alarm. "Deputy, you seem to be bleeding from somewhere."

A fresh tide of embarrassment washed over Rachel, and she braced herself for his scorn. "My foot. I stepped in a little battery acid."

Tigre scrambled to look before Rachel finished speaking. He grasped her right ankle and raised her foot, so that her leg flexed at the knee. His low voice warmed with a tone of encouragement. "Let's keep this elevated, shall we?"

Still lying on her stomach, Rachel propped herself up on her elbows and twisted to watch him over her shoulder. Her bruises protested the movement, but she ignored the pain. "It probably looks worse than it really is, since I tore the blister open."

Again, Tigre appeared to ignore her. He snatched the phone off the desk and punched a number with his thumb. In spite of his haste, his expression was serene. He pressed the phone to his ear with his shoulder, then pulled a small spray tube from his pocket.

Rachel felt both reassured by his competent manner and resentful that he seemed unaware of her words. "Doctor DeFlora, I—"

Tigre spoke to someone on the other end. "Hello, Burke. Tigre." Moving economically, he sprayed foam onto his hands and worked it over his skin to form gloves. "Got another third-degree acid burn. Bring some wheels to the desk. Stat." He set the phone on the floor.

Disbelieving, Rachel stared at Tigre. "But it doesn't hurt that much," she protested. "It can't be that bad."

Tigre met her gaze fleetingly, and he lifted one corner of his mouth. "I'm afraid I can't concur with your diagnosis, Doctor Ajmani. The caustic agents in chemical batteries imported from Kam inflict rapid and progressive tissue damage."

"But—" Rachel floundered for an argument. "But I—"

Tigre returned to his scrutiny of the burn, using both hands to tilt her foot to the light, studying it intently. "Where did this happen?"

Resigning herself to procedure, Rachel laid her head on her folded arms. "In Station Central, not far from the rec room."

Tigre carefully spread her toes, evidently checking for more blisters. "And about how long ago was this?"

In spite of annoyance and discomfort, Rachel let her eyes drift shut. "I don't know. Maybe fifteen or twenty minutes."

Tigre's tone remained calm and nonjudgmental. "Why didn't you tell us right away that you were burned?"

Rachel felt suddenly detached and remote. The tile floor was as comfortable as a mattress. "Tried to." One corner of her mouth was pressed against her arm, and her words came out slurred. "Then more important things came up."

"Ah, yes," Tigre said mildly. "Posting sentries on your dangerous alien criminal." He gently raised her other foot for inspection. "Get any juice on this one?"

"No." Rachel felt as if all her muscles were melting like wax, and she struggled to shake off sleep. "You think that I don't care about Meris, but you're wrong. I'm terribly worried about her."

"I see."

"And I don't think that Meris is a criminal. Not a professional, anyway. She doesn't take care of herself the way a real operator would." Rachel searched for the right words, needing to explain. "I think she's desperate. I think she's trapped in some far-reaching scheme. And I think that we're trapped in it, too." Tigre was silent, and Rachel realized how she must sound. "You think I'm crazy."

Tigre cleared his throat. "When was the last time you got any sleep, Deputy?"

A disjointed sense of desperation seeped into Rachel's thoughts. She had to make him understand. "Don't patronize me. I'm telling you that the Jadamii is at the root of something big. Bigger than the World Council. Bigger than Starcatcher."

Tigre's voice took on a practiced note of reassurance. "I promise we'll take good care of the Jadamii." He softly patted the sole of her uninjured foot. "We'll take good care of you, too."

The sound of running feet pounded the air. Rachel dragged her eyes open. A medic she did not recognize raced toward them, pushing a gurney.

Humiliation swept over Rachel, and she sighed deeply. "I can walk."

Tigre laughed under his breath. "I hope you never encounter an insurmountable obstacle, Deputy. You'd shatter like glass."

Tigre and Burke wheeled Rachel into a room along one of the side corridors. Lying on her stomach under a stiff sheet, Rachel felt wide awake and lucid after the indignity of being loaded onto the gurney. She propped herself up on her elbows, glancing around at the tile walls and white supply cupboards. "This isn't going to take long, is it?"

Tigre strode to a cupboard and keyed open its lock. "No, Deputy," he said in a preoccupied tone, "not long at all."

"Good. Because we still have a number of issues to resolve." Rachel cleared her throat. "Tell me more about Brontos."

"Sorry, Deputy, I can't talk now." Tigre gave her a sly grin. "I'm with a patient."

"Very funny." Grudging amusement pulled Rachel's mouth into an unwilling smile. *I probably deserved that.*

Tigre tossed a quick look over his shoulder at Burke. "Go ahead."

"Yes, Doctor." Burke guided the gurney toward a large metal sink equipped with several faucets and hoses.

A slight uneasiness rose up in Rachel as she recalled her basic first aid. "You're going to flood the burn."

"That's right," Burke replied amicably. He smoothly swung the gurney around so that Rachel's feet hung over the edge of the sink and she faced the middle of the room.

Rachel's heartbeat picked up speed. *Relax*, she told herself. *Just breathe.* The shoe in her pocket gouged her hip. Surreptitiously, she shifted her weight and tugged some slack into her uniform tunic, trying to get the shoe out from beneath her tunic without calling attention to her furtive movements.

Burke gently clasped the ankle of her burned foot. Rachel expected him to start the irrigation, and she stiffened every muscle in her body to keep from flinching.

"Did I startle you?" Burke asked in a calm, friendly voice. "I'm sorry." He eased a plastic sheet under her injured right foot and draped it over the left. "There. That will protect you from splashing, in case there's any live acid left in the burn."

"Sorry," she muttered. "Guess I'm a bit tense."

Burke switched on a bright lamp over the sink. "You're doing just fine."

His words failed to soothe Rachel. Annoyed by her own jumpiness, she twisted to watch over her shoulder.

Moving quickly, Tigre carried a tray of surgical instruments to the sink. "Remember, gloves first," he murmured to Burke. "And goggles, too. Where are they?"

"Sorry, Doctor," Burke hastily turned from the sink. "I'll get them."

"Hurry, please." Tigre crossed to the gurney's other end and crouched to meet Rachel eye to eye. "Listen, Deputy," he said, his expression grave. "I'll have to perform a debridement, which means I'll excise the damaged tissue from the burn to provide a clean base for regeneration. In order to make sure that you stay comfortable, I'd like to give you more than a local." He held up a disposable inhaler in its protective pouch. "Just a little Tri-Omega."

A faint touch of panic squeezed Rachel's heart, and she stared at the inhaler's pink cartridge. She remembered reading about the stuff, how certain fringe groups on the Freeholds claimed it induced prophetic visions. "Isn't that a hallucinogen?"

Tigre shook his head and spoke with exaggerated patience. "No, Tri-Omega only blocks pain. Some people report euphoria; others fall into a light doze and have pretty dreams. It's safe. I've administered it for years as an alternative to a general anesthetic."

Rachel regarded the inhaler dubiously, thinking about her brother's dependency on euphorics. "I don't know. . . ."

Tigre sighed. "Deputy, you don't have to take the Tri-Omega, if you don't want. I just thought you'd prefer it, since it wears off quickly and usually has fewer side effects than a sedative."

An odd sense of entrapment tightened the muscles at the nape of Rachel's neck. She realized that he was right; a sedative might incapacitate her for hours, and she didn't have the time, but she most emphatically did not want to take the Tri-Omega. It sounded no better than the stuff that led to her brother's early death.

Tigre drew his brows together in concern and mild irritation. "It's completely up to you, Deputy. Tell me what you want."

Rachel's heart beat in slow, hard strokes. Her actual problem, she supposed, was in relinquishing control to an opponent. However, she wanted Tigre to trust her, so she needed to prove her confidence in him. "You're the doctor," she replied. "I'll take the Tri-Omega, if you recommend it."

Tigre's brow relaxed. "Good," he said, clearly relieved. He straightened from his crouch and ripped the sterile wrapper from the inhaler.

Burke spoke from the sink. "I've got the goggles, Doctor. I put yours on the counter."

"Thanks." Tigre lifted the inhaler to the level of his eyes and carefully adjusted the dosage trigger. "Burke, maybe you ought to check the clamp on that hose before you start. We don't want another accidental shower, do we?"

Burke's murmured reply was lost in the sudden clatter of running water. Alarmed, Rachel clutched the gurney's rough sheet in both fists and clenched her jaw.

Tigre patted one of her fists. "Relax, Deputy. You're going to be fine." He settled the inhaler over her nose. "You know the routine, I'm sure. Take a deep breath through your mouth, exhale completely, then slowly draw in through your nose. Ready?"

The inhaler felt unpleasantly rubbery against her skin, but she went through the breathing sequence as directed. On her second inhalation, Tigre released the Tri-Omega. The mist had a faintly citrus scent, and it induced an immediate dizziness. Rachel bit her lips, regretting her decision to take the drug.

Tigre removed the inhaler and tossed it into a trash bin. "Go ahead, Burke. I'll engage the monitor."

At once, Burke turned the spray of water onto the burn. Expecting furious pain, Rachel drew a ragged breath. The dizziness intensified, as if fed by the rush of oxygen; it overwhelmed every other sensation and set the room spinning. Floundering for self-control, Rachel let her head fall forward onto the gurney's thin pillow.

"Good," Tigre said approvingly. His voice seemed flat, as if he spoke from the end of a cotton-lined tube. "Good. Just relax." He positioned the monitor next to the gurney and keyed in activation codes. "Okay, Burke, we're up."

"Monitor tracking is clear, Doctor," Burke answered. "Pulse reads ninety."

"Ah, good."

Miserably, Rachel opened her eyes again. Tigre lifted one corner of his mouth in a half-smile and patted her shoulder. "You're going to be fine, Deputy." He moved out of her sight to join Burke at the sink.

Vertigo gave the room another violent spin. A chilly mist of perspiration formed on Rachel's upper lip, and her stomach tensed with nausea. She closed her eyes again and settled her head on the pillow.

The spray of water felt prickly against her burned skin, but she could not tell whether the water was hot or cold. She wondered how the drug cushioned her from the pain when, aside from the dizziness, she felt none of the reported effects, not even sleepiness. *Maybe it's not working.*

The water's force lessened a bit. Burke asked quietly, "Like this?"

"Good," Tigre murmured. "Hold steady for a second, I want to clip that."

Troubled by their exchange, Rachel hoped they would wait to start cutting until the drug took full effect. Her hands turned cold, and she slipped them under her throat to warm them.

A flurry of lurid images skittered through her mind. Mouths spewed vomit. Entrails spilled from torn bodies. A woman's blood-smeared head bounced down a staircase. Her heart chilling in horror, Rachel fought to redirect her thoughts. *After this, need to call Wu. Wonder if he's found Bailey.*

The nightmare images gave way to a view of a tiny, dimly lit room stacked with broken shipping canisters. Startled by its clarity, Rachel held the mental picture and studied it.

The configuration of the room's curved walls suggested to her that she viewed the interior of a ship. A tarp lay on the trash-littered floor. At first, she only noticed that the rough fabric was stiff with filth, then she saw that the tarp enshrouded a Human form. As she watched, a man's hand extended from under the tarp's edge. The hand, lean and bronze-colored, rolled palm up, as if in entreaty. A bracelet of woven rags, like the kind worn by Freeholders, encircled the sinewy wrist. The long fingers twitched feebly once, then stilled.

A sensation akin to an electric shock jolted through Rachel's body. Heart racing, she opened her eyes and gasped for air. The monitor emitted a high-pitched cheeping. Wildly, she twisted to look over her shoulder.

Burke glanced at Tigre. "Doctor, pulse is one-twenty."

Tigre ripped off his wet gloves and pulled off his goggles. His brows drew together tightly in an expression of angry worry as he studied Rachel. "Deputy Ajmani—" He moved to crouch by her end of the gurney. "What's the matter?"

Desperately, Rachel tried to catch her breath. She scrabbled through her mind for the words she needed, finding it difficult to speak. "I saw a man," she whispered. "I saw him lying in garbage."

Tigre's graceful features smoothed in sympathetic understanding. "Ah, yes, that sounds frightening." His low voice held no hint of condescension. "You had a bad dream."

Maddened by her own inability to communicate, she shook her head violently. "No, no. I saw him die!"

Tigre had red indentations on his nose and cheeks from the goggles, and his silky hair was disheveled. "It sounds like you're upset. Most people feel happy when they take Tri-Omega."

Rachel's sense of horror faltered. She recalled using the

inhaler, breathing the lemon-scented mist. "Oh," she said softly. "I'm drugged."

Tigre's face lightened a bit. "That's right," he said encouragingly. "Try to remember that. And try to think of pleasant things. The monitor's alarm went off because your heart thought you were in danger. Try to relax, Deputy. Tell your heart it's safe. Okay?"

A strange wonder eclipsed Rachel's anxiety. She settled her head on the pillow. *Tell your heart it's safe.*

Tigre leaned closer and studied her face. "Okay?"

Serenely, Rachel met his gaze. He had very long lashes, she noted, and his hair sparkled with iridescent highlights. She smiled up at him, certain she needed to tell him something; explain to him why it was nice for the Rofan to bite, or inform him of the connection between Brontos and Starcatcher, or describe how Prudence Clarke invented the flight. "The gems of the Orient blend with the color of your hair—black as the reasons for night."

Tigre's mouth fell open, and he slowly straightened.

Burke cleared his throat. "What did she say?"

Tigre shrugged and puffed out his cheeks. "I'm not sure."

Burke gave a low, disapproving whistle. "Tigre, just how much T-O did you give her?"

"Level four." Tigre spread his hands. "Just a normal dose."

Contentedly, Rachel closed her eyes. She had quoted the wrong poem, but she was nonetheless certain that Tigre understood her secret message.

"Pulse is slowing," Burke reported in a carefully neutral tone. "Down to one hundred."

"Good." Tigre rejoined Burke at the sink. He dropped his voice to a murmur. "You know what happened, don't you? She fought it. I've never met anyone so recalcitrant. Why does she turn everything into a battle?"

Distantly amused by his question, Rachel smiled privately. She wondered what Wu would say about her experiences with Tigre. "What doesn't kill you," she said aloud, "will wake you up."

Tigre chuckled softly.

Yes. He understands.

The room began to spin again, slowly and lazily. Filled

with tranquillity, Rachel recalled the backyard swing of her childhood. She used to twist the ropes, then let the swing whirl her around while she looked straight up into the oak tree's branches.

Somehow, both Wu and Tigre were on the swing with her. Still smiling, Rachel drifted into a dream of spinning sunshine and fluttering leaves.

CHAPTER ELEVEN

RIFE MEIER lay belly down on the dusty floor of the ventilation shaft. He stared into the surrounding darkness and strained to listen for pursuit over the thunder of his laboring heart, trying to make out the thump of running feet or the crash of a forced entry hatch. He only heard his partner, Jardín Azul, crawling up the shaft behind him, the glide of fabric against skin, and the hissing echo of her breath.

Rife brushed his sweat-soaked, golden hair from his eyes. *It's all going wrong.* They had failed to plant the burn-out chip in Port Station's main generator, and their most recent foray onto Dock Two had nearly resulted in capture. Worst of all, a lunatic Freeholder named Bailey Rye had added an unnecessarily complex spin to their plan to discredit and destroy Councillor Weber.

Wiping his wet upper lip on his sleeve, Rife struggled to catch his breath. Jardín had insisted upon involving the Freeholder, and so Bailey knew everything from timetables to methods. But as far as Rife was concerned, Bailey's knowledge posed a definite threat to the mission. Thinking over the last few hours, he wondered if their recent failures were due to the Freeholder's interference.

He could not tell Jardín of his suspicions, since she inflicted dire punishments for doubting her decisions. Usually, she had sex with another man, and made Rife watch. Just the mere thought caused misery and rage to boil up to the surface. Rife narrowed his gray eyes. *If she does that with the Freeholder, I'll kill him.*

Jardín wriggled up beside Rife and pressed the length of her petite body against his. He turned on his side to give her more room, and she snuggled her cold face into the crook of his neck, convulsed with silent laughter.

Nerves. Closing his eyes, hiding in his own darkness, Rife passed a tender hand over Jardín's braided hair, then pulled her into a close embrace. For a long time, he simply held her, wondering why he loved her, knowing that he needed her.

Jardín was the only one who could control him, could somehow bend his rage to her will. She had taught him, a wolf, how to behave like one of the sheep. It added spice to the inevitable moment when he turned on some trusting fools and punished them for their gullibility.

Jardín had a personal mission to free humankind from slavery, starting with the elimination of the corrupt Councillor Weber, though Rife did not understand how sabotage and mass murder would accomplish Jardín's goals. *Don't care.* He bent his nose to her hair, inhaling her scent. *Only want to be with you.*

Slowly, Jardín's hysteria subsided. "That," she gasped, "was close."

Rife pressed his lips against her ear. "This place stinks," he breathed. "I hate it."

He felt Jardín smile against his throat. "Then you won't mind," she whispered, "if I blow it out of the sky?"

"Mind?" Rife repeated softly. "Not at all. In fact, I'll help you." He added, knowing it would please her: "Especially if you plan to blow Glee Weber along with it."

"Blow her to hell," Jardín said. "Count on it." She snatched a kiss, and her lips were like ice. "Time to move. Bailey's waiting for us."

The Freeholder's name raised a stinging welt of jealousy, and Rife abruptly released Jardín. "I suppose."

Jardín chuckled. "You hate him, don't you?"

"I didn't say—"

"You didn't have to," she whispered. "But, Rife, we needed him."

"Did we?" Rife tried to keep resentment out of his tone. Bailey had provided crucial surveillance equipment for Operation Starcatcher, though where a Freeholder might have gained access to such advanced technology was beyond comprehension. "I still say we could have done that trace-and-erase program ourselves."

Jardín's hands groped caressingly over his chest. "Bailey knows that we intend to expose Councillor Weber, to turn the Starcatcher ordeal against her."

It was a nonanswer. Pushing aside the pleasure that her touch induced, Rife sighed. "And what doesn't Bailey know?"

"That his death will incite the Freeholds to rise up against the World Council."

Rife drew a breath to answer, then paused. *I should have known. She always has more than one reason for anything she does.* "We'll have to link his death back to Weber."

"We will."

"Bailey's a lot smarter than he looks. How can we set it up without arousing his suspicion?"

"He already suspects." Jardín's unusually sweet tone dripped with mockery. "Bailey's a *shana*; he walks every path."

A sudden shudder climbed Rife's spine. Each Freehold community had a *shana*—part witch doctor, part clown—an individual gifted with the ability to travel the intertwined "paths" of past, present, and future. "I didn't—" Rife swallowed. "I didn't know that Bailey was a *shana*."

Jardín's voice hardened. "Don't tell me you believe in that garbage."

Rife opened his eyes again, vainly attempting to meet Jardín's gaze in the darkness. "I spent a couple of months on a Freehold, and I saw what *shanas* can do. One old woman told the elders about some experiments I had planned for a few of the settlement's obnoxious brats. She gave them details of things that existed only in my head."

Jardín snorted. "She was guessing."

Wanting to make her understand, Rife blindly reached out and clasped her shoulder. "If Bailey's a *shana*, then we don't stand a chance against him. He can see what we think before we think it. He's . . . dangerous."

Jardín jerked away from his touch. "He's a nitwit."

"He might act like one, but if he finds out—"

"He isn't going—"

"—he'll stop us. Maybe kill us." Rife struggled not to reach out for Jardín again. "Freeholders aren't the same passive sheep as everyone else, don't have the same brainwashed reflexes. And *shanas* are even more dangerous than—"

"Don't worry." Jardín pressed cold fingertips to Rife's lips and whispered silkily, "I've got everything under control."

"Do you?" Rife thought about their recent near capture, convinced now that Bailey was behind it. "We're so close to the end. We can't let him stop us."

"He won't," she said. "Trust me."

Though it took only a few minutes, the return trip to their hideout in a storage bay seemed to stretch into hours. By the time they emerged from the shaft, Rife shook with anxiety and barely suppressed rage.

Bedrolls, supplies, and Bailey's assortment of computerized surveillance equipment ranged around the scuffed metal walls. Bailey sat cross-legged in the center of the shabby compartment. His wild mop of red curls and brightly colored Freeholder's garb contrasted sharply with the hard-worn technology of his surroundings. A makeshift tripod of cable ratchets perched on the floor in front of him, upholding a corroded piece of deck plate that held glowing incense nuggets. Tendrils of fragrant smoke hung in the air over Bailey's head. His eyes opened slowly, empty of expression.

Uneasily, Rife glanced at Jardín. She smiled at the Freeholder and said, "What are you doing?"

Bailey spoke in a dreaming tone. "Rachel is walking the path of many futures. One holds my death as a captive of Phi-Nurians. I'm watching myself die through her mind."

Rife's skin prickled, but he forced himself to approach the seated figure. "Bailey, it's not a good idea to burn things on a space station. Too many flammable chemicals and—" Rife abruptly recognized the scent drifting up from the tripod as a powerful hallucinogen common on the Freeholds. "Verdad." He turned toward Jardín. "Nuggets of the concentrated resin. He'll be looped for hours."

Jardín smiled contemptuously. "Well, so much for our all-seeing, all-wise, and extremely dangerous *shana*."

Rife stared at Bailey. "I don't get it. He said he needed to go somewhere important. Why would he burn Verdad?"

Jardín giggled. "Perhaps," she said, "he was acting under the influence of that alien sedative I put in his water."

Surprised, Rife jerked his gaze to his partner. "You drugged him?"

"With Phenox. It's reported to have an interesting effect on Humans. Such a powerful euphoric that we can do anything to him and make him love it." Jardín wrinkled her nose mischievously. "I told you I had everything under control."

Relieved and filled with admiration, Rife shook his head. "You," he said, "are absolutely amazing."

From the floor, Bailey gave a low, disapproving whistle and murmured: "Tigre, just how much T-O did you give her?"

Jardín crossed to a pack by her bedroll, pulled out a pair of socks, and tossed them to Rife. "Here. Tie him up. Just in case he tries anything."

Rife caught the socks, then frowned down at Bailey. "Tigre?" The name tugged at his memory, raising images of blood-soaked rubble. "Who's Tigre?"

"Hey," Jardín said, "try not to breathe any more of that stuff. I need you clearheaded."

Suddenly realizing his own growing dizziness, Rife kicked over the tripod, then crushed out the smoldering incense under his boots. It felt good to stomp on something. "Better recycle the air in here," he advised. "Unless you want all three of us to have visions."

Kneeling in front of Bailey, Rife heard Jardín go to the main vent and turn up the fan. His hair stirred in the strong draft as he studied Bailey's remote expression. "Hey, *shana*," he asked in a casual tone. "Who's Tigre?"

Bailey smiled serenely. "The peacock's exaltation, the millet fox's brilliance, the gems of the Orient."

Anger sparked through Rife. "Come on, I know you understand me." He roughly grabbed Bailey's sinewy forearms. The Freeholder wore a wide bracelet of plaited rags around one wrist. Rife frowned at the eccentric piece of jewelry, then shrugged, deciding it would be too much trouble to remove. He picked up a sock. "Who's Tigre?"

"My *boku*. My teamer."

Thinking over the reply, Rife knotted the sock around Bailey's wrists. He did not know what *boku* meant, but "teamer" was a common expression in the Northern Freeholds, an affectionate term for the man with whom one shared a wife. "So . . . he's on your team?" Completely revolted, Rife yanked the knot in the makeshift bonds tighter. He could not imagine willingly sharing Jardín with another man. "Part of that old-fashioned, group marriage thing, huh?"

Behind him, Jardín said, "Hurry up. I need your help with these batteries."

"Almost done." Rife wrapped the other sock around the Freeholder's wrists. "Tigre," he mused aloud. "Why does that name bother me?"

"I don't know," Jardín said with poorly concealed impatience. "The name's not that unusual."

Images flashed through Rife's mind: clouds of dust, rubble, crushed human bodies. "Brontos."

Jardín inhaled sharply. "What?"

Rife abruptly made the connection. He remembered a young doctor with a torch in one hand and a scanner in the other, nimbly climbing through the debris, searching for survivors. Rife glanced over his shoulder at Jardín. "He was the surgeon on Brontos: Doctor Tigre DeFlora."

Jardín paused in the act of stooping over a crate of batteries. Her delicate brows drew together in a scowl of concentration. "And now he's here? On Port Station?"

Rife's lips slowly parted. It was a huge leap in logic, but it made a horrible kind of sense, and it was just the sort of shifty double cross that Glee Weber loved to pull. "Maybe I inhaled too much Verdad, but . . ."

"If that doctor is on the station—"

"—he might remember us, and that could pose a problem. Or, at least, he'd remember me, since I actually spoke to him several times." Rife smiled grimly. "Do you suppose Weber—?"

"Wouldn't put anything past that bitch." Jardín abandoned the batteries and quickly crossed over to the equipment and tapped into station records. A holographic screen leaped up, shimmering like a small campfire. It cast glowing rainbows across Jardín's face as she searched through personnel files. "Damn. He's here."

The surgeon's image appeared, overlaid by the standard ID grid showing his height and body measurements. Tigre was not a big man, but perfectly proportioned. He turned in a circle, for the benefit of the cameras, then tilted his head and smiled.

Jardín froze the screen. "I don't remember him."

"I do," Rife said. "Vividly. He saved me from taking a nasty fall." The smell of blood and dust returned to Rife, accompanied by the sensation of gravel sifting away under his boots and the memory of a sudden, hard grip on his arm. "You were working the other end of Starcatcher, as the observer. I was with Fred, setting traps."

Jardín set the image on replay and watched Tigre turn around over and over again. "What gorgeous eyes." She licked her teeth. "And what a nice ass."

Jealousy simmered through Rife, but he made himself grin. "The idiot doctor probably saved my life. And I was the one who killed all his friends. Pretty funny." Rife returned his attention to Bailey. "And he's your husband, is he?"

"Not my husband. My *boku*," Bailey explained in a distant voice. "My best friend. My other me. We share our woman's love."

"Hmm," Jardín said, sounding as if she considered the man a matrimonial prospect. "According to his file, Doctor DeFlora is unmarried."

Wanting to hurt someone, Rife snatched a handful of Bailey's red curls and yanked his head back. "You said he was your teamer."

Bailey gazed up at him, smiling softly. "He is. Just doesn't know it yet. It's a possible future."

Rife released him, snorting in disgust. "You make me sick."

Jardín was reading from a secondary screen. "This is interesting. You know, the World Health Agency has been petitioning to place a surgeon on Port Station for the last— oh, four years."

"Yeah, I know." Rife studied Bailey, wondering how much pain it would take to cut through his drug-induced euphoria. "Feeble politics. For the last two decades, the Agency's been trying, ever so politely, to weaken the World Council's power base."

"DeFlora's only been here a few days." Jardín raised her

head and looked at her partner. "Guess which member of the World Council granted the petition? And handpicked DeFlora from a slate of sixty-three candidates?"

Rife peered at her. "Glee Weber?"

"Glee Weber."

The hair on Rife's nape stirred. "Then it's no coincidence. She's onto us." He crossed to Jardín and sat down beside her on the dirty floor. "She'll have him testify against us, all the while claiming she didn't know how far we would take things on Brontos."

"Maybe." Jardín steepled her fingers in thought. "But it says here that DeFlora was the legal ward of one Richard Wagasi—the Agency's vice director."

"So she's trying to throw candy to the Agency?"

"Possibly. Or maybe she just wants us to dispose of sweet little Doctor Tigre."

"What?"

Jardín raised her brows. "One more victim of Rachel Ajmani's incompetence."

Rife nodded, trying to follow her line of reasoning. "Unless we shift the blame?"

Jardín smiled. "Right. Pin the blame on Weber. Make it seem like a cover-up for her part in the Brontos disaster. Which will set the Agency against the Council in a more forceful way."

Again filled with admiration, Rife kissed her cheek. Her skin felt smooth and cool against his warm lips. "Perfect."

Jardín frowned thoughtfully up at DeFlora's holograph. "I wonder. . . ." She turned her head, narrowing her eyes, and regarded the Freeholder. "Bailey. I believe that it's time to go meet your friend. Where is he?"

Bailey raised his hands and stared quizzically at his bound wrists. "Socks," he said. "That's not right. Socks go on your feet."

Jardín sharpened her tone. "Where is your friend, Bailey? We want to find him."

"Her." Bailey dropped his hands onto his lap. "My friend is Meris of Jada. I want to take her home to Hoshino Uta."

Rife exchanged glances with Jardín. "An alien?" He drew his brows together. Aliens were not allowed on Earth. "You want to take an alien back to your home Freehold?"

Bailey nodded, closing his eyes. "Meris needs a safe place. So the World Council won't get her." He abruptly slumped sideways onto the floor. "Need to . . . need . . ."

Jardín sprang to her feet and strode to Bailey. "Wake up." She kicked his leg. "Why is the World Council after your friend?"

Bailey sighed groggily. "The key . . ." He rolled onto his back, sweat bathing his face. "She is . . . the key to all power. . . ."

Jardín put her hands on her hips and chewed her bottom lip. "The key to all power?"

Rife climbed to his feet and joined Jardín. "It could mean anything."

Bailey opened his eyes and looked up at them. "It means power over all the galaxy."

Jardín turned her bright gaze to Rife. "Sounds interesting."

Rife blinked in surprise. "I thought you didn't believe in *shanas*."

"I don't. But the Jadamii might be useful." Jardín crouched and lifted Bailey's head. She stroked strands of red hair from his face. "Tell me," she coaxed seductively. "Tell me about Meris."

Rife trembled with jealousy. "He's out of his mind on Verdad. Remember what he said about the doctor? We don't know if he's talking about the present or—"

Sweat beaded on Bailey's forehead and dripped from the tips of his hair. He met Rife's gaze. "Your death is planned." Then his eyes fluttered shut and his body went limp.

Rife shivered with an unexpected touch of cold, but he tried to speak lightly. "Planned, huh?" He hunched his shoulders. "That's good. I'd hate to die by accident."

Jardín let Bailey's head drop to the deck plates and straightened from her crouch. "Wake him up."

"How?"

"I don't care. Just do it. I have more questions for him."

Pleasure thrilled through Rife, and he rolled up his sleeves. Bailey would pay for the way Jardín had touched him. "This should be fun."

Jardín's voice hardened. "I said to wake him up, not kill

him. And don't do anything that will look suspicious on his autopsy."

"But—"

"After we're done with him, we'll stuff him into a canister and send him to the Phi-Nurians. As a gift from Weber."

"To the Phi-Nurians?"

"Yes. But he'll die in transit. A tragic life-support failure."

"A possible future." Rife studied Bailey's unconscious figure, then grinned. "Maybe the Phi-Nurians will eat him."

"Whatever they do, the councillor will be implicated." Jardín's brown eyes seemed to look inward. "We also need to find out what we can about that Jadamii. And Doctor Tigre DeFlora."

On the threshold of Medica's staff lounge, another flashback caught Tigre. Cold sweat filmed his skin, causing his scrubs to stick to his back, and his heart raced.

Brontos.

The generator had crashed in the middle of the night shift, and the backup power hesitated a crucial three seconds before kicking on. Time enough for the joints in the main shaft's support system to go unstable.

Tigre relived the moment when the air pressure fluxed with a hollow boom that he felt to his bones. Terror flashed through him, even though he knew that the intense memory was triggered by stress and lack of sleep. He pressed his clammy forehead to the cool metal of the doorframe. In his mind, he saw swirling dust lit by the glare of sodium lamps. "Shit," he whispered. "Shit, shit, shit."

"Doctor?"

Tigre lifted his head. He saw no rubble, no dead and dying friends. Mismatched, comfortably worn furniture crowded Medica's staff lounge. Candid shots of the medics, technicians, and their families adorned the walls. In its niche by the door, a brewer steamed.

Nothando sat alone at a corner table, hunched over a cup of tea. Worry lined her eyes. "Doctor DeFlora, are you all right?"

Tigre made himself straighten. "Lousy headache," he lied. "And when you're off duty, it's 'Tigre.' Remember?"

Nothando's gaze lost its anxiousness, and she gave him a slow, tired smile. "Yes, Tigre." She made his name sound like a formal title. "What's up?"

Tigre hardly knew where to start. An armed and dangerous sociopath served as the station's warden. An unconscious Jadamii lay in the main recovery unit. The new head surgeon in Medica was suffering from post-traumatic stress disorder. And worst of all, the vice director of the World Health Agency, Doctor Wagasi, had sent a message that he would be arriving on the station in a short time.

At the age of sixteen, Tigre had lost his parents and little sister, surviving a car accident that they did not. His paternal uncle, Doctor Richard Wagasi had taken him in, and it was under his mentoring that Tigre pursued a career in medicine. After the Brontos tragedy, Doctor Wagasi had been adamantly opposed to Tigre accepting the Earth Port position. *Old fire-breather's checking up on me.*

Tigre carefully crossed to an armchair near Nothando's table and sank into it. "What's up?" he repeated wearily. "Not me."

Nothando's eyes crinkled at his feeble joke. "Serves you right for ignoring my advice," she said in a motherly tone. "I told you to get some sleep."

Tigre returned her smile, desperately wishing that a nap truly were the answer to everything. "Well, I tried," he said. "But little Saja ripped off her patch, and Paul needed help with her. Then another damned acid burn came in. Then I had to check on the patient from Jada."

Nothando's expression turned serious. "How is she?"

Turning his face away, Tigre shrugged. "We've got the bleeding stopped, but she's still unresponsive. Scanner trackings aren't worth a damn." Sinking into bone-deep weariness, he closed his eyes and rubbed them. Red dust seethed through his inner vision; he could smell it, taste it, feel its sandy drag over his skin. "I don't know if Meris is sleeping or dying. I just don't know."

Nothando made a gentle, pensive noise. "You're eating your heart out, aren't you?"

The dust sifted into his lungs and coated his throat. "Yeah," he said thickly. "I guess." He opened his eyes, forcing himself to return to the moment. *Stupid bastard. Snap out of it.*

"Maybe you ought to take something for that headache."

"Not a chance," Tigre said darkly. "The road to hell is paved with self-medication."

Nothando chuckled.

The taste of dust faded, and an older memory surfaced. Once again, he was sixteen, sitting in roadside grit, cradling his dying sister in his arms, not knowing what to do. Tigre shifted in his chair and glanced at Nothando. "I just hate feeling helpless."

"I know what you mean." She propped her chin on her fist. "It's difficult enough to keep Humans from dying. But to treat an alien . . ."

Hippocrates had admonished physicians to "do no harm." Meing's Vow opened with the declaration: "All compassion must be action."

"I just want to, by God, *do* something, you know?"

"I know."

Swallowing, Tigre looked at Nothando and deliberately changed the subject. "Tell me, how did things go with the transport? Any problems?"

Nothando shook her head. "No, it went smoothly. The families and the ambulatory patients were already on the dock, so it was only a matter of wheeling the stasis units aboard and waving good-bye." She dropped her gaze, brushing imaginary crumbs from the tabletop. "The easiest and saddest thing I've done in days."

The weight in Tigre's chest grew heavier. Most of the acid burns caused by the leaking batteries had been minor; but one faulty battery had exploded, seriously injuring several people. He nodded and clasped his hands between his knees, wondering what to say. The victims had been strangers to him, but they were his staff's friends and colleagues. "It's been rough."

Nothando sighed and toyed with her teacup. "I heard a lot of news on the dock. I ought to take a walk out there more often. Those techs know all the gossip."

"Oh?" Tigre's empty stomach clenched. He glanced at the brewer, wondering if a little tea would head off nausea. It was time for the evening meal, but he found the thought of food unbearable. "Hear anything really juicy?"

"Well . . ." Nothando dropped her voice to a confidential level. "They say that the new head of Medica threatened to bring charges against Warden Jackson."

"Really?" Then her words sank in, and Tigre turned to stare at her. "What?"

Nothando's eyes creased in a sudden smile. "They say that you marched into Checkpoint and called Wu Jackson an incompetent piece of shit."

"Oh. Yeah. That." Tigre slumped back in his chair. It seemed like an event from another lifetime, less real than the memories of Brontos, and he was not proud of his behavior. He had received that communication from his Uncle Richard shortly before storming Checkpoint, and Tigre had vented his displaced resentment on Wu. "I was sort of . . . angry."

"Wish I'd been there." Nothando spoke in a tone of warm approval. "And when you kicked Rachel Ajmani out of Medica."

Thoughts of the deputy raised an inner tangle of impatience, admiration, and embarrassment. The knot of emotions rolled through Tigre, absorbing his sense of unfocused guilt and replacing it with wholesome vexation. Pressing both hands to his forehead, he struggled for adequate words. "Rachel Ajmani is—impossible. You know that, don't you? The woman's an absolute menace."

"She's accustomed to having her own way." Nothando's smile turned faintly malicious. "So? Did she leave on her own? Or did you have to use a tranquilizer dart?"

Tigre grinned in spite of himself. "Neither. She had a third-degree acid burn on her heel."

Nothando stiffened and set down her cup. "Rachel did? She was the burn?" Her voice grew sharp with indignation. "I knew something was wrong. I just knew it!"

Feeling oddly rueful, Tigre touched the tips of his middle finger and thumb together to indicate the burn's circumference. "This big, and spreading like crazy."

Nothando slapped the tabletop in exasperation. "I asked her quite specifically if she was all right. She brushed me off. Then she argued with me about removing the staffers."

Taking perverse pleasure in Nothando's reaction, Tigre felt the tight muscles in his neck loosen. He folded his arms behind his head and arched his back in a stretch. "Ah, yes.

She argued with me, too. She even argued with the T-O and went a little hyper on us. She calmed down right away, but I thought Burke was going to shit seashells.''

Nothando spread her hands helplessly. "You said it: She's impossible."

Suddenly feeling restless and a bit hungry, Tigre levered his body out of the chair and strode to the brewer. "I don't understand her. Why is she like that?"

"I've known Rachel for twenty years, and I still haven't figured her out." Nothando propped her chin on a fist and gazed musingly into the empty air in front of her. "I remember when they deputized her. You've heard the story, haven't you?"

Shaking his head, Tigre folded his arms and leaned against the wall. "Spill the dirt."

Nothando glanced at the door, as though checking for possible eavesdroppers. "Rachel started at Port Station as a service tech."

Tigre's eyes grew wide. He had assumed Rachel's position had been a political appointment. "You mean, she was just a mechanic?"

"Just a mechanic," Nothando repeated. "Her second day on the job, a Phi-Nurian went berserk with a hand cannon and opened fire on a crowded catwalk."

"Oh, fantastic," Tigre dryly. "I suppose Rachel Ajmani single-handedly saved the day."

Nothando chuckled. "Of course."

Disconcerted, Tigre studied her. "You're joking."

Nothando shook her head emphatically, still smiling. "Rachel convinced the Phi-Nurian that her little particle welder was actually a lethal weapon. She had the Phi-Nurian disarmed and calmed down before the staffers arrived."

Thunderstruck, Tigre stared at Nothando. He imagined the scene with Rachel dressed in a tech's insulated coveralls, brandishing a six-inch welder like a sword. The crablike Phi-Nurian cowered against a pyramid of shipping canisters; its eyepad held no more emotion than a patch of moss, and it gripped a smoking gun in one of its four clawed hands. "When did this happen? I don't recall hearing about it on the news."

Nothando took a leisurely sip of her tea. "Let's see. It

happened back in '11. You would have been, what? Eight years old?"

The brewer peeped to announce the completion of its cycle. Smiling, Tigre set his cup under the spout and turned the spigot. "About that."

Nothando swallowed the last of her tea and leaned back in her chair. "The Phi-Nurians do this sort of thing far too often," she said. "They claim they can't help it. They also claim they can't help pooping on the floor." She snorted. "I think they don't even try."

Tigre picked up his cup and inhaled the fragrance of spiced tea. As he understood it, most of the difficulties with Phi-Nurians stemmed from their limited vision and their dependence upon olfactory signals, but he did not want to give Nothando a lecture on xeno-neurology. "Well," he said mildly, "different species are bound to have different customs."

Nothando gazed into her empty teacup, eyes distant with thought. "I suppose," she said, but sounded unconvinced.

"I'm actually looking forward to meeting a Phi-Nurian. And a Rofa."

"The Rofan offer a different set of problems," Nothando said. "When you finally get time to look over the records, you'll find a lot of treatment reports for bites and scratches."

"Hm." Tigre pressed his lips together. He had been briefed on some of the station personnel's sexual experimentation with the Rofan. "I reviewed them on the trip up here. Didn't see any serious injuries mentioned."

"The Rofan consider Humans beneath their dignity when it comes to dueling. At least, that's what I've been told." Nothando paused, seeming lost in her thoughts again. "A few months ago," she said slowly, "Checkpoint called us down to collect the body of a Rofa. Apparently, its shipmates killed it and tossed its corpse out onto the dock just before debarkation."

Nodding, Tigre remembered skimming the report. "Hours dead, I understand. And bled dry from multiple stab wounds."

"It was horrible. Just horrible." Nothando sat up stiffly and rubbed her face. "Remind me, sometime, and I'll take you to deep storage. We have four unclaimed Rofan bodies in stasis down there.''

Something in her listless tone brought the full sense of the crime's reality to Tigre. Feeling suddenly cold, he envisioned an industrial-type stasis bin heaped with dead Rofan. "Four of them," he murmured. He recalled the beautiful creature lying unconscious in one of Medica's beds. He pictured again her delicate, webbed ears and the silver sheen of her pelt. "Let's hope we don't add a Jadamii to our collection.''

CHAPTER TWELVE

TIGRE SHUFFLED down Medica's main corridor with his workboard under his arm. The panic attacks had faded under his growing exhaustion, but he still felt the swirl of dust against his skin whenever he closed his eyes.

The brief refreshment of his cup of tea with Nothando had wilted rapidly in the following hours of acid burns and equipment-related injuries. Interspersed throughout the emergencies were the normal cases a doctor might expect during the early evening shift on a busy station: one of the clerical staff sprained her ankle, a dock tech threw out his back, a new arbitrator developed a severe allergic reaction to Rofan dander. Through it all, Tigre found that his thoughts increasingly revolved around the couch in his office, and even the chance of opening himself to another flashback did not feel like a deterrent.

Five minutes. Lie down. Close my eyes. Just five minutes.

Passing the reception area, Tigre noted the empty chairs and smiled wearily at Burke, who manned the desk. "A lull."

Burke smiled back. "Going off duty?"

"I wish. Doing rounds."

All the patients, of course, were under monitor surveillance, but there were certain things a machine simply could not anticipate, perceive, or provide. The primitive interface of human senses remained at the core of medical attention.

Tigre turned down a side corridor filled with recovery

rooms. Moving as quietly as possible, he eased open Saja's door. The little girl lay asleep in the crib. A quick glance at the monitor revealed her condition as normal. He approached and studied her face. Her color looked good, and her breathing seemed deep and untroubled. All she really needed, he reflected, was for her mother's shift to end so she could go home.

Tigre withdrew, scribbling a note on his workboard, and crossed to the next room. Rachel also slept, though the Tri-Omega must have long since worn off. It had been not quite three hours since he performed the debridement. He frowned at the monitor. Her temperature seemed a little elevated. He hesitated, trying to decide whether to wake her.

Rachel's expression appeared stern in sleep, as if she were involved in an act of concentration, and it conveyed to Tigre the effects of enormous exhaustion. He judged it best to allow her to rest. *Give the regeneration a better chance.*

He turned to go, and Rachel sighed. He looked her way, but she had settled again. Her hair lay everywhere, spilling over the pillow in a riot of black curls.

Black as the reason for night. Tigre tried to recall the rest of Rachel's quote. *Something about Oriental jewels?*

After a long moment, Tigre realized that he was staring at his sleeping patient in a rather inappropriate manner. Turning away, he jotted a note on his workboard regarding Rachel's temperature and his preference that she be left resting.

Bracing himself, Tigre crossed to Meris' room. He checked the monitor readings on his workboard to verify that the Jadamii still slept, then opened the door.

The room smelled of her: a clean, furry scent that reminded Tigre of puppies. He realized that Meris was not an animal, but the comparisons continued to form in the back of his mind.

Meris lay on her side, filling the narrow bed. Long, fine whiskers covered her face and sprouted copiously from her oversized ears. *Lynx.* Dark shades of charcoal patterned the sleek, silver fur around her eyes and snout. *Wolf.* Broad, sloping shoulders and muscular arms gave evidence of a physique designed for climbing. *Orangutan.* The full mane extended down her spine in a narrowing fringe, then seemed to disappear until it burst into flower as a tuft at the tip of her tail. *Lion.*

Stepping closer, Tigre turned his attention to her injuries. Her hands lay open and relaxed, displaying the smooth, leathery palms. The hand with the ripped-out claw still rested on its elevation of pillows; the pad beneath it was clean with no evidence of further bleeding or seepage. In spite of the extra webbing between the fingers and the peculiar avenues of tendons for retractable claws, Meris' hands did not give the impression of paws. *Human.*

Tigre grimaced at the thought, feeling it a kind of bigotry. *No, not Human. Alien.*

He looked at the monitor, which had been set to provide a holographic display. The readings for pulse and respiration meant nothing to him, except as verification that her condition had not changed. There seemed to be evidence that she had broken her left leg at some time in the past; and she had some lingering traces of particle activity, possibly from an extended period in stasis.

The glowing projection of her supine form also indicated two areas of her body where temperatures remained consistently above the rest: her hand, and her shoulder. Automatic magnifications of the injuries popped up every few seconds, highlighting inflamed tissues and tendons, warning of possible permanent damage.

Tigre jotted notes onto his workboard. The information obtained from the scanner was illegal by Galactic Trade Association laws, and he might face future sanctions, but he could not bring himself to care. If they could learn anything that might help Meris, then he considered it worth whatever censure he provoked.

He needed help processing the information. Whether it was ethical or not, he had to pipe everything down to colleagues on Earth. Medica simply was not equipped for intensive research or laboratory analysis. As much as he dreaded the impending arrival of Doctor Wagasi, he knew his superior would offer whatever backing he needed to get the job done.

Tigre resumed taking notes while he walked to the door. With his head down, he nearly collided with someone coming into the room. "Pardon—" The bright green and blue of a Safety uniform splashed across his vision, and he jerked his attention up from his workboard.

Two staffers, a man and a woman, regarded him warily.

Tigre scowled. It was because of Warden Jackson and his minions that Meris suffered her current state. Tigre crowded the interlopers back into the hallway, shut the door, and silently glared.

The male staffer, a young fellow with golden hair, cleared his throat diffidently. "Doctor DeFlora?" He paused and glanced at his partner, as if for permission, then continued in an apologetic tone. "I don't suppose you remember me. I, uh, I was—" He gestured helplessly. "I was on Brontos when . . ."

Tigre recognized him then as one of the survivors who had helped with the rescue efforts. "Oh." It occurred to him that the staffer might be in Medica for treatment and not to interfere with Meris. "Oh, yes, of course." Tigre forced a smile. "Although I'm afraid I never learned your name."

The staffer shrugged one shoulder, swallowing. "There wasn't really time for introductions." He offered his hand. "Rife."

Trapped by routine courtesy, Tigre shook his hand. "Pleasure."

Rife gestured toward the woman. "This is my partner, Jardín."

Tigre nodded courteously, then looked at Rife. "What can I do for you?"

"Well . . ." Rife exchanged glances with his partner again. "You see—"

Tigre took in Rife's obvious discomfort. "Is this something you'd rather discuss privately?"

Rife drew in a deep breath, seeming at a loss. "I—"

Tigre tilted his head, keeping his voice neutral. "Is this about Brontos?"

"A little." Rife sighed. "I don't know what to do. This is just such a . . . such a mess."

Jardín crooked her brows worriedly and touched Rife's shoulder, then turned her anxious gaze to Tigre. "Maybe we ought to talk. If you have a minute?"

Smiling reassuringly, Tigre motioned to the empty room next to Meris'. "A minute."

The staffers, after a third exchange of glances, entered the room. Tigre followed them in and closed the door, mentally reviewing Medica's stock of mild tranquilizers. "What's troubling you?"

Rife slumped down onto the edge of the bed. "A little of everything, I suppose. And I don't know what to do."

Jardín folded her arms and leaned against the wall. "The warden ordered us to move the detainee back to her holding cell."

What? Tigre drew a breath to protest.

Rife spoke first. "But that's the wrong thing to do, I know. I *know* that. I mean, she's still out cold, isn't she?"

"Yes." Tigre looked back and forth between the two staffers, suddenly understanding their dilemma. "But you'll get in trouble with Warden Jackson if you don't follow through."

Rife sighed ruefully. "Lots of trouble. And then he'll just send someone else to do the job."

The woman nodded. "Or come and do it himself."

Tigre folded his workboard against his chest. "I won't let him."

Rife grimaced. "Doc, I'm afraid the warden's not too reasonable, at the moment. He's started carrying a pistol, you know. And, frankly, I'm scared to death of him." Rife made another of his loose-boned gestures. "I don't know anything but working in space, and I had a really hard time getting another post after Brontos. I only got this job because Councillor Weber put in a good word for me."

Tigre nodded. "I had the same problem, and the same solution. Without Councillor Weber's intervention, I'd still be—" A new thought occurred to him. "The councillor is visiting Earth Port right now, isn't she?"

Rife nodded. "She's here with the Xeno-Relations Committee. I thought about paying my respects, but then I was afraid she'd see what a mess everything is in and—"

"—want to help?" Tigre finished. "What's wrong with that?"

Rife drew his brows together in obvious confusion. "Help?"

Jardín straightened away from the wall. "You mean, go over Warden Jackson's head?"

"Exactly."

Rife swallowed hard and dropped his gaze to the floor. "We can't do that," he said in a small voice. "What if he finds out?"

Tigre scowled. "So what if he does? He's not God."

Jardín shifted closer to Rife. "Doctor, you don't know what you're saying. On this station, the warden is—"

Tigre spoke flatly. "I'm not afraid of Wu Jackson."

Rife raised his head and stared at Tigre for a long moment. "I remember—" he started, paused, then continued in a shyly admiring tone. "I remember you on Brontos. You never slowed down, you never rested. When everyone else collapsed from exhaustion, you just kept working."

Tigre flinched inwardly. The memory was a nightmare to him, his actions then based on sheer terror. "Don't make it sound so damned heroic," he snapped. "I just did my job."

Rife grinned. "Sure, Doc."

Tigre sighed, wondering how much time the whole process would entail. "All right, I'll take responsibility for going over the warden's head. In fact, I'll call the councillor myself and arrange for—"

Jardín looked alarmed. "Oh, you can't do that!"

Rife broke in. "Call the councillor, she means."

Fighting irritation, Tigre looked back and forth between the two. "What are you talking about?"

Rife shrugged widely. "The communications links are tapped. If you make a call, everyone on the station will know, especially all the merchant clients. I think we'd better contact her in person."

Jardín looked worried. "What if the warden sees us going aboard *Gaia's Love*?"

Tigre fumbled for clear thought. "So what if he does?"

Rife drew his brows together pensively. "It might be a little—" He chewed his bottom lip a moment. "Doc, would you consider taking a back route to Councillor Weber's ship?"

Tigre stared at him. "Back route?"

"It wouldn't take any longer," Rife said hurriedly. "In fact, it might prevent a delay."

Tigre hesitated, and suddenly the problem snapped into comfortable parameters in his mind. Regardless of the fact that it involved somewhat clandestine activity, the true issue was simply to provide the best care for a patient.

Contacting Councillor Weber would resolve several problems at once, and Tigre had to admit that he wanted to talk to her again. He had warm memories of the woman's compassion and intelligence. "Of course," Tigre said. "Let me talk to my people. I'll need to let them know that I'll be off duty for a couple of hours."

Rife smiled. *At least this little operation went according to plan.*

Rife helped Jardín seal the hatch, then he straightened and turned to the doctor. "Home again," he announced.

Tigre glanced around their hideout, appearing to take in the shabby walls and dirty floor. His expression turned dubious. "I don't think—"

Moving fast, Rife punched him in the gut.

Tigre doubled over.

Rife's smile widened. He loved how it felt, using his strength and speed against an unwary opponent. Without pausing, Rife followed his punch with a blow from his knee to ensure that Tigre had the breath knocked out of him. Then Rife grabbed the surgeon's arm and shoulder and slammed him backward into a bulkhead.

Tigre's head and back hit the metal surface with a dull boom. He made a strangled noise and sagged to the deck plates.

Served him right, Rife thought with contempt, for being so gullible.

Tigre clutched the back of his head. "What—?"

Grinning, Rife slapped him hard across the face. "Shut up."

Tigre's cheek turned bright red, clearly displaying Rife's handprint.

Pleased by that, Rife decided to make an identical mark on the other cheek. He grabbed the collar of Tigre's scrubs.

Jardín spoke coolly from behind Rife. "Don't hit him again. We need him to make a phone call."

For a fleeting moment, Rife considered disobeying. He could claim he had started the blow before she said anything. The idiot more than deserved it.

"Rife. . . ."

Reluctantly, Rife abandoned his intention. He flung Tigre to the floor, sat on him, and pinned his arms behind his back. "Very well," he said sullenly. "Give me something so I can tie him up."

"Socks?" she suggested archly.

Rife glanced up at her, took in her mischievous expression, then grinned in spite of himself. "That's wrong," he said, sharing the joke. "Socks go on your feet."

Tigre abruptly twisted beneath him, evidently attempting to throw him off-balance.

Amused, Rife pushed him down again. "Pathetic."

Tigre snarled wordlessly and continued to struggle. He snatched an arm free and tried to lever himself off the floor.

Rife chuckled and caught the errant limb. With mocking gentleness, he pulled it back. "Now, now," he scolded. He pressed Tigre's wrists against the small of his back. "Wriggling around like that only makes me grouchy. And, believe me, you don't want to make me grouchy."

Jardín giggled. She rummaged through her equipment pack and pulled out a cartridge of Phenox. "Don't tie him up. Let's use this."

Rife shook his head in admiration. "You're incredible."

Jardín crossed to him and then knelt, planting one knee on Tigre's head. "Thank you."

Rife held their victim motionless and watched as Jardín pressed the injector against Tigre's neck. It hissed as the drug went in. Tigre shouted in fear and rage.

Jardín smiled slightly, then met Rife's gaze.

Jardín. Breathing harshly, knowing only that he wanted her, Rife leaned closer and claimed her cool, sweet lips in a kiss.

For a few moments, she gave herself fully to him, opening her mouth and welcoming his tongue. Then she slowly withdrew and sighed. "We don't have time—"

Desire warred with the knowledge that she was right. "But it's been so long—"

Regret filled her lovely eyes, and she pressed a fingertip against his lips. "And we still have so much to do."

Rife bowed his head in concession. "I know. I just wish—" He broke off and gestured to the man they sat upon. "What next?"

"Well," Jardín said in a mock serious tone, "I think now we need Doctor DeFlora to start being just a bit more cooperative."

Tigre squirmed beneath Rife. "You're insane," he moaned softly. "You're both . . . both . . ."

Jardín stood, and her gaze traveled speculatively down the length of Tigre's body. "Doctor, I'm going to call Medica. I want you to tell your people that Rife and I will be there shortly, and that it's perfectly all right for them to release the Jadamii into our custody. You understand?"

Tigre shifted miserably beneath Rife, and sweat bathed his too-pretty features. "Go—" He seemed to choke on his own breath, then grimaced and clenched his jaw. "Go to hell."

Rife's anger flared. He grabbed fistfuls of Tigre's hair. "Listen, you little—"

Jardín extended one dainty foot and tapped Rife on the shoulder. "No. Not like that."

Rife glanced up at her.

Her expression was inward looking, predatory. "Doctor. I advise you to do as I ask. Otherwise, you won't like the consequences."

Though he was obviously succumbing to the Phenox, Tigre's eyes lit with defiance, and he compressed his lips in a silent refusal.

Jardín smiled. "Very well." She turned a meaningful gaze to Rife. "Take off his clothes."

Tigre fought to stay calm, tried to analyze his situation and formulate a means to escape, but his thoughts swam in every direction like a school of frightened fish.

"Oo," Rife cooed in a mocking echo of Jardín's words. "Take off his clothes. He'll enjoy that."

No! Tigre tried to voice his protest, but his breath caught in a sob of rage. *No, you bastard!*

In a sickening parody of tenderness, Rife rolled him onto his back, then pulled him up to gather him warmly into his arms. "I don't really go for men, but I think I could make an exception for you."

Tigre gnashed his teeth. "No!"

"I bet," Rife murmured into his ear, "that you're even more beautiful naked—"

"Bastard!"

"—than you are in these dirty scrubs." Rife slipped a

hand under Tigre's tunic and began an intimate exploration. "Oh," he breathed. "So soft."

In horror, Tigre felt his body responding pleasurably to Rife's attentions. "That drug—" He twisted to look at Jardín. "What the hell—?"

"Phenox," she supplied in a courteous tone. "Aliens use it. Nice stuff, don't you think? Goes far beyond an aphrodisiac."

Tigre stared at her. "You—?"

"Mm." Rife gently pulled his tunic off over his head. "I don't think you needed the Phenox. You love this, don't you? Too bad that Freeholder isn't here."

"N–no, stop it." Tigre tried to push Rife away, but his strength was gone. "Stop. . . ."

Jardín crouched down beside him. "If you really don't like what Rife is doing," she said reasonably, "then all you have to do is make that call."

"No!"

Rife carefully laid Tigre back on the floor. "No," he crooned. "You don't want me to stop." He pulled off Tigre's shoes and caressed his bare feet. "You're just pretty all over, aren't you?" He chuckled ruefully. "I never dreamed I'd ever say that to another man."

Heart laboring, Tigre turned his face to the wall. *No!*

Still laughing softly, Rife brushed his fingers along Tigre's erection. "You'll be more comfortable without anything on, won't you?"

Shame scalded Tigre.

Jardín also laughed. "Make the call, silly. It's all you have to do."

"That's right," Rife agreed. He tucked his fingers under the waistband of Tigre's pants. "Although I'm kind of enjoying this, it's really taking a lot of our valuable time."

Tigre closed his eyes, trying to distance himself from the physical pleasure. *No. I won't let you do it. Won't let you make me want it—*

A metallic crash split the air.

Tigre's eyes flew open, and he jerked his head toward the sound.

A dozen or so staffers charged through the hatch.

Rife gasped and jumped to his feet. "Shit!"

Thinking only to prevent Rife's escape, Tigre lunged to the side and grabbed his ankle. Rife kicked him in the shoulder, freeing himself. Tigre flew backward and hit the deck plates. A blazing hot sensation flashed through his shoulders and head. It should have been pain, he realized, but instead it simply felt startling. His vision blurred.

Booted feet rang on the metal floor. Staffers shouted, and there was another metallic crash.

Feeling weak, Tigre pushed himself up into an unsteady crouch.

A woman knelt in front of him. "Doctor?" She wore a blue and green uniform like Jardín and Rife, but her eyes were filled with obvious concern. "Are you all right?"

Tigre yearned to collapse against her, press his face into the warmth of her neck, explore her soft skin with hungry lips. "Don't—" Tigre shrank back. "Don't touch me."

The staffer studied him for a moment, then her attention obviously caught on the empty Phenox cartridge on the floor. She abruptly stood. "Warden!"

Confused, Tigre twisted to glance around the storage bay.

A group of staffers clustered at the bottom of a ladder that extended to a hatch near the ceiling. One staffer stood at the top of the ladder, clearly attempting to key in the code to unlock it. In sick despair, Tigre realized that Jardín and Rife had evaded capture.

Wu stood to the side, talking on his phone, but he nodded toward the staffer beside Tigre, indicating that he heard her call.

Tigre's vision blurred again, and he rubbed the back of his head. It felt so strange, the not-pain. His fingers came away wet, and he examined them, blinking hard to focus. Red smeared his fingers. *Blood.* He regarded it without agitation. *Scalp wound.*

Tigre glanced up.

Instead of the female staffer, Wu knelt in front of him. Tigre wondered when the exchange had taken place, and why he had not noticed it. Then the answer occurred to him, and he spoke without meaning to. "They drugged me."

Wu nodded soberly. "With Phenox, yes. We need to take you back to Medica."

"Am I going to die?"

"I was dosed with it once, and I'm still here," Wu said. "But you're not going to feel like yourself for a little while."

Tigre groped for more words. "They were going to—" He glanced down at himself, half-dressed and shamefully aroused. "They—they wanted the Jadamii. Wanted Meris. And I wouldn't—wouldn't let them—wouldn't—"

Wu picked up Tigre's tunic, shook it out, and held it up. "Here. Get dressed. You'll feel better."

Tigre accepted the offered garment and slipped it on over his head. "Might have a concussion. Vision keeps blurring."

Wu's voice turned raw. "Because you're crying."

"Am I?"

"What did they do to you? Can you remember?"

Of course, I can remember. Tigre drew a breath to say that, but then paused. The memories were jumbled and fading fast. "He hit me, Rife did. Couple of times, I think." Moisture ran down his cheeks. Surprised, Tigre rubbed it away with the back of his hand. A detached portion of his mind took an analytical interest in the fact that Wu was correct; he was, in fact, weeping. "And he called me things. And he said that—that—" It was too wrenching, and he could not bring himself to repeat it. "And something about a Freeholder." He wiped his eyes again and glared at Wu. "But I don't know any Freeholders."

Wu's expression darkened. "I do, unfortunately." Then he smiled at Tigre. "But don't worry about anything Rife and Jardín said, all right? They just wanted to make you feel bad."

"I know." Tigre wondered if he ought to resent being patronized, but the emotion refused to come. He shifted, preparing to stand, but lost his balance and fell against Wu. "Sorry." He started to push himself away, then became intensely aware of how warm and solid Wu felt, how good he smelled. Tigre clutched the other man. "Sorry," he whispered. "Sorry—"

Wu helped him stand, then very carefully disengaged from his grasp. "Can you walk? Or shall I call for a stretcher?"

Relief and gratitude flooded Tigre. Wu was not going to call him names, even though he might deserve it.

"Walk," Tigre said. He wanted to be under his own power. He gazed at Wu, helplessly searching for some way to express the magnitude of what he felt, to say how wrong he had been. He wanted to offer a thousand thanks and apologies, but the words would not come. "I can walk."

CHAPTER THIRTEEN

IT WAS MIDNIGHT when Tigre returned to his office. He closed his office door and leaned against it. After several hours of solicitous medical treatment, he could no longer bear his medics' sympathetic scrutiny; he simply wished to be left alone. *They don't know. Don't understand.*

According to all available data, the psychoactive effects of Phenox on Humans appeared to dissipate in ten to twelve hours. In two out of the seven reported cases, there were aftereffects of headache, nausea, and urinary tract irritation. None of the literature, however, told Tigre how to deal with the accompanying emotions, or how to heal from the bitter sense of shame.

Like warfare and public executions, sexual assault was a thing of Earth's turbulent past. He wished he could step outside himself to gain some distance and a clear perspective. He realized on an intellectual level that he was the victim of an antique crime, but Rife's mocking voice continued to echo in his memory, accusing him of willingly participating in the act.

"But you don't want me to stop, do you?"

Tigre flinched inwardly and dropped his face into his hands. Worst of all, in his current state, he was useless as a physician. The slightest personal contact induced quivering arousal, and then overwhelming shame. He did not even feel it was safe for him to observe in person. The most he could offer was to stay close at hand in Medica in order to provide technical advice to his staff.

Tigre lowered his hands and stepped away from the door. His medics had treated the scalp wound and the many bruises Rife had inflicted, erasing every physical trace of the abuse, but they could do nothing to heal the true damage.

Sighing, he glanced at his surroundings and wondered how to stay occupied while waiting for the Phenox to wear off. *Ten to twelve hours.*

Though small, his office contained both a miniature kitchen and a private washroom that could be neatly concealed behind a sliding partition. Dirty mugs cluttered the kitchen's tiny counter, and a pair of surgical scrubs festooned the shower door. Its surface littered with hard copies and rice chip crumbs, a plasti-board desk of modest proportions sat facing the door. A couch upholstered with a brocade of curling ferns stood along the wall opposite the kitchen; a neon-orange thermal blanket marred its elegant appearance. *Ought to tidy up.*

Tigre's personal workboard lay in the midst of the mess on his desk. Its screen glowed a soft blue, indicating standby mode. Shaking his head at his own carelessness, he crossed the room to shut it down.

Tigre's workboard was an older model, inherited from his late father, about the size of a clipboard and as thick as a man's thumb. Durable hedgewood sheathed the outer casing, evincing the modern taste for disguising technology whenever feasible. With its filigreed corner protectors and red-gold graining, it resembled nothing so much as an ornate picture frame.

Lines of legal prose filled the screen, an authorization document that permitted Medica's staff to observe the Jadamii under a scanner. At the bottom of the screen, like a finger of lightning, burned the jagged signature of Wu Jackson.

Guiltily, Tigre recalled his childish behavior with the warden, the threats and the insults. Gazing down at the signature, he spoke without meaning to. "And then . . . you saved me."

Startled by his own whispered voice, Tigre found his

breath catching in his throat. He was overwrought, he knew. He needed to calm down, clean up, then sleep off the Phenox. Wallowing in emotion would accomplish nothing.

Unbidden, the memory of collapsing against Wu returned. Tigre relived his weakness, his humiliation, his vulnerability, and Wu's restraint and compassion.

"Saved me," Tigre murmured, "twice."

A peculiar mix of conflicting emotions crowded his thoughts, and he shied away from them without looking at any too closely. Taking refuge in simple activity, Tigre keyed the document into the station's central computer records. His workboard obligingly produced another file.

It was the message from Richard Wagasi, his uncle and direct superior within the World Health Agency. Tigre had received it just before going to Checkpoint to confront Wu. Frowning, he reread it.

> *Coming for a visit. Bringing the whole family.*
> *We're all very proud of your efforts. Keep up the*
> *hard work. We're behind you every step of the way.*
> *Uncle Richard.*

Tigre swallowed, suddenly realizing that he had misunderstood. Clearly, Doctor Wagasi had heard about the tapped communication links and had disguised his message as a personal letter. When Tigre had first read it, the entire tone of the thing had sent him into a frothing rage. *We're behind you every step of the way.* Smiling slightly, Tigre saved the letter and shut down his workboard. He glanced over the desk, wondering where to start with the mess, and his gaze fell upon a book. "What the—?" Like a distant memory from years in the past, he suddenly recalled requesting the print job from the station's library files. Someone must have brought the hard copy to his office during the several hours that he was busy with the endless stream of patients.

Tigre picked up the book and turned it over in his hands. *The Collected Flights of Prudence Clarke.* An ancient photograph of a woman's face stared up at him from the cover. Limp strands of brown hair hung past her shoulders, and her features were heavy to the point of coarseness, but her pale blue eyes held a compelling blend of wisdom and sadness.

In his edgy emotional state, it took him a few moments to realize that it was the poet, Prudence Clarke.

"Ah, yes," Tigre murmured. He had looked up the poem Rachel quoted while under the influence of Tri-Omega. He had liked it, wanted to read more, and so had decided to order a copy of the book for his office. "The color of your hair, black as the reason for night."

His mood softening, he opened the volume and flipped through the pages, letting his gaze wander over the preface. The editor lamented Clarke's death; murdered by a stranger for the pittance of money she carried.

Tigre reflected that since the poet had died at the end of the twentieth century, over four hundred years in the past, she was spared from the coming devastation. She never knew about the plagues, the massive genocide of the Atrocity, or the Last War; but she also never knew a world at peace, or that her poetry would someday be read aboard a space station. *The real tragedy isn't when she died, but when she lived.*

Filled with melancholy, he turned the pages until he found an excerpt from her journal.

> *When I am dead, I shall miss hammocks in the rain and collie dogs. I'll miss the sharp scent of tomato plants, tire tracks in the snow, the tender flesh between my fingers, and the taste of buttered corn. I'll miss the endless, aching search for a reason to search when I am dead.*

Tigre's sadness deepened, and the unfamiliar heaviness of tears gathered in his chest, constricting his heart and choking his breath. "Murdered by a stranger." He turned away from his desk and paced erratically around his office. "And did he pretend to be a friend? Did he lure you away to somewhere dark and far from help? Did he—?" Tigre's eyes burned, and his vision blurred. "Did he take . . . more than your money?"

With a shaky sigh, he returned the book to his desk. "Losing my grip," he muttered. "Talking to myself, crying over dead poets. . . ."

He drifted to the kitchen nook, then wondered why. "Tea," he told himself. "You wanted tea."

"Wanted tea?" he echoed, keying the brewer into action. "What I really want is for the Phenox to wear off. Don't know why the Rofan like this stuff. It's pure shit."

He crossed to the couch and picked up the thermal blanket. "Pretty effective on pain." He folded the blanket, trying to ignore how soft and warm it felt. "Got rid of that damned headache."

He set the neatly folded blanket on the arm of the couch. "Effective on Humans. Maybe just effective on me. Who knows what it would do to someone else? Or to a Rofa?"

Tigre recalled Nothando's statement that four unclaimed bodies of murdered Rofan rested in the station's deep storage. He sat on the edge of the couch and slumped back against the cushions, wondering if the Rofan grieved as Humans did. If there were children or mates at home, asking for news, waiting for a voice at the door.

The phone on his desk trilled, and the sound slapped away Tigre's mental fugue like a dash of ice water. He rose from the couch and strode to the desk. Since the call came in on his direct line, he knew it was one of his medics. In seconds, his imagination teemed with fifty possible emergencies and the swift response necessary for each.

Tigre reached the phone on its second ring and snatched it off his desk. "Yeah?"

"Doctor?" Wu sounded uncharacteristically subdued. "Did I wake you?"

Irritation and relief spun through Tigre. "I thought you were one of my medics. I thought this was an emergency."

"It is."

"What?"

"May I speak with you?"

Tigre's heart picked up tempo. "Of course. Where are you?"

"Just stepping off the lift into Medica."

Tigre started for the door. "Are you injured?"

"No." The tautness eased from Wu's voice, and he chuckled. "At least, not yet. May I meet with you privately?"

The purring laughter sent an unwelcome shiver of pleasure through Tigre. "My office," he snapped. "Door's unlocked."

"This won't take long."

"Good." Tigre hung up and tossed the phone onto his desk. "Shit."

Arousal crackled through him, intensifying every sensation and coloring it with eroticism. The slide of the cotton scrubs against his skin, the rush of air into his lungs, even the pressure of his feet against the floor, everything boosted his already charged excitement.

"Oh, shit." Tigre bolted into the washroom, snatched up his bathrobe, and shrugged it on over his scrubs. That helped disguise the most obvious sign of arousal, but he still felt oddly vulnerable. He crossed to his desk, sat down behind it, and fired up his workboard again. It was juvenile behavior, he knew, to pretend to be involved in research; but he needed as many barriers between himself and Wu as he could find. Hurriedly, he brought up a random pharmacological study, then sat and waited.

After a few moments, the door opened slightly. "Doctor?" Wu said. "Are you—?"

Tigre began to tremble, but he kept his voice low and calm. "Come in."

Wu stepped through the door. He wore a bright blue and green parka, his black hair was disheveled, and he seemed flushed and sniffily, as if returning from a walk in the snow. "Thanks for seeing me," he said. "Phones are useless—all tapped."

The air felt as rich and intoxicating as wine. Wu's eyes were fathomless, deep. Tigre jerked his attention away from the other man and focused blindly on the dry text in front of him. "Not a problem. Just catching up on my journals. What's with the winter gear?"

"We had a riot on Dock Two."

Tigre dropped the pretense of reading and jerked his gaze to Wu. "What?"

"A riot." Wu unfastened his parka and rested his hands on his gun belt. "No casualties, this time. We closed trading on the upper level before any of the arbitrators got hurt. And I've dialed down the heat on the lower level, to discourage casual activity, but there's still some looting."

Tigre stared at him in disbelief. "Looting? You mean, stealing?"

Wu gave him a lopsided grin. "Yup. Stealing."

"But that's—that's—" Tigre noticed Wu's expression. "What the hell are you smiling at?"

"You," Wu said, eyes sparkling. "Just you."

"Don't patronize me." Tigre surged to his feet. "How the hell did you let a riot start on—?"

"How?" Wu interrupted, chuckling. "I had over half my staffers out hunting for you."

Tigre's anger faltered. He folded his arms and stared down at his desk.

"It's all about numbers, you see," Wu continued in a warm tone. "Fifty staffers, total. Three injured. Nineteen certified for xeno-relations, and only seven of them licensed to carry stingers. All of them have been on duty for at least forty-eight hours."

Tigre sighed heavily. "All right, I just—"

"Five hundred and sixty-nine aliens on Dock Two, with more arriving within the hour. Leaking chemical batteries everywhere. A couple of terrorists on board, a missing Freeholder, and an unconscious—"

"That's enough," Tigre said sharply. "I understand."

"Do you? Then put your people on emergency standby."

"Are you nuts? We've been in emergency mode for two days." Tigre glared at Wu. "And while I'm reminded of it, what possessed you to allow the likes of Jardín and Rife aboard the station? Those two must have enough treatment profiles to fill a library."

"Quite possibly," Wu said. "But how would I know that? I don't have access to the medical records of private citizens."

"But you—"

"In fact, I don't have the authority to prevent any Human from boarding the station. Aliens, yes. But Humans are out of my jurisdiction."

It made perfect sense, but it was not what Tigre wanted to hear. "How convenient."

"Doctor," Wu said in a low, provocative tone, "are you trying to pick a fight with me?"

Am I? Tigre thought dizzily. *I honestly don't know what the hell I'm trying to do.*

"It's just that I know a lot of other people who pick fights when they're exhausted."

"Really? And what about when they're doped with Phenox?"

Wu drew a breath, then appeared to change his intended words. "You're miserable, aren't you?" he asked in a serious tone. "Just keep in mind that you're not yourself."

Tigre snorted. "Thanks. That helps."

Wu sighed. "Sorry. Fresh out of wisdom." He turned toward the door. "I'd better go catch Jardín and Rife before they blow up the station."

"Blow up the—?" And then Wu's words fully sank in. Tigre's breath caught in his throat. He recalled Rife in the debris of the main shaft on Brontos. "Like Brontos?"

Wu paused and regarded him. "That's my guess."

Tigre wanted to argue, wanted to shout, but something in Wu's eyes stopped him. "We—" he swallowed against a sudden dryness in his throat. "We need to evacuate the station."

"How about what happened on Brontos?" Wu regarded him sidelong. "Numbers again, Doctor. I don't want to be cruel, but how many escape pods malfunctioned?"

"Shut up."

"Kids, mostly, right?"

Tigre's eyes burned. They had kept information of that tragedy from the rescue workers for several days. In an instant, he relived the moment when someone broke the news to him. He turned his back to Wu. "Are you done?"

"Just remembered something." Wu's voice softened. "You threatened to report me to Earth-side authorities. Have you sent that message yet?"

Tigre flinched inwardly, but kept his back turned. "No." Tears rolled down his cheeks, but he could not brush them away without Wu seeing. "I'd have to report you to my superiors at the Agency first."

"Even better."

Tigre frowned but resisted the urge to turn. "Stop clowning around."

"I'm serious," Wu said mildly. "The Agency operates independently of the World Council. Just be careful how you phrase your message. Our valued merchant clients will be reading every word."

"You want . . . me to report you?"

"Begging you, actually."

Reluctantly, Tigre glanced over his shoulder. "Why?"

Seeming to take no notice of the tears, Wu beamed at him. "Because it's all my fault." He turned toward the door. "And now, I must be off. Have some looting to squelch. Ta."

"Wait," Tigre blurted.

Wu paused and raised his brows inquiringly.

Tigre had no idea what to say next. His gaze fell on his workboard, triggering a memory of the Jadamii's authorization form. "What about Meris? Shouldn't we have a guard on her?"

"Ooo, yes." Wu grinned wickedly. "Thanks for reminding me. I brought Benjy along, and he's stationed outside Meris' door. Your people are outraged. Not only is his presence in Medica a direct contradiction of your specific orders, Doctor, but he's also a recovering patient. He ought to be in bed. Shocking breach of protocol. Intolerable, really."

Unwilling amusement joined Tigre's emotional mix of grief, irritation, and drug-induced desire. He laughed. "I'll put that in my report."

"Please do." For the first time, Wu's smile reflected in his eyes. "And kindly refer to me as a 'gun-toting maniac.' I've always wanted to be called that."

"I'll consider it."

"Thank you." Wu opened the door. "One more thing. Stay away from Councillor Weber."

"What?"

"I have every reason to believe that she holds the end of Jardín and Rife's leash."

Shock held Tigre motionless.

Wu nodded. "Be safe."

The door closed. Wu was gone.

Alone in his office, Tigre said: "You, too." A hundred questions belatedly occurred to him. He should have asked about Councillor Weber's connection to Jardín and Rife, why they were after Meris, and what Wu had experienced with Phenox.

Something else nudged the back of Tigre's mind, and he frowned in thought. "What about the Freeholder?"

His phone rang. Tigre snatched it up. "Yeah?"

Nothando sounded harried. "Doctor, I hate to bother you, but the warden has—"

"Brought a staffer? Yes, I know." Tigre cleared his throat. "And be careful what you say, I understand that the station's merchant clients are monitoring all our calls."

"Oh, but—"

"Though I can't imagine that they find our conversations interesting." Tigre crossed to the kitchen and poured his long-neglected tea. "We ought to start broadcasting radio dramas, or opera, and really give them something entertaining to—"

"Uh, Doctor," Nothando interrupted hesitantly. "One of the staffers is—"

"—a recovering patient, yes." Tigre raised the cup and inhaled the tea's fragrant steam. "Don't let him lift anything heavy, will you? And get him a chair."

"Very well." Nothando sounded disconcerted. In the background, a man was describing how he had gashed open his hand on a gantry's drive train. "What about the staffer outside your door? Does she get a chair, too?"

Tigre blinked. "Outside—?" He went to the door, opened it, and peeked out.

A grim-faced woman in blue and green turned to him and nodded respectfully. "Doctor."

"Ah," he said. She wore her long hair in a shining braid over one shoulder, and her skin was exceptionally smooth and creamy. She smelled wonderful. "What's your name?"

"Rosita. Staffer Oso's my partner."

Tigre smiled. "Very pleased to meet you. Feel free to get a chair, if you tire of standing. Also, you and your partner are quite welcome to use the lounge here in Medica—there's always tea or coffee ready."

Rosita nodded curtly and returned her attention to the empty air in front of her. "Thank you."

Tigre closed the door. "Nothando?"

"Yes, Doctor?"

"Anything else to discuss?"

"No, Doctor," she said. "At least, nothing that can't wait until you're fully . . . rested."

"Well, call if anything does come up."

"Thank you, Doctor. Good-bye."

"Good-bye." Sipping his tea, Tigre carried the phone to his desk and set it next to his workboard. A sudden yawn caught him, and he realized his own exhaustion. "Eight hours of sleep sounds good," he murmured. "And when I wake up, the Phenox will be gone. Almost."

"And then," he continued, "maybe I won't talk to myself anymore. Or feel like snuggling up against innocent passersby."

Tigre left his unfinished tea on the desk, crossed to the couch, and sat down. "Riot on Dock Two." He tried to grasp the ramifications of the words, but coherent thought eluded him. He decided it would be best to wait before sending another message to Doctor Wagasi. "Not thinking too clearly."

Tigre propped his elbows on his knees, letting his hands hang limp, and studied the kitchen and washroom. He wondered if he ought to clean up before he took a nap, but the thought of disrobing proved uncomfortable.

"Could eat something, I suppose." His gut rumbled at the thought of food, but then he recalled that he had given away all the soup and applesauce from his private cache to Nothando and the others. "Maybe I still have a sack of rice chips."

Tigre shifted his weight, preparing to stand. As he braced his arms, one hand sank into the soft blanket. His resolve melted, and he stretched out sideways onto the couch. The brocade felt cool and soothing under his cheek. A profound sense of relief washed over him, and he closed his eyes. He thought indolently about pulling the blanket over himself, but it seemed like too much work.

He floated on the edge of sleep. All the tension slid from his legs and shoulders. Sighing deeply, he rolled onto his back and draped an arm over his eyes. "Sleep first," he muttered. "Then . . ." *Then eat and shower.* He sighed again. *Better plan.*

His office door buzzed. A silent moan of despair welled up within Tigre. He searched his mind for the appropriate phrase. "Come in."

Someone entered the room, walking quietly. Tigre yawned and tried to think of something friendly to say. "You caught me," he murmured. "I hope to God this isn't another damned chemical burn." He lifted his arm away from his eyes and smiled at his guest.

Deputy Rachel Ajmani stood in the middle of his office, studying him with an unreadable expression.

CHAPTER FOURTEEN

L YING FLAT on his back on the couch, Tigre gazed up at Rachel. Her Port Authority uniform was sweat-stained and wrinkled, her long hair hung in tangles, and her expression conveyed nothing but disapproval. She smelled delicious, however. Battling the Phenox's influence, Tigre tried to pull his thoughts together. "Oh." He groped for more to say. "It's you."

Rachel lifted one brow in eloquent reply and shifted her attention to the mess in his office. She inspected the piles of hard copy on his desk, the dirty cups on the kitchen counter, and the pants over the top of the shower door.

Hoping his arousal was not as evident as it felt, Tigre sat up and rubbed the back of his neck. "Sorry. That didn't come out right." He sighed. "I merely meant that I wasn't expecting you."

Rachel turned her hard stare on him. "So I gathered," she said with ominous calm. "Your medics told me you were busy."

Heat touched Tigre's cheeks. "Well," he explained rue-fully, "most of them are old enough to be my parents. Sometimes they get a bit . . . protective."

"I must also say," Rachel continued, "that I don't ap-preciate the necessity of forcing my way past a staffer in order to—"

Tigre held up his hand. "Not my idea. Argue the point with Warden Jackson."

Rachel regarded him narrowly. "Warden Jackson?" she repeated slowly. "What's going on?"

"Nothing, Deputy. I just—"

"Why was Rosita given orders to let no one through? Are you under house arrest?"

Tigre drew a breath to explain, then found himself reluctant to mention his abduction or the Phenox. "Warden Jackson is also rather protective. He seems to think I'm in danger."

Surprise flashed over Rachel's features, and her frown softened. "Hmm," she said dryly. "I can relate to that."

Avoiding her gaze, Tigre glanced toward the floor and noticed her bandaged foot. With a vast sense of relief, he seized the opportunity to change the subject. "You know, Deputy, you really ought to keep that elevated."

Rachel drew a deep breath and let it out in an exasperated sigh. "I'm fine."

Irritation tangled with Tigre's surging arousal, sparking the need to move, and he hoisted himself off the couch. "Deputy Ajmani, may I respectfully point out that the last time you claimed to be 'fine,' you were lying on the floor—"

"Doctor—"

"—with bloody matter oozing from the ripped blisters of an acid burn." Afraid his gaze might linger on Rachel's shapely bosom, Tigre folded his arms and forced his eyes to meet hers. "Not only that, but you underwent surgery a few hours ago. So you are not 'fine.' "

Rachel also folded her arms, mirroring his stance. "I'm not here to discuss my foot."

An odd amusement seeped into Tigre's annoyance, and he wondered if the effects of Phenox made the argument so pleasurable, or if he simply enjoyed battling Rachel. "Oh, really?" he said with a slight smile. "Just wait until it swells up like a blowfish."

Rachel assumed an implacable expression. "Doctor De-Flora," she said quietly, "I will not tolerate any further delays. I insist that you provide me with a full report on the detainee's condition."

Tigre inwardly braced for extended combat, then noticed

the exhausted sag of Rachel's shoulders. She was trying to do her job, he suddenly realized, in spite of pain and weariness. Shamed, he crossed to his desk. "Very well, Deputy. But it may take a little time." He pulled the chair out and patted its upholstered back. "Have a seat."

Rachel studied him for a long moment, then limped around the desk.

Hastily, Tigre strode to the couch and snatched the blanket from it. He hovered as Rachel settled into the chair, then he bundled the blanket into a makeshift pillow and put it on the desktop. "Recline the chair," he ordered, "and rest your foot on this."

Moving with studied deliberation, Rachel obeyed. "There." Her mouth thinned in a chilly smile. "Are you satisfied?"

"No," Tigre grumbled. "I want to take a quick look at your dressing." Careful not to touch her more than necessary, he peeled back the adhesive tabs on the bandage, then leaned to study his work. The patch that sealed the regeneration gel into the debridement still held tight. The skin around the patch appeared red and irritated, but he judged it was not excessive enough to warrant further treatment. Placated, Tigre rewrapped the bandage and pressed the tabs down. "This isn't a walking cast, you know."

Rachel shifted impatiently. "Tell me about the detainee. Is she still bleeding?"

Tigre felt another flash of amusement, along with simmering resentment at the implied doubt of his competency. "No." He switched on his workboard and logged his examination of Rachel's dressing. "Of course not. I'm a doctor. I've taken Meing's Vow. I would never stand by and allow a patient to bleed to death." He sent his notation to Medica's records, and then raised his eyes to Rachel. "Any other questions?"

Rachel's gaze traveled over his face. She drew a breath to speak, then seemed to reconsider her words. "Is she still sedated?"

Feeling suddenly warm, Tigre bent over his workboard again, wondering if the drug-induced arousal somehow showed in his expression. "I believe so," he said. The controls on his workboard were the old, simple, on-screen variety. Using the point of his stylus, he tapped into Medica's scanner system. "Let's take a look."

The Jadamii's holographic image appeared in the air over the workboard's screen. Tigre and his staff had positioned Meris on her side, bracing her with cushioned supports in an attempt to ease the strain on her inflamed shoulder. Her injured hand rested on a clean towel, raised above her torso by a stack of pillows. Her eyes were closed, and her webbed ears drooped, limp and unresponsive. "Yes. Still sedated."

Rachel struggled to lean closer, trying to sit up in the reclined chair. "I can't see."

"Sorry." Tigre adjusted the image so it hung in the air vertically, and then he enlarged it until Meris appeared as long as his forearm. He glanced at Rachel. "How's that?"

Rachel's eyes widened in obvious shock and distress. "Oh, God," she breathed. She pressed both hands to her temples and slowly shook her head. "Oh, God."

Taken aback, Tigre returned his gaze to the scanner image, wondering what caused such an emotional response. He cleared his throat. "Deputy, you seem upset."

Rachel's voice was thick. "During the arraignment, Meris was so frightened that she hid under her bunk. I wanted her to trust me . . . and look what I've done to her." Rachel lowered her hands, clearly struggling to regain composure. "Is she going to be all right?"

Nudged by his own sense of inadequacy, Tigre shrugged one shoulder. "I wish to hell I knew."

"Doctor—"

"I don't know what I'm doing." Tigre tried to speak calmly. "I don't know anything about Jadamiin physiology or Jadamiin drugs. If I did, I—" He barely managed to prevent the whole story of his experience with Phenox from spilling out. "All I can do, Deputy, is make a few cautious guesses."

"I understand," Rachel said, offering a commiserating smile. "It's difficult to work in ignorance."

Tigre liked her smile, liked the way it warmed her features and brought sparkles to her dark eyes. Desire shimmered through his body. "Deputy, I—" *No. Stop.* Tigre swallowed hard and jerked his gaze back to the workboard. "—I want to show you something." He brought up vital signs as a multicolored graph over the patient's head. Tigre studied the display intently. While the numbers themselves made no sense, he noted that they demonstrated almost no variation over the previous hours. "Ah, yes. Look at this. Vital signs have remained steady."

"Is that good?"

"Absolutely." Tigre grinned ruefully. "At least, I hope so."

Rachel stirred and made a thoughtful noise. "Wu said she hurt her shoulder. Just how serious is the injury?"

"Let's take a look." Tigre adjusted the scanner to an internal, cross section view, changing the image to a computer simulation in shades of blue and gray.

Fascinated in spite of everything else, Tigre leaned closer to the hologram. A few of the organs, like the oversized lungs, were self-evident; but most were unidentifiable. More research was definitely called for, and he could hardly wait for Doctor Wagasi to arrive and review the collected data.

Rachel stirred. "Doctor?"

"Sorry." Tigre returned to the present. With the tip of his stylus, he pointed out three pulsing objects in the hologram, two in the chest and one in the pelvic region. "These, we're pretty sure, function as hearts." He indicated an area above one of the hearts and magnified it. "Here's where the injury occurred. Looks pretty good, though. Swelling has gone down, and the scanner isn't issuing emergency warnings anymore."

"Thank God," Rachel said in a tone of vast relief. "Does that mean she won't face disability?"

Tigre nodded. "As far as I can tell." He pointed to the vital signs chart again. "And look here—I did a special scan. This is an extremely high level of residual particle activity. Meris has spent at least ten years in stasis."

Rachel gripped the arms of the chair and tried to sit forward. "A special scan? Why?"

Surprised, Tigre glanced at her. *Perceptive question, Deputy Ajmani.* "When Safety first brought her in, there were no personal records. We discovered the particle levels when we tried to verify gender."

Rachel's teeth flashed white in a sudden smile. "Typical Human preoccupation."

Tigre found himself grinning in return. "Ah, yes. Strange

creatures, we Humans. This single-minded concern for reproductive functions must be what separates us from the
other sentient species in the galaxy."

"Well, not quite." Still smiling, Rachel steepled her fingers and rested her chin on the point. "In my experience,
our one distinctive trait is this: Adult Humans will always
attempt to rescue someone in danger, even at the cost of
their own lives." Her expression grew somber. "That, Doctor, is what separates us. You'll never see Rofan or Phi-
Nurians behave like that." She nodded at the scanner
image. "Or even, I suspect, the Jadamiin."

A shadow fell over Tigre's mood, and he turned to watch
Meris' pulsing hearts. He thought about the murder of Prudence Clarke, dead Rofan stored away like surplus grain,
and Rife's cold hands.

Rachel sighed. "Sorry. I didn't intend to give a xenology
lecture." She shrugged wearily. "I'm really not thinking too
clearly at the moment."

Tigre could not bring himself to look at her, afraid of
what she might read in his eyes. "I know what you mean."
Moving slowly, he tapped off the scanner link, switched off
his workboard, and set down his stylus. "Well, Deputy, I
guess that concludes my report."

"Thank you, Doctor."

Tigre did not want her to leave. Searching for words, he
sat down on the edge of his desk and frowned at the space
over Rachel's left shoulder. "I wish we knew more. We
desperately need some solid information."

"When dealing with aliens," Rachel said quietly, "solid
information is hard to get." She drummed her fingers on
the arms of the chair. "I'm glad that you reconsidered posting a staffer on Meris. Because, as pitiable as she seems
now, she'll become an instant danger once she awakens."

Tigre tensed, waiting for Rachel to ask again why a
staffer stood guard on his office. "Yes. Wu . . . convinced
me." He recalled again his urge to collapse against Wu, to
allow another man's strength to support him. The memory
raised an echo of Rife's voice: *"I don't usually go for
men. . . ."*

"Convinced you?"

"Yeah." Uneasy, Tigre slid off the edge of the desk and

turned away. "You know, I was wrong about him. Or, rather, partially wrong."

"Pardon?"

Tigre adjusted his robe and retied the belt. "I called him incompetent. He's not."

"Agreed."

Struggling against his own confusion, Tigre glanced over his shoulder. "But I still believe that he's dangerous."

"Dangerous?" Rachel folded her hands into a single fist and rested her chin on them. She appeared thoughtful, not angry, and her voice was calm. "If you mean that he's capable of taking strong measures, then I would have to agree. Yes, Wu is extremely dangerous."

No, that's not what I meant. "Strong measures?" he repeated bleakly. "Like tying up and drugging a Jadamii?"

Rachel bowed her head, slid her hands up over her eyes, and spoke as if reciting items on a list. "Meris had escaped her cell. Wu and his team couldn't subdue her. Meris attacked them." Rachel paused. "And Wu didn't want to shoot her."

Tigre's heart began to pound. "Shoot—?" Again unable to face Rachel, he turned away and paced blindly toward the door. "Do you mean that shooting Meris was actually an option?"

Rachel spoke in a calming tone. "It might have been best for him if he had shot her. It would have been perfectly legal self-defense. As things stand, Wu's career is in jeopardy. If Meris dies, and if Jada chooses to press for extradition, then his life may be over as well." Rachel's voice began to tremble, and she paused to clear her throat. "In a way, you might say that Wu risked his life to save her."

Tigre's anger faded, lost in a swelling sense of confusion and shame. He raised his arms over his head and pressed his forehead and hands against the door. The cold, metal surface smelled faintly of disinfectant. Evoked by sensory stimuli, an intense memory rose up of the bleak and chilly infirmary at his last post on Brontos.

He recalled the beige walls, the dented supply cupboards passed down from the machine shop, and how the aroma of onion soup always drifted through the air vents from the colony's main kitchen. Above the storm of strong emotion

and the throbbing heat of Phenox, hovered the simple longing for something familiar, for the plain and everyday details of ordinary life. The words of Prudence Clarke
returned to him. *When I am dead, I shall miss hammocks
in the rain and collie dogs.*

"Doctor?" Rachel's voice held an unexpected gentleness.
"Are you . . . all right?"

Just as abruptly as it came, the tide of confusion and
self-doubt swept away, leaving Tigre shaken and exhausted.
Still unable to look at Rachel, he dropped his arms and
stood up straight. "I'm sorry." He struggled to regain his
dignity. "I've been on the station for only three days, and
I've seen nothing but one emergency after another. I
haven't slept, I can't recall my last meal, and at any moment my staff and I may be called to a disaster on the
outer docks." He sighed and rubbed his aching neck. "This,
of course, is no excuse for my rotten behavior. I'm sorry."

"I'm sorry, too," Rachel said softly. "I never—" She
paused and sighed. "I'm just as concerned for Meris as
you are."

"I know." Feeling inwardly bruised, Tigre turned to face
Rachel. He groped for the thread of their previous conversation, but he could not recall what he had been ranting
about. *Maybe it's time you gave some thought to your patient.* "It's past midnight. You ought to eat something." He
tried to rephrase it as an invitation and not a medical order.
"Would you care to join me?"

"Thank you. That sounds wonderful." Rachel chuckled
ruefully. "I can't remember my last meal, either. I think it
was grapes."

Tigre's knees went weak at the thought of fresh fruit. He
crossed to the kitchen, opened the pantry cupboard, and
studied the contents. The rice chip bag contained a gram
of pulverized crumbs, but a dozen cartons of Naranha
brand liquid diet supplement remained on the shelf. "Deputy, if you like—"

"Please," she interrupted softly. "Stop calling me that.
My name is Rachel. Call me Rachel."

Startled by her request, Tigre found himself once more
unable to look at her. He pulled two cartons of Naranha
out of the cupboard and poked around the counter for a

couple of relatively clean cups. "Very well, Rachel," he replied briskly. "You can call me . . . Doctor."

She was silent.

Aghast that she took him seriously, Tigre glanced over his shoulder and blurted: "I'm joking."

Rachel wore a wicked grin. "I know." She spoke in a warm, provocative tone. "And I like it."

Scalding heat flooded Tigre's face and throat. He opened the Naranha with shaking fingers, wondering if Rachel were involved in a romantic relationship. He suspected not, since no one had made inquiries or had come to visit her after the surgery.

Tigre tried to imagine Rachel as a lover, and the heat flashed down his spine to his groin. He froze, lips parted, panting silently. *Stop it, you idiot, she's a patient.* Forcing himself to move, he poured the liquid supplement into two mugs and turned the conversation back to a safe topic. "So. Do you have any questions about your own medical status?"

"As a matter of fact, I do." Rachel's voice retained its oddly flirtatious quality. "Would you say that my reaction to the Tri-Omega was normal?"

Expecting her to ask about recovery time or the regeneration process, Tigre was caught off guard. He placed the mugs of Naranha in the warmer and set its timer, searching for a truthful reply that would not cause unnecessary worry. "Your initial response was somewhat unusual," he said casually, "but other than that, I'd say you fell within the range of normal experiences."

"Really?"

Keeping his expression bland, Tigre turned to look at her and shrugged. "You appeared rather agitated at one point, and you spoke of watching someone die. I assumed that a long-buried memory had resurfaced."

"No, it was—" Rachel laughed, shaking her head, and made a dismissive gesture. "I don't know what it was. I thought that maybe I was hallucinating."

Tigre resisted the urge to echo her laughter, wanting her to take him seriously. "Maybe you were. Just how long had you gone without sleep?"

Rachel lifted her chin and regarded him from the corners

of her eyes. "Same as you. Three days. I hope you aren't planning to have Burke give me a gurney ride back to bed."

Not yet. First, I want you to get a little nourishment. Tigre folded his arms and leaned his shoulder against the wall. "I ask only because you seemed a bit . . . off-balance . . . even before the Tri-Omega. Remember? You said that Meris was at the center of some enormous galactic plot."

Rachel passed a hand through her hair, looking pensive. "Well, it's most likely that she is. Perhaps I didn't phrase it clearly, but the statement was based upon informed speculation. It wasn't the product of sleep deprivation." She made a self-deprecating noise. "Although the fact that I spoke of it while lying on Medica's floor might have obscured its credibility."

"Ah, yes," Tigre conceded. "Just a little." He studied Rachel and reminded himself that she measured her professional experience in decades; he had been only a child of eight the day she relieved a crazed Phi-Nurian of its hand cannon.

An almost overwhelming urge to ask for her advice swept over him. He wanted to tell her about his brush with Jardín and Rife, to ask her about the dead Rofan in station's deep storage, to find out what happened during a dockside riot. He swallowed and took a deep, steadying breath. *She's a patient. Remember that. A patient. Stop putting yourself before her needs.* "Did I answer your question about the Tri-Omega?"

Rachel's smile turned ironic. "Not precisely. But then, I haven't asked you the real question." She paused and seemed to consider how to continue. "Maybe it wasn't a hallucination."

"Pardon?"

Rachel laughed and shook her head. "I don't know what to call it. It wasn't a dream, and it certainly wasn't a memory. It felt like a vision. Like I saw something real."

At a loss, Tigre stared at her. "A vision?"

Rachel let her head fall back against the chair's cushion. "I know it sounds strange. Believe me, I'm not what you'd call a mystic. But I saw a man lying in the hold of a ship, and he was dying."

"At a guess, I'd say it was a product of displaced anxiety." Tigre rubbed the back of his neck. "Can you give me a few more details? How exactly does this appear?"

Rachel replied without hesitation. "I'm standing in the doorway of a hold compartment. The bulkhead curves up into a low ceiling." Her hands traced a shape in the air, and her dark eyes seemed unfocused as she described the mental picture. "In fact, it looks like the hold of a BRD freighter. There are a lot of broken shipping canisters on the floor, along with mounds of garbage. A man is lying in the filth, he's covered with a dirty tarp, and he's dying." She grimaced and glanced at Tigre. "Just thinking about it makes my heart race again."

"Well, of course, it does," he said calmly. He knew that the last thing his patient needed was to feel anxiety about feeling anxiety. He maintained a conversational tone to assert that her reaction was normal. "It sounds like a disturbing thing to see."

Rachel shifted restlessly in the chair. "It doesn't make sense," she said slowly. "Phi-Nurians would never come aboard an Earth ship like a BRD. Small rooms make them nervous. But only a Phi-Nurian would treat a Human like that. The Rofan would make a clean job of the poor fellow under the tarp, not leave him to die alone. I can't—" She stopped abruptly and shook her head.

With the same care that he used with a surgical laser, Tigre asked another question. "How do you know there's a man beneath the tarp?"

Rachel's voice was tense. "One of his hands is reaching out from under it. He's got a rag bracelet, like the kind they wear on Freeholds."

Tigre's pulse lurched. Trying to disguise his sudden uneasiness, he rubbed his chin. *Freeholder?* "Ah, I see." With effort, he kept his voice empty of anything but casual curiosity. "What do you suppose it means?"

"I—" Rachel paused and her brows shot up in obvious surprise. "Bailey Rye!"

"Pardon?"

"Bailey Rye." Rachel settled back in the chair and crossed her legs at the ankles. "Our translator for Meris. He's a Freeholder," she explained. "He turned up missing after the arraignment, and we're not sure where he is. I've been terribly worried about him, and it all boiled over when I took the Tri-Omega. As you said: displaced anxiety."

For a moment, Tigre stood motionless, suddenly troubled and unsure of the cause. *A missing Freeholder?*

Someone had spoken of a Freeholder. *Was it Wu? Or Rife?*

The timer chimed. Tigre opened the warmer and lifted out the steaming mugs of Naranha. The wholesome smell of oranges filled the air, and Tigre's stomach whined with hunger.

"So, it's that," Rachel continued dryly, "or I've gone crazy."

Feeling strangely paternal, Tigre carried the mugs to the desk. "You are not crazy. You are merely exhausted, starved, and recovering from surgery." He handed a mug to Rachel. "Careful, it's pretty warm."

Looking doubtful, she sniffed the creamy concoction. "What is it?"

Tigre blew into his mug. "Naranha liquid diet. We give it to patients who can't tolerate solid food. Or to deputies who don't have time to eat a real meal." He sat on the edge of his desk and took a cautious sip. "You can drink it cold, but I think heating the stuff makes it more satisfying."

Rachel tasted it and raised her brows appreciatively. "Not bad." She smiled at him. "Thank you. Tigre."

He grinned back. "You're welcome. Rachel." Then it struck him that he had gained ascendancy over the Phenox. He still felt the physical arousal; and, though it might influence his thoughts and emotions, it no longer controlled him. *Like working with a headache.*

The crippling sense of shame had also vanished, and Tigre supposed he owed the return of his self-respect to Rachel's presence. She was a beautiful woman, desirable in every way, but he had not behaved inappropriately. The Phenox would not make him commit a sexual assault.

Tigre raised his mug, and the words of Prudence Clarke returned to him. "Here's to hammocks in the rain and collie dogs—" His throat constricted suddenly, and he could not finish. *—I'll miss them when I'm dead.*

Rachel tilted her head and regarded him curiously. "Pardon?"

"Nothing." He grinned and shrugged to cover his abrupt sense of distress.

Rachel raised her mug. "Be safe."

The shadow over Tigre's mood darkened. He thought about the riot on the outer docks, Rife's ugly wishes, and Jardín's soulless laughter. *Bailey Rye, a missing Freeholder.* Filled with dread, Tigre touched his cup to Rachel's and spoke the pledge as if it were a powerful ward against evil. "Be safe."

CHAPTER FIFTEEN

CONCHA REMOVED the headset, rubbed her tired eyes, and glanced at the clock. *Two in the morning.*

Since the disastrous meeting with Khanwa in Checkpoint, when the Rofa exposed her participation in Operation Starcatcher, she had been locked in her quarters aboard *Gaia's Love*, monitoring Earth Port's communication channels. She hoped to regain Rachel's trust by finding clues to Professor Rye's whereabouts.

Concha climbed stiffly out of her chair and stretched. Her fingers brushed the ceiling, and she smiled grimly. *At least, I have the proper tools.*

Borrowed without permission from the auxiliary communications room, equipment filled her tiny cabin aboard *Gaia's Love*. Naked receiver panels, lifted from consoles, lined the floor in two neatly cabled ranks. Display units and control pads covered the recessed bunk, and a holographic projector cast its shimmering light through the open door of the water closet.

Since the rest of Councillor Weber's staff deemed Concha beneath notice, it had been a simple matter to move the equipment to her cabin. Even when the ship's purser, Terrell, spotted her lugging a monitor along a corridor, he had clearly assumed her to be carrying out an assigned task. He had brushed past with the comment: "When you're done with that, come find me. I have another cleaning job for you."

The primary challenge had been rerouting the power links to draw directly from the station, so that the ship's command staff did not detect her illegal activities.

Concha had decided that if all the aliens at dock were tapping the station's phones, then one more set of Human ears would not matter. Sifting through Safety's messages, she quickly picked up coded phrases that would mean nothing to the Rofan or Phi-Nurians. "Special project" referred to some kind of search, Concha deduced; and the replies to the frequent requests for the time relayed station coordinates, probably for the location of leaking batteries.

Or for Jardín and Rife, she thought glumly. Worry for her friends added an extra dimension of urgency to her research.

Concha also monitored all ships' transmissions, sliding them through translation programs as needed, and paying particular heed to messages posted to Rachel's board.

Most were routine business, though Captain Akya averaged a message every few minutes, alternating between questions in regard to legal studies and strident demands for Bailey's return.

You're not the only one who wants that Freeholder. Concha settled into her chair again. *I've got a few questions for Professor Rye, myself.*

Surveying Rachel's earlier messages, Concha noted again the intriguing entry from an inbound Kamian freighter: "I grasp the stars and take the light to heart." She hunched her shoulders in thought. Every message received an alphanumeric log number when posted, but there was a gap in the sequence after the Kamian entry. "Strange," Concha murmured. "I wonder what happened?"

Concha pulled on the headset and picked up a control pad. She tried searching various files for deleted messages, but without results. Then she ordered a search for the missing entry based on its log number, and the computer asked for the password to Rachel's private files.

"Oh, she moved it." Using stolen clearance, Concha overrode the password request. The screen abruptly changed from plain text on a blank background to a pretty font overlaying a watercolor of a garden. Concha scrolled through letters from friends until she found the missing log entry.

It appeared to be a mundane copy of an invoice for a canister of polished rocks. "Why would Rachel—?" Concha drew her brows together. She recalled the transaction with Captain Khanwa, and how Rachel had bartered for the Rofa's cooperation. However questionable the exchange, the invoice itself could hardly qualify as personal. "A keepsake, perhaps?"

Troubled by the ramifications of that notion, Concha reached for the control pad again to close the message, then her gaze caught on the signature line. Instead of its name, Khanwa had written: "Danger Starcatcher Here."

A flash of heat and queasiness struck Concha, and she relived the moment when Khanwa had accused her of plotting Rachel's downfall. "Not true," she muttered. She closed the personal log, her fingers trembling, and returned to her review of station business. "Starcatcher is a legitimate—"

She broke off as a new realization hit. "Stars. . . ."

I grasp the stars and take the light to heart.

Concha slowly closed her eyes in growing disbelief. The Rofan knew about Starcatcher; and, evidently, so did the Kamians. "Who else?" she whispered. "Were Councillor Weber and I the only ones who thought it was a secret?"

One of the displays chirped, indicating a message of interest. Concha blinked and glanced at it. The Phi-Nurian diplomats were thanking Councillor Weber for her gift.

Concha frowned. "Gift?" She scrolled back through the records of *Gaia's Love* and found no mention of it. She tapped into the station's files and discovered that a canister had been delivered to the Phi-Nurian ship within the last hour. An attached notice from station logistics apologized for the six-hour delay caused by security issues on the dock. "What the—?"

Councillor Weber's personal seal graced the consignment orders. Concha studied the time stamp and shook her head. "Impossible," she murmured. "She was in an emergency meeting. She couldn't have—"

A new message flashed on Rachel's board, this time from Captain Khanwa.

Urgent. Deputy Ajmani. Come to berth B-5. Must discuss missing cargo. A list of statistics followed, describing the canister in question.

The net weight matched Bailey's. Concha's breath caught in her throat as she cross-checked the serial numbers. They matched that of the canister delivered to the Phi-Nurians. She jumped to her feet. "Bailey!"

The lift doors opened onto a set of air locks that station personnel had dubbed the "front porch." Feeling acutely self-conscious in her borrowed overalls, Concha stepped off the lift amid a half dozen dock techs. Her plan was to follow them out, then slip away to talk to Khanwa about Starcatcher and Bailey's location.

One of the techs, a young man with a narrow face, glanced up at a red light over the air lock door. "Oh, no," he groaned. "The dock is closed again?"

Everyone echoed the groan and headed for the Operations booth. Perforce, Concha stayed with the group, wondering what to do next.

People in coveralls and parkas crammed the tiny room. The scents of strong coffee and Human sweat filled the air, along with the barnyard odor of aliens. The young man repeated his question, "Closed again?"

Everyone in the booth answered in unison: "Closed again." General laughter ensued.

Trying to evade notice, Concha lingered near the door. The question-and-answer exchange was part of station culture, indicative of the personnel's unity. They all knew each other. *But I'm an outsider.*

"What's happened this time?" asked a woman from Concha's group. "Anyone hurt?"

Responses broke out from all over the booth.

"No."

"Don't think so. Safety just—"

"Bunch of Rofan running loose in the lower storage units, I heard."

"—kind of glad to warm up. It's *cold* out there."

A one-way window ran along the booth's right wall. None of the techs seemed interested in the view, but Concha drifted closer to look.

Dock Two looked much different than on her previous

visit. Harsh light blazed down from the emergency flood-lights on the ceiling, high above the metal deck. Catwalks, gantries, access ramps, and support girders blocked the illumination so that some areas of the dock were swathed in shadow. Large pallets filled with freight canisters further disrupted sight lines. The dock no longer held an air of bustling commerce, but seemed a deserted and dangerous place.

Someone stirred just behind Concha, and she glanced over her shoulder.

The Ops manager settled into her console with a steaming cup of coffee. She appeared young, around Concha's age, with a smooth complexion and shaved scalp; but her eyes seemed bruised and lined with fatigue. " 'Lo." She offered Concha a limp smile. "Afraid you missed all the excitement."

Concha copied the woman's casual tone. "Oh, well. There's always next time."

"Probably won't have long to wait." She pulled on her headset and lowered her voice, tinting it with warning. "I saw you earlier, you know, with Deputy Ajmani."

Concha gazed at the ops manager, noticing the protective anger behind the exhaustion in her eyes, and judged her an ally. She extended her hand. "Concha Singh."

"Lafiya DuChamp." Lafiya shook her hand without warmth. "You're that councillor's aide."

"No." The word spoke itself. Concha drew a breath to explain, then mentally shrugged. It was about to be true. Once Councillor Weber learned of her exploits, Concha would be dismissed. For some reason, the notion failed to trouble her. "No," Concha repeated firmly, "I'm Rachel's friend."

The wariness remained in Lafiya's expression. "Really?" She folded her arms. "How is she?"

"Still resting in Medica." Concha recalled hacking into Doctor DeFlora's files. "The surgery went well, though she had quite a chunk taken out of her foot."

Lafiya glanced away and said woodenly: "That battery acid is nasty stuff."

Concha nodded and dropped her voice to a confidential murmur. "Actually, I'm trying to run an errand for Rachel. She needs some information from the ship at berth B-5."

Lafiya raised her cup and spoke behind its cover. "Khanwa?"

"Yes."

"The honorable captain's been trying to get a message through all night, if I'm not mistaken." Lafiya gave her a sidelong, knowing glance. "Over and over, members of Khanwa's crew keep breaking dock curfew. Safety takes them to Checkpoint, calls the captain, and the captain has to go in person to sign for their release."

"So it's important." Concha turned to look out the window. The berth numbers stenciled onto the bulkheads were faded and hard to read. "Where do I find him?"

"Him?" Lafiya repeated archly. "Captain Khanwa is hardly a 'him,' in any sense of the word."

Heat touched Concha's cheeks, remembering the Rofa's sexual forwardness. "Berth B-5."

"Just this side of Section Four."

"Where?" Concha's breath raised steam on the window. "Which one is—?"

"See that mobile crane? The one with its front all smashed in?" Lafiya murmured. "That's B-5, right behind it."

Concha flicked her gaze to the crane. It was mounted on a platform, and it looked as if its operator had driven it into a wall. "What happened to it?"

Lafiya gave a strained laugh. "Phi-Nurians. About twenty of them, I'd guess, rolled it back and forth. Bashed its nose against the section support." She snorted. "I can't remember the last time something like this happened. At least, no one was hurt."

Two staffers in blue and green parkas glided out from behind a stack of pallets. Both wore their hoods up, so their faces were hidden, but their every movement conveyed caution.

Startled, Concha turned to Lafiya. "What are they doing?"

Lafiya shrugged one shoulder, though her expression turned alert. "Not sure. Safety's been sneaking around out there for the past twenty minutes like a bunch of kids playing hidey-tag. I bet they're looking for someone."

A sick wash of sweat enveloped Concha. She returned her attention to the staffers in time to see them disappear down an interior ramp. The shadowy dock was once again empty of Human activity. She wondered if Safety were searching for Bailey, but somehow doubted it. *Jardín and Rife. Safety must be closing in on them.*

The sick feeling spread to Concha's gut. Cool, ironic Jardín; warm, generous Rife; they would face more than a dismissal from the councillor's service. Life on a penal farm seemed their likely fate, perhaps accompanied by personality restructuring.

Heart hammering, Concha strode to the door.

"Hey," Lafiya said, "If you're going back to Checkpoint, would you—?"

Concha pushed through the doorway and let it close behind her, sealing off the rest of Lafiya's question. Instead of turning toward the lift, she went to the first air lock and tapped in the override, again using stolen clearance. For a tense moment, she feared the codes had been changed, then the hatch unlocked and opened for her.

What am I doing? The air temperature plunged on the other side of the air lock, and she paused to pull gloves out of her coverall's pockets. Her hands shook so hard, it was difficult to draw the gloves over her fingers. *What the hell am I doing?*

She had to get to Khanwa before Safety arrested her. If she put up a fight, then perhaps that would offer enough of a distraction to draw the hunt away from Jardín and Rife.

Not allowing herself to think beyond that, Concha keyed the override to the second air lock, and shoved at the latch. The door slid open, admitting a rush of frigid air. Concha clenched her jaw to keep her teeth from chattering. *Just keep moving.* She stepped out onto the dock and let the door slide shut behind her.

The cold stung her nose and bit the skin on her bare head. While chilly, the dock's climate had not been so uncomfortable on her previous visit. She recalled thinking it somewhat foolish when she had read that Warden Jackson had dialed down the heat in an attempt to discourage casual looters. It did not seem foolish anymore. The cold was piercing.

The Ops booth sat just behind her, and Concha imagined the techs preparing to bodily drag her from the dock. She glanced over her shoulder to the window. From the outside, it appeared to be a highly polished, black lacquered panel. The reflection of a young woman in tech's coveralls regarded her with a gravely determined expression. Concha nodded briskly to the invisible watchers and turned to go.

Pulling up her hood, she tried to recall the path she needed to take. Khanwa's ship was berthed with floor level access, instead of at some midpoint along the high dock wall among all the repair skiffs and power tugs.

Debris covered the dock's floor. Pallets full of cargo sat where the techs had evidently left them at the riot's inception. Quite a few of the canisters were broken. A few feet away, fluffy strands of packing material spilled over the deck plates, mingling with the shiny remains of expensive Kamian computer components.

Heart pounding, Concha walked toward Khanwa's berth. The dock seemed eerily silent without the overhead rumble of the main gantry, and her booted footsteps rang loudly on the metal floor. *Keep moving,* she reminded herself. *Don't have much time.*

Listening both for the scrabble of Phi-Nurian claws and the sound of Human pursuit, Concha rounded a tall stack of pallets and walked into someone dressed as a staffer.

He whirled, then froze. "Concha?"

Concha drew a breath to speak, then recognized Rife's voice.

Jardín appeared from between two stacks of canisters. "Careful," she muttered. "We may be watched. Pretend you don't know us."

Relief assailed Concha. "But I—"

Rife's blue eyes sparkled, and he gave her a secret smile from within the depths of his hood. "Back away a few steps," he advised. "And point to something, like you're trying to explain."

Concha obediently backed up. "Point to what?"

"The broken crane," Jardín said. "And perhaps shake your head."

Concha pointed at the crane and shook her head, miming denial for the benefit of possible watchers. "I've been worried about you two," she murmured. "You're in trouble, aren't you?"

Rife chuckled. "We were in trouble from the start," he said. "But, yes, it appears the warden has forgotten he's supposed to be assisting us."

Concha clenched her gloved hands into fists. "What can I do to help you?"

"Nothing," Jardín said calmly. "Forget about us. It's too late."

"But I can't just—"

"What," Jardín interrupted, "are you doing out here?"

Trying to rescue you. "I need to talk to Captain Khanwa. I think he has information about a missing translator."

Rife glanced at Jardín, then peered at Concha, speaking slowly. "Please . . . please tell me . . . you're not talking about Bailey."

Confused, Concha stared at him. "I think that the Phi-Nurians have him, but I'm not—"

"Yes," Jardín interjected. "Bailey is on the ambassadors' ship. He asked us to smuggle him on board. And since he's working for Councillor Weber, we—"

Her confusion mounting, Concha struggled with a wash of conflicting emotions. "Wait a minute. He works for the councillor?" She glanced back and forth between her two colleagues, her agitation mounting as the pieces to the puzzle scattered and re-formed in her mind. "Oh, hell!" She raised her fist and prepared to strike the stack of pallets. "Oh, bloody hell!"

Rife grabbed Concha's hand, preventing the blow. "Easy," he said in an understanding tone. "Don't hurt yourself."

Concha could barely refrain from shouting. "I wish someone had told me—"

Jardín spoke in a level tone. "Bailey's location is a rather sensitive issue. Why did you say that Khanwa might know about it?"

Concha tried to match the other woman's calm, but her voice shook badly. "That Rofa knows everything. He—it—even told Rachel about Starcatcher."

"Starcatcher," Jardín repeated pensively. "Strange how our primary mission has become nothing more than a nuisance."

Rife cleared his throat. "We should keep moving," he said. "Maybe we ought to escort you to Khanwa's ship."

Concha nodded. "It's this way," she pointed. "B-5."

Rife and Jardín flanked her, and they walked across the dock together.

"So," Jardín murmured. "You think Khanwa knows that Bailey is aboard the Phi-Nurian ambassadors' ship?"

Concha nodded. Her cheeks felt stiff with the cold. "His—its—message mentioned missing cargo."

"Hmm," Rife said politely. "Maybe Khanwa actually wants to discuss missing cargo. There's been a lot of looting, you see."

"I suppose that's possible," Concha said. "But his—its—message followed closely after the Phi-Nurians' response to Councillor Weber's gift." Concha's nose began to run, and she tried to sniff without drawing obvious attention to it. "If I can work out that the canister's net weight matched Bailey's, then I suppose Khanwa could as well."

Jardín made an approving noise. "Aide Singh, I do believe you've been involved in illegal information gathering."

Concha tried to smile, but her face felt too cold. "Bailey's all right, isn't he? I mean, the canister's delivery was delayed."

"Well," Rife said ruefully, "I certainly hope so. Seems like nothing is going according to plan."

"He's fine." Jardín's tone conveyed nothing but calm confidence. "We rigged him up with enough life support that the canister could be spaced without causing him harm."

Doubtfully, Concha recalled the canister's dimensions and wondered what sort of system they used. "If you're sure—"

"He's fine," Jardín repeated, with a trace of a smile. "The worst thing Bailey will suffer from is a double charley horse from having those long legs of his folded up for so long."

Relieved, Concha returned the smile. "So why is Bailey on the Phi-Nurians' ship?"

"Sorry," Jardín said. "We're not at liberty to discuss that."

"Oh." Concha gave up trying to be discreet about her drippy nose and sniffed loudly. "Does it have something to do with Meris?"

Jardín stopped and laid a delaying hand on Concha's arm. "What do you know about Meris?"

Concha shrugged. "She's a stowaway Jadamii. Though she claims she has no idea how she got aboard the *La Vaca*."

Rife had paced a few steps ahead, and he stopped to glance back over his shoulder. "Stowaway?" he echoed. "Why would a Jadamii sneak aboard an Earth freighter?"

Concha sniffed again, with weak results, and was forced to dab at her nose with the sleeve of her coveralls. "'Scuse me," she said, feeling like an idiot. "I don't know. Didn't Bailey tell you? He knows her from before, though I can't imagine how a Freeholder ever managed to meet a—"

Jardín and Rife exchanged glances. Concha broke off and stared at her colleagues. *They didn't know that?* A fierce trembling that had nothing to do with the cold seized Concha. *What is Bailey planning?*

"I think," Jardín said slowly, "that we should watch our step with Khanwa. If you don't mind, Concha, maybe you should let me do the talking."

They skirted the shoulder-high barricade that separated one loading area from the next, and crossed to the access hatch.

Once there, Rife stationed himself back to back with Jardín, keeping watch over the dock behind them. Jardín reached for the intercom's controls, but before she touched the panel, the hatch shot open. Startled, Concha flinched.

Khanwa stood in the air lock. "Ah," it sounded pleased, looking past Jardín and directly at Concha. "Pretty Human is here. Was hungry for you." Khanwa beckoned invitingly. "Come play in my bed. Let me eat you all up."

In spite of the dock's freezing cold, Concha felt her face go hot with mingled anger and embarrassment.

Jardín spoke in an authoritative tone: "Captain Khanwa, Earth Port Safety has issued—"

Khanwa turned its gaze to her. "—issued pictures of you and your friend." It raised its voice. *"Kaja!"*

Something crashed behind them. Concha whirled.

All over the loading area, canisters exploded open to reveal Rofan crew. They were all armed with knives, and they closed in around the three Humans.

Concha stood rooted. *What?*

Rife knocked down the Rofa closest to him with a vicious kick to the head. At the same instant, Jardín turned and grabbed Concha's elbow and shoulder. Though uncertain of Jardín's plan, Concha offered no resistance. Jardín threw her into Khanwa.

Surprise was quickly followed by alarm, as Concha slammed into the Rofa's solid body. Head, shoulder, and hip met in a jarring crash of bone on bone, and pain flashed like sparks across Concha's vision. Khanwa grunted at the impact and lost its balance. They fell together to the floor, and Concha's knee connected with a metal deck plate. For a moment, the agony was so intense that all other sensation faded from her consciousness.

Khanwa growled and shifted beneath her.

Awareness returned, and Concha rolled to her feet. Fire lanced through her knee, but she ignored it, sweeping the dock with her gaze. The Rofa that Rife had kicked sprawled motionless on the floor. Jardín and Rife were gone, but the other crew members were disappearing down an interior cargo ramp, presumably in pursuit.

On the verge of panic, Concha scrambled around the loading area's barricade. She dithered for a moment, but realized that she couldn't catch up with Jardín and Rife, and so sprinted toward the Operations booth. Behind her, Khanwa shouted for her to come back, and she quickened her pace. *What's going on?* Concha tasted blood as she ran and realized that she had bitten her lip in the fall. *Why did Jardín do that?*

Ahead of her, an access hatch abruptly slid open, and a dozen Phi-Nurians rushed into the loading area. Concha yelped and changed course. Damaged canisters lay in heaps to her right, and she swerved toward them, hoping the Phi-Nurians had not noticed her.

A broken pallet leaned crookedly between two leaking canisters of peaches, cutting across Concha's path. She turned to backtrack, then heard the sound of Phi-Nurian claws on the deck plates. *Hell!* She dived under the leaning pallet and wormed her way past it, only to discover a dead end. A wall of undamaged plastic crates offered no passage.

Concha twisted in the confined space to turn around, then sat still for a moment to listen for pursuit.

Claws scrabbled around the outside of her hiding place,

and a Phi-Nurian vocoder produced a sustained, low buzz. Pulse beating in her throat, Concha pulled herself into a tighter crouch and peered out past the pallet.

A Phi-Nurian scuttled into view, walking on all six feet. It held its head close to the floor, and its mandibles clicked open and shut in clear agitation. It appeared to be following the trail of her scent.

In spite of the cold, sweat sprang out beneath Concha's coveralls. Her thoughts scattered into random flashes of image and memory: her mother's careworn smile, red holly-hocks glowing against a cloud-laden sky, the caress of warm lake water. She wanted desperately to awake and find the whole trip a nightmare, for her life to be once again normal and full of promise.

On the other side of the pallet, the Phi-Nurian appeared to weave, trying to bring her into better focus with its single eyepad. "See you," it buzzed. It stretched one arm under the pallet, but could not reach her. "See-you-see-you-see-you."

Concha had read about Phi-Nurian psychology and how to deal with one of the aliens in a state of frenzy. All she needed to do, she knew, was to make it think, to present a problem or a threat that would engage its rational mind.

The Phi-Nurian lunged against the pallet, the extended claw snapping in an effort to grab her. Concha pressed her back against the crates, and suddenly realized that she was breathing in faint screams. *Idiot.* She clamped her lips together, though it made her more aware of her trembling jaw. *Don't panic. Think.*

A shrill cry came from above Concha's head. She tore her eyes from the threatening claw to glance up. A small figure clad in layers of bright Rofan tunics stood atop the crates behind her. "Hah! Stinky thing!" It charged the Phi-Nurian, nimbly leaping down the unsteady slope of damaged shipping containers. "Get 'way from cargo!"

Clearly startled, the Phi-Nurian reared and scuttled backward. The little Rofa paused on one of the leaking canisters and crouched in a menacing posture, brandishing a shard of jagged plastic in one fist, wielding it like a sword. "I, Jhaska, defend this cargo!"

The Phi-Nurian's vocoder transmission sputtered, and the

buzzing gained a deeper tone. "Threats. . . ." The word was scarcely discernible, buried in a harsh buzz. "Violence. . . ."

Lost in terrified uncertainty, Concha gripped the edge of the pallet in front of her. *Oh, God, what do I do?*

The Phi-Nurian lunged forward and snatched at Jhaska. The little Rofa stabbed at the attacking claw, then danced to the side. "Hah!" Jhaska's tone was jubilant. "Missed!"

The Phi-Nurian made another grab and caught Jhaska's sleeve. "Kill!"

As if performing a long-practiced move in a game, Jhaska twisted out of the captured tunic and leaped to another canister.

The Phi-Nurian seemed unaware that it held only an empty garment. "Kill!" It shook the tunic so hard the fabric cracked like a whip. "Kill, kill, kill!"

Jhaska hissed and chittered, eyes bright, and crouched as if to leap forward into battle.

Concha swallowed hard against the knot of fear in her throat. "Hey," she called softly. "Jhaska?"

The Rofa's ears twitched, and it flicked its challenging gaze to her. "Cargo thief!"

"No," Concha said hastily, holding up her hands. "I'm a friend."

"Liar!" Jhaska pointed its makeshift sword at her. "Get 'way from cargo!"

The Phi-Nurian flung the tunic aside and lunged for Jhaska again. In its effort to reach the Rofa, it crashed against the pallet, causing it to ram Concha backward against the stack of crates. Pain exploded from the back of her head, and her vision dissolved into red sparks.

The pallet's weight prevented breath. Concha blindly shoved at it, with a strength lent by panic, and managed to move it enough to breathe.

"Kill!" the Phi-Nurian buzzed. "I shall kill!"

Pulse lurching, Concha looked for the direction of attack. Both the Phi-Nurian and the young Rofa were out of her line of sight. *Oh, God, no!*

Bracing her back against the crates behind her, Concha pushed the pallet away enough to squeeze out from behind it. "Jhaska!"

The two had moved away from the pile of damaged

cargo to a clear area. The Phi-Nurian made repeated, lunging strikes with its claws. Jhaska defended itself with fearless and utterly ineffectual stabs of its sword; only the little Rofa's speed prevented it from being caught.

Concha pawed through the debris around her for something to use as a weapon, but everything seemed either too flimsy or too heavy. Past caring, she grabbed a handful of plastic strapping. "Hey," she shouted. Not allowing herself to think, she bolted toward the Phi-Nurian, whirling the floppy straps over her head like a lariat. "Get away from that kid!"

The Phi-Nurian paused in its attack and dropped into a crouch, appearing to forget about the Rofa. Panting with obvious exertion, Jhaska continued stabbing at the nearest claw.

Afraid the Phi-Nurian would return to its attack on Jhaska, Concha rushed right up to it and lashed it across the carapace with the straps.

The vocoder sputtered. Then the Phi-Nurian grabbed the straps and yanked them out of Concha's grasp. She did not let go in time, was pulled off-balance, and fell to her hands and knees. The agony of her tortured joints was so intense it brought a surge of nausea. Panting, she scrambled out of immediate reach. "Oh, God. . . ." Concha did not know if she were praying or cursing. "Oh, God. . . ."

"Kill!" The Phi-Nurian shook the straps. "Kill!"

A buzzing crack sounded from the far end of the dock, loud enough to set off echoes in the overhead support struts. The Phi-Nurian paused. Three more reports followed. A woman shouted something.

Distracted, Concha kept backing away from her attacker while trying to see the cause of the commotion. The noise possessed a vaguely electrical quality. "What's that?" she blurted.

The Phi-Nurian answered, its vocoder transmitting in a normal tone: "That's a hand cannon."

Concha gaped at her former attacker.

"It shoots particle bolts." The Phi-Nurian dropped the straps, clearly returning to a rational state, and turned away. "It's very dangerous here. I advise you to take cover."

Concha continued to stare in disbelief as the Phi-Nurian scuttled away. "But—"

Two more shots echoed over the dock. A Rofa screamed. Humans shouted. In the distance, several staffers ran toward the trouble.

Coming to herself, Concha glanced around for the young Rofa, but did not see it anywhere. "Jhaska?" She turned in a frantic circle, scanning the surrounding debris. "Where are you?"

Another crack from a hand cannon split the air, closer this time.

Limping, Concha skirted the pile of damaged canisters. "Jhaska," she called, trying to lure the Rofa to her. "I'm going to steal your cargo."

A series of shots occurred. Vertical lightning sizzled, and a crate next to Concha exploded into plastic splinters.

She whirled and ran. A few yards away, a metal ladder led up to the system of catwalks. Feeling exposed, she dashed for it and grabbed the bottom rung. For a moment, she hesitated, glancing back over her shoulder, torn between fear and the longing to protect Jhaska.

A Phi-Nurian ran from a stack of crates, its vocoder emitting nothing but noise. It carried a large gun, and when it saw her, it stopped to take aim.

Concha gasped and scrambled up the ladder, booted feet slipping in her haste.

A loud zap slapped the air. A particle bolt struck the ladder, and the metal rungs quivered under Concha's hands. *Nonconductive. Thank God.*

Panting, she reached the first level of the catwalks and pressed her back against the bulkhead. The Phi-Nurian was just beneath her, and she hoped the catwalk's metal floor was nonconductive also.

There was an access hatch about twenty feet to Concha's left, but she could not read its registry board from her current position. Feeling exposed, keeping her back pressed against the bulkhead, she inched her way toward the hope of real shelter. *Please let them be Human. Please. . . .*

The registry board was blank and dark. Concha grimaced. "Damn," she whispered. "Now what?"

The catwalk extended the length of the dock, jogging at

random intervals to avoid power conduits. Storage bays and ramps that served to accommodate the movement of light cargo further disrupted sight lines. Deep shadows cast by overhead supports and occasional clusters of equipment offered hiding places for more attackers. In spite of the bone-numbing cold, sweat ran down Concha's sides and slicked her chapped face.

Someone, Human or Rofan, ran along the catwalk above her. Concha nearly called out, then reconsidered the wisdom of drawing attention to herself.

More shots echoed over the dock. Concha flinched and ran, praying incoherently that she would be harder to hit as a moving target.

A man shouted. Concha thought it was her name. She scrambled up a ramp to the next level.

In the storage bay ahead of her, a Phi-Nurian leaped up from behind a cluster of cable spools. It pointed the wide muzzle of its hand cannon at her. Tiny red lights twinkled on the weapon's targeting scope. Struck by utter disbelief, Concha froze.

"Move!" roared the man.

Blindly, Concha whipped around and took the ramp in a shoulder dive. The hand cannon crackled. A particle bolt screamed along the dock wall to her left in a shower of sparks. Panting, she rolled to her feet and resumed running.

Twenty feet ahead of her, a covered ladder led down to another catwalk. Wu Jackson's face appeared above the ladder's shaft. "Hurry!"

A gasp of desperate relief burst from her. She pushed herself for more speed.

The Phi-Nurian fired again. The particle bolt hit a curved support rod overhead and splintered into a shower of miniature lightning. Wildly, Concha jerked away from it. Her balance failed. She fell heavily against the catwalk's railing, smacking her ribs on the metal bars. Sharp pain erupted from her side, and she doubled over.

Wu shouted a wordless warning. The hand cannon crackled. Light, white and dazzling, filled Concha's eyes. Something buzzed past her ear like an enormous wasp. Confused and blinded, she clung to the railing.

In the next instant, searing agony flashed in a straight line along her cheekbone and above her ear. Concha dropped to her knees and slapped her hands over the injury. *It shot me!*

The catwalk's floor thundered. In horror, she realized that Wu had left his safe position and was running toward her. "No!" She struggled to rise. "Stay back!"

The Phi-Nurian fired again. Dazed with pain and blinded by red haze, Concha pulled herself into a shaky crouch.

Wu called to the Phi-Nurian. "Earth Port Safety. Drop your weapon." His voice was tight and menacing. "Drop it, or I'll shoot."

Concha wobbled to her feet. Her sight cleared a bit, but she was unable to run. Terrified, she waited for the Phi-Nurian to finish her off.

A warm arm wrapped around her shoulders. Wu's voice was raw with concern. "You okay?"

Every breath stabbed her side like a knife. Gasping, she leaned into him. "Just peachy."

The Phi-Nurian scuttled to the top of the ramp and waved the hand cannon excitedly. "I shall kill two Humans," it buzzed. It reared up on its back limbs in a posture of exaltation. "Kill two!"

Desperately, Concha glanced at Wu.

Wu kept his eyes on the Phi-Nurian and raised his free arm to display the laser pistol in his grip. Without seeming to take aim, Wu squeezed off six rapid shots.

Hissing, prismatic beams of light flashed around the Phi-Nurian's feet. The floor smoked and bubbled where each beam struck. The Phi-Nurian shrieked and danced backward on all six legs.

"Freeze!" Wu ordered.

The Phi-Nurian scuttled to a standstill, but its claws opened and closed restlessly.

Wu motioned with the pistol. "Drop your weapon." He hardened his voice. "Drop it, or I'll kill you."

The Phi-Nurian flexed its mandibles and slowly stood up on its back legs again. "You lie," it scoffed. "Humans don't kill."

Wu's voice suddenly returned to its usual facetious tone. "Maybe you're right. But I have no targeting scope. What if I fire again and hit you by accident?" He raised the pistol, obviously taking careful aim. "If I kill you, I will feel . . . bad."

All the Phi-Nurian's claws opened. The hand cannon fell to the floor and tumbled down the ramp.

Numbly, Concha stared at the weapon. A dull roar filled her ears, and her vision darkened. The pain in her side and face faded away, enveloped by soothing warmth. Unconsciousness claimed her.

CHAPTER SIXTEEN

A HARSH, ammonia-laden smell stung Concha's nostrils. The enfolding darkness withdrew a bit, and she became aware of lying prone on a hard, unyielding surface. The air felt warm. Calm, human voices murmured in the background.

Concha wanted to return to sleep, but something rigid pressed against her nose. Distantly, she realized that it seemed to be the source of the disagreeable odor. She twisted her head away, but the offending object followed.

"Ah, good." The young man's voice sounded relieved. "She's coming around."

Concha's sinuses began to burn from the smell. She jerked her head in the other direction. After a moment, the thing pressed against her nose again.

"Concha?" Wu spoke from nearby. "Can you hear me?"

Feeling pestered, Concha scowled. "What?" The source of the odor removed itself. She opened her eyes, blinking.

A beautiful young man leaned over her. Expecting to see Wu, Concha gazed up at the graceful contours of the stranger's face, unable to recall ever meeting him. "Oh—" She swallowed. "You—?"

"Doctor Tigre DeFlora." He seemed to attempt a smile, but the resulting grimace drew lines of exhaustion around his mouth and eyes. "How do you feel?"

"I—" From flat on her back, Concha glanced around at their surroundings, trying to place the white plasti-board walls and storage cupboards. From the look of the furniture, she deduced that they were in an office, and that she seemed to be lying on a desk. "I don't—"

Wu leaned against the wall nearest her feet. His blue and green parka hung open, and his hair looked windblown. "There you are," he said, tilting his head. "Welcome back."

Concha cleared her throat. "Where are we?"

Wu gave her a tired grin. "Checkpoint. Otherwise known as Doctor DeFlora's Traveling Medicine Show and First Aid Emporium." His smile turned gentle. "I guess you don't remember the ride up in the lift. You were phasing in and out on me."

Concha creased her brow. Recent memories crowded her mind, but they seemed as fragmentary and disjointed as scenes from a nightmare. She thought she recalled a Rofan child and a Phi-Nurian with a hand cannon. "Did—?" She hoped she did not sound too confused. "Was I dreaming, or did a Phi-Nurian shoot at us?"

Wu's smile faded. "You weren't dreaming."

Tigre studied her intently. "How does your face feel?"

Concha raised her hand to her cheek and encountered the silken surface of a regeneration patch. "Fine," she said, surprised. "It doesn't hurt at all."

"Good." Tigre straightened and capped the tube of smelling salts. "The burn itself was superficial, which means it probably hurt worse than something more serious." The chair of the desk, pushed against the wall beside the door, held a medical kit. Tigre turned to it and tucked the tube inside. "I dusted an analgesic into the patch, so that should keep it from smarting for a while."

Concha dropped her hand from her face and met Wu's gaze. "I was lucky."

Wu shrugged one shoulder. "We were both lucky, more or less."

Concha slowly sat up and let her legs hang over the edge of the desk. The pain in her ribs and knees blazed into new fire. "My face," she said dully, "is the only thing that doesn't hurt."

Tigre did not look at her. "The scanner picked up a variety of minor contusions. I can give you something for the discomfort, if you want."

Ashamed of complaining, Concha shook her head. "No, thank you. If nothing's broken, then . . ." Her gaze returned to Wu. "Out on the dock . . . I thought I heard screaming. Was anyone injured?"

Wu pressed his back against the wall, his expression turning bleak. "Some casualties among the merchant clients. And two of my staffers are going home in stasis."

Tigre twisted to look over his shoulder. "I've already told you. They'll be fine." His tone held an odd note of hostility. "Stop blaming yourself for every shitty thing that happens on this station."

A soft light filled Wu's eyes, and he chuckled. "You're so sweet."

"Shut up."

Embarrassed by the exchange, Concha glanced out the office's open door. A tech hurried by, carrying a jug of drinking water. A Port Authority deputy, whom Concha identified as Sonría Omar, passed in the other direction, speaking adamantly into her phone: "No . . . no . . . no!"

The purposeful activity outside burned away the last of Concha's mental fog, and her sense of urgency returned. She glanced at Wu. "I need to talk to Deputy Ajmani."

Tigre spoke without turning around. "She's resting, as you should be."

Wu made an inquiring noise. "Resting, huh? And just how, Doctor, did you manage to persuade Rachel Ajmani to take a nap?"

"It wasn't easy."

"I daresay. What did you use? A blunt instrument?"

Tigre's back and shoulders stiffened. "No," he snapped. "A warm protein and carbohydrate solution."

Certain that she had missed something, Concha frowned at Tigre's back. "Then Rachel—?" she paused and corrected herself. "Deputy Ajmani is all right?"

Tigre bent over his medical kit, seeming intent upon rearranging the contents. "Rachel is exhausted and on the verge of physical collapse. She fell asleep on the couch in my office."

Wu stirred. "How . . . cozy."

Clearly ignoring Wu's remark, Tigre looked over his shoulder at Concha. "Leave Rachel alone. She's done more than her share."

"But I need—"

"Sorry," Tigre interrupted, "but it's time to think about what Rachel needs."

Chastened, Concha hunched her narrow shoulders and stared at her hands. A scorch mark from a particle bolt marred the cuff of her coveralls. She touched the melted fabric with trembling fingers. *I'm such an idiot.*

"Now, now," Wu said. "Let's not get grumpy. I think we've all had a bad day, Doctor."

Concha lifted her gaze to Wu. There were so many things she wanted to say to him, so much gratitude and relief and guilt to express, but all that came out was: "I almost got you killed."

Wu smiled at her as if she were a small child. "I wouldn't say that."

A lump formed in Concha's throat, and she could not speak. She clenched her jaw, staring at Wu, and wondered how he was able to forgive her.

His back still turned, Tigre said: "Sounds like I missed a lot of excitement." His tone was casual, empty of its earlier hostility. "What happened, Concha?"

Having a question to answer somehow seemed to unlock her voice. "Wu risked his life to rescue me."

"Well, maybe." Wu shrugged modestly. "Actually, I think our Phi-Nurian friend was merely toying with you." He slid to the floor and leaned back against the wall. "It had a targeting scope, remember? It could've hit you with the first shot, but it wanted to scare you for a while."

Tigre finally turned around, his brows rising in obvious consternation. "What?" He glanced back and forth between Concha and Wu. "Scare her? I don't understand."

Wu drew up one knee and rested his folded hands on it. "Oh," he said cheerfully, "Phi-Nurians enjoy that sort of thing. They're rather timid, by nature, so when they have an enemy at a disadvantage they can't resist the opportunity to gloat." He raised his brows. "What wretched and pathetic lives they must lead. At times, I truly pity them."

Concha ran her thumb over the scorch mark on her sleeve. She remembered how the Phi-Nurian had paused in its attack to taunt them, giving Wu the chance to draw his pistol. "Is that why you didn't shoot it?"

"Shoot it?" Wu chuckled. "Aide Singh, the day I can't out-intimidate a Phi-Nurian is the day I resign."

Tigre picked up his medical kit and sat down in the chair, awkwardly holding the kit on his lap. "I heard a story—" He paused, and his voice gained a quality of shyness. "Is it true about Rachel? Did she really disarm a Phi-Nurian with a—?"

"Particle welder?" Wu finished. "Yes. She did." He closed his eyes and seemed to seek a softer spot on the wall to rest his head. "Of course, from then on, we could not permit our techs to openly carry welders on Dock Two. The Phi-Nurians considered them weapons."

"But how—?" Tigre shook his head, seeming baffled. "I guess I'm trying to visualize the showdown. Didn't the Phi-Nurian try to shoot her?"

Concha nodded, remembering her own incredulous reaction the first time she had read the report. "It shot her in the chest and left her for dead."

Tigre's eyes widened. "What?"

"Yup," Wu said sleepily. "But, you see, Rachel had been working on the coupling for a docking ratchet. She still wore a protective jacket from using the welder. Impervious to radiant energy and—"

Tigre nodded impatiently. "Yes, yes, I know. I have to wear one for certain surgical procedures."

Concha had never considered the similarities of laser scalpels, welders, and hand cannons. "Really?"

Smiling, eyes still closed, Wu raised his uniform tunic to reveal a padded garment beneath. "I have to wear one all the time." He dropped the tunic and yawned. "Anyway, the particle bolt didn't even touch Rachel. She just played possum and let the Phi-Nurian crawl over her. When it turned its back, she jumped up and took it by surprise."

Tigre slowly shook his head. "That was really . . . reckless. How has she managed to survive this long?"

Irritated, Concha glared at Tigre. "It was brave, not reckless. Rachel saved a lot of lives, and she—"

From his spot on the floor, Wu broke into a sudden fit of laughter. Far different from his usual purring chuckle, it escaped from him in squeaking gasps that seemed to shake his entire frame. "You—" He paused as if battling to catch his breath. "You two—"

The sound of a scuffle broke from the hallway outside. "Hey!" a woman protested.

A small figure in a blue and green Safety parka rushed into the room. It positioned itself in front of Tigre, then turned its back to him and assumed a defensive crouch. Concha's heart leaped in relief. *Jhaska!*

A staffer appeared on the threshold; her broad face wore a harried expression.

With obvious effort, Wu pulled himself together. "Hello, Shoko," he said. "Having fun?"

The staffer, Shoko, made an exasperated noise. "I'm sorry, Wu. The little stinker moves like an eel."

The individual in the parka yanked back the hood to reveal a triangular, minklike face. Concha smiled at the little Rofa. "Jhaska, I'm so glad you're—"

Jhaska sinuously twisted its upper body around to study her with bright, unfriendly eyes. "Who you?"

Since the youngster did not seem to recognize her, Concha decided that she would refrain from identifying herself as the "cargo thief." "I saw you out on the dock, and I—"

Jhaska turned away from her and grunted dismissively.

Stung, Concha tightened her lips. *Rofan gratitude.*

Tigre glanced back and forth between the two Safety people, and his expression grew ironic. "Aren't there some snipers or looters for you to chase? Do you have to pick on a scared little kid?"

Shoko smiled thinly and folded her arms. "Scared? Does that pint-sized hooligan look scared to you?"

Wu sighed. "Now, now," he murmured, "let's remember to play nice."

Jhaska clutched Tigre's sleeve. "Tig-Tig," it said in a scratchy voice. "Tig-Tig, I want to stay here with you."

Shoko beckoned gently. "Come along, Jhaska," she coaxed. "I'll give you something to eat."

Jhaska glared at her with undisguised suspicion, and its tiny ears flicked flat. "No!"

Tigre looked down at Jhaska. "Listen to me." His Trade was textbook perfect, and his voice was warm and steady. "Are you hungry?"

Jhaska tilted its head and regarded him sidelong. "Maybe," it conceded craftily. "Just a little bit."

Tigre's face seemed to light up with affection and amusement. "What would you like to eat?"

"Shez," Jhaska answered at once. "I want shez."

"What?" Tigre glanced helplessly at his fellow Humans.

Wu beamed. "Peaches," he supplied. "The Rofan adore peaches."

Jhaska bounced as if to punctuate its affirmation. "Yes! P'shez!"

Wu smiled up at Shoko from his place on the floor. "See what you can find, hmm? We'll keep an eye on Jhaska for a couple of minutes."

Shoko nodded unenthusiastically. "Yes, sir."

"You might try asking a few of the arbitrators," Wu continued. "Some of them keep fruit on hand to give as incentives."

Shoko nodded. "Right." She turned to go.

Tigre smiled at Shoko. "And thank you."

Shoko shrugged. "Hey, anything for interspecies goodwill." She strolled out the door, and her voice came back from the hallway. "Little stinker."

Jhaska peered after Shoko. "I can stay here?"

Concha glanced at Wu. "May I ask?" She dropped her voice and spoke in Earth Standard. "How did you catch Jhaska?"

Jhaska swiveled its head around and looked at Concha. "What you say 'bout me?"

Wu shifted his weight, as if preparing to stand, then seemed to reconsider. He settled his back against the wall once more, shoulders sagging. "We suggested to our spirited little friend that it had earned the adult right to be arrested."

Concha smiled. "Clever."

Wu shrugged wearily. "Not really. We should have left Jhaska on the dock. The Rofan are furious with us for touching their baby. They don't believe we rescued it, and they're accusing us of abduction and torture."

Concha's heart sank. "Oh."

Jhaska raised its voice. "Speak Trade!"

Smiling, Tigre patted the Rofa's back. "Calm down. They're only discussing how you came to be here.

Jhaska snaked around from Tigre's chair, jumped onto

the desk, and thrust its face into Concha's. Its round eyes were bright. "I was in a fight," it declared. "A big, big fight!"

Concha's pulse picked up tempo, and she was unsure whether to be amused or afraid. Jhaska smelled warm and young, like a puppy; but she reminded herself that it was an unpredictable Rofa. *Don't back away.* "I'm impressed," she said. "You're very brave."

"I know," it replied in a matter-of-fact tone.

Tigre laughed softly. "Jhaska, come here."

The Rofa's small ears flicked flat in obvious annoyance, but it jumped from the desk to stand once again beside Tigre's chair.

Tigre pulled one corner of his mouth up into a rueful grin. "I feel like I've adopted a little brother or sister," he said. Then added in Standard: "Nice to have family again."

Jhaska abruptly slammed its shoulder into Tigre's arm. "Speak Trade!"

"Hey!" Tigre's tone was a mix of exasperation and laughter. He pulled the hood down over Jhaska's face.

Jhaska flung the hood back. "Hey!" it cried, exactly mimicking Tigre, and added defiantly. "I'll bite you!"

"Oh, you will?" Tigre taunted in Trade. "I don't think you're fast enough." His hand flicked out and tapped Jhaska's nose. The Rofa snapped at his fingers, but Tigre deftly whipped his hand away. The needle-sharp teeth closed on air. "See? Too slow."

Once again, Concha felt a blend of alarm and amusement. She knew surgeons had to take care of their hands, and she was certain Tigre did not realize how a Rofa's mind worked. *He may be his own next patient.* "Ah—?" She glanced at Wu.

Wu sat with his head settled back on the wall behind him. His forearm rested on his raised knee, and his hand hung limp in the air. He watched Tigre tease Jhaska, and an indulgent smile slowly lifted just the corners of his mouth.

Tigre made a series of swift feints, and Jhaska snapped at all of them. "See? See?" Tigre laughed. "You're not fast enough." He made a lightning move and tapped Jhaska's nose again. The Rofa squealed, eyes bright, and bobbed its head.

Someone shuffled up the hallway and paused in the door.

Concha jerked her attention away from Tigre and Jhaska and glanced over.

Deputy Sonría Omar stood on the threshold. A bland smile spread across her face, and she put her hands on her hips. "Someone just carried a basket of fresh peaches into Checkpoint's main office," she drawled in Trade. "I wonder who they're for?"

Jhaska jumped off the cot and stood up straight. "Me!" Its little ears shifted forward. "The p'shez'zez are for me!"

Tigre climbed to his feet, picking up his medical kit. "That was quick."

Sonría shrugged. "No doubt the station's arbitrators are anxious to maintain friendly relations."

Jhaska pulled at Tigre's sleeve. "Tig-Tig, let's go."

Tigre drifted to the door, and Sonría stepped aside for him. He paused and looked back at Concha, and his beautiful face hardened in a stern expression. "Get some rest."

Wondering when she would find the time, Concha nodded.

His gaze flicked to Wu. "That goes for you as well."

Jhaska jumped up and down, obviously wild with impatience. "Tig-Tig, I'm hungry." It leaped into the air, bulky parka and all, and sinuously spun in a circle before it landed. "Hungry, hungry, hungry!"

"Calm down." Tigre led Jhaska out of the room. "Stay here with me. This way."

Jhaska's voice echoed from the hallway. "P'shez'zez! A basket of p'shez'zez for Tig-Tig and me!"

Sonría leaned her shoulder against the wall. "Cute kid. Looks like it's decided to worship Doctor DeFlora."

Wu stirred. "Who wouldn't?"

Smiling inwardly, Concha found herself agreeing.

Sonría dropped her voice. "But the doctor shouldn't be here."

"Really?" Wu said. "Tell him that. I dare you."

Sonría folded her arms. "Do you think it's wise? To let him near Jhaska?" She gave Wu an intensely significant look. "Isn't he still . . . under the influence?"

Crooking her brows, Concha wondered what Sonría meant.

"He's fine," Wu said. "I think Jhaska actually helps him. Reminds him that he is, after all, still in control of himself."

Sonría appeared unconvinced. "Yes, but—"

"The difference between *having* feelings and *acting* upon feelings." Wu shrugged loosely. "Jhaska's good therapy."

Sonría regarded Wu narrowly. "And what about you? The way you've been teasing him. . . ."

"Oh, I'm good therapy, too. He needs someone to rudely reject. Someone safe."

"Safe?"

Wu spoke mildly. "For now."

Sonría gave a noncommittal grunt and turned her attention to Concha. "How do you feel?" Her tone was dry and kindly. "I hear you stepped too close to a particle bolt."

Embarrassed, Concha resisted the urge to touch the patch on her face. "Oh," she said casually, "I'll live."

Though Sonría's outward manner seemed more relaxed than Rachel's, her gaze was filled with the same quality of shrewd assessment. "You're lucky. The first time a Phi-Nurian took a potshot at me, it blew off my left leg at the knee. I spent a total of five months in a regeneration tank."

"Tut, tut," Wu scolded facetiously. "Tell her a nice story. What about the time you chased a Rofan drug smuggler across the bridge of the loading gantry?"

"Oh, sure," Sonría said. "Make fun of me. And all the while you've been out playing on Dock Two, I've been in Checkpoint trying to keep all our respective hides in one piece." She shuffled to Tigre's abandoned chair and sat down. "Oh, that feels good." She sighed deeply. "When was the last time you two listened to the bulletins?" She slid her eyes in Concha's direction. "And don't pretend you haven't hacked into the station's system."

Heat jumped to Concha's face, and she knotted her fingers together. "It's been . . . a while," she confessed.

"Same here," Wu volunteered blithely. "I turned off my phone out on the dock so it wouldn't ring and betray my hiding place—I mean, my position."

Sonría slouched back in the chair and folded her hands over her stomach. "Then let me fill you in."

Concha glanced back and forth between the two and started to slide off the desk. "I should leave and allow you to—"

"Stay," Sonría said. "You'll probably want to make a report on this."

"Yes, Deputy." Confused and suddenly worried, Concha returned to her seat. "Thank you."

Sonría nodded politely, then looked at Wu. "There's been a new development. We traced Rachel's leaking battery to a new case just shipped in last week."

"Mm." Wu narrowed his eyes. "Same as the one that exploded."

"Right," Sonría said. "In fact, we discovered that every battery in the case had sprung a leak."

Shocked, Concha pressed her knuckles against her lips. In an instant, she mentally reviewed her knowledge of chemical batteries. The ingenious Kamians manufactured them, using a process that sandwiched together superconductive metals to form the plates. The plates were immersed in hyperreactive solutions that were capable of generating a charge strong enough to power heavy machinery for extended amounts of time, even in the cold of space.

"Wait a minute," Concha blurted. "What about the failsafes?" As she understood it, the barriers that prevented the electrolytes and ionizers from combining were carefully designed to self-seal in the event of accidental puncture. There were also, she recalled, cells of neutralizing solution that rendered everything inert if the outer casing became compromised. "I mean—"

Sonría shrugged. "Damaged in transit, we're guessing. The Kamians aren't known for defective merchandise."

"But—" Concha shook her head tightly. "If only one battery in the case had detonated, it could have set off a chain reaction among the others. The resulting explosion would have ripped a hole in the station's hull."

Sonría nodded in agreement. "Boom."

Concha shifted edgily, certain that the batteries were not damaged in transit. *Why would Kamians sabotage a case of batteries?* Her hands began to tremble, and she recalled the message left for Rachel. *I grasp the stars and take the light to heart.*

Wu's dark eyes were alert and interested. "They would have seen us in the night sky over Paris. And we were all saved from certain death because Rachel Ajmani put her foot in it." He glanced at Concha, and gave her a humorously whispered aside: "She does this sort of thing all the time, you know. It's spooky."

Though still anxious, Concha dredged up a smile for him.

Sonría cleared her throat. "Next item: Dock Two remains clear. All the client ships are in the process of filing vouchers for the release of their personnel from detention. With a notable exception." Sonría paused and glanced at Concha. "The Phi-Nurians armed with the hand cannons have refused to identify their ship. Not only that, but none of the ships currently at Port will claim these individuals."

Wu frowned and thoughtfully stroked an imaginary mustache. "An interesting problem," he said. "I hate interesting problems." He regarded Sonría mildly. "The brigand who attacked us had posted itself beside the access to the diplomats' ship. Did you ask Their Excellencies if they were missing members of their entourage?"

Sonría gave him a blank stare. "I can't. They're still aboard *Gaia's Love* in that closed-door meeting with Deputy Jimanez-Verde and the World Council committee."

Concha struggled to keep a professional demeanor, but the trembling in her hands moved up her arms and into her shoulders. For the first time, it hit home that Councillor Weber sat in the ship's conference room with a delegation from Phi-Nu. She thought about the crate delivered to the Phi-Nurians' ship, and how its net weight matched that of Professor Rye.

Wu pursed his lips. "I recommend that you relay the inquiry to Lois when the meeting breaks."

Sonría smoothed her long hair back from her face. "My instructions to that effect are already pending. I'll let Lois decide on protocol." She cleared her throat. "Now it's your turn, Warden. I'll take your report on the impostors."

" 'Kay." Wu raised his voice. "Computer, please close the office door."

The door hummed and slid shut. Concha looked at Wu and found him studying her. After a prolonged pause, he spoke: "We took Jardín and Rife into custody during the riot."

Inwardly reeling, Concha looked back and forth between the two Port officials. "What?" she blurted, and then struggled to cover her reaction. "I mean—"

Wu continued to study her. "With all the other problems at hand, we've had a rough time sparing the people to track them down."

Concha spoke carefully, no longer certain where her loyalties rested. "I don't understand."

"Don't you?" Wu's tone gained a hostile quality. "Well, neither do I."

Sonría spoke deliberately. "Starcatcher. Warden Jackson briefed me on it earlier." She fell silent and gazed for a long moment at Concha. "What a mess."

Concha swallowed, trying to think. "I'm not—"

Sonría continued. "Your friends, Jardín and Rife, have racked up quite a list of charges. Besides kidnapping and assaulting Doctor DeFlora, they've harassed numerous station personnel. Additionally, they've tampered with safety and environmental systems, threatened the lives of merchant clients, and touched off a dockside riot of unprecedented proportion."

But they were acting under orders! Concha's protest died before it reached her lips. "Doctor DeFlora?"

Wu rubbed his hands together in facetious glee. "I can hardly wait to have a little chat with Jardín and Rife." He glanced at Sonría. "I suppose it's against the rules to make them share a detention cell with Phi-Nurians?"

Sonría gave a snort of laughter. " 'Fraid so."

"Damn." Wu scratched the back of his head. "What if I accidentally forgot the rules?"

"Hmm." Sonría smiled unpleasantly. "Well, we all have little memory lapses."

Wu turned his glittering gaze to Concha. "That reminds me," he said, "of something I forgot to tell you earlier. Aide Singh, you're under arrest."

CHAPTER SEVENTEEN

CONCHA STARED at Wu, her mouth working inarticulately, her mind blanking in fear.

"Unless," Wu continued in a sugary tone, "unless there's something you want to tell us?"

Concha shivered and hugged her folded arms close. Sweat left sticky trails down her sides, and her pulse throbbed in her ears.

"You realize, of course," Sonría said, "that no one involved will escape unscathed." She sighed and shook her head irritably. "I suppose, on the political level, it's been a long time in coming. But I really wish it had waited until after I retired."

Concha swallowed against the sudden dryness in her throat. "What do you mean, that Jardín and Rife . . . assaulted Doctor DeFlora?"

Wordlessly, Wu pulled a recorder out of his pocket. He aimed it at a blank area of the wall and keyed it on. A flatly lit projection began to play, all random movement and sound, and then the image coalesced into sense. Medics were treating a man with a battered face. "That's enough," the man said in a miserable tone, attempting to push their hands away. Both eyes were blackened and blood ran down his forehead. "Just . . . just leave me alone."

Wu froze the image. "That, believe it or not, is our beautiful Doctor DeFlora. His medics did a good job of patching him up, don't you think? There's not a trace of a bruise remaining on his face."

Her heart pounding, Concha stared. "What happened to him?"

"Jardín and Rife lured him to an isolated part of the station. Then they beat him up, drugged him, and . . . molested him."

"What?" Shock made it hard to breathe. Concha gazed helplessly at Wu. "That's impossible. It has to be a mistake. They would never—"

"No mistake. We caught them in the act."

Concha's throat contracted, and she remembered their actions on the dock. "But why would they do something like that?"

"You tell me." Wu's eyes glinted feverishly, and he shut off the recording. "How do any of their actions pertain to Starcatcher?"

"I think—" Concha's voice sounded thin and far away to her own ears. "I don't think Jardín and Rife are working on Starcatcher anymore."

Wu gestured encouragingly. "Go on."

"She—" Concha swallowed again, trying to remember the exact words. "Jardín told me that the Starcatcher mission had become a nuisance."

Sonría made an interested noise. "When was this?"

"Out—" Concha started to gesture toward the dock, then realized she did not know in what direction it lay, and let her trembling hand fall to her lap. "Out on the dock. When I went to talk to Captain Khanwa."

Sonría and Wu regarded her silently, clearly waiting for her to continue.

Concha drew a deep breath, and then started from the beginning. She outlined her time spent observing Rachel, her hours spent in clandestine surveillance efforts aboard *Gaia's Love*, Councillor Weber's alleged gift to the Phi-Nurians, Khanwa's resulting message, and her conversation with Jardín and Rife on the dock. "So," she finished, "I really don't know what's going on, but I'm beginning to think it has something to do with Meris."

Wu made a pleased noise. "Very nice." He turned off the recorder with a flourish. "And because you've been so helpful, I hereby unarrest you."

Concha stared, only at that moment realizing that he had recorded her confession. "You—?" She drew an unsteady breath and pulled herself together. "I didn't tell you all that as some sort of plea bargain. I told you because it's the right thing to do."

"Of course," Wu purred.

"It's true!"

Sonría shifted. "As I see it," she said, "we have two separate problems: Starcatcher and Meris. Starcatcher was a plot to destroy Rachel's credibility." She tossed Concha a dark glance. "Not only is Starcatcher illegal and unethical, it's a dreadful waste of time and resources. Your boss could have saved herself the trouble if she'd simply *asked* Rachel whether or not she wanted to sit on the World Council. I suspect the answer would have been 'no.'"

Startled, Concha sat upright. "What?" she said. "How could Rachel ever turn down such an opportunity?"

"Opportunity?" Sonría drawled. "You mean, for power?" She made a hissing noise of dismissal. "It's that sort of thinking that got us into this mess, isn't it?"

"Not for power," Concha protested. "But to do good. To make a difference. To try—"

"Save the rhetoric."

"But—"

Wu cleared his throat. "I agree with you, Concha. But it's a moot point now."

Feeling defeated, Concha gazed at him, trying to find words.

Sonría nodded slowly. "And we can't forget Meris. That Jadamii, along with Trabail Rye, seems to be connected to the shutdown of Igsha Reey Port." She narrowed her eyes in thought. "Warden, I suggest you have that chat with Jardín and Rife now."

Concha's heart hammered. Trying to disguise her nervousness, she glanced surreptitiously around Checkpoint's detention area, remembering her earlier visit with Rachel. Unlike then, however, all the cells but one were unoccupied. The largest held three Phi-Nurians, complaining at the top of their vocoders of mistreatment. The restraint field that encircled them shimmered in opalescent hues, indicating it was on at full force.

Concha followed Wu past the detention area. Thinking that Jardín and Rife would be held in one of the cells, she felt a flash of confusion when Wu turned up a narrow corridor filled with what appeared to be offices. The odor of Phi-Nurians faded somewhat, replaced by the scent of coffee and warm metal. Wu led the way to a small office along a side corridor.

Modesto and Chen stood guard just inside the door. The staffers wore grim expressions, and they held drawn stingers on Jardín and Rife. Still dressed in Safety uniforms, the prisoners sat on the floor, hands bound behind their backs. A small table to the side held a bewildering array of items sealed in clear, plastic bags.

Jardín no longer seemed confident and detached, but rather tired and anxious. Rife kept his head bowed, his golden hair screening his face.

A deep shock surged through Concha, and an involuntary noise of pity escaped her. She forced herself to remember what they had done to the doctor and how they had left her at Khanwa's mercy, but the feeling of friendship refused to fade.

Wu sauntered forward to stand over the prisoners. "So we meet again."

Jardín did not look up, but stared in disinterest at the air in front of her. "Warden." Her tone was flat. "I presume this farce means our deal is off."

"Oh, this is no farce," Wu said matter-of-factly. "This is the real thing."

Jardín's mouth twitched in contempt. "The real thing," she echoed. "The real thing."

"And Tigre DeFlora," Wu continued, "was never part of our deal."

Rife stirred. "All those others . . . so easy. . . ." He raised his face and looked up at Wu. A strange light burned in his blue eyes. "All those others . . ."

Concha tried to stop trembling, but the shaking in her arms and shoulders grew worse. There was something wrong with Rife; she could see it clearly, and she wondered why she had not noticed it before. *He's insane.*

Rife continued: "Everyone else that we locked in closets, they cooperated. They did what we told them, because they thought we were staffers." He shrugged. "Sheep. So respectful of authority that they don't even recognize an unreasonable demand. But Tigre was different, right from the start. Trouble."

Jardín scowled. "Shut up."

Rife gave no sign he heard. "A lot of trouble. And I guess—I guess—" His expression melted into sorrow, and he suddenly seemed very young. "I guess I got carried away. I do that sometimes. I can't help it."

Concha's hands turned icy, and she clenched them into fists. *He's doing it again. Saying what we want to hear.*

Wu gazed down at him. "Carried away?" he repeated in a gentle, deadly tone. "Sometimes I get carried away, too."

"Is Tigre—?" Rife paused and swallowed. "Is he going to be all right?"

"Don't." Wu's voice dropped to a whisper. "Don't you . . . dare . . . ask such a question."

Rife sighed and dropped his head again. "You want to hit me, don't you?" he asked dully. "Go ahead."

In the next instant, Wu lunged for Rife. Moving with unbelievable speed, he grabbed a fistful of Rife's uniform, dragged him to his knees, and then savagely punched him in the face. Rife fell backward, landing heavily on his bound arms. Blood welled up from his nose and mouth.

Horrified, Concha stood rooted.

From his place by the door, Chen inhaled through his teeth. "Warden!"

Wu glanced back at his staffer, brows raised. "What?" he asked mildly. "He gave me permission."

Lying as he had fallen, Rife began to giggle. "Warden Jackson, you—" Blood drooled from his lips. "You're a lot stronger than you look."

"Oh, yes," Wu agreed. "Meaner, too."

Jardín did not so much as glance at her partner. Her cool gaze flicked over her surroundings, studying the staffers with drawn stingers, Concha, and the scuffed bulkheads with the same weary indifference. "This is pointless," she said. "We were just following orders."

Cold perspiration dotted Concha's upper lip, and she wrapped her arms tightly around herself, unable to stop shaking. Jardín and Rife had been nice to her, and so she had trusted them and thought of them as friends. *Just one of the sheep.*

Filled with self-loathing, and trembling so badly that she could scarcely walk, Concha turned away toward the table. For a long moment, she stared blindly at the bagged items on display.

Wu spoke from beside her. "Interesting, huh?"

Concha jumped before realizing that he had joined her at the table.

Speaking softly, Wu pointed. "The stuff in this corner is what they had on them. The rest we took from their hideout."

For the first time, Concha really looked at the captured belongings. Some things seemed merely personal: a comb, packets of towelettes, candy. Quite a few items, however, she recognized as tools for working on field system circuitry. During her stint as a pilot, she had frequently used such implements for minor ship repairs.

Wu raised his brows at Concha. "Quite a collection," he murmured. "Your two friends were prepared for anything, weren't they?"

One of the tools was a miniature particle welder, a metal cylinder just slightly longer and thicker than a writing stylus. Concha recalled seeing Jardín working on it aboard *Gaia's Love*. The tip of the welder bore the blue-green oxidation of recent use.

An abrupt shudder shook Concha. A particle beam could be phased to pass through certain materials, allowing one to weld broken connections within a sealed unit. *The batteries.* "Warden," she whispered, her throat gone dry. "I think—"

Wu regarded her alertly. "Yes?"

Concha licked her lips, wondering if the logic was only obvious to her. "The batteries—" Her pulse pounded in her throat. "The batteries could have been sabotaged by someone using a welder."

Wu frowned. "What?"

Concha's voice shook, but she plowed on. "One well-placed shot. It would cook the neutralizer and nick a conductive plate just enough to initiate a corrosive reaction. And all the damage would be invisible to the naked eye."

Wu's face emptied of emotion. He turned back to Jardín and Rife and studied them with cold detachment.

Rife struggled upright and threw a worried look at Jardín. She continued to ignore him.

Wu lifted the bagged welder from the table and peered at its tip. His voice was colorless. "The batteries."

Jardín's expression conveyed nothing but boredom. "Pretty circumstantial, Warden," she said. "And I hope this doesn't place Concha under suspicion, since she seems to know the technique."

Concha's throat closed in terror.

With elaborate care, Wu returned the welder to the table. His hands dropped to his gun belt. "Concha's time during the period in question is accounted for. There are witnesses." His voice was soft, menacing. "She has an alibi. You do not."

Jardín's eyes narrowed as she evidently realized her error in speaking.

For a moment, no one moved. The sound of Jhaska's delighted squeals drifted from the direction of Checkpoint's main area, followed by a burst of Human laughter.

Wu's black eyes glittered as he regarded Jardín and Rife with reptilian intensity. "Those leaking batteries," he whispered, "sent some of my friends back to Earth in boxes."

Jardín returned Wu's stare without wavering. Her delicate mouth slowly curled into a smile of contemptuous triumph.

Concha's heart beat in slow, hard strokes, and perspiration rolled down her sides.

At that moment, Sonría strolled into the office. Her expression evinced its usual calm. "Sorry, I was delayed," she said to no one in particular. She studied the prisoners, gaze lingering on Rife's bloody mouth, then gave Wu a very direct glance. "Warden. You have a call in the outer office."

Wu's narrowed eyes flicked to Sonría. For a moment, he glared without evident recognition, then his hands relaxed off his gun belt. "Deputy Omar," he said without warmth.

"Better hurry," Sonría prompted and folded her arms. "I'll take over with this."

Concha blinked in disbelief. *She's dismissing him?*

Wu hesitated a long moment, seeming to search Sonría's face, then turned on his heel and headed for the door. As he passed the table holding the confiscated tools, he gestured toward the welder. "Take good care of that." His

tone was tight. "The civil authorities will want to see it."
He strode through the door without looking back.

Sonría watched Wu leave, then turned to the staffers
holding the stingers. "Chen, Modesto, put your weapons
away." Smiling unpleasantly, she looked Jardín and Rife
over. "Kids, you're in a lot of trouble."

Concha glanced at Jardín, and was startled to find the
woman studying her. She saw no reproach in Jardín's gaze,
only cool analysis, as if her colleague were a stranger memorizing her face.

An abrupt feeling of alarm tightened the muscles in Concha's shoulders. She backed away a few steps, then turned
and followed Wu.

The corridor outside the detention area was empty. Ventilators whispered near the ceiling, and voices echoed from
Checkpoint's outer offices. Concha wandered up the hall
until she came to an intersection. To her left lay private
offices and meeting rooms. An open space lay to her right,
filled with desks and monitoring equipment manned by
three tired-looking staffers. Beyond it all, tucked away in
a corner, was a modest lounge area. The vid played a program on equatorial butterflies. Tigre and a couple of medics
sat on the tattered chairs and watched Jhaska eat a juicy
peach.

A brewer sat near the monitor area on a low table. Wu
stood beside it, alone. He braced himself with one rigid
arm against the wall, head bowed.

Still hugging herself, Concha moved to stand beside him.
Once there, she realized that he might not want company.
She swallowed hard to keep from blurting something
pointless.

Wu spoke without raising his head. "I lost my temper."
His tone was colorless. "Thank God, Sonría chased me
out."

Concha hunched her shoulders. "Maybe—" She paused,
not knowing what to say, wanting to apologize for all her
blundering. "Maybe I was wrong. About the welder and
the batteries, I mean."

Wu lifted his face, his expression open and oddly vulnerable. "No," he said softly. "I'm sure you're correct."

Concha licked her dry lips. She found she did not want

him to believe her. She wanted him to argue against her theory.

"It's only hard to credit," Wu continued, "because we've been taught that we've outgrown violent crime. That it no longer occurs."

Concha sighed unsteadily. "Do you suppose Councillor Weber planned it all?"

Wu drew a breath to speak, but seemed to reconsider his words. His eyes betrayed an inner turmoil, a sudden welling of some long-hidden pain. "Maybe."

Feeling inadequate, Concha chewed the inside of her cheek.

Wu flicked his glance away from her, as if he realized he exposed too much feeling. He gestured airily to the nearby brewer. It murmured to itself, surrounded by an assortment of mismatched mugs. "I always come to the brewer when I'm in trouble." He picked up a mug. "A holdover from childhood, perhaps. When I was small, I always ran to the kitchen to talk to my grandmother. I suppose this is the closest approximation." He filled the mug and offered it to Concha. "Here. Have some of Checkpoint's lovely, terrible coffee."

Concha accepted the mug. "Thank you." She lifted it to inhale the steam, studying him furtively as he poured coffee for himself. His habitual smile was back in place, but Concha thought she still detected pain in his eyes. "Maybe—" She hesitated, fearful of sounding too familiar. "Maybe you ought to talk to someone."

Wu briskly squirted honey into his coffee from a sticky looking dispenser. "Maybe," he agreed cheerfully.

Some of the tension eased from Concha's tight shoulders. She leaned back against the wall and sighed. "Too bad you can't call Rachel. Talking to the one you love is a—"

Wu froze in the act of reaching for a bamboo stirrer and regarded her sidelong. "Excuse me?"

Confused, Concha stared back at him. "Pardon?"

"Are you suggesting that I have feelings for Deputy Ajmani?"

At a loss, Concha gestured helplessly. "But you do, don't you?"

Wu threw a hasty glance over his shoulder, and then leaned toward her. "Whatever you think you've observed,

I prefer that you not repeat it to anyone else. Not even to Rachel." He spoke quietly and without heat. "It could raise serious questions about my professional integrity. Or what's left of it. Understand?"

Mortified, Concha clutched her cup with both hands. "I'm so sorry," she stammered. "I didn't mean to—" She swallowed and attempted to sound like a grown woman instead of an awkward child. "It just seemed so obvious."

Wu slowly raised his brows. "Ob . . . vious?

Heat beat in Concha's face. "I mean—"

Wu burst into sudden laughter and shook the stirrer at her like a scolding finger. "Aide Singh, allow me to explain something: I am never obvious. At least, not by accident." He stirred his coffee and took a hearty swallow. "And I have to say, that while your deductive abilities show some promise, your tact borders on the nonexistent."

Confused and still embarrassed, Concha shook her head. "I don't—I mean—tact—?"

"Unbelievably tactless." Wu beamed at her. "However, you also have a puzzle-solving mind."

Concha shrugged tightly, certain that the compliment was only intended to set her at ease. "Not really."

"Yes, really." Wu took another deep swallow of coffee. "You were the one who figured out the connection between the leaking batteries and the particle welder, not me."

Concha shook her head. "But it was ob—"

"Aack! Don't use the 'o' word!"

Concha smiled in spite of herself. "It only occurred to me because I got shot at. I was thinking about radiant energy beams." She carefully touched the patch on her burned cheek and recalled her harebrained mission to talk to Khanwa. "I'm usually wrong when I put things together. I add one plus two and get twelve." She had no more to say, but Wu seemed to wait for her to continue. "I told you why I walked out onto Dock Two on the eve of a riot. I thought Captain Khanwa had some information regarding Professor Rye's disappearance." She snorted in self-derision. "Turns out I was laughably wrong."

Wu shrugged. "But you are not the perfect and godlike being that I am. You are entitled to make mistakes."

"Thanks."

"All teasing aside, you really ought to consider applying for a position at Port Station. I'm betting you'd make bronze rank within two years, and jade rank in another two." Wu raised his brows at her. "Deputy Jimanez-Verde will retire sometime in the next ten years. One of the silver deputies will move up, which will leave a vacancy for you."

A faint sense of panic seized Concha at the thought of a deputy's looming responsibilities. "I couldn't—two years—?" Again, she struggled for articulate speech. "I'm not ready for—"

Wu's smile softened. "Life isn't about being ready. We aren't born ready. And we certainly don't die—"

A staffer at a nearby monitor swiveled in his chair to face them. "Wu," he called in a quiet, urgent voice. A holographic projection of Earth Port slowly revolved in the air behind him. "I think you'll want to see this."

Wu raised his brows. "Oh, goody." He headed for the monitor and made an encouraging motion for Concha to follow. "Do come. I might need your brain."

Uncertain, but curious, Concha trailed after him.

The image seemed to hang from the ceiling like a curtain; a miniature station hovered in the air at eye level. Concha studied the holograph. Four arms radiated out from the station's central hub, and the arms connected the two concentric rings that contained the living quarters and the docks. Clusters of ships, mostly deep space freighters, obscured the station's appearance of a wheel within a wheel.

The staffer at the monitor, an older man with grizzled hair and a worried line over his brows, glanced up at her from his chair.

Wu gestured with his coffee cup. "Kepler, this is Concha Singh, Deputy Ajmani's new personal aide. Concha, meet Kepler Thai, Checkpoint coordinator." He peered at the image revolving in front of him. "What's up?"

Kepler touched a control, and the little station stopped spinning. He pointed with the tip of his stylus to a ship in final docking maneuvers. "The emissary of the Rofan Legitimacy has arrived. It's slotted to the berth adjacent to the Phi-Nurian ambassadors."

Forgetting herself in her fascination, Concha leaned to study the ship. It looked about the size of a private cruiser, she decided, big enough for six people to travel in comfort.

The swept-back wings and needle nose meant it doubled as an atmospheric craft, and its white paint job with the glittering gold trim hinted at wealth and prestige. Recalling her own days of running a shuttle to the Moon, she watched the ship make a tidy docking and felt a sudden envy of its pilot. "Now that," she said, "is a pretty bird."

Kepler tossed her an amused glance, eyes crinkling, then turned to Wu. "Docking Control reports that every Rofan vessel at port has hailed the new arrival. No reply from the emissary."

Wu nodded and stroked his upper lip. "This could easily become the party of the year." His gaze seemed to travel past the station's image and seemed to rest on the young Rofa in the lounge area.

Jhaska sat beside Tigre, licking peach juice off its fingers. It still wore the borrowed Safety parka, and its narrow face appeared sleepy and contented.

Wu glanced at Kepler. "What about our little friend's ship, the *Qusho*? Are they still threatening to battle their way into Checkpoint?"

Kepler shrugged one shoulder. "Deputy DelRio has been talking to them. He's calmed them down, somewhat, but they still want to come fetch their child. They're demanding that we open the dock to them." He cleared his throat. "I suggest that Doctor DeFlora try talking to them. He seems to get along with the Rofan."

"Hmm." Wu took a sip of coffee and rocked back on his heels. "It's definitely worth considering. I suspect that the good doctor is just fierce enough to make a Rofan captain back down." Wu returned his attention to the holograph. "Funny, isn't it," he said in a preoccupied tone. "After a hundred years of being snubbed by the Legitimacy, we're suddenly honored with a visit."

Concha recalled that in the past, the Rofan Legitimacy had refused to acknowledge any communication from the World Council. Every query, plea, and warning met with a blank wall of silence. The only contact between Humans and Rofan that approached official status was the meetings of Port Authority deputies with freighter captains.

She tried to follow Wu's thoughts, wondering what he saw in the emissary's visit. The Rofan and the Phi-Nurians were the only oxygen breathers who traded with Earth, and suddenly both governments sent official representatives. *We even have a Jadamii*, she thought wryly.

A deep uneasiness took hold of Concha. Councillor Weber was meeting with the Phi-Nurian delegation, and she wondered if the Rofan emissary would join the meeting.

Wu continued to study the emissary's ship, thoughtfully rocking from heel to toe. "Our friend from the Legitimacy," he said finally. "It hasn't talked to anyone?"

Kepler shook his gray head emphatically. "No one. Not even during docking. It handled the whole procedure via computer."

"Strange." Wu finished his coffee. "Did Docking Control notify the emissary that it would have to remain on board until we reopened the dock?"

Kepler shrugged. "Yes, but even that didn't raise a response."

"More strangeness." Wu glanced at Concha. "Most self-respecting Rofan would have been enraged by such news."

Concha glanced at the ship beside the emissary's and found the familiar, blocky shape of an Earth freighter. Startled, she pointed. "The Phi-Nurians came in this? An old, BRD light cargo transport?"

Kepler looked up at her, his expression glum. "They said they wanted something inconspicuous."

"Oh," Concha murmured without thinking. "Maybe that's why they wanted Bailey. To make repairs, or something."

Kepler tilted his head. "Pardon?"

Concha shrugged. "Bailey—Professor Rye—designed the BRD. Did you know that? He was only four, and he—"

Wu raised his brows at Kepler. "It seems that Bailey Rye is aboard the Phi-Nurian diplomats' ship."

Concha shifted uneasily. "Jardín and Rife told me that Bailey works for Councillor Weber. And that he asked to be smuggled aboard the Phi-Nurian ambassadors' ship."

Wu blew out his cheeks. "They lied to you. Bailey most definitely does not work for the World Council." He smiled grimly. "And though our young genius doesn't have the common sense God gave a rabbit, I doubt he'd place himself at the mercy of Phi-Nurians. He's an idiot, but he's not stupid."

Kepler raised a forestalling hand. "Wait a minute," he protested. "Are you saying—?" He looked back and forth between Wu and Concha. "What are you saying? That Their Excellencies are holding Bailey hostage?"

Wu raised his brows. "Well, it's just a hypothesis. At the moment, however, it's all we have."

Concha gripped her coffee cup in both hands, her mind racing. She recalled her earlier work with Rachel, and the sound of Bailey's recorded voice, carefully enunciating the words of the arraignment in Farnii. "Warden, what if—" She gestured helplessly. "What if Bailey has his own agenda regarding the Jadamii?"

Wu pressed the palms of his hands together, eyes narrowing in thought. "Oh, dear," he sighed. "This is all beginning to make horrible sense."

Kepler, still looking doubtful, reached for a headset. "Shall I contact Deputy Jimanez-Verde's office?"

"Please do." Wu clasped his hands behind his back. "Have a priority advisement relayed to Lois the instant she leaves the meeting. Also obtain a permit to search Their Excellencies' ship."

Kepler nodded. "Right away." He pulled on the headset and tapped in a code on his console.

Wu crossed to an unmanned console and set down his coffee cup. Then he took off his parka, hung it over the chair, and sat down. His eyes were bright as he brought the console out of standby mode.

Concha followed Wu. "Do you really think Bailey's in danger?"

Wu tapped in a string of commands. "I think it's a possibility we can't afford to ignore." He smiled up at her. "Let me show you something." He keyed in a long code, and a new image shimmered down from an overhead projector. The life-sized holograph displayed a teenaged youth dressed in the traditional garments of a Northern Freeholder: patchwork kimono, a collection of bright scarves, and a cloak called a *jude*.

Concha gazed at the image. "Is that Bailey?"

Wu leaned back in the chair and folded his arms. "Yup. From the first time we met."

Concha noted that, even as a youth, Bailey did not possess the well-fed face and figure that constituted his culture's ideal of masculine beauty. Though his hair was not yet dyed an unnatural shade of orange, adolescence exaggerated characteristics that were already unusual. His spare body seemed mostly leg, and his convex profile made his face appear camel-like.

Bailey spread his hands in a questioning gesture and waggled his long, tapering fingers. "Turn around?" he asked someone off camera. He slowly spun in a move from an old folk dance, arms waving like the windblown branches of a tree. He laughed, teeth flashing white against bronze skin. "There," he said in a mischievous tone. "How was that?"

Wu froze the image and pointed to a wide, woven band around Bailey's sinewy wrist. "Still wearing the same rag bracelet."

Concha nodded and continued to study the holograph. Wu had stopped the motion at a point that locked Bailey's limbs in awkward angles and turned his smile into a contorted grimace.

A deep chill invaded Concha, and she suddenly pictured Bailey as a victim of a violent accident. *What if the Phi-Nurians hurt him?* She restlessly drummed her nails against her coffee cup. "Can't we do something?" she asked.

Wu glanced up at her. "You mean break onto the ship, guns ablaze, and rescue the lad? I'd love to, but I'm afraid they'd kill him." His smile turned tight. "We'll have to be sneaky."

Kepler, at his console, hastily pulled off his headset and whirled around. "Wu. They've left *Gaia's Love*. Deputy Jimanez-Verde, the World Council committee, and the Phi-Nurian ambassadors are all on their way to Checkpoint detention."

Wu climbed to his feet, a malevolent glitter in his eyes. "How delightful. Let's go welcome our guests, hmm?"

Concha glanced nervously around the detention area, but she did not see Jardín and Rife. She relaxed fractionally, relieved she did not have to face Jardín's unnerving stare.

The Phi-Nurians in the cell seemed calmer. They no longer frantically paced or complained, but buzzed in quiet conversation. The cell's white tile floor was covered in

dung. Someone had sprayed the air with citrus-scented de-
odorizer, but Concha still detected a stink like dog feces.

Wu positioned himself in a corner, wearing an odd little
smile of anticipation. He pulled out his pistol and adjusted
the setting, then returned the weapon to its holster with a
confident pat.

Human and Phi-Nurian voices echoed in the hall that led
from the lifts. Concha's pulse picked up speed, and she
moved to stand beside Wu. "Wish Rachel were here,"
she muttered.

Wu kept his gaze fixed upon the doorway, but he chuckled softly. "Me, too."

Gold rank Deputy Lois Jimanez-Verde strolled into the
detention area, leading a procession of Human and Phi-
Nurian diplomats. The head of Port Authority was in her
mid-eighties but wore her white hair in a close-cropped
style favored by much younger women.

Five Phi-Nurians stalked in behind her, their clawed feet
clattering on the tile floor. Unlike others of their species,
the diplomats wore clothing. Long-sleeved garments in
shades of green and brown encased their crablike bodies.
Intrigued, Concha wondered if the attire was intended as a
compliment to Humans. *Or maybe it's just to keep their
dung off the floor.*

The World Council committee followed last, two men
and two women, most looking exhausted and uneasy. The
exception was Councilior Weber.

Even after a grueling round of meetings, Glee Weber
appeared immaculately groomed and elegantly composed. She wore her shining hair swept back in a bun,
which was still perfectly in place. Her makeup looked
fresh, and her expression was set in an unfailing smile.
She gave every appearance of matching her public relations profile; and Concha, even though she knew better,
longed to cast herself upon the councillor's fabled compassion. She stepped forward when Councilior Weber
glanced her way, but her employer's eyes looked past her
without recognition.

Feeling miserable, Concha stepped back to Wu's side.

Lois made a slow gesture, indicating their surroundings.
"This is Safety's detention area." She spoke Trade, and her

tone was unruffled. "Ambassador Pikros, please identify the individual you seek."

The leader of the Phi-Nurian diplomats wordlessly marched up to the cell and peered in. The detainees fell silent and became motionless.

Concha found herself holding her breath. She thought the cell's occupants seemed afraid of Pikros; too afraid to allow their primitive "under-minds" to throw them into a frenzy. Beside her, Wu casually rested his hands on his gun belt.

Pikros returned to Lois. "I grow weary of your pretenses," it buzzed harshly. "You know the one we want is not here."

Councillor Weber stepped forward. "With all due respect, we've been through this argument before. If Your Excellency will only describe to us in plain language—"

Pikros cut in. "Unnecessary. You have full knowledge of the one we want. Stop denying it."

Councillor Weber's manicured brows lifted in a show of gracious surprise. "I'm telling the truth. I have no idea for whom you are looking."

Wu cleared his throat. "Excuse me," he said cheerfully. "Lois, may I speak?"

Pikros reared back in obvious affront and turned to Lois. "Who is that person?"

Lois smiled at the assemblage, an unreadable expression in her eyes. "Your Excellencies, allow me to present Wu Jackson, warden of Earth Port Safety."

Wu made a deep and very proper bow. "I'll be brief: I know who you're looking for."

Concha, though startled, kept her face blank. She was entirely unable to tell if he were bluffing or not.

Weber and the other councillors exchanged baffled glances. Pikros approached Wu, mandibles clicking in agitation. "Then I demand that you deliver this person to me at once."

Wu smiled sweetly. "No."

Pikros waved all four of its clawed hands in the air. "This is an outrage!"

"Not at all. I simply see no benefit in granting your request."

"You are placing at risk," Pikros warned, "the continued goodwill of our species."

"Oh, I doubt it." Wu rocked back on his heels. "Your species needs us. You've built your economy upon Earth's trade, and you don't dare lose our patronage. Everyone knows that." His tone turned thin. "And besides, from the Human point of view, the behavior of you and your companions does not seem motivated by goodwill. You have performed an action that we construe as hostile."

Pikros froze for a moment. "What action?" it asked warily.

Wu's eyes narrowed, and his grin widened. "You *know* what you did."

Terrified by Pikros' close proximity, Concha struggled to maintain her neutral expression.

Pikros' buzzing voice lost its arrogant edge and became placating. "A lamentable misunderstanding. We assumed that, since the creature arrived as a gift from the World Council, we were free to do with it as we wished."

Councillor Weber seemed ready to interrupt, but Lois made a warning gesture. The councillor subsided, looking dissatisfied.

Concha's breath caught in her throat. *Bailey. They mean Bailey.*

Wu nodded. "Most lamentable," he agreed. "It occurs to me that an emissary from the Rofan Legitimacy has just arrived in Port. Perhaps it would be more to my benefit to offer the person you want to the emissary?"

"No, no, no!" Pikros abandoned its quiet tone. "You fool, you don't know what such an action would precipitate. As we speak, Jada and Igsha Reey are poised on the brink of interstellar war."

Again, Councillor Weber seemed ready to speak, but Lois waved her to silence.

"Oh, really?" Wu asked brightly. "Interstellar war? Why should I believe you?"

Pikros slipped all four of its clawed hands into the sleeves of its garment and seemed to try for an air of dignity. "I refuse to bandy words with you. I demand that you immediately hand over Meris of Jada."

Wu shook his head. "Ambassador, you're in no position

to make demands. Return Bailey Rye to me, alive and un-injured. Then, maybe, I'll consider negotiating with you." His hands tightened on his gun belt. "Remember that you're at a disadvantage."

Pikros pulled two of its hands from the concealing sleeves. One hand held a short-barreled gun. "Perhaps," it said, aiming the gun at Wu's head, "you are mistaken."

Chapter Eighteen

THE PHI-NURIAN'S tone turned silken. "Perhaps," it said, "you are the one at a disadvantage." Pikros' grip on the gun remained firm; its aim at Wu's head unwavering. "This unsightly knob atop your body . . . it encases your brain, does it not?"

Concha froze, scarcely daring to breathe. Anything, she knew, might startle Pikros into firing. From the corner of her eye, she saw the four members of the World Council exchange panicked glances. *Don't*, she begged them silently. *Don't say a word.*

The Phi-Nurians in the cell cowered against the far wall. The four members of Pikros' diplomatic party stood in a cluster, clawed hands opening and closing restlessly. Clearly fearless, Lois watched everything from her place in the center of the room.

Wu's stance also seemed relaxed and confident. His shoulders were straight, and his hands rested lightly on his gun belt. His eyes sparkled with an odd amusement as he studied the Phi-Nurian's weapon. "What is that thing?" he asked casually. "It can't be a hand cannon, because we scanned you for those when you debarked."

Pikros reared its crablike body into a fully upright position. "Your inadequate equipment could not detect a weapon such as this."

"No energy fields, I suppose." Wu's tone was purely conversational, as if he were alone in the room with Pikros.

"Looks a little like an old-fashioned projectile gun. What's it fire?"

Pikros' voice turned unabashedly boastful. "Metal pellets."

"Primitive."

"Effective."

Wu grinned suddenly. "It would have to be. No Phi-Nurian can hit the wide side of a Kamian tanker without the aid of a targeting scope."

"From this proximity," Pikros buzzed, "I doubt I will miss."

Concha's pulse pounded in her ears. She could not grasp Wu's motive for taunting an armed Phi-Nurian. *He's practically dared it to shoot.* She flicked her gaze around the detention area. Six staffers were all that Wu could spare from the crises-ridden outer docks. They stood near the doorways, faces tense. One staffer, the brawny Chen, held a drawn stinger.

Wu slowly released his grip on his gun belt. The fingers on his right hand subtly flexed with a quality of anticipation. "It doesn't matter," he said calmly. "You're outnumbered. Pull that trigger, and you'll die."

The party of Phi-Nurian diplomats stirred edgily. Councillor Weber shifted and drew a breath to speak. Lois frowned a warning to remain silent. The councillor obeyed, her perpetual smile slipping away into an expression of frustration.

Pikros clicked its mandibles. "If I die, I will not be alone in death. This gun contains twenty rounds of ammunition. In a room such as this, full of your tender-bodied species, there is no need for a targeting scope." It gestured broadly with its middle set of limbs, and its tone became conciliatory. "But, come, be reasonable. Count the cost. All that we require is the release of Meris of Jada into our custody. Threatening each other serves no purpose."

Pursing his lips, Wu seemed to consider Pikros' words. "What about the Human aboard your ship? Will you release him unharmed?"

Pikros' buzzing voice softened to a purr. "Of course."

"Oh—" Wu sighed, and his shoulders slumped. "Very well. You win. We'll give you Meris."

Concha fought to keep her expression neutral. *What the hell are you doing?*

Pikros' claws snapped in obvious excitement. "Then surrender Meris at once." Its buzzing voice turned harsh and exultant. "At once! At once!"

Wu's eyes glinted. "We have Meris in a highly restricted area of the station. A place where no Phi-Nurian may enter. I'll send some of my people to bring Meris to you. Then—"

"No!" Pikros interrupted scornfully. "I hold the gun. I am the one who decides where we shall and shall not go. And I say that you shall take us to Meris."

Concha tensed, suddenly understanding that Wu had manipulated the Phi-Nurian into making its rash choice. He was trying to separate the hostile aliens from Lois and the councillors, but such a maneuver would place him in an extremely risky position. *Careful.*

"Take you?" Wu repeated doubtfully. "It's a terrible breach of procedure, but I suppose I have no choice.

"No." Pikros gestured with its gun. "You do not."

Councillor Weber whirled toward Lois. Her colleagues reached to restrain her, but she shouldered away their hands. "Deputy," she barked, "I protest—!"

Pikros jumped, clearly startled. It spun toward the councillor.

Everything seemed to happen in an instant.

A loud crack split the air, like the close report of thunder. Councillor Weber fell backward against a wall. Her mouth flew open in shock. Bright red blood splattered over her chin.

Concha felt as if time stopped. She stood frozen, staring, trying to make sense of what she saw. There was a ragged hole in the councillor's chest, torn flesh tangled with shredded clothing. Realization jolted through Concha. *It shot Glee!*

At the same moment, a powerful blow struck Concha's side and flung her to the floor. The hard tiles jarred every bone in her body. For a panic-stricken second, she thought she also had been shot. A flash of blue and green caught the edge of her sight, and she realized that Wu had pushed her from the line of fire.

A man screamed, voice cracking. Terror jerked along

Concha's nerves. She scrambled into a crouch and glanced around at the flurry of movement.

Two of the committee, blind to danger, rushed to kneel beside the fallen Councillor Weber. A staffer shoved her way in between Lois and the Phi-Nurians. Other staffers drew their stingers. The detainees in their cell huddled motionless and silent, still too frightened to fall into a frenzy.

In a movement too rapid for Concha's eyes to follow, Wu drew his laser pistol. "Freeze!" he ordered.

Pikros whipped toward Wu, gun raised.

Wu fired point-blank at Pikros' midsection. Hissing light scorched the air.

Concha expected to see the Phi-Nurian collapse. Instead, Pikros waved its claws in triumph. "Your paltry energy weapons will have no effect upon me," it buzzed. It once again aimed its gun at Wu's head. Its voice turned frenzied, irrational. "I shall kill you! Kill you, kill you!"

In a flash, Concha saw why the Phi-Nurians wore clothing. "Shields!" she called. "They've got shields!"

Wu was already moving as she spoke. He gripped the claw that held the gun and jerked it toward the ceiling. At the same time, he brought his pistol butt down in a hammer blow on the dull gray organ that served as Pikros' eye.

The Phi-Nurian's six limbs jerked in spasms, and it toppled over backward. Thick, black matter from the eye slopped onto the floor. The limbs went rigid. Pikros lay motionless.

Numb with shock, Concha stared at the body. *It's dead. He killed it.*

The four remaining members of the ambassador's party all pulled guns from their sleeves.

All over the room, staffers scrambled to place themselves between the committee and the Phi-Nurians. Wu stood firm. He held Pikros' captured weapon in both hands, and his round face wore a grim expression. "Drop your guns," he ordered. "Or I'll shoot."

The Phi-Nurians froze in seeming indecision.

Wu raised the gun, elbows straight. "I'm not bluffing, so don't try me. I've got nineteen rounds left, and I don't need a targeting scope."

For a moment, Concha thought they would surrender.

But from the cell, one captive Phi-Nurian burst into a loud stream of buzzing noise.

As a group, the ambassadorial party whirled and opened fire on the detainees. The first victim seemed to explode in a splash of black blood; fragments of its limbs and carapace flew in every direction.

Concha screamed in horror, but could not hear her own voice over the roar of weapons.

Still moving in unison, the ambassadors turned and bolted toward the door that led to Checkpoint's offices, firing as they ran.

With an oath, Wu flung himself to the floor and rolled into a crouch. Arms rigid, he swung his aim to follow the Phi-Nurian's retreat. He fired, and the gun roared. The shot struck the foot of a fleeing Phi-Nurian, and its claw burst into tarry fragments. The alien stumbled and dropped down to its middle set of limbs. It fired wildly over its shoulder.

A staffer took the shot in his thigh. He spun into a fall, his leg laid open like an anatomical cross section.

The Phi-Nurians scrabbled down the hallway toward Checkpoint offices, firing behind them to prevent pursuit.

Concha's breath came in ragged gasps, but her mind raced ahead of her fear. She realized that the Phi-Nurians were bearing down upon a handful of unarmed medics.

Wu rushed toward the door. "Chen, get everyone out of here," he ordered. "The rest of you, follow me. Keep low." He dived into the hall.

Concha scrambled after him, thinking only that she needed to help.

A staffer near Concha gripped her shoulder and pulled her toward the wall. "Hey," he hissed in protest. "Stay back. You're unarmed."

Irritated, she shook his hand off. "So are you."

Shots rang out ahead of them, and a man gave a staccato cry of agony.

Concha's breath caught in her throat, and she looked down the hall.

Wu had reached the end where it branched into two directions. Gripping the Phi-Nurian gun in both hands, he edged around the corner to his left, into Checkpoint's monitor area. Concha expected him to order the aliens to drop their weapons. Instead, he opened fire, squeezing off three rapid shots.

The Phi-Nurians returned fire. Bits of the wall and ceiling near Wu burst into dust.

Wu flung himself back around the corner. "They're coming!"

The Phi-Nurians charged past the end of the hall with the ear-shattering roar of weaponry.

The wall beside Concha took a peppering, and it exploded into splinters of plasti-board. Acting on pure instinct, she tucked herself into a shoulder roll.

A woman shouted from nearby. Concha pulled herself into a crouch and wildly glanced around.

Three Phi-Nurians clattered down the hall's right branch, heading into the complex of offices and meeting rooms.

Wu sprinted after them, along with two of his staffers. The other two staffers rushed into the monitor area to the left. Heart lurching, Concha followed them.

A Phi-Nurian lay on the floor in front of the brewer, its six limbs still jerking in death spasms. Black blood spotted the tile all around it.

In the lounge area in the far corner, a young medic peered out from behind a chair. Her eyes were wide and blank with shock.

Kepler sat on the floor, slumped against the main monitor console. His breath came in gasps, and he clutched his bleeding shoulder in one hand. His gaze rolled to Concha. "Secure—" His voice broke, and he grimaced in pain.

From the other side of Checkpoint came the roar of gunfire and Human cries of agony and terror. Concha's blood turned to ice.

One of the staffers slapped her partner's arm. "Come on," she shouted. "Let's go!"

They both ran toward the battle.

Frantically, Concha called after them. "Wait! I need—!"

Kepler struggled to pull himself straight. "Secure— Have to—"

Concha scrambled to his side. She could not believe the staffers had left her alone with a wounded man. *Damn them*, she swore silently. *Idiots! Damn them, damn them, damn them!* Like a still life from another place and time,

Wu's empty coffee cup sat on the monitor's control board. His blue and green parka still hung over the chair. She snatched it free and hastily bundled one sleeve into a pad. "Medic!"

Blood welled up over Kepler's fingers and spread through his uniform tunic in a growing stain. She pulled his hand away and pressed the makeshift pad against his torn shoulder. Kepler, eyes squeezed shut, gnashed his teeth in agony. Concha maintained firm pressure. She was no expert, but she knew he was losing blood fast. "Hey!" she shouted, her voice cracking like a whip with fear and desperation. "We need a medic! Fast!"

Kepler grabbed her wrist, his fingers sticky with his own blood. "Secure area." His voice was hoarse. He nodded toward a headset that lay on the floor just out of reach. "Tell . . . secure area." He feebly shook her wrist. "Hurry!"

Concha was unsure of the procedure he ordered, but she was positive she did not want to release the pressure on his wound. "It's all right." She was surprised at the confidence in her own voice. "Wu is handling everything."

Tigre slid into a crouch by Kepler's side. The front of his lavender tunic was wrinkled and smudged with red, as if someone had clenched it in a bloody fist. His fine-boned, beautiful face was serene. "Ah, yes," he said softly. "Let's see what we have here."

For a moment, Concha simply stared at him in equal parts of surprise and relief.

A senior medic dressed in blue knelt beside Concha and placed her hands on the makeshift pad. "I'll take over."

Coming to herself, Concha backed away to get out of the doctor's light. Kepler seemed unaware of Tigre and the medic. He kept his gaze on Concha and nodded weakly toward the headset. "Tell—" He swallowed. "Tell Environment . . . seal area." His eyes seemed feverishly bright. "Secure—"

Concha raised her hands in a calming gesture. "It's all right. I'll take care of it," she promised. "You let Doctor DeFlora help you. Okay?"

The opposite end of Checkpoint was ominously silent. Feeling exposed, Concha cautiously rose to her feet, crept to where the headset lay, and picked it up.

From the new angle, she could see the floor behind the desks. A few yards away, a staffer lay on her side, staring at Concha. It was Shoko, who had found peaches for Jhaska. She lay with her head on her arm, her body relaxed.

Concha, glad to see someone she knew, drew a breath to speak. Then she noticed that the back of Shoko's head was the wrong shape, and that bloody clots filled her hair. Her brown eyes were dull. Blood brimmed in the cup of her ear.

Tears blurred Concha's vision, and she gagged. She whirled toward the doctor and tried to voice a cry for help.

Tigre seemed to sense her gaze and glanced over his shoulder. Concha, mouth working noiselessly, pointed to Shoko. Tigre's expression remained calm. He silently shook his head and returned his attention to Kepler.

Concha's heart sank. She understood Tigre's refusal. *He's already seen her. She's beyond help.*

The headset in Concha's hand chirped. A man on the other end spoke in a rising tone of worry. ". . . respond, Kepler. Checkpoint, are you there?"

Feeling numb, she pulled on the headset. "Checkpoint."

The man made a weak little noise of relief. "Who is this? Is this Shoko?"

"I—" Tears welled up again. Concha had to swallow.

The man's voice grew tight. "Checkpoint? What's going on? Talk to me, Checkpoint. Someone punched in an emergency code."

"This is Concha Singh." She glanced down at her coveralls and found them smudged with blood and dusted with plasti-board powder. "Deputy Ajmani's temporary aide."

"This is Rudy Sheng, Environmental Control. What's going on over there?"

Near the lounge, a medic knelt beside an injured colleague, holding his hand and murmuring encouragement. In front of the brewer, the Phi-Nurian's body lay still and rigid. "We have a crisis in progress. Kepler wants you to secure the area immediately."

"Well," Rudy said doubtfully, "what area? I'm afraid I need specifics. Is Kepler there?"

A Human shout echoed from across the hall, followed by a blast of gunfire. Heart skipping, Concha ducked down behind the monitor's bulky console. "Checkpoint! Secure Checkpoint now!"

Rudy cleared his throat. "You sure about that? It'll cut you off from help for about thirty minutes. The fail-safes, you know."

Phi-Nurian claws rattled up the hallway. "I kill," it buzzed. "I kill! I kill!"

Concha's mind raced in circles. The thirty-minute time lag, she knew from research, was built into the station's system to prevent massive depressurization. If she ordered the area sealed, she locked them all in with the Phi-Nurians. *Kepler's orders,* she reminded herself. "Seal Checkpoint," she said. "Do it!"

A single Phi-Nurian burst into the monitor area. "I kill!" Its voice was discordant with frenzied exaltation. "I kill!"

Concha hazarded a glance from around the console. Kepler, Nothando, and Tigre sat on the floor in plain sight. They had nowhere to take cover.

The Phi-Nurian charged up to them. Mandibles flexing in excitement, it reared up on its back two legs. "I shall kill three Humans." It raised its gun. "Kill!"

Tigre flung himself over his patient. "No!"

Without a second thought, Concha leaped to her feet and threw the headset at the Phi-Nurian. The light, plastic item struck close to its eyepad. The Phi-Nurian scuttled back a few steps.

Wu's coffee mug sat on the console's control board, within easy reach. She snatched it up and pitched it at the Phi-Nurian. "Leave them alone!"

The heavy ceramic mug hit the eyepad squarely. The soft, gray tissue immediately darkened as if bruised. Shrieking like tortured metal, the Phi-Nurian clumsily wheeled around to flee. It started toward the hall that led to the detention area. Its gun went off and blew a hole in a nearby wall twice the size of a dinner plate.

In an instant, Concha recalled the people in the detention area, the head of Port Authority and the wounded staffer. "Oh, no," she muttered. She grabbed up the monitor's chair. "Hey, you!" She had to keep the Phi-Nurian distracted until Tigre and the others found cover. "Stay right there."

The Phi-Nurian whipped around. It weaved as it stood, as if it tried to bring her into focus with its injured eye. Panting, Concha charged forward with the chair raised high. She closed the distance between them in three long strides.

The Phi-Nurian brought up its gun.

Concha swung the chair like a bat, putting all her strength into the blow.

The Phi-Nurian jerked backward, and the chair missed it entirely.

Off-balance, Concha struggled to redirect her swing.

The Phi-Nurian fired.

Concha felt the chair ripped from her hands in an explosion of plastic splinters. She twisted her face away, protecting her eyes.

The alien caught her arm and shoulder in two of its clawed hands. "Caught you!" it buzzed. "Kill you!"

Concha struggled to tear free from its crushing grip. "I won't let you hurt them," she said through gritted teeth. She did not care that her words made no sense, that she was the intended victim. She repeated the phrase over and over, raising her voice in a defiant chant, twisting, jerking, and kicking. "I won't let you hurt them! I won't let you hurt them!"

The Phi-Nurian shook her like a rag. Her head snapped back and forth. Unconsciousness threatened, and dancing pinpoints of light filled her vision.

It flung her away. Concha spun helplessly and tumbled to the floor, momentarily blinded. Her hands encountered a fabric-covered bulk. An acrid stink assaulted her nose, and Concha realized she had landed near the dead Phi-Nurian.

The sound of running Human feet pounded the air. On her hands and knees, Concha looked up to see two staffers dash into the area from the direction of Checkpoint's offices. A wave of desperate relief washed over her.

The Phi-Nurian whirled toward the staffers.

Concha frantically ripped the gun from the dead alien's claw. "No!" She held it in both hands, elbows straight, following Wu's example. The gun was heavier than it looked, and its handle felt greasy. "Don't move, or I'll shoot!"

Rearing up on its lower limbs, the Phi-Nurian clicked its

mandibles. "None shall be spared!" It raised its weapon, weaving to bring its victims into focus. "All shall die!"

The staffers made no move to take cover or defend themselves. In a flash of sudden horror, Concha recognized Jardín and Rife. They stood frozen, staring at their assailant, faces blank with shock.

Afraid that the Phi-Nurian would fire, Concha aimed at a spot on the wall far above where it stood. She recalled how Wu had disarmed the dockside sniper with a series of warning shots. Concha gritted her teeth and pulled the trigger. A loud crack split the air. The gun's recoil knocked her from her knees to her backside.

Fragments of the wall showered down, glittering on the alien's garb. "Die!" it buzzed. "You will die!" It jerked the barrel of its gun toward her and fired. Three blasts wildly swept the area, striking walls and lounge furniture.

Concha scrambled to her feet and took aim at the alien's midsection. Tigre and the others were in point-blank range, and she knew she had to disarm it. *It may not miss next time.* "Drop your weapon," she commanded. "Throw it down on the floor, or I'll kill you."

The Phi-Nurian hesitated, mandibles flexing. "You don't have a targeting scope," it pointed out.

"I don't need one," she replied. She braced her arms to fire. "Hold the gun, and you die. Throw it down, and you live. Decide!"

The Phi-Nurian's middle set of limbs went limp. It tossed down its weapon with obvious reluctance. "Live," it buzzed sullenly. "I want to live."

Braids flying, Jardín leaped for the surrendered weapon. Before Concha realized the other woman's intention, Jardín snatched up the gun and whirled toward the Phi-Nurian.

The alien shrank against the wall.

Tigre, from his place on the floor, flung out his hand in entreaty. "No! Don't!"

Jardín fired.

The blast swept away the bruised eyepad and the powerful mandibles. Black Phi-Nurian blood and tissues spattered the wall. Limbs jerking horridly, the body slumped to the floor.

Rife stared at the murdered alien. "Jardín—"

Jardín grabbed his wrist and yanked him toward the hall.
"Come on!"

A chill fury seized Concha. She redirected her aim at
Jardín. "Stop. You're not going anywhere."

"Oh, no?" Jardín paused, her expression challenging.
"Go ahead. Kill me. I dare you." She spread her arms,
offering herself as a target. "I've given you permission.
Do it."

Rife tore his gaze from the Phi-Nurian with obvious effort and looked at his companion. "Jardín—" His voice
quavered. "Jardín, what are you doing? This wasn't—this
isn't part of the plan."

In the room behind Concha, the brewer went into a heating cycle, purring away as if everything were normal. From
his place by the monitor console, Kepler made a breathless
noise of pain. Someone near the lounge area vomited in a
series of choking hiccups.

Concha's entire body ached. The gun seemed an increasingly heavy weight to support with her rigid arms, and the
muscles in her narrow shoulders burned with strain. She
kept her attention riveted upon Jardín, wondering why Environmental Control had not sealed off Checkpoint.

Jardín studied Concha. "You can't do it, can you?" A
chilly smile spread over her delicate features. "You don't
have the nerve to shoot me." She made a noise of contempt. "Weak. Just like all the rest."

His battered face lined with anxiety, Rife made an attempt to pull his arm from his partner's grasp. "Jardín,
we need—" He swallowed and his tone became pleading.
"Please. The ship, Jardín, let's go." He turned his frantic
gaze to Concha. "You have to help us."

"Shut up, Rife." Jardín's voice held a poisonous tone.
"Just shut up."

Concha thought she saw an opportunity to stall the two
until help arrived. "What are you talking about?" She met
Rife's gaze, trying to look earnest. "What ship?"

From around the corner of the hall to Checkpoint offices,
a flash of blue and green caught Concha's eye.

Wu glided soundlessly into the monitor area. His uniform
was liberally splashed with blood, and one sleeve appeared
to be soaked. Blood plastered his hair to his forehead and
striped the left half of his face.

He held a drawn stinger in his hand, rather than a Phi-Nurian gun, and all three of the stinger's charge lights glowed amber, indicating it was set to deliver a debilitating shock. Wu's expression was alert, predatory.

Concha flicked her gaze back to Rife and hoped she had not betrayed Wu's presence. *Need to keep up the distraction.*

Rife's eyes took on a feverish glaze. "An escape ship. Ready to go. Help us, and we'll let you come along."

Wu continued his stealthy approach toward Jardín and Rife from behind.

Concha cleared her throat, fighting to keep her tone neutral. "I still don't understand."

Jardín giggled suddenly. The uncharacteristic laughter made Concha's stomach turn cold. "I'm not leaving until the job is done. Until I've taken care of that Jadamii."

Wu silently picked his way through chunks of plasti-board and the shattered remains of the chair. He positioned himself behind and to the side of Jardín and Rife, so that Tigre and the others were out of his line of fire. He spoke in a calm, everyday voice. "Her name is Meris."

Jardín jumped like startled cat. She whirled toward him, trying to keep everyone in sight. Rife stared at Wu, frozen in surprise.

Wu's dark eyes glinted from his mask of blood, but his tone became peculiarly gentle. "Meris. Just so that you know that you're planning to murder a person."

Jardín raised her captured gun. "I don't care what you call it," she replied sweetly. "It has to die. And I'm the only one with the courage to take action."

Wu tilted his head. Fresh blood trickled from his scalp and rolled down his face like tears. "There are many kinds of courage, my dear. The Rofan call their greatest act of bravery *eykhrru-rru*, which is submitting to the inevitable. We Humans call ours 'self-sacrifice.'"

Jardín drew her brows down. "What are you babbling about?"

"Sorry," Wu said softly. "I guess you would have to be Human to understand." He whipped his stinger up, aiming at Jardín.

Rife gasped and threw himself between Jardín and Wu. "No!"

At the same instant, Jardín fired.

A loud crack shattered the air. The blast caught Rife in the back. A corona of blood flew from the wound, and the front of his shirt bellied out like a sail full of wind. Rife's brown eyes went wide with shock and reproach. Blood erupted from his mouth as he pitched forward into Wu.

Jardín immediately spun on her heels and bolted toward the detention area.

Concha's awareness returned like the slap of icy water. She raced forward in pursuit.

Jardín flew ahead of her down the hall, arms pumping and braids bouncing. Concha's longer legs gave her the advantage. She began to close the distance.

Abruptly, the lights in Checkpoint pulsed off and on. The next second, the clangorous sound of an alarm bell spilled through the air. Concha recognized the signal for emergency containment procedures. She had only thirty seconds before the section partitions closed.

At the doorway to the detention area, Jardín turned and took aim.

Narrow lips compressed, Concha stopped. She gripped the gun in both hands and fired three times into the wall beside Jardín. Plasti-board exploded in a glittering cloud of dust and needle-sharp splinters.

Jardín flung herself away from the stinging debris, shrieking like a panther. Concha dived forward. She grabbed Jardín by one shoulder and spun her around. "All right, you." She shoved the muzzle of her gun into the soft flesh under Jardín's chin. "It's time you learned your limits."

Jardín gazed up at her, eyes bright and fearless. Her dainty mouth twisted into a smile, and she raised the gun in her hand to Concha's head. "You better pull that trigger. Because I don't have limits."

Concha's heart lurched, and her grip tightened on the gun's greasy handle. She looked straight into Jardín's eyes. *Do it,* she ordered herself. *Do it!*

"Too late," Jardín said. She squeezed the trigger. An impotent click sounded in Concha's ear.

Jardín's smirk vanished.

Checkpoint's lights pulsed again and the alarm changed to a buzzer. Concha recognized the warning that the section seals were about to close.

With a strength belied by her size, Jardín jerked herself free and swung her empty gun like a club.

The blow caught Concha on her burned cheekbone. Pain exploded like a white light behind her eyes. She fell to her knees.

Jardín ripped the gun from her hand. Wildly, Concha snatched after it. "No!"

Jardín made a contemptuous noise and sprinted away into the detention area.

The hallway spun in dizzying circles. Pain induced a spasm of nausea. Concha gagged, and a burning thread of bile rose in her throat. She swallowed hard and climbed to her feet. She had to stop Jardín. *Had the chance. Should've shot her.*

Clenching her teeth against the pain in her head, Concha staggered into the detention area. The stench from the Phi-Nurian bodies was almost unendurable. Chunks of plasti-board debris soaked in puddles of red and black blood.

All alone, Chen stood in front of the sealed door that led to Station Central. His face was a landscape of frustrated anger.

Concha's heart fell. She braced herself against the wall, panting. "She's gone, isn't she? She got away."

Chen made a motion as if he prepared to kick the door, but stopped himself with obvious effort. "Yes." His voice was thick with self-disgust. "I let her run right past me."

Strong hands pulled Concha away from the wall and turned her around. Wu gripped both her shoulders and peered into her eyes. Blood ran down his face from his sticky hair. His uniform was so soaked with blood she could smell it. "Are you all right?" His voice was raw. "Did she hurt you?"

Wretchedly, Concha forced herself to meet his gaze. "I let her get away. I had the chance to shoot her, and I didn't do it." She swallowed. "She's going to Medica. She'll kill the detainee. She'll kill anyone who tries to stop her. And we're trapped in Checkpoint." She put her hands on Wu's shoulders, so that they stood in each other's clasp. He no longer seemed an enigma to her. His playful humor, his unrequited love for Rachel, and the way his ferocity was yoked to compassion, all seemed comfortingly familiar. "What are we going to do?"

Wu lifted just the corners of his mouth. "We shall do," he said softly, "as we must." He released her with a gentle pat and turned away.

Concha slumped against the wall and closed her eyes. She saw again Jardín's face with its rosebud mouth and delicate bones. A scorching anger rose up within her, and her pulse pounded in her ears. *Next time*, she vowed silently. *Next time, I'll kill her.*

CHAPTER NINETEEN

RACHEL JERKED awake from a deep sleep, her heart hammering. Splintered images from a nightmare flashed through her mind: the cramped hold of a ship, the tarp-enshrouded figure on the filthy floor.

Battling a sense of suffocation, Rachel pushed away the blanket and sat up. Sweat soaked her long hair and her rumpled uniform. She rubbed her forehead with a shaking hand and sighed. The nightmare was merely a holdover from the Tri-Omega, but she could not fathom her own strong reaction to the images. *Seems so real.*

Pain pulsed in her injured right foot, and all her joints felt gritty with fatigue. Grimacing, she carefully shifted to lean against the back of the sofa.

Tigre's homelike office seemed less cluttered. A pair of pants no longer decorated the washroom. The counter in the kitchen nook was free of Naranha cartons, and all the cups hung on a rack. Evidently, Tigre had tidied up, and she found it disconcerting to think of him silently clearing things away while she slept.

Rachel remembered her earlier discussion with him; his abrupt bursts of temper, his sly humor, and his moments of touching vulnerability. She liked the shrewd, measuring quality in his gaze and the unruffled manner with which he handled a crisis. She also, she decided, liked the way he never backed down from a fight. A slow smile spread across Rachel's face as she recalled her attempt to confront him while he treated her for the burn. *Sorry, Deputy, I can't talk now. I'm with a patient.*

A clock on the wall by the door read early morning, which meant she had slept for several hours. Wu's report, she judged, had undoubtedly reached Lois' desk. Once free of the XRC meeting, there was every possibility that Lois would suspend Wu. Rachel guessed that there was also a fair chance Lois might remove her from the Jadamii's case.

Rachel reached for the familiar weight of the phone in her pocket, intending to call for an update. She pulled out a canvas shoe. She stared at it for a blank moment, until she recalled handing her phone to the maintenance tech. Exasperation cleared her mind like a strong cup of coffee, and she shoved the shoe back into her pocket.

Glad that Tigre was not around to fuss, she carefully climbed to her feet. Keeping her injured heel off the floor, Rachel limped a few steps to the desk. Her heart pounded from the minor effort, and dozens of aches came alive all over her body. She looked for the phone, but the desk held only a small lamp and a globular fidget-toy filled with red crystals. It was logical, she realized, for Tigre to take his phone with him.

Although her burned foot throbbed, Rachel cautiously shifted more weight to it. The added pressure actually brought a little relief. She judged she could walk as far as Medica's main desk if she moved slowly. Once there, she would rest, use the phone, and make an informed plan.

The office door was about five steps away. Rachel gathered her strength. The last thing she wanted was for Tigre to return and discover her sprawled on the floor. Tightening her mouth in a grim smile, she limped to the door and opened it.

The hall outside seemed deserted. Rachel paused, leaning against the doorframe to catch her breath. The smell of antiseptics rose up from the gray floor tiles, and the odor of regeneration compounds filled the air. At the end of the hall to her left, sat Medica's desk. It appeared unstaffed at the moment, so there was no officious medic around to argue that she ought to be in bed.

As in most parts of the station, sturdy handrails lined the walls. Rachel gripped the nearest one and hobbled toward the desk. Burning pain erupted from her sore shoulder, rivaling the discomfort in her injured foot. Irritated by her body's protests, she drove herself to keep moving. *Just a bit stiff, that's all.*

Ahead of her, she noticed that the desk's chair was pushed back at an awkward angle, as if someone had left it in a hurry. She forced herself to a quicker pace, wondering if there were an emergency with the Jadamii.

From somewhere in Medica, a child abruptly shrieked. Rachel started violently. "What the—?"

The child burst into forlorn sobbing, and Rachel recalled the little girl with the bandaged forehead. *Saja Mead.* "Poor thing," she muttered.

Rachel limped to the end of the hall and paused in Medica's central area. From where she stood, she could see down the other two halls. She glanced around for medics and staffers, but Medica seemed empty. Saja's heartwrenching cries were the only sound. Rachel felt a touch of panic. *Where is everyone?*

"Tigre?" Rachel called softly. "Burke? Nothando?"

"Mama!" Saja wailed. "Mama!"

Muffled by a closed door, a man raised his voice in an angry shout. Rachel swung her head around, trying to determine his location. She could not make out the words, but she was positive she recognized Benjy's booming baritone.

"Hello?" Rachel listened, but no reply came. "Benjy?"

Saja's weeping echoed through the empty halls. Panting, Rachel limped toward the desk. A peculiar mingling of smells hung in the air. It reminded her of the repair docks and the familiar stink of coolants and hyper-fluids. She gripped the edge of the desk for support and looked for the phone.

It still sat on the counter, but the lower part of the handset was a singed puddle of melted plastics and components. At a complete loss, Rachel stared at the damage. It looked to her like a welder mishap. She drew her brows together. "What's going on?"

Saja's cries became a rhythmic keening, desperate and imploring. Rachel tore her gaze away from the phone and threw a wild glance up the hall. "Doctor DeFlora?" she called. "Tigre?" She waited two heartbeats for an answer, and then raised her voice to a dockside bellow. "Hey! Is anyone taking care of the baby?"

Saja screamed in raw terror. "Mama!"

Lashed by pity and a sudden sense of disaster, Rachel strode awkwardly up the central hall in the child's direction. "I'm coming, Saja." She tried to sound cheerful and reassuring. "Don't cry. Aunt Rachel's coming."

Pain lanced up from her injured foot, and she felt as if she had sand in all her joints. Grimly, she pushed herself to move faster.

From the other side of Medica, Benjy's deep shout echoed with one clear word, furious and terrified: "No!"

Heart lurching, Rachel froze.

A sharp explosion rocked the air.

Rachel whirled toward the sound. "Benjy!"

Behind her, Saja gave a long, high-pitched screech. Torn by indecision, Rachel glanced back at the child's room. "Damn!" She turned and broke into a limping run toward Saja.

The weeping seemed to grow louder as Rachel reached the door. Saja stood clutching the side of the crib. Her round face was creased with tragedy, and it streamed with tears. A bandage saturated with dark green regenerative agents stuck to her forehead. When she saw Rachel, she raised her little arms over her head. "Up!" she sobbed. "Up!"

Filled with compassion, Rachel limped to the crib and lifted Saja out. "I know, I know," she murmured. "It's scary to be all alone."

Saja's body felt tense, and her bare arms and legs were cold to the touch. Rachel pulled the blanket from the crib and wrapped it around her.

Benjy had sounded frightened. *What the hell could scare Benjamin Oso?* The explosion should have drawn help, but Rachel did not hear running feet or anyone calling medical orders. *Now I'm scared.*

Rachel smiled at Saja and patted her back. "There we go. Is that better?"

Saja regarded her rescuer with wide, brown eyes. Her sobbing turned to low moans of desperate relief. Rachel gently brushed back the wisps of silky hair that stuck to the little girl's cheeks. "Do you remember me, Saja? Hmm?" She kept her voice soft. "I'm Aunt Rachel. I live next door."

Saja's tear-filled gaze traveled over Rachel's face. Her weeping faded to hiccupping gasps.

Rachel carefully shifted her hold on the child so that her good leg took the extra weight. "What a big girl," she murmured. "What a big, brave girl you are." She checked Saja's diaper and was relieved to find it dry. "Oh, good."

A changing table beside the crib held a dispenser full of disposable wipes. Rachel pulled one out and dried Saja's wet face. "Doesn't that feel better?"

Saja studied Rachel with a grave expression of doubt. "Mama," she said. "Want Mama."

"I know you do, sweetie." She tugged the blanket to cover more of Saja's legs. "Let's go find Mama," she suggested briskly. She pulled out a few more wipes to take along and turned toward the door. *Let's go find anyone.*

There was a shadowy flicker of movement in the hallway, as if someone had quickly stepped away from the entrance. Rachel caught only a sense of mass and height. She paused. "Benjy?" There was no answer. Warily, she edged to the door. "Someone there?"

The hall outside was deserted. Rachel's skin prickled, and she pulled Saja closer. Equipment beeped from somewhere in Medica, but she heard no Human voices. Cautiously, she slipped out the door, keeping her back to the wall. If the Jadamii was loose, she knew the safest thing for Saja would be to get her out of Medica.

The child squirmed and made a noise of protest. Rachel bent her head to Saja's ear. "Shhh. We need to be quiet." Ignoring the pain in her foot, she sidled down the hall.

The lift lay just beyond the main desk, at the junction

of the three corridors. Cautiously, she approached the area.

Saja tugged at the badge on Rachel's sleeve. "Dis?" Her sweet voice echoed. "Dis?"

Hastily, Rachel pulled the badge from its magnetic holder and handed it to the child. "Shhh," she whispered. "You can hold this, but you need to be quiet. Okay?"

Saja accepted the badge with an air of wounded dignity, and she studied its blue and green enameled surface with halfhearted interest.

Hoping the child would stay occupied and silent, Rachel resumed her careful journey to the lift. The beeping equipment seemed to be located in the last room at the end of the hall. The door was open. Rachel knew it had been closed when she passed it on her way to Saja.

Rachel scowled in thought. She did not want to place Saja at risk, but she could not ignore the possibility that a friend might be lying unconscious in the room. Steeling herself, she crept to the door and glanced around.

The beeping issued from a monitor stationed beside a narrow examination table. Pillows and cushions were strewn over the floor, but the room was empty. Cold settled into Rachel's gut. Tigre, she recalled, had braced Meris on her side with cushions to ease the strain on her shoulder. *And now she's prowling through Medica.*

Rachel eased away from the door and leaned back against the wall. Her thoughts raced in wild circles. A few more steps would bring them to the end of the hall, the main desk, and the lift. She studied the open area, knowing that she did not have the strength for a sprint. *We'll be a slow-moving target, visible from every hallway.*

Saja abruptly burst into song, chirping wordless, staccato notes like a sparrow. Rachel's heart leaped into her throat. She hastily pressed her fingertips to the little girl's mouth. "Shh, shh, Saja!" she whispered urgently. "We have to be quiet."

Saja squirmed and twisted her face away. "No!"

Perspiration misted Rachel's upper lip. She renewed her hold on Saja and limped to the end of the hall, abandoning stealth.

The smell of burned plastics still hung in the air near

the desk. Rachel glanced down the other hallways. They appeared empty.

Teeth clenched, Rachel hobbled toward the lift, pushing herself for speed. Searing pain shot up from her foot, climbing the tendons in her leg and setting fire to her hip and lower back. Grimly, she concentrated on each awkward step. *Move,* she urged herself. *Keep moving.*

The melted plastic from the phone had congealed in sooty drips down the desk's front panel. Overhead, the mobile of pastel geometric shapes spun in serene self-orbit, powered by the warm draft of the air vent. Saja raised both hands, pointing. "Pree'y," she said in a tone of wonder. She patted Rachel's cheek, obviously trying to draw attention to her discovery. "See? Pree'y."

Rachel's breath came in dry rasps. "Yes, sweetie," she panted. "It's pretty."

A dark blot lay on the floor near the lift. At first, Rachel thought it was more melted plastic from the phone. As she limped closer, however, she noticed its cratered appearance. Raising her eyes from the floor, she saw the dark substance sandwiched between the lift doors. She shambled to a halt and stared. Someone had welded the doors shut.

Rachel's heart beat in slow, hard strokes, and sweat rolled down her face. For a moment, she studied the damage without moving. It was a neat job, she observed, done by someone who knew how to handle a particle beam. She glanced to the door of the emergency hatch, a few yards away, and found that it was welded shut also.

Saja tenderly daubed at Rachel's face with her blanket. Her wide eyes were filled with sympathy. "No cwy," she said earnestly. "No cwy."

Touched by the child's concern, Rachel smiled at her reassuringly. "I'm all right." Her voice was hoarse with exhaustion. "Aunt Rachel never cries."

"Oh," Saja said. She matter-of-factly offered the badge. "Dis."

"Thank you," Rachel whispered and absently dropped the enameled disk into her pocket. Trying to catch her breath, she returned her attention to the lift doors. She could not grasp the motivation for such an action, unless the Jadamii was more interested in vengeance than escape. *Doesn't make sense.*

Saja stirred restlessly. "Mama. Want Mama."

"I know, sweetie." Rachel patted the child's back. "I know." She glanced down all three hallways, wondering where she could find a safe place for Saja. She was running out of strength, and she knew that if Tigre or Benjy were able to help, they would have already done so. Lashed into an abrupt decision, she started toward Tigre's office. *His door locks from the inside, I think.*

Saja pointed at the melted phone as they passed the desk. "Dis?"

Resigned to the knowledge that she could not keep the child silent, Rachel spoke in a whisper, hoping Saja would imitate. "That's the phone. Someone broke it."

"Bwoke," Saja chirped. "Uh-oh."

The hall seemed endless, Tigre's office an impossible distance away. Rachel's arms trembled with fatigue, but she maintained her hold on Saja as an act of fierce determination.

She had no doubt that Wu was working on a rescue at that moment. All she needed to do, until help arrived, was to keep her little friend from meeting the Jadamii.

Medica's tile floor was hard and cold. Every step jarred Rachel to the bone, but she pushed herself to move faster. She could rest when she got to Tigre's office, Saja would be safe there. Sweat soaked Rachel's hair and dripped down her face; her breath whistled through her clenched teeth.

"Uh-oh." Saja patted Rachel's face with the blanket.

Not wanting to worry the little girl, she smiled. "Aunt Rachel is tired."

"An' Way-toe."

A sudden warmth surrounded Rachel's heart, easing the burden of her exhaustion and pain. She hobbled the last few yards to Tigre's office. "Here we are, Saja," she panted. "All safe and sound."

Without warning, the office door flew open. A young woman in a blue and green Safety uniform darted into the hallway. She aimed a large gun at Rachel, arms braced to fire.

Rachel stopped. Years of experience caused her to speak in a calm, rational tone. "Don't shoot."

The young woman appeared petite to the point of

frailty, and she wore her black hair in short, girlish braids. She maintained her threatening stance. "Ajmani."

In an instant, Rachel took in the stranger's familiarity with a weapon that most Humans only saw in historical dramas. She also noted the woman's singular lack of concern for a helpless child. In the next moment, Rachel recognized Jardín. Fear iced her blood, but her instincts warned her to appear confident, and she narrowed her eyes. "*Deputy* Ajmani."

A faint smile curled Jardín's dainty mouth. "*Deputy* Ajmani." She slowly lowered the gun, but kept both hands on the grip. "You're the one who killed a Phi-Nurian with a particle welder. I've heard of you."

Rachel did not bother to explain that she had merely disarmed the sniper, not killed it. "I'm flattered."

The hand cannon looked unwieldy in Human hands. Rachel remembered Benjy's shout and the thunderous sound that followed. The chill in her bones deepened as she realized she faced an enemy far worse than any alien.

Saja pointed at the weapon. "Dis?" Her pure, clear voice was filled with uncertainty. "Dis?"

Jardín raised her delicate brows as she looked Rachel up and down. "I had no idea," she said sweetly, "that the duties of a silver rank deputy included baby-sitting."

Rachel pointedly ignored the gibe. "I don't believe," she replied, meeting Jardín's gaze, "that weapon is standard issue."

Jardín's smile widened. "We haven't met," she said. "But I'm sure you've heard of me. Jardín Azul, World Council operative." She abruptly giggled. "Deputy Ajmani, I must say you're not at all what I expected."

Rachel drew a breath to retort, then noticed the small particle welder tucked under Jardín's belt. The welder's tip was encrusted with the oxidation of recent use.

Saja stirred. "Mama," she said fretfully. "Want Mama."

Rachel gently patted the child's back, but kept her attention on Jardín. "And you're not what I expected," she replied calmly. "Where is everyone?"

Jardín gave her a sidelong glance. "That's none of your concern, Deputy."

"I think it is," Rachel said. "I heard a gunshot. Are Benjy and the others all right?"

Jardín smiled and lifted her chin. "I think, at this point, you should worry more about yourself." She paused and added silkily: "Deputy."

Concealed in the folds of Saja's blanket, Rachel's hands clenched into fists. However, she knew that to engage Jardín in verbal combat would only place Saja at risk. "I won't offer any resistance," she said quietly. "You have the gun."

Jardín smirked. "And I have the guts to use it."

Rachel could not imagine anyone firing a gun as an act of courage. Violent behavior was a form of insanity that the Human race had outgrown. The person she faced was some sort of throwback to a barbarous past. "I'm sure."

Jardín abruptly brought the hand cannon to bear on Rachel, slapping the metal against her palm in a business-like manner. "Give me your phone."

Rachel's instincts red-lighted. Jardín's manner betrayed a clear need to dominate. *But she doesn't want it to be too easy.* "It's in my pocket." Rachel reached for it, moving carefully, and pulled out her shoe. She stared at it, as if perplexed. "Oh. That's right. I gave my phone to Larry."

Jardín growled. "Don't play with me!"

"I'm not." Rachel dropped her shoe and then patted her pocket to prove it was empty. "I don't have a phone. I don't have anything with me." She paused, and added earnestly, "It's been a very bad day."

Jardín made another animal-like noise of frustration and roughly searched Rachel's pockets herself. Rachel went cold inside with rage, feeling Jardín's hands on her, knowing it was intended as a kind of violation.

Evidently satisfied, Jardín stepped back. "Pathetic," she said. "I expected more from the great Deputy Ajmani."

Rachel could not trust herself to speak.

Saja, perhaps sensing the tension, began to whimper. "Mama!" She clutched Rachel's neck. "Want Mama now!"

Jardín's smile turned poisonously sweet. "Well, Deputy, I won't keep you any longer from your . . . duties." She gestured with the gun toward Tigre's office, and her voice cracked like a whip. "Get in there."

Rachel glared, compressing her lips, but did not offer

an argument. There was nothing she could do, she realized, to help Benjy or Tigre. She hobbled to the door, trying not to seem too eager, and opened it.

"You stay in there until I come and get you," Jardín ordered. "Understand?" She started to close the door to Tigre's office, and then paused. "I mean it, Deputy. Stay in here." She nodded at Saja and added, "I'd hate for any harm to come to that precious baby girl."

The door shut.

For a moment, Rachel stood with the crying child in her arms and trembled.

"Mama," Saja sobbed.

The door's control panel hung on the wall in easy reach. Rachel slapped open the cover and keyed the lock.

Saja clutched the neck of Rachel's uniform in both hands. "Want Mama."

Rachel's arms shook with fatigue. "Mama's coming." Afraid she would drop the child, she hobbled to Tigre's desk. She deposited Saja in the bowllike chair and locked it back in a reclining position. The chair's high sides made it a safe and, she hoped, inescapable nest. "There we are." She dried Saja's eyes with a wipe and smoothed back her hair. "You're all right," she said. "You're all right."

Saja reached for Rachel with both hands, her expression stricken. "Up! Want up!"

The fidget-toy on Tigre's desk caught Rachel's attention. She picked it up and displayed it. "Look, Saja. What's this?"

Saja's gaze rested on the crystal-filled globe. She seemed fascinated in spite of her distress, and her sobbing faltered.

Encouraged, Rachel tilted the globe. The loose, red crystals inside rattled and sparkled. "Ooo," she said with the dry remains of her voice. "Pretty."

Saja swallowed her tears and reached for the toy. "Dis?" she asked doubtfully. "Dis?"

Rachel handed the globe to Saja. "Pretty." She listened for gunfire, unable to clear from her mind the image of Jardín stalking Meris through Medica. *Or perhaps Jardín is the prey.*

Rachel tucked the blanket more securely around the child. "Saja, are you thirsty? Do you want a drink of water?"

Saja tore her gaze away from her new toy, looked up at Rachel, and spoke one clear word: "Juice."

Rachel gently dried a stray tear on Saja's cheek. Tigre kept the Naranha in his kitchen cupboard, and she supposed Saja would like its orange flavor. "All right. Aunt Rachel will bring some juice."

Though so exhausted she could scarcely move, Rachel limped to the kitchen. She recalled Benjy's shout and the explosive gunshot. There was every chance that her friend lay wounded or dead. She again saw Meris cowering under the bunk in her cell, and then remembered the fleeting shadow outside Saja's room. Rachel's gut twisted with helpless anxiety. She selected a carton of Naranha from the cupboard and lifted a clean cup from the rack, forcing herself to concentrate on the problem at hand. *Saja. Think about Saja. Jardín threatened to return.*

The seal on the Naranha proved stubborn, and Rachel fumbled to peel it back. She knew that Jardín would have to cut through the, lock mechanism with the welder to get through the door. Rachel would have ample time to put Saja in the washroom, where she would be less likely to fall victim to a stray shot. Then Rachel would be free to jump Jardín and take away the gun. *Have to do it. If she takes us hostage, she might be able to bargain her way off the station.*

"Mama?" Saja's pure voice quavered.

Alarmed that the child would begin to cry again, Rachel spoke reassuringly. "Mama's coming." She opened the carton, trying to think of a distraction. "Saja, what does the doggy say?"

"Goggy?" Saja repeated.

Rachel poured the Naranha into the cup. Tigre had heated the liquid, she recalled. "What does the doggy say?" She eyed the warmer. Though she found the thought horrible, she considered throwing boiling water in Jardín's face. *Would even the odds.* "Does the doggy say 'bow-wow'?"

Behind her, Saja said in a rapturous tone: "Goggy! Gog-gog-goggy!"

Shaking with fatigue, Rachel turned with the cup in her hand. "What does the kitty—?"

Meris stood in the doorway of the washroom, only a few feet from Saja's chair. Her lustrous silver pelt bristled, and her webbed ears were folded back like the horns of an owl.

Saja reached for the alien. "Goggy," she crooned.

Glaring at Rachel, Meris flexed her clawed hands and growled.

CHAPTER TWENTY

TIGRE SHUFFLED down an empty corridor in Check-point. Perspiration and dried blood stained his rumpled scrubs, and his slender shoulders sagged with exhaustion.

Around him lay Safety's complex of meeting rooms and offices. Holes gaped in the plasti-board walls, and gritty debris crunched under his feet. The odor of feces and vomit hung in the air, along with a harsh stink that he always associated with Human fear.

His dirty hair slid limply into his eyes. He brushed it back and noticed for the first time the tremor in his hands. *Damn.*

The crisis in Checkpoint was over, and the section partition had reopened. Tigre knew that, like his medics, he ought to return to his quarters to rest. But with the Phenox finally gone from his system, he felt restless, and there was no way to usefully expend his nervous energy. The dead and seriously wounded were all packed into stasis, and those with minor injuries were farmed out to the doctors of various ships at port. *Nothing you can do. Nothing.*

Tigre rounded a corner. The smell of Phi-Nurian dung abruptly closed in around him. It was so strong it made his throat ache. Narrowing his eyes against the stench, he studied the nearby doorway of a darkened office. *In there.* He moved to the door and glanced in.

The room was an unadorned cube like all the others in

Checkpoint, with a small desk and chair in one corner. The sheet-covered bodies of the Phi-Nurian diplomats lay in a row on the floor. Unprepared for the sight, Tigre swallowed hard. He had not realized that their remains were still in Checkpoint.

A man dressed in black stood in the deep gloom near the far wall, arms folded and head bowed.

For a moment, Tigre simply stared. The surreal quality of the scene made him doubt what he saw, and he waited for the figure to fade into a jumble of shadows.

The man stirred and lifted his face. A steeply angled beam of light from the hall traced the firm line of his jaw and his high cheekbones. It was Wu Jackson.

Tigre drew a breath, but then could not think of anything to say.

Wu met Tigre's gaze. "I had to stop them. I didn't know what else to do." His tone was flat, colorless. "They were killing my friends."

Tigre's mouth went dry. "I know."

Wu maintained his unwavering regard. His dark eyes held an unreadable expression.

Tigre jerked his attention away from Wu and studied the Phi-Nurians' inert forms. He found no sorrow for them within his heart, only a bleak relief that they would not hurt anyone else. "I know," he said again.

Skirting the bodies, Wu moved toward the door. His rolling walk was soundless.

Tigre, uneasy, backed away a step.

Wu emerged from the room. Without the shapeless Safety uniform and its padded undergarment, he no longer looked plump and rather soft. The tighter fit of his black tunic emphasized the solid muscles in his chest and shoulders. "Doctor."

Tigre's heart began to pound. Annoyed with himself for allowing Wu to intimidate him, he folded his arms. "Why," Tigre said tightly, "aren't those bodies in stasis?"

Wu paused a long moment before he answered. "That would be illegal, according to Galactic Trade Association laws. We do not have their permission."

Tigre snorted. "Ridiculous."

Wu tilted his head. "Doctor, you shouldn't be here. You ought to return to your quarters."

Tigre frowned. "I think," he said, "I'm a little too old to be sent to my room."

Wu's voice was toneless. "I mean that you need to rest."

Tigre shifted. He wanted nothing more than to leave Checkpoint, but he could not forget the hostages in Medica. "Too keyed up to sleep."

Wu gave no sign that he heard. He glanced down at Tigre's arm. "What happened to you?"

Tigre followed his gaze. A mottled band of bruises darkened his right forearm. For a moment, he could not recall what caused it, then an image from the blurred memories of triage surfaced in his mind. A staffer with a chest wound had gripped him with the desperate strength of the dying. "A patient did this." He held his arm out to the light and turned it as if displaying a bracelet. "I've had much worse, believe me. Frightened people often clutch their rescuers. Instinct."

Wu's mouth slowly contorted into a grimace of deep pain. "Instinct," he repeated hoarsely.

Completely taken aback, Tigre froze. He suddenly recalled that Wu had recently witnessed the violent deaths of longtime friends and colleagues. *And he saved your life, you self-absorbed bastard.*

Looking at the situation from a new perspective, he wondered what caused Wu to linger over the Phi-Nurians' bodies, if he regretted the necessity of taking strong action. Tigre groped for the right words. He laid his left hand over the patch of bruises on his arm, measuring his fingers against it. "Actually," he said in a casual tone, "you might say I did this to myself. If I could have talked to him, calmed him down, he would have let go." He paused, wanting to choose his words carefully. "But I yanked myself free and shut the lid on his stasis unit. Other people needed me. There just wasn't time."

Wu's breath roughened, and he glanced away. "I . . ." He swallowed and bowed his head.

Tigre forced himself to remain silent. It was Wu's turn to talk.

Wu sighed. "This . . . whole thing." He gestured loosely to the offices around them. "I overheard one of the councillors calling it a massacre. But I don't think it was anything so simple. What occurred here was a collision of instincts."

Tigre waited.

Wu's gaze drifted to that darkened office. "Phi-Nurians go berserk when they're threatened. And if they gain the advantage, they kill. They can't help it, it's hardwired into their brains. They'll even attack their own kind." He paused and returned his attention to Tigre. "The trick is to get them at a disadvantage and keep them talking. To present an intellectual threat that engages their rationality."

Tigre nodded, recalling Concha's valiant actions.

Wu glanced down at Tigre's arm. He lifted his hand, but stopped short of touching the mottled skin. "There wasn't time."

"No, there wasn't. But you—" Tigre struggled to keep his voice steady. "You saved a lot of lives."

Wu flicked his gaze to Tigre's and held it. "Maybe."

Tigre found himself staring into eyes filled with fathomless depths of sorrow, pride, and cunning. Again, his heart began to beat in rapid strokes, and he remembered again why Wu inspired such fear in him. *Dangerous man.*

"Or maybe," Wu continued quietly, "I've sealed the fate of our species. Have you considered that, Doctor?"

An odd chill settled in Tigre's gut. "What do you mean?"

Wu jerked his head toward the darkened office. "Do you realize that this may be our future? That our species will once again know warfare as a daily reality?" He narrowed his eyes. "Think about it. There are only three other oxygen-breathing species in the galaxy. In a single day, we have managed to create a diplomatic catastrophe with each."

"But you—"

Wu shook his head. "I've played this game a long time, Doctor, and I recognize the early signs of disaster. As Rachel said, we're becoming boxed into a set of limited choices. Someone has engineered this entire disaster. Someone who wants Earth estranged from Jada, Igsha Reey, and Phi-Nu."

Tigre drew a breath to argue, then paused. He recalled Rachel sprawled on Medica's floor, insisting that the Jadamii had embroiled them in a wide-reaching galactic plot. "Rachel said—" It occurred to him that she might be dead, and he had to swallow hard before he could speak. "She told me that Meris was at the root of something big. That the poor Jadamii was desperate, trapped." He sighed. "I'm

afraid I didn't give her words much credence at the time.
I thought it was the sleep deprivation talking."

Wu's eyes glinted. "Rachel Ajmani is no fool. What else
did you two discuss over your warm carbohydrates?"

Tigre sighed and passed a hand through his dirty hair.
He wished he did not find Wu so unnerving. "I'm not sure
how much I can tell you without breaking patient confiden-
tiality. We didn't—"

A staffer rounded the corner at the end of the hall. He
was a young fellow with straight black brows and a somber expression.

When he saw Wu and Tigre, he froze.

Wu slowly raised his hands, palm out, to the level of his
shoulders. "Hello, Rico," he said in a friendly tone. "Nice
to see you."

Rico's face went blank with disbelief. "Warden. What are
you doing here? You're supposed to be in your quarters."

Wu shrugged lightly. "I broke out."

Tigre frowned. "What are you talking about?"

Wu glanced at Tigre. "Well, you see, I've been suspended from duty. Placed under arrest, actually."

Tigre wanted to shout, but the word came out a strangled
whisper. "What?"

Wu curled up just the corners of his mouth. "You
heard me."

Rico was obviously distressed. "Why did you do this,
Warden?" His voice climbed an octave. "Don't you realize
how much trouble you're in?"

"Of course, I do," Wu said gently. "So much trouble that
a little more won't make any difference."

Tigre felt the blood rush to his face on a tide of anger.
"Wait just a goddamned minute! In trouble? What the hell
for?" He glared at the young staffer. "For saving our col-
lective backsides?"

Rico swallowed. "Doctor DeFlora, it isn't—"

Tigre swung his arm in a violent gesture of contempt. "Is
the head of Port Authority out of her mind? The wolves
are loose in the fold, and she chains the dog in his kennel?
What in the name of bloody hell does she—?"

Wu sighed elaborately. "Doctor, please don't shout. I
happen to have a rather notable headache."

Tigre, heart hammering, folded his arms. "Oh, I am so sorry," he said in a tone of heavy sarcasm. "Do you want something for the pain?"

Wu's crafty smile softened, and he regarded Tigre with unmistakable amusement. "No, thank you. I already drank a shot of whiskey." His voice gained a strangely intimate quality. "Although I wish you could give me just a fraction of your energy. You, Doctor, are a blazing ball of fire."

Tigre scowled. "And you," he snapped, "are a lagoon filled with piranha."

Rico cleared his throat. "Excuse me. Warden, I think you'd better come with me to see Chen." Wearing a tortured expression, he unclipped the stinger from his belt and aimed it at his senior colleague. "Please. Don't make me use this."

Tigre followed Rico and Wu into Safety's main monitor area. Like the rest of Checkpoint, the plasti-board debris covered the tile floor. Holes gaped in the walls, and the pieces of a shattered chair lay in a heap beside one of the desks. Puddles of blood, both red and black, laced the air with the stink of death.

In spite of the mess, the area seemed crowded with people. Technicians encircled the damaged main monitor console, shaking their heads over bullet-riddled control boards. A few bleary-eyed staffers manned the auxiliary consoles. In a far corner, several grim members of station maintenance unpacked cleaning equipment from a large utility cart. Deputy Sonría Omar leaned over Chen's shoulder, pointing to something on a monitor screen.

Wu walked into the center of the room. Though he kept his hands raised, he appeared to be cheerful and unembarrassed by the situation. Rico, still holding the stinger, looked as ashamed as a dog caught chewing a sofa pillow.

People glanced up, and a tense silence fell over the area. Sonría straightened slowly and folded her arms. "Wu."

Wu beamed at her. "Hello, Sonría. Sorry I'm late."

A sudden hysterical impulse to laugh seized Tigre, and he pressed the back of his hand against his mouth to stifle it.

Chen stood up from his position at the console. He glanced around at the staring personnel and spoke in a mild tone. "All right, folks. Let's remember to concentrate." He waited until everyone returned to work, then sauntered toward Wu.

Sonría joined him, a scowl darkening her wide face. "Wu, what are you doing here?"

Tigre spoke without thought. "What the hell do you think he's doing here? Did you honestly expect him to sit on his ass and watch the station fall apart?"

Wu stirred. "Doctor . . ."

Sonría looked Tigre up and down, and something relented in her gaze. "No," she said in a dry, motherly tone, "I just didn't expect him to get caught." She laid an arm along his shoulders with easy familiarity and gave him a slow smile. "Doctor, you look worse than I feel. When was the last time you got any sleep?"

Tigre, caught off guard, stood rooted. He knew he ought to pull away, but he found the simple, physical contact infinitely comforting. He had forgotten how it felt to be touched without arousal. "I'm all right."

Sonría snorted. "If I miss too much sleep, I start seeing pink snakes come out of the walls."

The last thing Tigre had expected was any sort of commiseration, and it was almost too much for him. He had to swallow before he could speak. "I'm fine."

Chen, forehead puckering with worry, planted himself in front of Wu. "Will you please put your hands down?" he said. "You're making everyone nervous."

Wu clasped his hands behind his back. "Sorry."

Chen sighed and glanced at Rico. "Keep it short, please."

Rico cleared his throat. "There's not much to tell. I found him in the Delta Section, talking to Doctor DeFlora. He said he broke out of his quarters."

Wu rocked back on his heels. "I'm such a rascal."

Chen regarded him with disapproval, then turned to the staffer. "Thanks, Rico. Good job. I'll handle it from here."

Rico threw an apologetic glance at Wu and nodded. "Yes, Chen." He turned and walked out of the area.

Chen watched him go, then flicked his gaze to Wu. "You find this all very amusing, don't you?"

Wu gave a burst of laughter. "No, not really."

"It's sheer hell for us, you know," Sonría said calmly.

"Watching you destroy your career. Do you know what Rachel would say about your recent adventures?"

Wu shrugged. "The last time I spoke with our esteemed Deputy Ajmani, she promised to make me climb all eight hundred and forty-three steps of the Last War Memorial on my hands and knees while she followed behind, kicking my ass."

At the mention of Rachel's name, something tightened in Tigre's chest. He looked at Sonría. "What's going on with the situation in Medica?" His voice sounded pathetically young and uncertain to his own ears, and he tried to roughen it. "No one has told me a damned thing, and I'm getting tired of it."

Sonría gave him a gentle pat on the arm and released him. "There isn't much to report, Doctor. Deputy Jimanez-Verde is handling the case herself, and she'll update us when she has news." She paused and added reluctantly, "Last I heard, they were still trying to cut their way into Medica. Jardín has evidently welded shut all the doors, and Lois' crew is having a bad time trying to override the safeguards."

Tigre struggled to grasp the full scope of her words. "But—" He gestured helplessly. "I'll admit I'm no expert, but wouldn't it behoove us to move as fast as possible? That madwoman has had the free run of my department for nearly forty minutes. What if—?"

Chen interrupted. "Doctor, we are all doing everything we can. I promise we'll inform you as soon as we get into Medica." He turned to Wu and tapped him on the chest. "And you, please stay where I can see you. You try to leave the area, and I'll be forced to toss you into a detention cell. Understood?"

Wu made an elaborate gesture of obeisance. "Of course."

Chen turned on his heel and stalked back to his console. Tigre glared after him. *Bastard.*

Wu regarded Sonría, his eyes full of alert interest. "So. Any word from Benjy or Rosita? If Meris wakes up while they're trying to cope with Jardín—"

Sonría shook her head, avoiding Wu's gaze. "No. We can't raise a response from anyone in Medica."

Wu's tone became subdued. "That's . . . not good."

Tigre recalled the two Safety staffers, the man with the booming baritone and the pretty woman with a long braid over one shoulder. "Why are we just standing here? We've got to do something."

The predatory light rekindled in Wu's eyes. "I agree, Doctor. There's an access tube that runs from level three to the big storage closet in Medica. You create a diversion, and I'll make a run for it."

Irritated that Wu never seemed to take him seriously, Tigre folded his arms. "I'll do better than that," he snapped. "I'll go down that damned access tube myself. Where's the hatch on level three?"

Wu shook a scolding finger. "No, no, Doctor. Jardín has a Phi-Nurian shoot-n-go-boomer. You leave the gunplay stuff to me, is that clear?"

Sonría gave Wu a dour smile. "Keep talking like that," she drawled, "and I'll put you in detention."

Tigre's mind abruptly veered to consider the possibilities. "We keep the pharmaceuticals in that supply closet. I could—"

Wu folded his arms. "No."

"—find something to use on Jardín. Hell, even a snootful of Tri-Omega would—"

Wu rounded on him, his eyes wide and ferocious. "No!"

Tigre's pulse jumped with excitement, and he ignored Wu's glare. He turned to Sonría; certain she would see the logic of his plan. "I wouldn't even have to get that close to her," he explained. "And if she's hurt anyone—"

Sonría shot Wu an unfriendly glance, then smiled at Tigre. "Doctor," she said gently, "I don't think you realize just how tired you are. I understand that you're worried, but I think you need to get a little rest. Go back to your quarters. I promise we'll call as soon as—"

Tigre shook his head, trying to find the right words. "I can't. Don't you see? I need to help."

Sonría sighed and rubbed the back of her neck. "I know how you feel," she said wearily, "but there isn't—" She paused and her brows went up. "Well, I do have one problem that may interest you, Doctor. One small problem."

Tigre spread his hands. "But what about—?"

Sonría gestured to the lounge area in the corner and its

modest grouping of well-worn furniture. "To be precise, one small Rofa."

Thunderstruck, Tigre clutched the top of his head. He had assumed Jhaska had been returned to its ship. "You mean Jhaska?" He headed for the lounge. "Damn it, why didn't anyone tell me—?"

Sonría followed him. "We have a delegation from its ship demanding entrance to Dock Two. They want to come and retrieve Jhaska themselves."

Wu chuckled. "Ah, yes. Rofan pride. They must always take what is theirs."

Smashed peaches and the broken shards of coffee cups covered the floor of the lounge. A couch sat against one wall, and two deep armchairs faced each other over a low table.

The couch had apparently sustained several direct hits when the Phi-Nurians sprayed the room with gunfire. Stuffing blossomed from holes in its canvas covering.

Jhaska lay curled in a tight ball on one of the chairs. It still wore a blue and green Safety parka, a gift from Shoko, who had died in the shooting. The parka's hood was pulled down over Jhaska's face.

Filled with concern, Tigre knelt beside the chair. "Jhaska?"

The hood stirred, and a scratchy voice answered. "Tig-Tig."

A sour odor like bile tainted the air. Sonría moved to stand beside the chair, and Wu joined her. "We found the kid hiding behind the couch," she said.

Tigre nodded, suddenly remembering. "Shoko told Jhaska to take cover there when the trouble started."

"Good thinking," Sonría said, "but I'm afraid all those peaches didn't agree with its digestion."

Tigre pulled back the hood. Jhaska's face rested in a fresh puddle of vomited fruit. Its eyes were squeezed shut, and its small ears drooped.

Tigre carefully slid one hand under Jhaska's head and raised it from the mess. "Easy, now," he murmured. He gently wiped the child's mouth with the hem of his tunic. "What's the matter, Jhaska? Does your tummy hurt?"

The round eyes opened, bright with pain. "Hurts, Tig-Tig."

Sonría made a sympathetic noise. "Poor kid."

Wu strode to the utility cart and pulled off a handful of cloth towels. He brought them back to Tigre and offered them without comment.

Tigre did not look up. "Thank you." He laid one of the folded towels over the puddle of vomit and settled the child's head onto the clean, dry surface. The hood of the parka seemed to have escaped getting soiled, and he pushed it out of the way. "Jhaska, do you hurt anywhere else?"

Jhaska closed its eyes again. "No."

Tigre tenderly smoothed the russet fur between Jhaska's ears. He noticed that the young alien's nose leather did not have its usual pink-orange color, but instead appeared gray. "Deputy Omar. Tell me again why we can't take Jhaska back to its ship."

Sonría sighed. "Rofan psychology. Has something to do with gift giving and obligation. If we carry Jhaska down to them, we'll be offering a deadly insult."

Wu cleared his throat. "A double insult. Because we're giving back something we took."

Tigre glanced up at Sonría. "Then why not let them come up? Good God, do you really think they want to cause trouble?"

Sonría smiled thinly. "They're carrying knives."

Tigre shrugged. "So?" he said irritably. "Tell them to leave their cutlery at home."

Sonría rubbed the back of her neck again. "Doctor, it isn't that simple. This situation has already escalated into a legal—"

Tigre felt his face turn hot with rage. "Look," he interrupted in an elaborately rational tone. "We have a sick and frightened child on our hands. I'll give you just three minutes to get Jhaska's parents up here, or I'll personally carry the kid down to Dock Two."

Sonría sighed wearily. "Doctor—"

From the monitor area, Chen called in a low, urgent voice. "Sonría."

She turned to go. "Excuse me, Doctor."

"Three minutes," Tigre repeated.

Sonría walked away, giving no sign that she heard. Tigre returned his attention to his young patient. Jhaska's breath seemed to come in bursts of shallow panting. Tigre mentally cursed his lack of knowledge.

Wu strolled to the couch and studied it with speculative interest. "Hmm." He pushed the large piece of furniture away from the wall and looked over the area behind it. "Doctor." His voice was unusually somber. "I'm afraid we may have a big problem."

Still kneeling beside Jhaska, Tigre frowned up at him. "What now?"

Wu moved to crouch at Tigre's side. "I don't like the look of our little friend's former hiding place. Perhaps you'd better check to see if Jhaska stopped a bullet."

For a moment, his words made no sense to Tigre. "What?" He glanced down at Jhaska and noticed the way it clutched its hands to its abdomen. *Oh, God.* He drew a deep breath and assumed his professional mask of serenity. "Jhaska, I want to look at your tummy."

The child curled into a tighter ball. "No," it whimpered.

Tigre began to unfasten the bulky parka. "Jhaska, let go of your tummy for just a minute. I need to look at it."

Jhaska snarled. "No! I'll bite you!"

Tigre continued to work. "You can't, remember? I'm too fast for you." He tried to ease Jhaska's hands away. "I won't hurt you. I promise. I just want to make you feel better."

Jhaska emitted a puppylike whine of pain and terror.

Wu bent close to the child's ear. "Jhaska," he said softly. "Are you old enough for bravest-brave? For *eykhrru-rru*?"

Jhaska's round eyes snapped open. "Yes! I was in a big—" Its voice broke and it grimaced. "—big fight!"

Wu held out his hands. "Then let Tig-Tig look at your tummy, and we'll see how hard you can squeeze my fingers. Okay?"

Jhaska took a few gulping breaths, as if steeling itself, then snatched at Wu's hands.

There was a damp-looking rip in the parka. Tigre's heart sank, but he kept his voice steady. "Good, Jhaska. This won't take long."

A shadow fell over them as Sonría returned to the chair. "Hey," she said in a scandalized tone. "What the hell are you doing?"

Tigre swiftly finished unfastening the parka. "Deputy." He did not bother to look up. "Get out of my light."

Jhaska wore a bewildering assortment of clothing beneath the coat: loose trousers, three tunics of differing lengths, and two vests. Each garment was densely embroidered; each stained with runny, ocher-colored matter.

Wu made a noise of mingled anger and pity. "Gut shot."

Tigre did not know what to think. "Maybe. But it doesn't smell like a bowel perforation. And there's not nearly enough blood. All the same, better get a stasis unit in here."

"We can't," Sonría protested. "We don't have permission."

A sudden clatter of discussion and questions broke out in the monitor area as people realized the situation. Tigre kept his attention on Jhaska. "I don't care." He quickly pushed away the parka's bulk to check the child's back for an exit wound. "I doubt Jhaska's parents will care either."

Sonría's voice was thick with obvious distress. "Doctor. The Rofan don't believe in medical intervention. You know that. You also know that you have no legal right to render treatment."

Tigre slipped his hands over the embroidered clothing, feeling for telltale dampness, and encountered only dry fabric. *Good. I hope.* "Calm down, Deputy. I'm only making an assessment." He pulled the parka back into place. "Okay. I'm done looking, Jhaska. You were very brave."

Jhaska's small ears flicked. "I know." It released Wu's fingers and once again pressed its hands to its stomach.

Wu cleared his throat. "Just how bad is it?"

Tigre picked up a towel and tried to clean off the sticky matter. *How the hell should I know?* "Difficult to say without a scanner. The kid's obviously in a lot of pain. Wish I could get it undressed completely." He cast a cold eye at Sonría, who stood clutching the back of the chair. "Deputy, where is that stasis unit?"

Jhaska made a soft, breathless noise of misery. Its lips rolled back, revealing rows of needlelike teeth. Wu hesitantly laid a hand on its thin shoulder. "Easy, little friend."

Sonría, leaning on the chair, sighed and shook her head. "Doctor, we can't put Jhaska into stasis. Trade laws forbid any such—"

Tigre scrambled to his feet, his pulse lurching. "Deputy Omar, I don't give a—" He fought for control. "I don't care what the Galactic Trade Association laws dictate. Do you want Jhaska to die? Do you want that on your conscience?"

Sonría closed her eyes and bowed her head. "Wu. Please explain to him."

Wu looked up from his place beside Jhaska. "Don't blame 'Ría. None of this is her fault." His expression seemed open and oddly vulnerable. "Don't you see? We're boxed in. Anything we do, any decision we make, will be wrong. Our fate was sealed the moment we rescued Jhaska from Dock Two."

Tigre frowned down at Wu. "What?"

"I mean," Wu said, "that the Rofan would have been pleased and proud if we had allowed their child to die in combat. But, being Human, we couldn't let that happen." His voice softened, pleading. "Don't you see? It's another collision of instincts."

His frown deepening, Tigre folded his arms. "The only thing I see is that we're wasting time. Get a stasis unit in here. And call Jhaska's ship, tell them to prepare for surgery."

Wu's voice was raw. "Doctor, for the last time: The Rofan don't practice medicine. They don't believe in it."

Everyone in the monitor area, staffers and maintenance people, stood staring at the argument. It took every bit of Tigre's will to prevent himself from shouting. "That's insane."

"No," Wu said gently. "It's not insane, or wrong, or misguided. It's alien."

Chen strode over to the lounge area. His heavy shoulders were hunched, and his forehead was lined with worry. "Doctor, I understand your concern. I also realize that you're fond of Jhaska. But there's nothing you can do. Nothing."

A deep trembling seized Tigre. Once again, he was only sixteen, sitting by the roadside, helpless to stop his little sister from dying. "But—"

Chen spread his hands. "I don't expect you to like it. No Human wants to let a child die. But we haven't got a choice in this matter." He stepped around the chair and stood towering over Tigre. "Now. We'll soon have a delegation of angry Rofan on our hands. So I think you'd better say good-bye to Jhaska. And then, I think you'd better leave Checkpoint."

Wu stirred. "Chen . . ."

"I mean it. If you refuse to leave, I'll have you arrested and confined to quarters." Chen nodded to a nearby staffer. "Blanca, please escort Doctor DeFlora to the lift."

A thickset young woman stepped forward and regarded Tigre doubtfully. "Doctor?"

Tigre's throat closed. He glanced down at his young friend. Seemingly oblivious to the Humans around it, Jhaska coiled itself into a tighter ball. It gave a bubbling sigh and whispered: *"Eykhrru-rru."*

CHAPTER TWENTY-ONE

TIGRE KNELT beside Jhaska's chair. The young Rofa seemed pitifully small, nearly lost in the voluminous bulk of its Safety parka. Its tiny ears lay flat, and its eyes remained squeezed shut. Though unsure if the child were aware of him, Tigre leaned close. "Jhaska? Did you say something?"

Jhaska's lips twitched, and it whispered a short phrase.

Every joint in Tigre's body ached with exhaustion, and he struggled to keep his voice steady. "Speak Trade, Jhaska. I can't understand you."

Wu, also crouched beside the chair, shifted slightly closer to Tigre. "My Rofan is pretty sketchy." His eyes filled with concern. "First, it said *'eykhrru-rru.'* Then I think it said it was cold."

Tigre drew his brows together. "Cold?" He threw a glance of reproach at Chen, who stood over him like a mountain. "Hear that? The poor kid may be going into shock."

Chen closed his eyes wearily. "Doctor, please—" He paused and sighed. "Just say good-bye to Jhaska, and then leave Checkpoint. Don't force me to arrest and detain you."

The staffer, Blanca, rested her hands on her weapon belt, her expression turning alert.

For a moment, a sense of defeat held Tigre motionless.

He gazed up at Chen, remembering his little sister's death and searching for something to say.

Wu cleared his throat. "Chen—"

Tigre rose slowly to his feet. He glanced around the monitor area, noticing the exhausted sag in Sonría's face and the stricken expressions of the staffers and techs. It suddenly occurred to him how he must appear within the context of the blood-splashed walls and shattered equipment—disheveled, smeared with vomit and blood, crazed from lack of sleep.

As if prompted by the new perception, a vivid image of Rachel sprang to mind. He remembered her uncombed hair, rumpled uniform, and the dark smudges of exhaustion under her eyes. She had come to help, and he had tried to expel her from Medica. His past actions suddenly seemed the purest idiocy. He wondered what she thought of him, and if he would ever have the chance to offer his hand in apology. *Sorry, Rachel. Now I understand.*

Tigre lifted his chin and met Chen's gaze. "I'm not going anywhere." His mouth went dry, but he forced himself to continue. "So I guess you'll have to arrest me."

"No," Wu said calmly. "He can't do that." He looked up at Chen. "I've been trying to tell you. You don't have the authority to issue orders to Doctor DeFlora. Or to place him under arrest." He returned his attention to Jhaska, and passed a gentle hand over the Rofa's sleek head. "Medica's head surgeon is answerable only to Deputy Jimanez-Verde."

Tigre blinked and glanced down at Wu. He was entirely aware of the parameters of his rights and privileges, and he knew that outside of Medica he was subject to the direction of any ranking Port Authority official.

Chen's weary frown faded into a stare of consternation. "What?"

Wu shrugged casually and glanced at Sonría. "Tell him."

Sonría shook her head and passed her hand through her hair. "I don't know," she said tiredly. "Not my area. But it sounds stupid enough to be on the books."

Chen recovered his scowl, but seemed confused. "I'm not sure—"

Snatching at the unexpected reprieve, Tigre once again knelt beside Jhaska's chair. The little Rofa's nose leather seemed to be an unhealthy shade of blue-gray, and its breath hissed between its bared teeth. Tigre mentally groped for some method of offering aid and comfort that would not be considered a medical procedure. "Jhaska, just try to relax." He gently patted the child's narrow shoulder. "I'm going to take good care of you."

From a console in the monitor area, a staffer shot to his feet. "Deputy Omar. Dock Two's on the phone."

Sonría whipped around. "What is it?"

The staffer's face was tense. "The contingency from Jhaska's ship—"

"What's the matter?" She strode toward the staffer. "Did they finally decide to shoot their way in?"

The staffer shook his head. "They've called the Rofan emissary's ship."

Wu puffed out his cheeks. "Oh, dear."

Chen gave Tigre a warning look and headed toward Sonría, motioning for Blanca to follow. "Any response from the emissary?" He joined the others at the console, and the conversation turned muted.

Wu studied Jhaska, his eyes dull. "Boxed in. All of us. And the innocent are the first to suffer."

Trying to disguise his own hopelessness, Tigre raised his brows. "And everyone says that I'm the one who needs to get some sleep. You sound like you've been narcotized. Snap out of it."

Wu regarded him somberly for a moment, then gave him a faint smile. "Sweet-talker."

Jhaska shivered and curled into a tighter ball.

Tigre picked up a fresh towel and dabbed at the traces of vomit around the child's mouth. "Jhaska? Can you hear me? It's Tig-Tig."

Jhaska's round eyes flicked open, then squeezed shut again. "Cold."

Tigre gently pulled the parka's hood up over the child's head. "Is that better? Do you want a blanket?"

Jhaska sighed. *"Eykhrru-rru."*

Baffled, Tigre threw a glance at Wu. "Was that a yes?"

"Hard to say." Wu tilted his head. "The Rofan are difficult to understand. All in all, I prefer dealing with the Phi-Nurians."

"Not me. I've never been shot at by a Rofa."

Wu's tone was mild. "Doctor, you *are* a Rofa."

Tigre scowled and returned his attention to Jhaska. "If the Rofan don't practice medicine as we do, then getting permission—"

"They don't practice medicine at all."

Tigre narrowed his eyes. "You keep saying that, but I don't know what you mean."

"Yes, you do. You've read the studies and the cultural briefs, but you're choosing not to remember the plain facts." Wu looked him straight in the eye. "The Rofan do not practice medicine."

"Are you trying to tell me they don't even perform the most basic first aid?"

Wu nodded. "Exactly."

Tigre spread his hands. "What about a minor abrasion? Wouldn't they try to stop the blood? Apply pressure?"

Wu smiled gently. "No."

Tigre drew a breath to speak, then could not think of anything to say. Wu was right, of course, he had read all the literature. He just did not want to believe that it applied in the case of Jhaska.

"The Rofan are not Human beings," Wu said. "It's just that simple . . . and just that complicated."

"But—" Tigre searched his mind for a half remembered fragment of conversation. "You told me that Deputy Omar once chased a Rofan drug smuggler across the bridge of a loading gantry. If they use drugs, they must—"

Wu's smile turned grim. "Drugs are only for recreational purposes. A means for adventure. I've never heard of a Rofa taking something for a headache." He sighed. "Every now and then, we find a Rofan body on the dock. The victim always bears multiple stab wounds, and the Rofan always claim it was the loser in a private dual. But I can't help wondering if these cases are actually a matter of euthanasia."

Tigre's gut turned cold, recalling the Rofan cadavers in storage. He studied Jhaska's narrow face, with its clenched teeth and tightly shut eyes. "Well," he said. "I'm not going to let that happen."

A spark of approval lit Wu's gaze. "If anyone can change the Rofan mind-set, Doctor, it's you."

Tigre glanced to where Chen and Sonría huddled over a console, then whispered: "Is that why you lied?"

Wu pressed his fingertips to his throat in a facetious gesture of genteel reproach. "Why, Doctor, whatever do you mean?"

"You told Chen that he couldn't arrest me." Tigre forced himself to meet Wu's gaze. "If you have some reason for keeping me in Checkpoint—"

"Maybe," Wu said in a cozy tone, "I just like to look at you."

It occurred to Tigre that Wu resorted to flirtation whenever he did not want to answer a particular question. "And maybe you'd better stop saying shit like that."

Wu laughed. "Maybe." He threw a casual look around the room and lowered his voice. "So. Assuming you get permission to treat Jhaska, how will you proceed? Plan on unanesthetized surgery?"

Tigre narrowed his eyes. "Of course not. Drugs, remember?" He wondered what the Rofan used recreationally. Abruptly, a whole host of problems loomed in his mind, and his hands turned icy. *Shock, toxemia, secondary infections. Oh, God.* He cleared his throat. "Just getting the kid into stasis is the first priority. Surgery is one thing. Reviving a Rofa from clinical death is an entirely different matter."

Wu shrugged. "I'm not trying to discourage you, Doctor, but have you really thought this through? Considered every angle?"

Tigre snorted. "Hell, no! What good would that do?"

Chen called out from the monitor area. "Wu." His voice was low and urgent, and his forehead creased with anxiety. "A moment, please?"

Wu tossed Tigre an impish grin. "This is where it starts to get fun. Hang on tight." He swiftly rose to his feet and strode to Chen.

Tigre returned his attention to Jhaska. The child still breathed in jerking gasps. "Jhaska, can you hear me?" He laid a gentle hand on its shoulder. "It's Tig-Tig."

Jhaska's small ears flicked. "Hurts bad."

Tigre leaned closer. "I want to make you feel better, Jhaska."

"Eykhrru-rru."

A deep shudder welled up from within Tigre, and he had to swallow before he could speak. "I don't know what that means. Speak Trade."

Jhaska opened its round eyes. "Means no more fight. Means—be the most brave." It licked its dry lips. "Thirsty."

"I know." Tigre searched for the right words. "But I need to make your tummy better before I can give you a drink."

With obvious effort, Jhaska raised its head a bit. "Better?" it asked suspiciously. "How—?" It broke off in a burst of convulsive coughing.

Inwardly cursing, Tigre slid one hand under Jhaska's head to steady it. More sour-smelling fluid came up, along with a few fibrous lumps of partially digested peaches. Tigre threw a ferocious glance toward Sonría in the monitor area. "Deputy! I need that stasis unit."

She did not turn to look, but Wu swung around and headed back for the chair. He still wore that odd, anticipatory smile. "Doctor." He crouched beside Tigre. "We have a huge problem on its way to Checkpoint."

Tigre's eyes blazed. "I don't give a damn about—" Then Wu's words sank in. "Jhaska's parents are coming?"

"Parent. Escorted by shipmates and one distinguished emissary of the Rofan Legitimacy." Wu sighed airily. "Of course, the emissary seems to be what the Rofan call a *gukka*, a professional duelist. So the entire situation has gained a whole new outlook."

Jhaska's vomiting subsided, and the child broke into panting. Tigre settled its head back onto the chair's cushion and reached for a clean towel. He tried to follow Wu's line of thought, but could not imagine the implications. "So? What are you saying?"

Wu handed him the towel, and his smile turned ferocious. "Get ready for another fight, Doctor."

Tigre scowled and began to wipe Jhaska's mouth. "Are you trying—?" A shadow fell over him, and he glanced up.

Chen loomed above him. "We need to move Jhaska to a secured area."

Tigre narrowed his eyes. "Pardon?"

Chen looked unhappy, but determined. "The Rofan are on their way, since they insist upon coming to retrieve the child. But there's no reason why we can't pick the location. I want Jhaska moved to the detention area."

For a moment, Tigre glared up at him in silence, too angry for coherent thought. Then he returned his attention to cleaning Jhaska's face. "No."

Chen's tone was stern. "Doctor, you can't—"

Tigre carefully laid the vomit-smeared towel to one side and rose to his feet. "I have had," he said quietly, "just about enough of you." Chen drew a breath to speak, but Tigre jerked his hand up. "It may be true that I can't legally treat Jhaska, but I'll be damned if I'm going to stand by and allow you to exacerbate a critical injury."

Chen drew his heavy brows together. "Doctor—"

"Shut up," Tigre snapped. "Until Jhaska's parent arrives, the only move I want that kid to make is to the interior of a stasis unit."

Chen's face turned red. "Now, hold on—"

Wu cleared his throat. "Chen. Don't bother to argue."

Chen spread his hands, and his voice rose in pitch. "Do you want a repeat of the Phi-Nurian incident? Hostile aliens running wild through the nerve center of Safety?" He gestured toward the offices down the hallway. "We have a room full of dead diplomats—"

Tigre's heart lurched. "Shut the hell up!"

Wu rose smoothly to his feet. He wore his habitual smile, but there was a hard glint in his eyes. "Calm down, both of you." He laced his fingers together and pressed down on the top of his head. "Chen. Six angry Rofan are bringing a hired duelist—a *gukka*—to Checkpoint. I recommend that you clear the area of all these innocent bystanders while you have the time. Hmm?"

Chen nodded, his forehead again creased with anxiety. "Right." He glanced significantly at the surgeon.

Tigre folded his arms. "Don't look at me like that. I'm staying to cheer for the *gukka*."

Chen frowned, but turned away. Tigre glared after him, clenching his jaw to keep it from trembling.

Wu drew close, but made no move to touch him. "Chen's not a bad fellow," he murmured. "He's just scared to pieces."

Tigre smiled bitterly. "Aren't we all?"

Jhaska gave a breathless whimper of misery. "Tig-Tig . . ."

Tigre knelt beside the chair. "I'm here, Jhaska. Don't worry."

Jhaska licked its lips. "Water."

Hating his own helplessness, Tigre laid a hand on the child's shoulder. "The people from your ship are coming for you. They'll be here soon."

Jhaska opened its eyes. They were bright with unmistakable pain. "Eeya?" it whispered. "My giver . . . coming?"

Tigre, at a loss, looked at Wu.

"Parent."

Tigre kept his voice warm and reassuring, "Yes, and she—" The Rofan, someone once told him, resented Human gender labels. "Your giver's bringing lots of others. Even an emissary from the Legitimacy. A *gukka.*"

Jhaska's ears lifted. "Dútha!" Its voice gained strength. "Big, big Dútha!"

Wu bent close. "Jhaska, do you know the emissary?"

Jhaska raised its head. "Everyone know," it said. "Legit'macy—only one *gukka*: Dútha."

Wu puffed out his cheeks. "Oh, goody."

Jhaska let its head sink to the cushion, but it kept its bright eyes on Wu. "Dútha," it said darkly, "will bite you."

All over the monitor area, techs and maintenance people hastily gathered up their equipment. Sonría stood in front of an auxiliary console, keeping her eyes on a monitor screen and holding a headset to her ear. Tigre glanced uneasily at Wu. "Is it—?" He paused, disliking the nervous quality in his voice. "Was Chen right? Is this going to be a repeat of the Phi-Nurian incident?"

Wu's dark eyes held a preoccupied expression, as if he plotted a chess gambit. "I hope not."

"That," Tigre said flatly, "is not reassuring."

Wu smiled gently. "Doctor, we have at least two hostage situations on the station at this time. The Phi-Nurians still have Bailey aboard their ship, and Jardín still has everyone in Medica. It makes me angry, and I'm a sweet-tempered fellow." He patted Jhaska's shoulder. "How do you think the Rofan are feeling?"

Jhaska laid its small ears flat. "Speak Trade."

Tigre sat back on his heels, trying to assimilate the new

information. His own exhaustion, long denied, suddenly threatened to overwhelm him. He glanced down at his young friend. "Jhaska—"

The Rofa peered up at him from the folds of the parka's deep hood. An abrupt sense of Jhaska's otherness seized Tigre, and he no longer saw the child as a fur-covered Human.

Jhaska was critically wounded, no doubt bleeding internally, but had not lapsed into unconsciousness. It was in extreme pain, alone among aliens, and yet seemed fearless.

"*Eykhrru-rru*. It means never being afraid, doesn't it?" A nebulous understanding formed in Tigre's mind; he caught a glimpse of a calm, strong society where personal suffering was a matter of sinewy indifference. "You fight to win. But if you can't win, you don't continue to fight in fear. You surrender in pride and courage. Is that right?"

"Yes, yes! *Eykhrru-rru*—" Jhaska broke off in a dry cough. "Bravest-brave. . . ."

Wu, still crouched at his side, regarded him with undisguised approval. "Very good, Doctor," he said warmly. "You may have a glowing future in Xeno-Relations."

Heat rose up in Tigre's face, and he jerked his eyes away from Wu. He did not understand why the unexpected praise rattled him so much. *Bastard.*

Chen strode to the lounge area. "The Rofan are on the lift." He hovered over Tigre and folded his arms. "Doctor, I'd feel more comfortable if you stepped away from Jhaska. There might—"

Wu rose to his feet. "Did Deputy DelRio persuade the surviving members of the World Council committee to stay out of this?"

Chen shook his head tightly. "Those idiots are on the lift, too. And I don't have enough people up here if there's trouble."

Wu gave him a crooked smile. "You have me."

Chen drew down his heavy brows. "I ought to place you in a cell."

A collection of voices near the entry snatched Tigre's attention. Two members of the World Council, middle-aged women in saris, led a group of Rofan into the monitor area. A jade rank Port Authority deputy and a tired-looking staffer brought up the rear. The councillors and the Rofan all seemed to be talking at once, and no one seemed to be listening to what another said.

Tigre slowly straightened and gazed in fascination. The adult Rofan wore layers of embroidered clothing like Jhaska, but there was nothing soft or cute about their triangular faces. Their muzzles bore the white cross-hatchings of old scars, and a hostile light filled their beady eyes.

Among the Rofan glided a creature that Tigre mistook at first glance for a Jadamii. It wore no clothing except for an unadorned loincloth, and around its neck hung fine chains loaded with bells, sparkling stones, and talismans. "Oh," Tigre breathed, "what—?"

"The emissary," said Wu in an undertone, "is evidently not one of the childbearing gender."

Tigre stared. Unlike the other Rofan, its ears were large and pointed, and its silky pelt shaded from fawn to white at the throat and breast. Tigre mentally fumbled with the concept of seven distinct genders, trying to fit the emissary into a recognizable sexual identity.

Wu cleared his throat. "Doctor," he murmured. "In this situation, prolonged eye contact could be misconstrued as an invitation to fight."

Tigre jerked his gaze away. "Sorry." Heat touched his cheeks, and he recalled Rachel's words. *Typical Human preoccupation.*

The Rofan spread out, swaggering through the area, inspecting the damage. A few of them shouldered aside Safety personnel and boldly toyed with the main monitor's control panel. Two of them walked along the walls, scuffing through the plasti-board dust, kicking aside larger pieces of debris. The councillors followed after them, pleading with them to refrain. Tigre noticed that none of the station's people attempted to speak to the Rofan or resist their investigation. He glanced at Wu.

Wu seemed relaxed and alert, watching the activity with what seemed to be only casual interest.

Jhaska's head bobbed up, and it shook back the hood. Its round eyes were feverish with excitement. "Eeya!" It called. "Eeya-ya!"

One of the Rofa at the monitor console twisted around

and stared in Jhaska's direction. Its gaze met Tigre's, and its small ears flicked flat.

Tigre hastily lowered his eyes. Wu, standing near, whispered, "Quiet. Don't speak first."

Eeya strode directly to Jhaska. The child reached for it, breaking into a halting narrative in its native tongue. Tigre moved wordlessly aside, and Eeya gathered Jhaska into its arms.

The emissary watched from the middle of the room, calmly ignoring the councillor who plied it with questions.

Jhaska, sighing, laid its head on its giver's shoulder. The adult's expression betrayed no Human emotion of love or worry, but it folded the child close.

Tigre swallowed painfully. He desperately wanted to urge for a stasis unit, but he remembered Wu's instruction.

Eeya stared at him for a moment without moving, and then it looked down at the chair. The towel still lay over the puddle of vomit. With its free hand, Eeya flicked the towel aside and studied the mess of partially digested peaches. It lifted its eyes to Tigre, and something softened in its gaze. "Name's Eeya."

Tigre suddenly realized he was holding his breath. He gulped air and let his shoulders lower. "I'm Doctor Tigre DeFlora." He resisted the urge to offer his hand. "Are you Jhaska's giver?"

"Yes." Eeya's tone held an edge of impatience, as if Tigre had asked something foolish. "Of course."

Tigre tried to pull his thoughts together, wondering how he could explain Jhaska's injury to someone entirely unfamiliar with medicine. "I'm not certain if—"

Jhaska interrupted with another gasping outburst. Its giver inclined its head and listened patiently to the child, making no attempt to hush or calm it.

Tigre paused uncertainly and glanced toward Wu for coaching. Wu's gaze was locked on something in the room beyond. Tigre turned.

The emissary strolled toward them. It studied the damaged equipment and the bloodstained walls with an air of knowledgeable interest.

The councillor at its elbow began to follow it. "Honorable Dútha," she said, "please give me just a moment of—"

Sonría stepped forward, took the woman's arm, and whispered something vehemently in her ear.

Dútha crossed to stand beside Eeya. It studied Tigre with an openly curious expression.

Wu stirred and stepped closer to Tigre.

Jhaska finished speaking with a dry cough, then seemed to go limp. Ears drooping, it laid its head on its giver's shoulder. Eeya raised its eyes and regarded Tigre with an appraising stare. "Jhaska says that you move too fast to bite."

Memories of playing with Jhaska surfaced, and Tigre had to swallow in order to speak. "And your child is . . . courage itself."

Eeya grunted. "I know." It glanced toward the damaged main monitor console. "Big mess. Phi-Nurians blasted the shit out of this place."

"Nothing we can't fix," Tigre said, trying to keep the tremor out of his voice. He gestured casually toward Jhaska. "Speaking of repairs, it's about time we got the child into surgery. Don't you think?"

Eeya snarled and took a half step back. "No."

Wu cleared his throat. "Doctor, what are you—?"

Tigre flung him a silencing glance, then looked at Eeya. "Why not? There's nothing to be afraid of, just a simple procedure."

Eeya said stonily. "It is not our way."

Tigre spread his hands. "You mean you don't have a doctor?" He tapped his chest with clenched fists. "I could perform the surgery. It's probably only a bowel perforation. Even if—"

Eeya took another step back. "No."

Tigre struggled to find words. "Maybe you don't understand the situation. Without prompt attention to this injury, Jhaska may die."

Eeya cuddled its child closer and turned away.

Tigre lurched forward. "Wait! I—"

Dútha blocked his path. Tigre tried to step around it. "Excuse—"

Dútha caught him by both shoulders and stopped him.

Tigre found himself staring into alien eyes. He read in them intelligence, sophistication, and a certain dark amusement. Sheer surprise made him freeze in its grip. All around the room he heard the gasps of Human reaction, and he abruptly realized his danger. *Dútha*, Jhaska had said, *will bite you.*

Dútha spoke without heat. "You are fortunate that I understand you mean no harm." Its voice was low and full of rough music. "A *gukka* with less discernment or pride might have broken your skull."

Tigre's heart slammed against the wall of his chest, but he made no attempt to pull free. "Of course, I intend no harm. I just want to help Jhaska."

"No one may help Jhaska now, but Jhaska."

Tigre trembled with frustration. "You're wrong. I can help."

Dútha studied him a long moment. "You don't understand, do you? This is our way. It will test the little one's will to live."

Tigre's voice rose in volume. "Will to live? Jhaska's got enough will for ten people! That is not the problem." He tightened his jaw and spoke through clenched teeth. "The problem is that chunks of metal have ripped holes in the kid's gut. The problem is that you're standing in my way. Now take your hands the hell off me and—"

Dútha maintained its powerful grip. "I will release you when we have reached an understanding."

Tigre paused to catch his breath and collect his thoughts. Beyond Dútha, he saw Eeya move to stand by the door. "Tell me something. When an important piece of equipment on your ship breaks, do you throw it away or repair it?"

Dútha's tone was patient. "We repair it, if we can. But a loading winch is not the same as a child. Machinery has no soul."

Tigre's voice cracked. "That's exactly my point!" He distantly recognized that he had lost his self-control, but he plowed on. "How can you let someone like Jhaska, all that spirit and curiosity and love—how can you let it die? For no more reason than some sort of cold philosophy?" He swallowed hard. "Don't the Rofan love their children?"

"Of course, we do. Of course." Dútha raised its chin and addressed someone behind Tigre. "You. Come. Restrain this brave one until we leave. I have no desire to hurt it."

Strong Human arms encircled Tigre from behind. "Easy,

now, Doctor," Wu murmured. "You'd better stay with me."

Suddenly furious, Tigre twisted wildly. "Let go!"

"Not just yet." Wu possessed unexpected agility and balance, easily countering Tigre's desperate efforts to free himself. "I think you need to calm down."

Dútha cautiously backed away a few steps, then made a slight, formal bow. "Doc-tor. I hope we shall meet again soon. I wish to continue our . . . philosophical discussion."

Tigre abruptly noticed all the other Rofan gathering around Eeya at the door. The group watched Dútha, evidently only waiting for the *gukka* to finish its business.

Cold horror robbed Tigre of the energy to struggle, and he realized he only had moments in which to change Eeya's mind. "Wait," he called to the giver. "Just think about what I've said. Please."

Dútha turned to go, then paused. It pulled a tinkling talisman on a chain from around its neck. "Here. Take this." The *gukka* pressed the piece of jewelry into Tigre's hand. "You need it. You're crazier than I am."

Distracted, Tigre barely glanced at the object. It seemed to be a thimble-sized bell of gray metal. "But I—"

Dútha turned and swaggered to the door without a backward glance.

Jhaska, still wrapped in the Safety parka, rested unmoving in its giver's arms. The little Rofa's eyes were shut, and its jaw hung slack. Eeya tenderly pulled the hood over Jhaska's face.

Tigre's vision clouded, and the parka's blue and green blurred with the bloodstained walls of Checkpoint. "Please! At least—" He swallowed painfully against the rising knot in his throat. "At least put Jhaska into stasis. What harm could it do?"

The Rofan left Checkpoint, followed by the subdued councillors and their handlers.

Tigre strained against Wu's grip, calling out after Eeya. "Don't let Jhaska die!" Scalding tears welled up and ran down his cheeks. "Don't throw away your child!"

Wu's voice was tight. "Doctor, please calm down."

Tigre flung his whole weight forward in an attempt to break away. "Let go of me!" he roared. "Let go!"

"No." Wu spoke softly into his ear. "You let go. We have a lot of other people who need your help. Remember your patients in Medica?"

Tigre stopped struggling, paralyzed by rising despair. *Oh, God.*

Wu's encircling arms shifted subtly from a restraining hold to a warm embrace. "You can't do anything more for Jhaska. Just let go, dear friend. Let go."

Tigre lowered his head and gritted his teeth to keep from sobbing out loud. All his walled-off emotions broke to the surface, his anger for the acid-burn victims, his helpless concern for Meris, and his horror over the Checkpoint massacre. *Nothing you can do. Nothing.* "Rotten bastard," he said thickly.

In an abrupt return to his playful persona, Wu delivered a noisy kiss to the back of Tigre's head. "I love you, too."

The facetious response halted Tigre's descent into a personal hell. He sputtered in protest and violently shook his head. "Cut it out!"

Wu released him with a pat on the shoulder. "I think you're okay now."

"Goddamned right, I'm okay!" Tigre jerked his filthy clothing straight and glared around the room. He expected to see everyone staring at him in worried shock, but the expressions he saw seemed to convey wonder and admiration.

Sonría approached him with an approving grin. "That was amazing!" She glanced at Chen. "Have you ever seen anything like it?"

Chen shook his head. "They were as tame as lambs."

Tigre scowled. "What the hell are you talking about?"

Sonría planted herself in front of Tigre, hands on hips. "You had an emissary of the Legitimacy, a Rofan *gukka*, eating out of your hand." Her grin widened. "They didn't even threaten retribution. It's unheard of. How did you—?"

Her jubilation cut Tigre. He held up a hand. "Don't. Please. I—" His throat tightened, and he saw Jhaska's face again. He forced himself to speak gently. "I've just lost a patient."

Sonría's smile faltered. "Oh. Yes. I'm sorry."

Wu picked up a clean towel and offered it to Tigre. "Here. Dry your eyes. Blow your nose. We have work to do."

Tigre bundled away his grief, as he had countless times before, until there was leisure to mourn. He still held Dútha's gift, so he slipped the chain around his neck to free his hands and took the towel. "Thanks."

Chen raised his brows doubtfully. "You're not actually going to wear that thing, are you? You don't know what it means."

Wu rocked back on his heels. "Means: 'Watch out. Here comes one mean badass.' "

Tigre dabbed at his nose with the towel, not really wanting to touch himself until he cleaned his hands. His fingers were sticky with Jhaska's blood and vomit. "Need to scrub," he muttered. "God only knows what kind of bugs I'm carrying."

He glanced down at the chair, and studied the sad mess of partially digested peaches. Between one breath and the next, a sudden idea seized him. *Specimen.* He raised his trembling hands and gazed at them in rising excitement. "Someone, find a few specimen bags for me."

Chen exchanged glances with Wu and Sonría, and then blinked at Tigre. "Pardon?"

Tigre's heart began to pound, his mind racing. Eeya might change its mind. "Hurry!" He hastily pulled his tunic off over his head and peered at the slimy patch of Jhaska's vomit. "Autolysis—cell decay. We don't know how quickly this stuff will break down; better get it all into stasis fast."

Sonría cleared her throat. "Doctor—" Her voice held a tentative quality. "Are you okay?"

"Fine." Tigre glanced up at her and saw the anxious cast of her brows. He flicked his gaze to Chen and found sad sympathy. "Stop looking at me like that. I'm fine." He gestured with his tunic. "I want to take specimen samples. It may be the only opportunity we have to collect—"

Sonría laid her arm along his bare shoulders. "Sure, Doctor. I understand," she said kindly. She tossed Wu a meaningful stare.

Wu stepped forward, his face oddly impassive. "I have an idea. Let Chen call the lab in Environmental Control. They can handle everything."

"Sure," Sonría said encouragingly. "Let them take care of it for you. That way you can get a little rest."

Irritation battled with grief in Tigre's mind, and he slowly shook his head. "I haven't cracked, so you can stop trying to humor me. Surely you can see how important this is."

"Of course." Wu's tone was colorless. "In fact, maybe I'd better take you to the lab immediately. Hmm?" He slipped his arm around Tigre's waist and led him away from the deputy. "Come on, Doctor."

Sonría's voice was gentle. "And try to get some sleep."

Tigre frowned back at her. "Damn it, I'm fine." He tried to pull away from Wu, but the other man maintained his grip. "Let go."

Wu led him firmly to the door. "Just as soon as I'm sure you won't fall over."

The hall outside Checkpoint was only a few yards long, and it ended with the doors to a lift. Wu, still holding Tigre, touched the lift's control panel.

Tigre again tried to wrench free, and the little bell around his neck chimed. "Let go of me, I said! Just who the hell do you think—?"

The lift doors opened, and Wu hauled him inside.

"Hey! You can't—!"

The doors whisked shut, and the lift lurched into motion. His heart hammering, Tigre ripped free and whirled to face Wu. He found himself staring straight into eyes as bright and predatory as any Rofa's.

Wu smiled tenderly. "Well, Doctor. You got me out of Checkpoint, so I'll give you a choice. Either you can spend an indeterminate amount of time locked in a closet, or you can come with me to the access hatch on level three. I'm going to Medica."

CHAPTER TWENTY-TWO

MERIS CROUCHED in the doorway of the washroom, her webbed ears folded back and clawed hands raised in obvious warning.

Rachel stood motionless in the little kitchen area, still clutching the cup of Naranha. In spite of the danger, a swarm of details choked her mind; and she became intensely aware of her injured foot's throbbing pain, the not-quite-orange smell of Naranha, and her desire to hear Wu's voice again.

Think, she urged herself, trying to grapple with simple facts. She was locked in Tigre's office with a defenseless child and a dangerous alien. *Can't grab Saja and run. Jardín is out there.*

Meris narrowed her gray-green eyes. She no longer fit Rachel's memory of the frightened detainee who hid under her bunk, or the pitiable figure lying unconscious in Medica. Meris appeared self-controlled, powerful, and capable of inflicting serious bodily harm.

Rachel swallowed hard.

Meris hissed. Her silver-and-charcoal pelt fluffed out, and the tuft at the end of her tail bristled.

Saja, ensconced in Tigre's bowl chair, reached for the Jadamii. "Goggy!" Saja said in an ecstatic tone. A smile lit her round, sweet face. "Gog-gog-goggy!"

Meris flicked her gaze to the child. Her hand flexed.

Rachel felt as if her heart stopped. "No!" The word came

out a dry whisper. She flung herself forward. "No!" Her
legs buckled with her first step, and she fell to the floor,
landing heavily on her hands and knees. The blow sent
crushing pain through all her bones, and she gnashed her
teeth to prevent herself from crying out. The cup of Naranha tumbled over the carpet, slopping orange drink. Rachel
flung the hair out of her eyes and threw a wild glance at
Meris.

Meris gazed down at her, unmoving.

Rachel, gasping for air, stretched out her hand in entreaty. "No." Sweat spangled her upper lip. "Please. . . ."

Meris' ears lifted. She regarded Rachel for a long moment, then somberly offered her hand. "Up."

Her heart pounding, Rachel stared at Meris.

Meris spread her whiskers. "Do you understand me?"
She spoke Trade with a Rofan accent. Her voice was low,
genderless, and full of a dry resonance that tickled the ear.
"Let me help you up."

Rachel forced herself to speak. "Thank you." Hesitantly,
she took Meris' hand. The palm was warm and hairless,
and it felt surprisingly Human.

Meris raised Rachel to her feet and studied her calmly.
"I know you, I think. You are the deputy who ques-
tioned me."

"Yes." Rachel cautiously brushed her hair back with a
shaking hand. Her injured foot sent searing pain up the
tendons in her leg; and her shoulder, wrenched from her
earlier fall, felt as if it were on fire. She took a few unsteady
steps to Tigre's desk and gripped the edge. "I'm Deputy
Rachel Ajmani."

"My name is Meris." She glanced around the office,
studying Saja, the plasti-board desk, and the brocade-
covered couch. She gestured gracefully toward the door.
"Is it locked?"

Rachel abruptly shivered. "Yes."

Meris reached for her again. "Are you certain you can
stand unaided?"

"I'll be all right," Rachel said automatically. "I'm just
tired."

Saja opened and closed her little hands in a beckoning
gesture. "Come-come," she crooned. "Come, goggy."

Meris looked at Saja again, and a myriad of whisker-like

vibrissae stood up all over her face. "I had no idea," she said, "that Human children were so beautiful." Her ears curled forward in obvious fascination. "Is it yours?"

Rachel paused. "I am," she said, "responsible for her safety."

"She's hurt," Meris pointed out.

"She fell down and bumped her head." Rachel watched Meris for signs of agitation. "Do you remember that? They carried her past your cell."

"Ah, yes," Meris said. "I suppose I went a bit mad. Jadamiin babies only cry when they're in terrible pain, so I thought someone was torturing a child." She held out her left hand, displaying the injured finger with the missing claw. "I hurt myself."

"I know. I—" A sudden wonder seized her. *She was trying to rescue Saja?* Rachel had to clear her throat. "I was worried about that. How is your shoulder?"

"A little sore." Meris returned her attention to Rachel. "You're hurt, too."

Rachel glanced down at her foot. The bandage was dirty and torn. *This is not,* Tigre had told her, *a walking cast.* She met Meris' gaze. "We've all been facing difficulties, it seems."

"So it does," Meris said. "What's happening aboard your station? Rebellion? Mass hysteria? I witnessed one of your guards forcing two of its associates into a closet at gunpoint. When I tried to intervene, it shot at me."

Relieved to hear that Benjy might be unharmed, Rachel sat down on the edge of the desk. *Tried to intervene?* She sighed, wondering how she could explain Jardín without increasing misunderstanding. "I'm sorry. That individual is not station personnel. I don't know who she is, or how she managed to—"

"By all Paths, that creature is armed with a Phi-Nurian scattergun," Meris interrupted. "Are you positive the door is secured?"

"Yes," Rachel said. The word came out a harsh croak, and she cleared her throat. "We're safe. Help is on the way."

Meris peered at her. "Deputy, you seem more than tired. Are you sick?" She pointed at the couch. "Perhaps that bed-thing might be a more suitable resting place?"

Saja made an impatient noise, still reaching toward Meris. "Want up!"

"I—" Rachel had to clear her throat again. "I want to stay near Saja."

Meris flicked her tail. "Ah," she said wisely. "You don't trust me."

"Forgive me if I seem discourteous," Rachel replied with the dry remains of her voice. "But I have no reason to trust you." She edged around the desk to place herself between Meris and the child. "Why didn't you tell me during the arraignment that you could speak Trade?"

Meris considered her answer for a long moment. "If you don't trust me, then why are you asking me questions?" Her tone was mild. "You won't believe me, no matter what I say."

Rachel wearily raked her tangled hair away from her face. Meris responded in an entirely different manner than a timid Phi-Nurian or a belligerent Rofa. *Careful.* "I am trying," she explained, "to find a reason to trust you. I want to understand you."

Meris spread her webbed ears in obvious curiosity. "Trust? Understanding?" She held out her hands, as if weighing the words. "These are not the same things." She gestured smoothly toward the door. "I understand that guard out there with the Phi-Nurian scattergun. It wants to kill me."

Saja climbed up the side of the bowl chair and balanced precariously on its edge. "Goggy!" she cried insistently. "Goggy!"

Meris made a wordless noise like a sneeze that somehow sounded both exasperated and amused. "By all Paths, Deputy." She swept past Rachel and caught hold of Saja before she fell. "Pay attention to the baby."

Saja's soft, brown eyes filled with joy. "Up," she piped and raised her hands above her head. "Want up."

"How charming." Meris calmly lifted Saja out of the chair and settled her comfortably in her arms, moving with the practiced ease of someone who handled small children every day.

Heart pounding, Rachel drew a breath to protest.

Meris met Rachel's gaze. "I shall not," she stated deliberately, "harm the little one. I would never do such a thing."

Rachel licked her dry lips. "You might not intend to hurt her," she began cautiously. "But if—"

Meris made a fluid gesture of dismissal with her free hand. "Deputy, I grow weary of your suspicion. Reconcile yourself to the fact that I share your concern for the child." She pointed to the chair. "Now, sit. Restore your inner balance. I believe in civilized behavior, whatever the circumstances."

Rachel hesitated, but could find no clear argument. Keeping her eyes on Meris, she limped to the chair, tilted it down, and sank into it. The muscles in her legs twitched with the sudden release of tension, and she doubted she would be able to stand again.

"Good," Meris said approvingly. She carefully deposited Saja onto Rachel's lap. "I hope you trust me now?"

Saja's little face darkened with frustration. "No!" she protested and tried to squirm away from Rachel's grip. "Want down!"

Rachel struggled to control Saja with what remained of her failing strength. "Come on, sweetie," she murmured. "Be a good girl for Auntie Rachel."

"She's probably tired," Meris observed. "And hungry." She strolled to the couch, her slightest movement filled with self-aware poise. "I didn't speak Trade earlier," she said suddenly, "because I could not. I didn't remember learning it." The blanket hung in a tangle over the arm of the couch. She picked it up, shook it out, and glanced over her shoulder at Rachel. "I only remember it at this time because I'm under the influence of Phenox."

Rachel, distracted with Saja, tried to grasp Meris' meaning. "The drug made you remember?"

Meris' tone was patient. "It isn't easy to explain." She returned to the chair, carrying the blanket. "Phenox is a strange substance, and its effects vary with the dosage." She wrapped the blanket around Rachel and Saja, carefully smoothing and patting. "We used it in ancient times for guarding sacred or dangerous knowledge."

Taken aback by the Jadamii's motherly behavior, Rachel said, "I'm sorry. I still don't understand."

Meris gracefully knelt beside the chair. "Phenox somehow alters the memory processes in the brain. I only have access to certain memories while the drug peaks in my system. In a short while, I'll fall into another deep sleep. When I awake, I'll have no recollection of this time." She hesitated. "Nor will I be able to speak any language but my native Farnii."

"But—" Rachel drew her brows together and fumbled to think through Meris' words. "That means we won't be able to communicate again."

Meris spread her ears wide. "You have a translator. During the arraignment, he spoke for you."

Rachel abruptly recalled that Meris and Bailey knew each other. "Yes. Well. That's another problem." She studied Meris' face, watching for a reaction. "Bailey's missing."

Meris rose to her feet and turned away, hunching her shoulders. "By all Paths."

Rachel continued carefully: "He doesn't seem like the sort to disappear. There are a lot of Rofan at port; I hope he didn't become involved in a duel by accident."

Meris did not turn around. "A duel?" Her tufted tail sank to the floor, and she gave a soft moan of unmistakable despair. "It's surprisingly easy."

Saja stopped wriggling and regarded Meris doubtfully. "Goggy?" She turned her soft brown eyes to Rachel. "Goggy cwy?"

Rachel smiled sadly, and ran the tip of her little finger through the child's fine hair. "Yes, sweetie."

Ears drooping, Meris wandered to where the cup lay on the floor. "What was this?"

"Fruit drink." Rachel's voice came out a dry wheeze, and she cleared her throat. "For Saja." She nodded toward the kitchen area. "There are more cartons of the stuff in that big cupboard, if you want any."

Meris, moving as if in pain, picked up the cup. "I will get some more for Saja." She carried the cup to the sink and selected a clean one from the rack. Ears lifting slightly, she glanced over her shoulder at Rachel. "Perhaps you might try finding another translator from among the Rofan at port? Some of them know a smattering of Farnii."

Rachel let her head fall back against the chair, hiding her interest in the conversation's turn. "No. Rofan freighter captains trade in information as much as cargo. It didn't seem like a good idea to broadcast your presence on the station."

Meris cautiously opened the cupboard. "I was thinking of more responsible individuals, like representatives of the Legitimacy. They are selected for their discretion and honesty."

Saja squirmed. "Mama," she said fretfully. "Want Mama."

Rachel patted the child's back and wondered what track Meris' mind followed. "I'm sure," she said, "they are exemplary individuals. But the Rofan Legitimacy never sends representatives to Earth Port."

Meris, pulling a carton of Naranha from the cupboard, paused. "Never? Do you mean there isn't one here currently?"

"Not—" Rachel's voice faded out, and she had to clear her throat. "Not as far as I know."

Meris seemed to remember the carton in her hand. She set it on the counter and closed the cupboard door. There was a tentative quality in the way she moved, as if she were not certain which surfaces were solid.

Rachel watched, all instincts alert. "Were you expecting to find the Legitimacy aboard the station?"

"I—" Meris lowered her head. "Yes," she answered softly. "I was supposed to meet my friend, Dútha." She picked up the carton of Naranha and neatly opened it. "But now, I'm afraid . . . they've killed Dútha."

Rachel's pulse jumped. "Who?"

Meris poured the drink into the clean cup. She seemed to concentrate on the small chore, as if it enabled her to keep talking. "Dútha's superiors within the Legitimacy."

Rachel slowly straightened in her chair. "Meris," she said steadily, "maybe you should start at the beginning."

Meris slumped against the counter. "I can't. I don't know the beginning." She gazed at Rachel. "Dútha knew all that."

Seeking to shock Meris into revealing more, Rachel said: "According to rumor, you're a criminal wanted by the Legitimacy."

Meris' head jerked back in unmistakable surprise. "Me?" She raised both hands, fingers spread. "That isn't true. I didn't even want to come to Eartha, but Dútha—" She stopped.

Rachel nodded. "Go on," she urged softly. "I want to help."

"Why?" Meris' webbed ears rolled back. "You are neither kin nor an ally."

Rachel ran her hand through her hair. "Because we Humans consider it civilized behavior. Think about it. We haven't mistreated you, and yet you're in a great deal of trouble for attacking a crewman on the *La Vaca*."

"That was an accident," Meris said. "The creature startled me, and I thought it meant me harm."

"You should not," Rachel pointed out, "have been on the ship at all. Fraud and assault are serious criminal charges."

Meris' ears lifted. "Really? And if I decide to press countercharges? Or are you going to claim that the guards who tied me up and drugged me are not station personnel?"

Rachel compressed her lips. *You've got me there.* "I'm willing to consider," she replied smoothly, "that there may be mitigating circumstances on both sides."

Meris studied Rachel for a long moment. "Very well, then," she said calmly. She carried the Naranha over to the chair and handed it to Rachel. "Dútha thought it had something to do with . . . an artifact."

Saja reached for the cup. "Juice."

Rachel let the little girl hold the cup while she steadied it. "Artifact?"

"An ancient relic of Jada." Meris crouched down beside the chair. "Archaeologists recovered it from the bottom of the ocean, and it's written in an obscure dialect of a dead language." She spread her hands. "It defies translation. It's a historical curiosity, a bone for scholars to gnaw."

Saja took three noisy gulps, then pushed the cup away. "All done."

Rachel set the Naranha on the desk, trying to force her tired mind to focus. "And the artifact, is it responsible for the upheaval on Igsha Reey's Port Station?"

"Dútha thought so." Meris' tone held conviction. "And that *gukka* was no fool. Dútha said—" She paused and spread her hands. "Deputy, I don't know how to make you understand. Dútha was the one who knew all the details."

Rachel drew her brows together in thought, certain she was missing something obvious. "But, Meris, how did you become involved in this?"

Meris' ears drooped. "Dútha rescued me. I—" She seemed unable to speak. "It's a very long story, but I found myself alone and helpless aboard Igsha Reey's station. Dútha saved my life. Stepped in and—" She gently touched Rachel's hand. "Deputy, have you ever pledged friendship with a Rofa?"

Somewhat uneasily, Rachel recalled Khanwa's passionate declaration. "Just recently."

"Then you have yet to learn the true nature of the Rofan," Meris said softly. "Let me simply say that Dútha was braver and truer to me than kin. That *gukka* rescued me from my captors and smuggled me aboard a freighter from Eartha."

Rachel tried to sound polite. "How did Dútha do that?"

Meris made a dismissive gesture. "Some Kamian gadget. It used static electricity, I think." She picked up her tail and tenderly brushed its tuft against Saja's nose. "Dútha promised to meet me at Earth Port. If Dútha is not here, then I must fear the worst."

Saja laughed with delight. "Tick-ol, tick-ol."

Rachel had to swallow before she could speak. "Don't give up hope. Maybe your friend was delayed. Dútha could be arriving as we speak."

"Maybe." Meris did not sound cheered. "But I was drugged with Phenox when I met Dútha. I can't remember Dútha, or what my friend did for me, unless I'm between sleeps. That's why I was so desperate to escape the freighter, why I hurt that person. I had to get to Dútha."

Sympathy squeezed Rachel's heart. "Can't you take more Phenox?"

"Of course." Meris' tone was patient. "But I can't keep taking it, sleeping my life away. And it—" She paused. "I once took too much, and it erased all my memories. I'm afraid of doing that again."

Rachel searched for the right words. "But Dútha will remember you. Dútha will still be your friend."

"Yes." Meris slowly rose to her feet. "As we say on Jada, friendship is—"

Someone pounded on the office door. Rachel started violently. Meris leaped sideways, and her ears flashed back.

Jardín's voice came through the speaker on the door's control panel. "Ajmani. Open up."

Rachel sat in tense silence and slowly turned her eyes to Meris.

Saja waved at the door. "Hello? Hello? Come in."

"Answer me," Jardín demanded. "I'm not playing a game."

Meris, pelt bristling, crept closer to Rachel. "By all Paths, who is that?" she whispered. "What does it want?"

Rachel's heart picked up speed. "It's Jardín. The one with the gun."

Jardín's tone gained an ominous edge. "I can cut my way in, you know. Open the door now, Ajmani, and that little girl won't get hurt."

Tigre stared around himself in rising wonder. He stood beside Wu on an entry platform inside the station's walls, at the junction of a vertical and a horizontal access tube.

Tigre had expected dirty, dimly lit shafts, but everything was clean and bright. Each tube, five feet wide, had a mirrored panel running down its length beside the ladder rungs. Lamps spread a haze of golden light; a soft roar filled the air, like the amplified whisper in a seashell.

"My God," Tigre murmured. "This place is beautiful."

A map of the access network hung on the wall beside the hatch. Wu studied it intently, tracing a red line with his thumbnail. "Isn't it, though?" He glanced at Tigre, his eyes sparkling. "Aren't you glad you came along?"

"Sure." Oddly embarrassed by his admission, Tigre looked away from Wu and found himself gazing at his own reflection in a mirror panel. The golden light bleached the pants of his lavender scrubs to white and made his blue-black hair shine like silk. Smudges of exhaustion darkened the tender flesh under his eyes, and a mottled band of bruises encircled his right forearm. He was shirtless, and Dútha's bell hung over his heart, its gray metal warmed by his skin.

Wu gently patted Tigre's bare shoulder. "Ready, Doctor?"

Tigre returned his attention to Wu and folded his arms. "More than ready."

Smiling, Wu dropped to his hands and knees and slid feetfirst into the downward tube. Holding the top rung of the ladder, he beamed up at Tigre. "Follow me, Doctor."

Tigre wiped his sweating, filthy palms on his scrubs and climbed in after Wu. The rungs were covered with textured material that offered a firm grip, and Tigre found the descent surprisingly easy.

The hatch above him hummed shut. The soft roar of air ceased.

"A bit of advice." Wu's voice set off whispering echoes along the tube. "Don't look down. Use the mirror to check my position, it's less distracting."

"Okay." In spite of exhaustion and grief, a peculiar excitement warmed Tigre's blood. He glanced at the mirror and found that he could see Wu clearly.

Wu caught his eye and grinned. "Hello," he said cheerfully. "I'm going to set a fairly quick pace, but let me know if you get tired. We've got the rough equivalent of twenty stories to climb, so we can't wear ourselves out before we get to Medica."

Tigre involuntarily glanced down the shaft. It seemed to end at another hatch thirty feet below. He suddenly realized just how narrow the tube was, and how far it would be if he fell. *Oh, God.* A sudden sweat sheathed his bare chest and back, but he forced himself to keep moving. *Don't look down, stupid.* He looked up at the top of the shaft.

Instead of the hatch, he saw a large ventilation fan, with curling blades like scimitars. It turned slowly, spanning the diameter of the tube. Tigre squinted up at it, wondering why he had not noticed it before. As he watched, it began to turn faster. Tigre stopped climbing, seized by a sudden sense of dread.

Without warning, the fan fell. Its whirling blades picked up speed as it dropped toward them.

Tigre's warning cry dried in his throat. He clutched the rungs and tried to tuck in his head.

Wu's voice was soft. "Doctor. You okay?"

Heart hammering, Tigre clung to the ladder. Nothing happened. After a few moments, he cautiously raised his head and glanced up the shaft. The fan was gone. Breathing raggedly, he stared at the hatch. *What the hell?*

Wu cleared his throat. "Doctor?"

"Fine," Tigre said. "I'm fine." His voice sounded thin and scared to his own ears. "I just—" He swallowed, and a fresh tide of cold perspiration washed over him. "Almost slipped."

"Don't worry." Wu's tone held an odd gentleness. "I won't let you fall."

Tigre felt each stroke of his heart jolt through his body. "Thanks," he muttered. Gritting his teeth, he resumed his downward climb. He recalled Deputy Omar's joking reference to hallucinations induced by sleep deprivation. *Pink snakes. I'm seeing goddamned pink snakes.*

"Still glad you came along?" Wu asked brightly.

Tigre scowled at the other man's reflection. "I hope you realize," he said, "that I came because I wanted to."

Wu beamed at him. "Oh, of course."

"I mean that you wouldn't have had to lock me in a closet," Tigre continued, "because I wouldn't have reported you."

Wu chuckled. "I know. And that's exactly why I would've locked you up. You would have made yourself an accessory."

"Hey," Tigre protested. "I can make my own decisions."

"I know that. You're here, aren't you?"

Tigre drew another sputtering breath, then paused. *What the blazes am I arguing about?* He urged his tired mind to focus on the situation at hand. "What I don't understand," he said, "is why Deputy Jimanez-Verde is wasting her time trying to cut into Medica. Why didn't she just send someone down this tube?"

"She did," Wu said cheerfully. "Me."

Tigre glanced at Wu's reflection in the mirror. Wu still wore a smile.

"But," Tigre stammered, "she had you arrested."

"Exactly. And suspended from duty. So the station isn't liable for any illegal action I take."

A fresh chill invaded Tigre, and his hands turned clammy. A long fall of a different sort presented itself to his awareness. "Aw, hell." He kept his tone casual. "I think I just stepped into a bigger pile of shit than I realized."

Wu laughed kindly. "That's the trouble with making your own decisions. But don't worry. I've kidnapped you, remember?"

I won't let you fall. Tigre, feeling strangely shy, smiled at Wu. "Thanks," he said softly, "but I think you're in enough trouble. And I'm not helpless, you know."

"I realize that, Doctor. You're clearly a force to be reckoned with," Wu said. "No wonder that *gukka* was so impressed."

Tigre did not want to think about his confrontation with Dútha, or his failure to save Jhaska's life. "He just considered me too small and insignificant to be a worthy opponent."

Wu paused before speaking. "So. You've decided that Dútha is male. Interesting."

Tigre frowned. "What the hell do you mean by that?"

"Nothing. Except . . ." Wu cleared his throat. "Dútha said it wanted to see you again. When it invites you to meet with it, will you go?"

"Probably."

Wu's tone gained a tentative quality. "What if the invitation is sexual?"

Tigre swallowed hard. "Pardon me?" He fought against the impulse to stop and think. "Is that likely?"

"Well. Yes."

An unexpected heat rose up in Tigre's face and throat, but he forced himself to continue his downward climb. Once again, he mentally fumbled with the concept of Rofan gender. It had been easy for him to see Jhaska as a sexless individual, but Dútha was a different matter.

Tigre suddenly wondered if the *gukka* were, in fact, a female. It put everything, the confrontation, Dútha's patience, the gift of jewelry, in a different perspective. "So, if I—?" Then he belatedly deciphered Wu's tone of voice, and he inhaled though his teeth. "Then has a Rofa ever—" He searched for a tactful word. "—propositioned you?"

Wu chuckled. "Yes."

Tigre's curiosity reared. He had read the report on some of the station personnel's sexual experimentation, but the documentation had not given names. He needed to swallow again before he could speak. "But how—?"

"Well, it's a matter of—" Wu stopped and made a

pleased noise. "Oh, goody. We're at the first hatch." He patted the back of Tigre's calf. "Don't climb down any farther, Doctor. I need room to maneuver."

Tigre stopped and glanced down at Wu. "So what happened with the Rofa? Was it angry when you refused the offer?"

Wu held the ladder with one hand and leaned out toward a small control plate. He did not look up at Tigre. "Who said that I refused?"

Tigre's lips parted in surprise, and he struggled to find words. Entirely unbidden, a vivid fantasy flashed through his mind of tumbling among pillows with Dútha. Shaken and confused by his own thoughts, Tigre scowled. "You made love with a Rofa? That was stupid."

Wu pressed a command on the control plate with his thumb. "Really?" He chuckled. "Doctor. You are the one with a Rofan bell around his neck."

Tigre's face grew hot. "Just what," he asked grimly, "are you implying?"

"Don't get mad again," Wu said in a friendly tone. "You're always getting mad at—" He paused and peered at the control panel. "Hmm." He pushed the command a second time.

Tigre watched him. "What's wrong?"

Wu pouted. "Interestingly, it's locked."

Tigre tightened his grip on the ladder. "You mean we can't get through?"

"Maybe." Wu keyed in a string of numbers, then pressed his palm against a sensor grid. "Let's see if I've still got clearance." The hatch at his feet slid to the side, and a warm draft billowed into their tube. Wu sat down on the floor and swung his legs through the opening. He grinned up at Tigre. "Follow me, Doctor."

Tigre waited until Wu was through the hatch before he started down. "What was that all about?" he demanded. "Why haven't they removed your code from the system?"

Wu laughed. "Oh. They probably thought they did. But I, sneaky reprobate that I am, have more than one code."

Following Wu's example, Tigre got down on the floor and slid his feet through the hatch. He glanced upward, letting his gaze travel the length of the access tube to the top. He flinched inwardly, afraid the spinning fan would appear again, but he saw nothing except the hatch. "What if we get stuck in here?" he asked. "What if they find your other codes, and we're trapped between two locked hatches?"

"That's an interesting question," Wu replied cheerfully. "And I don't want to think about the answer."

Tigre snorted and eased his aching body through the opening. "How far did you say we had to go?"

"About twenty stories. Most of it straight down." Wu's voice set off whispering echoes. "Think you can make it?"

Tigre clenched his jaw. Memories of his time on Brontos surfaced, and he recalled five days of backbreaking rescue efforts with minimal food and rest. Compared to hauling bodies from rubble, the climb down to Medica was a long nap in a soft bed. "Make it?" he replied. "Do I have a choice?"

Wu laughed gently. "You could wait for me here."

"Oh, yes. Very amusing." When Tigre gripped another rung on the ladder, he encountered something sticky. He peered at his already filthy fingers and discovered traces of a black substance. "Oh, damn it," he muttered.

"Pardon?"

Tigre grimaced. "Sorry. I just seem to be tracking shit everywhere."

"Ah," Wu said. "I've noticed it, too. So I don't believe it's from your shoes."

Tigre paused, gripping the rung with one hand, and wiped his fingers on his soiled scrubs. "God, I want a shower."

"I don't believe," Wu continued, "that it's from my shoes, either."

"Oh?" Tigre said absently.

"So you know what this means, don't you?"

Tigre drew his dark brows together, trying to follow Wu's drift. "What?"

"Someone has come through here before us. Someone, it seems, who was recently in Checkpoint."

It took Tigre a moment to unravel the implications of Wu's statement. "Oh," he said uncertainly. "Is that bad?"

"Hope not."

Feeling chastened, Tigre tried to pull his thoughts together. "So what are we going to do?" He gazed at Wu's reflection and hoped he was not asking ridiculous questions. "I mean, who do you suppose is ahead of us? Jardín?"

"Maybe. Maybe not."

"Do we keep going?"

Wu sighed. "Oh, yes. We keep going. We just watch out for traps."

Tigre nodded. The slight movement made the lamps' golden light smear the air with red trails of fire. *I'm losing it. Can't think straight.* "What kind of traps?"

Wu made a noise of facetious protest. "Please, Doctor. That's another interesting question."

"Yes, but—" Tigre abruptly noticed his own reflection in the mirror. There were dark shadows under his cheeks, and his eyes appeared sunken. *I look like a corpse.* Rattled, he groped for the thread of conversation. "Maybe they're on another errand, and they're not headed to Medica at all."

"Maybe," Wu said. His voice took on an anxious shading. "Doctor, are you sure you're all right? You don't seem like yourself."

"Well . . ." Tigre was not sure what to say. "I've been on my feet for three days." He changed the subject. "So. What's the plan when we get to Medica?"

"I don't have a plan yet. I need to see what the situation is when we get there." Wu paused and cleared his throat. "You sure you're all right? You don't . . . sound . . . so good. Maybe I ought to drop you off at the next access."

The muscles in Tigre's shoulders tightened. "No, you can't do that!" He struggled to modify his desperate tone. "Someone might be injured. You can't help them and deal with Jardín at the same time. And besides—" His reasoning hit a brick wall, and he floundered for the end of his sentence. "I can take something. When we get to the supply closet in Medica, I mean."

"Oh?" Wu asked guardedly. "What? A stimulant?"

"Better." Tigre tried to sound authoritative. "Seroplex. Chemical sleep."

"Seroplex?" Wu's tone was openly exasperated. "Isn't that just the prescription form of 'Jaz'? I know pilots who take that stuff. It's highly addictive and ought to be restricted."

"But I won't take enough to—" Tigre glanced in the

mirror. Something hovered behind him that looked like a ball of burning rags. It floated just behind his head, giving off a roiling cloud of golden smoke. *A trap!*

Tigre's heart lurched. With a wordless cry, he twisted around to face the threat. Both feet slipped off the ladder as he turned, and his chin slammed down on one of the rungs. Pain flashed through his jaw and seemed to explode in the back of his head. He felt himself falling backward, and he realized with a shock that he had lost his grip on the ladder.

Tigre tasted blood. His entire body throbbed with pain.

Wu's voice was close to his ear. "Tigre?" He sounded strangely frightened. "Can you hear me? Wake up."

Tigre opened his eyes. Details presented themselves in slow procession as reality took shape around him. He was standing on the floor of the tube; collarbone, belly, and thighs pressed against the rungs of the ladder. Wu stood behind him, using the length of his body to keep him upright. Tigre moaned and raised his head. "Oh, God."

"Tigre?"

Moving carefully, Tigre shifted to support his own weight. "I'm okay." Nausea swept through him. He closed his eyes again and rested his sweating forehead on a rung. "What happened?"

"You slipped." Wu's voice was shaky with obvious relief. "And I think you hit your head. You blacked out for a minute."

"Oh, God." Tigre swallowed. "I'm sorry. I'm so sorry."

Wu cleared his throat. "Could have happened to anyone." He gently patted Tigre's bare shoulder. "Good thing we were near the end of the tube, though. I don't think I could have carried you much farther."

Tigre cautiously opened his eyes. His chin was sticky with blood, and he dabbed at it with the back of his wrist. "Yeah," he said thickly. "Good thing." He glanced in the mirror. Wu wore a strained expression, and perspiration rolled down his face. "You okay?"

Wu grinned faintly and shrugged. "Twisted my ankle. I'll live."

Tigre turned to face Wu. In the tube's narrow confines, they stood mere inches apart. He gazed into the other man's eyes, and for the first time he simply saw another Human. "You should have just let me fall."

Wu's voice was soft. "Oh, I would never do that."

Tigre sighed. "Do you realize," he said, "just how many times you've saved my life today?"

Wu dropped his gaze. "I'm not keeping score."

His words seemed to vibrate in the air after he spoke them. Tigre felt their meaning with his whole body, as if from the shock of physical impact. He studied Wu's face, searching for a way to answer.

Even in the pervasive golden light, Wu's visage seemed pinched and white. Sweat rolled from the tips of his hair and soaked into his black tunic.

Tigre narrowed his eyes. "Your ankle," he said slowly. "Are you sure it's just twisted?"

Wu shrugged again. "Maybe sprained. It's not—"

Tigre knelt, ignoring the protest of his wrenched muscles, and tucked his slender frame into a compact crouch.

Wu stood with all his weight on his left foot. His right foot puffed around the edges of his shoe. Carefully, Tigre lifted the trousers' cuff and rolled down the sock. Wu's ankle was bloated and purple. *Aw, hell.*

"If you're rested, Doctor," Wu said, "we ought to get moving again."

"Your ankle doesn't look so good." Tigre spoke calmly, falling into his professional manner. "We'd better wrap it with something to give it a little support. I don't suppose you're wearing a belt?"

"Sorry."

Tigre tugged at the knot on his scrub pants until it came loose and pulled the tie all the way out. It provided him with less than a yard of a narrow fabric strip. "I'll try using this . . ." Abruptly, the full scope of the situation hit him.

He had been willing to take any risk to rescue the people trapped in Medica. But he realized at that moment that he could save no one: not Jhaska, or Rachel, or Wu. *And the Agency might denounce me. This will just kill Uncle Richard.* Aware of his own long silence, Tigre pushed away his despair and drew a steadying breath. "I hope you're happy." He spoke in a carefully cheerful tone. "Now my pants are going to fall off."

Wu laughed weakly. "All part of my master plan."

Tigre patted Wu's good leg. "Hey, maybe you ought to sit down. This may—"

"Don't have time," Wu interrupted. "We've got to get to Medica."

Tigre gazed up at him. "Wu. I think there's a good chance your ankle is broken. Are you trying to tell me that you can't feel the rough edges of bones grinding around in there?"

"No, dear friend." Wu ducked his head to wipe his sweating face on the sleeve of his black tunic. "I'm trying to tell you that we don't have time."

"But your by God ankle is—"

Moving like a striking snake, Wu bent down and snatched the tie from Tigre's hands. "Give me that." He looked down at Tigre with an expression of amused exasperation. "I'll wrap up my own ankle. You go to Medica."

"What?" Tigre stared up at him. "I can't leave you alone."

"Yes, you can." Wu reached into the pocket of his trousers and pulled out a shiny, black object. He offered it to Tigre. "And take this with you."

It took Tigre a few moments to recognize the item in Wu's hand. It was a laser pistol. Tigre recoiled. "No. Put that thing away."

Wu gave no sign he heard. He continued to hold the pistol in front of Tigre's eyes. "Look for injured station personnel. If Jardín gets anywhere near you, shoot her."

"I refuse," Tigre said evenly, "to even touch that thing." He looked up at Wu, meeting his gaze squarely. "I'm a doctor. Remember? I've taken Meing's Vow. I'm sworn to save lives, not end them."

"I'm not recommending that you shoot to kill."

Tigre narrowed his eyes. "And now that I think about it, you were suspended and placed under arrest. Where did you get a pistol?"

Wu grinned. "Stole it from the room where they laid out the Phi-Nurian bodies." He offered the pistol again. "Take it, Tigre. Think of it as a long-range scalpel."

Tigre shook his head adamantly. "Absolutely not. There's nothing you can say—" Without thinking, he ran his filthy hands through his hair. His fingers were still encrusted with Jhaska's vomit, and the faint scent of peaches drifted to him. For a moment, he froze, crouched at Wu's feet. "You're right. I'm wasting time." His words seemed to form in his mind as he spoke them, and he wondered if he were an idiot or a hero. "I won't take the pistol. But I—" *Oh, God, help me.* "—I will go to Medica."

CHAPTER TWENTY-THREE

MERIS CROUCHED on the floor behind the desk, her pulse thrumming in her ears. She battled against her own powerful instincts, resisting the urge to hide, reminding herself of her place upon the Three Great Paths. *Dútha died to save me. I cannot let it be in vain.*

With an intensity born of love and sorrow, Meris wished for her friend's living presence. *You promised to be at my side.* But now she was alone among aliens, trapped in a cramped and smelly compartment on a space station, cornered by an assassin. Worst of all, she possessed only a brief period of unbroken memory while the Phenox peaked in her system. Soon she would fall into another deep sleep; and when she awoke, if she survived, she would have no recollection of her family's treachery or her desperate flight to Eartha Port Station.

From the hallway outside came the voice of Jardín, the one with the gun. Meris spread her webbed ears wide and listened intently. She could not understand Jardín's words, but obvious threat edged her tone. Meris clearly heard her pace back and forth just beyond the door, her shod feet scuffing the tiled floor.

Rachel sat bolt upright in her chair. She also seemed to be listening to Jardín, though Meris detected no movement of the Human's small ears. A pungent wave of Rachel's fear scent washed through the air, and she protectively folded her arms around the small child on her lap.

Innocent of danger, Saja tried to wriggle free. Though an alien, the child's smooth hide and wide eyes held infinite appeal; her beauty made Meris view the odorous, damp, and graceless adult in a more forgiving light.

Jardín stopped her incomprehensible ranting.

The skin on Meris' scalp tightened, causing her mane to rise up in hackles. "What is she saying?" she whispered to Rachel. "What does she want?"

Visible traces of moisture spangled Rachel's upper lip. "She's insane," the deputy breathed. "She says if I don't hand you over, she'll kill Saja."

"Kill?" Meris echoed in disbelief. "How? You said the door was secured. You said we were safe!"

Jabbering cheerfully, little Saja lifted a corner of her blanket and attempted to dry Rachel's wet face.

"She's got a welder. She'll try to cut her way in." Rachel's gaze darted to every corner of the room as if searching for a way to escape. "We have to stall her until help arrives."

Meris also looked around but saw nothing to reassure her. The room reflected the geometric architecture of which the Humans seemed so fond—all straight lines and hard edges. The furnishings were bulky and unrefined, and every surface exuded the musky scent of Humans. A desk and chair sat in the middle of the floor, an upholstered bedlike thing stretched along the right wall, and to the left was an area that seemed to be a miniature galley.

The different spaces, along with an adjoining sanitation facility, suggested to Meris that the room was intended for both living and working. The idea of such multiple functions was depressingly efficient, and it only reaffirmed the rumors that Human society was utilitarian and conformist. *And only one door! By the Three Great Paths, what kind of room has only one door?*

The stink of melting metal assaulted Meris' nose, burning through the scent of terrified Human. She peered over the top of the desk. A smoldering spot of orange light appeared along the edge of the door, near its latch plate. "All Paths," she hissed.

A cup, still full of Saja's beverage, sat in the middle of the desk. Meris snatched it up and strode to the door. The orange light grew brighter, wreathed in wisps of bitter smoke.

Thinking only in terms of dousing a fire, she tossed the contents of the cup onto the welder's hot spot. A hissing crackle cut the air. Startled, Meris dropped the cup. White sparks danced over the latch plate. From the other side of the door, Jardín screamed with frustration and fury, sounding more like an animal than a sentient being.

Panting, Meris backed away and glanced toward the desk. Rachel leaned forward in her chair, her eyes wide. Saja pointed and asked something in a worried tone.

From the hall outside came the sound of scuffling and muffled thumps. Meris spread her ears and extended the vibrissae on her brow. "Rachel," she whispered. "I think she's throwing herself against the door."

"Temper tantrum." Rachel's voice was soft but filled with unmistakable satisfaction. "I'll wager that your little trick fused the lock mechanism. Probably blew the power cell in her welder, too."

Hope surged through Meris, and she lifted her tufted tail. "Really? We're safe?"

A sudden roar like thunder shattered the air. The door boomed and shivered in its frame.

"All Paths!" Meris flung herself to the floor and scrambled for refuge behind the desk.

Little Saja shrieked and began to wail. Rachel clutched the child to her. Meris heard their hearts beating, a rapid and arrhythmic thumping. "Rachel, are you all right?"

Rachel swallowed with a sticky noise. "She shot at the door."

Liquid ran freely from Saja's eyes and nose, and the visible dampness on Rachel's face began to drip. In a distracted flash of random thought, Meris decided it was some sort of survival trait for Humans to exude moisture when in danger.

Jardín hammered on the door and shouted Rachel's house name as if it were a curse. "Ajmani!"

Instinct reared again, batting aside Meris' terror. Acting upon the overwhelming impulse to protect Saja, Meris stalked to the door. She did not know the full capabilities of a scattergun, but she thought it prudent to prevent Jardín from firing again. Motioning for Rachel to remain silent, she spoke in Trade to the enemy outside. "Keep shooting." She tried to sound cool and dangerous, like Dútha. "Go on. Waste all your ammunition."

There was silence from Jardín. Meris tensed. "Do you understand me?"

"Ajmani?" Jardín's voice held an uncertain note, but she replied in Trade. "Is that you?"

Meris' webbed ears flicked back. "The deputy can't talk to you now."

"You—?" Jardín paused, and her tone softened. "Have I the honor of addressing Meris?"

Meris flexed her clawed hands. *Pathless monster.* "Yes. Whatever honor that would mean to a Human."

"Esteemed Meris." Jardín's voice turned as light and sweet as a bell. "I am so relieved to find you unharmed."

Meris settled one shoulder against the wall beside the door, half turning so she could see Rachel for guidance. "Oh?" she said dryly. "Really?"

Rachel leaned forward in the chair and whispered, "What are you doing?"

Meris lifted her chin and mouthed a single word: "Stalling."

"Please," Jardín continued, "come out of that room. There isn't much time before the others arrive. We have to hurry, or we won't make our escape."

"What are you talking about?" Meris tried to sound disdainful. "What others?"

Jardín's voice rose in pitch. "Station Safety. They're after you. We've got to get away. If they find you here, they'll kill you."

Meris laid her ears back. She could not recall ever hearing a more ludicrously transparent lie. *But, of course, she believes I've just harmed a Port Authority deputy.* "Forgive me for mentioning this," she said with mocking courtesy, "but I recognize your voice. I saw you in the hallway. You wore an Eartha Port Safety uniform."

"It's a disguise, nothing more." The pitch of Jardín's voice grew higher. "Please. You have to trust me."

"You also, if I'm not mistaken, shot at me."

"But I didn't mean to. You startled me."

The skin over Meris' back tightened, and the hackles marched down her spine. She recalled how Jardín had turned to face her, how slowly and carefully she had raised her weapon. *By all Paths, just how stupid do I seem?* "Liar."

"You have to believe me," Jardín said earnestly. "Come out of there. Hurry!"

Meris wrinkled her nose. "You," she said, "are not only a liar, you are also a bore."

Jardín's voice rose in desperation. "I'm telling the truth. We've got to get out of here."

Meris narrowed her eyes, thinking of Bailey and his promises to help. "Then persuade me. Tell me why you are placing yourself at risk for a stranger. What value does my life have for you?"

From outside the door, Jardín gave a wordless shout of frustration and rage. "Open up!" Her voice was raw. "Do you hear me?"

Rachel stirred uneasily, but Meris raised her hands in a reassuring gesture. "Go away," she called to Jardín. "You're scaring the baby."

"I'm warning you," Jardín said hoarsely, "you'll be sorry you didn't cooperate."

"I doubt it." Meris studied the door. It appeared sound, showing no signs of buckling or perforation. Moving with extreme caution, she placed the palms of her hands against its surface and exerted slow pressure. The door shifted minutely, as if crooked in its frame. *Damaged.* "I'd rather take my chances with station Safety."

Jardín made a disgusted noise. "They'll torture you, you know. They'll do anything to gain information about the Artifact."

Meris' breath caught in her throat, and she tried to recall what she had told Rachel. "Information? About the Artifact?" she repeated. "That doesn't make sense." She turned to face Rachel and phrased her words for the deputy's benefit. "Why would they torture me for that? Anyone can get a copy. By all Paths, we hand them out to Rofan tourists!"

"Fakes," Jardín said contemptuously. "I'm talking about the original Artifact. Someone has translated it."

Rachel's eyes narrowed, and she seemed to regard Meris with suspicion.

Meris' silvery pelt fluffed out in terrified anger. "You're

mad," she told Jardín. "It's an archaeological curiosity, nothing more."

There was a thump on the door, as if Jardín had punched it. "Liar," she snapped. "I spoke to someone who knew all about it. The Artifact was only partially translated, but even so, its meaning was clear."

"Translated? The Artifact?" A thread of bile rose in Meris' throat. Dútha had tried to tell her as much, but she had remained unconvinced. "Impossible."

"The perfect tool for galactic conquest," Jardín said grimly. "The Artifact is a set of calculations regarding the nature of time. It even contains details on the structure of black holes." She paused. "Information that every government in the galaxy will want to obtain at any cost."

Meris stood frozen, her thoughts racing in frantic circles. *Can it be true?*

"Do you understand?" Jardín continued relentlessly. "You are the only Jadamii who can read it. You're a catalyst for galactic war."

"Me?" Meris stammered in genuine confusion. "I'm not a catalyst for anything!" She approached Rachel, spreading her hands in entreaty. "I'm an old, old Jadamii. I spend my days drinking sweetleaf tea and taking care of my children's children."

Rachel leaned forward in the chair. "Jardín," she called. "Who translated the Artifact?"

There was a brief pause. "Ajmani?" Jardín's voice warmed with satisfaction. "I thought you were listening."

"Who?" Rachel repeated.

"He's here on the station. Perhaps you've met him," Jardín replied. "He's a *shana* on the Hoshino Uta Freehold, and a genius with languages."

Rachel carefully climbed to her feet and settled Saja in the chair. "Bailey." She leaned on the desk, bracing herself with trembling arms. "His name is Bailey Rye, and he seems to be missing. Do you know where he is?"

Jardín made a disgusted noise. "Ask your friend, Meris."

Meris moved to face Rachel across the desk. "She's lying. Lying about Bailey and the Artifact," she whispered. "You have to believe me."

Rachel met her gaze squarely. "Why didn't you tell me everything about the Artifact?"

"Because I don't think it's true." Meris hunched her shoulders. "But I guess the truth doesn't matter. We are all grinding toward a war over a set of equations that does not, in fact, exist."

The door rattled as if Jardín hammered it with the butt of her gun. "Ajmani, you have to listen to me," she shouted. "Meris knows how to read the Artifact. Once the World Council tortures the rest of the translation from her, what will they do with that knowledge?"

Meris ran a dispirited hand through her mane. "I don't know what to say. How to make you believe me."

Without warning, vertigo seized her. A deep hum filled her ears, and the room seemed to spin. Fearing a fall, she hastily lowered herself to the floor. She recognized the dizziness; the Phenox was wearing off. *All Paths, not now!*

Rachel knelt in front of her. "Meris? What's wrong?"

The hum became a physical sensation in the back of her head. "Jardín is lying. The Artifact is harmless. And I don't know where poor Bailey is." Struggling for words, Meris repeated: "Poor Bailey."

Rachel put her hands on Meris' shoulders, and her gaze seemed both anxious and compassionate. "It's all right," she said. "I believe you."

Jardín pounded on the door. "Ajmani! Do you hear me?"

The humming enveloped Meris' skull, and her vision blurred. "It's over. The Phenox is failing. When I wake up—if I wake up—I won't remember any of this."

"What do you mean?" Rachel asked softly. "You won't remember anything?"

Meris tried to explain one last time. "When I awake, my most recent memory will be . . . a weeping Human child . . . rage . . . and guards drugging me." She pressed her hands to her temples, trying to stay focused. Rachel drew a breath to speak, but Meris raised a forestalling hand. "Please. While we have time. There is something I once told Dútha, and I want to say it to you."

Jardín hammered the door again. "Do you hear me, Ajmani?"

The humming began to travel down Meris' spine. "On Jada, we follow the Three Great Paths: Hand, Mouth, and Eye. But I know of a Fourth Path—" Shadows loomed within her mind, but she fought to keep speaking. "Friendship."

"Meris—"

"Please," Meris entreated. "I shall forget. You must remember it for me."

From the other side of the door, Jardín spoke in a tone of ominous quiet. "Meris. Come out now, and I'll make it quick and painless."

Meris found herself sliding into a reclining position. "Tell Dútha—tell—" The shadows deepened. "I—I— *I—love*—"

Darkness claimed her.

Tigre slid through the hatch and into the unlit supply closet. The comforting and familiar smell of regeneration compounds welcomed him. Too shaky to stand, he crept forward on his hands and knees, wearing nothing but his underwear and Dútha's bell. His scrub pants, missing their drawstring, had quickly become a dangerous liability in his long climb, and he had discarded them at one of the hatches. *Shit, it's cold in here.*

Storage cupboards lined the closet's walls; and a rack by the door held three, prepacked emergency kits. Tigre paused and peered up at the cupboards, trying to decipher the content tags by the golden light from the access tube. After three hectic days in Medica, he knew where they kept most of the equipment, but the pharmaceutical stores were unexplored territory.

For a moment, the search to find the supplies he needed seemed an impossible task. He sat on the floor in a boneless slouch, shivering with exhaustion in the chill air. A single phrase from the journal of Prudence Clarke ran repeatedly through his mind, as it had since he left Wu. *When I am dead, I shall miss hammocks in the rain and collie dogs.* The words no longer held any rational meaning for him; they were simply a mantra that measured his every breath.

A storage cupboard sat in front of him. Listlessly, he pressed his thumb to the sensor pad on the door's lock. It peeped, and the door slid open to reveal tidy stacks of clean scrubs. He dragged one of the garments from the cupboard and shook it out. It was a tunic, but he could not ascertain its color in the dim, golden light. He pulled it on over his head. The thing fit his slender frame like a tent, but he felt a bit more oriented to his own identity. *Almost as good as a bath*. He rummaged through the cupboard until he found a pair of pants. Feeling as awkward as a three year old, he pulled them on and tied the drawstring.

Using the cupboards for handholds, Tigre hauled himself to his feet. A box of sterile wipes sat on a nearby counter. He carefully cleaned his hands, then methodically began to open door after door. In the second cupboard, he found the inhalers and transdermic injectors; in the fourth, he discovered the drugs he wanted. With shaking hands, he loaded a Seroplex cartridge into an injector and set the dosage for maximum. He pulled aside his tunic and shoved down the waistband of his pants to expose his right hip. Clenching his jaw, he pressed the injector to his bare skin and pulled the trigger.

The Seroplex burned as it entered his body. Tigre bit his lips, waiting for it to take effect. The drug was not a stimulant, but a chemical simulation of sleep, and he calculated it would keep him on his feet for another twelve hours. "Come on," he whispered impatiently. "Start already."

As if cued by his words, nausea swept through him in a massive flux. Tigre pressed his sweating forehead against the cool surface of a cupboard and closed his eyes. *When I am dead*— The air turned hot, then cold. His stomach heaved. "Oh, God," he panted softly. "Oh, God—" The blood in his brain seemed to turn effervescent. The tickling, champagne effect bubbled away his distress and left him with an altogether wholesome sense of well-being.

Tigre opened his eyes and raised his head. Though still physically exhausted, he felt mentally exhilarated, as if fresh from a strenuous workout. "Damn," he whispered. He stared with reverence at the empty cartridge in the injector. "This stuff is good."

From somewhere in Medica came a woman's incoherent shout. Tigre's heart lurched. He snatched up an inhaler, jammed a Tri-Omega cartridge into its chamber, and strode to the door. The shouting continued. He pressed his ear against the door and listened. It did not sound like Rachel's voice, but it occurred to him that where there was smoke, there was fire. *And where there's an argument, there's Deputy Ajmani*.

He holstered the inhaler in the waistband of his scrub

pants, hoping the tunic was voluminous enough to conceal it in case Jardín happened to spot him. The medical kits that hung in the rack by the door were black canvas bags about the size of a loaf of bread. Tigre unhooked one and slipped its padded strap over his left shoulder. Heart pounding, he opened the door a crack and peeked out.

The light in the hallway outside seemed dazzling. Tigre paused, waiting for his eyes to adjust. The woman still shouted. Echoes distorted most of her words, but he thought she demanded entrance to somewhere. Forcing himself into professional calm, he slowly opened the door and edged into the hall.

Medica's white walls and gray-tiled floor seemed like home. Tigre softly shut the closet door and made sure of the kit's strap. The woman stopped shouting and lowered her voice. Only then did he recognize the sweetly venomous tones of Jardín Azul, and it sounded as if she were in the left corridor where his office was located.

Swallowing hard, Tigre crept across the floor to the opposite wall and pressed his back against it. He stood in the central corridor. If Jardín happened to glance around the corner, he would have no place to take cover.

The door to an examination room was about six feet away. Tigre sidled toward it, his breath sounding loud to his own ears.

A figure in coveralls stepped out of the room and aimed a gun at his head.

Tigre froze.

The person lowered the gun. It was Concha.

Tremors crawled over Tigre's body. He struggled to refrain from collapsing in relief.

Concha, her narrow face as tense as a fist, made a brusque gesture for him to keep quiet.

Tigre nodded, meeting her gaze dispassionately. She was the one, he deduced, who had left the tracks in the access tube. He studied her, noting that she still wore the regeneration patch on one cheek; smudges of exhaustion darkened the skin under her eyes. She slowly looked him up and down, and he realized that he still had blood on his mouth from his fall in the tube and that bruises still ringed his right forearm.

Concha grimly motioned him into the examination room.

Moving carefully, Tigre crept up the hall and through the door. Concha crowded in after him and pressed her mouth against his ear. Her whisper was fierce. "What the hell are you doing here?"

"Wu sent me," he breathed.

Concha scowled. "What's that supposed—?" She froze for a moment, as if listening. Tigre did not hear anything, but Concha pushed herself away from him. "Stay here," she hissed.

Tigre drew a breath to protest, but she slid out the door and into the hall.

Cautiously, Tigre padded to the door and looked out.

Concha, back to the wall, worked her way up the corridor.

Tigre watched, fighting an idiotic urge to go after her. She had a Phi-Nurian gun, and she planned to use it. Less than an hour ago, the thought would have been unimaginable. At the moment, shooting Jardín seemed only expedient. Horrified with himself, Tigre tried to shake the idea away.

Concha was nearly to the end of the hall. She held the gun in a businesslike manner with both hands. He had refused a weapon from Wu, citing his sacred vows as a doctor. Tigre's throat tightened. If he allowed Concha to shoot Jardín, he was as liable as if he pulled the trigger himself.

When I am dead . . .

Jardín's voice continued to come as an echoing murmur. He could pick out isolated words. She seemed to be talking about cutting something.

Concha reached the end of the hall. Medica's front desk sat just behind her, and beyond that stood the lift. She paused, as if gathering her resolve, and raised the gun with both hands to the level of her heart. Pulse beating in his throat, Tigre clutched the strap of his kit.

Concha whipped around the corner and fired. The gun's roar split the air.

Tigre lunged toward her. "No!"

A second blast followed as Jardín returned fire. Concha tumbled backward and hit the front desk. She slumped to the floor, leaving a bright smear of blood on the desk's tiled face.

Tigre sprinted up the hall. The inhaler of Tri-Omega fell

out of his waistband, and the kit's strap dropped from his shoulder. "Stop it!" His voice was a raw scream. "Jardín, don't—"

A third shot shattered the air. It hit the top of the desk, just over Concha's head. Dust and tile chips flew.

Tigre burst past the end of the hall. He slid into a crouch at Concha's side, hoping to shield her from another barrage, and looked over his shoulder.

Jardín, gun in hand, braids flying, raced toward him. She still wore her counterfeit Safety uniform, and her heart-shaped face seemed an unfeeling mask of stone.

Consumed with fury, Tigre flung out his arm in an imperious gesture of command. "Enough!" he shouted. "No more—"

Jardín, several yards away, skidded to a halt and raised her gun.

From behind him, in the direction of the lift, came the high-pitched whine of machinery. Tigre did not trouble to look toward the noise, knowing the desk blocked his view. Instead, he turned his attention to Concha. She lay on her side, her arms limp. Blood soaked the front of her uniform and trailed from her nose and mouth.

Jardín launched herself at him and grabbed the neck of his tunic. "Get up," she ordered. She jammed the hot muzzle of the gun into the tender flesh of his throat. "Move."

Tigre, glaring at her, rose to his feet. "I need," he said through clenched teeth, "to get her into stasis."

Jardín's delicate mouth twisted into a smile. She turned the gun on Concha, taking obvious aim at her head. "Cooperate, Doctor. Or she'll be too dead to revive."

Tigre met her eyes and read serious intent in them. "Understood."

Another burst of noise came from the lift. Jardín gathered a fresh grip on his tunic and dragged him in the direction of his office. "Come on." She moved the gun to a spot between his shoulder blades and pushed him along in front of her. "And don't get any heroic ideas. I'll blow you in half."

Shaking with rage, but knowing better than to offer a struggle, Tigre allowed her to herd him to the door of his own office. Safety was cutting through the lift doors; all he had to do was keep Jardín busy. It was time for what the

Rofan called *eykhrru-rru,* surrender without fear. "Listen," Tigre said steadily, "there's got to be a better way. Just let—"

Jardín gave no sign she heard him. "Hey, Ajmani." Her light, sweet voice was exultant. "We have visitors. One of them is still alive." She jabbed Tigre in the spine with her gun. "Say hello to Deputy Ajmani."

Scorch marks defaced the office door, and a small particle welder lay on the floor nearby. Tigre folded his arms to hide his trembling hands. He recalled his first conversation with Concha concerning the similarities of welders and scalpels. He noticed that the welder's tip was melted, useless. *Overloaded the power cell.* "Rachel?" He tried to sound confident and reassuring. "Are you all right?"

"Tigre?" Her voice was a strained whisper. "What happened? Who died?"

He licked his dry lips. "I don't know. She's—" The lie choked him, and he had to swallow. "A dock tech, I think. I've seen her before, but I don't know her name."

There was a long pause. "Oh," Rachel said softly.

"Concha Singh," Jardín supplied. "She may be revivable. If you don't waste any more time."

The high-pitched whine sliced through the air again, and the lift doors rattled. Jardín raised the muzzle of her gun to the nape of Tigre's neck. "Ajmani, they've almost cut their way in. You're running out of time and options. Open the door, and no one else will die except that alien menace. Refuse to cooperate, and this very beautiful man will be a red splash on the—"

"No, Rachel!" Tigre interrupted wildly. "Don't do it!"

The lift doors rattled again. Jardín shoved him into the wall, then spun him around to face her and pinned him with her body. "I don't want to kill you," she whispered, her breath hot in his ear. "It would be such a waste."

Tigre's blood jumped. Though he loathed her, he could not ignore the tight fit of their hips or the firm thrust of her small breasts. Arousal flared.

Jardín gave a throaty laugh. "Well," she said archly. "I wish I had more time."

Panting, Tigre closed his eyes, sickened by his own body's appalling betrayal. *Is it the Seroplex? A Phenox flashback?* The fire in his loins seemed to borrow power from his helpless rage. He wanted to hurt her, to batter her senseless. Tears squeezed from the corners of his eyes. "God—" Bile choked him. "God damn you."

The lift doors clattered and boomed. Jardín gently traced the line of his cheekbone with the muzzle of her gun. "No time," she murmured. "Too bad."

Tigre twisted his face away and looked toward the desk. Concha's body lay in a spreading pool of blood.

Jardín shoved herself away from him, backing up several feet. "Time's up, Ajmani," she called. "You've got to the count of three to open the door." She raised the gun in both hands and aimed at Tigre's chest. "One, two—"

A hissing beam of rainbow light lanced Jardín's right knee. She shrieked, dropping the gun, and fell to the tiled floor. She clutched her wound, then cried out again as she burned her hands on her own cooked flesh.

Tigre whipped toward the direction of the shot.

Wu sagged against the wall, his laser pistol in his hand. Sweat soaked his black tunic, and his eyes seemed glazed with pain.

The lift doors ground open. A dozen staffers in vivid green and blue charged into Medica.

Jardín made an animallike snarl of rage and scrabbled for her gun.

Wu fired again. The laser bolt struck her chest with a sickening crackle. A charred, bloodless spot no bigger than a thumbprint appeared over her heart. Jardín's body jackknifed, then went limp.

The staffers scattered. One of them found Concha and shouted for a stasis unit. Several rushed toward Wu and Tigre.

Wu dropped his pistol and put his hands up, though his gaze remained fixed on Tigre. "You okay?"

Unable to speak, Tigre nodded.

Wu sighed and sagged against the wall.

CHAPTER TWENTY-FOUR

TO RACHEL, the corridors of Medica seemed cold and gray. Stasis units waited on two gurneys near the lift doors. Light gleamed on their black lacquered surfaces, and the field indicators on their control plates glowed amber.

Rachel stood beside the unit that held Concha's body. She faced the wall, head bowed, arms limp. She wore her own rose-pink bathrobe over a patient's white gown, and her black hair hung in a long braid, still damp from a recent shower. In spite of painkillers and a fresh bandage, her injured foot throbbed in time to the leaden beat of her heart. Rachel welcomed the pain. Without it, she feared exhaustion would distance her from recent events, steal her ability to grieve.

Someone approached from behind. "Rachel?" Nothando, the senior medic, laid a gentle hand on her shoulder. "Are you going to be all right?"

Rachel lifted her head and turned.

Like everyone else on Medica's small staff, Nothando seemed worn to the bone. "I'm sorry about Concha. I heard she was a friend." Genuine concern suffused her lined face. "This must be very difficult for you."

Rachel swallowed against the swelling knot in her throat. "Yes," she whispered. "I—" She was grateful that Benjy and the rest of Jardín's prisoners were unharmed, but sorrow eclipsed her relief. She could not shake the feeling that she was to blame for Concha's death. *I pushed her away, didn't trust her.* "Yes. Difficult."

Nothando lightly patted her shoulder. "Is there anything I can do for you?" she asked. "Anything you want?"

Rachel's throat constricted painfully. She looked away from Nothando's sympathetic gaze and focused on the stasis unit's amber indicators. "I—" Her voice came out a rasping croak. She needed to file a confidential report with Lois concerning the World Council's recent actions. She shook her head. "Just want to stand here," she whispered. "For a little while."

"Of course," Nothando said. "If you think of anything you need, I'll be right over there at the main desk. Okay?"

Rachel's eyes stung. The amber lights seemed to blur and spread. Not trusting herself to speak, she nodded.

"Anything at all." Nothando turned away and walked to the desk.

Rachel blinked hard to clear her vision. The tears were ridiculous, brought on by a childish gratitude for Nothando's kindness. She would weep for Concha, but never for herself.

From her place by the lift, she could see down each of Medica's three corridors. Called in to help the flagging staff, doctors from the various ships at Earth Port conferred with each other in small clusters. Two technicians squinted and poked at the latch assembly on Tigre's office door, and another attempted to scrape melted phone components from the surface of the main desk. Her expression stony, a woman from Maintenance ran a floor cleaner back and forth over the spot where Concha had died.

Rachel twisted her face away. According to Tigre, Jardín would live; her recovery was a matter of simple organ replacement. Concha was dead, however, beyond any regenerative procedures.

Rachel rested her hand on the stasis unit, remembering the aide's youthful swings from confidence to shattered insecurity, her leaps of intuition, and the wounded reproach in her eyes when faced with Rachel's distrust. *Concha.*

The lift doors opened, and Tigre stepped out. He wore a fresh set of lavender scrubs, and his blue-black hair looked clean and dry. Rachel caught the scent of citrus soap and sandalwood. Tigre carried a printed copy of a scanner image, and he studied it with a fierce scowl of concentration. Briskly, he strode past her without raising his head.

Rachel cleared her throat. "Rough day." It was a stupid thing to say. She tried to find more words, but failed.

Tigre turned and looked at her, and it seemed to take a moment for recognition to hit. "Rachel?" His frown melted, and his tone became too gentle. "You ought to be resting. Why aren't you in bed?" He glanced toward Nothando at the desk. "Let me get—"

Rachel touched his shoulder to reclaim his attention. "No, I—" The sound of her own voice stopped her. It was cracked, hoarse, thick with unshed tears.

"What is it?" Tigre asked softly, obviously misreading her sudden silence. "Do you need something to help you sleep?"

Afraid his kindness would destroy her fragile composure, Rachel shook her head. "No," she whispered. "I need . . . answers."

The worry faded from Tigre's eyes, and he regarded her with his teeth set askew. "I'm being a pain in the ass, aren't I?" He folded his arms. A small bell hung around his neck on a fine chain, and it chimed with his movement. "I hate it when people mother me, and now I'm doing it to you. Sorry."

Rachel swallowed and looked away. "Don't worry about it."

"Hey." Tigre gripped her arm just above the elbow and shook it a little. "I'm on my way to the staff lounge for a cup of spice tea. Come with me. I don't have many answers, but I've got a lot of questions."

Rachel hesitated. She did not want to leave Concha, it felt disloyal; but she realized that standing beside a stasis unit would accomplish nothing. "Questions," she repeated, her voice fading in and out. "Sometimes," she said, "enough questions can equal an answer." She briefly rested her fingertips on the glowing indicators. *Good-bye, Concha.* Straightening her shoulders, she turned to Tigre. "I need to find Lois. I've got to make a report."

"Make it later," he said with friendly arrogance, motioning to the left corridor. "Come on. The lounge is this way."

Rachel sighed.

Tigre casually offered his arm for support. "Here." His manner was so matter-of-fact, that Rachel slipped her hand around his arm without resentment. "Thanks."

Together they walked toward the lounge. Tigre matched her pace, sauntering along at her side without a hint of solicitous concern. As they approached his office, Rachel recalled their hasty meal of Naranha, and how he made her keep her foot elevated. "Admit it," she croaked. "The spice tea is just a sneaky ploy to make me rest."

"Of course it's sneaky. I'm a doctor."

Rachel wanted to smile, but found she could not. She desperately wanted to see Wu again, but he had been taken away by Safety before her release from the locked office. "Where are they holding Wu? Do you know?"

"I've just left him," Tigre said. "He's in custody aboard the *La Vaca.*"

Rachel suspected that Wu's placement on that particular ship was not a coincidence. A nagging anxiety faded from the back of her mind, and she knew that he would be safe with Captain Mendez. "*La Vaca?*"

Tigre slid a look in her direction. "They have a much more expensive and versatile welder than I do," he said in a casual tone. "I convinced them that the *La Vaca* was the only logical choice."

"You—?" Rachel finally managed a weak smile. "Thank you. How is he doing?"

"He was still a little groggy when I left, but the procedure went quite well. I left him asleep in sick bay, under the care of an old schoolmate of mine, Doctor Sang." Tigre held up the scanner print he carried, an image of bones done in shades of smoky blue. "See? This is a portrait of Wu's ankle."

Rachel peered at it, though she had no idea what to look for. "Is it broken?"

"Yes." Tigre gave her a lopsided grin. "But it didn't stop him from climbing down twenty stories through an access tube. Frightening man."

Rachel abruptly realized she saw no staffers in the corridors. "Where's Meris?" She stopped and twisted to look around. "Is anyone with her?"

"She's fine. Sleeping off the Phenox," Tigre said. "I've got her back in her old room with no less than six people keeping watch." He tilted his head, and the bell around his neck chimed. "She's in much better shape than you, Deputy Ajmani."

Rachel reached for the bell and lifted it to the light. It seemed to be made of pewter, and it was inscribed with flowing script. "Pretty." Narrowing her eyes, she tried to read the writing. "I've seen something like this before, but I can't remember where."

Tigre shifted self-consciously. "Around the neck of a Rofan *gukka*?"

Rachel stared at him. "A what?"

Tigre shrugged, and a faint flush stole over his cheeks and throat. "A *gukka* gave it to me. The emissary from the Legitimacy. Dútha."

The name ripped through Rachel like a spear of lightning. She clutched Tigre's slender shoulders in both hands, scarcely able to articulate. "Dútha?"

"Well, yes," he said, obviously taken aback by her intensity. "Why? Do you know him?"

"I—" Rachel struggled to think. "When did you speak to him? Is he still at Port?"

Tigre carefully pulled himself free from her grasp. "I assume he's still here." He regarded her doubtfully. "He said he wanted to meet with me again."

Rachel turned around. Hanging onto the handrail for support, she started toward the lift. According to Meris, Dútha possessed detailed information that would throw light on the recent events at Earth Port. "I've got to talk to him."

"Hey," Tigre protested gently. He stepped in front of her, blocking her path. "It's time for tea. And maybe a sandwich, since it's time for lunch, and we've both skipped breakfast."

A rising sense of urgency made it difficult to choose words. "Tigre, this is important. I need to—"

"You need to rest and eat," Tigre interrupted, his voice soft and earnest. "Rachel, you're on the brink of collapse.

You've gone for days without real sleep, and it's a miracle you—"

Rachel peered at him. "I've had a lot more sleep than you." For the first time, she noticed his energetic manner. "You took something, didn't you?"

"Rachel—"

"You did." Rachel clasped his shoulders again, recalling the street names of the stimulants Sasha had favored. "What was it? 'Dragonfire'? 'Jaz'? 'White Light'?"

"Seroplex," Tigre said with an oddly defiant glint in his dark eyes. "A prescription form of Jaz."

"Give me some."

"No," Tigre said flatly. "Absolutely not. I only took it because lives were at stake."

Rachel tightened her hold, digging her fingers into his shoulders. "I'm in the same position. I'm the only one who—"

"Rachel—"

She thrust her face close to his. "This is big," she said through clenched teeth. "I can't say more until I report to Lois, but the lives of billions may hang in the balance."

Tigre's eyes widened. "Rachel, what are you saying?" he whispered. "What's going on?"

"I need—" From the corner of her eye, Rachel saw the worried stares of medics. She lowered her voice. "I need to stay on my feet, keep my head clear." She searched for some sure, persuasive argument, but found only the simplest words. "Help me, Tigre. Please."

Once again in uniform, Rachel paused inside the Ops booth on Dock Two's upper level. The tiny room smelled of strong coffee and Human sweat, but the chair at the control console stood empty. Rachel frowned and looked at Tigre. "I don't like this." Her voice came out a hoarse croak. "There ought to be someone on duty."

Tigre smiled tightly. "Seems like every department is shorthanded."

Rachel sat down in the chair and keyed her access code into the console. She marveled at how clearheaded she felt, without the jittery edge she associated with stimulants. A large, one-way window beside the door provided a wide view of the dock. "There it is," she said. "Are you sure you're up to this?"

The dock appeared to be a long hallway, slightly curved, so that only two thirds of the section partition at the other end was visible. Access hatches lined the walls on both sides. Glowing registry boards beside every hatch announced each vessel's name, planet of origin, corporate affiliation, and itinerary. The booths of licensed arbitrators, islands of polished wooden counters and stained-glass partitions, occupied the floor's center section.

The upper dock had not escaped the violence. Scorch marks from particle weapons defaced the white walls. Broken glass and bits of smashed furniture littered the floor. The fountains all stood dry. In the midst of the riot's debris, Rofan traders quarreled with arbitrators and each other.

"I can handle it." Tigre glanced at Rachel. "How do you feel?"

Her injured foot still ached, and grief weighted her spirit; but it was good to be back in familiar surroundings. "Wish my voice were better." Rachel shrugged one shoulder. "But, other than that, I feel surprisingly normal. I can't believe I'm drugged."

"Well, you are," Tigre said dryly. "And you'll believe it when the hangover hits."

Rachel brought up the Dock Master's grid. It hovered above the console, a vertical lattice of blue lines. A flashing message at the top declared the entire length of Dock Two closed for safety reasons. Rachel narrowed her eyes. "There's an awful lot of activity out there for a closed dock. It doesn't make sense."

Tigre snorted. "Wu's not in charge."

"But Lois is out there, according to her office. I can't imagine her tolerating this circus." Rachel pointed to the top of the grid. "Damn. Dútha's ship is berthed at the other end. Beside the Phi-Nurian ambassadors." She stood up and limped to the door. "Should have used the other entrance. Now, we've got to hike."

Smiling grimly, Tigre joined her at the door. "I'm ready."

They stepped onto the dock. Rofan voices filled the air with echoing shouts. To her left, a freighter captain stood locked in debate with a red-faced arbitrator. "I don't care," the Rofa said, its small ears flat. "I'm keeping the bonus. Stinking port is responsible for damages, not me."

Rachel grasped Tigre's arm and guided him around the argument. "Let's steer clear of trouble," she muttered. "I don't like the mood out here."

Tigre made a noise of protest and glanced at her wildly. "But aren't you going to help? That Rofa—"

"—is within its rights," she interrupted. She did not have time to explain the arbitration system to him. "Come on." She led him toward the dock's far end. "We need to find Lois and Dútha."

Tigre flung an anxious glance over his shoulder. "But it's yelling at that man."

"Yelling is not against the law," Rachel replied absently, her mind on other concerns. At the end of the dock ahead, she noticed that Safety had the area around the Phi-Nurian ambassadors' ship cordoned off. Lois would be there, in the thick of things. Rachel hoped she could speak to her superior before the situation grew worse.

Tigre stared up at the ceiling. "How—?" He spread his hands. "How is cargo loaded onto ships? I thought I'd see conveyors and cranes."

Rachel pointed at the floor. "All that is done on the lower level. We conduct business up here."

"Ah." Tigre paused, then cleared his throat. "But how—?" He stopped talking and froze, staring straight ahead. "Dútha."

Rachel followed his gaze. A Rofa wearing a loincloth strolled toward them, and the other Rofan made way for it with notable courtesy. Instead of the red-gold pelt of the childbearing gender, the individual's coloring shaded from fawn to cream at its throat. Its ears were large and triangular, rather than small and round. Over its right arm, it carried a stained and tattered Safety parka.

Rachel managed to avoid staring, though she had never seen a Rofa quite like it, and she wondered about its gender. "Is . . . 'he' . . . Dútha?"

Tigre did not seem to hear her. "Oh, God," he said unsteadily. "He's got Jhaska's coat."

Taken aback, Rachel laid a hand on his shoulder. "What's wrong?"

Tigre's fine-boned features seemed tight with inner pain. "Oh, God," he whispered brokenly, "I can't—"

Dútha stopped in front of Tigre. The *gukka* wore a large, sheathed knife on his belt. Rachel's heart began to pound.

It occurred to her that Rofan surrounded them, and they were far from help if a misunderstanding arose.

Dútha extended the parka to Tigre. "The little one wished for you to have this," he said solemnly, "as a remembrance."

Moving stiffly, Tigre took the parka and folded it against his heart. "Is Jhaska—?" He swallowed hard and bowed his head. "Did Jhaska die?"

Dútha studied him a long moment, his gaze bright and discerning. "I don't know," he answered finally. "The ship left port before the end."

Tigre sighed and looked up. "So there may be hope."

"No," Dútha said, his tone somehow both harsh and compassionate. "No hope."

Troubled by Tigre's grief, Rachel stood motionless, scarcely able to breathe.

Tears glittered in Tigre's dark lashes, but his chin came up. "I don't care. I will keep hope—" With a dramatic sweep, he flung the parka around his shoulders and pulled it on. "—and remembrance."

Around them, Rofan merchant captains and their crew continued to loudly wrangle. They gave no sign of interest in Dútha's discussion, but Rachel noticed that they were careful not to come too close.

With startling familiarity, Dútha touched the bell that hung over Tigre's heart. "You're wearing it."

"Yes. Although, I—" Tigre swallowed hard. "I wonder about its significance."

Dútha seemed unaware of anyone but Tigre. "Significance?" His graceful ears swept up, alert and upright. "It's the bell of *Hjeina*."

Tigre tried to repeat the word. "Hay—?"

Dútha coughed the initial consonant from the back of his throat. "*Hjeina*."

"And what," Tigre asked, "is a *Hjeina*?"

"Many, many things." The Rofa's voice was rough but richly vibrant. "*Hjeina* is the first and last letter of the alphabet. It is a term of affection applied to children. It is the name of an ancient hero, a *gukka* who fought only one enemy." He paused, studying Tigre. "It is your name, if you claim it."

Curiosity tugged at Rachel, and she recalled what Bailey had said about an insane deity.

Tigre crooked his brows. "But I'm not—" He sighed and shook his head. "I'm not a warrior. I'm a healer. You know that, don't you?"

Dútha touched the bell again and made it chime. "Yes. I know. But I don't understand." Thoughts moved in the Rofa's dark eyes, as he obviously considered his next words. "You intervene to . . . prevent death."

"That's right," Tigre said. He also seemed unaware of Rachel or the surrounding clamor of the dock. "I'm a surgeon, someone who's trained to repair injuries to the body."

One of Dútha's ears folded back. "And are you able to . . . prevent death . . . always?"

Tigre swallowed. "No. Sometimes the damage is too extensive, or I can't begin treatment in time."

Dútha raised his index finger and seemed to point to two separate spots in the air. "So some live. And some die. That sounds unjust." He laid back both ears and narrowed his eyes, but his manner appeared thoughtful rather than hostile. "Tell me. In the cases where you are able to prevent death, how do you decide whether or not to intervene?"

Rachel's breath caught in her throat as a new understanding of Rofan society opened within her.

"Whether or—?" Tigre stared at the Rofa a moment, then spread his hands. "We always intervene."

Dútha stared back. "Why?"

"I—" Tigre seemed to search for words. "I've taken a vow never to turn aside from anyone who needs my help."

Dútha inclined his head. "I have taken a similar vow. That is how I became involved with that child's giver. *Gukkan* has three duties: to defend their own honor, to fight for those who cannot, and to end needless suffering."

For a moment, Tigre stood frozen, staring. "Jhaska?" he breathed. "You would have ended Jhaska's suffering?"

"Yes." Dútha's tone was gentle. "And I offered, but the little one's giver refused my assistance."

Tigre folded his arms and bowed his head. His silky hair swung forward to veil his eyes. "I don't understand," he said thickly. "All Jhaska needed was a minor surgical procedure. . . ."

"How can you speak so casually," Dútha asked, "of such gross injustice? It's horrible."

Tigre jerked his head up. "Horrible?" His eyes were filled with unshed tears, and his voice was raw. "How dare you—"

Suddenly coming to herself, Rachel cleared her throat. "Tigre," she began softly, "don't—"

Tigre turned to her. "Tell him, Deputy, about the stasis bin in the station's deep storage. Filled with Rofan bodies." He covered his eyes with one hand. "Horrible," he whispered. "Horrible."

Dútha glanced at her, ears lowering a bit. "Bodies?" he asked. "What bodies?"

Rachel met his gaze squarely. "Unclaimed bodies." Her voice came out a harsh croak. "For years, we've filed inquiries with the Legitimacy, asking how to properly dispose of them. To date, we've received no reply."

Dútha wrinkled his nose and flicked his fingers in a gesture of dismissal. "Dispose of them any way you wish."

Rachel raised her brows. "Are you speaking on behalf of the Legitimacy?"

Dútha bared his teeth in a chilling parody of a Human smile. "As always."

Tigre jerked his head up, eyes blazing. "I want them!" He glared at Dútha. "Give the bodies to me."

The Rofa peered at Tigre. "*You* want them?" he repeated doubtfully. "You're not going to eat them, are you?"

Tigre recoiled. "No!"

"Our species," Rachel interjected smoothly, "does not customarily eat the flesh of sentient beings."

Tigre folded his arms. "I promise," he said unsteadily, "that the bodies will be treated with utmost respect."

Dútha's shoulders twitched. "Treat the living with respect. Treat the dead any way you find necessary."

"Are you giving them to me?" Tigre persisted.

Dútha flicked his fingers again. "Yes, yes." For the first time, an edge of impatience crept into his voice. "I did not come here on behalf of the dead. Do as you wish."

Tigre bowed. "Thank you," he said softly. "You have given me something of great value."

Dútha wrinkled his nose, but his ears lifted. "You are a strange creature. I'll wager that even your own kind finds you so."

Tigre threw Rachel a measuring glance. "Oh, yes."

Rachel cleared her throat. "Honorable Dútha, it is urgent that I speak to you in private."

Dútha turned his gaze to her, his eyes filled with both menace and dark amusement. "And why," he asked, "should I find you worthy of my attention?"

Rachel spread her hands. "Because there is a Fourth Path," she whispered. "The Path of Friendship."

For a long moment, Dútha stood motionless. "Meris," he breathed. "You have Meris."

"Meris," Rachel corrected gently, "is our honored guest." She glanced pointedly at the shouting mob of traders and arbitrators surrounding them. "Forgive me, honorable Dútha, but I fear we cannot speak freely here. If you—?"

Dútha gestured abruptly. "Take me to her."

"Of course." Rachel paused, then continued reluctantly. "The knife on your belt. I can't allow you to carry it."

Tigre turned on his heel to face her. "Rachel," he said in a scandalized tone. "This isn't the time to—"

"I understand." Without a trace of hostility or reluctance, Dútha pulled the knife from its sheath and offered the hilt to Rachel. "Keep it safe for me."

Caught completely off guard, Rachel's first impulse was to refuse the weapon. She had heard stories about *gukkan* and their knives. She held out her hand, and Dútha laid the hilt across her palm. "I'll take care of it," she promised, "until you return to your ship." Carefully, she put the knife in the pocket of her uniform.

Dútha silently touched his fingertips to his eyes.

Heart pounding, Rachel indicated the hatch just beyond the next ship. "This way, if you please." Not looking to see if they followed, she turned and started walking.

At the neighboring berth, ropes strung through plastic pylons separated the area around the Phi-Nurian ambassadors' ship from the rest of the dock. A lone and obviously uneasy staffer stood on duty by the access hatch within the secured space. A middle-aged woman in a floral-print sari paced back and forth over the center of the floor, talking on a phone and gesturing emphatically. Rachel recognized her from previous audits. *Councillor Phong. Oh, no.* Near the door of the dock's exit hatch, silver rank Deputy Alfstan DelRio watched the councillor, his expression tense and unhappy.

Rachel narrowed her eyes and studied the scene. "What in God's name is going on?" She unhooked a rope from a pylon and motioned Dútha and Tigre through. "This isn't the proper procedure for—"

Councillor Phong seemed to notice their intrusion. Still talking on the phone, she snapped her fingers at Alfie and made a peremptory gesture for him to get rid of them.

The deputy stiffened in affront but strode toward Rachel.

Rachel limped forward to meet her colleague halfway.

"Alfie," she whispered hoarsely. "Where's Lois?"

Alfie's breath was rough with barely suppressed fury, though clearly not directed at Rachel. "Councillor Phong has just relieved Deputy Jimanez-Verde of her duties." He glanced at the *gukka* and bowed in polite acknowledgment. "Honorable Dútha."

Dútha did not reply. His dark gaze traveled with speculative interest over the Phi-Nurians' access hatch.

Rachel stared at Alfie. His words seemed pure nonsense. "When did this happen?"

Alfie's mouth tightened. "About twenty minutes ago. There was an argument over proper procedure."

Dútha suddenly spoke, seeming to address no one in particular. "In times of crisis," he said in a mild tone, "disobedience is sometimes the only course of true loyalty."

A deep foreboding seized Rachel. She turned to the Rofa and searched his face, remembering that he might be on the run from political enemies. "Are you—?"

A few yards away, the access hatch to the Phi-Nurians' ship slid open.

The staffer beside the hatch drew her stinger and flung a wild glance their way. "Get back!"

Councillor Phong called shrilly to the staffer. "Hold your fire!"

A Phi-Nurian scuttled onto the dock, its clawed feet scrabbling on the tiled floor. It charged past the staffer and took its stand near the center of the secured area, brandishing a scattergun. The light gleamed dully off its mottled brown carapace, and its mandibles flexed in agitation. "All will stop," it buzzed in stilted Trade. "None will move." It took aim at the nearest person: Tigre. "Drop your weapons, or I kill."

Tigre froze, but his eyes blazed with suppressed fury.

The staffer cautiously set her stinger on the floor.

Rachel spoke calmly, knowing she had to prevent the Phi-Nurian from descending into a frenzy. "That weapon is useless. We outnumber you."

The Phi-Nurian turned the gun on her. "No talk," it said. "Just bring Meris."

Councillor Phong turned toward Rachel. "Quiet," she commanded. "I'm in charge of this—"

The Phi-Nurian whirled toward the councillor.

Tigre flung himself forward. "No!"

Without thinking, Rachel also lunged to intercede. "Tigre! Don't—"

Moving with incredible speed, Dútha slammed his body into her. They crashed to the floor in an ungainly sprawl. *His knife,* she thought frantically. She struggled to throw the Rofa off. *He's after his knife!*

A loud blast split the air. With brutal force, Dútha shoved her to the floor again. Pain lanced through her already injured shoulder, and warm blood soaked her uniform. Stunned and breathless, Rachel fought for consciousness.

Tigre cried out in a wordless shout of rage and horror.

"Be silent," the Phi-Nurian ordered.

Rachel tried to lift her head to see, but it was pinned beneath one of the *gukka's* arms. Gasping for air, she shifted feebly to free her right hand. Dútha lay motionless atop her, his muzzle pressed against her neck. Liquid spread over Rachel's throat and seeped into the collar of her uniform. Between one heartbeat and the next, the chill realization hit that he had used his body to shield her. "Dútha?" she breathed. Fumbling, she raised her hand to the wetness around the Rofa's mouth. "Honorable Dútha?"

"Let go!" Tigre bellowed. "Let go of me, you—!"

Dútha drew a choking breath. His lips moved against

Rachel's fingers, but she could not discern what the Rofa attempted to say.

The Phi-Nurian's claws rattled on the floor, accompanied by the sound of scuffling shoes. "Let go of me!" Tigre's tone was ferocious, entirely empty of fear. "Damn it—" He broke off, panting in exertion.

The Phi-Nurian raised its voice. "Meris," it buzzed. "You will bring Meris."

Something struck flesh with a palpable thump. Tigre gave a breathless gasp of pain.

At the sound, Dútha's arms and shoulders went rigid, as if he prepared to rise. More thin Rofan blood washed across her throat and soaked her uniform. "Dútha," she whispered. "Don't—"

With a bubbling snarl, Dútha jerked himself to the side so he no longer pinned her.

Heart pounding, Rachel twisted to look at Tigre. Searing pain flashed through her shoulder, and she swallowed against sudden nausea.

"Meris," the Phi-Nurian repeated. "I will not go without Meris."

Tigre struggled against the Phi-Nurian's grip. It had him just above one elbow, and it shook him like a doll.

Councillor Phong clutched both hands over her heart, her face crumpled with horror.

Holding her wounded shoulder, Rachel scrambled to her feet. She forced her voice to its carrying dockside bellow. "Stop!" She lunged toward the Phi-Nurian. "Do you hear me? Stop that!"

The Phi-Nurian turned the scattergun on her, but it quit shaking Tigre. He sagged to his knees, gasping for air, his brows drawn together in silent fury.

The Phi-Nurian clicked its mandibles excitedly. "You." It motioned to Rachel with its gun. "You come, too."

Tigre made a noise of enraged protest. "No!" he rasped. "You can't take her. She's hurt."

The Phi-Nurian reared up exultantly, obviously lost in frenzy. "*Can* take," it jeered. "*Will* take."

Rachel seized the opportunity. "I'm too important," she argued. "You can't take me." She waved at Tigre. "Take him. He's nothing."

The Phi-Nurian flung Tigre away like a scrap of paper. "Nothing."

Relief soared through Rachel.

Tigre gracefully rolled to his feet. For a moment, it seemed he would launch himself at the Phi-Nurian. Then his gaze fell on Dútha's bleeding form, and he slid into a crouch beside him.

Thinking only to prevent the Phi-Nurian from taking more hostages, Rachel lurched toward it. It gripped her arm and injured shoulder in two of its clawed hands. Rachel's agony was so complete that it shut down hearing and sight in a roaring, red vortex.

The Phi-Nurian buzzed something in triumph. Rachel struggled to remain on her feet, knowing that her continued survival hinged upon keeping her wits about her.

The Phi-Nurian dragged her toward the hatch of its ship. Rachel fought to regain her vision.

"No!" Tigre shouted. "Stop it. Don't let it take her. She's been shot!"

Rachel jerked her face toward the sound of his voice. The red haze parted, and she saw him beside Dútha. Tigre held one of the Rofa's hands, as if attempting to find a pulse.

For a moment, Rachel met Tigre's gaze. She read his horrified shock of realization, that she was trading herself for him. She tried to convey with her eyes that this was the way she wanted it.

"Meris," the Phi-Nurian buzzed. "Bring Meris. I give this one back. No more talk."

The hatch closed.

CHAPTER TWENTY-FIVE

TIGRE KNELT beside Dútha. The Rofa lay on the floor of Dock Two, thin blood soaking the cream-colored fur at his throat.

Chaos surged around them. From the corner of his eye, Tigre caught sight of frantic movement, Humans rushing to take cover, Rofan boarding their ships. Over the background roar of shouts, he heard Deputy DelRio issue a string of terse commands to the staffers, ordering them to clear the dock.

Tigre's hands trembled with equal portions of terror and volcanic rage, but he kept his attention on Dútha, maintained his calm expression. "Easy," he murmured. "You're wounded. Lie still."

Dútha opened his eyes. His ears flicked weakly. "Meris," he said in a bubbling whisper. "Tell Meris . . . I . . ."

"Just try to rest." Worried about blood loss, Tigre carefully probed the Rofa's throat with his fingertips. "Let me—"

With startling speed, Dútha thrust his muzzle down and snapped at the doctor's fingers.

Tigre whipped his hand away just in time. "Hey!"

Dútha's eyes gleamed. "Jhaska right," he said. "Too . . .fast to bite. . . ."

Somewhere not far away, Deputy DelRio and Councillor Phong engaged in a heated debate. "You have to listen to me," the deputy said, obviously struggling for self-control. "You're dealing with an alien, a Phi-Nurian, not a Human. You can't—"

"How dare you lecture me," Councillor Phong retorted, her voice low and furious. "How dare you question my decisions!"

Tigre's shoulders tightened. He recalled his past argument with Rachel, how he had brushed aside her knowledge and experience.

Dútha's ears sagged. "Meris—"

Tigre bent close. "You have to let me help you." He searched for reasoning the Rofa would accept. "You said you could not abide unnecessary suffering; but if you die, thousands of innocent people will endure—" He broke off. *Keep it simple.* "Meris needs you. My friend Rachel needs you."

Dútha rolled his head toward the hatch of the Phi-Nurian's ship. "Rachel." He tried to get up, then settled back to the floor with a groan. "Not let . . . take Knife-Bearer. . . ." He closed his eyes. "You go. Fight for Rachel."

Tigre found the idea intensely appealing. He clenched his jaw. "I can't. I'm a healer, not a fighter."

Dútha licked his teeth. "You . . . Hjeina."

Tigre crooked his brows, uncertain how to respond. "Hjeina" meant so many different things to the Rofan. Dútha might be calling him a child or a mythic hero.

A staffer suddenly crouched beside them, a tired looking fellow whom Tigre recalled from Checkpoint. "Doctor?" Rico's tone was urgent. "Do you need help?"

Tigre spoke without thought. "Get a stasis unit over here. Fast."

Rico glanced down at Dútha, then turned a worried stare to Tigre. "Do we have permission?"

Despair threatened, but Tigre bent closer to Dútha. "Will you allow me to help you?"

Dútha gave a bubbling sigh. "Ship." He fumbled at his belt and pulled off a palm-sized metal disk. "My ship." He awkwardly pressed the disk into Tigre's hand. "I give you."

Rico's expression went blank. "That's an entry key. It just gave you its ship!"

Tigre's heart sank. "But I don't want your ship, Dútha. I want to—" He tried to remember how the Rofa had phrased it. "I want to intercede, prevent you from dying."

Dútha licked his teeth again. "Thirsty."

Tigre shuddered, remembering how Jhaska begged for water. "Dútha," he said. "Please. Think of me as—as a mechanic. Let me repair the damage to your body."

"My body?" Dútha wrinkled his nose. "You want?"

"I want to—"

"Yes. Do. . . ." The Rofa flicked his fingers dismissively. ". . . as you . . . wish. . . ." He gave a final sigh and lay still.

Tigre's throat tightened. *He gave me his body.* His vision blurred with sudden tears. "Oh, God—"

Beside him, Rico drew an explosive breath and scrambled to his feet. "Hey," he called to another staffer. "Bring that stasis unit over here. Hurry!"

Tigre jerked his chin up and drew a breath to speak, but the words would not come. Rico had no way of knowing what Dútha had meant, that he had actually refused assistance.

Tigre sat frozen, heart pounding, torn with indecision.

Two staffers ran to them, pushing a coffinlike stasis unit. One of them looked down at Dútha and blinked in confusion. "But . . . it's a Rofa."

"It gave verbal authorization," Rico said. "I'm a witness."

Tigre swallowed. *Tell them. Tell them now.* Without consciously making a decision, he shifted around to give them room and slipped his hands under Dútha's head. "Keep him level, please," he directed calmly. "I'll hold his head steady."

Working together, the four of them loaded Dútha's limp body into the stasis unit. Tigre engaged the power and watched the indicators light up. All the while, he waited for remorse to attack, for something within him to condemn his actions.

"Take him to Medica?" one of the staffers asked.

Tigre stood up slowly.

Near the hatch to the Phi-Nurians' ship, Councillor Phong and Deputy DelRio's confrontation escalated into a shouting match. "Do you want to be placed on suspension as well?" she demanded. "Do you?"

Tigre folded his arms, hugging the bulk of Jhaska's Safety parka close to him. If Wu were present, he would know what to do, but Wu was under treatment on board one of the ships at port. "No," Tigre said. "Medica doesn't have the right equipment. We're going to the *La Vaca*. They have just what we need."

With the raw scream of metal on metal, the door to the hold rolled shut.

Rachel lay on the filthy floor, breathing through her clenched teeth. Her neck and back ached from the Phi-Nurian's rough handling, and the fire in her wounded shoulder blazed hotter with every stroke of her heart. Even as she struggled against physical pain, however, the Seroplex kept her mind clear and her thoughts focused.

Nearby, someone sighed.

Rachel lifted her head slightly and listened. The hold was silent. She shook the hair from her eyes and peered into the surrounding shadows, wondering if the sound had been an echo of her own breath.

Shattered freight canisters crowded the limited floor space, and the bulkheads curved overhead to create a low ceiling. The cramped, dimly lit compartment was typical of the old BRD cargo ships, and it matched the scene from her vision exactly. It occurred to her in a distant, abstract way that she ought to be surprised by this, but her mind closed around the realization without protest. The air, dense with the odor of Phi-Nurian dung, possessed a heavy quality that made her wonder about the oxygen level. "Bailey?"

Moving carefully, she pushed herself into a loose crouch. Blood soaked her uniform over her right shoulder, warm near the wound, clammy around the edges. Gingerly, she pulled aside her collar to check the damage. The flesh looked chewed, but she could move her right arm with a manageable amount of pain. Dútha had pushed her aside to take the brunt of the blast; she had caught only a few fragments of ammunition. She remembered what Meris had said about him. *Braver and truer than kin.*

Without warning, Wu filled her thoughts. His wicked grin, the glint in his eyes, his purring chuckle; even the dry, sweet scent of his hair returned to her with the full power

of reality. She wondered why he came to mind at such a
time, and the answer to that rang with the clarity of a bell.

She wanted to see him again, to have him near, and to
tell him so. It went beyond desire or romantic love. Wu
was her partner, her ally, her only home. *Braver and truer*—

A faint, wordless whisper drifted to her ears.

Rachel's heart leaped, and she lifted her head. "Bailey?"
The word came out a harsh croak.

Only silence answered her. Rachel wobbled to her feet,
the sudden eruption of pain in her shoulder causing her to
gag a bit. She swallowed hard. "Bailey? Is that you?"
Frayed bits of metal cable littered the floor, and she cautiously edged through them, uncertain of her balance.
"Bailey?"

A large crate sat in the middle of the hold, its plastic
sides seamed with cracks. Behind it lay a motionless figure
enshrouded in a filth-encrusted tarp.

Horror shocked through her. Rachel fell to her knees
and ripped back the heavy canvas.

Bailey lay curled on his side, and his long, henna-tinted
hair obscured his face. His hands were tied together in front
of him, though it appeared that he had partially freed his
right wrist from its bonds.

Rachel hastily brushed Bailey's wild curls aside. A collection of rainbow-hued scarves festooned his throat, but one
was tied as a murderously tight gag over his nose and
mouth. His eyes were shut, his face slack.

"Hang on, Bailey." Fumbling with both hands, Rachel
peeled the gag away. "Breathe, sweetie, breathe."

Bailey drew a deep, croupy breath.

"You're all right," Rachel told him, praying it was true.
She wanted to push him onto his back, but did not know
what other injuries he might have sustained. "Take it easy."

Bailey's bonds appeared to be some sort of synthetic fabric. She tried to work the knots loose, but they were too
tight. Remembering Dútha's knife, she pulled it out of her
pocket and used it to saw through the fabric. *Socks?* Rachel
tossed them aside and picked up Bailey's hands. Heavy rag
bracelets around his wrists seemed to have prevented
chafing; she rubbed his chilly fingers to stimulate circulation. "Are you with me, Bailey?" she rasped. "Can you
wiggle your thumbs?"

Panting, Bailey opened his eyes and looked up at her.

Again, Rachel experienced a sudden mental jolt that felt like recognition. She froze, gazing into a face that seemed as familiar as her own reflection in a mirror. *What is it? Why does he affect me like this?* Shaking off her confusion, Rachel patted his cheek. "Can you hear me? Are you hurt? Say something."

A rusty noise escaped Bailey's throat. "Zo, Rachel."

Relieved laughter threatened, and she had to swallow before she could speak. "Hello, yourself."

Bailey drew a breath to speak, then broke into a violent fit of coughing.

Alarmed, Rachel slipped a hand under his head to offer support. "Take it easy," she said again. "Everything is going to be all right."

"Out." Bailey's voice was a dry squeak. "We've just got to—" He burst into another round of coughing.

Rachel spoke with long-rehearsed, professional confidence. "Don't worry. I'll do everything I can to get you out of here."

Bailey weakly tried to push himself up. Rachel helped him sit and settled him back against the crate. His gaze settled on her bloody uniform. "Hurt?"

"It's minor."

Bailey swallowed. "Hold," he whispered. "Unheated."

Rachel glanced around at the broken containers with a new eye. They all bore the unmistakable signs of thermal stress, the cracks caused by rapid heating and cooling of materials not intended for changing extremes. Evidently the hold was unheated in transit. If the ship left dock before they escaped, they would freeze to death in minutes.

"I see what you mean," she said. She returned Dútha's knife to her pocket. "You take it easy," she said and climbed stiffly to her feet. "I'll attempt to—"

Bailey made a papery sound. Rachel paused and looked over her shoulder, and he nodded toward the far bulkhead. "There," he croaked. "Tools."

Rachel raised her brows doubtfully, but edged her way through the litter to investigate. A pile of items lay on the floor beside a ripped duffel bag, and it took her a moment to recognize them as personal belongings. She saw clothing, the shattered remains of a recorder, toiletries, and a canvas tool pouch. She bent down and picked up the pouch. It was empty. "Bailey—" She scrabbled through the clothing. "I don't—" Her fingers encountered small, metal objects, and she pulled a probe and a miniature cutter into the light. "Ah, here we are. Just what I needed."

Bailey struggled to stand. "Let me—" He cleared his throat, and his voice became stronger. "Let me help."

Feeling strangely detached from her body, as if she operated it by remote control, Rachel regained her feet and started for the door. "Save your strength," she advised, forcing her own voice to function. "I was working on these old BRD's while you were just a kid." She knelt beside the door and glanced over at him. "See what the Phi-Nurians have left of your stuff."

Bailey shuffled to where the ruined duffel bag lay and made a miserable noise. "What a mess." He crouched down and began to gather his things. "Why did they do this?" he asked with innocent reproach. He heaped everything in the center of his cloaklike garment, tied it up with a belt, and somehow strapped it over his shoulders like a backpack. "They didn't have to do this."

"Could've been worse." Rachel returned her attention to the bulkhead on the right side of the door's frame. She recalled with satisfaction that the control board for the lock mechanism was in an easy place to access. She switched on the cutter and pressed it against the bulkhead. "This is going to cause a red light on their Ops console. That means one of them may show up before I'm finished."

"There's only one of them left." Bailey made his way through the garbage and squatted beside her.

A thin curl of white smoke drifted up from the cutter's tip. Rachel edged it down slowly, making a neat incision in the bulkhead. "Only one?" she repeated. "Are you sure?"

Bailey shrugged. "That's what it told me. And it was very angry, so I don't think it was lying." He awkwardly pulled a scarf from around his neck and used it to tie back his hair. "It came in here, and it told me that all the others were dead, and that now it was alone. And it kicked me." He paused a moment, then added: "My leg still hurts."

Once more, the odd sense of familiarity stole over Rachel. She flicked her gaze to him, again wondering why she responded to him so strongly. Beneath a forelock of his cascading curls, his eyes were copper-colored, large and full-lidded. *Because he's beautiful?* She returned her attention to her work. "There may be only one left," she said, "but it still has a scattergun."

"I'm not scared," Bailey replied. "Not as long as you're here."

Rachel smiled tightly, thinking of Wu again. "Thank you very much," she said, "but the first rule is: Always be scared." She shifted her grip on the cutter and began a slice at a right angle to the first. "By the way, I've been worried about you."

"I know," Bailey said in a warm tone. "I was in your mind."

"In my—?" Rachel forced herself to pay attention to her work. "What are you talking about?"

"I slowed my bodily functions when they loaded me into the crate. Suspended animation, they used to call it. I can live for three days in that state." He flexed his fingers, evidently to encourage circulation. "I suppose the Phi-Nurian thought I was dead. That's why it took you; it needed another hostage."

Rachel suddenly remembered how frustrating it was to try conversing with Bailey. "What do you mean, that you were in my mind?"

"My body was shut down, so my soul walked freely," Bailey replied. "When they operated on your foot, they gave you Verdad, and so I could enter your mind." He paused, then said: "I'm a *shana*. I walk every Path. You have the potential to be a *shana*, too, otherwise you couldn't have read my thoughts."

Rachel drew her brows together. She remembered that certain individuals on the Freeholds claimed to experience drug-induced psychic perceptions. "Bailey. I don't believe in that mind-reading stuff. And they gave me Tri-Omega, which you would have known if you had actually been in my mind."

Bailey's tone remained friendly. "It's the same drug. Just different names." He laughed. "I know lots of poetry, but you don't. And yet, you quoted Prudence Clarke to Tigre:

The peacock's exaltation,
The millet fox's brilliance,

The gems of the Orient
Blend with the color of your hair—
    black as the reasons for night."

Rachel's hand slipped, and the cutter made a jog in its incision. "How—?" Heat rose up in her face, and she flicked her gaze to him. "How do you know about that?"

Bailey's wide mouth stretched in a generous smile. "I can't think of a single, logical explanation. Can you?"

Rachel thinned her lips and returned her attention to the cutter. *Beautiful, but obnoxious.*

"Hey," Bailey said in a wounded tone. "Are you mad at me?"

"No." Rachel heard the sharpness of her own voice and tried to soften it. "No," she said again, more gently. She shifted the cutter's direction to start the final leg of the triangle. "I'm terrified. And I think we need to concentrate on staying alive, not—" She shook her head. "I'm just scared. That's all."

"Oh," Bailey said sadly. "I'm sorry. I didn't mean to—"

"Your leg," Rachel interrupted. "How bad is it?" She glanced at him. "Think you'll be able to run?"

Bailey rubbed the outside of his thigh. "Sure. It's only bruised." He raised his brows and regarded her doubtfully. "What about you? Will you be able to run, Rachel?"

Her neck and back ached, her foot throbbed in time with her heartbeat, her shoulder felt as if it were impaled by a spear of fire, and she had a rotten headache. Rachel grinned in spite of herself. "If that Phi-Nurian shows up with its gun, I'll run like a rabbit."

Bailey giggled.

Rachel finished the final incision, leaving the top point of the triangle uncut. She turned off the tool and handed it to Bailey. "Okay. Here's where the trouble starts." She wiped her slick hands on her trousers and took a steadying breath. "Go stand over on the other side of the door, out of the way, in case it shoots. When the Phi-Nurian shows up, you—"

Bailey extended his left wrist. "Look. I wanted to tell you earlier. I have a weapon."

Frowning, Rachel studied his wrist. He wore a wide rag bracelet that covered most of his left forearm. The cufflike piece of jewelry consisted of embroidered and tasseled canvas inset with a Y-shaped piece of filigreed metal. "What are you—?"

Bailey lifted the metal piece. As if springdriven, it snapped up against his left palm. Rachel abruptly realized that the bracelet was a slingshot. In a series of neat, swift movements, Bailey pulled a marble-sized ball of ammunition from a concealed pouch in the cuff and nestled it against the slingshot's band.

"See?" he said. "We're armed, too. You've got Dútha's knife, and I've got this."

Rachel cleared her throat. "It's very pretty. But we need to—"

Bailey stood up. Holding the slingshot sideways with his left arm rigid, he drew back on the band as if drawing a bow, stretching its three-inch length to an incredible degree. "I'm ready," he said. "Go ahead and short out that relay on the door's panel. Just don't get in my line of fire. I don't want to kill the wrong person."

Rachel narrowed her eyes and studied the Freeholder. His stance and expression all conveyed expertise with the weapon in his hand. She discarded her notion that the slingshot was merely a toy. "Killing the Phi-Nurian," she said quietly, "should be our last resort."

Bailey raised his brows. "I understand, Rachel. But it might be necessary."

"The situation is bad enough without adding to the fatalities."

"I'm sorry," he said earnestly. "I don't want to kill it. I truly hope we escape the ship without it trying to stop us. But I don't think my hope is terribly realistic. Do you?"

"If this Phi-Nurian is the only one left," Rachel argued, "then it's the only who can corroborate Meris' story. And to confess that the Phi-Nurian government risked diplomatic catastrophe to get their claws on one stowaway Jadamii." She lifted her hands, palms up, pleading. "There are clouds of war on the horizon, Bailey, and the wind is blowing in our direction. Don't invite the lightning. Don't—"

An echoing hum vibrated through the ship's hull. Rachel recognized the noise immediately. Their captor had powered up the ship's hyperspace drive.

Bailey's eyes widened. "Why is it prepping for a jump?"

Rachel returned to the cut she'd made in the bulkhead. "I'd say our Phi-Nurian friend has just found a way to hold the entire station hostage. 'Deliver Meris, or you all die.' " Carefully, she bent the triangular flap of metal up to expose the control panel's guts. "With any luck, it will be so busy arguing with Docking Control that it won't notice one more red light on its Ops board." She picked up the probe and peered into the hole. The reassuringly familiar grid of standard G-H Bontelle circuitry met her sight. She poised the probe's tip over the lock relay. "Get ready to run," she warned. "The hatch to the upper level access is to the right."

"I know that," Bailey said tensely. "Don't cut the lights."

"Don't be insulting." Rachel firmly pressed the probe's tip against the lock relay. A series of miniature sparks danced over the panel, and the door shot open.

With his slingshot still drawn, Bailey cautiously edged through the door and glanced around. "All clear so far," he whispered. "Come on."

Rachel rose to her feet and limped after him. The Phi-Nurians had torn out the bulkheads of the hold compartment across from their former prison, creating a wide passage quite different from the BRD's original cramped layout. Their captors had not bothered to add cosmetic touches to their remodeling, and the jagged ends of support struts thrust up through the deck plates. She caught Bailey's eye and jerked her head toward the outer hatch, just a few yards away.

Bailey nodded, sweat spangling his upper lip.

Heart pounding, Rachel cautiously made her way to the hatch and studied its control panel. Amber warning lights glowed to indicate the hatch was sealed and ready for debarkation. *Oh, damn.*

Bailey backed toward her, still holding his weapon ready. He glanced anxiously at the panel. "Now what?" he whispered. His breathing seemed ragged. "I hope you're not thinking of trying to override the controls."

Rachel jammed the end of the probe under the panel's cover plate. "No choice." Using the probe as a lever, she pried the metal plate away from its housing in the bulkhead.

Bailey issued a wordless hiss of protest.

"Stay alert," Rachel ordered. "I'll try to engage a repair program, make it think this whole mess is only a test."

Claws scrabbled in the passage to their left. The Phi-Nurian rounded the corner, gun drawn. It paused when it saw them, weaving to bring them into focus.

Desperately, Rachel brandished the probe as if it were a laser pistol. "Throw down your weapon," she commanded, "or I'll shoot."

The Phi-Nurian raised its gun and fired. The blast hit the bulkhead and the open control panel. Bits of metal and plastic exploded in every direction.

Rachel threw herself away from the flying debris and rolled to the floor. "Bailey!" she shouted. "Run!"

The air split with a sound like the crack of a whip.

Rachel scrambled into a crouch and looked up.

The Phi-Nurian stood rigid, its upper limbs straight and stiff. There was a small hole in the middle of its eyepad. Blood, thick and black, dribbled from the wound and down over its mandibles. The alien's limbs jerked in horrible spasms, and it fell over backward.

Bailey slowly lowered his slingshot. His eyes widened with horror. "Oh, God."

Rachel climbed to her feet and limped to the Phi-Nurian's body. Carefully, she disengaged the gun from its clawed hand; nerve spasms might cause it to fire.

Bailey's voice was unsteady. "It's dead. Isn't it?"

Rachel straightened and met Bailey's gaze. "Yes. You killed it."

Bailey recoiled as if she had slapped him. "But I—" His mouth worked inarticulately for a moment. "I couldn't let it hurt you."

"Justified self-defense." Sick and sad, Rachel turned away. "Come on. We need to get to the bridge and notify the station."

In the air lock of the *La Vaca*, Tigre waited beside Dútha's stasis unit. Rico had left him to return to more pressing duties; and, deprived of the need to appear calm, Tigre found himself giving way to anxiety.

With a thump of shifting pressures, the hatch slid open. The ship's surgeon, Arthur Sang, stood in the corridor beyond, his broad face creased with obvious worry. "Tigre!" He rushed into the air lock. "I heard about the incident with the Phi-Nurian. Let's get you—"

Tigre gripped his friend's shoulders. "No time," he interrupted. "Rachel. It's got Rachel."

"What?" Arthur's concern slid into confusion. "But you—"

Tigre forced himself to slow down, to remember that Arthur only wished to help. "I'm fine for now. Just a little shaken."

"A little—?"

"That's a joke, Arthur. A joke."

Arthur stared at him for a few moments in silence, then sighed. "A possible spinal injury isn't a joke. You might have any number of—"

"I know." Tigre nodded toward the stasis unit. "But first things first. I need you to take this patient for me, and then I need to talk to Wu Jackson." He pushed the unit out of the air lock and aboard the ship, then paused. "Where is he? I suppose he's confined somewhere."

"No." Arthur folded his arms. "Right now, he's dining with the captain."

Tigre froze, gazing helplessly at Arthur. *Dining . . . ?* Abruptly, the universe shifted back into recognizable shape, and he was once again in a world where Human beings trusted one another and behaved with kindness.

Arthur tilted his head. "Tigre?"

"Sorry." Tigre passed a shaking hand through his hair. "I just realized how much I'd let the World Council get to me."

Arthur smiled slightly, but his expression conveyed no humor. "The World Council, eh? How much do you know about the current crisis?"

Tigre shrugged. "More than I want to."

Arthur crossed to the stasis unit and braced his arms to help push. "Let's get your patient to sick bay. Then I'll take you to the captain. I think she'll want to talk to you."

"But Rachel—"

At the end of the corridor, a lift door opened and Captain Marj Mendez stepped out. Wu followed her.

Tigre felt a surge of relief. "There you are!"

Wu smiled and sauntered toward him. Though a pressure

cast encased his ankle, he seemed to have no trouble walking. "Ah, Doctor, glad you're here. This will save some time."

Marj nodded, seeming grimly satisfied. "No more messing around."

Wu beckoned for Tigre to come with him to the air lock. "Shall we go?"

"Go?" Tigre echoed. "Go where?"

"To rescue Rachel."

Without another word, Tigre turned and followed Wu to the air lock.

They did not speak again until they were aboard the station and on a lift for Dock Two.

Wu cleared his throat. "Is Rachel badly injured?"

"I don't know." Tigre did not want to think about the last time he saw Rachel or the look in her eyes. "Her shoulder was bleeding, but she was still conscious."

Wu kept his gaze fixed on the lift doors. "What about you?"

"I'm conscious, too. Just barely."

Wu did not look at him, seeming to wait.

Tigre sighed in irritation. "Headache," he snapped. "Possible whiplash. Nothing of immediate concern. How's your ankle?"

"Good." Wu leaned against the wall, still wearing a preoccupied expression. "Just fine."

"Are you in pain?"

"Do you care?"

"What kind of question is that?" Tigre folded his arms. "Of course, I care." His own words seemed freighted with deeper meaning, and he tried to amend them. "I mean, I care—" He could think of nothing else to say.

For the first time, Tigre recognized his feelings for Wu. Too intense for mere friendship, the strange bond seemed closer to gratitude than desire; felt more like rage than romantic interest. "I care . . . about you." The words seemed both momentous and trivial. Irritated by his inability to express himself, he added: "I think I've fallen for you. Really pisses me off."

"Oh?" Wu's tone remained colorless. "Somehow, you didn't strike me as the type."

"I'm not, you infuriating piece of shit!"

Sighing, Wu closed his eyes. "Doctor, you should know better. Shared danger, rescue, mutual suffering, it all creates a certain type of delusion. And the fact that—"

"Don't play amateur psychiatrist with me!"

"—that you were the victim of a sexual assault only adds a poisonous spin to the whole thing. It's some sort of syndrome. I can't remember the clinical term for it."

"Love?"

"Tigre." Wu's tone held infinite weariness. "You do not love me."

"Yes, I do, you bastard," Tigre said hotly.

"You don't even know me."

"I know you well enough." He lunged for Wu and gripped his shoulders. "And when this is all over, I'm going to kick your ass!"

Wu's remote expression melted into a sardonic smile, and he finally met Tigre's eyes. "Get in line. Rachel has a prior claim."

Tigre's heart thundered. Beneath his fingers, Wu's shoulders felt warm and strong. He ordered himself to let go, but found that he could not bring himself to release his hold on the only anchor he possessed. "Rachel?"

"Don't tell me that you love her, too?"

"Yes, I do."

"Doesn't that make things rather complicated?"

Instinct warned Tigre to show no hesitation. "I suppose," he said levelly. "But I'm not afraid of complexity."

"I see. And when this is all settled, should the three of us run away to a Freehold and get married?"

"Very well."

Wu's brows shot up. "I was asking sarcastically."

"Too late. Proposal submitted and accepted." Tigre's breath roughened as conflicting urges warred within him. He wanted to collapse against Wu and allow himself to be held, but he also wanted to punch him in the mouth. Appalled by both desires, Tigre somehow discovered the strength to push himself away. "Any other feeble protests?"

"I guess not." Wu made a hapless gesture. "But how do you plan to convince Rachel?"

"Easy. Let it be her idea." Wanting to reach out to Wu,

Tigre folded his arms. "Now, will you answer my god-damned question? Are you in pain?"

"Rather significantly." Wu's gaze seemed to travel over Tigre's face. "But so are you. I really wish I hadn't asked you to come."

No longer intimidated by the dark cunning in those eyes, Tigre met them unflinchingly. "Rachel's wounded, remember? I just happen to know a little first aid."

Wu looked away again, turning his attention to the lift's control panel. "I've set it for an express trip to Dock Two's lower level, but it will take a few minutes. Let's hope we don't face resistance when we arrive."

Tigre's frown deepened. "What do you mean?"

Wu raised his brows. "If Councillor Phong discovers our attempt to rescue Rachel, she might try to interfere."

Given what Tigre had already witnessed, Wu's concerns seemed more than reasonable. "I suppose," he sighed. "But I really don't get it. What does the World Council have against Rachel?"

A series of expressions shifted across Wu's face. He glanced at Tigre sidelong. "You shouldn't ask that question. Unless you're very careful, just knowing about the game makes you a player."

"I don't give a damn."

"Ah. Well, then—" A peculiar smile lifted just the corners of Wu's mouth. "Well, then, I would venture to guess that in this particular case, it isn't Rachel they want kept as hostage. It's Professor Bailey Rye."

Tigre frowned. "The translator? Why?"

"There are a lot of reasons." Wu's tone became soft, tender. "You see, I've been lying low, observing this game for a very long time."

Tigre suddenly found it hard to breathe as a few more things about Wu began to make sense.

"Bailey," Wu continued in that deceptively gentle voice, "may be much more than a xeno-linguistic expert. You ever hear of an organization called *Ōkaze*?"

Tigre shook his head. "Sounds like something from one of the Northern Freeholds."

"Yes, it does, doesn't it? *Ōkaze* liberates political prisoners and offers them sanctuary in the Freeholds."

"Political prisoners? What do you mean by—?"

"Almost anyone sentenced to life on a penal farm."

"But—" Tigre intended to argue that the internees on penal farms were dangerous individuals who posed a threat to society, but recent events made him pause to rethink his understanding. "Oh."

"Of course, the World Council finds this bothersome to an extreme degree." Wu lowered his gaze, seeming to look inward. "By all reports, the *Ókaze*'s leader is a brash youth who styles himself 'Shiro.' A silly boy. Smart enough, I suppose, but prone to impetuous stunts."

"And you think—" Tigre licked his dry lips. "You think Bailey is this Shiro person?"

"I think the World Council does. Councillor Weber probably did. And Councillor Phong—" Wu lifted his eyes. "—seems quite determined to have him eliminated."

Tigre hunched his shoulders. It explained why the councillor had suspended the head of Port Authority and ignored the advice of Deputy DelRio. "But Bailey might have nothing to do with *Ókaze*!"

"True." Wu tilted his head with an air of consideration. "But one must ask oneself what business Bailey—a Freeholder—has at Earth Port. And why was he at Igsha Reey Port when it shut down? His activities raise a whole series of interesting questions, and you know how much I hate interesting questions."

Feeling sick, Tigre recalled Rachel's concern over the possibility of galactic strife. "What about Rachel? Is she involved?"

Wu's voice turned bleak. "Rachel." Anguish surfaced in his eyes, along with carefully contained rage. "Our esteemed Deputy Ajmani is far, far too honest for such things."

"But Councillor Phong doesn't know that!"

"Again, true. If Rachel's still alive, she is in grave peril, as much from the machinations of the World Council as from her captors." Moving casually, Wu reached into a pocket and pulled out a gun.

Tigre straightened in alarm. "Where the hell did you get that?"

"The honorable Captain Mendez loaned it to me." Wu carefully checked the weapon's settings. "Almost there.

Brace yourself. We may have to wade through a welcoming party."

A thread of bile burned in the back of Tigre's throat, sheer terror; but he forced himself to speak calmly. "I'm ready."

The lift slowed. Tigre swallowed loudly.

"Scared?"

"Hell, yes!"

"Good." Wu's grin became a fierce display of teeth. "Me, too."

CHAPTER TWENTY-SIX

THE BRIDGE retained the structure typical of the old BRD freighters, consisting of a boxy room fronted by a curved viewing bay. Since the ship was moored on the outer ring, a vista of the station's exterior filled half the viewing bay; an airless landscape of docking gantries and berth couplings lit by the harsh glare of floodlights. The other half presented a field of stars that appeared to sweep by in a parade as the station rotated.

Rachel paused to catch her breath, resisting the urge to press her hands against her shoulder wound. It flared with searing pain at her slightest movement, somehow pulling threads of fire through the muscles in her neck and arm.

The Phi-Nurians had torn out the chairs, but the operational consoles looked fundamentally unaltered. Bailey edged onto the bridge, pushing aside broken plastic with the toe of his boot. "What a mess." In spite of his wild curls and Freeholder's garb, the gaze he cast at the consoles' controls was sharp and discerning, not the bewildered look of a farm boy. Red lights pulsed in warning from every board. A stream of instructions spilled from the communications console; the station warning all ships to clear Dock Two. "Rachel," he said tensely. "I don't like this."

"Me either." She limped to the main console, glanced over the controls, and found most of them locked into safety override positions. "This doesn't make sense." Keeping her eyes on the displays, she twisted toward communications, reaching for the station link. "Better inform Docking Control that we—"

Rachel's groping fingers encountered jagged edges. She jerked her gaze to the console and discovered the entire control panel smashed and its indicators dead. "What the hell is—?" She tried to open a channel, gingerly pressing the shattered code keys. A fat spark crackled against her fingernail. More startled than hurt, Rachel whipped her hand away. "Damn!"

Evidently the only functioning component of the communications system, the station-line speaker continued to broadcast the crisp voice of the Docking Control Chief, Brian Stanislav, as he assigned lanes to the hastily debarking ships. She scowled, wondering how to reach anyone on station to advise them of their current situation. *This is the last time I loan anyone my phone.*

"Rachel!" Bailey leaned over an auxiliary console, frantically attempting to key in a command. "We're cycling toward a jump sequence! Forty seconds!"

Rachel's heart started racing, and she lunged for the pilot's controls. If the ship kicked into hyperspace while still at dock, the generated fields would shred the station like wet paper. Her plan had been to debark and pilot the ship to a safe distance before the jump cycle completed, but there was not enough time. "Engaging all-system abort code."

"No!" Bailey crossed the bridge in two strides and grabbed her hands. "You can't do that!"

"Let go!" Rachel furiously wrenched free of his grip. "Are you mad?"

"If you cut the particle regulators during a sequence, the engines will tip over into critical!"

"I know that!" Fingers shaking with fury, Rachel punched in the standard six-digit code, hoping the relays were not too fried to obey. "But it will spare the station."

The ship shuddered as the abort command worked its way through all the main functions. The overhead lights flickered and went to emergency battery power. Rachel blew out her cheeks in relief. With luck, Chief Stanislav would recognize the shutdown as a signal and wait for them to finish their escape.

Clearly aghast, Bailey stared at her. "You've cut life support!"

"We won't need it." Rachel grabbed his arm and yanked him toward the door. "We're leaving."

"But—"

"Hurry! Before Docking Control jettisons the ship." Rachel pushed him through the door and gave him a shove. "That way. To the end of the hall, and then right. Run!"

Bailey cast a reproachful look over his shoulder and broke into a graceful lope. "The hatch is the other way," he called. "Why are we—?"

Rachel ran after him, trying to ignore the biting pain in her injured foot. She did not have the breath to remind him that their captor had undoubtedly damaged the upper level hatch when it shot out the control panel. "Lower level hatch," she panted. "Move!"

They reached the end of the hall and turned right. Beside the lift, a covered service ladder descended to the lower deck. Bailey gripped the top rung and waited for her to catch up, his youthful face tense with worry. "Rachel, you going to make it?"

Every breath pulled at her wounded shoulder. "Move!" she ordered hoarsely. Sweat rolled down her face. "Go!"

Bailey scrambled down the ladder. Rachel followed him, forcing herself to climb carefully. He stopped and waited for her at the bottom. Rachel wanted to shout for him to run, but she did not have the breath.

In the next instant, her feet slipped from their rung, and her arms jerked straight with the burden of her full weight. Fire lanced her wounded shoulder. As if from a great distance, she heard Bailey shouting something, but his words made no sense. She lost her grip and fell in a heap on the deck.

The blow smacked all the air from her lungs. With a desperate sense of drowning, Rachel fought to inhale. The inrush of oxygen seemed to increase her ability to feel pain, and the agony in her foot and shoulder burned with white-hot intensity. Shadowy haze filled her vision. She knew she had to stand, but could not remember how.

"Rachel!" Bailey dropped to the floor beside her. "Are you all right?"

The shoulder wound reopened, and warm blood soaked into her uniform. Seeming to float beyond the reach of her body's torment, Rachel's mind clicked to the only logical conclusion: Bailey had to leave her. Unable to speak, Rachel pointed toward the lower level hatch.

Bailey scrambled to his feet, bent, and scooped her up into his arms. Pain flared up her spine, and she gagged.

"It's okay," he murmured. "I got you." He carried her like a child to the hatch.

The air turned chill. Rachel shivered. Without life support's constant input of heat, the temperature on the ship would quickly become as cold as space.

Still holding her, Bailey awkwardly keyed the command on the hatch's control plate. "Will this work? I don't—"

The lights abruptly dimmed, and the hatch slid to one side. Rachel swallowed against rising nausea. "Go!" she choked. "Go!"

Bailey shifted his hold on her and sidestepped into the air lock. The cold intensified. It knifed into Rachel's lungs with every breath. The three steps to the next hatch seemed an impossible distance.

His teeth chattering, Bailey carried her forward and reached for the control plate. "Why—?" He tapped the command. "—so cold?"

The hatch shot back. Brutally frigid air blasted over them from the darkness beyond. Lit by glaring lights, gantries arched away in the distance.

Lost in perfect horror, Rachel could only stare. *Space!*

Bailey hauled her through the hatch. The familiar thunder of metal deck plates greeted her ears, and she realized that they had not stepped into space. *Dock Two.* Relief accomplished what pain and fear had failed to do; robbed Rachel of her self-control. She let her head fall against Bailey's shoulder and dissolved into helpless giggles.

The doors to the lift shot open.

Tigre flattened himself against the wall, expecting a barrage of laser fire.

Gun ready, Wu rolled out of cover and took aim.

Sweat rolled down Tigre's face. His heart beat in hard jolts.

From outside the lift, a woman spoke. "Thank God, it's you!"

His expression going blank, Wu slowly lowered his gun and stepped out of the lift. "Lois? What are you doing here?"

Tigre cautiously peered around the edge of the door. The silver-haired and venerable Deputy Jimanez-Verde was lowering her laser pistol. "Come with me," she said. She turned and strode toward the Operations booth. "We don't have much time."

Wu followed without a backward glance. Feeling shaky and weak from the aftermath of his adrenaline surge, Tigre trailed after them.

Dock Two's Operations booth seemed full of people. Tigre recognized Deputy DelRio and Deputy Omar; but there was also a sandy-haired fellow in a black Docking Control uniform, and a young woman dressed in a cargo tech's blue coveralls.

"Honorable Deputies." Wu nodded. "Brian. Lafiya."

Lois turned to Wu and laid her hands on his shoulders. "How did you—?" Then her gaze fell on Tigre. "Doctor DeFlora."

Tigre stared at her uncertainly. "Deputy Jimanez-Verde. I heard you were under arrest. What's going on?"

Lafiya, the young woman at the control console, jumped to her feet. "They're out!"

There was a general rush to the window.

"I see them," Deputy Omar said. "Professor Rye is carrying Rachel."

Lois whirled. "Brian, jettison the ship."

Brian did not look happy. "But, Deputy, it may not clear the gantries."

"Do it!"

Tigre squirmed through the press of bodies to get to the window. "Rachel?" The dock was a mess of debris and equipment, banded by black shadows. "Where is she?"

Deputy DelRio pointed to a high catwalk. "There. See them?"

Tigre saw nothing except heavy machinery, but he headed toward the door. "Come on."

"Doctor," Lois said. "The temperature out there is well below freezing. We've got—"

Tigre did not pause. "Then bring blankets. Hurry."

*   *   *

Bailey murmured in her ear, sounding frightened. "Rachel?"

Ashamed, she fought to compose herself, gritting her teeth to prevent them from chattering. "Yes?"

"Didn't you feel that?"

Rachel raised her head and gazed into his copper-colored eyes. Again, a strong sense of connection stole over her. "Feel what?"

"The floor shook."

"Really?" The cold made breathing painful. "No doubt, control jettisoned the ship." Though the effort made her nauseated, Rachel twisted her head around to get her bearings.

They stood on one of the high catwalks. The nearest exit hatch was down three zigzag flights of metal stairs and twenty feet across the floor. Debris from the riot still covered the deck plates, and she guessed that the heat had been turned down to discourage looting. All equipment stood silent, and the registry boards of the nearby berths were ominously dark. Only Dútha's ship still lay at dock, the other vessels had evidently cast off to escape destruction.

Rachel felt Bailey's arms tremble, and she recalled that he had been through some rough treatment as well. Though much younger, he was not inexhaustible, and she feared his strength would give out. "Put me down."

Bailey staggered and clutched her more tightly to his chest.

At first, Rachel thought he meant to argue, then she realized that the catwalk shook.

"What—?" Bailey suddenly sounded quite young and frightened. "What's happening?"

The answer clicked into Rachel's brain as if from an outside source. "Ship snagged on a docking gantry."

The lights pulsed off and on. A high-pitched alarm bell split the frigid air; the thirty second warning for section closing. The station had initiated emergency containment procedures.

Rachel pointed toward the staircase. Bailey had to get off the dock before the partition sealed. If the imminent explosion of the Phi-Nurian ship did not blow the dock to vacuum, he would freeze to death during the thirty-minute delay before the seal opened. "Leave me—" Rachel's voice came out in a breathless whisper. She cleared her throat. "Go."

Below, the exit hatch shot open. Tigre hurtled onto the dock.

"It's him," Bailey gasped. "It's Tigre."

Horror lent power to Rachel's voice. "No!" she shouted hoarsely. "Go back!"

Tigre's face flashed up to her. "Rachel!" He darted toward the stairs, weaving to avoid equipment. "Get her down here! Hurry!"

"She's hurt," Bailey called. He started toward the end of the catwalk, staggering with obvious fatigue. "She can't walk."

Tigre did not slow when he hit the stairs, and his boots clattered on the metal steps as he took them two at a time. "Keep moving," he called. "Station's jettisoned the ship, but it hung up on a gantry. We've got to get off this dock!"

Rachel pushed at Bailey's chest. "Leave me!"

"You're so stubborn." Bailey laughed breathlessly. "Why do I always fall in love with the stubborn ones?"

Tigre appeared at the top of the stairs and sprinted up to them. Frost from his steaming breath clung to his long lashes. "Less than . . . thirty seconds," he panted. He pulled off his parka as he jogged beside Bailey and tucked it around Rachel. "Hurry!"

As they reached the top of the stairs, the lights pulsed again and a loud buzzer sounded. The section partition rolled down like a metal curtain, cutting them off from the exit hatch.

They stood at the top of the stairs in a huddle.

The alarm stopped. Silence yawned. Rachel stared at the partition. *Sealed in.*

Bailey cleared his throat. "That's not good. Is it?"

"No," Rachel said. Her mind clicked through a series of survival maneuvers. There was no way to protect themselves from the explosion, but they ought to find some way to generate warmth. She twisted in Bailey's arms. "Put me down."

Bailey made a disappointed noise, but carefully set her on her feet. The parka slid off and fell on the floor. Rachel hissed in shock as the frigid air hit her, freezing the fresh blood on her uniform.

With an inarticulate oath, Tigre hastily snatched the parka up and bundled it around her. Something that looked like a disk of gold filigree fell out of the pocket and hit the floor plates with a bell-like chime.

Bailey picked up the disk and turned it over in his long fingers. "A Rofan entry key?"

Tigre scowled. "Dútha's ship."

Not knowing whether to laugh or swear, Rachel stared at Tigre. "Dútha's ship?" She pointed at the registry board beside them. "You mean this one?"

"I—"

Rachel grabbed the key from Bailey, took two limping strides to the access hatch, and shoved the key into the scanner. The hatch promptly opened with a rush of blessedly warm air. "Inside," she ordered.

The three of them crowded into the air lock. Bailey shut the hatch, then turned to Rachel with a worried expression. "I've seen Dútha in action. I'm not sure how a *gukka* of such renown will respond to three uninvited—"

"He gave me his ship," Tigre interrupted.

"He?" Bailey echoed. "You mean Dútha?"

Tigre's voice dripped with contempt. "Yes."

Bailey's eyes narrowed in his first display of temper, and he also adopted a hostile tone. "Can you pilot it?"

"No. Can you?"

"Yes."

Running low on patience, Rachel shoved Bailey toward the inner hatch and croaked: "Then do it."

Without a word, Bailey keyed the override, and the hatch shot open. He hurried onto the ship. Rachel took a step to follow and nearly fell. Tigre threw a supporting arm around her and helped her over the threshold.

They immediately entered the ship's living quarters, which seemed to consist entirely of a single compartment with a galley and a recessed bunk. "Huh," Tigre said. "Cozy."

"Dútha—" Rachel fought for breath. "How's Dútha?"

"Fine."

"But—"

Bailey glanced over his shoulder. "This way. Hurry."

Following Bailey, they stumbled onto the bridge. The view screen covered the whole forward wall, and there appeared to be only two seats. Bailey flung himself into one and powered on the restraints. "You'll have to share," he said, his hands dancing over the control panel in front of him. "Hurry and get situated."

Racked with pain, Rachel clambered into the copilot's couch and rolled onto her side to make room for Tigre. He seemed to hesitate a moment, but then climbed in and spooned up against her. Rachel fumbled with the controls on the arm of the couch and managed to get the restraint mesh in place. "Secured," she croaked for Bailey's benefit. "Move."

"Aye, aye," Bailey said cheerfully. "Moving." The view screen flashed with differing images of Dock Two's exterior, and then paused. A dilapidated BRD freighter dangled from the end of a gantry. "There it is." Bailey opened a communications channel. "Zo, Docking Control? Are you reading me? This is Pilot Bailey Rye aboard the . . . uh . . . well—"

"This is Chief Stanislav of Docking Control. You're cleared. Disengage and follow the designated coordinates on your—"

Wu broke in. "Do you have Rachel and Tigre?"

In spite of pain and the moment's danger, at the sound of his voice, the tension and distress faded from Rachel's thoughts. She smiled softly. *Wu.*

Bailey tossed her a quick grin. "Yup. They send their warmest regards." He returned his attention to the BRD. "Chief, I'm going to get that hunk of garbage off your pretty dock."

"Negative." Brian's tone was implacable. "Follow the designated coordinates."

Bailey closed communications. "What a grouch." He looked at Rachel. "We can tug that BRD off the station and boost it toward open space."

Tigre made a noise of protest. "That's a pretty delicate operation, isn't it?"

Bailey set his long jaw in a stubborn expression. "I designed this bird. I can fly it."

Rachel studied him, weighing the alternatives. If the

Phi-Nurians' ship blew while still tangled with the gantry,
there was no telling the extent of damage and loss of life
it might cause. "Worth a try," she whispered and nudged
Tigre with her elbow. "Permission granted, Shipmaster
DeFlora?"

"What?" Tigre said tensely.

"Your ship." Though unable to see his face, Rachel
caught his surprised intake of breath. "Do it?"

"Hell, yes," Tigre said. "Do it."

"Aye, aye." Bailey stretched his mouth into an enthusiastic grin and set his hands on the controls. "Doing it."

The ship made final disengagement from the station with
a barely perceptible shudder. Feeling helpless, Rachel split
her attention between the view screen and Bailey.

With feathery touches to the thrusters, Bailey maneuvered the ship close to the BRD and matched the station's rotation.

"Damn," Rachel whispered in admiration.

Tigre snorted softly. "Show-off."

Carefully, Bailey extended a magnetic mooring lock, as
if preparing to dock with the BRD. The lock struck its
target with a dull boom that shook the ship. "Easy, now,"
Bailey murmured. He urged the ship to ease away from
the dock with a series of fluttering thrusts. "Be a good girl
for Daddy."

The screech of metal on metal vibrated through the hull.
It stopped suddenly, and they were free, pulling the BRD
with them. "Ah," Bailey said in a triumphant tone. "Here
we go."

Rachel exhaled her long held breath. "God. . . ."

Tigre stirred against her. "Did we do it?"

Bailey laughed, his teeth flashing by the light of the view
screen. "We sure did!" He appeared to reset the thrusters'
controls. "Hang on!"

In the next instant, the ship dived away from the station,
still dragging the BRD with it. Rachel instinctively clutched
the arm of the couch. She felt Tigre muffle his cry of surprised fear against the back of her head. " 'S okay," she
whispered to him. "Under control."

The ship rolled, picking up velocity. Inertial compensa-
tors moaned in strain. "Come on, little girl," Bailey said.
"You can do it."

Rachel's vision filled with pinpoints of light. *No. Can't faint now.*

Bailey released the BRD from the magnetic lock and then sent the ship into another dive. "Just like a slingshot," he announced. "Whee!"

Fighting against sudden nausea, Rachel forced her eyes to keep focused on the view screen. The BRD shot away from the station. "Tra—" She paused to swallow. "Trajectory?"

Bailey laughed again, clearly pleased with himself. "BRD is headed for open space."

Tigre panted in Rachel's ear. "Is everything all right, then? Did we do it?"

"We did," Bailey said.

"Is it over?" Tigre's tone darkened. "No more hotshot pilot shit?"

"No more. Promise." Bailey's eyes seemed to disappear into the creases of his wide smile. "It's all over, except for the part where everyone yells at me." He reopened the communications channel. "Listen."

The irate voice of Chief Stanislav filled the bridge. "—irresponsibility! Do you read me? Twenty-seven violations of station—"

Still grinning, Bailey settled back in the pilot's couch and put his hands behind his head. "Reading you, Chief, go ahead."

"—traffic procedures, and twelve violations of galactic—!"

"Why, yes, we'd love to return to dock," Bailey said. "Please issue approach coordinates."

Wu broke in. "Rachel? Tigre?"

Behind her, Tigre raised his head. "We're here," he called. "Rachel's wounded. Would you tell what's-his-name to stop pounding his chest and let us dock?"

Rachel drew a breath to protest that she was fine.

At that moment, a blaze of light ripped across the view screen. The filters immediately damped it down, and the onboard computer replaced the shadowy image with a simulation. Communications dissolved into static.

With a startled hiss, Bailey leaped from his relaxed posture to reach for the controls. "That was fast," he said. "Glad we put some distance on it."

Tigre tightened his hold on Rachel. "I thought you said it was over!"

On the screen, the BRD broke into pieces.

"Debris?" Rachel croaked. "Tracking?"

Bailey made an unhappy noise. "Best guesses only. The explosion's interrupted all transmission frequencies."

"What?" Tigre said. "What the hell is going on?"

Bailey kept his eyes on the screen. "The BRD blew up. The blast is interfering with sensor signals, so we can't see what's actually happening. We have to rely on the computer to speculate for us." He gestured toward the image in front of them. The BRD looked like a peony shedding its petals. "Based on all combined factors, the computer's telling us what is *probably* happening."

"Little pieces," Rachel whispered. "Should be all right."

"Yup," Bailey said thoughtfully. "Given the strength of the explosion—"

Tigre squirmed, obviously impatient. "But what about particle fields? What about—?"

"Shields," Rachel whispered. She dropped her head onto the couch and closed her eyes. "Station . . . ships . . . all shielded."

"Rachel's right," Bailey said. "We'll be fine, unless we get hit with something big."

"But," Tigre said, "isn't there anything we can do?"

"Not a thing." Bailey chuckled gently. "Except take a nap, since we can't dock until the sensors are back on-line."

Sleep sounded good to Rachel, but the Seroplex kept her mentally alert in spite of her body's raging fatigue. She wondered how Wu was feeling, and if his ankle hurt as much as her foot.

Tigre shifted restlessly again.

For the first time, Rachel became aware of the source of his discomfort. "Um . . . Tigre?"

Self-loathing filled his voice. "Sorry."

Rachel glanced down at her filthy uniform, knowing she reeked of blood, Phi-Nurian dung, and sweat. "Flattered," she whispered. "Really."

Tigre sighed in an unhappy manner, but seemed to relax somewhat.

Rachel wondered if Wu would be jealous if he saw them. *Probably not. He'd probably just want to join us.* She raised her gaze and found Bailey watching her with a gentle smile. "What?"

"Nothing." He tapped in a command on the control panel. "Let's investigate Dútha's taste in music. Perhaps if we—"

Meris' voice came over the speakers, and she spoke in Trade. "I'm telling you that the Artifact is nothing more than a historical curiosity."

With an explosive oath, Bailey slapped at the controls, and the speakers went silent.

Shocked, Rachel struggled for words.

Tigre stirred behind her. "What was that? It sounded like a—"

Rachel cleared her throat. "Meris."

Bailey chuckled, though his laughter seemed forced. "That was a Rofan soap opera. In the next twenty seconds, I'll wager, all the characters will engage in rampant, seven-way sex."

"It was Meris." Rachel met Bailey's gaze and held it. "I already know she speaks Trade. And I know she's talking about the Artifact."

"But—"

"Play it."

With clear reluctance, Bailey restarted the recording. Dútha's voice filled the bridge. "You know, the Legitimacy has ordered me to return you to Jadamiin custody. I believe this is tantamount to a death sentence. Both sides of your family would benefit from having you eliminated. Once you achieve the status of goddess, there's no risk of the equations falling into the wrong hands, and they can accuse the other side of your murder."

Bailey inhaled sharply through his teeth.

Rachel frowned, remembering what Meris had told her while they were trapped together in Medica.

Tigre shifted restlessly. "What are they talking about?"

Rachel shook her head. "Listen."

Dútha continued: "And if I thought that the current crisis could be dealt with so simply, I would obey my superiors' orders to return you."

"Oh," Tigre said softly. "Is that why Jardín and Rife—?"

"Shh."

Dútha's tone turned thoughtful. "—I believe that your death would resolve nothing."

Meris said something in Farnii.

Dútha sounded darkly amused. "Don't thank me yet. It isn't over. And you may not like the course I take to preserve your life." There was a pause, filled with the whisper of fabric. "To start, we need to find the mathematician responsible for partially deciphering the equations. Who is it? Do you know?"

Bailey tilted his head, frowning in apparent bewilderment. "Mathematician?" he whispered. "But that's not right, it's a—"

"Listen," Rachel said. "Just listen."

It sounded as if a scuffle occurred, then Dútha spoke in a tone of clear regret. "I wish there were another way, dear friend."

Meris sounded terrified. "Poison?"

"I would never be so cruel," Dútha said. "It's Phenox."

"No," Meris whispered. "Please. . . ."

"Don't be afraid," Dútha murmured. "When you wake up, you'll have a friend by your side."

Silence fell. The recording clicked off.

Bailey looked at Rachel. "So. She really was drugged against her will."

"Sounds—" Rachel's voice cracked, and she had to finish in a dry rasp. "Sounds that way."

"Sounds," Tigre said grimly, "like you need to stop talking and rest."

Abruptly, the view screen cleared.

"Finally!" Bailey lunged for the controls. "Let's get this little bird back to her nest." He flicked the station link. "Docking Control? Zo? Do you read me?"

"Reading you." Chief Stanislav's tone conveyed enormous relief. "You ready to come in out of the cold?"

"Yes, please."

"We're slotting you to Dock One. Follow the designated coordinates."

"Aye, aye. Following." Bailey's long-fingered hands danced over the controls. "Can't wait for a hot bath and a nice cup of tea."

Behind Rachel, Tigre drew a deep breath, then released it without speaking.

Rachel hesitated. "Tigre?"

"I just—" He swallowed loudly. "Is it over? Is everything all right now?"

Rachel thought of the World Council's machinations, Meris' plight, and her own impending dismissal. "Of course," she whispered. "It's all right."

Bailey gave them both a wide grin. "Oh, it's more than all right. Guess who's in final approach to the station?"

Tigre sounded impatient. "Who?"

Bailey brought up a listing of ships on the main view screen, enlarged it, and then highlighted several ships. "Doctor Richard Wagasi of the World Health Agency. Twyla Binks, an elder of the Freehold Cooperative Association. Vulana Garcia of the World Council's Internal Affairs Bureau. And Miles Glockner, head of Global Disaster Services."

Tigre made a strange noise of mingled exasperation and relief. "Doctor Wagasi? He's finally here? About time."

Bailey's grin widened. "A formidable individual."

Tigre snorted. "That's putting it nicely. The World Council better watch their backs."

"Exactly." Bailey reset the thrusters and turned the ship. "All our worries are over."

Letting her eyes finally fall shut, Rachel smiled softly. Bailey might be correct. With so many independent and powerful observers aboard the station, Councillor Phong and the other members of the XRC would have to tread carefully. No doubt an investigation would take place, and Councillor Weber's Starcatcher plot would finally be brought to light.

Pressed against Tigre's warmth, Rachel drifted into a light doze, dreaming of Wu.

CHAPTER TWENTY-SEVEN

TIGRE WANDERED into his office, closed the door, and dimmed the lights. For a moment, he simply stood in the middle of the room, drinking in the silence.

The last several hours seemed steeped in unreality. The arrival of Richard Wagasi and a swarm of public officials had broken the World Council's stranglehold on the station.

Tigre had given a detailed report to a committee composed of doctors and disaster relief representatives, and recounting events drove home the realization of how much had happened in the space of a day. It had been less than twenty-four hours since Rachel limped into Medica with a chemical burn.

And now Rachel, Wu, Bailey, and Meris were all recovering comfortably in Medica. Tigre had been fed supper and ordered to rest. It was all precisely the way it was supposed to be.

"But why," he whispered into the silence, "do I feel like I'm waiting for something?"

Tigre looked around his office, studying the cheap desk, the brocade of curling ferns on the couch, and the pure lines of kitchen cupboards. Everything reflected back his own sense of anticipation. It was as if a life-changing revelation hovered near the ceiling, ready to fall like rain.

Distantly, Tigre recognized the Seroplex as the cause of his mental state. The drug still worked at full force within him, its presence like the low thrum of a powerful engine in his mind.

As if triggered by his heightened awareness, his exhaustion abruptly became too insistent to ignore. His lower back ached, and his legs wobbled. Tigre shuffled across the room and settled onto the couch. Letting his head fall against the cushions, he closed his eyes. He waited for drowsiness to steal over him, wanting to lose himself in the warm comfort that bordered the edge of sleep. Instead, a barrage of images rattled through his mind. He saw torn flesh, acid burns, shattered bones, and the shocked expressions on the faces of the dead.

Heart pounding, Tigre sat bolt upright. "God!"

The bell around his neck chimed with the sudden movement. Tigre clutched it in his fist to silence it. He did not want to see Dútha's eyes again, or imagine the Rofa's body in a stasis unit. He started to pull the chain from around his neck, but froze. *Coward. Can't face your own decision.*

Tigre opened his hand and gazed down at the bell. He picked out the symbol for *Hjeina* from the flowing script, recalling that it was both the first and last letter of the Rofan alphabet. He seized upon the symmetry, the pure, circular illusion of beginning and end, of life and death. He suddenly thought he understood why Dútha had called him *Hjeina*, the *gukka* who fought one enemy.

One enemy: Myself.

Time seemed to stop. Trapped in the moment, Tigre found himself unable to move past his new insight. A chill emptiness descended upon him; and he realized that in the vast panorama of the universe he was nothing but an infinitesimal, pulsating sack of mucus and gristle.

His office door opened a crack. From the hall outside, a shaft of light spilled across the floor. "Zo?" Bailey said hesitantly. "Tigre?"

The Freeholder's voice induced a rush of difficult emotions. Tigre had to swallow before he could speak. "Come in."

Bailey stepped into the office, staring around with widened eyes. "Tigre?" The light caught in his wild curls and turned them into a nimbus of red-gold. "Where are you?"

Tigre tried to gather the strength to stand, but failed.

"Sorry," he said. "The light dial is on the panel by the door. Please turn it up, if you want."

Bailey glanced at the panel, then feigned startled alarm and jumped sideways like a spooked horse. "Aha," he said playfully. "There it is!" He turned up the light and grinned at Tigre. "And there you are! I—" His hands flew to his mouth. "Oh, I'm sorry. Were you asleep?"

Tigre shook his head. "No." He managed a weak smile. "Just sitting and thinking."

"In the dark?" Bailey sauntered across the room and sat down on the couch. "Why? Are you sad?"

Although somewhat taken aback, Tigre found that he liked Bailey's peculiar directness. "Sad, yes," he confessed. "And too jazzed to sleep." He gestured to the air around them. "Too much of the universe in my head."

Bailey nodded, the corners of his eyes crinkling with a rueful smile. "Cosmic episode." He settled sideways on the couch so that he faced Tigre. "The existential quandary magnified exponentially."

Tigre laughed softly. "Exactly."

Bailey planted his elbow on the back of the couch and rested one cheek against his fist. "Sometimes I hear people grieve over the loss of those shining moments in their lives, when suddenly everything makes sense. They see how the universe is one harmonious event, and that everything is beautiful and good. And then, in a tragic instant, it's all gone." He chuckled. "And they never realize how narrowly they've escaped a personal trip to the innermost circle of hell, because that's all their moment of enlightenment was. The prelude to a cosmic episode."

Tigre also twisted sideways on the couch. "Really?" He wanted Bailey to keep talking, wanted the voice, with its musical accent, to hold at bay all his memories of the dead. "Don't you think that's a bit cynical?"

Bailey shrugged one shoulder lightly. "Maybe," he said. "But I fall victim to a cosmic episode at least once a month, and oneness with the universe is merely a warning sign. If I'm not careful, I lapse into a catatonic state in which I'm aware of only two things: My own utter insignificance, and the fact that somewhere out there is a black hole twisting time and space into . . . something else. The way a spindle twists wool into yarn." He shuddered elaborately. "Horrible!"

Tigre's exhaustion took on a cozy feeling, the conversation reminding him of late night bull sessions with his friends in medical school. Settling his head against the cushions, he lazily traced the outline of a fern with an index finger. "So you're saying that true enlightenment doesn't exist?"

"Of course, it exists," Bailey replied. "But it comes as the answer to a question."

Startled, Tigre jerked his eyes to Bailey's face. "The answer—?"

"Socrates taught through questions. And, for thousands of years, students of Zen gained enlightenment by contemplating a koan. 'What is the sound of one hand clapping?'"

"So simple." Somewhere near his heart, Tigre felt wonder open like a rose. "The answer to a question."

"Yup." Bailey sprang to his feet and wandered inquisitively around the office. "And true enlightenment doesn't go away. And it isn't rare, it happens over and over again. It's actually just the awareness of the infinite cycle of revelations that make up our lives. It's the heart of all art and music and—" He paused by the desk and picked up *The Collected Flights of Prudence Clarke*. "—poetry. It's the soul of friendship." He hugged the book to his chest, regarding Tigre with sudden shyness. "Sorry," he said hesitantly. "I talk too much."

"Not at all."

Bailey hunched his wide shoulders. "You're very kind, but you shouldn't encourage me. I can get awfully weird, sometimes."

"Don't be so hard on yourself."

Bailey turned the book over in his hands and studied the poet's photograph on the cover. "Prudence. Such a sweet face." He let the book fall open. "This is one of my favorite passages."

Tigre leaned his head on the cushion again. "Read it."

Bailey shifted self-consciously, but obeyed. "'When I am dead, I shall miss hammocks in the rain and collie dogs. I'll miss the sharp scent of tomato plants, tracks in the snow, the tender flesh between my fingers, and the taste of buttered corn.'" He raised his eyes to Tigre and finished in a somber tone. "'I'll miss the endless, aching search for a reason to search when I am dead.'"

Tigre's tranquil mood dissolved into memories of Concha, Dútha, and poor Jhaska. He bowed his head, unable to bear the other man's gaze.

Bailey's voice was soft. "I'm sorry. I made you sad again." He sat down on the couch beside Tigre. "What's wrong?"

Tigre shrugged and shook his head, not sure he could trust himself to speak without tears. He grieved not only for the ones who died, but also for Dútha; the one who chose not to live.

Bailey reached for the bell that hung over Tigre's heart. It chimed at the touch of his fingers. "This is quite an item," he said reverently. "Probably from the third century of the To'a'sha Dynasty on Igsha Reey. A museum piece."

Tigre felt an odd sting of jealousy that Bailey knew so much. "Dútha gave it to me," he said thickly.

"Another generous gift. More valuable than the ship."

Scalding tears filled Tigre's eyes. He kept his face averted. "Really?"

Two tears fell on Bailey's hand, but he gave no sign he noticed. "A Rofa," he said, "would normally pass something like this on to its offspring, not an alien. You must have impressed Dútha."

Tigre clenched his teeth. "He said—" His voice broke, and he had to swallow before he could speak. "He said: 'You'll need it. You're crazier than I am.'"

Bailey laughed gently. "Rofan humor."

Humiliated by his tears, Tigre tried to pull himself together, dragging his sleeve across his eyes. "I'm sorry. I don't usually fall apart like this with a complete stranger."

"But I'm not a stranger," Bailey said. "I'm your new friend."

"Careful." Sniffing, Tigre dredged up a smile. "You may regret declaring yourself. I can be a mean little turd."

Bailey stood up and strode to the kitchen area. "That's all part of your medical training, isn't it?"

"Very funny."

Bailey glanced over the counter. "Where do you keep your wipes? One of us has got to blow his nose."

"In the washroom, I think." Tigre tried to stand, but his

legs did not have the strength to lift his body. He sank back onto the couch. "To your left."

Bailey opened the door and whistled in admiration. "Quite a set of amenities. Wish I were the head of Earth Port Medica." He picked up a box of wipes on the edge of the sink and carried it back to the couch. "Which reminds me. I actually had a reason to visit you."

Tigre took one of the wipes and blew his nose. "What's the problem?" he asked. "Your leg giving you trouble?"

"My leg's okay. Thanks." Bailey grinned and settled sideways on the couch again. "I need your permission to do something with Meris."

Tigre tilted his head. "Do?" he echoed. "Do what?"

Bailey fished something out of a pocket and handed it to Tigre. It was a small, brown bottle with a handwritten label.

Tigre held the bottle between his thumb and forefinger and peered at the eccentric lettering. "B-r-g-m-t?" He looked at Bailey. "What is this?"

"Bergamot." Bailey's tone was enthusiastic. "I thought we could use it to reassure Meris, make us seem less alien."

Tigre raised his brows. "How?"

"Simple." Bailey leaned forward. "We just apply a little around her nose while she's still asleep, and then wear the scent ourselves when she wakes up. That way we'll smell familiar to her, like members of her family or something."

Tigre scratched the back of his head, trying to phrase his question tactfully. "Don't they do that with . . . dogs?"

"I don't know," Bailey replied earnestly. "Do they?"

"I mean . . ." Tigre worked hard to prevent himself from sounding too skeptical. "Do you really think it will work with Meris?"

Bailey shrugged. "My neighbors do something like this to coax their ewes to adopt orphaned lambs."

"Yes, but—"

Bailey raised his hands in concession. "I know that Meris isn't as feebleminded as a sheep, but instinct is instinct. And the Jadamiin depend upon olfactory and auditory signals more than they do visual cues."

Tigre opened the bottle and sniffed the contents. A fresh, soapy scent filled his nose. "Nice," he said. "It doesn't have an alcohol base, does it?"

"No. Oil."

Tigre capped the bottle and handed it back to Bailey. "Well," he said, "I don't suppose it can hurt anything. But let me talk it over with Rachel before we go ahead with it. Meris is her client."

Bailey brightened. "Okay. Thanks!"

Tigre grinned at the other man's excitement. "What if Meris doesn't like the smell of bergamot? What if—?"

The door buzzed.

Tigre cleared his throat. "Come in."

The door opened. Wu Jackson limped over the threshold and turned to speak to someone outside. "Just a few minutes alone, if you please?"

A man murmured assent.

Wu nodded. "Thank you, Chen." Moving stiffly, he closed the door and turned toward the couch. A bulky pressure wrap encased his right ankle, and he wore a ratty brown bathrobe. His face seemed unusually pale.

Distressed, Tigre gripped the arm of the couch and prepared to climb to his feet. "Wu. What the hell are you doing out of bed?" He tried to find the necessary coordination to stand, but then found himself wallowing fruitlessly in the cushions. "You walk on that ankle, and it will swell up like a—!"

Wu did not seem to hear Tigre. He stood in the middle of the room and regarded Bailey with a cold, measuring stare.

Tigre abruptly fell silent. He remembered seeing that expression on Wu's face before. *Uh-oh.*

Bailey appeared oblivious to his peril. He remained in his relaxed sprawl beside Tigre, grinning up at Wu. "Zo, Jackson-san. Long time, eh?"

Wu folded his arms and tilted his head. "Professor Rye." His tone was empty of any humorous shading. "You've pulled some idiotic stunts in the past, but tampering with the machinations of Glee Weber was—"

Bailey burst into laughter. "I know," he confessed. "It was pretty stupid."

"It was worse than stupid," Wu said contemptuously. "You put the entire station at risk."

Bailey shrugged one shoulder. "I'm flattered, Jackson-san, but you're giving me too much credit. Earth Port was already at risk. According to your reports, it's been at risk for over a year."

Heart thumping, Tigre raised both hands to forestall the exchange. "Wait a minute," he protested. "What are you talking about?" He glanced back and forth between Bailey and Wu. "Do you two know each other?"

"We've met." Wu limped to Tigre's desk and sat down on one corner. "Professor Rye is an agent for . . . certain powerful political entities in his Freehold."

"Agent?" Bailey made a noise that was half laughter and half exasperation. "You make it sound so shadowy. I'm actually more of a technical adviser." He shrugged one shoulder. "Same as you."

Tigre stared at Wu. "You—?" *The answer to a question.*

"No," Wu said coldly, "not the same." He kept his eyes on Bailey. "There is no one like you. No one to match your intellect—"

Bailey slowly climbed to his feet and regarded Wu reproachfully. "What?" he said in a tone of bewilderment. "What are you saying?" He shook his head and spread his hands, as if at a loss for words. "Just what do you think I am?"

"—and no one who can stop you." Wu paused and added in a pleasant voice: "Except me. I ought to kill you."

For a heartbeat, Bailey stood motionless. Then the innocent hurt faded from his brown eyes, replaced by an expression of fierce intensity. "Oh. Well. That would solve everything, wouldn't it?"

Tigre's blood chilled, and he swallowed hard. *Damn.*

Wu folded his arms. "Tell me, Professor Rye. You knew exactly what Jardín and Rife were capable of. Why did you infiltrate their operation?"

Bailey shrugged. "Someone had to."

"Did you learn anything useful?"

Bailey passed a hand through his unruly curls. "No," he admitted ruefully. "As you said, it was a stupid thing to do." He suddenly grinned. "No one can match my intellect."

Wu's eyes glinted. "And what if Deputy Ajmani had died trying to save your butt?"

Bailey sobered. "She didn't."

Wu slid off the edge of the desk and advanced upon Bailey, every move filled with steely menace. "What if she had? What if they had cut her up alive like they did that poor fellow who—?"

"That wasn't my fault!" Bailey shouted. "I never—!" His gaze locked on Tigre, and he fell silent.

Tigre abruptly became aware of himself again. He was hunched forward, clutching the arm of the couch. Sweat rolling down his sides, he struggled to find words, but could think of nothing to say.

Wu turned to look at him, and his gaze softened. "Tigre—"

Tigre licked his dry lips. "What are you two fighting about?"

Wu puffed out his cheeks. "I'm not sure." He limped to the couch and sat down next to Tigre. "I'm just tired."

Bailey stood with his arms hanging listlessly at his sides. "Jackson-san," he sighed and shook his head, "what do you think I've done? Do you think I've sold you and Rachel to the World Council?"

"No, Professor Rye." Wu laced his fingers together and pressed his hands to the top of his head. "You may be an idiot of unprecedented proportions, but you're not stupid."

Bailey grinned. "Thanks."

Tigre peered up at Bailey. His mind, buzzing with too much new information, zigzagged from thought to thought like a bee blundering through a rosebush. "Jardín." He spoke without meaning to. "Did you know her?"

Folding his long legs, Bailey sat down on the floor. He tilted his head, and regarded Wu and Tigre with an appraising stare. "Well. Yes and no."

Wu adjusted the belt on his bathrobe, paying elaborate attention to the task. "Confession is good for the soul, Professor Rye."

Chewing his bottom lip, Bailey studied Wu. "Part of my . . . duties," he said finally, "is to keep an eye on potential troublemakers. Jardín Azul and her followers are at the core of a spreading underground movement of isolationists."

Tigre narrowed his eyes. "Underground movement? Like *Ókaze?*"

"Different goals," Bailey said. "Jardín's group wants Earth to withdraw from outside contact."

Tigre frowned in thought. "They aren't the only ones. There are a lot of people proposing isolation. And I have to admit that some of their arguments make sense in the light of current events."

Bailey shook his head adamantly. "Impossible. We can't go backward."

"That sounds a little odd," Tigre said, "coming from a Freeholder."

"Even on the Freeholds, we move forward. We just limit the use of technology, and we maintain the old ways." Bailey pulled his legs into a full lotus. "It's like enlightenment. A new awareness cannot be lost."

Wu stirred. "What does this have to do with Jardín?"

Bailey laid his hands, palms up, on his knees. "She had begun to promote the Freeholds as the models for a new Earth society. A concept that appeals to outsiders who, begging your pardon, have absolutely no idea what life on a Freehold is like. And so—" He sighed. "And so I arranged a meeting, pretended to be a sympathizer, and offered to help with their plan to expose and discredit Councillor Weber."

"And?" Wu prompted.

Bailey raised his brows. "She drugged me with Phenox, picked my brain, and then threw me to the Phi-Nurians." He paused. "Jackson-san, you and I are alike in many ways. We have both managed to resist the universal conditioning that creates cooperative and law-abiding individuals. And we are both capable of ignoring any legal restriction if it prevents us from the action we deem necessary." He laughed softly. "But I'm too much of a ninny to be terribly dangerous, and you are governed by love."

Wu nodded. "Jardín doesn't suffer from those limitations."

"No," Bailey said sourly. "She's smart, she's capable of anything, and she's convinced that our little planet would be a much better place if only she were in charge."

Wu rolled his eyes and puffed out his cheeks. "And in five short months, she'll be out of regeneration."

"But not out of treatment," Tigre pointed out. "She's killed so many people that she's due for at least three years of personality restructuring."

"Hopefully, we'll have a plan to deal with her by then."

Wu patted Tigre's shoulder and climbed to his feet. "I should be going," he said heavily. "Before Chen starts to think I'm up to something nefarious."

Tigre struggled to stand. "Let me help you."

Wu chuckled. "No, thanks. You're in worse shape than I am." He reached into a fold of his bathrobe, pulled out a laser pistol, and handed it to Tigre. "An early birthday gift."

Tigre gaped at the weapon, robbed of words, the Seroplex making him wonder if Bailey had somehow known all along that Wu was armed. *Is that why he answered our questions?*

"You're welcome." Wu kissed the top of Tigre's head and limped to the door. "I have to go and appear before the kangaroo court. I don't know if I'll be back."

Tigre tried to sort through his seething emotions. "What are you talking about?"

"Our so-called rescuers have started the process of placing blame. Things may get ugly." Wu stopped with his hand on the latch. "Hang onto that gun. If they try to implicate Rachel, grab her and get to the *La Vaca*."

In silent reply, Tigre closed his fingers around the pistol.

Wu looked at Bailey. "Thanks for the information." He paused, an unreadable expression on his face. "Keep an eye on things, hmm?"

Bailey nodded solemnly.

Wu left without looking back.

Bailey gazed in the direction of the closed door for a long moment, then turned toward Tigre. "I have never," he stated, "been so frightened in my whole life."

Tigre hefted the weapon and distantly recalled his own fear of Wu. "He can be intimidating."

"That's an understatement." Bailey pressed both hands to his face. "I thought he was going to kill me."

Still emotionally entangled in Wu's farewell, Tigre answered absently. "Well. He didn't."

Bailey closed his eyes and shook his head. "Everyone I've met on Earth Port Station seems big and dangerous— Sonría Omar, Rachel Ajmani, Alfstan DelRio, Wu Jackson. It feels like wading through grizzly bears. How can you stand it?"

"The bears are my friends."

"Friends." Bailey glanced at Tigre and smiled softly. "If I lived on the station—" He broke off, his gaze suddenly unfocused.

"Yes?"

Bailey blinked and seemed to return to himself. "Sorry," he said. "What were we talking about?"

Tigre wearily passed a hand through his hair. "I'm not sure."

The book of poetry still lay on the desk. Bailey strolled over and picked it up. "Death, wasn't it? And grief."

Tigre shifted uncomfortably, and Dútha's bell chimed. "Actually," he said, "I think it was Meris and bergamot."

Bailey studied him for a moment and seemed to reconsider his intended words. "Yes. Well. I suppose I ought to let you rest." He awkwardly handed the Prudence Clarke book to Tigre. "Here."

"Thanks." Tigre took the book with his free hand. "I guess I could use a little time alone. I think the Seroplex is wearing off."

"I understand." Bailey wandered to the door, face averted. "See you later?"

Tigre pulled his mouth into a stiff smile. "Of course."

Bailey stepped into the hall and closed the door behind him.

Alone, Tigre sat motionless, holding a pistol in one hand and poetry in the other. He waited for the events of the day to replay in his head, or for despair to swoop down on dark wings, but his mind remained clear.

He studied the picture of Clarke, noting the sadness in her smile and the wistful intelligence in her blue eyes. He found himself wishing he had known her. It seemed unjust that she was dead, when she so clearly appreciated the everyday details of life.

Tigre bowed his head. He listened to the echoes of recent events within himself, recalling the wounds and the suffering, but also the unexpected acts of compassion and heroism.

"How do you know when to intercede?"

"We always intercede," Tigre whispered.

"It comes as the answer to a question."

The silence around him seemed to ring like a bell. "I'm

going to do it." He settled back in the cushions, knowing he could at last sleep. "I'm going to revive Dútha."

Rachel lay on a hard, narrow bed in one of Medica's rooms. Thinking that she caught a whiff of something other than antiseptics in the air, she slowly opened her eyes and found herself facing a blank wall. The scent was somehow both dry and sweet, like cured hay, and she knew that her best friend was near. "Wu."

"Rachel," he complained, "I wish you wouldn't do that. It's spooky."

Smiling, Rachel turned her head on the pillow to look at him. "Sorry."

Wu limped from the doorway to the bedside chair and sat down with a sigh. "Ooo, that feels wonderful." He tilted his head and studied her. "How are you?"

The combination of Seroplex and euphorics made it hard to keep her eyes open. "Full of Tri-Omega. According to Bailey, I ought to be able to see the future." She blinked at him. "What about you? Are you supposed to be walking around on that ankle?"

Wu gestured airily. "Important things to do. Secret, Safety warden type stuff."

Rachel languidly ran her hand over the blanket and let her smile widen. "You needed to get up and use the loo?"

"Well. Yes." Wu tightened the tie on his old, brown bathrobe. "Plus, I chatted for a moment with Tigre."

Rachel's eyes drifted shut, but she forced herself to keep talking. It felt so good to have him there. "Oh? A friendly chat?"

"Mostly." Wu chuckled. "He's such a . . . stimulating fellow."

She recalled what Tigre had said about Wu. "He's afraid of you."

Wu snorted. "That little shit," he said flatly, "isn't afraid of anything."

Something in his voice made her drag her eyes open. She studied his face, its moods and expressions more familiar to her than her own. "Warden Jackson," she said. "You really are in love with him."

Wu's mouth fell open, and his eyes widened in obvious

shock. "Rachel—" An odd pain filled his gaze, and he seemed unable to continue speaking.

Worried that she had hurt him, Rachel reached out and took his hand. "Sorry," she said softly. "I was just teasing."

"No," Wu replied. "You're right."

"Good. I enjoy being right." Rachel forced herself to speak lightly. "But don't get the idea that I'm giving you up. You're mine."

Wu took her hand in both of his. "Rachel, I—"

Chen appeared in the doorway, wearing his perpetual, anxious frown. "Wu?" he said uneasily. "They've called again. They're tired of waiting."

Wu carefully returned her hand to the bed, treating it like fragile porcelain. "Waiting," he repeated softly.

A faint alarm penetrated her drugged haze. Rachel tried to prop herself up on her elbows, but could not gather the strength. "Who's waiting? What's going on?"

Wu stood up. Although the inner pain was unmistakable in his eyes, he gave her a wicked smile. "Oh, they say they just want to take my statement. But I think they're going to spank me."

Rachel grinned at him. Wu had been in trouble before, once suspended for ninety days. She would wade into the fray, she decided, after she dealt with Meris' case. "Spanked? Wish I could watch."

Wu made a prim noise of facetious outrage. "You're horrid." He turned and limped to the doorway where Chen waited.

"Don't forget our date," she said. "The Last War Memorial."

"I'll bring a picnic lunch." He started to go.

Rachel did not want him to leave. "Wu?"

He paused and leaned against the doorframe.

"Everything's going to be all right?" Rachel had not intended to make it a question, a plea for reassurance.

Wu's smile softened. "Everything," he replied tenderly, "will be just peachy." He raised his hand, palm out, and spread his fingers. " 'Bye."

" 'Bye," she echoed.

Wu limped out into the hallway. Chen gave Rachel a respectful nod and followed him.

Utter exhaustion suddenly engulfed Rachel, and she sank

back onto the pillow. She ought to rest for a few hours, she knew, while Meris still slept. *Just a quick nap.*

Rachel closed her eyes. She tried to mentally outline a report on Meris, but her thoughts kept sliding in other directions.

She remembered meeting Wu for the first time, when he was still Checkpoint Coordinator, and how she had liked him immediately. She recalled the party where he danced on a table with a rose in his teeth, the year he became addicted to chess and began a running game with nearly everyone on the station; the day he illegally smashed open a load of crates from a Phi-Nurian freighter and proved them full of pirated computer components.

She did not mind that he loved Tigre, she decided. *I love Tigre, too.*

Sleep claimed Rachel. In dark dreams, she wandered through a strange city built into the walls of a canyon, searching along its empty streets for Wu.

CHAPTER TWENTY-EIGHT

ON THE EDGE OF waking, eyes still closed, Meris heard the voices of children. For a moment, she simply listened to the carefree chatter. *How sweet.* She sighed, drawing closer to consciousness, and the scent of fresh herbs followed the breath.

Abruptly, Meris realized that the children spoke a strange language, and the whole nightmare of her current plight returned to her. *That screaming baby!* Her eyes flashed open. *I must save—!*

A Human child crouched in front of her, studying her face with wide eyes.

Panic forgotten, Meris froze. Far from the loathsome aspect presented by adult Humans, the engaging little creature possessed a dry and soft-looking hide. Its black mane hung in loose curls to its shoulders, and its features conveyed only innocent fascination. Slowly, it extended a small finger and touched her nose.

"Greetings," Meris whispered in Farnii. "What's your name?"

The child crinkled its eyes and squealed in delight.

"Charming." Meris carefully sat up and glanced around. She was in the middle of a room filled with plush pillows and bright colors. On the floor nearby, four other children played together with peculiar toys, indicating total immersion in their game. "Utterly charming."

The translator, Bailey, knelt by the wall nearest the door.

Meris regarded him quietly. "I heard someone torturing a child."

Bailey ducked his head in a brief bow. "No, Mother of Multitudes. Human children weep even if they are only slightly injured. What you heard was someone carrying a child with a mild injury past your door."

Meris flattened her ears. "Are you telling the truth?"

"I swear it, Mother of Multitudes."

"Then why—?"

The Human child crawled into her lap and snuggled up against her.

Meris' anger evaporated. She gently wrapped her arms around the small figure.

Bailey spoke in an earnest tone. "It was a terrible misunderstanding, that's all."

"Misunderstanding," Meris repeated absently. She lowered her nose to sniff the child's sweet scent. "What is my little friend's name?"

Bailey blinked. "I don't know her name."

"Well," Meris said, wrinkling her nose at him. "Ask her. Then tell me. You're a translator, after all."

Rachel drifted back into consciousness. A foul-tasting paste coated her mouth, and a headache pounded against her temples. She opened her eyes. The soft white light of Medica seemed painfully harsh. She squinted up at the ceiling and tried to marshal her thoughts, but motion near the door caught her attention.

Tigre stood on the threshold. "Rachel?" He seemed uncharacteristically subdued. "May I come in?"

She rolled her head on the pillow to look at him. The slight movement ignited the muscles in her neck and back. Pain reared in her wounded shoulder. Rachel clenched her teeth. "Of course."

Tigre approached the bed, carrying two mugs of steaming liquid. His lavender surgeon's scrubs looked fresh, and his silky hair was clean, but his dark eyes seemed glassy with pain. He set the mugs on the bedside table, moving with elaborate care. "How do you feel?"

"Fine."

"Oh, really?" Tigre's expression softened in a sudden smile. "When I woke up, I discovered that someone had tied a knot in my spine just between the fifth and sixth vertebrae."

"Well," Rachel admitted reluctantly. "I do have a . . . rather severe headache."

"How's the shoulder?"

"Much better than my head."

"Ah, yes. The many joys of a Seroplex hangover," Tigre said ruefully. "Wish I could give you something for it." He snorted. "Hell, I wish I could give myself something for it, but further medication only postpones the backlash."

The situation with Meris returned to the forefront of Rachel's thoughts. "What time is it?" She struggled to sit. "How long have I slept?"

Tigre slid an arm under her shoulders and helped her up. "About forty hours."

Thunderstruck, she stared at him. "What?"

"About forty hours," Tigre repeated. "It's Thursday, a little after midnight. I've been up for less than an hour."

"But—" Rachel floundered helplessly for thought. "But I had things to do. Meris—"

Tigre raised a hand. "It's okay, Rachel. Meris is fine. They gave her case to someone else."

"But—" Bitter disappointment welled within her, worse than any physical pain. "But why? Why didn't they wake me up?"

Tigre raised his brows. "Wake you?" he asked incredulously. "How?"

Rachel pressed her palms against her throbbing temples. "I don't know, I—" She tried to find words that did not sound trivial or complaining. "I just—" She swallowed. "I've worked so hard on this case."

"I understand," Tigre said softly.

"And Dútha?"

"Everything's taken care of. Stop worrying." He handed her a mug from the table. "You need something in your stomach. Drink this."

Rachel took the warm mug and regarded the thick, pale orange liquid inside. "Naranha?"

"What else?" Tigre sat down in the chair beside her bed and picked up the other mug. Every move he made indicated that he felt as awful as she did. "One of my medics brought down a little soup, but it made me puke. This liquid diet stuff is the only thing that sounded good."

Rachel's gut clenched in sympathetic nausea, but she took a sip of Naranha. The mild orange flavor brought back memories of sitting in Tigre's office, discussing Jadamiin physiology, drug-induced visions, and Wu Jackson. "What's going on with Wu?"

"Well," Tigre sighed. "I don't know how to tell you this, but Wu's in a lot of trouble."

Rachel's heart sank, but she kept her expression calm. "Wu has been in trouble several times before. It more or less goes with the job."

He—" Tigre broke off and stared gloomily into his mug. "The Interim Committee held a hearing."

"Interim Committee?" Rachel repeated. "Is that what our independent observers are calling themselves?"

"Yes. I glanced over the transcript a few minutes ago, and Wu took responsibility for everything."

Making a mental note to look at the transcript as soon as possible, Rachel took another small sip of Naranha. "Has he been charged yet?"

"No. I don't think so." Tigre's voice was unsteady. "But I'm still worried."

Rachel started to remind Tigre that Wu could not be charged for simply doing his job; but then it occurred to her that if other members of the World Council were also involved in the conspiracy, it would make sense for them to divert attention from themselves by finding a scapegoat.

Tigre pressed a hand to his forehead and seemed to fight for composure. "Here I go again," he said. "Loading you with problems. I can't—"

"It's all right," Rachel interrupted. "I asked." Grateful for the generous length of her patient's gown, she slowly and carefully shifted so that her legs hung over the edge of the bed. The slightest movement brought shocks of pain to her throbbing head. "Who's handling Meris' case?"

"Deputy Omar." Tigre took a swallow of Naranha and grimaced. "Bailey's helping."

"Oh, dear. Poor 'Ría."

Tigre lowered his voice. "You know, Rachel, there's more to Bailey than he seems. He's——" Tigre drew his brows together. "Different. And I don't mean that he's a genius." He sighed. "I sound crazy."

"No." Rachel forced herself to take another sip of Naranha. "Trabail Rye is definitely a young man to watch. I'd like to think we can trust him, but I—" Afraid to say too much, to embroil Tigre in her own doubts, she broke off. *I don't like his role in translating the Artifact.* "I'm not sure."

Tigre carefully set his mug on the table. "Wu said—" With a sudden gasp, he pressed his arms against his stomach and hunched forward in his chair. "Shit!"

Alarmed, Rachel extended a hand. "Are you all right?"

"Yeah. Stomach cramp." Inhaling through his teeth, Tigre straightened. "Wu accused Bailey of being an agent for some sort of odd Freeholder hegemony, and Bailey more or less admitted it." His brow furrowed in an anxious scowl. "Rachel, why would the Freeholds need, or even want, such an individual? The Freeholds are supposed to be politically neutral, so why would a Freeholder work against the World Council?" He paused and added: "It scares me."

Avoiding Tigre's gaze, Rachel looked down into her mug. "Wu would be shocked to hear you say that."

Tigre did not seem to hear her. "He tried to warn me about the politics involved. I'm sorry I didn't listen."

With a strange sense of impending disaster, Rachel glanced up at him. She did not want Tigre's speculations to lead him into trouble, into the dark waters. If the World Council were corrupt, if it were engaged in a clandestine war with the neutral and independently governed Freeholds, then there was no telling what it would do to someone who asked the wrong questions.

"Don't worry about it too much," Rachel said and made herself smile. "And remember what we've just been through. Dealing with Jardín is enough to make anyone paranoid. Don't you agree?"

Tigre did not return her smile. "I suppose." He rubbed his forehead. "I hope it's only the hangover that's making me see monsters, but I can't help thinking about Bailey. Wu didn't trust him. Not completely, anyway. And as far as I'm concerned, Wu is God."

"Don't tell him that. He's already too—"

Soft voices drifted from the hallway outside the room,

and two people appeared in the open doorway. The man wore lavender surgical scrubs. Middle-aged and dignified, he gave the impression of someone accustomed to being obeyed. The woman appeared to be in her thirties, and she wore a dark green pilot's jumpsuit. She caught Rachel's gaze and gave her a friendly smile.

The man cleared his throat. "Excuse us for interrupting."

"Oh." Tigre climbed to his feet, seeming uncertain. "Doctor Wagasi."

Though feeling self-conscious in her gown, Rachel beckoned. "Please come in."

"Thank you." He favored Tigre with a sternly paternal look. "And it's 'Uncle Richard' when you're off duty, remember?"

Tigre clearly remained ill at ease. "Yes, Uncle Richard."

Still smiling, the woman approached Rachel and extended her hand. "Vulana Garcia. I'm very pleased to meet you, Deputy."

"Pleased to meet you, too." Rachel shook the offered hand, liking Vulana's warmth and directness. "You're with the World Council's Internal Affairs, aren't you?"

"That's right." Vulana laughed and gestured at her jumpsuit. "Sorry about the fashion statement, but I didn't have time to pack before I was called away."

Richard tilted his head and studied Rachel. "Deputy Ajmani, how do you feel?"

"Well, I—"

"Lousy," Tigre cut in, sounding far angrier than was warranted. He whirled toward Vulana. "She feels like crap. So whatever you want from her, just—"

Vulana stared at Tigre, obviously taken aback.

Mortified, Rachel sighed. "Tigre. Calm down. And let me speak for myself, please." She smiled at Vulana, and then looked at Richard. "I have a blinding headache, which I've been told is a Seroplex hangover."

Richard nodded in a sympathetic manner. "Quite painful, yes." He studied the monitor beside her bed. "Your temperature is somewhat elevated. How's the shoulder?"

Rachel flexed it gingerly. Pain flared behind her collarbone and lanced through her temples. "Sore, but usable," she said. "Quite frankly, my head hurts more."

Richard frowned at Vulana. "Perhaps your questions will need to wait."

Rachel wondered if this might be an opportunity to help clear Wu of impending charges. "Questions?" Moving cautiously, she set her cup of Naranha down on the bedside table. "I can try to give you some answers. I'm well enough for that."

Vulana raised her brows anxiously, pulling a small recorder from her pocket. "We just need clarification on a few points. I can come back for your statement later."

Tigre clenched his fists. "No. This is insane. She's sick." He turned his gaze to Rachel, and his expression turned imploring. "You need to rest."

Unable to fathom his peculiar behavior, Rachel smiled reassuringly. "This will only take a few minutes, I'm sure. I promise to rest afterward."

Tigre looked stricken. "But—"

Richard dropped a fatherly hand on his shoulder. "Perhaps you'll step outside with me a moment? I have a few questions of my own about your other patients."

Giving every appearance that he was abandoning Rachel to certain death, Tigre followed his superior out the door.

Filled with concern, Rachel watched him go.

Vulana hesitated, still holding her recorder. "If you're sure you feel well enough?"

Sudden nausea flooded Rachel. She smiled weakly. "Of course."

Instead of sitting down, Vulana went to the door and beckoned. A tense-looking young man in a black uniform stepped into the room. Vulana nodded toward him. "Deputy, please allow me to introduce Miles Glockner from Global Disaster Services."

Rachel smiled. "Pleased to meet you."

Miles did not return the smile. "Deputy."

Vulana started the recorder. "Let's begin, shall we?"

Miles folded his arms. "Deputy Ajmani." In stark contrast to Vulana, his manner was utterly cold and impersonal. "Tell me. Who made the decision to have the Jadamii incarcerated in the station's martial arts arena?"

Rachel blinked at him, expecting any question but that. "I did."

Vulana cleared her throat. "Warden Jackson says that it was his decision."

The pain in Rachel's head increased until she thought it might split open like an overripe melon. "It was not. It was my decision entirely." Afraid they might slap Wu with a charge of perjury, she added: "There was a great deal of discussion over the matter, so perhaps the warden doesn't remember where the final responsibility rests."

Vulana and Miles exchanged glances. Vulana switched off the recorder.

Disconcerted, Rachel raised her brows. "Is that all you wanted to know?"

"It is." Miles approached the bed and stood over her. "Deputy Ajmani, you have confessed to placing a violent alien in close proximity to the station's child care facilities. You're hereby under arrest for child endangerment."

Stunned, Rachel stared up at him, unable to find words.

Miles regarded her with an implacable expression. "Come with me. You are to be held in the station's detention block, pending a formal arraignment."

His head throbbing, Tigre followed Richard down the main corridor of the *Caduceus*, flagship of the World Health Agency. At any other time, he would have been excited to be on board and eager to talk to the onboard physicians, but his thoughts remained centered on Rachel. *Shouldn't leave her alone.*

Richard paused before a hatch, keyed it open, and entered. "Please, come in."

Tigre crossed the threshold and glanced around the well-appointed office. A huge desk faced the door. Behind it, a faux window displayed the view of a country garden complete with birds and butterflies. "Nice."

Richard gestured to a set of heavily upholstered lounge chairs in front of the desk. "Have a seat. I'll start some tea."

Tigre crossed to one of the chairs and sat on the edge. He found the thought of tea both appealing and revolting. "Please don't go to any trouble."

"No trouble at all." Smiling slightly, Richard picked up a palm-sized workboard from the desk and handed it to Tigre. "Here. Take a look at this."

Suppressing a grimace of nausea, Tigre took the workboard off standby. A rust-colored holograph leaped up from the screen. "What the—?" Swarms of peculiar objects hung motionless in the column of light. "What is this?"

Richard keyed a control on the desk, and a brewer rose from below a sliding panel. "Blood cells."

"Blood—?" Tigre's breath abruptly caught in his throat. His fingers trembling, his headache forgotten, he rotated the image and increased the magnification. Some of the cells seemed to be dividing three ways, in a manner of mitosis very different from that of Humans. "Rofan blood?"

Chuckling, Richard started the brewer. "I'm guessing that their chromosomes come in sets of three. Instead of 'X' and 'Y,' they have 'X,Y, Z.'" He gestured toward the holograph. "These are a preliminary scan. From the specimen provided by that Rofan child."

Sudden grief flashed through Tigre, but he kept his voice steady. "Jhaska."

"Yes, thank you. Jhaska." Richard casually leaned a hip against the desk and tilted his head. "Perhaps that would make a fitting name for the new facility. 'The Jhaska Memorial Institute of Xeno-biology.'"

"Perhaps." Then the words sank in, and Tigre stared at Richard. "What?"

"Funding is already approved." Richard appeared to be fighting back an enormous smile. "I want to appoint you as head of research."

"Me?" Tigre's heart began to pound, and a flood of eager thoughts filled his mind. "Why me?"

"Because Dútha authorized *you* to render treatment."

"But—"

"However, you cannot reasonably expect to revive Dútha without concrete knowledge of Rofan physiology. As the physician in charge, you'd be able to guide the research along the most expedient path."

Tigre returned his attention to the holograph, desperately trying to think. He had hoped the Agency would see the value of further research, but he had expected more resistance. *Too easy. Too good to be true.*

"You realize, of course, that this is only the beginning." Richard's tone gained enthusiasm. "If other Rofan follow Dútha's example and seek medical aid, this may lead to

the establishment of a secondary medical facility aboard
Earth Port Station. Perhaps even to the founding of a uni-
versity on Igsha Reey."

Tigre groped for the bell that hung over his heart. *Except
Dútha didn't authorize treatment.* Awareness of the pain in
his head returned. *After I revive him, he'll kill me.*

The brewer finished its cycle, and Richard poured two
cups of tea. "The possibilities are endless."

Feeling a stir of something akin to panic, Tigre smiled
weakly and set the workboard down on the desk. "Uncle
Richard, could I have a little time to think about it?"

Richard handed him a cup of tea. "What is there to think
about?" He settled into the chair next to Tigre's. "This isn't
nepotism. You're the only one for the job, and you know it."

Tigre lifted his cup and inhaled the fragrant steam.
"Mmm, menthol and . . . lemon?"

Richard smiled. "Special blend. Try it. I guarantee it will
make you feel much better."

Cautiously, Tigre took a sip. There was a medley of other
flavors beneath the dominant overtone of menthol. He
could not quite place all the ingredients, but they did not
upset his stomach. "It's good. Thank you."

"You're most welcome," Richard said. "May I venture
to guess that your reluctance stems from the current situation? And from your concern for your friends here? You
don't want to gain a reward from your shared ordeal, especially not if they may face disciplinary measures."

Tigre nodded and took another sip of tea. It made his
sinuses tingle, but seemed to bring a little relief to his headache. "I'm worried about Rachel, and . . ."

"Warden Jackson?" Richard held his cup in both hands
and regarded Tigre with paternal exasperation. "He's been
cleared and exonerated, of course. And what possible
charges could Deputy Ajmani face? Has she committed
any crime?"

Tigre set down his cup. "Of course not. I just—" He
gripped his forehead, trying to think straight. "This is just
happening so fast."

Richard grunted. "You think that now, but wait until
you're knee-deep in research."

Tigre drew a breath to reply, then held it. *What the hell
am I arguing about?*

He had promised himself that he would revive Dútha, and his Uncle Richard was very generously providing the means to get the job done. Heading up a research project for a new institute would also boost his medical career. There was no logical reason to refuse. *He's right. I just don't want to leave Rachel and Wu.*

Richard studied him, his expression softening with affection. "And, besides, I'd like to have you on Earth. I'm getting too old to travel light years every time I want to share a new tea recipe."

Tigre smiled. He owed it to Dútha, to his Uncle Richard, and to himself to leave the station for a new post. "I think that 'The Jhaska Memorial Institute of Xeno-biology' is the perfect name." In a sense, he owed it to Jhaska, as well, so that his young friend's death would not be meaningless "And I'd be honored to head the research."

Rachel sat on Checkpoint's hard tile floor and leaned against the cool wall of her cell. She still wore only her patient's gown, but they had allowed her a thermal blanket for warmth. The pain in her shoulder and head was bearable if she kept perfectly still. Mercifully, the detention area contained no other prisoners at the moment.

One of Miles Glockner's men from Global Disaster Services stood guard outside the cell. Station personnel walked through on a regular basis, and they all murmured a respectful greeting to Rachel as they passed.

A blond with a beetling brow, the guard scowled at them, clearly wishing he could order them to refrain from speaking.

Rachel's lips twitched. *Pathetic. Someone like you can't intimidate people who are accustomed to aliens.*

Lafiya DuChamp strode into the area. When she saw Rachel, she paused for a moment, and her features turned brick red. "Deputy Ajmani!"

Her voice stabbed through Rachel's head, and she grimaced. "Please don't shout. It makes me see stars."

"I thought this was just a stupid rumor!" Lafiya crossed to the guard. "Why the hell is she locked up? She's hurt and sick."

The guard glared at her, a muscle in his jaw jumping.

Obviously undaunted, Lafiya glared back. "Who's responsible for this? I want a name."

"Miles Glockner." The guard seemed to think he had scored a point. "Director of Global Disaster Services."

Lafiya's brows lowered. "Global—?" She set her hands on her hips. "This isn't the 'globe.' You're all out of your jurisdiction."

In spite of the headache, Rachel smiled.

Lafiya made a pointedly respectful bow in Rachel's direction, then turned on her heel and stalked away. "I'll be back in a minute."

Rachel watched her go, wondering what she intended to do. *Hope she doesn't land in trouble.*

As Lafiya left, a young staffer named Rico escorted two Rofan into the area. The guard stiffened alertly.

The Rofan were dressed in the garb of the Northern Freeholds. One Rofa had the sleek, auburn hide of the childbearing gender; the other had a silky coat of black and gold. Both wore baggy trousers over patchwork kimonos, and it took Rachel a long moment to recognize Akya and Khanwa.

They swept up to the cell and stared at her.

Rachel gazed back at them. It was startling to see Rofan in Human garb. They seemed more like creatures from a fairy tale than aliens, and she concluded that Bailey's influence had led them to adopt Freehold-style attire. "Honorable Captains," she said, finally remembering to speak. "Please forgive me for not rising."

"Humph." Akya sat down on the floor, and tilted its small, round ears. "We shall join you." It noticed Khanwa was still standing and gestured impatiently. "Sit-sit-sit-sit!"

Khanwa obeyed, keeping its orange eyes fastened on Rachel. "Deputy Aja-mani. You don't smell the same. Are you sick?"

"Just a little," she said. "A reaction to a drug. Nothing to worry about."

"Ah, a bad dose." Khanwa visibly relaxed. "It once happened to me on a dull trip to Kam. I couldn't stop shitting for three days."

Rachel fought the impulse to smile. "Yes. A . . . bad dose."

Khanwa leaned forward and said in a cozy tone: "I could

come in there. Lick you all over. Make you feel so good, you wiggle like a—"

The guard swallowed audibly. "Now—now, hold on," he protested. "I don't think—"

Ignoring the guard, Akya pulled a paper fan from its sleeve and opened it with an authoritative snap. "Deputy Aja-mani, I have reviewed your case in detail. In my expert opinion, the charges brought against you are—"

The guard turned his scowl to Rico. "Excuse me, but why did you bring these things in here?"

Akya paused. "We are not 'things.'" It did not look at the guard. "You are a bigot. Unless you apologize immediately, I'll make a formal complaint against you."

The muscle in the guard's jaw flexed rhythmically. "Get them out of here," he told Rico, "or I'll have you charged with contempt."

Fanning itself, Akya also turned to look at Rico. "You're a witness."

Rico nodded. "I am."

Akya glanced up at the guard. "You cannot order us out of here. We are serving as legal counsel to Deputy Aja-mani." It bared its teeth in a parody of a Human smile. "And your threat toward this dutiful Safety staffer implies that my associate and I did not come here of our own volition, but were somehow coaxed here in an attempt to harass you."

The guard's face darkened to an ugly shade of maroon. He snapped a glance toward Rachel, as if daring her to comment.

Rachel returned his gaze coolly. "The honorable captain is quite correct. Almost everything you say substantiates an attitude of bigotry."

With a series of jerking movements, the guard unclipped the phone from his belt. "We'll see about that," he said. "I'm calling for backup."

Akya slapped its fan shut and pointed it at the guard. "Do so," it said imperiously. "Bring someone of intellect and authority."

At that moment, Lafiya returned, leading a group of three Freeholders. "Here." She gestured toward Rachel. "You see?"

The Freeholders, a woman and two men, studied the entire detention area, and their expressions slowly settled into troubled frowns. Slim and elegant in her flowered kimono, the woman stepped forward and looked at the guard. "Zo, Bruce."

"Twyla."

Bruce. Rachel glanced up at the guard. Knowing his name somehow made him seem more Human.

Twyla gracefully motioned toward Rachel. "Did Miles really order this?"

"Yes," Bruce said tightly.

Twyla stepped closer, tilting her head. "But Deputy Ajmani is still recovering from several injuries."

"I know," Bruce said, his voice rising to a shout. "You don't think I know that?"

For the first time, Rachel saw the anxiety and guilt behind his angry manner. *Poor fellow. Out of his depth.*

Bruce continued: "You think I'm enjoying myself? I'm only following orders." He broke off, panting, then spoke in a quieter tone. "Ten hours ago, an earthquake hit Nuevo Chimbote. Just about leveled the city. I should be *there*, digging out survivors, not *here*—"

Akya reopened its fan. "Only following orders." It looked at Rachel. "Humans, it seems, blindly follow the orders of their superiors, even if the orders are cruel or unreasonable."

Too weary to argue, Rachel shrugged her uninjured shoulder. "Perhaps."

"I'll wager," Akya said, "that you allowed yourself to be placed in this cell. That you walked in without a struggle."

Rachel sighed. *"Eykhrru-rru."*

"Mm." Akya peered at her over the top of its fan. "You are truly a *gukka* with words."

Twyla turned to one of her entourage. "Call Miles. Try to talk some sense into him."

"Right." Pulling out a phone, the man turned away and left the detention area.

Akya resumed fanning itself. "As I was saying, in my expert opinion, the charges against you are not only ludicrous, but tainted with xenophobic bigotry."

Nausea swept over Rachel, and she once again settled her pounding head against the cool wall. "Really?" she said politely. "How so, honorable Captain?"

"Meris of Jada is like a goddess to her people. She is the Mother of Multitudes. To consider her a ravening beast, capable of attacking children, is not only an insult to her, but to the Jadamiin as a species." Akya slid its glance to the Freeholders. "Surely you don't mean to suggest that the Jadamiin are nothing but animals?"

Twyla bowed, then knelt on the floor. "Certainly not, honorable Captain," she said. "That is why Meris of Jada is now at liberty within the station's nursery."

In spite of her physical misery, Rachel smiled. "Good. She'll like that. She adores kids."

From her place by the door, Lafiya suddenly strode forward. "So the charges of child endangerment are false!"

"No," Rachel said reluctantly, afraid that the blame would resettle upon Wu. "When I made the decision to detain Meris in Station Central, I didn't know that she wasn't a danger. In fact, when Wu pointed out how close her enclosure was to the nursery, I brushed aside his concerns."

Lafiya appeared crestfallen. "Oh."

Rachel felt as though she'd been unkind. "Sorry."

Akya growled. "Deputy Aja-mani, as your attorney, I must advise against making such statements in front of so many witnesses."

"Sorry."

"Sorry is not—" Akya paused. "Many witnesses." It abruptly stood and pointed at Lafiya. "You. You are Deputy Aja-mani's friend?"

Lafiya clenched her fists. "Goddamned right, I'm her friend!"

"Good. Then you will assist in organizing a community pardon for Deputy Aja-mani."

Lafiya drew her brows together. "A what?"

Akya closed its fan and tucked it into the sleeve of its kimono. "If every adult aboard the station votes to pardon Deputy Aja-mani, then she will be cleared of the charges."

Twyla cleared her throat. "It isn't that simple," she said. "Everyone must give a valid reason *why* she ought to be pardoned. They must give one example of a deed that demonstrates her high character, a deed that they witnessed personally."

Lafiya grinned suddenly. "Easy."

Twyla looked disconcerted.

Lafiya spread her hands. "The only tricky part will be picking just one example."

An ache formed in Rachel's throat. "Lafiya—"

Still smiling widely, Lafiya bowed and turned to go. "See you in about twenty minutes."

Rachel stared after her, unable to speak.

Akya motioned impatiently for Khanwa to rise. "Come-come-come-come!"

Khanwa rose and headed for the door, then paused and looked at Akya. "We do it now, don't we?"

"Of course." Akya bowed deeply to Rachel. "Excuse us, please. We will see you later."

Khanwa also bowed, less expertly, though clearly the Rofa had been practicing. "Yes, later," it purred. "And maybe I'll bite you."

They swaggered out of the area. Grinning, Rico nodded to Rachel and followed them.

The ache in Rachel's throat intensified, and moisture leaked from the corners of her eyes. *Brave and truer than kin.*

Twyla sighed in obvious pity. "You feel unwell, don't you?"

Rachel wiped at her tears with the sleeve of her patient's gown. "Oh, it's not that," she said, and laughed shakily. "It's just that I've never had a Rofa tell me 'good-bye.'"

CHAPTER TWENTY-NINE

MERIS STOOD in an air lock of the *La Vaca* with Bailey and Captain Mendez. Seeking to comfort herself, Meris clasped her tail to her chest and stroked its tufted tip. She peered down the chill interior of the docking tube, then turned her gaze to Captain Mendez. "Couldn't we board in the usual way?"

The captain regarded her steadily with sharp blue eyes. "I've already explained. Someone might be watching. We're very lucky that the Rofan emissary's ship was reassigned to the next berth when it returned to dock."

"Too lucky for coincidence," Meris pointed out. "And if someone as simpleminded as me would think so, then a clever enemy would have no trouble seeing the connection."

"True," said Captain Mendez. "But by then, you'll be out of their reach."

Bailey gestured down the tube. "I'll go ahead and open it up." He crossed the threshold and strode toward the other ship's hatch, pulling on heavy gloves as he went. His boots rang hollowly on the floor.

Shivering her fur, Meris returned her attention to the captain. "But why can't I stay with you? I'm sure Deputy Omar would understand. And maybe even Deputy Ajmani."

Captain Mendez folded her arms. "Believe me, my crew and I would love to keep you aboard. But we would die, trying to protect you. You stand a better chance of surviving in a Freehold."

"Are you sure?"

"As sure as I've ever been of anything. And that's saying a lot." Captain Mendez grunted and looked down the tube to where Bailey worked on the hatch. "I pity any fool who picks a fight with a Freeholder. Particularly, *that* Freeholder."

Meris lowered her voice to a murmur. "Are you sure he's trustworthy?"

"Yes." The single, unadorned word conveyed total conviction. Captain Mendez offered her hand. "Good-bye, Meris. I'd always wanted to meet a Jadamii, and I'm honored that the privilege included meeting you."

Compelled by courtesy and gratitude, Meris briefly gripped the captain's hand. "The honor was all mine. You've been more than kind, and I don't know how to thank you."

Captain Mendez folded her arms again and glanced away. "Thank me by staying alive. And do what Bailey says."

"I hope we meet again someday."

"So do I."

Bailey got the hatch open and looked over his shoulder. "Mother of Multitudes?" he called. "Are you ready?"

Terror raised the ruff of fur along Meris' spine. "Yes." She cast one last look at Captain Mendez. "Good-bye." Not allowing herself to hesitate another moment, she started briskly down the tube. Twenty steps took her to Bailey's side, and he ushered her into the airlock.

Closing the hatch, he looked over his shoulder at her. "It will warm up in a short while."

Meris did not feel especially cold, but she nodded politely. "Most gracious."

"Most honored."

Meris listened to the air system go through its cycle. "Are you certain that this is permitted?" she asked. "Dútha won't mind?"

"Of course not. Dútha is a dear friend of yours who wants you to be safe."

The hatch of the air lock slid open. Meris stepped through. The stark, colorless interior of Dútha's ship appeared exactly as it had when she last saw it, though the odor of Humans overlaid the Rofa's warm scent. Unpleasant memories returned, and Meris felt her ears fold back.

Bailey secured the hatch. "I think it's best if we take off right away."

"Very well." Meris recalled the Phenox injection, and her mane bristled. *Dútha is a friend?* Her gaze landed upon the disarranged bunk. She strode to it, snatched up a blanket, and sniffed it. Her own scent clung to the surface. Horror crept through her mane, raising it into a stiff crest. *I was in Dútha's bed?*

Bailey headed for the bridge. "This way, if you please. We don't have much time."

Insides churning, Meris followed him. "Wait. I don't understand—"

Bailey was already in the pilot's couch, powering on the restraints. "Dútha gave this ship to an associate. And I'm . . . borrowing it."

Meris stood locked in fear and confusion, clutching the back of the copilot's couch. "But Dútha drugged me."

Bailey's long fingers scuttled over the controls. "I can explain that. Please, trust me, Mother of Multitudes."

Repelled by the speed of his movements, Meris turned her head away. She wondered if she had been foolish to believe Captain Mendez.

Suddenly, Meris' recorded voice filled the air: *"I've missed you terribly, without knowing why. Only that something important was gone from my life."* Dútha replied: *"They wouldn't let me near you. I didn't know how to get a message to you."*

Meris whirled, ears flashing forward. "What is that?"

Bailey did not look up from his departure preparations. "Dútha recorded your conversation while you were under the influence of Phenox. It will answer most of your questions." The view screen abruptly flashed into a flight schematic. "I can play it for you as we travel. But we have to leave. And *now*."

Sick with worry, Meris climbed onto the copilot's couch and tried to get comfortable. "But won't my enemies just follow me to Earth?"

Bailey finally looked at her. "Our planet is not without

defenses. Just because we're not warlike, doesn't mean we're an easy target." He paused and seemed to consider his words. "And I've submitted false readings to the system relays. As far as any watchers are concerned, this ship is on autopilot and bound for Igsha Reey."

Meris raised her ears. "You can do that?"

"Oh, yes." Bailey pointed to a button on the arm of her couch. "Please engage your restraints."

Meris pressed the button, and the mesh slid into place. "But what about your World Council? Didn't you say that they were after me, too?"

"Some of them. But most members of the World Council are decent people, and I think they'll take steps to protect you." Bailey returned his attention to the ship's navigational controls. "However, it's best if we get you to a Freehold as quickly as possible."

Meris shifted again on the strange contours of the couch and pulled her tail to the side. "Very well."

A metallic clang vibrated through the ship. "Mooring locks disengaged," Bailey said. "Hang on, Mother of Multitudes. We're going to Earth."

Rachel woke abruptly from a light doze, to find a group of people standing over her. Momentarily too disoriented to recognize faces, she stared up at them wordlessly.

A woman crouched in front of her. "Deputy?"

Then Rachel recognized Lafiya. "Oh, I'm sorry, I didn't—"

"You're free." Lafiya gestured to the people around her. "The community pardon went through."

Rachel felt disconnected from herself, as if a dense shadow lay over her heart, smothering her emotions. She peered up at the ring of smiling faces, spotting Noni Mead, Saja's mother; Carl, the gantry operator; young Jordie, from the maintenance crew; the Phi-Nurian, Captain Deiras; and Akya, still dressed as a Freeholder and exuding an air of supreme self-satisfaction. "You mean—?" She searched for words, the implications expanding in her mind and crowding her thoughts. "You mean everyone—?"

"Uh-huh." Lafiya grinned suddenly. "Everyone aboard good ol' Earth Port Station."

Den stirred. *"And* the merchant clients."

"Oh, yes," Lafiya added hastily. "And all our valued merchant clients."

The magnitude of their concern and support penetrated and dissolved the dark sense of separation. Rachel's vision blurred with sudden tears. "I—I don't know how—" She had to swallow. "Thank you."

Akya also crouched beside her. "The Interim Committee, particularly those associated with the World Council and Global Disaster Services, were reluctant to accept the validity of the pardon. But the Freeholders insisted that—" Akya broke off and studied her with a discerning gaze. "You don't smell right. You're ill."

Lafiya stared at the Rofa, then turned her attention to Rachel. "What?" She laid a callused hand against Rachel's cheek. "Deputy, you're burning up."

Rachel attempted to smile. "I'm fine, really. I never get sick."

Lafiya twisted to look over her shoulder. "Hey, Nothando!"

"I'm fine," Rachel repeated. "Just a little tired."

Nothando moved to the front of the crowd, nervously avoiding the aliens, and bent to study Rachel. "Deputy? Shall I call for a gurney?"

"Please don't." Rachel looked up at her. "Where's Tigre?"

Nothando's expression turned sad. "Doctor DeFlora was unexpectedly called back to Earth. He left with Doctor Wagasi."

The disappointment bit deep. "He didn't say good-bye."

"No." Nothando's tone was gentle. "He didn't say good-bye to anyone."

Fear colored Rachel's sadness. "Where's Wu?"

Nothando smiled slightly. "Under quarantine, in his quarters. Seems he picked up a mild viral infection."

Akya stood and carefully backed away. "Maybe you caught the same thing, Deputy Aja-mani?"

Rachel tried to stand, but her limbs felt too weak to support her. "No, I just need to—"

Nothando glanced at Lafiya. "You touched her. Be very sure to wash your hands as soon as possible."

Suddenly seized with the urge toward hysterical laughter,

Rachel shook her head. "Don't believe this. Burned, drugged, shot, beaten, and nearly blown up. And now, I'm *sick*?"

Lafiya said, "Don't forget arrested and incarcerated."

"Thank you."

Nothando looked thoughtful. "We'll need to run a few tests, but—"

"I don't believe this!"

Lafiya gave her a wolfish grin. "Could be worse, Deputy. You could be quarantined with Wu."

Rachel drew a breath to retort, and then paused. "Actually," she said, "that sounds better than sitting on a hard floor in Checkpoint detention."

Chuckling, Nothando straightened and pulled out her phone. "I'll call for a gurney."

Rachel slumped against the wall in a facetious display of defeat. "Yes, I suppose you'd better." After a brief internal struggle, she added: "And see if Wu's in the mood for company."

"Deputy?"

"What doesn't kill you," Rachel said, "will wake you up."

Meris stood frozen. Behind her sat the ground car, its metal surface reassuring and solid against her back. Around her spread the alien landscape of Earth, all swathed in a deepening blue twilight.

Several hours earlier, they had left Dútha's ship in an underground hangar located in a weedy and empty field. The gravel road was the only sign of civilization; no buildings broke up the surrounding masses of vegetation, no generators hummed from beneath the ground. *Such isolation.*

A bank of tall grass bordered the road, and beyond that loomed a dense growth of the towering plant life that Bailey called *treez*. Though familiar with their appearance from the long car ride, Meris found the height of *treez* unnerving. Jada's cold and rocky surface supported mostly lichens, wiregrass, and a small variety of ferns. She did not like giant plants, she decided, and the climate that fostered such malignancies must be barbarous in the extreme.

Bailey, beside her, drew in and released a noisy breath. "Ah," he said enthusiastically. "Fresh air."

It stank of moist rot. Meris fought against the impulse to cover her nose.

Bailey stepped off the road and into the knee-high grass. An invisible cloud of whining insects rose around him. Absently waving them away from his face, the Human turned to her. "Here we are," he announced. "Beautiful, isn't it?"

Meris nodded her head. According to her observations, the gesture signified either agreement or respectful consideration of another's words. "Yes," she lied politely. "Very pretty."

Bailey smiled. She reminded herself that it was a friendly expression, in spite of the alarming display of flashing teeth. The Human made an expansive, beckoning motion with both arms. "Follow me, if you please."

Meris could not bring herself to step off the road. "What about the car?"

"Leave it. I've set the timer. It will drive itself back to the airfield." A small wind sprang up. It played with the wild curls of his mane and made the tall grass rustle. "The sky's clouding over. Let's get under the *treez* before the rain starts, eh?"

Meris glanced up involuntarily. All she saw was darkness. *The sky? He can see the sky?* "What do you mean?"

"Rain," he repeated, sounding bewildered. "You have rain on Jada."

"Snow, mostly." Meris returned her attention to him. "Just how far does your vision extend?"

Bailey hunched his shoulders briefly. "Depends. Why? Is there—?" He paused and studied her for a moment. "Oh. Mother of Multitudes, are you nearsighted?" He tilted his head. "Can you make out the treetops?"

Meris squinted upward. Most of the leafy branches faded into shadowy obscurity. "Some of them."

Bailey smiled again. "We'll see about fitting you with glasses—corrective eyewear. But in the meantime, I'll try to remember that you can't see as far as I can." He walked backward a few steps. "This way, please. We have a long hike to my house."

The thought of stepping into the bug-infested vegetation raised the hair on her shoulders. Meris dug her toes into the warm, dusty gravel. "Are you quite certain," she asked, "that you obtained the proper clearance to bring me to

Earth? I thought your species doesn't allow aliens on its home world."

Bailey spread his hands. "I'm a Freeholder. We Freeholders don't believe in unnecessary laws." He tilted his head. "Meris. What's the matter? Are you frightened?"

Affronted, Meris glared at the Human. "Don't be insulting. I'm not frightened, I'm—" *Repelled.* "I want you to do me the courtesy of keeping me informed. I want to know of the risks."

"I'm sorry," Bailey said softly. "I didn't intend to be a bad host." He extended his hand, palm up. "Please. Walk with me. I swear that my only intention is to protect you from danger."

Meris hesitated. The wind picked up intensity and set the leafy branches of the surrounding *treez* into dancing motion. She found herself surprised by the suppleness of the enormous plants; the swaying limbs possessed an undeniable grace. The wind blew away the fetid odor of rot in a bracing, ozone-laden rush. The clean air seemed to evaporate her uneasiness. Meris stepped off the road and grasped Bailey's hand.

Rachel lay on her cot in Wu's quarters. Her nose ran constantly, her throat hurt, and a persistent cough made conversation difficult; but she could not recall ever feeling so cozily happy and contented. Wu was there, sharing illness and quarantine, and Rachel felt as if she were on a leisurely vacation. Smiling, she rolled her head on the pillow to look at him.

Wu sat on his bed, propped up by a heap of cushions, listening to Chen on the phone and making interested noises. He looked exhausted. His nose was red and starting to peel, and he appeared to be breathing through his mouth. He caught her studying him and winked.

Not wishing to distract him, Rachel crooked three fingers in a playful wave, then sat up to reach for her cup of cooling tea on the bedside stand.

Since the station assigned living space according to the size of the family, rather than an individual's position, Wu's quarters held barely enough room for a bed and a desk. Snapshots of friends covered the walls, and a *faux* window of a cityscape hung over the headboard. A brewer and small vid sat on the desk. Rachel's cot took up all the available floor space, but that offered no real difficulties; neither of them did much except blow their noses, drink gallons of tea, and talk on the phone.

Rachel emptied her cup, then refilled it from the brewer, which sat within easy reach. Her phone rang, and she had to grope for it among the blankets before answering it. "Ajmani."

"It's Lafiya."

Rachel smiled. "Oh. Hello."

"I've been deputized." Lafiya spoke in a tone of facetious exasperation. "Deputy Jimanez-Verde called me into her office and saddled me with a bronze rank."

Rachel's smile widened, recognizing the modesty behind Lafiya's manner. "Good." She picked up Wu's cup, warmed it with more tea, and returned it to the bedside stand. "Congratulations, Deputy DuChamp."

Lafiya sighed. "I don't deserve this."

"Ah, but you do." Rachel's nose began to drip, and she hastily reached for a wipe. "No more loafing around the Ops booth, I'm afraid."

"Deputy Jimanez-Verde said—" Lafiya paused, and her tone became shy. "—she said that I'd start out as your assistant."

"Is that so?" Recalling her own recent discussion with Lois, Rachel held the folded wipe against her nose. "Now that you mention it, I guess I could use the help. I hope you make good coffee."

Lafiya laughed. "It's better than Wu's."

Bailey talked as they traveled. His soft voice blended with the patter of rain as he explained the sounds, sights, and smells of his world. Meris' last vestige of uneasiness died under an avalanche of exhilarated curiosity. Alien words and concepts crowded her mind, and she gained expanded understanding of the meanings behind Bailey's gestures and facial expressions. She pelted him with questions, and his every answer inspired a hundred new questions.

They paused to rest at the top of a steep hill. Bailey pointed down the slope, into the forested darkness. "Not much farther, and we'll hit the path to Hoshino Uta. We'll make better progress then."

"Hoshino Uta," Meris repeated, tasting the sounds. "Ooo-tah."

"That's where I live. The oldest and most beautiful settlement in the whole Freehold."

Meris gazed down through the frolicking branches of the trees as if she could see the settlement. "What lovely names your people give to places. What do they mean?"

Bailey shouldered his pack and started down the hill. "Well, the Freeholds are all named in honor of the Winter Star, which isn't actually a star."

Meris followed him, picking her way through the undergrowth. "No?"

"Nope," Bailey said. "It's a comet. But our ancestors didn't know that, as they were left uneducated in the aftermath of the Last War. So they declared the new star's arrival the signal of a new era of peace on Earth." He glanced over his shoulder at her. "Hoshino Uta doesn't translate into Farnii very well. It means something like 'Melodic Chant of the Star.'"

"Ah." Meris again marveled at Bailey's ability to see stars with the naked eye. She wanted to ask about the comet's orbit, his ignorant ancestors, and the Human concept of peace. She reluctantly stuck to the topic of names. "Hoshino Uta." She flicked her ears and added impulsively, "I like saying that."

Bailey let his head fall back and made a prolonged, musical sound. She remembered him uttering a similar string of wordless noises on several past occasions, but none with such variation. "I—" He appeared to have difficulty catching his breath. "I'm glad you—"

Meris drew close and peered at him. "What's the matter? Are you having respiratory spasms?"

Smiling, Bailey shook his head. "No. It's all right. I'm only laughing."

"Pardon?"

Bailey sighed and passed a hand through his unruly mane. "I guess I should have explained it before. Humans laugh. It's an intricate, nonverbal form of communication, and we use it to convey feelings too complex for words." He spread his hands. "Usually, laughter expresses amusement and delight. It means we're happy."

Meris tilted her head. "It seems involuntary."

"Sometimes it is." Bailey bared his teeth in a wide smile. "Human infants laugh before they can talk. Maybe it was our species' first language."

"Ah," Meris said. "I think I understand. It takes the place of mobile ears and a tail."

Bailey laughed again. "You may be right." He hitched the pack up on his shoulder and started down the hill. "Let's go," he said. "The sooner we get home, the sooner we can rest."

With a sigh, Wu clicked off his phone. "Oh, goody."

Rachel set aside a printed report and looked over to him. "What's the matter?"

"Hasn't made the news yet, but Councillor Phong has been cleared of any collusion in the Starcatcher conspiracy." Wu picked up his tea, then appeared to change his mind and returned it to the bedside stand. "Glee Weber is the only member of the World Council who's been charged. And she's dead."

Rachel thought of Concha, and anger stirred within her. "So no one will be held responsible?"

"Well, I hate to sound like a skeptic, but—" Wu paused to blow his nose. "—but I'm afraid that the corrupt members of the World Council have had plenty of time to cover their tracks. If anyone faces punishment, it will be the innocent."

Rachel frowned. "Then it was all for nothing."

"Perhaps. Perhaps not. Some of the former victims of Starcatcher have already been released from penal service." Wu slumped back against his pile of cushions. "And Chen says there's talk of creating a system of checks against the World Council's power. Popular opinion is all for calling upon the Freeholds to mediate."

Rachel's hands began to shake, and she clenched them into fists. *Too late for Concha.*

Wu spoke gently. "Hey. . . ."

"I don't understand," Rachel said. "I don't understand people like Weber. Why would someone with so much power engage in such malicious and petty schemes?"

Wu picked up his tea and took a slow sip. "I'm glad you don't understand," he said. "The day you do, is the day you should step down from authority."

"It's all pointless, in the end. What did Weber gain?"

"Exactly."

Rachel glared at him. "Stop trying to smooth my feathers."

"Sorry." Wu grinned at her. "Old habit."

Rachel drew a breath to speak, but her nose suddenly began to run. She snatched up a wipe to staunch the flow. "I've decided," she said, "that I don't like being sick."

"Dreadful, isn't it?" Wu set down his cup and pulled the blankets up to his chin. "I've dreamed for years of having you spend the night, but this isn't what I had in mind."

To Meris' relief, the rain stopped just as they reached the path, though the overhanging branches continued to drip on them as they traveled. Surfaced with crushed white rock, the path seemed to glow with its own light as it curved through the forest. It was broad enough to permit them to walk side by side, which facilitated their continuing conversation.

At one point, the forest opened into a wide clearing. Bailey stopped and spread his arms to the sky. "Ah," he said. "The Moon is so beautiful tonight. There were times over the past few months that I doubted I'd ever see it again."

Meris followed his gaze upward. She detected a hazy brightness in one part of the sky, but no details. "What does it look like?" she asked wistfully.

Bailey glanced at her, his brows raised. "You mean you can't even see the Moon? Oh, Meris—" His voice faded, and he broke into a fit of coughing.

Meris laid a hand on his shoulder and encountered wet fabric. "Are you all right?"

"Thank you," Bailey whispered. "I'm—" He coughed again, and then spoke in a huskier version of his normal voice. "I'm fine. Just have a sore throat. All the cold air on the station's unheated dock, and then talking."

"And the rain," Meris added. "Your clothes are soaked." She tilted her head and studied him. "Maybe you're sick. If you were Jadamiin, I'd say you were coming down with a case of the snots." She gently pressed two fingers against his nose pad. His skin felt chilly and damp, an unmistakable sign of incipient illness. "Your nose is cold."

Smiling, Bailey pulled her hand away and held it gently.

"You're very kind," he said, "but I don't get sick. I'm very resistant to disease, and I've received a thorough vaccination program against anything my immune system can't handle." He carefully squeezed her hand and released it. "I'll be fine. I don't have . . . whatever you said."

Though doubtful, Meris nodded. "Good. I sincerely hope you never experience the snots."

Bailey abruptly sneezed.

Meris paused and tilted her head.

Bailey's expression conveyed unmistakable astonishment. "I don't—" He sneezed again, and the convulsive jerk of his head flung his mane into his face.

"The snots."

Bailey brushed the curls away from his eyes and sniffed. "I'm not sick," he protested. His voice contained a peculiar resonance. "I'm just—"

"Your sinus cavities," Meris said, "sound like they're filling with mucus. Among the Jadamiin, that's a symptom of illness."

Bailey sniffed. "But I've never been sick before."

"Live long enough," Meris said dryly, "and you'll experience everything."

"But I—" Bailey peered at her worriedly. "Are the snots a serious illness? Are they contagious?"

Meris folded her ears back. "If you're wondering whether I've carried this malady to Earth," she said stiffly, "perhaps you should have considered that possibility before we made planet-fall."

Bailey spread his hands. "I'm wondering if I'm going to die," he answered. "Should I seek medical attention?"

He suddenly sounded very young. Meris lifted her ears. "No one on Jada has ever died of the snots," she said. "And if you're resistant to disease, then you may not have a bad case." She patted his wet shoulder. "Maybe I'm wrong, and you're not sick at all. But I think the sooner we get you warm and dry, the better off you'll be."

Rachel listlessly sipped her mug of warm Naranha, wishing she could taste it. The door panel buzzed.

Since Wu was taking a shower, Rachel set aside the Naranha and struggled up off her cot to answer. "Yes?"

"It's Sonría. Hope you weren't sleeping."

"No, I was awake." Rachel brushed the hair back from her face and stared at the door. "Is something wrong?"

"Not sure." Sonría kept her voice low, as if wary of listeners. "Is Bailey in there with you?"

Rachel blinked. "No. We're in quarantine, so—"

"I can't find him anywhere."

Alarm tightened Rachel's shoulders. "What do you mean?"

"He's missing. And that Binks woman from the Freehold Association is about to pee her kimono."

"Damn."

"Damn, indeed."

Running low on strength, Rachel sank to the floor and tried to think. "Have you tried Captain Akya's ship?"

"Yes. And Khanwa's. Binks is accusing Councillor Phong of abduction, and she's making noises about searching the World Council's ship."

Rachel's thoughts darkened. "That's not a bad idea. And maybe you ought to put a double guard on Meris, so she doesn't disappear either."

Sonría chuckled humorlessly. "Already took care of that. I've got her aboard the *La Vaca*."

Nodding to herself, Rachel propped one shoulder against the wall. Marj Mendez could be counted upon. "Good thinking."

"Are you sure you don't know where Bailey is?"

"Sorry." Closing her eyes, Rachel sorted through ideas. "What about Dútha's ship? Have you tried there?"

After a long pause, Sonría said, "I hope Bailey wasn't aboard that thing. Though, now that I think about it, he hasn't been seen since it took off."

"Took off?"

"Yeah. Docking Control says the ship was set on some sort of preprogrammed schedule to automatically return to Igsha Reey."

"What?" Rachel's eyes flew open. "But Dútha gave it to Tigre."

"Can't help that. It's gone."

"But it can't be. Dútha wouldn't—" Rachel began to cough and could not continue.

Sonría made a sympathetic noise. "I'll let you go back to bed. If you think of anything, give me a call, okay?"

"'kay."

"Be safe."

"You, too." Rachel crept back to her cot. Feeling cold, she wrestled her way under the blankets and reached for her phone.

Wu stuck his head out from the washroom. "Someone at the door?"

Nodding, Rachel keyed the *La Vaca*'s number. "We've got another disaster brewing."

Wu whined like a puppy. "I'll dry off." He disappeared into the washroom.

A grumpy woman answered. "*La Vaca*. Watch officer."

"Deputy Ajmani," she whispered hoarsely. "I need to talk to the captain."

The officer's voice warmed. "Ah, Deputy, I'm really sorry, but the captain's engaged. Shall I leave a message that you called?"

For a moment, Rachel thought about insisting on being put through, but she didn't wish to interfere in Sonría's investigations. "Please. Tell her that it's important."

"My pleasure, Deputy."

"Thank you." Rachel clicked off, then sat holding the phone, lost in thought. The World Council members aboard the station were under scrutiny, so it made no sense for them to abduct Bailey. And if Bailey had wandered aboard Dútha's ship, he was more than capable of overriding the automatic program. *Unless he was injured. Or dead.*

Wrapped in his robe, Wu emerged from the washroom. "What's going on?"

Rachel regarded him somberly. "Trouble in paradise."

Bailey's condition continued to worsen as they walked. He sneezed, shivered, and coughed up phlegm. His voice dried to a painful croak, but he kept talking.

The trees thinned, as they continued, and the undergrowth became a carpet of grass. Meris gazed around in rising excitement. "Are we almost there?" she asked. "Is it far to Hoshino Uta?"

Bailey nodded. "This is Riguchi Park," he whispered, his voice completely gone. His shoulders sagged, and it seemed a great effort for him to continue walking. "We'll get to my house in just a few minutes." He pointed listlessly. "The gate is just ahead. Can you see it?"

Meris peered into the darkness ahead. "No." The wind blew toward them, carrying a myriad of scents. She lifted her nose and drank it in. "I smell water, pine trees, and Humans." A fragment of tinkling music drifted to her. She spread her webbed ears wide and listened for more. "How large is the settlement?"

"Pretty big," Bailey replied. "Population is about twelve thousand."

Meris glanced at him. "You think that's big?"

Bailey shrugged. "For a Freehold settlement, it's huge."

Two tall shapes flanked the path in front of them. At first, Meris thought they were trees; but as they walked closer, she realized that they were pillars. "The gate," she said. "That's the gate, isn't it?"

"Yes." Bailey sighed. "Home again."

The pillars seemed to be fashioned of the same white stone used on the path. They rose in unadorned symmetry, evincing the stark, geometric design that humans preferred. Meris drew close to one and ran her hands over its surface. The stone felt pleasantly cool with a smooth finish. "What do you call this stuff?"

"Limestone." Bailey laughed faintly. "There's another name for your collection."

"Names," Meris murmured. She turned to Bailey. "I've never asked you. What does your name mean?"

"It's old," Bailey said. "And it has several meanings. My real name is 'Trabail,' which means something like 'the pain of birth.' But everyone calls me 'Bailey,' and that means a 'strong wall,' or 'a place of refuge.'" He paused and cleared his throat. "And I hope that is what I shall always be to you, Meris: Sanctuary from all harm."

He seemed quite sincere. Meris took his hand. "Most gracious."

They walked together through the gate. The path continued for a short distance, gently sloping down to a wide platform with high metal railings. Meris gripped the top rail and peered over the edge. As far as she could see, they hung over a dark void filled with the distant rush of water. "Is this it?" she asked. "Where are the buildings?"

"All around us," Bailey said in a hoarse whisper. "You mean you can't see them?"

He sounded so distraught that Meris patted him on the shoulder. "Don't fret," she said. "I hear the river. Does it have a name?"

Bailey sniffed and wiped his nose on his sleeve. "Rana."

"Rana," Meris repeated, liking the rolled 'r.' "I can't see it from here, but it has a beautiful voice."

"Tomorrow," Bailey whispered, "we'll get you fitted with glasses, so you can see properly."

Meris slid her hand from his shoulder and grasped his arm above the elbow. "Come on, my young friend," she coaxed. "Show me where you live. It isn't far, is it?"

Bailey gestured weakly to the left. A ramp led away from the platform into darkness. They followed it, walking side by side down its gentle incline. The ramp took them to another platform, a short flight of stairs, and a zigzag turn. Small, glowing lanterns cast pastel pools of pink, lavender, and green over their feet. "Pretty," she commented approvingly. "Very pretty."

Bailey nodded, made a squeaking attempt at speech, then gestured helplessly and fell silent.

After a few minutes of travel, Meris realized that the interconnected ramps were actually a street system that worked its way across and down the wall of the canyon. Fragrant pine trees occasionally leaned over the railings, their branches hung with banners and tinkling chimes. She spread her ears and vibrissae in an involuntary reaction of delight. Sounds came to her from everywhere, and she heard the murmur of water, dreamlike music, and the haunting call of some night bird. "This is incredible," she whispered. "But where are all the people? Why haven't we met anyone?"

Bailey sniffed. "The way . . . has been cleared," he breathed. "Out of respect for you."

Meris nodded. "Ah."

They made another sharp turn, and Meris found herself facing the forested canyon wall. A building nestled among the whispering pines. She stopped and stared. Balconies, colonnades, and elaborately gabled porches flowed in liquid asymmetry from one level to another, all connected by sweeping flights of stairs. Banners and bells hung from every prominence. Sweet-smelling plants spilled like living draperies from window boxes. Small lamps poured jewel-bright, amber light over the walkways.

Lost in rising wonder, Meris struggled to find words. "Is this—?" She tore her gaze away from the structure and turned to Bailey. "Is this a house?"

Bailey nodded. "Just the outside," he whispered. "Rooms . . . dug into the rock." He turned away. "So tired."

Wu listened to Rachel repeat everything she'd heard from Sonría. He pulled at his lower lip, drawing his brows down in thought. "What a mess," he said finally. "But I rather suspect that Bailey is still aboard the station. He's not an easy fellow to render helpless."

"Jardín did it."

"No, Bailey allowed her to do it. He's an idiot."

Rachel pulled out a fresh wipe for her nose. "So fill me in. Where do you think he is?"

"Hiding." Wu smiled unpleasantly. "Trying to make waves. Perhaps attempting to pin the well-deserved blame on Councillor Phong."

"Hmm." Rachel could imagine Bailey employing such tactics, and later strolling out of a deep storage bay, protesting that he had been lost. "Rather underhanded, isn't it?"

"Perhaps."

Rachel dabbed gingerly at her sore nostrils. "I hope some Phi-Nurians don't have him."

"Chen says that our Phi-Nurian merchant clients are terrified that they'll be barred from Earth Port. They're on their best behavior, and haven't so much as pooped on the floor in the past twelve hours." Wu fussed with his blankets. "I wish we could teach the World Council such nice manners."

"Agreed."

"And my nose hurts," Wu said, as if continuing the topic. "And my throat hurts. And I ache all over."

"Me, too."

"Let's hunt down Councillor Phong and sneeze on her."

Dwellings continued to present themselves as Bailey and Meris traveled to the floor of the canyon. Each house was unique, and Meris marveled over the Humans' endless inventiveness. The murmur of the river grew louder as they walked, and the air became laden with moisture.

Bailey's house sat on the canyon floor, surrounded by a grove of pines. Like the others, it was partially built into the wall of rock, but it also included a thatched and woodtimbered extension of generous proportions.

Meris followed Bailey up a neat path of stepping-stones to the door. Containers of night-blooming flowers filled the air with a sweet scent that mingled with the aroma of pine and river. Bailey paused with his hand on the door latch and looked at her. In spite of his ill health, he seemed pleased and excited. "Here we are," he whispered, smiling. "Hope the raccoons haven't taken over."

Bailey opened the door, swung it wide, and gestured for Meris to precede him over the threshold.

Hearts pounding, Meris stepped into the house. She found herself in small room with a ceiling so high it exceeded her vision. To her right, a circular staircase coiled up into the shadows. In front of her and to the left, arched doorways opened into rooms beyond. A large, round table sat in the center of the room, covered with a variety of peculiar items. Over the table hung a cascade of something that seemed to be composed of vines and leaves. Only stale odors filled the still air, and Meris detected no other presence within the house. She glanced at him. "You live here alone?"

Bailey stepped in behind her and fumbled with a control plate on the wall beside the door. "Yes," he whispered and pressed a button. "Alone."

Pink and gold light flooded the room. Meris turned and saw that the thing over the table was actually a cluster of lamps, fashioned of some golden metal to resemble a flowering vine. Its mirrored leaves cast both shadows and spangles of light over the walls and gleaming staircase.

"All Paths," Meris breathed. She cautiously padded forward over the shining floor, trying to look in every direction at once. Detail after detail grabbed her attention; overhead galleries lined with ornate banisters, the elegant carving on the table's pedestal, the faceted glass in the window over the door. Though undeniably alien, Meris found the decor sophisticated, gracious, and incredibly beautiful. "I had no idea," she said. "I thought—" She glanced at Bailey. "I expected something more . . . primitive. Not this—" She gestured to their surroundings. "Luxury."

Bailey dropped his pack to the floor and sighed with heartfelt relief. "Luxury?" he repeated in his voiceless whisper. He kicked off his shoes and wiggled his toes. "Thank you for the compliment, but my home is—" He broke into a violent fit of coughing.

Meris went to him and put her hands on his shoulders. "That's enough, my young friend," she said crisply. "No more talking. I'm putting you to bed. Just point the way, and I'll take care of the rest."

CHAPTER THIRTY

RACHEL LAY on her stomach on the floor of Wu's quarters, her chin propped on both fists. Wu lay facing her in the exact same pose, his dark eyes fixed on the chessboard between them.

Rachel's cot was folded up and leaning against the door. Over Wu's bed, the *faux* window presented its cityscape bathed in the deepening dusk of an impending summer storm. Thunder rumbled in the distance, and lights began to twinkle in the nearby skyscrapers.

Rachel struggled to keep her mind on the game. She recalled the last several days as a battle against rising frustration, and only Wu's presence made the situation bearable. Though their symptoms had subsided, an overly cautious Nothando refused to release them from quarantine. They spent a great deal of time talking to colleagues on the phone.

Rachel received nothing but evasion whenever she tried to contact Captain Mendez. Her mother was still sulking and would not return any of her calls. Rachel also had made numerous attempts to get in touch with Tigre, still in transit to Earth aboard the *Caduceus,* but he never answered the messages she left. Wu had no luck reaching him, either. She hoped he was not ill.

Bailey remained missing, which was also a cause for worry. A search of Councillor Phong's quarters aboard *Gaia's Love* turned up recorded conversations that linked her to a conspiracy against the sovereign neutrality of the Freeholds. She was currently under arrest and being held in Checkpoint detention.

Deputy Jimanez-Verde had made inquiries via hyperlight transmission to Jada and Igsha Reey, but every communication was met with silence. Phi-Nu had denied any responsibility for the Checkpoint massacre, declaring that the individuals who instigated the violence had been criminals and had acted without governmental knowledge or approval.

On Earth, investigation after investigation opened as more evidence of World Council corruption came to light. It appeared that the late Councillor Weber had been involved in more than the Starcatcher conspiracy, and that blackmail and misappropriation of funds would be added to the list of posthumous charges.

Wu quietly cleared his throat. "So?" he prompted. "What are you going to do?"

Rachel sighed. "I don't know. If the World Council falls, we may be facing a global economic crisis. I've been thinking that even if they close down Port Station, a lot of companies may choose to remain in operation. I suppose I could sign on with someone like Mendez y Mendez." She ran her hand through her hair in distraction. "And I've got a little money saved. I could get my own ship and start up a courier service."

Wu grinned. "Sounds like fun," he said. "But I was talking about the game. It's your move."

"Oh." Rachel glanced down at the board and saw an opening. Since they were playing "Ricochet," the sides of the board were a deflective surface for any diagonally moving piece. She picked up her queen, bounced it off her home rank, fired it off the right side, and knocked over Wu's king. More thunder rumbled from the *faux* window. "Check and mate."

"Hey!" Wu cried in mock protest. "You can't do that. That's sneaky."

Rachel smiled triumphantly. "Thank you. I had a good teacher." She reached for the teacup at her elbow and found it empty. "Time to make more tea. I think that should be the loser's chore."

Wu's brows shot up. "Loser? Are you calling me a loser?"

"Yes."

"Just asking." He climbed to his feet and beamed down at her. "Any preferences? How about some coffee?"

"I don't—"

Set to monitor certain broadcasts, the vid on the desk peeped and turned itself on. Rachel sat up and fixed her gaze on it.

An image appeared, that of the World Council's logo, the Earth encased in a diamond. A woman's disembodied voice announced in dulcet tones that the following was a brief update of the Port Station hearings. Filled with sudden apprehension, Rachel wrapped her arms around herself and hunched her shoulders.

The World Council chambers supplanted the logo. Rachel saw the curved table, around which sat roughly a third of the one-hundred-and-fifty-member Council. They slouched in their chairs, their faces sagging with exhaustion.

A holographic image filled the space beside the witness' podium. A slender figure in a richly embroidered dashiki, projected twice as large as life, stood glaring at the councillors. "Today," said the announcer, "the World Council sat in session for fourteen hours." The cameras pulled in for a close-up of the witness, and Tigre DeFlora's fine-boned face filled the vid screen.

Rachel's pulse raced, and she rose to her feet.

Wu breathed some soft word and joined her at the desk.

Tigre's eyes glinted with suppressed ferocity. He made a defiant, sweeping gesture with one arm, and the sleeve of his dashiki painted the air like a banner.

Recalling what he had endured, Rachel could guess what he said and why he seemed so angry.

"Among others," the announcer continued, "the Council heard testimony from Port Station's former head surgeon, Doctor Tigre DeFlora, via hyperlink transmission." The picture faded to the World Council's logo. "We will bring further updates as they become available." The vid clicked off.

Rachel stood unmoving, barely aware of her surroundings. A thousand tiny memories from the crisis with Meris swarmed through her mind, biting and stinging like gnats. "Not much of an update," she said. "But then, they never are."

"He looked good," Wu murmured. He reset the brewer and started it. "I suppose he told them all to go to hell."

. . . the gems of the Orient blend with the color of your hair—black as the reasons for night. "Oh?" Though hurting, Rachel made herself smile. "I thought he only said that to people he liked."

Wu chuckled. "Such a stimulating fellow."

"I miss him."

"So do I."

Rachel continued to stare at the dark vid. "I wonder why he won't return our calls?"

"My fault, I suppose. I couldn't give him what he wanted."

Rachel turned to Wu. She read pain and sorrow in his eyes. With no other thought but that she loved him, she slipped her arms around him and pressed her lips to his.

Wu drew in a deep breath of obvious surprise but did not pull away.

Rachel pressed closer, sliding her hands into his hair. His lips tasted of sweet, spiced tea.

Wu cradled her face in his hands, moving his mouth hungrily against hers. He breathed in sighs.

After an eternity, Rachel paused for oxygen. She pressed her forehead against his, so they were nose to nose. "You know," she murmured. "I think I've always wanted to do that."

Wu's smile was as soft as a caress. "What a coincidence," he said. "I think I've always wanted you to do that, too."

Rachel's phone chimed. Wu made a disappointed noise and slowly released her.

Still quivering from his kiss, Rachel picked her phone up from the floor and answered it. "Ajmani."

The woman on the other end sounded angry. "Rachel? Is that you?"

Recognizing the voice, Rachel closed her eyes. "Yes, Mother. It's me."

"Rachel?"

"Yes, Mother."

"Well, why didn't you say so?"

Rachel sighed. "Who else calls you 'Mother?' "

"I'm surprised that *you* do," her mother snapped. "The

way you ignore me. I think you must hate me. You want me to die, so you can—"

Rachel pinched the bridge of her nose and tried to change the subject. "I'll be home on furlough in a few weeks."

"What?"

"I said that I'll be coming home soon."

"Well, what for?" Her mother's voice dripped with sarcasm. "I know it's not to see me."

Wearily, Rachel fought for self-control. "Why do you say things like that?"

"Well, it's the truth, isn't it?"

"Mother—"

"Isn't it?"

Tears stung Rachel's eyes, and she struggled to keep the angry hurt out of her voice. "Yes, I suppose it is."

"You hate me."

"Yes, I suppose I do."

Her mother actually sounded pleased. "That's a fine way to talk."

"Thank you."

"You're just like your father. You want me to die. Go ahead and say it."

Rachel started to comply, then paused. *This is how you drove Sasha to his death.*

Wu drew close again, studying her face with a worried expression. "Rachel?" he whispered. He reached over to touch her hand. "Hey?"

"Go on," her mother said in a rancorous tone. "Say it."

His fingers felt warm on the back of her cold hand. Rachel's distress eased away. She smiled at Wu and closed her fingers around his. *Truer than kin.*

"Say it," her mother demanded. "I want to hear you sat it."

In command of herself again, Rachel cleared her throat. "Mother, you sound upset. Call me back when you've calmed down."

"Say it, say it, say—!"

Rachel cut the connection.

Wu regarded her solemnly, tightening his grip a little. "Trouble in paradise?"

Rachel put the phone in her pocket. "I want a new mother."

"I would be glad to share mine with you." Wu still looked serious, and he clasped Rachel's hand in both of his. "I would be . . . honored."

It took a moment for the full meaning of his words to sink in. "Wu. . . ."

"Please. Think about it."

"I don't have to." Rachel found herself smiling so hard it hurt. "My answer is 'yes.' "

Meris carried a bowl of soup into the main room, which was part of the wood-framed structure that extended from the rock-hewn portion of the house. Though accustomed to living underground, Meris found that she preferred the more alien, wooden portion of the house. She liked the feel of the smooth boards beneath her feet, the prevailing scent of pines through the many windows, and the way her vision disappeared into the upward shadows of the thatched roof.

Lying upon layers of futon, Bailey opened his bleary eyes and rolled his head on the pillow to look at her. The tender skin around his nostrils was raw and peeling, and his lips were cracked. Meris could not recall ever seeing a more painful case of the snots. "Sit up," she commanded gently. "I've brought you something to eat."

"I'm not—" Bailey broke into a fit of coughing.

Meris set the tray down beside the bed, nudging aside a stack of books. "Doctor Harada said you had to keep your strength up," she reminded him. "And the soup will soothe your throat." She went to the window and pushed aside the paper-covered shutters. The yellow sunlight of Earth poured into the room, falling over the blue-and-white bedcover and bringing a rich sheen to the dark woodwork. She turned to face Bailey.

He sat up stiffly. "Nothing tastes good," he complained in a harsh croak. "In fact, nothing *tastes*."

Meris returned to the bed and tidied the clutter around the tray. "You'll like this," she promised. *I hope.* She rearranged his pile of folded handkerchiefs, put his workboard on standby, and moved the radio to within easy reach. "I think I'm developing a knack for Freehold cookery."

Bailey lifted the lid of the lacquered bowl and studied the thick, brownish contents. "What is it?"

"Wasabi and raisin soup."

"Mm," he said noncommittally. He picked up the bowl and sniffed the contents.

Meris' tail sank. "You like raisins. You said they were good for you."

Bailey gave her a weak smile. "Yes. They are." He raised the bowl to his mouth and took a tiny taste. His brows shot up. "Hey!"

Meris lifted her ears. "Do you like it?"

"Yup." He took a bigger mouthful and swallowed it with gusto. A sheen of perspiration formed under his eyes. "I can taste it," he declared. "Hot and sweet."

Relieved, Meris sat down on the floor beside the futon. She arranged herself in a dignified, yet casual, pose with her weight on one hip and her legs curled to the side. "I said you'd like it."

Bailey set down the bowl and reached for his stack of handkerchiefs. "Whoo!" he said gleefully. "It's cleaning me out." He blew his nose with an extended, hornlike blast. "This is wonderful. I can almost breathe. Thank you!"

"Not quite the response I anticipated," Meris said dryly, "but you're welcome, nonetheless." She reached over and turned on the radio. "It's almost time for that gardening program. Today, they're going to describe easy ways to attract songbirds."

Bailey picked up his bowl of soup. "I have to tell you, Meris. I've enjoyed the last few days. Even with the snots, I—" He froze, staring at her, his mouth hanging open. "What did you just say?"

Confused, Meris tilted her head. She had no idea what he meant. "You're welcome?"

Bailey sat bolt upright. "Songbirds!" He hastily set the soup aside and threw back the covers. "You've learned *Hongo*!"

Meris blinked. *Hongo* was the local dialect. "I have?"

Bailey crouched on the floor in front of her, a feverish brightness in his eyes. "You have." He spoke in *Hongo*. "You understand me perfectly, don't you?"

Meris spread vibrissae wide in astonished delight. "Yes," she said. "Yes, I do."

"How long?" Bailey made a movement as if he intended to clutch her shoulders, but then seemed to stop himself. He clasped his hands together. "How long have you known?"

Meris shrugged and tried to recall. "It's been gradual," she said. "Watching vid broadcasts, I just began to understand more and more of what was said."

Bailey's tone turned reverent. "Incredible." He leaned closer, peering at her as if seeing her for the first time. "Humans possess the ability to learn a language without the benefit of translation, but it takes them much longer to become proficient." His nose began to run. He absently wiped it with the back of his hand. "I'd heard rumors that the Jadamii absorbed languages quickly, but to witness it myself—"

Amused, Meris laid a kindly hand on his shoulder. "Bailey, child, use a handkerchief." She motioned toward the futon. "And get back into bed. You're making a big fuss over nothing."

"Nothing?" Bailey gazed up at her. "But this is—"

"Normal. Absolutely normal." It was funny to see him so excited over the most commonplace ability. "Now, get back under the blankets and eat the rest of—"

He clambered over to the radio. "This is only local programming." He switched stations. "This is the global mesh. They broadcast in Standard. Can you—?"

A female announcer spoke in a language quite different from *Hongo* or Trade. Meris picked out isolated phrases such as "World Council," "special report," and "Port Station."

Bailey drew his brows together and turned up the volume.

Meris studied his expression alertly. "What's going on?"

Bailey cleared his throat. "Evidently, we've missed a lot of excitement. An investigative committee has just concluded a hearing on World Council corruption." He spoke in a distant tone, as if busy with his own thoughts. "Tomorrow, they'll vote."

"Vote?" Meris echoed. "Vote on what?"

Bailey narrowed his eyes, though he appeared to gaze upon

some inner image. "Whether or not to start a rash of impeachment proceedings." He stood up and turned to her. "I've been incredibly stupid. Because of me, they're about to throw away the good with the bad." He started for the door.

"Bailey," Meris said, "where are you going?"

"Need to get cleaned up," he muttered. "I've got to make some calls."

Rachel awoke and opened her eyes. The window's simulation of dawn cast pink and gold light over Wu's tiny quarters, and the recorded sounds of early traffic drifted through the air.

Wu lay behind her, his body cupped around hers, his breath soft on her shoulder. It felt natural to have him there, as if they had always shared a bed. The chessboard still lay in the middle of the floor, though partially covered by their discarded clothing. She smiled drowsily and rolled over to face him.

Already awake, Wu grinned at her. "Morning."

"Morning," she purred. She ran her fingers through his hair. "I could just eat you for breakfast."

Wu laughed in uncomplicated happiness. "I won't put up a fight."

Rachel gave him a lingering kiss, then very gently bit his bottom lip. "Guess what I'm in the mood for?"

Wu raised his brows and pursed his lips. "Do tell."

Rachel chuckled. "I want to—"

From somewhere in the pile of clothes, a phone went off.

Wu sighed. "Oh, goody, I think it's mine." He climbed out of the bed and fished through the garments. "Thank heavens, someone called me, just when Rachel was about to suggest something naughty." He held up the phone and stared at it blankly. "Oh, it's yours." He handed it to her, sighing again, and ambled off into the washroom. " 'Scuse me. Need to pee."

Grinning, Rachel keyed her phone on. "This is Ajmani."

The station's computer clicked as it verified her identity, then spoke in its genderless voice: "Priority message relay from inbound Kamian freighter 2624 to Deputy Rachel Ajmani." The computer clicked off, and a Kamian vocoder whispered: "'I grasp the stars and take the light to heart.'" The computer clicked on. "Awaiting instructions."

Rachel's hands turned cold. "Reply."

"One moment, please." The computer issued a series of high-pitched beeps. "Connection established."

Fighting for calm, Rachel said, "This is Deputy Ajmani of Earth Port Authority."

"Zo, Rachel!" Bailey said. "Long time, eh?"

Rachel's lips parted, but words failed to come.

"Hellooo? You there?"

Though still feeling stunned, Rachel found her voice. "Bailey! Where the hell are you?"

"Hoshino Uta." Bailey sounded pleased with himself. "Things on the station were getting sticky, so I brought Meris here for safekeeping."

"You—?" Rachel recovered enough from her surprise to start thinking again. Her inability to reach Captain Mendez by phone suddenly made sense. "Wait. Don't say any more. This call may be—"

"Don't worry. Our conversation's totally secure and encrypted in ten different ways."

"Encrypted?" Rachel slowly climbed to her feet. "Then that earlier call from a Kamian freighter was you?"

Bailey chuckled ruefully. "Yes, sorry about that. I needed to run a test. Had to make sure I could fool the relays and mask a ship's true heading."

Wu came out of the washroom. "I heard Bailey's name. Is that him on the phone?"

Rachel nodded and beckoned him closer. "Is Meris all right?"

"Perfectly fine," Bailey said. "She loves it here."

Wu drew near, and Rachel tilted the phone so he could listen and speak.

Bailey continued in an earnest tone: "I would have called sooner, but I've been ill. Meris says it was 'the snots.' "

"Wu and I were quarantined," Rachel said. "Nothando told us it was some sort of opportunistic virus."

"Well," Bailey said, "considering what we'd endured, I suppose our immune systems were low on power. Did Tigre get sick, too?"

Wu cleared his throat. "We saw him on a news broadcast, and he looked quite well."

"You—?" Bailey seemed taken aback. "You haven't spoken to him?"

Rachel exchanged glances with Wu. "No. He's on his way back to Earth, and we can't seem to reach him."

"That's a bit . . . worrying. I'll see what I can find out." Bailey sniffed. "Excuse me. My nose keeps running."

Mentally sorting through her list of unanswered questions, Rachel said, "Tell me about the Artifact. What is it? And why are so many people after Meris because of it?"

"The Artifact," Bailey said, "is an archaeological relic that predates Jada's current recorded history. In an article I published in *Xenos* last year, I used it as an example of the bias that a translator must avoid bringing to any work." He paused and sighed. "To put it briefly, I took the same text and provided three varying and equally valid translations. One was a hymn to the sun. One was a record of war. And one was a set—"

"—of equations," Rachel finished, "dealing with the structure of time and space."

"It was brilliant," Bailey said hotly. "And I should have won the Weinreich Award."

"But—" Rachel tried to sort through the conflicting stories. "What does it have to do with Meris?"

"Certain factions on Jada wanted her to translate the Artifact, and others wanted to prevent her from doing so. The translation in my article was entirely a work of fiction, but, taken out of context, it provided a plausible-looking excuse to murder her." Bailey sniffed again. "And that would have caused a revolutionary war on Jada."

"War?" Rachel repeated numbly.

"Right," Bailey said. "Someone wanted the people of Jada to rise up against their High Assembly. Not only that, but they tried to turn the Rofan Legitimacy against itself. And they attempted to arrange for the Phi-Nurians to be barred from every port in the galaxy."

Wu spoke in a flat tone. "Do you have any proof of this, Professor Rye?"

"What sort of proof do you need?" Bailey's voice was edged with challenge. "What about our issues with the World Council? Bad timing, eh?"

Thoughts whirling, Rachel ran a hand through her hair, trying to think of any political agency capable of such wide-ranging interference. "But why? What would anyone gain by causing so much conflict?" And then the answer occurred to her. "Trade."

Wu looked at her, clearly startled. "Pardon?"

Rachel's voice came out in a dry whisper: "The Kamians."

"Just so." Bailey paused and blew his nose. "Like an opportunistic virus."

"Wait." Wu paced away a few steps. "Now, wait. I can't believe the Kamians would do that."

Evidently, Bailey heard him. "You don't have to believe it's the Kamians. You can believe it's the Phi-Nurians or the Rofan, if you find that easier. Or you can attribute the whole mess to the ghosts of those who died in the Last War. Placing blame, at this point in the game, is worse than foolish."

Rachel drew her brows together. "What are you getting at?"

Wu returned to her side and settled his head against hers to listen to the phone.

Bailey sighed, suddenly sounding weary. "I don't know. Nothing is ever certain. Perhaps it's all a coincidence, but I don't like the idea that we're all being dragged along by the same avalanche."

Rachel closed her eyes. "So what do you suggest that we do?"

"Seek peace," Bailey said.

The connection broke.

Rachel slowly lowered the phone and turned her eyes to Wu. He slipped his arms around her.

"I'm glad you're here," she said, finding comfort in his solid warmth. She supposed she needed to somehow get a message to Lois and inform her of Bailey's whereabouts. "About what Bailey said, what do you think we ought to do?"

Wu kissed her ear, then whispered into it: "Watch and wait."

Rachel's phone chimed again. She jumped and nearly dropped it, then keyed it on. "Ajmani."

Nothando spoke hesitantly. "Good morning, Deputy. I hope I didn't wake you."

"No." Rachel straightened alertly. "Are we out of quarantine?"

Nothando's voice turned warm. "You are. And free to return to duty."

Rachel tried to sound enthusiastic. "That's wonderful. I'll be sure to pass the news along to Wu. Thank you."

"You're welcome. Be safe."

"You, too." Rachel clicked off the phone and checked the time. "Forty-five minutes to get ready."

Wu kissed her shoulder. "I heard that. Sounds like vacation is over."

"Afraid so."

Wu released her with obvious reluctance. "See you after our shift is over?"

"Of course." Rachel smiled, finding herself happy in spite of doubt and the threat of future turmoil. "My quarters, this time."

Seated at a small desk in his cabin aboard the *Caduceus*, Tigre closed down his workboard and rubbed his forehead. *So tired.*

Hard copies and data chips covered the surface of his desk, evidence of his preparatory work on Rofan physiology. The ship would reach Earth in two days, and he had to be ready to make a presentation before the Agency's Planning Commission. Tigre slumped back in the chair. He closed his aching eyes, but still saw floating images of Rofan protein chains.

With nothing to distract him, all his hovering regrets settled upon his soul. He wished he had defied the Port Authority officials and put Jhaska into stasis. He wished he had stopped Concha from facing Jardín. And he desperately wished he could talk to Rachel and Wu again.

They had tried to get in touch, but he had refused to take their calls or to return their messages. Fear lay at the back of his actions. He could lie to everyone else about Dútha's authorization for treatment, but he knew that Wu and Rachel would drag the truth from him. Too much hinged upon the lie.

Tigre shifted and prepared to stand, but the required effort suddenly seemed too great. "God, I'm tired." He rested his head on the desktop and thought about the daunting challenge of getting ready for bed. Then he thought about the cartridge of Seroplex he had hidden in his desk drawer. "Shit."

It would be foolish to use it. He had no idea how he might get more to stave off the hangover. Uncle Richard would be furious to know that he had it. *But I need to finish the presentation.*

The intra-ship phone rang. Tigre groaned and picked it up. "DeFlora."

To his confusion, he heard a signal as if he had placed the call. He was about to hang up, when a woman answered.

"Ajmani."

Tigre gasped. "Rachel?"

"Yes? Who—?"

The connection crackled. "This is Wu."

His exhaustion forgotten, Tigre climbed to his feet. "What—? How—?"

Wu sounded surprised. "Tigre? Is that you?"

"Yes, of course, it's me," Tigre said, still baffled. "Are you aboard the *Caduceus*?"

"No," Rachel said, "we're still—" She paused, then spoke in a somewhat angry tone. "Bailey."

"Zo," Bailey said, sounding nervous. "Please don't be mad at me."

Tigre drew his brows together. "What the hell is going on?"

Wu chuckled. "Bailey's new hobby, it seems, is playing with communications systems."

Their voices, so familiar, raised a tide of longing within Tigre. He could imagine each one of them: Wu, grinning wickedly; Bailey, wearing an overly innocent expression; and Rachel, trying to look stern. "How—?" Then Tigre decided he did not really care how Bailey had managed to rig a hyperlink conference call to come in through the ship's phone line. "How is everyone?"

Rachel's tone turned warm. "We miss you. Why didn't you say good-bye?"

"Sorry." Tigre sat on the edge of his desk. "I know it was shitty of me, but I couldn't handle it."

Wu murmured. "I thought you wanted to run away to a Freehold."

Remembering his marriage proposal to Wu, Tigre felt his ears turn warm. "Well—"

Bailey broke in. "That was supposed to happen. It was the most probable future. I saw it."

Tigre's mouth fell open, and he struggled for comprehension. "What?"

"I saw it," Bailey repeated, obviously aggrieved. "You were supposed to come to Hoshino Uta, but you didn't. And now everything is messed up, and Rachel is going to marry Wu."

Stunned, Tigre lost the ability to form words. *Rachel—?*

Rachel spoke in a deceptively quiet tone: "Messed up?"

"Uh," Bailey said, "I didn't mean it the way it sounded."

Wu seemed amused. "Professor Rye, you're an idiot."

"I know."

Tigre pulled his thoughts together with effort. "Is it true? Rachel, are you going to marry Wu?"

"Yes," she said softly. "Yes, I am."

As if facing a medical emergency, Tigre slipped into his calm, professional manner. "That's wonderful news. I hope the two of you are very happy."

"Thank you," Rachel said. "That means a lot to me."

"Yes," Wu said, "thanks."

Bailey still sounded upset. "Rachel deserves more than one husband."

"Indeed," Wu said. "But I believe you'd have to duel Captain Khanwa for the position of second husband."

Stricken with a sudden fear that the topic would turn to Rofan, Tigre cleared his throat. "I hate to cut this short," he lied, "but I'm due at a meeting in a few minutes."

Bailey made a disappointed noise.

"Understood," Rachel said. "We're on duty in a few minutes, as well. Call us when you have time to talk."

"Please do," Wu said. "And be safe."

"You, too." Tigre had to swallow. "All of you." He cut the connection.

For a long moment, he stood motionless, staring down at the phone in his hand.

Sorrow gathered like a weight near his heart, choking his breath. He wondered why it hurt so much to lose Rachel and Wu, when he had only just met them. *Stupid. You don't have time to wallow in emotion.*

Tigre looked at the mass of work on his desk. Exhaustion swooped down upon him, and he swayed on his feet.

So much to do.

Without making a conscious decision, he sat down, un-locked the desk drawer, and pulled out a box of wrapped candies. He opened the box and dumped the contents onto the desk; the cloying odor of fruit and chocolate filled the air. The Seroplex cartridge lay amidst the bundles of bright paper.

Numbly, Tigre rummaged through the drawer until he found an injector. He fitted the cartridge into it, pulled down his waistband, and shot the Seroplex into his hip.

Liquid fire spread under his skin, and Tigre gasped. "God—!" His brain bubbled, and he thought he might black out. Then the misery faded, taking with it his sense of doubt and sorrow. Energized, alert, and filled with new enthusiasm, Tigre grinned at the empty injector. "Not too shabby."

The candy suddenly smelled luscious. He unwrapped a piece of chocolate-covered orange peel and ate it with full appreciation, then reactivated his workboard. Humming a little, he brought up the file on protein chains and looked over it with fresh interest. He would have to find a way to dispose of the injector, he thought idly, and to think of a method to secure more Seroplex.

Reviewing a report on the triple chromosome sets of the Rofan, Tigre unwrapped and ate another candy. "And, somehow, I'll . . ." Fiercely and defiantly happy, he licked chocolate from his lips. *Find a way to forget Rachel and Wu.*

Still preoccupied with the phone call to Tigre, Rachel stepped into Dock Two's Operations booth. Cargo techs in heavy coveralls filled the cramped space, and the odor of bad coffee hung in the air.

"Hey, hey!" someone cried. "There she is!"

Rachel looked around at all the grinning faces, knowing that every person there had voted for her pardon. "Yes," she said, feeling both honored and humbled. "Here I am, thanks to you."

"Welcome back." Fran Swanson, the senior cargo tech, crossed to her, carrying a cup of coffee. "Have you read the reports, Deputy? The Rofan have bought all the dummy cargo."

Rachel blinked at her. "What?"

Smiling, Fran handed her the coffee. "There's not a single canister left. It's the hottest commodity to hit the station in a decade. The arbitrators are rolling in revenue."

"If we were smart," someone said, "we'd pack up some more dummies to sell off."

"It's the mystery they like," someone else declared. "The Rofan just love to be surprised."

The general conversation veered into stories of Rofan idiosyncrasies. Relieved to escape the spotlight, Rachel strolled to the window where Lafiya stood.

Dressed in the indigo blue of her new Port Authority uniform, Lafiya beamed at her. "Good to see you, Deputy Ajmani. How are you feeling?"

"Just fine, Deputy DuChamp." Rachel returned the smile. "Anything I ought to know?"

Lafiya nodded toward the dockside activity. "We got word about an hour ago that Igsha Reey has reopened."

"Really?"

"Almost everyone is leaving." Lafiya shrugged one shoulder. "It's turned nice and quiet. Since they're all prepping for departure, they're too busy to duel or have frenzies. Safety is bored silly." She paused and directed her gaze pointedly out the window. "Speaking of Safety, I wonder what Warden Jackson is up to?"

Mood soaring at the mention of his name, Rachel followed Lafiya's gaze.

Wu stood in berth B-5's loading area, talking to Captain Akya and an assemblage of crew. Wu seemed to be pointing to something on top of a canister, but since his back was to the Ops booth, Rachel could not make out the details. Akya appeared fascinated and delighted. Its small ears were pricked forward, and its head bobbed.

"Yes," Rachel murmured, pulling out her phone. "Good question." She keyed Wu's code and watched him answer.

"This is Wu."

"What's this I hear about you marrying a Rofa?"

Lafiya snickered.

Wu turned toward the Ops booth and waved impishly "A rumor, nothing more," he said. "I'm already spoken for."

Rachel felt a sudden heat in her face and throat. "Better believe it."

"How's your day going?"

"I went to my office, but someone has buried my desk under a mountain of hard copies."

"Tsk-tsk. Think of wasted resources. Not to mention the fire hazard. I'll need to have a stern word with those responsible."

Rachel laughed. "Please do."

"So," Wu continued, "instead of digging out your desk, you decided that it was more important to reestablish your presence on Dock Two."

"And just in time, it seems. What are you doing?"

"Merely teaching the honorable Captain Akya to play chess. All in the name of interspecies goodwill, of course."

Rachel sipped her coffee. It was awful. It was wonderful. "Of course."

"Want to come watch?"

"Won't I be a distraction?"

"Yes. I may be forced to distract you back."

Rachel took another swallow of coffee. It felt good to be back in routine, to enjoy the trust and companionship of friends; and to know that, in spite of hardship and danger, certain things remained constant. "I think," she said, "that I could get used to being distracted. I think I may even get used to your coffee."

Wu chuckled. "I love you, too."

Uneasily, Meris studied the computerized display in front of her. Even after several intensive lessons, she found working with the Freehold's communications link a daunting prospect, especially since mistakes tended to be expensive. She turned on her stool to glance at Bailey. "I'm sorry, but I need help again."

"Don't apologize." He immediately set aside his book and climbed to his feet. "I like helping you."

Meris wrinkled her nose at Bailey, knowing he understood it as a smile.

They were in one of the house's rock-hewn rooms. Heavy matting covered the floor as a barrier against the chill, and shelves filled with books hung along the walls. Bailey called the room his library, though it also contained the commlink and a collection of deeply upholstered furniture.

Bailey bent over to peer at the display.

"I was looking up Prudence Clarke's poetry," Meris explained, "when the screen suddenly changed to this one. For no reason. I didn't touch anything."

Bailey wrinkled his nose at her. "It's nothing to worry about." He pointed to the top of the display. "See? It says 'new message.' It's just notifying you that you have a letter."

Meris abruptly recognized the screen. "Oh," she said, feeling foolish. She carefully tapped the command to take her back to the poetry. "Most gracious."

"Most honored." Bailey turned, then paused. "May I ask? Why the interest in Prudence Clarke?"

Meris raised her vibrissae in surprise. "Because of what you told me. About Earth Port Station and your message to Deputy Ajmani." Every day, Meris listened to the recording of her conversation with Dútha, hoping that it would trigger a memory. She found it troubling that the individuals whom she regarded as family back on Jada were those who had betrayed her; and her true friends were aliens. "I was curious, and I wanted to read the whole poem."

Bailey tilted his head. "Very well, though I don't know how much you'll understand."

He helped her find the poem she needed, and then assisted her in printing it out.

Meris read over the hard copy in growing bewilderment. "Well, you're correct. I don't understand. What does it mean?"

Bailey settled cross-legged on the floor beside her stool. "It's a flight, which is a poetic form that uses layers of images and details to describe an essentially indescribable moment of revelation."

Meris read the poem again, trying to find meaning in the singsong nonsense about rabbits and tears and stars.

"Personally," Bailey continued, "I think she's trying to capture the essence of perfect inner balance, the awareness of awareness."

Meris set the printout aside. "I think it's about nothing."

Bailey laughed. "Exactly." He stood and returned to his book.

I grasp the stars and take the light to heart. Meris tapped the command to check her mail. She wondered if it would make more sense if she could see the stars with her own eyes. Bailey had been working hard to develop a set of glasses for her, but he had yet to find a way for her to comfortably wear them.

The new message popped up. It was from Jada's High Assembly, and it simply read: *Mother of Multitudes, we entreat you, please return home. Those who wish you harm have been deposed. Your true children long for you.*

Meris' three hearts broke into an uneven gallop, and her mane stood up in bristles. She drew a breath to speak, then found no words.

Somehow, they had traced her location to Hoshino Uta. Meris clenched her hands, baring her claws. They had lied to her. Denied her mastery of her own life. Sealed her away from Dútha, her friend and mate.

Your true children long for you.

Behind her, Bailey laughed over something in his book. He did that from time to time, and always seemed unaware that he had made a sound.

Meris released her breath. Bailey was her child now, as dear to her as any tied by birth.

For a moment, she gazed at the message, trying to think. If she simply deleted it, they would send another. If she accused them, they would deny it. If she sent polite excuses, they would reply with polite arguments.

Her children wanted her dead, and all for the sake of a few fraudulent equations. For the sake of nothing.

The fur fluffed out all over her body. *Nothing.*

Bailey stirred behind her. "I'm hungry. Let's walk into town and get ice cream."

Meris enjoyed these evening excursions, even though she always drew staring attention from passersby. She loved strolling through the jewel-lit streets under the whispering pines, listening to the river's distant music and the rhythmic pulse of locusts, and finally stepping into the gaudy little shop filled with sticky, giggling children.

"Yes, let's do that," Meris said. "Just give me a minute to finish this."

"Take your time." Bailey stood and walked to the door. "I'll go and get ready."

Meris wrinkled her nose at him. He wrinkled his in response and left the room. She picked up the printout and carefully typed her reply to Jada.

I grasp the stars and take the light to heart. I walk like plush and teach the rabbits how. I weep sweet diamonds and drop the sparkles one by one. There is nothing to learn and I learn it very well. I stand alone and fill my arms with wind. I grasp the stars. I grasp the stars.

Bailey appeared in the doorway. "Ready?"

"Yes." Meris stood and sent her message on its way across the light-years. "I'm ready."

Julie E. Czerneda

Web Shifters

"A great adventure following an engaging character across a divertingly varied series of worlds."—*Locus*

Esen is a shapeshifter, one of the last of an ancient race. Only one Human knows her true nature—but those who suspect are determined to destroy her!

BEHOLDER'S EYE
0-88677-818-2
CHANGING VISION
0-88677-815-8
HIDDEN IN SIGHT
0-7564-0139-9

Also by Julie E. Czerneda:
IN THE COMPANY OF OTHERS
0-88677-999-7
"An exhilarating science fiction thriller"
—*Romantic Times*

To Order Call: 1-800-788-6262

Julie E. Czerneda

THE TRADE PACT UNIVERSE

"Space adventure mixes with romance...a heck of a lot of fun."—*Locus*

Sira holds the answer to the survival of her species, the Clan, within the multi-species Trade Pact. But it will take a Human's courage to show her the way.

A THOUSAND WORDS FOR
STRANGER
0- 88677-769-0
TIES OF POWER
0-88677-850-6
TO TRADE THE STARS
0-7564-0075-9

To Order Call: 1-800-788-6262

CJ Cherryh
EXPLORER

CJ Cherryh
Classic Series in New
Omnibus Editions

THE DREAMING TREE
Contains the complete duology *The Dreamstone* and
The Tree of Swords and Jewels.   0-88677-782-8

THE FADED SUN TRILOGY
Contains the complete novels *Kesrith*, *Shon'jir*, and
Kutath.   0-88677-836-0

THE MORGAINE SAGA
Contains the complete novels *Gate of Ivrel*, *Well of
Shiuan*, and *Fires of Azeroth.*   0-88677-877-8

THE CHANUR SAGA
Contains the complete novels *The Pride of Chanur*,
Chanur's Venture and *The Kif Strike Back.*
                                        0-88677-930-8

ALTERNATE REALITIES
Contains the complete novels *Port Eterntiy*, *Voyager in
Night*, and *Wave Without a Shore*   0-88677-946-4

AT THE EDGE OF SPACE
Contains the complete novels *Brothers of Earth* and
Hunter of Worlds.   0-7564-0160-7

To Order Call: 1-800-788-6262

Tanya Huff

The Confederation Novels

"As a heroine, Kerr shines. She is cut from the same mold
as Ellen Ripley of the *Aliens* films. Like her heroine,
Huff delivers the goods." --*SF Weekly*

VALOR'S CHOICE
0-88677-896-4
When a diplomatic mission becomes a battle for survival,
the price of failure will be far worse than death...

THE BETTER PART OF VALOR
0-7564-0062-7
Could Torin Kerr keep disaster from striking while escort-
ing a scientific expedition to an enormous spacecraft of
unknown origin?

To Order Call: 1-800-788-6262

DAW 19

C.S. Friedman

The Best in Science Fiction

THIS ALIEN SHORE 0-88677-799-2
A *New York Times* Notable Book of the Year
"Breathlessly plotted, emotionally savvy. A potent
metaphor for the toleration of diversity"
—*The New York Times*

THE MADNESS SEASON 0-88677-444-6
"Exceptionally imaginative and compelling"
—*Publishers Weekly*

IN CONQUEST BORN 0-7564-0043-0
"Space opera in the best sense: high stakes adventure
with a strong focus on ideas, and characters an intelligent reader can care about."—*Newsday*

THE WILDING 0-7564-0164-X
The long-awaited follow-up to *In Conquest Born*.

To Order Call: 1-800-788-6262